EVERYMAN,
I WILL GO WITH THEE,
AND BE THY GUIDE,
IN THY MOST NEED
TO GO BY THY SIDE

JONATHAN LETHEM

MOTHERLESS BROOKLYN

THE FORTRESS OF SOLITUDE

WITH AN INTRODUCTION
BY CHARLES YU

EVERYMAN'S LIBRARY
Alfred A. Knopf New York London Toronto

430

THIS IS A BORZOI BOOK
PUBLISHED BY ALFRED A. KNOPF

First included in Everyman's Library, 2024

Motherless Brooklyn
Copyright © 1999 by Jonathan Lethem

The Fortress of Solitude
Copyright © 2003 by Jonathan Lethem

Introduction copyright © 2024 by Charles Yu
Bibliography and Chronology copyright © 2024 by Everyman's Library

Motherless Brooklyn originally published in the United States by
Doubleday, a division of Random House, Inc., New York in 1999 and in
Great Britain by Faber and Faber Limited, London, in 2000. *The Fortress
of Solitude* originally published in the United States by Doubleday,
a division of Random House, Inc., New York, in 2003 and in Great
Britain by Faber and Faber Limited, London, in 2003.

everymanslibrary.com
www.everymanslibrary.co.uk

ISBN: 978-1-101-90848-8 (US)
978-1-84159-430-9 (UK)

A CIP catalogue reference for this book is available from the
British Library

Typography by Peter B. Willberg

Book design by Barbara de Wilde and Carol Devine Carson

Typeset in the UK by Input Data Services Ltd, Bridgwater, Somerset

Printed and bound in Germany by GGP Media GmbH, Pössneck

CONTENTS

INTRODUCTION

I'm a back-of-the-store guy. My dream: a large, dusty used bookshop. Shelves and shelves of trade paperbacks, pages not quite yellowing, maybe off-white. Vintages and anchors and penguins crammed against each other, mostly alphabetized, a bit of randomness tossed into the system by the intentional or careless hands of readers interested for a moment, and then not so much. Spine out. Only titles and author names visible, the bare minimum of information to go on. What are you going to pick? How are you going to spend your lunch break, your coffee break, the next two minutes or two hours or two weeks? Do you share this dream with me? If so, you know that the stakes are high. Choose correctly and you might find the holy grail. Here, alone, under fluorescent lights. A secret decoder ring, a magical object that unlocks your hidden powers. Somewhere in the slightly warped pages of your own private discovery, selected by whatever mysterious algorithm governs the whims and desires of the lonely browser, the desperate searcher, you will make your choice, consciously or otherwise. What are you looking for, back-of-the-store-guy, on a Saturday night, five minutes to closing? People outside on Telegraph are already drunk and heading for the next place. You're in the fiction section looking for something deeper, something special, preferably under ten bucks. You're in here because of the dream. Choose correctly and you might find a sentence that will change your life.

Jonathan Lethem is a rare writer. A back-of-the-store guy who ended up on the front tables, and then the front page of the book review. My own private secret decoder ring. I'm actually the guy who discovered Lethem. And then discovered all my friends and professors had beaten me to the punch. Not only is Lethem living the dream, for a certain kind of nerd (this one), he *is* the dream: outsider *and* insider. Standout *and* dropout. Fanfic as canon. Liner notes as literature. Before Reddit threads and Wikis, before message boards, there has always been this energy, back-of-the-store energy, the energy of people obsessing over details. Lethem has channeled that energy, harnessed it into a superhuman level of discernment, the power to make subtle distinctions, taxonomies, to catalog the world. Along with others in his cohort (Michael Chabon, Jennifer Egan, George Saunders, to name a few), Lethem helped to re-map contemporary fiction, erasing boundaries, revealing new rivers and streams, places with good vistas and fertile soil, places to build from and expand. Some time early this century, the capital of literary moved from realism to a far-flung outpost in the genres. Lethem was at the frontier.

*

But before he was a front-of-the-store author, he was the clerk in the stacks, and before that he was a boy growing up in a bohemian commune in Brooklyn, the son of Richard Brown Lethem, a painter, and Judith Frank Lethem, an activist; the latter Jonathan Lethem has described as "the most forceful and extraordinary person" that he knew. He was only fourteen when Judith died of a brain tumor; the profound loss was a formative event for Jonathan as writer:

What I do is use something tangible I can get hold of; often that's my mother's death. I think I've written about motherless children in many different ways and at different times . . . my mother . . . the one who seemed to hold everything together, and a great creator of meaning and feeling herself was lost. I didn't experience this as disenchantment; I experienced it as a confirmation: everything I've been warned about in the world can come all the way to you and reach you in your own center.

As a teenager, Lethem attended the High School of Music & Art in New York, where he published a zine and created animated films. In 1982, he matriculated at Bennington College in Vermont, intent on studying art. It was a lateral move. Lethem went from being a white kid in Gowanus to being a public-school kid in a private college where, surrounded by classmates who came from wealth and privilege, he was an outsider again. Realizing he wanted to be a writer, Lethem dropped out of Bennington in his second year. He hitchhiked across the country, ending up in Berkeley, California, where he worked at a number

Lionel in particular, this is hard – he's lost not only a benefactor but a shield, an insulating layer between himself and other people. Without Minna, Lionel and his Tourette's must now navigate their own way through the mystery. Retracing steps and piecing together clues. Paying visits to acquaintances, old and new, friendly and not-so-friendly. It's hard enough being a detective. For Lionel it's a uniquely difficult challenge being exposed to so much direct, unfiltered contact with all of the messy particulars of the world. As he says of himself, Lionel has not only Tourette's but also meta-Tourette's. Not just ticcing, but "[t]hinking about ticcing . . . mind racing, thoughts reaching to touch every possible symptom. Touching touching. Counting counting. Thinking thinking."

It's in that progression from touching to thinking, longing for "ritual contact just to make myself feel at home" that *Motherless Brooklyn* derives its energy, its brilliance and originality. For Lionel Essrog, language is always bubbling "inside . . . the frozen sea melting . . . too dangerous to let out." But it does come out, in spurts and squirts. And that's the issue. It's always there, underneath, pushing outward. The pressure has to go somewhere and it finds its conduit in language, a stream of words in search of a target. A detective looking for patterns in a world that seems to forever remain just out of grasp.

Constantly looking for meaning and, failing to find it, Lionel resorts to manufacturing it for himself. "Assertions and generalizations are . . . a version of Tourette's. A way of touching the world, handling it, covering it with confirming language." So too are conspiracies, "the making and tracing of unexpected connections a kind of touchiness, an expression of the yearning to touch the world, kiss it all over with theories, pull it close." This touchiness, this yearning can sometimes endear him to others – those who already love or tolerate him. More often, it makes people uncomfortable, preventing intimacy, deeper contact with others, with the world underneath the words, the connection he longs for.

So Lionel stays lonely. He has his moments, brushes with people who care for him (most of all, Frank Minna), who flirt with him, who want to use him. Music is a temporary reprieve, as are cheeseburgers and self-love. Lethem has said that, underneath, of bookstores, including Pegasus and Pendragon, landing finally at the venerable Moe's Books on Telegraph Avenue:

It was at Moe's, in that huge literature section, that I was constantly discovering all these forgotten authors that I ended up being powerfully influenced by. Just handling this ocean of different books – new and used, in and out of print, famous and forgotten – it was literature as this giant mosaic of texts and experiments and attitudes.

That influence can be felt in his early novels, written while Lethem was still working as a bookseller, including his *Gun, With Occasional Music* (which drew comparisons to Raymond Chandler and Philip K. Dick) and *As She Climbed Across the Table* (my first Lethem, I read most of it one afternoon in Berkeley while seated upstairs at Cafe Milano on Bancroft, stopping occasionally to watch two old men play chess; a quarter-century later, I still remember it as one of the books that made me want to write fiction.)

In 1996, Lethem moved back to New York City and began writing *Motherless Brooklyn*, the story of Lionel Essrog, a would-be detective with Tourette's syndrome, who is the character of his that Lethem has said he most identifies with. Through Lionel, compulsion becomes the engine of endless variation: an unceasing performance of manic improvisation. Lionel can't help but riff on anything and everything. For Lionel, the city and its inhabitants are an infinite source of surprise, epiphany and error, chatter and gossip, a never-ending stream of natural speech to be heard and misheard. In Lionel's mind, fragments of language evolve through recombination and mutation, branching out in new directions. Most of those directions trail off into nonsense, but a few wander their way into discovery, into new meanings.

Early on in the novel, Lionel loses his boss and mentor, Frank Minna. For Lionel, Frank is more than that: he's a kind of father figure, a protector to Lionel and the other Minna Men. With Minna gone, the center of their world has been removed, and Minna's acolytes spin centrifugally in different directions. Previously tethered to each other through employment and in their shared identity, the Minna Men find themselves alone. For

JONATHAN LETHEM

MOTHERLESS BROOKLYN
THE FORTRESS OF SOLITUDE

WITH AN INTRODUCTION
BY CHARLES YU

EVERYMAN'S LIBRARY
Alfred A. Knopf New York London Toronto

430

THIS IS A BORZOI BOOK
PUBLISHED BY ALFRED A. KNOPF

First included in Everyman's Library, 2024

Motherless Brooklyn
Copyright © 1999 by Jonathan Lethem

The Fortress of Solitude
Copyright © 2003 by Jonathan Lethem

Introduction copyright © 2024 by Charles Yu
Bibliography and Chronology copyright © 2024 by Everyman's Library

Motherless Brooklyn originally published in the United States by
Doubleday, a division of Random House, Inc., New York in 1999 and in
Great Britain by Faber and Faber Limited, London, in 2000. *The Fortress
of Solitude* originally published in the United States by Doubleday,
a division of Random House, Inc., New York, in 2003 and in Great
Britain by Faber and Faber Limited, London, in 2003.

everymanslibrary.com
www.everymanslibrary.co.uk

ISBN: 978-1-101-90848-8 (US)
978-1-84159-430-9 (UK)

A CIP catalogue reference for this book is available from the
British Library

Typography by Peter B. Willberg

Book design by Barbara de Wilde and Carol Devine Carson

Typeset in the UK by Input Data Services Ltd, Bridgwater, Somerset

Printed and bound in Germany by GGP Media GmbH, Pössneck

CONTENTS

his "books all have this giant, howling missing [center] – language has disappeared, or someone has vanished, or memory has gone" and this missing center is acutely felt by Lionel Essrog.

But occasionally, that missing center is located, briefly. In the form of Carlotta Minna, an "old stove" who cooks for her son Frank and his Minna Men, serves them "plates of sautéed squid and stuffed peppers," and who gives Lionel what he craves most in a motherless city – the touch of a mother:

> . . . Carlotta hovered . . . over the backs of our chairs . . . gently touching our heads, the napes of our necks. We pretended not to notice, ashamed in front of one another and ourselves to show that we drank in her nurturance . . . But we drank it. It was Christmas, after all.

*

In 2003, four years after *Motherless Brooklyn*, Lethem published *The Fortress of Solitude*. A chronicle of 1970s Brooklyn centered on Dean Street, a fictional neighborhood block and a cosmos, dense and rich with its own mythologies. A novel of breadth and depth, scope and intimacy, it's a story of friendship and love, of two boys, Dylan Ebdus and Mingus Rude, one white and one Black, their inner lives and outer ones, starting from their teenage adventures and following them on diverging paths through the decades.

If Lionel Essrog is the character with whom Lethem most identifies, then Dylan Ebdus is the one whose biographical details map most closely onto Lethem's own. A Jewish kid growing up in Brooklyn, an outsider. A visible target who retreats to his room, to music and comics. The parallels extend beyond Dylan to his parents, his father Abraham, an artist, and his mother, whose role in the novel is felt less as a character and more as an absence. In the 1970s, Lethem's own parents moved their family to Brooklyn, a section of northern Gowanus now known as Boerum Hill. As one of the few white kids in a then mostly Black and Puerto Rican neighborhood, Lethem was a visible outlier, bullied throughout his childhood. Like Dylan Ebdus, a teenage Jonathan Lethem sought refuge in music and comics. And books.

But where *Motherless Brooklyn* is circular, inward, relatively

compact ("wheels within wheels"), *The Fortress of Solitude* is sprawling, spanning decades, both coasts (east then west), with detours
to summer camp and then Camden (a fictional stand-in for Bennington College). It covers the idyllic (and not so idyllic) adolescent
years, a period of intense friendship and closeness between Dylan
and Mingus, years in which Dean Street seemed to be a whole
world unto itself. Afternoons with "dazing slackness." A period
when best friends are defined by secrets, and secret identities. A
period of magic. Years later, we catch up with the pair, their paths
having carried them away from each other. Dylan in California.
Mingus in and out of prison. The Dean Street they once inhabited
now gentrified. Lost to the past. We get a sense of this loss in the
words from Dylan, by then a music critic:

Voices in memory you can't name, rich with unresolved yearning: a
song you once leaned toward for an instant on the radio before finding
it mawkish, embarrassing, overlush. Maybe the song knew something
you didn't yet . . . By chance it goes unheard for fifteen years, until the
day when your own heartbreak unexpectedly finds its due date.

These two novels, each significant on their own, also fit snugly
under one cover. Although their Brooklyns are different (Minna's
Court Street, the "old Brooklyn, a placid ageless surface alive
underneath with talk" feels far from the Dean Street of Rude
and Ebdus and Woolfolk), the two works share more than a
common geography. *Motherless Brooklyn* and *The Fortress of Solitude*
could swap titles and the result would be equally fitting, if not
more so. Dylan and Mingus are both motherless. Lionel Essrog
has a solitary existence, trapped in the fortress of his own mind.
Music soothes his compulsions, eases the pressure, music that
"toyed with feelings of claustrophobic discomfort and expulsive
release . . . guitar and voice twitching and throbbing within obsessively delineated bounds, alternately silent and plosive." Listening to Prince, Lionel is "exempt from [his] symptoms." Music
also provides comfort and solace to Dylan Ebdus, who writes:

The voices of Barrett Rude Jr. and the Subtle Distinctions lead nowhere, though, if not back to your own neighborhood. To the street
where you live. To things you left behind.

INTRODUCTION

Both Dylan and Lionel share at their center an instability. That giant, howling, missing center. A common impulse or itch, a quality that turns them inward, wheels within wheels, distinctions on top of distinctions. A nervous energy, obsessive, forever searching. Back-of-the-store guys.

Lethem has said he's "always liked working from that sense of . . . license that the margins permit," visualizing himself "writing books that were meant one day to be dusty, forgotten volumes being encountered by intrepid browsers in a used bookstore." This volume you're holding is one of the many reasons why that's unlikely to happen. With fractal intensity and a seemingly encyclopedic mind, Lethem is a creator and protector of the forgotten. A possessor of secret powers. Through his work, we visit new spaces, spaces in the middle of a neighborhood block, or your best friend's bedroom, or a summer afternoon. In the words of Dylan Ebdus:

We all pined for those middle spaces, those summer hours when Josephine Baker lay waste to Paris . . . when a top-to-bottom burner blazed through a subway station, renovating the world for an instant . . . A middle space opened and closed like a glance, you'd miss it if you blinked . . . In the same spirit, on Rachel's principles, I'd been pushed out like a blind finger, to probe a nonexistent space, a white-boy integrating public schools which were just then being abandoned, which were becoming only rehearsals for prison. Her mistake was so beautiful, so stupid, so American. It terrified my small mind, it always had. Abraham had the better idea, to try to carve the middle space on a daily basis, alone in his room . . . We were in a middle space then, in a cone of white, father and son moving forward at a certain speed.

Reading Lethem transports me back to my own middle space. Berkeley, Saturday night at Moe's, five minutes to closing. Reading Lethem, it always seems possible I'm a detective on a case. It seems possible I am "first awake in the world, possible the world was new."

Charles Yu

SELECT BIBLIOGRAPHY

JOSEPH BROOKER, *Jonathan Lethem and the Galaxy of Writing*, Bloomsbury Academic, New York, 2019.

JAIME CLARKE, *Conversations with Jonathan Lethem*, University Press of Mississippi, Jackson, MS, 2011.

DAN FOX, "Jonathan Lethem's Not-Quite-Last Interview," *Substack*, Issue 34, December 17, 2023.

RIVKA GALCHEN, "In Between the Dream and the Doorknob: On Jonathan Lethem's Fictions," *Ecotone*, University of North Carolina, Wilmington, Vol. 5, No. 1, Fall 2009.

EVAN HUGHES, *Literary Brooklyn: The Writers of Brooklyn and the Story of American City Life*, Henry Holt, New York, 2011.

MATTHEW LUTER, *Understanding Jonathan Lethem*, University of South Carolina Press, Columbia, SC, 2015.

JAMES PEACOCK, *Jonathan Lethem*, Manchester University Press, Manchester, UK, 2012.

CARSTEN SCHINKO, *Sonic Fictions of America*, Universitätsverlag Winter, Heidelberg, Germany, 2021.

STACIE WILLIAMS, *Bizarro Worlds: Jonathan Lethem's The Fortress of Solitude*, Fiction Advocate, New York, 2018.

CHRONOLOGY

DATE	AUTHOR'S LIFE	LITERARY CONTEXT
1964	Born on February 19 in Manhattan; family soon moves to Kansas City, then Brooklyn.	Bellow: *Herzog.* Berne: *Games People Play.* Cheever: *The Wapshot Scandal.* Selby: *Last Exit to Brooklyn.* Thompson: *Pop. 1280.*
1965		Herlihy: *Midnight Cowboy.* Mailer: *An American Dream.* Wolfe: *The Kandy-Kolored Tangerine-Flake Streamline Baby.*
1966		Barth: *Giles Goat-Boy.* Capote: *In Cold Blood.* Pynchon: *The Crying of Lot 49.* Stout: *Death of a Doxy.* Susann: *Valley of the Dolls.*
1967		Levin: *Rosemary's Baby.* Manchester: *The Death of a President.* Styron: *The Confessions of Nat Turner.* Thomas: *Down These Mean Streets.* Thompson: *Hell's Angels.*
1968		Cleaver: *Soul on Ice.* Dick: *Do Androids Dream of Electric Sheep?* Derleth: *Wisconsin Murders.* Mailer: *Armies of the Night.* Updike: *Couples.* Vidal: *Myra Breckinridge.* Wolfe: *The Electric Kool-Aid Acid Test.*
1969		Angelou: *I Know Why the Caged Bird Sings.* Bradbury: *I Sing the Body Electric.* Greenlee: *The Spook Who Sat by the Door.* McPherson: *Hue and Cry: Stories.* Puzo: *The Godfather.* Oates: *Them.* Roth: *Portnoy's Complaint.*

HISTORICAL EVENTS

Warren Report into Kennedy assassination published. Civil Rights Act outlaws racial discrimination. Martin Luther King receives Nobel Peace Prize.

US bombs North Vietnam. Malcolm X assassinated.

Black Panthers founded, Oakland, California. Vietnam War: US planes bomb Hanoi and Haiphong. China: Mao launches Cultural Revolution, period of Red Terror (to 1976).

Racial violence in many US cities; President Johnson appoints commission to investigate causes. "Summer of Love," Haight-Ashbury, California. Six-Day War between Israel and Arab states. Che Guevara shot dead, Bolivia.

Student protests in US and throughout Europe. Martin Luther King Jr. and Robert F. Kennedy assassinated. Nixon elected US president. Shirley Chisholm first Black woman elected to US House of Representatives. Soviet invasion of Czechoslovakia.

Neil Armstrong first man on moon. US troops begin withdrawal from Vietnam. Woodstock rock festival attended by 400,000 in New York State. Harlem Cultural Festival holds six concerts with joint attendance of 300,000. The New York Mets win the World Series.

DATE	AUTHOR'S LIFE	LITERARY CONTEXT
1970		Dickey: *Deliverance*.
		Fo: *Accidental Death of an Anarchist*.
		Higgins: *The Friends of Eddie Coyle*.
		Márquez: *One Hundred Years of Solitude*.
		Morrison: *The Bluest Eye*.
1971		Blatty: *The Exorcist*.
		McCarthy: *Birds of America*.
		O'Connor: *The Complete Stories*.
		Stegner: *Angle of Repose*.
		Thompson: *Fear and Loathing in Las Vegas*.
1972		Calvino: *Invisible Cities*.
1973		Algren: *The Last Carousel*.
		Pynchon: *Gravity's Rainbow*.
1974		Benchley: *Jaws*.
		Heller: *Something Happened*.
		King: *Carrie*.
1975		Bellow: *Humboldt's Gift*.
		Doctorow: *Ragtime*.
		Stout: *A Family Affair*.
1976		Carver: *Will You Please Be Quiet, Please?*
		Haley: *Roots*.
		Selby: *The Demon*.
1977		Cheever: *Falconer*.
		King: *The Shining*.
		Morrison: *Song of Solomon*.
1978	Death of mother, Judith Frank Lethem.	Irving: *The World According to Garp*.
		Selby: *Requiem for a Dream*.
1979		Mailer: *The Executioner's Song*.
		Roth: *The Ghost Writer*.
		Sorrentino: *Mulligan Stew*.
		Styron: *Sophie's Choice*.
1980		King: *Firestarter*.
		Ludlum: *The Bourne Identity*.
		Robinson: *Housekeeping*.

CHRONOLOGY

US invades Cambodia. "Women's Strike for Equality," celebrating the fiftieth anniversary of women having the right to vote in the US with an estimated attendance of 50,000 in New York. Jordan: Black September conflict. Chile: Allende becomes world's first democratically elected Communist head of state. France: De Gaulle dies.

Voting age lowered to eighteen in US. India and Pakistan border disputes erupt into full-scale war.

US and USSR sign Strategic Arms Limitation Treaty (SALT I). Eleven Israeli athletes killed by Arab guerrillas at Olympic Village, Munich. Watergate scandal (to 1974): Democratic National Committee headquarters burgled. Shirley Chisholm first Black person to bid for the Democratic presidential nomination (is unsuccessful). *Ms.* magazine launched. Military coup in Chile: General Pinochet comes to power. Yom Kippur War; oil crisis. Supreme Court in US rules that abortion is legal and suspends capital punishment (until 1976). Mobile phones first marketed. Nixon resigns after Watergate scandal; Gerald Ford becomes US president.

Vietnam War ends. Bill Gates and Paul Allen found Microsoft.

Jimmy Carter elected US president. Chairman Mao dies. First Apple computer.

Elvis Presley dies. New York City struck by citywide blackout. Final episode of *Roots* airs, viewed in 36 million households.

Camp David Agreement signed by Carter, President Sadat of Egypt and Menachem Begin, Israeli prime minister.

Soviet troops occupy Afghanistan. Carter and Brezhnev sign SALT II. Shah of Iran forced into exile; Ayatollah Khomeini establishes an Islamic state; American embassy siege in Tehran. Margaret Thatcher becomes the UK's first woman prime minister.
Ronald Reagan elected US president. Iran–Iraq War begins (to 1988).

DATE	AUTHOR'S LIFE	LITERARY CONTEXT
1981		Carver: *What We Talk About When We Talk About Love.* Rushdie: *Midnight's Children.* Calvino: *If on a winter's night a traveler.*
1982	Enters Bennington College in Vermont.	Galeano: *Memory of Fire.* Walker: *The Color Purple.*
1983		Carver: *Cathedral.* Vidal: *Duluth.* Márquez: *Chronicle of a Death Foretold.*
1984	Drops out of college; goes to California.	Amis: *Money.* King & Straub: *The Talisman.* Updike: *The Witches of Eastwick.* Willeford: *Miami Blues.*
1985		Atwood: *The Handmaid's Tale.* Auster: *The New York Trilogy* (to 1986). DeLillo: *White Noise.* Ellis: *Less than Zero.* McCarthy: *Blood Meridian.* Levi: *If Not Now, When?*
1986		Amis: *The Moronic Inferno.* Hiaasen: *Tourist Season.* King: *IT.* Stead: *I'm Dying Laughing: The Humourist.*
1987		Ellroy: *L.A. Quartet* (to 1992). Morrison: *Beloved.* Turow: *Presumed Innocent.* Wolfe: *The Bonfire of the Vanities.*
1988		Chabon: *The Mysteries of Pittsburgh.* DeLillo: *Libra.* Harris: *The Silence of the Lambs.* Rushdie: *The Satanic Verses.*
1989	Publishes first short story.	Irving: *A Prayer for Owen Meany.* King: *The Dark Half.* Wolff: *This Boy's Life: A Memoir.*

CHRONOLOGY

Assassination attempt on Reagan, Washington. Sandra Day O'Connor first woman to serve on the US Supreme Court. Maiden voyage of Space Shuttle. Egypt: Sadat killed by Islamic fundamentalists. IBM Personal Computer launched.

Equal Rights Amendment does not meet requirement of 38 state ratifications, and is not adopted as a constitutional amendment. Beginning of 1980s stock market boom in US. Lebanese Civil War: multinational force lands in Beirut to oversee the PLO withdrawal from Lebanon. Falklands War between Argentina and UK.
US troops invade Grenada after government overthrown. Martin Luther King Jr.'s birthday becomes federal holiday. CDs launched.

Reagan re-elected in landslide. Indian prime minister Indira Gandhi assassinated. Famine in Ethiopia.

Reform begins in USSR under Mikhail Gorbachev, new general secretary of the Communist Party.

US bombs Libya. Gorbachev–Reagan summit. Nuclear explosion in Chernobyl, USSR. The New York Mets win the World Series.

Reagan makes Berlin Wall speech. World population reaches five billion.

George H. W. Bush elected US president. Soviet troops withdrawn in large numbers from Afghanistan.

Berlin Wall dismantled. Communism collapses in Eastern Europe. USSR holds first democratic elections. Tiananmen Square massacre in China. US troops invade Panama. Tim Berners-Lee publishes research paper proposing World Wide Web.

DATE	AUTHOR'S LIFE	LITERARY CONTEXT
1990		Byatt: *Possession*.
		Crichton: *Jurassic Park*.
		Pynchon: *Vineland*.
1991		Ellis: *American Psycho*.
		Gray: *Poor Things: Episodes from the Early Life of Archibald McCandless M.D., Scottish Public Health Officer*.
		Grisham: *The Firm*.
		Okri: *The Famished Road*.
		Smiley: *A Thousand Acres*.
1992		Grisham: *The Pelican Brief*.
		McCarthy: *The Border Trilogy* (to 1998).
		Tartt: *The Secret History*.
1993		Proulx: *The Shipping News*.
		Welsh: *Trainspotting*.
1994	First novel, *Gun, with Occasional Music* is published.	Grisham: *The Chamber*.
		Heller: *Closing Time*.
		King: *Insomniac*.
1995	*Amnesia Moon* (novel).	Ellroy: *Underworld USA Trilogy* (to 2009).
		Roth: *Sabbath's Theater*.
1996	*The Wall of the Sky, the Wall of the Eye* (story collection), wins the World Fantasy Award for best collection.	Atwood: *Alias Grace*.
		Palahniuk: *Fight Club*.
		Wallace: *Infinite Jest*.
1997	*As She Climbed Across the Table* (novel).	Bellow: *The Actual*.
		DeLillo: *Underworld*.
		Frazier: *Cold Mountain*.
		Pynchon: *Mason & Dixon*.
		Roth: *American Pastoral*.
1998	*Girl in Landscape* (novel).	Bolaño: *The Savage Detectives*.
		Morrison: *Paradise*.
		Roth: *I Married a Communist*.
1999	Publication of *Motherless Brooklyn*, which wins the National Book Critics Circle Award; *Kafka Americana*, with Carter Scholz (story collection).	Coetzee: *Disgrace*.
		Jin: *Waiting*.
		Southwell: *Conspiracy Theories*.
		Sontag: *In America*.
		Stephenson: *Cryptonomicon*.
		Whitehead: *The Intuitionist*.
2000		Brown: *Angels & Demons*.
		Hiaasen: *Sick Puppy*.
		Murakami: *Norwegian Wood*.
		Roth: *The Human Stain*.

CHRONOLOGY

Nelson Mandela released in South Africa. Boris Yeltsin elected first leader of Russian Federation after end of Communist rule. NASA deploys Hubble Space Telescope.
Gulf War begins. War breaks out in former Yugoslavia. Apartheid ends in South Africa. Bush and Gorbachev sign START arms reduction treaty. Clarence Thomas appointed to US Supreme Court.

Bill Clinton elected US president. Riots in Los Angeles.

Palestinian leader Yasser Arafat signs peace agreement with Israeli prime minister Yitzhak Rabin. World Trade Center bombing.
Mandela's ANC takes power after South African elections. Civil war in Rwanda. Russia takes military action in Chechen Republic. Jordan and Israel sign peace treaty.
Rabin assassinated in Israel. Oklahoma City bombing. Launch of eBay. First "Million Man March" held in Washington DC.

Clinton re-elected US president. UN adopts Comprehensive Nuclear Test Ban Treaty.

Hong Kong sovereignty given back to China by UK. Economic crisis: stock markets around the world crash, Dow Jones Industrial Average plummets. Death of Princess Diana in Paris. First public use of WiFi. "Million Woman March" held in Philadelphia.

Clinton impeached over sex scandal (acquitted 1999). Good Friday peace agreement in Northern Ireland. Google founded.

Ethnic Albanians attacked by Serbs in Kosovo; US leads NATO in bombing of Belgrade. Columbine High School shooting.

George W. Bush elected US president. Vladimir Putin succeeds Yeltsin as Russian president. Slobodan Milosevic's regime collapses in former Yugoslavia.

DATE	AUTHOR'S LIFE	LITERARY CONTEXT
2001	*This Shape We're In* (novella); editor of *The Vintage Book of Amnesia*.	Franzen: *The Corrections*. Moore: *Stupid White Men*. Russo: *Empire Falls*.
2002	Editor of *Da Capo Best Music Writing 2002: The Year's Finest Writing on Rock, Pop, Jazz, Country and More*.	Auster: *The Book of Illusions*. Carter: *The Emperor of Ocean Park*. Eugenides: *Middlesex*.
2003	Publication of *The Fortress of Solitude*, which becomes a *New York Times* bestseller.	Brown: *The Da Vinci Code*. Gibson: *Pattern Recognition*. DeLillo: *Cosmopolis*. Shriver: *We Need to Talk About Kevin*.
2004	*Men and Cartoons* (story collection).	Robinson: *Gilead*. Roth: *The Plot Against America*.
2005	Receives a MacArthur Fellowship; *The Disappointment Artist* (essay collection).	Didion: *The Year of Magical Thinking*. Ellis: *Lunar Park*. Ishiguro: *Never Let Me Go*. Koontz: *Velocity*. Larsson: *The Girl with the Dragon Tattoo*.
2006	*How We Got Insipid* (story collection); *Believeniks!: 2005: The Year We Wrote a Book About the Mets* (written with Christopher Sorrentino, as "Ivan Felt and Harris Conklin").	Adichie: *Half of a Yellow Sun*. McCarthy: *The Road*. Pynchon: *Against the Day*. Updike: *Terrorist*.
2007	*You Don't Love Me Yet* (novel); *Omega the Unknown* (comic); *The Light and the Sufferer* (film directed by Christopher Peditto, based on a story by Lethem).	Diaz: *The Brief Wondrous Life of Oscar Wao*. Klein: *The Shock Doctrine*. Russo: *Bridge of Sighs*.
2008		Robinson: *Home*. Roth: *Indignation*.
2009	*Chronic City* (novel).	Larsson: *The Girl Who Played with Fire*. Moore: *The Gate at the Stairs*. Roth: *The Humbling*.
2010	*They Live* (non-fiction/film).	Coover: *Noir*. Egan: *A Visit from the Goon Squad*. Ferris: *The Unnamed*. Larsson: *The Girl Who Kicked the Hornets' Nest*. Roth: *Nemesis*.

CHRONOLOGY

Al-Qaeda attacks New York's World Trade Center; US and allies take action against Taliban in Afghanistan. Wikipedia launched.

Bush creates Department of Homeland Security. Moscow theater hostage crisis.

US and British troops invade Iraq; Saddam Hussein captured.

Bush re-elected US president. Terrorist bombings in Madrid. Tsunami in Indian Ocean. Facebook launched.
Hurricane Katrina floods New Orleans. Rosa Parks dies. Terrorist bombings in London. YouTube founded.

Iran joins "nuclear club." North Korea tests nuclear weapon. Saddam Hussein sentenced to death.

Virginia Tech shooting. Bush reduces US forces in Iraq. Al Gore and UN climate scientists win Nobel Peace Prize. Nancy Pelosi elected first female Speaker of US Congress. iPhone introduced.

Barack Obama, Democratic senator from Illinois, elected first Black president of the United States. Collapse of Lehman Brothers triggers world financial crisis.
Ongoing world financial crisis. H1N1 ("swine flu") global pandemic. Barack Obama awarded Nobel Peace Prize.

Healthcare Reform Bill passed by President Obama. Deepwater Horizon (BP rig) oil spill in Gulf of Mexico. US combat mission ends in Iraq. iPad introduced.

DATE	AUTHOR'S LIFE	LITERARY CONTEXT
2011	Begins teaching position at Pomona College as the Roy Edward Disney '51 Professor of Creative Writing and Professor of English; speaks at Occupy Wall Street; *The Ecstasy of Influence: Nonfictions, etc.* (essay collection); *The Exegesis of Philip K. Dick* (edited by Lethem and Pamela Jackson); *The Epiphany* (short film by S. J. Chiro based on a story by Lethem).	Child: *The Affair.* Murakami: *1Q84.* Wallace: *The Pale King.*
2012	*Fear of Music* (non-fiction/music).	Leonard: *Raylan.* Robinson: *2312.*
2013	*Dissident Gardens* (novel).	Adichie: *Americanah.* Kimmel: *Angry White Men.* Laymon: *Long Division.* Saunders: *Tenth of December: Stories.* Tartt: *The Goldfinch.*
2014		Grossman: *A Horse Walks into a Bar.*
2015	*Lucky Alan and Other Stories.*	Franzen: *Purity.* Hannaham: *Delicious Foods.* Lee: *Go Set a Watchman.* Morrison: *God Help the Child.* Stephenson: *Seveneves.* Yanagihara: *A Little Life.*
2016	*A Gambler's Anatomy* (novel; published in the UK as *The Blot*).	Alderman: *The Power.*
2017		Auster: *4 3 2 1.* Diaz: *In the Distance.* Saunders: *Lincoln in the Bardo.* Strout: *Anything Is Possible.*
2018	*The Feral Detective* (novel).	Burns: *The Milkman.* Moshfegh: *My Year of Rest and Relaxation.* Wolff: *Fire and Fury.*
2019	Film of *Motherless Brooklyn*, screenplay by Edward Norton;	Jones: *An American Marriage.* Luiselli: *Lost Children Archive.*

CHRONOLOGY

"Arab Spring": protests and rebellions against repressive regimes across Middle East. Syrian Civil War begins. Osama Bin Laden killed by US Navy Seals. "Don't Ask, Don't Tell" policy repealed. Martin Luther King Jr. Memorial opens to the public. The Occupy Wall Street protest movement begins in Zuccotti Park, Manhattan.

Obama re-elected US president. Mars Science Laboratory ("Curiosity Rover") lands on Mars. Xi Jinping becomes General Secretary of Chinese Communist Party. Hurricane Sandy. Sandy Hook shooting. Trayvon Martin, 17 years old, shot and killed by police in Florida.
Edward Snowden leaks classified documents revealing mass surveillance by the US National Security Agency. Boston Marathon bombing. Black Lives Matter movement begins.

Russia annexes Crimea. ISIS declares Islamic Caliphate.

Iran agrees deal on nuclear program with world powers. Paris Climate Accord commits majority of countries to reducing greenhouse gas emissions. Islamic terror attacks in Paris. Refugee crisis in Europe. Supreme Court rules that all states must recognize same-sex marriage. Charleston Church shooting.

Donald Trump wins US presidential election. UK referendum on EU membership results in "Leave" vote. North Korea begins missile and nuclear testing. Coup in Turkey fails. National Museum of African American History opens doors to public.
Trump takes up office of president, promising to "make America great again." Xi Jinping granted second term as general secretary of Chinese Communist Party. North Korean crisis (to 2018).

"Trade War"; Trump imposes tariffs on imports from China. Trump announces his intention to withdraw the United States from the Iranian nuclear agreement but negotiates with North Korea's Kim Jong-un over denuclearization. #MeToo movement goes global. Meghan Markle marries Prince Harry.
Hong Kong protests (to 2020). President Donald Trump impeached. Amazon rainforest wildfires. North Korea nuclear negotiations continue

JONATHAN LETHEM

DATE	AUTHOR'S LIFE	LITERARY CONTEXT
2019 *cont.*	*More Alive and Less Lonely: On Books and Writers* (essays); awarded the Raymond Chandler Prize in Italy.	
2020	*The Arrest* (novel).	DeLillo: *The Silence*. Offill: *Weather*. Robinson: *Jack*.
2021		Everett: *The Trees*. Ishiguro: *Klara and the Sun*. Franzen: *Crossroads*. Mott: *Hell of a Book*.
2022		Hannaham: *Didn't Nobody Give a Shit What Happened to Carlotta*. McCarthy: *The Passenger*. Egan: *The Candy House*. Yanagihara: *To Paradise*.
2023	*Brooklyn Crime Novel* (novel).	Whitehead: *Crook Manifesto*.
2024	*The Collapsing Frontier* (stories and essays); *Cellophane Bricks* (art writings).	Márquez: *Until August*.

CHRONOLOGY

with no agreement. First COVID-19 case in Wuhan, China. Boris Johnson elected as prime minister in UK.

COVID-19 declared a pandemic by World Health Organization. Climate disasters continue: Australia fire season, US wildfires, droughts and tropical storms. George Floyd killed by police, triggering worldwide Black Lives Matter protests. Joe Biden elected as president; Kamala Harris elected first Black vice president of the US.

Trump supporters storm the Capitol building in protest of election results. US commits to rejoin Paris Climate Agreement. COVID-19 vaccine created. Last US troops withdraw from Afghanistan – Taliban take over country.

Russia invades Ukraine. Roe v. Wade overturned by Supreme Court; constitutional protections for abortion severed. Inflation rises worldwide. Protesters in Iran march against the country's treatment of women. Pakistan flooding crisis. Death of Queen Elizabeth II.

Turkey–Syria earthquake. 37-count indictment against former president Donald Trump; date of trial set. Coronation of King Charles III in UK. Israel–Hamas war – worldwide protests calling for ceasefire.

MOTHERLESS
BROOKLYN

For my Father

WALKS INTO

CONTEXT IS EVERYTHING. Dress me up and see. I'm a carnival barker, an auctioneer, a downtown performance artist, a speaker in tongues, a senator drunk on filibuster. *I've got Tourette's.* My mouth won't quit, though mostly I whisper or subvocalize like I'm reading aloud, my Adam's apple bobbing, jaw muscle beating like a miniature heart under my cheek, the noise suppressed, the words escaping silently, mere ghosts of themselves, husks empty of breath and tone. (If I were a Dick Tracy villain, I'd have to be Mumbles.) In this diminished form the words rush out of the cornucopia of my brain to course over the surface of the world, tickling reality like fingers on piano keys. Caressing, nudging. They're an invisible army on a peacekeeping mission, a peaceable horde. They mean no harm. They placate, interpret, massage. Everywhere they're smoothing down imperfections, putting hairs in place, putting ducks in a row, replacing divots. Counting and polishing the silver. Patting old ladies gently on the behind, eliciting a giggle. Only – here's the rub – when they find too much perfection, when the surface is already buffed smooth, the ducks already orderly, the old ladies complacent, then my little army rebels, breaks into the stores. Reality needs a prick here and there, the carpet needs a flaw. My words begin plucking at threads nervously, seeking purchase, a weak point, a vulnerable ear. That's when it comes, the urge to shout in the church, the nursery, the crowded movie house. It's an itch at first. Inconsequential. But that itch is soon a torrent behind a straining dam. Noah's flood. That itch is my whole life. Here it comes now. Cover your ears. Build an ark.

"Eat me!" I scream.

* * *

"Maufishful," said Gilbert Coney in response to my outburst, not even turning his head. I could barely make out the words – "My mouth is full" – both truthful and a joke, lame. Accustomed to my verbal ticcing, he didn't usually bother to comment. Now he nudged the bag of White Castles in my direction on the car seat, crinkling the paper. "Stuffinyahole."

Coney didn't rate any special consideration from me. "Eatmeeatmeeatme," I shrieked again, letting off more of the pressure in my head. Then I was able to concentrate. I helped myself to one of the tiny burgers. Unwrapping it, I lifted the top of the bun to examine the grid of holes in the patty, the slime of glistening cubed onions. This was another compulsion. I always had to look inside a White Castle, to appreciate the contrast of machine-tooled burger and nubbin of fried goo. Kaos and Control. Then I did more or less as Gilbert had suggested – pushed it into my mouth whole. The ancient slogan *Buy 'em by the sack* humming deep in my head, jaw working to grind the slider into swallowable chunks, I turned back to stare out the window at the house.

Food really mellows me out.

We were putting a stakeout on 109 East Eighty-fourth Street, a lone town house pinned between giant doorman apartment buildings, in and out of the foyers of which bicycle deliverymen with bags of hot Chinese flitted like tired moths in the fading November light. It was dinner hour in Yorktown. Gilbert Coney and I had done our part to join the feast, detouring up into Spanish Harlem for the burgers. There's only one White Castle left in Manhattan, on East 103rd. It's not as good as some of the suburban outlets. You can't watch them prepare your order anymore, and to tell the truth I've begun to wonder if they're microwaving the buns instead of steaming them. Alas. Taking our boodle of thusly compromised sliders and fries back downtown, we double-parked in front of the target address until a spot opened up. It only took a couple of minutes, though by that time the doormen on either side had made us – made us as out-of-place and nosy anyway. We were driving the Lincoln, which didn't have the "T"-series license plates or stickers or anything else to identify it as a Car Service vehicle. And we were large men, me and Gilbert. They probably thought we were cops. It didn't matter. We chowed and watched.

Not that we knew what we were doing there. Minna had

sent us without saying why, which was usual enough, even if the address wasn't. Minna Agency errands mostly stuck us in Brooklyn, rarely far from Court Street, in fact. Carroll Gardens and Cobble Hill together made a crisscrossed game board of Frank Minna's alliances and enmities, and me and Gil Coney and the other Agency Men were the markers – like Monopoly pieces, I sometimes thought, tin automobiles or terriers (not top hats, surely) – to be moved around that game board. Here on the Upper East Side we were off our customary map, *Automobile* and *Terrier* in Candyland – or maybe in the study with Colonel Mustard.

"What's that sign?" said Coney. He pointed with his glistening chin at the town house doorway. I looked.

" 'Yorkville Zendo,' " I read off the bronze plaque on the door, and my fevered brain processed the words and settled with interest on the odd one. "Eat me Zendo!" I muttered through clenched teeth.

Gilbert took it, rightly, as my way of puzzling over the unfamiliarity. "Yeah, what's that *Zendo*? What's that?"

"Maybe like Zen," I said.

"I don't know from that."

"Zen like Buddhism," I said. "Zen master, you know."

"Zen master?"

"You know, like kung-fu master."

"Hrrph," said Coney.

And so after this brief turn at investigation we settled back into our complacent chewing. Of course after any talk my brain was busy with at least some low-level version of echolalia salad: *Don't know from Zendo, Ken-like Zung Fu, Feng Shui master, Fungo bastard, Zen masturbation, Eat me!* But it didn't require voicing, not now, not with White Castles to unscrew, inspect and devour. I was on my third. I fit it into my mouth, then glanced up at the doorway of One-oh-nine, jerking my head as if the building had been sneaking up on me. Coney and the other Minna Agency operatives loved doing stakeouts with me, since my compulsiveness forced me to eyeball the site or mark in question every thirty seconds or so, thereby saving them the trouble of swiveling their necks. A similar logic explained my popularity at wiretap parties – give me a key list of trigger words to listen for in a conversation and I'd think about nothing else, nearly jumping out of my clothes at hearing the slightest hint of one, while the same task invariably drew anyone else toward blissful sleep.

While I chewed on number three and monitored the uneventful Yorkville Zendo entrance my hands busily frisked the paper sack of Castles, counting to be sure I had three remaining. We'd purchased a bag of twelve, and not only did Coney know I had to have my six, he also knew he was pleasing me, tickling my Touretter's obsessive-compulsive instincts, by matching my number with his own. Gilbert Coney was a big lug with a heart of gold, I guess. Or maybe he was just trainable. My tics and obsessions kept the other Minna Men amused, but also wore them out, made them weirdly compliant and complicit.

A woman turned from the sidewalk onto the stoop of the town house and went up to the door. Short dark hair, squarish glasses, that was all I saw before her back was to us. She wore a pea coat. Sworls of black hair at her neck, under the boyish haircut. Twenty-five maybe, or maybe eighteen.

"She's going in," said Coney.

"Look, she's got a key," I said.

"What's Frank want us to do?"

"Just watch. Take a note. What time is it?"

Coney crumpled another Castle wrapper and pointed at the glove compartment. "You take a note. It's six forty-five."

I popped the compartment – the click-release of the plastic latch was a delicious hollow sound, which I knew I'd want to repeat, at least approximately – and found the small notebook inside. GIRL, I wrote, then crossed it out. WOMAN, HAIR, GLASSES, KEY. 6:45. The notes were to myself, since I only had to be able to report verbally to Minna. If that. For all we knew, he might want us out here to scare someone, or to wait for some delivery. I left the notebook beside the Castles on the seat between us and slapped the compartment door shut again, then delivered six redundant slaps to the same spot to ventilate my brain's pressure by reproducing the hollow thump I'd liked. Six was a lucky number tonight, six burgers, six forty-five. So six slaps.

* * *

For me, counting and touching things and repeating words are all the same activity. Tourette's is just one big lifetime of tag, really. The world (or my brain – same thing) appoints me *it*, again and again. So I tag back.

Can *it* do otherwise? If you've ever been *it* you know the answer.

* * *

"Boys" came the voice from the street side of the car, startling me and Coney both.

"Frank," I said.

It was Minna. He had his trench-coat collar up against the breeze, not quite cloaking his unshaven Robert-Ryan-in-*Wild-Bunch* grimace. He ducked down to the level of my window, as if he didn't want to be seen from the Yorkville Zendo. Squeaky cabs rocking-horsed past over the pothole in the street behind him. I rolled down the window, then reached out compulsively and touched his left shoulder, a regular gesture he'd not bothered to acknowledge for – how long? Say, fifteen years now, since when I'd first begun manifesting the urge as a thirteen-year-old and reached out for his then twenty-five-year-old street punk's bomber-jacketed shoulder. Fifteen years of taps and touches – if Frank Minna were a statue instead of flesh and blood I've have buffed that spot to a high shine, the way leagues of tourists burnish the noses and toes of bronze martyrs in Italian churches.

"What you doing here?" said Coney. He knew it had to be important to not only get Minna up here, but on his own steam, when he could have had us swing by to pick him up somewhere. Something complicated was going on, and – surprise! – we stooges were out of the loop again.

I whispered inaudibly through narrowed lips, *Stakeout, snakeout, ambush Zendo.*

The Lords of Snakebush.

"Gimme a smoke," said Minna. Coney leaned over me with a pack of Malls, one tapped out an inch or so for the boss to pluck. Minna put it in his mouth and lit it himself, pursing his brow in concentration, sheltering the lighter in the frame of his collar. He drew in, then gusted smoke into our airspace. "Okay, listen," he said, as though we weren't already hanging on his words.

Minna Men to the bone.

"I'm going in," he said, narrowing his eyes at the Zendo. "They'll buzz me. I'll swing the door wide. I want you" – he nodded at Coney – "to grab the door, get inside, just inside, and wait there, at the bottom of the stairs."

"What if they come meet you?" said Coney.

"Worry about that if it happens," said Minna curtly.

"Okay, but what if—"

Minna waved him off before he could finish. Really Coney was groping for comprehension of his role, but it wasn't forthcoming.

"Lionel—" started Minna.

* * *

Lionel, my name. Frank and the Minna Men pronounced it to rhyme with *vinyl*. Lionel Essrog. *Line-all.*

Liable Guesscog.

Final Escrow.

Ironic Pissclam.

And so on.

My own name was the original verbal taffy, by now stretched to filament-thin threads that lay all over the floor of my echo-chamber skull. Slack, the flavor all chewed out of it.

* * *

"Here." Minna dropped a radio monitor and headphones in my lap, then patted his rib pocket. "I'm wired. I'll be coming over that thing live. Listen close. If I say, uh, 'Not if my life depended on it,' you get out of the car and knock on the door here, Gilbert lets you in, two of you rush upstairs and find me quick, okay?"

Eat me, dickweed was almost dislodged from my mouth in the excitement, but I breathed in sharply and swallowed the words, said nothing instead.

"We're not carrying," said Coney.

"What?" said Minna.

"A piece, I don't have a piece."

"What's with *piece*? Say *gun*, Gilbert."

"No gun, Frank."

"That's what I count on. That's how I sleep at night, you have to know. You with no gun. I wouldn't want you chuckle-heads coming up a stairway behind me with a hairpin, with a harmonica, let alone a gun. I've got a gun. You just show up."

"Sorry, Frank."

"With an unlit cigar, with a fucking Buffalo chicken wing."

"Sorry, Frank."

"Just listen. If you hear me say, uh, 'First I gotta use the bathroom,' that means we're coming out. You get Gilbert, get back in the car, get ready to follow. You got it?"

Get, get, get, GOT! said my brain. *Duck, duck, duck, GOOSE!*

"Life depended, rush the Zendo," was what I said aloud. "Use the bathroom, start the car."

"Genius, Freakshow," said Minna. He pinched my cheek, then tossed his cigarette behind him into the street, where it tumbled, sparks scattering. His eyes were far away.

Coney got out of the car, and I scooted over to the driver's seat. Minna thumped the hood once, as if patting a dog on its head after saying *stay,* then slipped past the front bumper, put his finger up to slow Coney, crossed the pavement to the door of One-oh-nine, and hit the doorbell under the Zendo sign. Coney leaned against the car, waiting. I put on the headphones, got a clear sound of Minna's shoe scraping pavement over the wire so I knew it was working. When I looked up I saw the doorman from the big place to the right watching us, but he wasn't doing anything apart from watching.

I heard the buzzer sound, live and over the wire both. Minna went in, sweeping the door wide. Coney skipped over, grabbed the door, and disappeared inside, too.

Footsteps upstairs, no voices yet. Now suddenly I dwelled in two worlds, eyes and quivering body in the driver's seat of the Lincoln, watching from my parking spot the orderly street life of the Upper East Side, dog-walkers, deliverymen, girls and boys dressed as grown-ups in business suits shivering their way into gimmicky bars as the nightlife got under way, while my ears built a soundscape from the indoor echoes of Minna's movement up the stair, still nobody meeting him but he seemed to know where he was, shoe leather chafing on wood, stairs squeaking, then a hesitation, a rustle of clothing perhaps, then two wooden clunks, and the footsteps resumed more quietly. Minna had taken off his shoes.

Ringing the doorbell, then sneaking in? It didn't follow. But what in this sequence did follow? I palmed another Castle out of the paper sack – six burgers to restore order in a senseless world.

"*Frank*," came a voice over the wire.

"*I came*," said Minna wearily. "*But I shouldn't have to. You should clear up crap on your end.*"

"*I appreciate that*," went the other voice. "*But things have gotten complicated.*"

"*They know about the contract for the building*," said Minna.

"*No, I don't think so.*" The voice was weirdly calm, placating. Did I recognize it? Perhaps not that so much as the rhythm of Minna's replies – this was someone he knew well, but who?

"*Come inside, let's talk*," said the voice.

"*What about?*" said Minna. "*What do we have to talk about?*"

"*Listen to yourself, Frank.*"

"*I came here to listen to myself? I can do that at home.*"

"*But do you, in fact?*" I could hear a smile in the voice. "*Not as often, or as deeply as you might, I suspect.*"

"*Where's Ullman?*" said Minna. "*You got him here?*"

"*Ullman's downtown. You go to him.*"

"*Fuck.*"

"*Patience.*"

"*You say patience, I say fuck.*"

"*Characteristic, I suppose.*"

"*Yeah. So let's call the whole thing off.*"

More muffled footsteps, a door closing. A clunk, possibly a bottle and glass, a poured drink. Wine. I wouldn't have minded a beverage myself. I chewed on a Castle instead and gazed out the windshield, brain going *Characteristic autistic mystic my tic dipstick dickweek* and then I thought to take another note, flipped open the notebook and under WOMAN, HAIR, GLASSES wrote ULLMAN DOWNTOWN, thought Dull Man Out of Town. When I swallowed the burger, my jaw and throat tightened, and I braced for an unavoidable copralalic tic – out loud, though no one was there to hear it. "Eat shit, Bailey!"

Bailey was a name embedded in my Tourette's brain, though I couldn't say why. I'd never known a Bailey. Maybe Bailey was everyman, like George Bailey in *It's a Wonderful Life*. My imaginary listener, he had to bear the brunt of a majority of my solitary swearing – some part of me required a target, apparently. If a Touretter curses in the woods and there's nobody to hear does he make a sound? Bailey seemed to be my solution to that conundrum.

"*Your face betrays you, Frank. You'd like to murder someone.*"

"*You'd do fine for a start.*"

"*You shouldn't blame me, Frank, if you've lost control of her.*"

"*It's your fault if she misses her Rama-lama-ding-dong. You're the one who filled her head with that crap.*"

"*Here, try this.*" (Offering a drink?)

"*Not on an empty stomach.*"

"*Alas. I forget how you suffer, Frank.*"

"*Aw, go fuck yourself.*"

"Eat shit, Bailey!" The tics were always worst when I was nervous, stress kindling my Tourette's. And something in this scenario was making me nervous. The conversation I overheard was too knowing, the references all polished and opaque, as though years of dealings lay underneath every word.

Also, where was the short-dark-haired girl? In the room with Minna and his supercilious conversational partner, silent? Or somewhere else entirely? My inability to visualize the interior space of One-oh-nine was agitating. Was the girl the "she" they were discussing? It seemed unlikely.

And what was *her Rama-lama-ding-dong*? I didn't have the luxury of worrying about it. I pushed away a host of tics and tried not to dwell on things I didn't understand.

I glanced at the door. Presumably Coney was still behind it. I wanted to hear *not if my life depended on it* so we could rush the stairs.

I was startled by a knock on the driver's window. It was the doorman who'd been watching. He gestured for me to roll down the window. I shook my head, he nodded his. Finally I complied, pulling the headphones off one ear so I could listen.

"What?" I said, triply distracted – the power window had seduced my magpie mind and now demanded purposeless raising and lowering. I tried to keep it subtle.

"Your friend, he wants you," said the doorman, gesturing back toward his building.

"What?" This was thoroughly confusing. I craned my neck to see past him, but there was nobody visible in the doorway of his building. Meanwhile, Minna was saying something over the wire. But not *bathroom* or *depended on it*.

"Your friend," the doorman repeated in his clumsy Eastern European accent, maybe Polish or Czech. "He asks for you." He grinned, enjoying my bewilderment. I felt myself knitting my brow exaggeratedly, a tic, and wanted to tell him to wipe the grin off his face: Everything he was seeing was not to his credit.

"What friend?" I said. Minna and Coney were both inside – I would have noticed if the Zendo door had budged.

"He said if you're waiting, he's ready," said the doorman, nodding, gesturing again. "Wants to talk."

Now Minna was saying something about ". . . *make a mess on the marble floor* . . ."

"I think you've got the wrong guy," I said to the doorman. "*Dickweed!*" I winced, waved him off, tried to focus on the voices coming over the headphones.

"Hey, hey," the doorman said. He held up his hands. "I'm just bringing you a message, friend."

I zipped down the power window again, finally pried my fingers away. "No problem," I said, and suppressed another *dickweed* into a high, chihuahuaesque barking sound, something like *yipke!* "But I can't leave the car. Tell my *friend* if he wants to talk to come out and talk to me here. Okay, *friend*?" It seemed to me I had too many friends all of a sudden, and I didn't know any of their names. I repeated my impulsive flapping motion with my hand, an expedient tic-and-gesture combo, trying to nudge this buffoon back to his doorway.

"No, no. He said come in."

". . . *break an arm* . . ." I thought I heard Minna say.

"Get his name, then," I said, desperate. "Come back and tell me his name."

"He wants to talk to you."

"Okay, *eatmedoorman*, tell him I'll be right there." I powered up the window in his face. He tapped again, and I ignored him.

". . . *first let me use your toilet* . . ."

I opened the car door and pushed the doorman out of the way, went to the Zendo door and knocked, six times, hard. "Coney," I hissed. "Get out here."

Over the headset I heard Minna shut the bathroom door behind him, begin running water. "*Hope you heard that, Freakshow,*" he whispered into his microphone, addressing me directly. "*We're getting in a car. Don't lose us. Play it cool.*"

Coney popped out of the door.

"He's coming out," I said, pulling the headphones down around my neck.

"Okay," said Coney, eyes wide. We were in the thick of the action, for once.

"You drive," I said, touching my fingertip to his nose. He flinched me away like a fly. We hustled into the car, and Coney revved the engine. I threw the bag of cooling Castles and paper wreckage into the backseat. The idiot doorman had vanished into his building. I put him out of my mind for the moment.

We sat facing forward, our car shrouded in its own steam, waiting, vibrating. My brain went *Follow that car! Hollywood star! When you wish upon a cigar!* My jaw worked, chewing the words back down, keeping silent. Gilbert's hands gripped the wheel, mine drummed quietly in my lap, tiny hummingbird motions. This was what passed for playing it cool around here.

"I don't see him," said Coney.

"Just wait. He'll come out, with some other guys probably." *Probably, gobbledy.* I lifted one of the headphones to my right ear. No voices, nothing but clunking sounds, maybe the stairs.

"What if they get into a car behind us?" said Coney.

"It's a one-way street," I said, annoyed, but glancing backward at this cue to survey the parked cars behind us. 'Just let them pass."

"Hey," said Coney.

They'd appeared, slipping out the door and rushing ahead of us on the sidewalk while I'd turned: Minna and another man, a giant in a black coat. The other man was seven feet tall if he was an inch, with shoulders that looked as though football pads or angel wings were hidden under his coat. Or perhaps the petite short-haired girl was curled under there, clutching the tall man's shoulders like a human backpack. Was this giant the man who'd spoken so insinuatingly? Minna hurried ahead of the giant, as if he were motivated to give us the slip instead of dragging his heels to keep us in the game. Why? A gun in his back? The giant's hands were hidden in his pockets. For some reason I envisioned them gripping loaves of bread or large chunks of salami, snacks hidden in the coat to feed a giant in winter, comfort food.

Or maybe this fantasy was merely my own self-comfort: a loaf of bread couldn't be a gun, which allotted Minna the only firearm in the scenario.

We watched stupidly as they crossed between two parked cars and slid into the backseat of a black K-car that had rolled up from behind us in the street, then immediately took off. Overanxious as we were, Coney and I had at some level timed our reactions to allow for their starting a parked car, and now they were getting away. "Go!" I said.

Coney swerved to pull the Lincoln out of our spot, batted bumpers, hard enough to dent. Of course we were locked in. He backed, more gently thumped the rear end, then found an arc sufficient to free us from the space, but not before a cab had rocketed past us to block the way. The K-car tucked around the corner up ahead, onto Second Avenue. "Go!"

"Look," said Coney, pointing at the cab. "I'm going. Keep your eyes up."

"Eyes up?" I said. "Eyes out. *Chin* up." Correcting him was an involuntary response to stress.

"Yeah, that too."

"Eyes open, eyes on the road, ears glued to the radio—" I suddenly had to list every workable possibility. That was how irritating *eyes up* had been.

"Yeah, and trap buttoned," said Coney. He got us right on

the tail of the cab, better than nothing since it was moving fast. "What about gluing your ears to Frank while you're at it?"

I raised the headphones. Nothing but an overlay of traffic sounds to substitute for the ones I'd blotted out. Coney followed the cab onto Second Avenue, where the K-car obligingly waited in a thicket of cabs and other traffic for the light to change. We were back in the game, a notion exhilarating and yet pathetic by definition, since we'd lost them in the space of a block.

We merged left to pull around the first cab and into position behind another in the same lane as the car containing Minna and the giant. I watch the timed stoplights a half mile ahead turn red. Now there, I thought, was a job for someone with obsessive-compulsive symptoms – traffic management. Then our light turned green and we lurched all together, a floating quilt of black- and dun-colored private cars and the bright-orange cabs, through the intersection.

"Get closer," I said, pulling the phones from my ears again. Then an awesome tic wrenched its way out of my chest: "*Eat me Mister Dicky-weed!*"

This got even Gilbert's attention. "Mister Dicky-weed?" As the lights turned green in sequence for us the cabs threaded audaciously back and forth, seeking advantage, but the truth was the lights were timed for twenty-five-mile-an-hour traffic, and there wasn't any advantage to be gained. The still-unseen driver of the K-car was as impatient as a cabbie, and moved up to the front of the pack, but the timed lights kept us all honest, at least until they turned a corner. We remained stuck a car back. This was a chase Coney could handle, so far.

I was another story.

"Sinister mystery weed," I said, trying to find words that would ease the compulsion. It was as if my brain were inspired, trying to generate a really original new tic. Tourette's muse was with me. Rotten timing. Stress generally aggravated tics, but when I was engaged in a task the concentration kept me tic-free. I should have done the driving, I now realized. This chase was all stress and no place for it to go.

"Disturbed visitor week. Sisturbed."

"Yeah, I'm getting a little *sisturbed* myself," said Coney

absently as he jockeyed for an open spot in the lane to the right.

"Fister—" I sputtered.

"Spare me," groused Coney as he got us directly behind the K-car at last. I leaned forward to make out what I could of the interior. Three heads. Minna and the giant in the backseat, and a driver. Minna was facing straight ahead, and so was the giant. I picked up the headphones to check, but I'd guessed right: no talk. Somebody knew what they were doing and where they were going, and that somebody wasn't even remotely us.

At Fifty-ninth Street we hit the end of the cycle of green lights, as well as the usual unpleasantness around the entrance to the Queensborough bridge. The pack slowed, resigning itself to the wait through another red. Coney sagged back so we wouldn't be too obvious pulling in behind them for the wait, and another cab slipped in ahead of us. Then the K-car shot off through the fresh red, barely missing the surge of traffic coming across Fifty-eighth.

"Shit!"

"Shit!"

Coney and I both almost bounced out of our skins. We were wedged in, unable to follow and brave the stream of crosstown traffic if we'd wanted to try. It felt like a straitjacket. It felt like our fate overtaking us, Minna's losers, failing him again. Fuck-ups fucking up because that's what fuckups do. But the K-car hit another mass of vehicular stuff parked in front of the next red and stayed in sight a block ahead. The traffic was broken into chunks. We'd gotten lucky for a minute, but a minute only.

I watched, frantic. Their red, our red, my eyes flicked back and forth. I heard Coney's breath, and my own, like horses at the gate – our adrenalinated bodies imagined they could make up the difference of the block. If we weren't careful, at the sight of the light changing we'd pound our two foreheads through the windshield.

Our red did change, but so did theirs, and, infuriatingly, their vehicular mass surged forward while ours crawled. That mass was our hope – they were at the tail end of theirs, and if it stayed densely enough packed, they wouldn't get too far away. We were almost at the front of ours. I slapped the glove-compartment door six times. Coney accelerated impulsively and tapped the cab in front of us, but not hard. We veered to the side and I saw a silver scrape in the yellow paint of the cab's bumper. "Fuck it, keep going," I said. The cabbie seemed to have the same idea anyway. We all screeched across Fifty-ninth, a madcap rodeo of cabs and cars, racing to defy the immutable law of timed stoplights. Our bunch splayed and caught up with the rear end of their splaying bunch and the two blended, like video spaceships on some antic screen. The K-car aggressively threaded lanes. We threaded after them, making no attempt to disguise our pursuit now. Blocks flew past.

"Turning!" I shouted. "Get over!" I gripped the door handle as Coney, getting fully into the spirit of things, bent topological probability in moving us across three crowded lanes full of shrieking bald rubber and cringing chrome. Now my tics were quieted – stress was one thing, animal fear another. As when an airplane lands shakily, and all on board concentrate every gram of their will to stabilize the craft, the task of imagining I controlled things I didn't (in this case wheel, traffic, Coney, gravity, friction, etc.), imagining it with every fiber of my being – that was engagement enough for me at the moment. My Tourette's was overwhelmed.

"Thirty-sixth," said Coney as we rattled down the side street.

"What's that mean?"

"I dunno. Something."

"Midtown Tunnel. Queens."

There was something comforting about this. The giant and his driver were moving onto our turf, more or less. The boroughs. Not quite Brooklyn, but it would do. We bumped along with the thickening traffic into the two dense lanes of the tunnel, the K-car safely tied up two cars ahead of us, its windows now black and glossy with reflections from the strips of lighting that laced the stained tile artery. I relaxed a bit, quit holding my breath, and squeaked out a teeth-clenched, Joker-grimacing *eat me* just because I could.

"Toll," said Coney.

"What?"

"There's a toll. On the Queens side."

I started digging in my pockets. "How much?"

"Three-fifty, I think."

I'd just put it together, miraculously, three bills, a quarter, a dime and three nickels, when the tunnel finished and the two lanes branched out to meet the six or seven toll booths. I balled the fare and held it out to Coney in a fist. "Don't get stuck behind them," I said. "Get a fast lane. Cut someone off."

"Yeah." Coney squinted through the windshield, trying to work an angle. As he edged to the right the K-car suddenly cut out of the flow, moving to the far left.

We both stared for a moment.

"Whuzzat?" said Coney.

"E-Z Pass," I said. "They've got an E-Z Pass."

The K-car slid into the empty E-Z Pass lane, and right through the booth. Meanwhile Coney had landed us third in line for EXACT CHANGE OR TOKEN.

"Follow them!" I said.

"I'm trying," said Coney, plainly dazed by this turn of events.

"Get over to the left!" I said. "Go through!"

"We don't got an E-Z Pass." Coney grinned painfully, displaying his special talent for rapid reversion to a childlike state.

"I don't care!"

"But we—"

I started to pry at the wheel in Coney's hands, to try and push us to the left, but it was too late by now. The spot before us opened, and Coney eased the car into place, then rolled down his window. I plopped the fare into his open palm, and he passed it over.

Pulling out of the tunnel to the right, we were suddenly in Queens, facing a tangle of indifferent streets: Vernon Boulevard, Jackson Avenue, Fifty-second Avenue. Et cetera.

The K-car was gone.

"Pull over," I said.

Chagrined, Coney parked us on Jackson. It was perfectly dark now, though it was only seven. The lights of the Empire State and the Chrysler loomed across the river. Cars whirred past us out of the tunnel, toward the entrance to the Long Island Expressway, mocking us in their easy purposefulness. With Minna lost, we were nobodies, nowhere.

"*Eatmepass!*" I said.

"They could of just been losing us," said Coney.

"I'd say they were, yes."

"No, listen," he said feebly. "Maybe they turned around and went back to Manhattan. Maybe we could catch them—"

"Shhh." I listened to the earphones. "If Frank sees we're off his tail, he might say something."

But there was nothing to hear. The sounds of driving. Minna and the giant were sitting in perfect silence. Now I couldn't believe that the man in the Zendo was the same as the giant – that garrulous, pretentious voice I'd heard couldn't have shut up this long, it seemed to me. It was surprising enough that Minna wasn't chattering, making fun of something, pointing out landmarks. Was he scared? Afraid to let on he was miked? Did he think we were still with him? Why did he want us with him anyway?

I didn't know anything.

I made six oinking sounds.

We sat waiting.

More.

"*That's the way of a big Polish lug, I guess,*" said Minna. "*Always gotta stay within sniffing distance of a pierogi.*"

Then: "*Urrhhf.*" Like the giant had smashed him in the stomach.

"Where's Polish?" I asked Coney, lifting away one earphone.

"Wha?"

"Where around here's Polish? *Eat me pierogi lug!*"

"I dunno. It's all Polish to me."

"Sunnyside? Woodside? Come on, Gilbert. Work with me. He's somewhere Polish."

"Where'd the Pope visit?" mused Coney. It sounded like the start of a joke, but I knew Coney. He couldn't remember jokes. "That's Polish, right? What's it, uh, Greenpoint?"

"Greenpoint's Brooklyn, Gilbert," I said, before thinking. "We're in Queens." Then we both turned our heads like cartoon mice spotting a cat. The Pulaski Bridge. We were a few

yards from the creek separating Queens and Brooklyn, specifically Greenpoint.

It was something to do anyway. "Go," I said.

"Keep listening," said Coney. "We can't just drive around
Greenpoint."

We soared across the little bridge, into the mouth of
Brooklyn.

"Which way, Lionel?" said Coney, as if he thought Minna
were feeding me a constant stream of instructions. I shrugged,
palms up toward the roof of the Lincoln. The gesture ticcified
instantly, and I repeated it, shrug, palms flapped open, grimace.
Coney ignored me, scanning the streets below for a sign of the
K-car, driving as slow as he could down the Brooklyn side of
the Pulaski's slope.

Then I heard something. Car doors opening, slamming,
the scuff of footsteps. Minna and the giant had reached their
destination. I froze in mid-tic, concentrating.

"*Harry Brainum Jr.*," said Minna in his mockingest tone. "*I
guess we're gonna stop in for a quick installation, huh?*"

Nothing from the giant. More steps.

Who was Harry Brainum Jr.?

Meanwhile we came off the lit bridge, where the notion
of a borough laid out for us, comprehensive, had been briefly
indulgeable. Down instead onto McGuinness Boulevard, where
at street level the dark industrial buildings were featureless and
discouraging. Brooklyn is one big place, and this wasn't our
end of it.

"*You know – if you can't beat 'em Brainum, right?*" Minna went
on in his needling voice. In the background I heard a car horn –
they weren't indoors yet. Just standing on the street somewhere,
tantalizingly close.

Then I heard a thud, another exhalation. Minna had taken
a second blow.

Then Minna again: "*Hey, hey—*" Some kind of struggle I
couldn't make out.

"*Fucking—*" said Minna, and then I heard him get hit again,
lose his wind in a long, mournful sigh.

The scary thing about the giant was that he didn't talk,
didn't even breathe heavy enough for me to hear.

"Harry Brainum Jr.," I said to Coney. Then, afraid it sounded like a tic to him, I added, "Name mean anything to you, Gilbert?"

"Sorry?" he said slowly.

"Harry Brainum Jr.," I repeated, furious with impatience. There were times when I felt like a bolt of static electricity communing with figures that moved through a sea of molasses.

"Sure," he said, jerking his thumb in the direction of his window. "We just passed it."

"What? Passed what?"

"It's like a tool company or something. Big sign."

My breath caught. Minna was talking to us, guiding us. "Turn around."

"What, back to Queens?"

"No, Brainum, wherever you saw that," I said, wanting to strangle him. Or at least find his fast-forward button and push it. "They're out of the car. Make a U-turn."

"It's just a block or two."

"Well, go, then. *Brain me, Junior!*"

Coney made the turn, and right away there it was. HARRY BRAINUM JR. INC. STEEL SHEETS., in giant circus-poster letters on the brick wall of a two-story plant that took up a whole block of McGuinness, just short of the bridge.

* * *

Seeing BRAINUM on the wall set off a whole clown parade of associations. I remembered mishearing *Ringling Bros. Barnum & Bailey Circus* as a child. Barnamum Bailey. Like Osmium, Cardamom, Brainium, Barnamum, Where'smymom: the periodic table of elements, the heavy metals. Barnamum Bailey might also be George and Eat Me Bailey's older brother. Or were they all the same guy? Not now, I begged my Tourette's self. Think about it later.

* * *

"Drive around the block," I said to Coney. "He's here somewhere."

"Quit shouting," he said. "I can hear you."

"Shut up so I can hear," I said.

"That's all I said."

"What?" I lifted an earphone.

"That's all I said. Shut up."

"Okay! Shut up! Drive! Eat me!"

"Fucking freakball."

The block behind BRAINUM was dark and seemingly empty. The few parked cars didn't include the K-car. The windowless brick warehouse was laced with fire escapes, wrought-iron cages that ran the length of the second floor and ended in a crumpled, unsafe-looking ladder. On the side street a smallish, graffitied Dumpster was tucked halfway into the shadow of double doorway. The doors behind were strapped with long exterior hinges, like a meat locker. One lid of the Dumpster was shut, the other open to allow some fluorescent bulbs sticking up. Street rubbish packed around the wheels made me think it hadn't moved in a while, so I didn't worry about the doors behind it. The other entrance was a roll-up gate on a truck-size loading dock, right out on the brightly lit boulevard. I figured I would have heard the gate sing if it had been raised.

The four stacks of the Newtown Creek Sewage Treatment Plant towered at the end of the street, underlit like ancient pylons in a gladiator movie. Fly an inflatable pig over and you'd have the sleeve of Pink Floyd's *Animals* album. Beneath its shadow we crept in the Lincoln around all four corners of the block, seeing nothing.

"Damn it," I said.

"You don't hear him?"

"Street noise. Hey, hit the horn."

"Why?"

"Do it."

I concentrated on the earphones. Coney honked the Lincoln's horn. Sure enough, it came through.

"Stop the car." I was in a panic now. I got out onto the sidewalk, slammed the door. "Circle slow," I said. "Keep an eye on me."

"What's the deal, Lionel?"

"He's here."

I paced the sidewalk, trying to feel the pulse of the blackened building, to take the measure of the desolate block. It
was a place made out of leftover chunks of disappointment,
unemployment and regret. I didn't want to be here, didn't want
Minna to be here. Coney paced me in the Lincoln, staring
dumbly out the driver's window. I listened to the phones until
I heard the approach of my own steps. My own heart beating
made a polyrhythm, almost as loud. Then I found it. Minna's
wire had been torn from his shirt and lay tangled in a little
heap on the curb of the side street, at the other end of the block
from the Dumpster. I picked it up and pushed it into my pants
pocket, then ripped the headphones off my neck. Feeling the
grimness of the street close around me I began to half-run down
the sidewalk toward the Dumpster, though I had to stop once
and mimic my own retrieval of the wire: hurriedly kneel at the
edge of the sidewalk, grab, stuff, remove phantom headphones,
feel a duplicate thrill of panic at the discovery, resume jogging.
It was cold now. The wind punched me and my nose oozed in
response. I wiped it on my sleeve as I came up to the Dumpster.

"You jerks," Minna moaned from inside.

I touched the rim of the Dumpster and my hand came away
wet with blood. I pushed open the second lid, balanced it
against the doorway. Minna was curled fetally in the garbage,
his arms crossed around his stomach, sleeves covered in red.

"Jesus, Frank."

"Wanna get me out of here?" He coughed, burbled, rolled
his eyes at me. "Wanna give me a hand? I mean, no sooner than
the muse strikes. Or possibly you ought to get out your brushes
and canvas. I've never been in an oil painting."

"Sorry, Frank." I reached in just as Coney came up behind
me and looked inside.

"Oh, shit," he said.

"Help me," I said to Coney. Together we pulled Minna up
from the bottom of the Dumpster. Minna stayed curled around
his wounded middle. We drew him over the lip and held him,
together, out on the dark empty sidewalk, cradling him absurdly, our knees buckled toward one another's, our shoulders
pitched, like he was a giant baby Jesus in a bloody trench coat
and we were each one of the Madonna's tender arms. Minna

groaned and chuckled, eyes squeezed shut, as we moved him to the backseat of the Lincoln. His blood made my fingers tacky on the door handle.

"Nearest hospital," I breathed as we got into the front.

"I don't know around here," said Coney, whispering, too.

"Brooklyn Hospital," said Minna from the back, surprisingly loud. "Take the BQE, straight up McGuinness. Brooklyn Hospital's right off DeKalb. You boiled cabbageheads."

We held our breath and stared forward until Coney got us going the right way, then I turned and looked in the back. Minna's eyes were half open and his unshaven chin was wrinkled like he was thinking hard or sulking or trying not to cry. He saw me looking and winked. I barked twice – "yipke, yipke" – and winked back involuntarily.

"Fuck happened, Frank?" said Coney without taking his eyes off the road. We bumped and rattled over the Brooklyn-Queens Expressway, rottenest surface in the boroughs. Like the G train, the BQE suffered from low self-esteem, never going into citadel Manhattan, never tasting the glory. And it was choked with forty- or fifty-wheel trucks, day and night.

"I'm dropping my wallet and watch back here," said Minna, ignoring the question. "And my beeper. Don't want them stolen at the hospital. Remember they're back here."

"Yeah, but what the fuck happened, Frank?"

"Leave you my gun but it's gone," said Minna. I watched him shuck off the watch, silver smeared with red.

"They took your gun? Frank, what happened?"

"Knife," said Minna. "No biggie."

"You're gonna be all right?" Coney was asking and willing it at once.

"Oh, yeah. Great."

"Sorry, Frank."

"Who?" I said. "Who did this?"

Minna smiled. "You know what I want out of you, Freakshow? Tell me a joke. You got one you been saving, you must."

Minna and I had been in a joke-telling contest since I was thirteen years old, primarily because he liked to see me try to get through without ticcing. It was rare that I could.

"Let me think," I said.

"It'll hurt him if he laughs," said Coney to me. "Say one he knows already. Or one that ain't funny."

"Since when do I laugh?" said Minna. "Let him tell it. Couldn't hurt worse than your driving."

"Okay," I said. "Guy walks into a bar." I was watching blood pool on the backseat, at the same time trying to keep Minna from tracking my eyes.

"That's the ticket," rasped Minna. "Best jokes start the same fucking way, don't they, Gilbert? The guy, the bar."

"I guess," said Coney.

"Funny already," said Minna. "We're already in the black here."

"So guy walks into a bar," I said again. "With an octopus. Says to the bartender 'I'll bet a hundred dollars this octopus can play any instrument in the place.'"

"Guy's got an octopus. You like that, Gilbert?"

"Eh."

"So the bartender points at the piano in the corner says, 'Go ahead.' Guy puts the octopus on the piano stool – *Pianoctamus! Pianoctamum Bailey!* – octopus flips up the lid, plays a few scales, then lays out a little étude on the piano."

"Getting fancy," said Minna. "Showing off a little."

I didn't ask him to specify, since if I had he'd surely have said he meant me and the octopus both, for the *étude*.

"So guys says 'Pay up,' bartender says 'Wait a minute,' pulls out a guitar. Guy gives the octopus the guitar, octopus tightens up the E-string, closes its eyes, plays a sweet little fandango on the guitar." Pressure building up, I tagged Coney on the shoulder six times. He ignored me, driving hard, outracing trucks. "Guy says 'Pay up,' bartender says 'Hold on, I think I've got something else around here,' pulls a clarinet out of the back room. Octopus looks the thing over a couple of times, tightens the reed."

"He's milking it," said Minna, again meaning us both.

"Well, the octopus isn't good exactly, but he manages to squeak out a few bars on the clarinet. He isn't going to win any awards, but he plays the thing. *Clarinet Milk! Eat Me!* Guy says 'Pay up,' the bartender says 'Just wait one minute,' goes in the back rummages around finally comes out with a bagpipes. Plops the bagpipes up on the bar. Guy brings the octopus over, plops the octopus up next to the bagpipes. *Octapipes!*" I paused to measure my wits, not wanting to tic out the punch line. Then I started again, afraid of losing the thread, of losing Minna. His eyes kept closing and opening again and I wanted them open. "Octopus looks the bagpipes over, reaches out lifts one pipe lets it drop. Lifts another lets it drop. Backs up, squints at the bagpipes. Guy gets nervous, comes over to the bar says to the octopus – *Accupush! Reactapus!* – says to the octopush, *fuckit,* says *gonnafuckit* – says 'What's the matter? Can't you play it?' And the octopus says 'Play it? If I can figure out how to get its pajamas off, I'm gonna fuck it!' "

Minna's eyes had been closed through the windup and he didn't open them now. "You finished?" he said.

I didn't speak. We circled the ramp off the BQE, onto DeKalb Avenue.

"Where's the hospital?" said Minna, eyes still shut.

"We're almost there," said Coney.

"I need help," said Minna. "I'm dying back here."

"You're not dying," I said.

"Before we get in the emergency room, you want to tell us who did this to you, Frank?" said Coney.

Minna didn't say anything.

"They stab you in the gut and throw you in the fucking garbage, Frank. You wanna tell us who?"

"Go up the ambulance ramp," said Minna. "I need help back here. I don't wanna wait in some goddamn walk-in emergency room. I need immediate help."

"We can't drive up the ambulance ramp, Frank."

"What, you think you need an *E-Z Pass,* you stale meat loaf? Do what I said."

I gritted my teeth while my brain went, *Guy walks into the ambulance ramp stabs you in the goddamn emergency gut says I need an immediate stab in the garbage in the goddamn walk-in ambulance says just a minute looks in the back says I think I've got a stab in the goddamn walk-in immediate ambuloaf ambulamp octoloaf oafulope.*

"*Oafulope!*" I screamed, tears in my eyes.

"Yeah," said Minna, and now he laughed, then moaned. "A whole fucking herd of 'em."

"Someone ought to put you both out of your misery," muttered Coney as we hit the ambulance ramp behind Brooklyn Hospital, driving against the DO NOT ENTER signs, wheels squealing around a pitched curve to a spot alongside double swinging doors marked with yellow stencil EMS ONLY. Coney stopped. A Rastafarian in the costume of a private security guard was on us right away, tapping at Coney's window. He had bundled dreadlocks pushing sideways out of his hat, chiba eyes, a stick where a gun should be, and an embroidered patch on his chest indicating his first name, Albert. Like a janitor's uniform, or a mechanic's. The jacket was too big for his broomstick frame.

Coney opened the door instead of rolling down the glass.

"Get this car out of here!" said Albert.

"Take a look in the back," said Coney.

"Don't care; mon. This for ambulances only. Get back in the car."

"Tonight we're an ambulance, Albert," I said. "Get a stretcher for our friend."

Minna looked terrible. Drained, literally, and when we got him out of the car you could see what of. The blood smelled like a thunderstorm coming, like ozone. Two college students dressed as doctors in green outfits with rubber-band sleeves took him away from us just inside the doors and laid him onto a rolling steel cart. Minna's shirt was shreds, his middle a slush of itself, of himself. Coney went out and moved the car to quiet the security guard pulling on his arm while I followed Minna's stretcher inside, against the weak protests of the college students. I moved along keeping my eyes on his face and tapping his shoulder intermittently as though we were standing talking, in the Agency office perhaps, or just strolling down Court Street with two slices of pizza. Once they had Minna parked in a semiprivate zone in the emergency room, the students left me alone and concentrated on getting a line for blood into his arm.

His eyes opened. "Where's Coney?" he said. His voice was like a withered balloon. If you didn't know its shape when it was full of air it wouldn't have sounded like anything at all.

"They might not let him back here," I said. "I'm not supposed to be here myself."

"Huhhr."

"Coney – *Eatme, yipke!* – Coney kind of had a point," I said. "You might want to tell us who, while we're, you know, waiting around here."

The students were working on his middle, peeling away cloth with long scissors. I turned my eyes away.

Minna smiled again. "I've got one for you," he said. I leaned in to hear him. "Thought of it in the car. Octopus and Reactopus are sitting on a bench, a fence. Octopus falls off, who's left?"

"Reactopus," I said softly. "Frank, who did this?"

"You know that Jewish joke you told me? The one about the Jewish lady goes to Tibet, wants to see the High Lama?"

"Sure."

"That's a good one. What's the name of that lama? You know, at the end, the punch line."

"You mean Irving?"

"Yeah, right. Irving." I could barely hear him now. "That's who." His eyes closed.

"You're saying it was someone named – *Dick! Weed!* – Irving who did this to you? Is that the name of the big guy in the car? Irving?"

Minna whispered something that sounded like "remember." The others in the room were making noise, barking out instructions to one another in their smug, technical dialect.

"Remember what?"

No answer.

"The name Irving? Or something else?"

Minna hadn't heard me. A nurse pulled open his mouth and he didn't protest, didn't move at all.

"Excuse me."

It was a doctor. He was short, olive-skinned, stubbled, Indian or Pakistani, I guessed. He looked into my eyes. "You have to go now."

"I can't do that," I said. I reached out and tagged his shoulder.

He didn't flinch. "What's your name?" he asked gently. Now I saw in his worn expression several thousand nights like this one.

"Lionel." I gulped away an impulse to scream my last name.

"Tourette's?"

"*Yessrog.*"

"Lionel, we're going to do some emergency surgery here. You must go wait outside." He nodded his head quickly to point the way. "They'll be needing you to handle some papers for your friend."

I stood stupefied, looking at Minna, wanting to tell him another joke, or hear one of his. *Guy walks into*—

A nurse was fitting a hinged plastic tube, like a giant Pez dispenser, into Minna's mouth.

I walked out the way I'd come in and found the triage nurse. Thinking *arbitrage, sabotage,* I told her I was with Minna and she said she'd already spoken to Coney. She'd call out when she needed us, until then have a seat.

Coney sat crossed-legged and cross-armed with his chin clamped up angrily against the rest of his face, corduroy coat still buttoned, filling half of a kind of love seat with a narrow shelfload of splayed dingy magazines attached to it. I went and filled the other half. The waiting area was jammed with the sort of egalitarian cross-section only genuine misery can provide: Hispanics and blacks and Russians and various indeterminate, red-eyed teenage girls with children you prayed were siblings; junkie veterans petitioning for painkillers they wouldn't get; a tired housewife comforting her brother as he carped in an unceasing stream about his blocked digestion, the bowel movement he hadn't enjoyed for weeks; a terrified lover denied attendance, as I'd been, glaring viciously at the unimpressible triage nurse and the mute doors behind her; others guarded, defiant, daring you to puzzle at their distress, to guess on behalf of whom, themselves or another, they shared with you this miserable portion of their otherwise fine, pure and invulnerable lives.

I sat still for perhaps a minute and a half, tormented images of our chase and the Brainum Building and Minna's wounds strobing in my skull, tics roiling in my throat.

"*Walksinto,*" I shouted.

A few people looked up, confused by my bit of ventriloquism. Had the nurse spoken? Could it have been a last name? Their own, perhaps, mispronounced?

"Don't start now," said Coney under his breath.

"Guywalks, walksinto, guywalksinto," I said back to him helplessly.

"What, you telling a joke now?"

Very much in the grip, I modified the words into a growling sound, along the lines of "*whrywhroffsinko,*" – but the effort resulted in a side-tic: rapid eye blinks.

"Maybe you ought to stand outside, you know, like for a cigarette?" Poor dim Coney was just as much on edge as I was, obviously.

"Walks walks!"

Some stared, others looked away, bored. I'd been identified by the crowd as some sort of patient: spirit or animal possession, verbal epileptic seizure, whatever. I would presumably be given drugs and sent home. I wasn't damaged or ailing enough to be interesting here, only distracting, and slightly reprehensible in a way that made them feel better about their own disorders, so my oddness was quickly and blithely incorporated into the atmosphere.

With one exception: Albert, who'd been nursing a grudge since our jaunt up the ambulance ramp and now stood inside to get away from the cold, perhaps also to keep a bloodshot eye on us. I'd given him his angle, since, unlike the others in the waiting room, he knew I wasn't the patient in my party. He stepped over from where he'd been blowing on his hands and sulking in the doorway and pointed at me. "Yo, mon," he said. "You can't be like that in here."

"Be like what?" I said, twisting my neck and croaking "*Sothisguysays!*" as an urgent follow-up, voice rising shrilly, like a comedian who can't get his audience's attention.

"Can't be doing *that* shit," he said. "Gotta take it else*where.*" He grinned at his own verbal flourish, openly pleased to provide this contrast to my lack of control.

"Mind your own business," said Coney.

"*Piece! Of! String!*" I said, recalling another joke I hadn't told Minna, also set in a bar. My heart sank. I wanted to barge in and begin reciting it to his doctors, to his white intubed face. "*String! Walks! In!*"

"What's the matter with you, mon?"

"WEDON'TSERVESTRING!"

I was in trouble now. My Tourette's brain had shackled itself to the string joke like an ecological terrorist to a tree-crushing bulldozer. If I didn't find a way out I might download the whole joke one grunted or shrieked syllable after another. Looking for the escape hatch I began counting ceiling tiles and beating a rhythm on my knees as I counted. I saw I'd reattracted the room's collective attention, too. *This guy might be interesting after all.*

Free Human Freakshow.

"He's gotta condition," said Coney to the guard. "So lay off."

"Well, tell the mon he best stand up and walk his condition out of here," said the guard. "Or I be calling in the armada, you understand?"

"You must be mistaken," I said, in a calm voice now. "I'm not a piece of string." The bargain had been struck, at a level beyond my control. The joke would be told. I was only a device for telling it.

"We stand up we're gonna lay a condition on *your* ass, Albert," said Coney. "You unnerstand that?"

Albert didn't speak. The whole room was watching, tuned to Channel Brooklyn.

"You gotta cigarette for us, Albert?" said Coney.

"Can't smoke in here, mon," said Albert softly.

"Now, that's a good, sensible rule," said Coney. " 'Cause you got all these people in here that's concerned about their *health.*"

Coney was occasionally a master of the intimidating non sequitur. He certainly had Albert stymied now.

"I'm a *frayed knot*," I whispered. I began to want to grab at the nightstick in Albert's holster – an old, familiar impulse to reach for things dangling from belts, like the bunches of keys worn by the teachers at St. Vincent's Home for Boys. It seemed like a particularly rotten idea right now.

"Afraid of what?" said Albert, confused, though understanding the joke's pun, in a faint way.

"Afrayedknot!" I repeated obligingly, then added, "Eatmestringjoke!" Albert glared, unsure what he'd been called, or how badly to be insulted.

"Mr. Coney," called the triage nurse, breaking the stalemate. Coney and I both stood at once, still pathetically overcompensating for losing Minna in the chase. The short doctor had come out of the private room. He stood behind the triage nurse and nodded us over. As we brushed past Albert I indulged in a brief surreptitious fondling of his nightstick.

Half a fag, that's what Minna used to call me.

"Ah, are either of you a relative of Mr. Minna's?" The doctor's accent rendered this as *misdemeanors*.

"Yes and no," said Coney before I could answer. "We're his immediates, so to speak."

"Ah, I see," said the doctor, though of course he didn't. "Will you step this way with me—" He led us out of the waiting area, to another of the half-secluded rooms like the one where they'd wheeled Minna.

"*I'mafrayed*," I said under my breath.

"I'm sorry," said the doctor, standing oddly close to us, examining our eyes. "There was little we could do."

"That's okay, then," said Coney, not hearing it right. "I'm sure whatever you can do is fine, since Frank didn't need so much in the first place—"

"*I'mafrayedknot*." I felt myself nearly choke, not on unspoken words for once but on rising gorge, White Castle-flavored bile. I swallowed it back so hard my ears popped. My whole face felt flushed with a mist of acids.

"Ahem. We were unable to revive misdemeanor."

"Wait a minute," said Coney. "You're saying unable to revive?"

"Yes, that's right. Loss of blood was the cause. I am sorry."

"Unable to revive!" shouted Coney. "He was re*vived* when we brought him in here! What kind of a place is this? He didn't need to be revived, just patched up a little—"

I began to need to touch the doctor, to deliver small taps on either shoulder, in a pattern that was absolutely symmetrical. He stood for it, not pushing me away. I tugged his collar straight, matching the line to his salmon-colored T-shirt underneath, so that the same margin showed at either side of his neck.

Coney stood in deflated silence now, absorbing pain. We all

stood waiting until I finally finished tucking and pinching the doctor's collar into place.

"Sometimes there is nothing we can do," said the doctor, eyes flicking to the floor now.

"Let me see him," said Coney.

"That isn't possible—"

"This place is full of crap," said Coney. "Let me see him."

"There is a question of evidence," said the doctor wearily. "I'm sure you understand. The examiners will also wish to speak with you."

I'd already seen police passing through from the hospital coffee shop, into some part of the emergency room. Whether those particular police were there to detain us or not, it was clear the law wouldn't be long in arriving.

"We ought to go, Gilbert," I told Coney. "Probably we ought to go right now."

Coney was inert.

"Problyreallyoughttogo," I said semicompulsively, panic rising through my sorrow.

"You misunderstand," said the doctor. "We'll ask you to wait, please. This man will show you where to go—" He nodded at something behind us. I whipped around, my lizard instincts shocked at having allowed someone to sneak up on me.

It was Albert. The Thin Rastafarian Line between us and departure. His appearance seemed to trigger comprehension in Coney: The security guard was a cartoon reminder of the real existence of police.

"Outta the way," said Coney.

"We don't serve string!" I explained.

Albert didn't look any more convinced of his official status than we were. At moments like this I was reminded of the figure we Minna Men cut, oversize, undereducated, vibrant with hostility even with tear streaks all over our beefy faces. And me with my utterances, lunges, and taps, my symptoms, those extra factors Minna adored throwing into the mix.

Frank Minna, unrevived, empty of blood in the next room.

Albert held his palms open, his body more or less pleading as he said, "You better wait, mon."

"Nah," said Coney. "Maybe another time." Coney and I both leaned in Albert's direction, really only shifting our weight, and he jumped backward, spreading his hands over the spot he'd vacated as if to say *It was someone else standing there just now, not I.*

"But this is a thing upon which we must insist," said the doctor.

"You really don't wanna insist," said Coney, turning on him furiously. "You ain't got the insistence required, you know what I mean?"

"I'm not sure I do," said the doctor quietly.

"Well, just chew it over," said Coney. "There's no big hurry. C'mon, Lionel."

MOTHERLESS BROOKLYN

I GREW UP in the library of St. Vincent's Home for Boys, in the part of downtown Brooklyn no developer yet wishes to claim for some upscale, renovated neighborhood; not quite Brooklyn Heights, nor Cobble Hill, not even Boerum Hill. The Home is essentially set on the off-ramp to the Brooklyn Bridge, but out of sight of Manhattan or the bridge itself, on eight lanes of traffic lined with faceless, monolithic civil courts, which, gray and distant though they seemed, some of us Boys had seen the insides of, by Brooklyn's central sorting annex for the post office, a building that hummed and blinked all through the night, its gates groaning open to admit trucks bearing mountains of those mysterious items called letters, by the Burton Trade School for Automechanics, where hardened students attempting to set their lives dully straight spilled out twice a day for sandwich-and-beer breaks, overwhelming the cramped bodega next door, intimidating passersby and thrilling us Boys in their morose thuggish glory, by a desolate strip of park benches beneath a granite bust of Lafayette, indicating his point of entry into the Battle of Brooklyn, by a car lot surrounded by a high fence topped with wide curls of barbed wire and wind-whipped fluorescent flags, and by a redbrick Quaker Meetinghouse that had presumably been there when the rest was farmland. In short, this jumble of stuff at the clotted entrance to the ancient, battered borough was officially Nowhere, a place strenuously ignored in passing through to Somewhere Else. Until rescued by Frank Minna I lived, as I said, in the library.

* * *

I set out to read every book in that tomblike library, every miserable dead donation ever indexed and forgotten there – a mark of my profound fear and boredom at St. Vincent's and as well an early sign of my Tourettic compulsions for counting, processing, and inspection. Huddled there in the windowsill, turning dry pages and watching dust motes pinball through beams of sunlight, I sought signs of my odd dawning self in Theodore Dreiser, Kenneth Roberts, J. B. Priestley, and back issues of *Popular Mechanics* and failed, couldn't find the language of myself, as I failed to in watching television, those endless reruns of *Bewitched* and *I Dream of Jeannie* and *I Love Lucy* and *Gilligan* and *Brady Bunch* by which we nerdish unathletic Boys pounded our way through countless afternoons, leaning in close to the screen to study the antics of the women – women! exotic as letters, as phone calls, as forests, all things we orphans were denied – and the coping of their husbands, but I didn't find myself there, Desi Arnaz and Dick York and Larry Hagman, those harried earthbound astronauts, weren't showing me what I needed to see, weren't helping me find the language. I was closer on Saturday mornings, Daffy Duck especially gave me something, if I could bear to imagine growing up a dynamited, beak-shattered duck. Art Carney on *The Honeymooners* gave me something too, something in the way he jerked his neck, when we were allowed to stay up late enough to see him. But it was Minna who brought me the language, Minna and Court Street that let me speak.

*   *   *

We four were selected that day because we were four of the five white boys at St. Vincent's, and the fifth was Steven Grossman, fat as his name. If Steven had been thinner, Mr. Kassel would have left me in the stacks. As it was I was undersold goods, a twitcher and nosepicker retrieved from the library instead of the schoolyard, probably a retard of some type, certainly a regrettable, inferior offering. Mr. Kassel was a teacher at St. Vincent's who knew Frank Minna from the neighborhood, and his invitation to Minna to borrow us for the afternoon was a first glimpse of the glittering halo of favors and favoritism that extended around Minna – "knowing somebody" as a life condition. Minna was our exact reverse, we who knew no one and benefited nothing from it when we did.

Minna had asked for white boys to suit his clients' presumed prejudice – and his own certain ones. Perhaps Minna already had his fantasy of reclamation in mind, too. I can't know. He certainly didn't show it in the way he treated us that first day, a sweltering August weekday afternoon after classes, streets like black chewing gum, slow-creeping cars like badly projected science-class slides in the haze, as he opened the rear of his dented, graffitied van, about the size of those midnight mail trucks, and told us to get inside, then slammed and padlocked the doors without explanation, without asking our names. We four gaped at one another, giddy and astonished at this escape from our doldrums, not knowing what it meant, not really needing to know. The others, Tony, Gilbert and Danny, were willing to be grouped with me, to pretend I fit with them, if that was what it took to be plucked up by the outside world and seated in the dark on a dirty steel truck bed vibrating its way to somewhere that wasn't St. Vincent's. Of course I was vibrating too, vibrating before Minna rounded us up, vibrating inside always and straining to keep it from showing. I didn't kiss the other three boys, but I wanted to. Instead I made a kissing, chirping sound, like a bird's peep, over and over: "Chrip, chrip, chrip."

* * *

Tony told me to shut the fuck up, but his heart wasn't in it, not this day, in the midst of life's unfolding mystery. For Tony, especially, this was his destiny coming to find him. He saw more in Minna from the first because he'd prepared himself to see it. Tony Vermonte was famous at St. Vincent's for the confidence he exuded, confidence that a mistake had been made, that he didn't belong in the Home. He was Italian, better than the rest of us, who didn't know what we were (what's an Essrog?). His father was either a mobster or a cop – Tony saw no contradiction in this, so we didn't either. The Italians would return for him, in one guise or another, and that was what he'd taken Minna for.

Tony was famous for other things as well. He was older than the rest of us there in Minna's truck, fifteen to my and Gilbert's thirteen and Danny Fantl's fourteen (older St. Vincent's Boys

attended high school elsewhere, and were rarely seen, but Tony
had contrived to be left back), an age that made him infinitely
dashing and worldly, even if he hadn't also lived outside the
Home for a time and then come back. As it was, Tony was our
God of Experience, all cigarettes and implication. Two years
before, a Quaker family, attendees of the Meeting across the
street, had taken Tony in, intending to give him a permanent
home. He'd announced his contempt for them even as he packed
his clothes. They weren't Italian. Still, he lived with them for a
few months, perhaps happily, though he wouldn't have said so.
They installed him at Brooklyn Friends, a private school only
a few blocks away, and on his way home most afternoons he'd
come and hang on the St. Vincent's fence and tell stories of
the private-school girls he'd felt up and sometimes penetrated,
the faggy private-school boys who swam and played soccer
but were easily humiliated at basketball, not otherwise Tony's
specialty. Then one day his foster parents found prodigious
black-haired Tony in bed with one girl too many: their own
sixteen-year-old daughter. Or so the story went; there was only
one source. Anyway, he was reinstalled at St. Vincent's the next
day, where he fell easily into his old routine of beating up and
befriending me and Steven Grossman each on alternating days,
so that we were never in favor simultaneously and could trust
one another as little as we trusted Tony.

Tony was our Sneering Star, and certainly the one of us
who caught Minna's attention soonest, the one that fired our
future boss's imagination, made him envision the future Minna
Men inside us, aching to be cultivated. Perhaps Tony, with
his will for his Italian rescue, even collaborated in the vision
that became The Minna Agency, the strength of his yearning
prompting Minna to certain aspirations, to the notion of having
Men to command in the first place.

* * *

Minna was barely a man then himself, of course, though he
seemed one to us. He was twenty-five that summer, gangly
except for a tiny potbelly in his pocket-T, and still devoted to
combing his hair into a smooth pompadour, a Carroll Gardens

hairstyle that stood completely outside that year of 1979, projecting instead from some miasmic Frank Sinatra moment that
extended like a bead of amber or a cinematographer's filter to
enclose Frank Minna and everything that mattered to him.

* * *

Besides me and Tony in the back of Minna's van there was
Gilbert Coney and Danny Fantl. Gilbert then was Tony's right
hand, a stocky, sullen boy just passing for tough – he would
have beamed at you for calling him a thug. Gilbert was awfully
tough on Steven Grossman, whose fatness, I suspect, provided
an uncomfortable mirror, but he was tolerant of me. We even
had a couple of odd secrets. On a Home for Boys visit to the
Museum of Natural History in Manhattan, two years before,
Gilbert and I had split from the group and without discussion
returned to a room dominated by a enormous plastic blue
whale suspended from the ceiling, which had been the focus of
the official visit. But underneath the whale was a double gallery
of murky, mysterious dioramas of undersea life, lit and arranged
so you had to press close to the glass to find the wonders tucked
deep in the corners. In one a sperm whale fought a giant squid.
In another a killer whale pierced a floor of ice. Gilbert and I
wandered hypnotized from window to window. When a class
of third- or fourth-graders were led away we found we had the
giant hall to ourselves, and that even when we spoke our voices
were smothered by the unearthly quiet of the museum. Gilbert
showed me his discovery: A munchkin-size brass door beside
the penguin diorama had been left unlocked. When he opened
it we saw that it led both behind and into the penguin scene.

"Get in, Essrog," said Gilbert.

If I'd not wanted to it would have been bullying, but I
wanted to desperately. Every minute the hall remained empty
was precious. The lip of the doorway was knee-high. I clambered in and opened the flap in the ocean-blue-painted boards
that made the side wall of the diorama, then slipped into the
picture. The ocean floor was a long, smooth bowl of painted
plaster, and I scooted down the grade on my bended knees,
looking out at a flabbergasted Gilbert on the other side of the

glass. Swimming penguins were mounted on rods extending straight from the far wall, and others were suspended in the plastic waves of ocean surface that now made up a low ceiling over my head. I caressed the nearest penguin, one mounted low, shown diving in pursuit of a delectable fish, patted its head, stroked its gullet as though helping it swallow a dry pill. Gilbert guffawed, thinking I was performing comedy for him, when in fact I'd been overwhelmed by a tender, touchy impulse toward the stiff, poignant penguin. Now it became imperative that I touch *all* the penguins, all I could, anyway – some were inaccessible to me, on the other side of the barrier of the ocean's surface, standing on ice floes. Shuffling on my knees I made the rounds, affectionately tagging each swimming bird before I made my escape back through the brass door. Gilbert was impressed, I could tell. I was now a kid who'd do anything, do crazy things. He was right and wrong, of course – once I'd touched the first penguin I had no choice.

Somehow this led to a series of confidences. I was crazy but also malleable, easily intimidated, which made me Gilbert's idea of a safe repository for what he regarded as his crazy feelings. Gilbert was a precocious masturbator, and looking for some triangulation between his own experiments and generic schoolyard lore. Did I do it? How often? One hand or two, held this way, or this? Close my eyes? Ever want to rub up against the mattress? I took his inquiries seriously, but I didn't really have the information he needed, not yet. My stupidity made Gilbert grouchy at first, and so he'd spend a week or two both pretending he hadn't spoken, didn't even know me, and glowering to let me know what galactic measures of pain awaited if I ratted him out. Then he'd suddenly come back, more urgent than ever. Try it, he'd say. It's not so hard. I'll watch and tell you if you do it wrong. I obeyed, as I had in the museum, but the results weren't as good. I couldn't yet treat myself with the tenderness I'd lavished on the penguins, at least not in front of Gilbert (though in fact he'd triggered my own private explorations, which were soon quite consuming). Gilbert became grouchy again, and prohibitively intimidating, and after two or three go-arounds the subject was permanently dropped. Still, the legacy of disclosure remained with us, a ghostly bond.

* * *

The last boy in Minna's van, Danny Fantl, was a ringer. He only looked white. Danny had assimilated to the majority population at St. Vincent's happily, effortlessly, down to his bones. In his way he commanded as much respect as Tony (and he certainly commanded Tony's respect, too) without bragging or posing, often without opening his mouth. His real language was basketball, and he was such a taut, fluid athlete that he couldn't help seeming a bit bottled up indoors, in the classroom. When he spoke it was to scoff at our enthusiasms, our displays of uncool, but distantly, as if his mind were really elsewhere plotting crossover moves, footwork. He listened to Funkadelic and Cameo and Zapp and was as quick to embrace rap as any boy at the Home, yet when music he admired actually *played,* instead of dancing he'd stand with arms crossed, scowling and pouting in time with the beat, his expressive hips frozen. Danny existed in suspension, neither black nor white, neither beating up nor beaten, beautiful but unfazed by the concept of girls, rotten at schoolwork but coasting through classes, and frequently unanchored by gravity, floating between pavement and the tangled chain-mesh of the St. Vincent's basketball hoops. Tony was tormented by his lost Italian family, adamant they would return; Danny might have coolly walked out on his parents one day when he was seven or eight and joined a pickup game that lasted until he was fourteen, to the day Minna drove up in his truck.

* * *

Tourette's teaches you what people will ignore and forget, teaches you to see the reality-knitting mechanism people employ to tuck away the intolerable, the incongruous, the disruptive – it teaches you this because you're the one lobbing the intolerable, incongruous, and disruptive their way. Once I sat on an Atlantic Avenue bus a few rows ahead of a man with a belching tic – long, groaning, almost vomitous-sounding noises, the kind a fifth-grader learns to make, swallowing a bellyful of air, then forgets by high school, when charming girls becomes more vital than freaking them out. My colleague's compulsion was terribly specific: He sat at the back of the bus, and only when every head faced forward did he give out with his masterly digestive simulacra. We'd turn, shocked – there were fifteen or twenty others on the bus – and he'd look away. Then, every sixth or seventh time, he'd mix in a messy farting sound. He was a miserable-looking black man in his sixties, a drinker, an idler. Despite the peekaboo brilliance of his timing it was clear to everyone he was the source, and so the other riders hummed or coughed reprovingly, quit giving him the satisfaction of looking, and avoided one another's gaze. This was a loser's game, since not glancing back freed him to run together great uninterrupted phrases of his ripest noise. To all but me he was surely a childish jerk-off, a pathetic wino fishing for attention (maybe he understood himself this way, too – if he was undiagnosed, probably so). But it was unmistakably a compulsion, a tic – Tourette's. And it went on and on, until I'd reached my stop and, I'm sure, after.

The point is, I knew that those other passengers would barely recall it a few minutes after stepping off to their destinations. Despite how that maniacal froglike groaning filled the auditorium of the bus, the concertgoers were plainly engaged in the task of forgetting the music. Consensual reality is both fragile and elastic, and it heals like the skin of a bubble. The belching man ruptured it so quickly and completely that I could watch the wound instantly seal.

A Touretter can also be The Invisible Man.

* * *

Similarly, I doubt the other Boys, even the three who joined me in becoming Minna Men, directly recalled my bouts of kissing. I probably could have forced them to remember, but it would have been grudgingly. That tic was too much for us to encompass then, at St. Vincent's, as it would be now, anytime, anywhere. Besides, as my Tourette's bloomed I quickly layered the kissing behind hundreds of other behaviors, some of which, seen through the prism of Minna's rough endearments, became my trademarks, my Freakshow. So the kissing was gratefully forgotten.

By the time I was twelve, nine months or so after touching the penguins, I had begun to overflow with reaching, tapping, grabbing and kissing urges – those compulsions emerged first, while language for me was still trapped like a roiling ocean under a calm floe of ice, the way I'd been trapped in the underwater half of the penguin display, mute, beneath glass. I'd begun reaching for doorframes, kneeling to grab at skittering loosened sneaker laces (a recent fashion among the toughest boys at St. Vincent's, unfortunately for me), incessantly tapping the metal-pipe legs of the schoolroom desks and chairs in search of certain ringing tones, and worst, grabbing and kissing my fellow Boys. I grew terrified of myself then, and burrowed deeper into the library, but was forced out for classes or meals or bedtime. Then it would happen. I'd lunge at someone, surround him with my arms, and kiss his cheek or neck or forehead, whatever I hit. Then, compulsion expelled, I'd be left to explain, defend myself, or flee. I kissed Greg Toon and Edwin Torres, whose eyes I'd never dared meet. I kissed Leshawn Montrose, who'd broken Mr. Voccaro's arm with a chair. I kissed Tony Vermonte and Gilbert Coney and tried to kiss Danny Fantl. I kissed Steven Grossman, pathetically thankful he'd come along just then. I kissed my own counterparts, other sad invisible Boys working the margins at St. Vincent's, just surviving, whose names I didn't know. "It's a game!" I'd say, pleadingly. "It's a game." That was my only defense, and since the most inexplicable things in our lives were games, with their ancient embedded rituals – British Bulldog, Ringolevio, Scully and Jinx – a mythos handed down to us orphans who-knew-how, it seemed possible I might persuade them this was another one, The Kissing Game. Just as important, I might persuade myself – wasn't it something in a book I'd read, a game for fevered teenagers, perhaps Sadie Hawkins Day? Forget the absence of girls, didn't we Boys deserve the same? That was it, then, I decided – I was single-handedly dragging the underprivileged into adolescence. I knew something they didn't. "It's a game," I'd say desperately, sometimes as tears of pain ran down my face. "It's a game." Leshawn Montrose cracked my head against a porcelain water fountain, Greg Toon and Edwin Torres generously only shucked me off onto the floor. Tony Vermonte twisted my arm behind my back and forced me against a wall. "It's a game," I breathed. He released me and shook his head, full of pity. The result, oddly enough, was I was spared a few months' worth of beatings at his hands – I was too pathetic and faggy to touch, might be better avoided. Danny Fantl saw my move coming and faked me out as though I were a lead-footed defender, then vanished down a stairwell. Gilbert stood and glared, deeply unnerved due to our private history. "A game," I reassured him. "It's a game," I told poor Steven Grossman and he believed me, just long enough to try kissing our mutual tormentor Tony, perhaps hoping it was a key to overturning the current order. He was not spared.

*   *   *

Meantime, beneath that frozen shell a sea of language was reaching full boil. It became harder and harder not to notice that when a television pitchman said *to last the rest of a lifetime* my brain went *to rest the lust of a loaftomb,* that when I heard "Alfred Hitchcock," I silently replied "Altered Houseclock" or "Ilford Hotchkiss," that when I sat reading Booth Tarkington in the library now my throat and jaw worked behind my clenched lips, desperately fitting the syllables of the prose to the rhythms of "Rapper's Delight" (which was then playing every fifteen or twenty minutes out on the yard), that an invisible companion named Billy or Bailey was begging for insults I found it harder and harder to withhold.

*   *   *

The kissing cycle was mercifully brief. I found other outlets, other obsessions. The pale thirteen-year-old that Mr. Kassel pulled out of the library and offered to Minna was prone to floor-tapping, whistling, tongue-clicking, winking, rapid head turns, and wall-stroking, anything but the direct utterances for which my particular Tourette's brain most yearned. Language bubbled inside me now, the frozen sea melting, but it felt too dangerous to let out. Speech was intention, and I couldn't let anyone else or myself know how intentional my craziness felt.

Pratfalls, antics – those were accidental lunacy, and more or less forgivable. Practically speaking, it was one thing to stroke Leshawn Montrose's arm, or even to kiss him, another entirely to walk up and call him Shefawn Mongoose, or Lefthand Moonprose, or Fuckyou Roseprawn. So, though I collected words, treasured them like a drooling sadistic captor, bending them, melting them down, filing off their edges, stacking them into teetering piles, before release I translated them into physical performance, manic choreography.

And I was lying low, I thought. For every tic issued I squelched dozens, or so it felt – my body was an overwound watchspring, effortlessly driving one set of hands double-time while feeling it could as easily animate an entire mansion of stopped clocks, or a vast factory mechanism, a production line like the one in *Modern Times,* which we watched that year in the basement of the Brooklyn Public Library on Fourth Avenue, a version accompanied by a pedantic voice-over lecturing us on Chaplin's genius. I took Chaplin, and Buster Keaton, whose *The General* had been similarly mutilated, as models: Obviously blazing with aggression, disruptive energies barely contained, they'd managed to keep their traps shut, and so had endlessly skirted danger and been regarded as cute. I needn't exactly strain to find a motto: silence, golden, get it? Got it. Hone your timing instead, burnish those physical routines, your idiot wall-stroking, face-making, lace-chasing, until they're funny in a flickering black-and-white way, until your enemies don policeman's or Confederate caps and begin tripping over themselves, until doe-eyed women swoon. So I kept my tongue wound in my teeth, ignored the pulsing in my cheek, the throbbing in my gullet, persistently swallowed language back like vomit. It burned as hotly.

* * *

We rode a mile or two before Minna's van halted, engine guttering to a stop. Then a few minutes passed before he let us out of the back, and we found ourselves in a gated warehouse yard under the shadow of the Brooklyn-Queens Expressway, in a ruined industrial zone. Red Hook, I knew later. He led us to a large truck, a detached twelve-wheel trailer with no cab in evidence, then rolled up the back to reveal a load of identical sealed cardboard crates, a hundred, two hundred, maybe more. A thrill went through me: I'd secretly count them.

"Couple you boys get up inside," said Minna distractedly. Tony and Danny had the guile to leap immediately into the truck, where they could work shaded from the sun. "You're just gonna run this stuff inside, that's all. Hand shit off, move it up to the front of the truck, get it in. Straight shot, you got it?" He pointed to the warehouse. We all nodded, and I peeped. It went unnoticed.

Minna opened the big panel doors of the warehouse and showed us where to set the crates. We started quickly, then wilted in the heat. Tony and Danny massed the crates at the lip of the truck while Gilbert and I made the first dozen runs, then the older boys conceded their advantage and began to help us drag them across the blazing yard. Minna never touched a crate; he spent the whole time in the office of the warehouse, a cluttered room full of desks, file cabinets, tacked-up notes and pornographic calendars and a stacked tower of orange traffic cones, visible to us through an interior window, smoking cigarettes and jawing on the telephone, apparently not listening for replies – every time I glanced through the window his mouth was moving. The door was closed, and he was inaudible behind the glass. At some point another man appeared, from where I wasn't sure, and stood in the yard wiping his forehead as though he were the one laboring. Minna came out, the two stepped inside the office, the other man disappeared. We moved the last of the crates inside. Minna rolled down the gate of the truck and locked the warehouse, pointed us back to his van, but paused before shutting us into the back.

"Hot day, huh?" he said, looking at us directly for what might have been the first time.

Bathed in sweat, we nodded, afraid to speak.

"You monkeys thirsty? Because personally I'm dying out here."

Minna drove us to Smith Street, a few blocks from St. Vincent's, and pulled over in front of a bodega, then bought us beer, pop-top cans of Miller, and sat with us in the back of the van, drinking. It was my first beer.

"Names," said Minna, pointing at Tony, our obvious leader. We said our first names, starting with Tony. Minna didn't offer his own, only drained his beer and nodded. I began tapping the truck panel beside me.

Physical exertion over, astonishment at our deliverance from St. Vincent's receding, my symptoms found their opening again.

"You probably ought to know, Lionel's a freak," said Tony, his voice vibrant with self-regard.

"Yeah, well, you're all freaks, if you don't mind me pointing it out," said Minna. "No parents – or am I mixed up?"

Silence.

"Finish your beer," said Minna, tossing his can past us, into the back of the van.

And that was the end of our first job for Frank Minna.

*   *   *

But Minna rounded us up again the next week, brought us to that same desolate yard, and this time he was friendlier. The task was identical, almost to the number of boxes (242 to 260), and we performed it in the same trepidatious silence. I felt a violent hatred burning off Tony in my and Gilbert's direction, as though he thought we were in the process of screwing up his Italian rescue. Danny was of course exempt and oblivious. Still, we'd begun to function as a team – demanding physical work contained its own truths, and we explored them despite ourselves.

Over beers Minna said, "You like this work?"

One of us said *sure*.

"You know what you're doing?" Minna grinned at us, waiting. The question was confusing. "You know what kind of work this is?"

"What, moving boxes?" said Tony.

"Right, moving. Moving work. That's what you call it when you work for me. Here, look." He stood to get into his pocket, pulled out a roll of twenties and a small stack of white cards. He stared at the roll for a minute, then peeled off four twenties and handed one to each of us. It was my first twenty dollars. Then he offered us each a card. It read: L&L MOVERS. NO JOB TOO SMALL. SOME JOBS TOO LARGE. GERARD & FRANK MINNA. And a phone number.

"You're Gerard or Frank?" said Tony.

"Minna, Frank." Like *Bond, James*. He ran his hand through his hair. "So you're a moving company, get it? Doing moving work." This seemed a very important point: that we call it *moving*. I couldn't imagine what else to call it.

"Who's Gerard?" said Tony. Gilbert and I, even Danny, watched Minna carefully. Tony was questioning him on behalf of us all.

"My brother."

"Older or younger?"

"Older."

Tony thought for a minute. "Who's L and L?"

"Just the name, L and L. Two L's. Name of the company."

"Yeah, but what's it mean?"

"What do you need it to mean, Fruitloop – Living Loud? Loving Ladies? Laughing at you Losers?"

"What, it doesn't mean anything?" said Tony.

"I didn't say that, did I?"

"*Least Lonely*," I suggested.

"There you go," said Minna, waving his can of beer at me. "L and L Movers, Least Lonely."

Tony, Danny and Gilbert all stared at me, uncertain how I'd gained this freshet of approval.

"*Liking Lionel*," I heard myself say.

"Minna, that's an Italian name?" said Tony. This was on his own behalf, obviously. It was time to get to the point. The rest of us could all go fuck ourselves.

"What are you, the census?" said Minna. "Cub reporter? What's your full name, Jimmy Olsen?"

"*Lois Lane*," I said. Like anyone, I'd read Superman comics.

"Tony Vermonte," said Tony, ignoring me.

"Vermont-ee," repeated Minna. "That's what, like a New England thing, right? You a Red Sox fan?"

"Yankees," said Tony, confused and defensive. The Yankees

were champions now, the Red Sox their hapless, eternal victims, vanquished most recently by Bucky Dent's famous home
run. We'd all watched it on television.

"Luckylent," I said, remembering. "Duckybent."

Minna erupted with laughter. "Yeah, Ducky fucking Bent!
That's good. Don't look now, it's Ducky Bent."

"*Lexluthor,*" I said, reaching out to touch Minna's shoulder.
He only stared at my hand, didn't move away. "Lunchylooper,
Laughyluck, Loopylip—"

"All right, Loopy," said Minna. "Enough already."

"*Lockystuff*—" I was desperate for a way to stop. My hand
went on tapping Minna's shoulder.

"Let it go," said Minna, and now he returned my shoulder
taps, once, hard. "Don't tug the boat."

* * *

To *tugboat* was to try Minna's patience. Any time you pushed
your luck, said too much, overstayed a welcome, or overesti-
mated the usefulness of a given method or approach, you were
guilty of having tugged the boat. *Tugboating* was most of all a
dysfunction of wits and storytellers, and a universal one: Anybody who thought himself funny would likely tug a boat here
or there. Knowing when a joke or verbal gambit was right at
its limit, quitting before the boat had been tugged, that was art
(and it was a given that you wanted to push it as near as possible
– missing an opportunity to score a laugh was deeply lame, an
act undeserving of a special name).

Years before the word *Tourette's* was familiar to any of us,
Minna had me diagnosed: Terminal Tugboater.

* * *

Distributing eighty dollars and those four business cards was all
Minna had to do to instate the four of us forever – or anyway,
for as long as he liked – as the junior staff of L&L Movers.
Twenty dollars and a beer remained our usual pay. Minna would
gather us sporadically, on a day's notice or no notice at all – and
the latter possibility became incentive, once we'd begun high

school, for us to return to St. Vincent's directly after classes and lounge expectantly in the schoolyard or recreation room, pretending not to listen for the distinctive grumble of his van's motor. The jobs varied enormously. We'd load merchandise, like the cartons in the trailer, in and out of storefront-basement grates all up and down Court Street, borderline shady activity that it seemed wholesalers ought to be handling themselves, transactions sealed with a shared cigar in the back of the shop. Or we'd bustle apartmentloads of furniture in and out of brownstone walk-ups, legitimate moving jobs, it seemed to me, where fretting couples worried we weren't old or expert enough to handle their belongings – Minna would hush them, remind them of the cost of distractions: "The meter's running." (This hourly rate wasn't reflected in our pay, of course. It was twenty dollars whether we hurried or not; we hurried.) We put sofas through third-story windows with a makeshift cinch and pulley, Tony and Minna on the roof, Gilbert and Danny in the window to receive, myself on the ground with the guide ropes. A massive factory building under the Brooklyn end of the Manhattan Bridge, owned by an important but unseen friend of Minna's, had been damaged in fire, and we moved most of the inhabitants for free, as some sort of settlement or concession – the terms were obscure, but Minna was terrifically urgent about it. When a couple of college-age artists objected to our rough handling of a pile of damaged canvases the firemen had heaped on the floor, he paced and seethed at the delay; the only meter running now was Minna's own time, and his credibility with his friend-client. We woke at five one August morning to collect and set up the temporary wooden stages for the bands performing in the Atlantic Antic, a massive annual street fair, then worked again at dusk to tear the stages down, the hot avenue now heaped with a day's torn wrappers and crumpled cups, a few fevered revelers still staggering home as we knocked the pine frames apart with hammers and the heels of our shoes. Once we emptied an entire electronics showroom into Minna's truck, pulling unboxed stereos off shelves and out of window displays, disconnecting the wires from lit, blinking amplifiers, eventually even taking the phone off the desk – it would have seemed a sort of brazen burglary had Minna not been standing on the sidewalk in front, drinking beer and telling jokes with the man who'd unpadlocked the shop gates for us as we filed past with the goods. Everywhere Minna connived and cajoled and dropped names, winking at us to make us complicit, and everywhere Minna's clients stared at us Boys, some wondering if we'd palm a valuable when they weren't looking, some trying to figure the angle, perhaps hoping to catch a hint of disloyalty, an edge over Minna they'd save for when they needed it. We palmed nothing, revealed no disloyalty. Instead we stared back, tried to make them flinch. And we listened, gathered information. Minna was teaching us when he meant to, and when he didn't.

It changed us as a group. We developed a certain collective ego, a presence apart at the Home. We grew less embattled from within, more from without: nonwhite Boys sensed in our privilege a hint of their future deprivations and punished us for it. Age had begun to heighten those distinctions anyway. So Tony, Gilbert, Danny and myself smoothed out our old antipathies and circled the wagons. We stuck up for one another, at the Home and at Sarah J. Hale, our local high school, a required stop except for those few who'd qualified for some special (i.e., Manhattan) destination, Stuyvesant or Music and Art.

There at Sarah J. we St. Vincent's Boys were disguised, blended with the larger population, a pretty rough crowd despite their presumably having parents and siblings and telephones and bedroom doors with locks and a thousand other unimaginable advantages. But we knew each other, kept an eye on each other, bad pennies circulating with the good. Black or white, we policed one another like siblings, reserved special degrees of scorn for one another's social or institutional humiliations. And there we mixed with girls for the first time, about as well as chunks of road salt in ice cream, though ice cream might be a generous comparison for the brutal, strapping black girls of Sarah J., gangs of whom laid after-school ambushes for any white boy daring enough to have flirted, even made eye contact, with one inside the building. They comprised the vast majority there, and the handful of white or Latin girls survived by a method of near-total invisibility. To pierce their cone of fear and silence was to be met with incredulous glares of resentment. Our lives are led elsewhere, those looks said, and yours ought to be too. The black girls were claimed by boy-friends too sophisticated to bother with school, who rode by for them at lunch hour in cars throbbing with amplified bass lines and sometimes boasting bullet-riddled doors, and their only use for us was as a dartboard for throwing lit cigarette butts, a frequent sport. Yes, relations between the sexes were strained at Sarah J., and I doubt any of us four, even Tony, so much as copped a feel from the girls we were schooled with there. For all of us that would wait for Court Street, for the world we would come to know through Minna.

* * *

Minna's Court Street was the old Brooklyn, a placid ageless sur-face alive underneath with talk, with deals and casual insults, a neighborhood political machine with pizzeria and butcher-shop bosses and unwritten rules everywhere. All was talk except for what mattered most, which were unspoken understandings. The barbershop, where he took us for identical haircuts that cost three dollars each, except even that fee was waived for Minna – no one had to wonder why the price of a haircut hadn't gone up since 1966, nor why six old barbers were working, mostly not working, out of the same ancient storefront, where the Barbicide hadn't been changed since the product's invention (in Brooklyn, the jar bragged), where other somewhat younger men passed through constantly to argue sports and wave away offers of haircuts; the barbershop was a retirement home, a social club, and front for a backroom poker game. The barbers were taken care of because this was Brooklyn, where people looked out. Why would the prices go up, when nobody walked in who wasn't part of this conspiracy, this trust? – though if you spoke of it you'd surely meet with confused denials, or laughter and a too-hard cuff on the cheek. Another exemplary mystery was the "arcade," a giant storefront paneled with linoleum, containing three pinball machines, which were in constant use, and six or seven video games – Asteroids, Frogger, Cen-tipede – all pretty much ignored, and a cashier, who'd change dollars to quarters and accept hundred-dollar bills folded into lists of numbers, names of horses and football teams. The curb in front of the arcade was lined with Vespas, which had been in vogue a year or two before but now sat permanently parked, without anything more than a bicycle lock for protection, a taunt to vandals. A block away, on Smith, they would have been stripped, but here they were pristine, a curbside Vespa showroom. It didn't need explaining – this was Court Street. And Court Street, where it passed through Carroll Gardens and Cobble Hill, was the only Brooklyn, really – north was Brooklyn Heights, secretly a part of Manhattan, south was the harbor, and the rest, everything east of the Gowanus Canal (the only body of water in the world, Minna would crack each and every time we drove over it, that was 90 percent guns), apart from small outposts of civilization in Park Slope and Windsor Terrace, was an unspeakable barbarian tumult.

* * *

Sometimes he needed just one of us. He'd appear at the Home in his Impala instead of the van, request someone specific, then spirit him away, to the bruised consternation of those left behind. Tony was in and out of Minna's graces, his ambition and pride costing him as much as he won, but he was unmistakably our leader, and Minna's right hand. He wore his private errands with Minna like Purple Hearts, but refused to report on their content to the rest of us. Danny, athletic, silent and tall, became Minna's trusted greyhound, his Mercury, sent on private deliveries and rendezvous, and given early driving lessons in a vacant Red Hook lot, as though Minna were grooming him for work as an international spy, or Kato for a new Green Hornet. Gilbert, all bullish determination, was pegged for the grunt work, sitting in double-parked cars, repairing a load of ruptured cartons with strapping tape, unfastening the legs of an oversize dresser so as to fit it through a small doorway, and repainting the van, whose graffitied exterior some of Minna's neighbors had apparently found objectionable. And I was an extra set of eyes and ears and opinions. Minna would drag me along to back rooms and offices and barbershop negotiations, then debrief me afterward. What did I think of that guy?

Shitting or not? A moron or retard? A shark or a mook? Minna encouraged me to have a take on everything, and to spit it out, as though he thought my verbal disgorgings were only commentary not yet anchored to subject matter. And he adored my echolalia. He thought I was doing impressions.

Needless to say, it wasn't commentary and impressions, but my verbal Tourette's flowering at last. Like Court Street, I seethed behind the scenes with language and conspiracies, inversions of logic, sudden jerks and jabs of insult. Now Court Street and Minna had begun to draw me out. With Minna's encouragement I freed myself to ape the rhythm of his overheard dialogues, his complaints and endearments, his for-the-sake-of arguments. And Minna loved my effect on his clients and associates, the way I'd unnerve them, disrupt some schmooze with an utterance, a head jerk, a husky *"Eatmebailey!"* I was his special effect, a running joke embodied. They'd look up startled and he'd wave his hand knowingly, counting money, not even bothering to look at me. "Don't mind him, he can't help it," he'd say. "Kid's shot out of a cannon." Or: "He likes to get a little nutty sometimes. Forget about it." Then he'd wink at me, acknowledge our conspiracy. I was evidence of life's unpredictability and rudeness and poignancy, a scale model of his own nutty heart. In this way Minna licensed my speech, and speech, it turned out, liberated me from the overflowing disaster of my Tourettic self, turned out to be the tic that satisfied where others didn't, the scratch that briefly stilled the itch.

"You ever listen to yourself, Lionel?" Minna would say later, shaking his head. "You really are shot out of a fucking cannon."

"*Scott Out of the Canyon!* I don't know why, I just – *fuckitup!* – I just can't stop."

"You're a freak show, that's why. Human freak show, and it's free. Free to the public."

"Freefreak!" I hit him on the shoulder.

"That's what I said: a free human freak show."

* * *

We were introduced to Matricardi and Rockaforte at their brownstone on Degraw Street one day in the fall, four or five months after meeting Minna. He'd gathered the four of us in the van in his usual way, without explaining our assignment, but there was a special degree of agitation about him, a jumpiness that induced a special ticcishness in me. He first drove us into Manhattan across the Brooklyn Bridge, then underneath the bridge, to the docks near Fulton Street, and I spent the whole time imitating the nervous jerks of his head as he negotiated traffic. We parked in the middle of a concrete yard in front of one of the piers. Minna disappeared inside a small, windowless shack made of corrugated steel sheets and had us stand outside the van, where we shivered in the wind coming off the East River. I danced around the van in a fit, counting suspension cables on the bridge that soared over us like a monstrous steel limb while Tony and Danny, chilliest in their thin plaid jackets, kicked and cursed at me. Gilbert was nicely insulated in a fake down coat which, stitched into bulging sections, made him look like the Michelin Man or the Red Queen from *Alice in Wonderland*. He stood a few feet from us and methodically tossed chunks of corroded concrete into the river, as though he could earn points by cleaning the pier of rubble.

Minna emerged just as the two small yellow trucks drove up. They were Ryder Rental vans, smaller than Minna's, and identically decorated, one pristine, the other dingy. The drivers sat smoking cigarettes in the cabs, with the motors running. Minna unlatched the backs of the trucks, which weren't padlocked, and directed us to move the contents into his van – quick.

The first thing I laid hands on was an electric guitar, one shaped into a flying V and decorated with enameled yellow and silver flames. A cable dangled from its socket. Other instruments, guitars and bass guitars, were in their hard black cases, but this one had been unplugged and shoved into the van in a hurry. The two trucks were full of concert gear – seven or eight guitars, keyboards, panels full of electronic switches, bundles of cable, microphones and stands, pedal effects for the floor, a drum kit that had been pushed into the truck whole instead of being disassembled, and a number of amplifiers and monitors, including six black stage amps, each half the size of a refrigerator, which alone filled the second Ryder truck and each took two of us to lift out and into Minna's van. The amplifiers and hard cases were stenciled with the band's name, which I recognized faintly. I learned later they were responsible for a minor AM hit or two, songs about roads, cars, women. I didn't grasp it then, but this was equipment enough for a small stadium show.

I wasn't sure we could fit the whole contents of the two trucks into the van but Minna only egged us to shut up and work faster. The men in the trucks never spoke or got out of the cabs, just smoked and waited. No one ever appeared from the corrugated shack. At the end there was barely room for Gilbert and me to crowd in behind the doors to ride with the band's calamitously piled equipment while Tony and Danny shared a spot up front with Minna.

We crossed the bridge back to Brooklyn like that, Gilbert and I fearing for our lives if the load shifted or toppled. After a few breathless turns and sudden stops Minna double-parked the van and freed us from the back. The destination was a brownstone in a row of brownstones on Degraw Street, red brick, stone detailing flaking to powder, genteel curtained windows. Some canny salesman had ten or twenty years before sold the entire block on defacing these hundred-year-old buildings with flimsy tin awnings over the elegant front doors; the only thing special about Matricardi and Rockaforte's house was that it lacked one of these.

"We're gonna have to take apart those drums," said Tony when he saw the doors.

"Just get it inside," said Minna. "It'll fit."

"Are there stairs?" said Gilbert.

"You'll see, you chocolate cheesepuffs," said Minna. "Just get it up the stoop already."

Inside, we saw. The brownstone which appeared so ordinary was an anomaly just through the doors. The insides – typical narrow halls and stairs, spoked banisters, high ornate ceilings – had all been stripped and gutted, replaced with a warehouse-style stairwell into the basement apartment and upstairs. The parlor floor where we stood was sealed off on the left by a clean white wall and single closed door. We ferried the equipment into the upper-floor apartment while Minna stood guarding the rear of the van. The drums went easily.

The band's equipment tucked neatly into one corner of the apartment, on wooden pallets apparently set out for that purpose. The upper floors of the building were empty apart from a few crates here and there and a single oak dining table heaped with silverware: forks, spoons in two sizes, and butter knives, hundreds of each, ornate and heavy, gleaming, bundled in disordered piles, no sense to them except that the handles all faced in one direction. I'd never seen so much silverware in one place, even in St. Vincent's institutional kitchen – anyway, those St. Vincent's forks were flat cutouts of dingy steel bent this way to make tines, that way to make a handle, barely better than the plastic "sporks" we were issued with our school lunches. These forks were little masterpieces of sculpture in comparison. I wandered away from the others and obsessed on the mountain of forks, knives and spoons, but especially those forks, as rich in their contours as tiny thumbless hands, or the paws of a silver animal.

The others shifted the last of the amplifiers up the stairs. Minna reparked the van. I stood at the table, trying to look casual. Jerking your head was good cover for jerking your head, I discovered. Nobody watched me. I pocketed one of the forks, trembling with lust and anticipation, joy in my fear, as I did it. I only just got away with it, too: Minna was back.

"The clients want to meet you," he said.

"Who's that?" said Tony.

"Just shut up when they talk, okay?" said Minna.

"Okay, but who are they?" said Tony.

"Practice shutting up now so you'll be good at it when you meet them," said Minna. "They're downstairs."

Behind that clean, seamless wall on the parlor floor lay hidden the brownstone's next surprise, a sort of double-reverse: The front room's old architecture was intact. Through the single door we stepped into a perfectly elegant, lavishly fitted brownstone parlor, with gold leaf on the ceiling's plaster scroll-work, antique chairs and desks and a marble-topped side table, a six-foot mirror-lined grandfather clock, and a vase with fresh flowers. Under our feet was an ancient carpet, layered with color, a dream map of the past. The walls were crowded with framed photographs, none more recent than the invention

of color film. It was more like a museum diorama of Old Brooklyn than a contemporary room. Seated in two of the plush
chairs were two old men, dressed in matching brown suits.

"So these are your boys," said the first of the two men.

"Say hello to Mr. Matricardi," said Minna.

"Yo," said Danny. Minna punched him on the arm.

"I said say hello to Mr. Matricardi."

"Hello," said Danny sulkily. Minna had never required
politeness. Our jobs with him had never taken such a drab turn.
We were used to sauntering with him through the neighborhood, riffing, honing our insults.

But we felt the change in Minna, the fear and tension. We
would try to comply, though servility lay outside our range of
skills.

The two old men sat with their legs crossed, fingers templed
together, watching us closely. They were both trim in their
suits, their skin white and soft wherever it showed, their faces
soft, too, without being fat. The one called Mr. Matricardi had
a nick in the top ridge of his large nose, a smooth indented scar
like a slot in molded plastic.

"Say hello," Minna told me and Gilbert.

I thought *mister catch your body mixture bath retardy whistlecop's
birthday* and didn't dare open my mouth. Instead I fondled the
tines of my marvelous stolen fork, which barely fit the length of
my corduroy's front pocket.

"It's okay," said Matricardi. His smile was pursed, all lips
and no teeth. His thick glasses doubled the intensity of his stare.
"You all work for Frank?"

What were we supposed to say?

"Sure," volunteered Tony. Matricardi was an Italian name.

"You do what he tells?"

"Sure."

The second man leaned forward. "Listen," he said. "Frank
Minna is a good man."

Again we were bewildered. Were we expected to disagree?

I counted the tines in my pocket, one-two-three-four,
one-two-three-four.

"Tell us what you want to do," said the second man. "Be
what? What kind of work? What kind of men?" He didn't

hide his teeth, which were bright yellow, like the van we'd unloaded.

"Talk to Mr. Rockaforte," urged Minna.

"They do what you tell them, Frank?" said Rockaforte to Minna. It wasn't small talk, somehow, despite the repetitions. This was an intense speculative interest. Far too much rested on Minna's reply. Matricardi and Rockaforte were like that, the few times I glimpsed them: purveyors of banal remarks with terrifying weight behind them.

"Yeah, they're good kids," said Minna. I heard the hurry in his voice. We'd overstayed our welcome already.

"*Orphans*," said Matricardi to Rockaforte. He was repeating something he'd been told, rehearsing its value.

"You like this house?" said Rockaforte, gesturing upward at the ceiling. He'd caught me staring at the scrollwork.

"Yes," I said carefully.

"This is his mother's parlor," said Rockaforte, nodding at Matricardi.

"Exactly as she kept it," said Matricardi proudly. "We never changed a thing."

"When Mr. Matricardi and I were children like yourselves I would come to see his family and we would sit in this room." Rockaforte smiled at Matricardi. Matricardi smiled back. "His mother believe me would rip our ears if we spilled on this carpet, even a drop. Now we sit and remember."

"Everything exactly as she kept it," said Matricardi. "She would see it and know. If she were here, bless her sweet pathetic soul."

They fell silent. Minna was silent too, though I imagined I could feel his anxiety to be out of there. I thought I heard him gulp, actually.

My throat was calm. Instead I worked at my stolen fork. It now seemed so potent a charm, I imagined that if I had it in my pocket I might never need to tic aloud again.

"So tell us," said Rockaforte. "Tell us what you're going to be. What kind of men."

"Like Frank," said Tony, confident he was speaking for us all, and right to be.

This answer made Matricardi chuckle, still toothlessly.

Rockaforte waited patiently until his friend was finished. Then he asked Tony, "You want to make music?"

"What?"

"You want to make music?" His tone was sincere.

Tony shrugged. We all held our breath, waiting to understand. Minna shifted his weight, nervous, watching this encounter ramble on beyond his control.

"The belongings you moved for us today," said Rockaforte. "You recognize what those things are?"

"Sure."

"No, no," said Minna suddenly. "You can't do that."

"Please don't refuse our gift," said Rockaforte.

"No, really, we can't. With respect." I could see this was imperative for Minna. The gift, worth thousands if not tens of thousands, must absolutely be denied. I shouldn't bother to form nutty fantasies about the electric guitars and keyboards and amplifiers. Too late, though: My brain had begun to bubble with names for our band, all stolen from Minna: *You Fucking Mooks, The Chocolate Cheeseballs, Tony and the Tugboats.*

"Why, Frank?" Matricardi. "Let us bring a little joy. For orphans to make music is a good thing."

"No, please."

Jerks From Nowhere. Free Human Freakshow. I pictured these in place of the band's logo on the skin of the bass drum, and stenciled onto the amplifiers.

"Nobody else will be permitted to take pleasure in that garbage," said Rockaforte, shrugging. "We can give it to your orphans, or a fire can be created with a can of gasoline – it would be no different."

Rockaforte's tone made me understand two things. First, that the offer truly meant nothing to him, nothing at all, and so it could be turned away. They wouldn't force Minna to allow us to take the instruments.

And second, that Rockaforte's strange comparison involving a can of gasoline wasn't strange at all to him. That was now exactly what would happen to the band's equipment.

Minna heard it too, and exhaled deeply. The danger was past. But at the same moment I turned a corner in the opposite direction. My magic fork failed. I began to want to pronounce a measure of the nonsense that danced in my head. *Bucky Dent and the Stale Doughnuts*—

"Here," said Matricardi. He raised his hand, a gentle referee. "We can see it displeases, so forget." He fished in the interior pocket of his suit jacket. "But we insist on a measure of gratitude for these orphan boys who have done us such a favor."

He came out with hundred-dollar bills, four of them. He passed them to Frank and nodded at us, smiling munificently, and why not? The gesture was unmistakably the source for Frank's trick of spreading twenties everywhere, and it instantly made Frank seem somehow childish and cheap that he would bother to grease palms with anything less than a hundred.

"All right," said Minna. "That's great, you'll spoil them. They don't know what to do with it." He was able to josh now, the end in sight. "Say thanks, you peanutheads."

The other three were dazzled, I was fighting my syndrome.

"Thanks."

"Thanks."

"Thanks, Mr. Matricardi."

"Arf!"

After that Minna got us out of there, hustled us through the brownstone's odd hallway too fast even to glance back. Matricardi and Rockaforte had never moved from their chairs, just smiled at us and one another until we were gone. Minna put us all in the back of the van, where we compared hundred-dollar bills – they were fresh, and the serial numbers ran in sequence – and Tony immediately tried to persuade us he should caretake ours, that they weren't safe in the Home. We didn't bite.

Minna parked us on Smith Street, near Pacific, in front of an all-night market called Zeod's, after the Arab who ran it. We sat and waited until Minna came around the back of the van with a beer.

"You jerks know about forgetting?" he said.

"Forgetting what?"

"The names of those guys you just met. They're not good for you to go around saying."

"What should we call them?"

"Call them nothing. That's a part of my work you need

to learn about. Sometimes the clients are just the clients. No names."

"Who are they?"

"They're nobody," said Minna. "That's the point. Forget you ever saw them."

"They live there?" said Gilbert.

"Nope. They just keep that place. They moved to Jersey."

"*Gardenstate*," I said.

"Yeah, the Garden State."

"*Garden State Brickface and Stucco!*" I shouted. Garden State Brickface and Stucco was a renovation firm whose crummy homemade television ads came on channels 9 and 11 during Mets and Yankees games and during reruns of *The Twilight Zone*. The weird name of the firm was already an occasional tic. Now it seemed to me that Brickface and Stucco might actually be Matricardi and Rockaforte's secret names.

"What's that?"

"*Garden State Bricco and Stuckface!*"

I'd made Minna laugh again. Like a lover, I loved to make Minna laugh.

"Yeah," he said. "That's good. Call them Bricco and Stuck-face, you goddamn beautiful freak." He took another slug of beer.

And if memory serves we never heard him speak their real names again.

* * *

"Makes you think you're Italian?" said Minna one day, as we all rode together in his Impala.

"What do I look like to you?" said Tony.

"I don't know, I was thinking maybe Greek," said Minna. "I used to know this Greek guy went around knocking up the Italian girls down Union Street, until a couple their older brothers took him out under the bridge. You remind me of him, you know? Got that dusky tinge. I'd say half Greek. Or maybe Puerto Rican, or Syrian."

"Fuck you."

"Probably know all your parents, if you think about it.

We're not talking the international jet set here – bunch of teen mothers, probably live in a five-mile radius, need to know the goddamn truth."

So it was, with this casual jaunt against Tony's boasts, that Minna appeared to announce what we already half suspected – that it was not only his life that was laced with structures of meaning but our own, that these master plots were transparent to him and that he held the power to reveal them, that he did know our parents and at any moment might present them to us.

Other times he taunted us, playing at knowledge or ignorance – we couldn't know which it was. He and I were alone when he said, "Essrog, Essrog. That name." He crunched up his mouth and squinted, as if trying to remember, or perhaps to read a name inscribed on the distant Manhattan skyline.

"You know an Essrog?" I said, my breath short, heart pounding. "*Edgehog!*"

"No. It's just— You ever look it up in the phone book? Can't be more than three or four Essrogs, for chrissakes. Such a weird name."

Later, at the Home, I looked. There were three.

* * *

Minna's weird views filtered down through the jokes he told and liked to hear, and those he cut short within a line or two of their telling. We learned to negotiate the labyrinth of his prejudices blind, and blindly. Hippies were dangerous and odd, also sort of sad in their utopian wrongness. ("Your parents must of been hippies," he'd tell me. "That's why you came out the superfreak you are.") Homosexual men were harmless reminders of the impulse Minna was sure lurked in all of us – and "half a fag" was more shameful than a whole one. Certain baseball players, Mets specifically (the Yankees were holy but boring, the Mets wonderfully pathetic and human), were half a fag – Lee Mazzilli, Rusty Staub, later Gary Carter. So were most rock stars and anyone who'd been in the armed services but not in a war. Lesbians were wise and mysterious and deserved respect (and how could we who relied on Minna for all our knowledge of women argue when he himself grew baffled and reverent?) but could still be comically stubborn or stuck up. The Arabic population of Atlantic Avenue was as distant and unfathomable as the Indian tribes that had held our land before Columbus. "Classic" minorities – Irish, Jews, Poles, Italians, Greeks and Puerto Ricans – were the clay of life itself, funny in their essence, while blacks and Asians of all types were soberly snubbed, unfunny (Puerto Ricans probably should have been in this second class but had been elevated to "classic" status single-handedly by *West Side Story* – and all Hispanics were "Ricans" even when they were Dominicans, as they frequently were). But bone stupidity, mental illness, and familial or sexual anxiety – these were the bolts of electricity that made the clay walk, the animating forces that rendered human life amusing and that flowed, once you learned to identify them, through every personality and interaction. It was a form of racism, not respect, that restricted blacks and Asians from ever being stupid like a Mick or Polack. If you weren't funny, you didn't quite exist. And it was usually better to be fully stupid, impotent, lazy, greedy or freakish than to seek to dodge your destiny, or layer it underneath pathetic guises of vanity or calm. So it was that I, Overt Freak Supreme, became mascot of a worldview.

*   *   *

I called the Brooklyn directory's Essrogs one day when I was left alone for twenty minutes in a warehouse office, waiting for Minna to return, slowly picking out the numbers on the heavy rotary dial, trying not to obsess on the finger holes. I'd perhaps dialed a phone twice at that point in my life.

I tried *F. Essrog and Lawrence Essrog and Murray and Annette Essrog.* F. wasn't home. Lawrence's phone was answered by a child. I listened for a while as he said "Hello? Hello?," my vocal cords frozen, then hung up.

Murray Essrog picked up the phone. His voice was wheezy and ancient.

"Essrog?" I said, and whispered *Chestbutt* away from the phone.

"Yes. This is the Essrog residence, Murray speaking. Who's this?"

"Baileyrog," I said.

"Who?"

"Bailey."

He waited for a moment, then said, "Well, what can I do for you, Bailey?"

I hung up the phone. Then I memorized the numbers, all three of them. In the years that followed I would never once step across the line I'd drawn with Murray or the other telephone Essrogs – never show up at their homes, never accuse them of being related to a *free human freak show*, never even properly introduce myself – but I made a ritual out of dialing their numbers and hanging up after a tic or two, or listening, just long enough to hear another Essrog breathe.

* * *

A true story, not a joke, though it was repeated as often, tugboated relentlessly, was of the beat cop from Court Street who routinely dislodged clumps of teenagers clustered at night on stoops or in front of bars and who, if met with excuses, would cut them off with "Yeah, yeah. Tell your story *walking*." More than anything, this somehow encapsulated my sense of Minna – his impatience, his pleasure in compression, in ordinary things made more expressive, more hilarious or vivid by their conflation. He loved talk but despised explanations. An endearment was flat unless folded into an insult. An insult was better if it was also self-deprecation, and ideally should also serve as a slice of street philosophy, or as resumption of some dormant debate. And all talk was finer on the fly, out on the pavement, between beats of action: We learned to tell our story walking.

* * *

Though Gerard Minna's name was printed on the L&L business card, we met him only twice, and never on a moving job. The first time was Christmas Day, 1982, at Minna's mother's apartment.

Carlotta Minna was an Old Stove. That was the Brooklyn term for it, according to Minna. She was a cook who worked in her own apartment, making plates of sautéed squid and stuffed peppers and jars of tripe soup that were purchased at her door by a constant parade of buyers, mostly neighborhood women with too much housework or single men, young and elderly, bocce players who'd take her plates to the park with them, racing bettors who'd eat her food standing up outside the OTB, barbers and butchers and contractors who'd sit on crates in the backs of their shops and wolf her cutlets, folding them with their fingers like waffles. How her prices and schedules were conveyed I never understood – perhaps telepathically. She truly worked an old stove, too, a tiny enamel four-burner crusted with ancient sauces and on which three or four pots invariably bubbled. The oven of this herculean appliance was never cool; the whole kitchen glowed with heat like a kiln. Mrs. Minna herself seemed to have been baked, her whole face dark and furrowed like the edges of an overdone calzone. We never arrived without nudging aside some buyers from her door, nor without packing off with plateloads of food, though how she could spare it was a mystery, since she never seemed to make more than she needed, never wasted a scrap. When we were in her presence Minna bubbled himself, with talk, all directed at his mother, banking cheery insults off anyone else in the apartment, delivery boys, customers, strangers (if there was such a thing to Minna then), tasting everything she had cooking and making suggestions on every dish, poking and pinching every raw ingredient or ball of unfinished dough and also his mother herself, her earlobes and chin, wiping flour off her dark arms with his open hand. She rarely – that I saw, anyway – acknowledged his attentions, or even directly acknowledged his presence. And she never once in my presence uttered so much as a single word.

That Christmas Minna had us all up to Carlotta's apartment, and for once we ate at her table, first nudging aside sauce-glazed stirring spoons and unlabeled baby-food jars of spices to clear spots for our plates. Minna stood at the stove, sampling her broth, and Carlotta hovered over us as we devoured her meat-balls, running her floury fingers over the backs of our chairs, then gently touching our heads, the napes of our necks. We pretended not to notice, ashamed in front of one another and ourselves to show that we drank in her nurturance as eagerly as her meat sauce. But we drank it. It was Christmas, after all. We splashed, gobbled, kneed one another under the table. Privately, I polished the handle of my spoon, quietly aping the motions of her fingers on my nape, and fought not to twist in my seat and jump at her. I focused on my plate – eating was for me already by then a reliable balm. All the while she went on caressing, with hands that would have horrified us if we'd looked close.

Minna spotted her and said, "This is exciting for you, Ma? I got all of motherless Brooklyn up here for you. Merry Christmas."

Minna's mother only produced a sort of high, keening sigh. We stuck to the food.

"*Motherless Brooklyn*," repeated a voice we didn't know.

It was Minna's brother, Gerard. He'd come in without our noticing. A fleshier, taller Minna. His eyes and hair were as dark, his mouth as wry, lips deep-indented at the corners. He wore a brown-and-tan leather coat, which he left buttoned, his hands pushed into the fake-patch pockets.

"So this is your little moving company," he said.

"Hey, Gerard," said Minna.

"Christmas, Frank," said Gerard Minna absently, not looking at his brother. Instead he was making short work of the four of us with his eyes, his hard gaze snapping us each in two like bolt cutters on inferior padlocks. It didn't take long before he was done with us forever – that was how it felt.

"Yeah, Christmas to you," said Minna. "Where you been?"

"Upstate," said Gerard.

"What, with Ralph and them?" I detected something new in Minna's voice, a yearning, sycophantic strain.

"More or less."

"What, just for the holidays you're gonna go talkative on me? Between you and Ma it's like the Cloisters up here."

"I brought you a present." He handed Minna a white legal envelope, stuffed fat. Minna began to tear at the end and Gerard said, in a voice low and full of ancient sibling authority, "Put it away."

Now we understood we'd all been staring. All except

Carlotta, who was at her stove, piling together an improbable, cornucopic holiday plate for her older son.

"Make it to go, Mother."

Carlotta moaned again, closed her eyes.

"I'll be back," said Gerard. He stepped over and put his hands on her, much as Minna had. "I've got a few people to see today, that's all. I'll be back tonight. Enjoy your little orphan party."

He took the foil-wrapped plate and was gone.

Minna said, "What're you staring at? Eat your food!" He stuffed the white envelope into his jacket. The envelope made me think of Matricardi and Rockaforte, their pristine hundred-dollar bills. Brickface and Stucco, I corrected silently. Then Minna cuffed us, a bit too hard, the bulging gold ring on his middle finger clipping our crowns in more or less the same place his mother had fondled.

* * *

Minna's behavior with his mother oddly echoed what we knew of his style with women. I'd say girlfriends, but he never called them that, and we rarely saw him with the same one twice. They were Court Street girls, decorating poolrooms and movie-theater lounges, getting off work from the bakery still wearing disposable paper hats, applying lipstick without missing a chew of their gum, slanting their heavily elegant bodies through car windows and across pizza counters, staring over our heads as if we were four feet tall, and he'd apparently gone to junior high school with each and every one of them. "Sadie and me were in the sixth grade," he'd say, mussing her hair, disarranging her clothes. "This is Lisa — she used to beat up my best friend in gym." He'd angle jokes off them like a handball off a low wall, circle them with words like a banner flapping around a pole, tease their brassieres out of whack with pinching fingers, hold them by the two points of their hips and lean, as if he were trying to affect the course of a pinball in motion, risking *tilt*. They never laughed, just rolled their eyes and slapped him away, or didn't. We studied it all, soaked up their indifferent femaleness, that rare essence we yearned to take for granted.

Minna had that gift, and we studied his moves, filed them away with silent, almost unconscious prayers.

"It's not that I only like women with large breasts," he told me once, years later, long after he'd traded the Court Street girls for his strange, chilly marriage. We were walking down Atlantic Avenue together, I think, and a woman passing had caused his head to turn. I'd jerked my head too, of course, my actions as exaggerated and secondhand as a marionette's. "That's a very common misunderstanding," he said, as if he were an idol and I his public, a mass audience devoted to puzzling him out. "Thing is, for me a woman has to have a certain amount of *muffling*, you know what I mean? Something between you, in the way of insulation. Otherwise, you're right up against her naked soul."

*   *   *

Wheels within wheels was another of Minna's phrases, used exclusively to sneer at our notions of coincidence or conspiracy. If we Boys ever dabbled in astonishment at, say, his running into three girls he knew from high school in a row on Court Street, two of whom he'd dated behind each other's backs, he'd bug his eyes and intone, *wheels within wheels*. No Met had ever pitched a no-hitter, but Tom Seaver and Nolan Ryan both pitched them after being traded away – *wheels within wheels*. The barber, the cheese man, and the bookie were all named Carmine – oh yeah, *wheels within wheels*, big time. You're onto something there, Sherlock.

By implication we orphans were idiots of connectivity, overly impressed by any trace of the familial in the world. We should doubt ourselves any time we imagined a network in operation. We should leave that stuff to Minna. Just as he knew the identity of our parents but would never reveal it to us, only Frank Minna was authorized to speculate on the secret systems that ran Court Street or the world. If we dared chime in, we'd surely only discovered more *wheels within wheels*. Business as usual. The regular fucking world – get used to it.

*   *   *

One day in April, five months after that Christmas meal, Minna drove up with all his windows thoroughly smashed, the van transformed into a blinding crystalline sculpture, a mirrorball on wheels, reflecting the sun. It was plainly the work of a man with a hammer or crowbar and no fear of interruption. Minna appeared not to have noticed; he ferried us out to a job without mentioning it. On our way back to the Home, as we rumbled over the cobblestones of Hoyt Street, Tony nodded at the windshield, which sagged in its frame like a beaded curtain, and said, "So what happened?"

"What happened to what?" It was a Minna game, forcing us to be literal when we'd been trained by him to talk in glances, in three-corner shots.

"Somebody fucked up your van."

Minna shrugged, excessively casual. "I parked it on that block of Pacific Street."

We didn't know what he was talking about.

"These guys around that block had this thing about how I was uglifying the neighborhood." A few weeks after Gilbert's paint job the van had been covered again with graffiti, vast filled-in outlines of incoherent ballooning font and an overlay of stringy tags. Something made Minna's van a born target, the flat battered sides like a windowless subway car, a homely public surface crying for spray paint where both private cars and bigger, glossier commercial trucks were inviolate. "They told me not to park it around there anymore. Then after I did it a couple of times more, they told me a different way."

Minna lifted both hands from the wheel to gesture his indifference. We weren't totally convinced.

"Someone's sending a message," said Tony.

"What's that?" said Minna.

"I just said it's a message," said Tony. I knew he wanted to ask about Matricardi and Rockaforte. Were they involved? Couldn't they protect Minna from having his windows smashed? We all wanted to ask about them and never would, unless Tony did it first.

"Yeah, but what are you trying to say?" said Minna.

"*Fuckitmessage*," I suggested impulsively.

"You know what I mean," said Tony defiantly, ignoring me.

"Yeah, maybe," said Minna. "But put it in your own words."
I could feel his anger unfolding, smooth as a fresh deck of
cards.

"*Tellmetofuckitall!*" I was like a toddler devising a tantrum to
keep his parents from fighting.

But Minna wasn't distractable. "Quiet, Freakshow," he said,
never taking his eyes from Tony. "Tell me what you said," he
told Tony again.

"Nothing," said Tony. "Damn." He was backpedaling.

Minna pulled the van to the curb at a fire hydrant on the
corner of Bergen and Hoyt. Outside, a couple of black men sat
on a stoop, drinking from a bag. They squinted at us.

"Tell me what you said," Minna insisted.

He and Tony stared at one another, and the rest of us melted
back. I swallowed away a few variations.

"Just, you know, somebody's sending you a message." Tony
smirked.

This clearly infuriated Minna. He and Tony suddenly spoke
a private language in which *message* signified heavily. "You
think you know a thing," he said.

"All I'm saying is I can see what they did to your truck,
Frank." Tony scuffed his feet in the layer of tiny cubes of safety
glass that had peeled away from the limp window and lay scattered on the floor of the van.

"That's not all you said, Dickweed."

That was the first I heard Minna use the term that would
become lodged thereafter in my uppermost tic-echelon: *dickweed*. I didn't know whether he borrowed the nickname or
invented it himself on the spot.

What it meant to me I still can't say. Perhaps it was inscribed
in my vocabulary, though, by the trauma of that day: Our little
organization was losing its innocence, although I couldn't have
explained how or why.

"I can't help what I see," said Tony. "Somebody put a hit on
your windows."

"Think you're a regular little wiseguy, don't you?"

Tony stared at him.

"You want to be Scarface?"

Tony didn't give his answer, but we knew what it was.

Scarface had opened a month before, and Al Pacino was ascendant, a personal colossus astride Tony's world, blocking out the sky.

"See, the thing about Scarface," said Minna, "is before he got to be Scarface he was *Scabface*. Nobody ever considers that. You have to want to be Scabface first."

For a second I thought Minna was going to hit Tony, damage his face to make the point. Tony seemed to be waiting for it too. Then Minna's fury leaked away.

"Out," he said. He waved his hand, a Caesar gesturing to the heavens through the dented roof of his refitted postal van.

"What?" said Tony. "Right here?"

"Out," he said again, equably. "Walk home, you muffin asses."

We sat gaping, though his meaning was clear enough. We weren't more than five or six blocks from the Home anyway. But we hadn't been paid, hadn't gone for beers or slices or a bag of hot, clingy zeppole. I could taste the disappointment – the flavor of powdered sugar's absence. Tony slid open the door, dislodging more glass, and we obediently filed out of the van and onto the sidewalk, into the day's glare, the suddenly formless afternoon.

Minna drove off, leaving us there to bob together awkwardly before the drinkers on the stoop. They shook their heads at us, stupid-looking white boys a block from the projects. But we were in no danger there, nor were we dangerous ourselves. There was something so primally humiliating in our ejection that Hoyt Street itself seemed to ridicule us, humble row of brownstones, sleeping bodega. We were inexcusable to ourselves. Others clotted street corners, not us, not anymore. We rode with Minna. The effect was deliberate: Minna knew the value of the gift he'd withdrawn.

"*Muffin ass*," I said forcefully, measuring the shape of the words in my mouth, auditioning them for tic-richness. Then I sneezed, induced by the sunlight.

Gilbert and Danny looked at me with disgust, Tony with something worse.

"Shut up," he said. There was cold fury in his teeth-clenched smile.

"Tellmetodoit, muffinass," I croaked.

"Be quiet now," warned Tony. He plucked a piece of wood from the gutter and took a step toward me.

Gilbert and Danny drifted away from us warily. I would have followed them, but Tony had me cornered against a parked car. The men on the stoop stretched back on their elbows, slurped their malt liquor thoughtfully.

"*Dickweed*," I said. I tried to mask it in another sneeze, which made something in my neck pop. I twitched and spoke again. "*Dickyweed! Dicketywood!*" I was trapped in a loop of self, one already too familiar, that of refining a verbal tic to free myself from its grip (not yet knowing how tenacious would be the grip of those particular syllables). Certainly I didn't mean to be replying to Tony. Yet *dickweed* was the name Minna had called him, and I was throwing it in his face.

Tony held the stick he'd found, a discarded scrap of lath with clumps of plaster stuck to it. I stared, anticipating my own pain as I'd anticipated Tony's, at Minna's hand, a minute before. Instead Tony moved close, stick at his side, and grabbed my collar.

"Open your mouth again," he said.

"Restrictaweed, detectorwood, vindictaphone," said I, prisoner of my syndrome. I grabbed Tony back, my hands exploring his collar, fingers running inside it like an anxious, fumbling lover.

Gilbert and Danny had started up Hoyt Street, in the direction of the Home. "C'mon, Tony," said Gilbert, tilting his head. Tony ignored them. He scraped his stick in the gutter, and came up with a smear of dog shit, mustard-yellow and pungent.

"Open," he said.

Now Gilbert and Danny were just slinking away, heads bowed. The street was brightly, absurdly empty. Nobody but the black men on the stoop, impassive witnesses. I jerked my head as Tony jabbed with his stick – tic as evasive maneuver – and he only managed to paint my cheek. I could smell it, though, powdered sugar's opposite made tangible, married to my face.

"*Stickmebailey!*" I shouted. Falling back against the car behind me, I turned my head again, and again, twitching away, enshrining the moment in ticceography. The stain followed me, adamant, on fire. Or maybe it was my cheek that was on fire.

Our witnesses crinkled their paper bag, offered ruminative sighs.

Tony dropped his stick and turned from me. He'd disgusted himself, couldn't meet my eye. About to speak, he thought better of it, instead jogged to catch Gilbert and Danny as they shrugged away up Hoyt Street, leaving the scene.

*   *   *

We didn't see Minna again until five weeks later, Sunday morning at the Home's yard, late May. He had his brother Gerard with him; it was the second time we'd ever laid eyes on him.

None of us had seen Frank in the intervening weeks, though I know that the others, like myself, had each wandered down Court Street, nosed at a few of his usual haunts, the barbershop, the beverage outlet, the arcade. He wasn't in them. It meant nothing, it meant everything. He might never reappear, but if he turned up and didn't speak of it we wouldn't think twice. We didn't speak of it to one another, but a pensiveness hung over us, tinged with orphan's melancholy, our resignation to permanent injury. A part of each of us still stood astonished on the corner of Hoyt and Bergen, where we'd been ejected from Minna's van, where we'd fallen when our inadequate wings melted in the sun.

A horn honked, the Impala's, not the van's. Then the brothers got out and came to the cyclone fence and waited for us to gather. Tony and Danny were playing basketball, Gilbert perhaps ardently picking his nose on the sidelines. That's how I picture it anyway. I wasn't in the yard when they drove up. Gilbert had to come inside and pull me out of the Home library, to which I'd mostly retreated since Tony's attack, though Tony had shown no signs of repeating it. I was wedged into a windowsill seat, in sunshine laced with shadows from the barred window, when Gilbert found me there, immersed in a novel by Allen Drury.

Frank and Gerard were dressed too warmly for that morning, Frank in his bomber jacket, Gerard in his patchwork leather coat. The backseat of the Impala was loaded with shopping bags packed with Frank's clothes and a pair of old leather suitcases that surely belonged to Gerard. I don't know that Frank Minna ever owned a suitcase in his life. They stood at the fence, Frank bouncing nervously on his toes, Gerard hanging on the mesh, fingers dangling through, doing nothing to conceal his impatience with his brother, an impatience shading into disgust.

Frank smirked, raised his eyebrows, shook his head. Danny held his basketball between forearm and hip; Minna nodded at it, mimed a set shot, dropped his hand at the wrist, and made a delicate O with his mouth to signify the *swish* that would result.

Then, idiotically, he bounced a pretend pass to Gerard. His brother didn't seem to notice. Minna shook his head, then wheeled back to us and aimed two trigger fingers through the fence, and gritted his teeth for *rat-a-tat*, a little imaginary schoolyard massacre. We could only gape at him dumbly. It was as though somebody had taken Minna's voice away. And Minna was his voice – didn't he know? His eyes said yes, he did. They looked panicked, as if they'd been caged in the body of a mime.

Gerard gazed off emptily into the yard, ignoring the show. Minna made a few more faces, wincing, chuckling silently, shaking off some invisible annoyance by twitching his cheek. I fought to keep from mirroring him.

Then he cleared his throat. "I'm, ah, going out of town for a while," he said at last

We waited for more. Minna just nodded and squinted and grinned his closemouthed grin at us as though he were acknowledging applause.

"Upstate?" said Tony.

Minna coughed in his fist. "Oh yeah. Place my brother goes. He thinks we ought to just, you know. Get a little country air."

"When are you coming back?" said Tony.

"Ah, coming back," said Minna. "You got an unknown there, Scarface. Unknown factors."

We must have gaped at him, because he added, "I wouldn't wait underwater, if that's what you had in mind."

We were in our second year of high school. That measure

loomed suddenly, a door of years swinging open into what had been a future counted in afternoons. Would we know Minna whenever it was he got back? Would we know each other?

Minna wouldn't be there to tell us what to think of Minna's not being there, to give it a name.

"All right, Frank," said Gerard, turning his back to the fence. "Motherless Brooklyn appreciates your support. I think we better get on the road."

"My brother's in a hurry," said Frank. "He's seeing ghosts everywhere."

"Yeah, I'm looking right at one," said Gerard, though in fact he wasn't looking at anyone, only the car.

Minna tilted his head at us, at his brother, to say *you know*. And *sorry*.

Then he pulled a book out of his pocket, a small paperback. I don't think I'd ever seen a book in his hands before. "Here," he said to me. He dropped it on the pavement and nudged it under the fence with the toe of his shoe. "Take a look," he said. "Turns out you're not the only freak in the show."

I picked it up. *Understanding Tourette's Syndrome* was the title, first time I'd seen the word.

"Meaning to get that to you," he said. "But I've been sort of busy."

"Great," said Gerard, taking Minna by the arm. "Let's get out of here."

* * *

Tony had been searching every day after school, I suspect. It was three days later that he found it and led us others there, to the edge of the Brooklyn-Queens Expressway, at the end of Kane Street. The van was diminished, sagged to its rims, tires melted. The explosion had cleared the windows of their crumbled panes of safety glass, which now lay in a spilled penumbra of grains on the sidewalk and street, together with flakes of traumatized paint and smudges of ash, a photographic map of force. The panels of the truck were layered, graffiti still evident in bone-white outline, all else – Gilbert's shoddy coat of enamel and the manufacturer's ancient green – now chalky black, and delicate like sunburned skin. It was like an X ray of the van that had been before.

We circled it, strangely reverent, afraid to touch, and I thought, *Ashes, ashes* – and then I ran away, up Kane, toward Court Street, before anything could come out of my mouth.

* * *

Over the next two years I grew larger – neither fat nor particularly muscular, but large, bearlike, and so harder for the bantamweight Tony or anyone else to bully – and I grew stranger. With the help of Minna's book I contextualized my symptoms as Tourette's, then discovered how little context that was. My constellation of behaviors was "unique as a snowflake," oh, joy, and evolving, like some microscoped crystal in slow motion, to reveal new facets, and to spread from its place at my private core to cover my surface, my public front. The freak show was now the whole show, and my earlier, ticless self impossible anymore to recall clearly. I read in the book of the drugs that might help me, Haldol, Klonopin, and Orap, and laboriously insisted on the Home's once-weekly visiting nurse helping me achieving diagnosis and prescription, only to discover an absolute intolerance: The chemicals slowed my brain to a morose crawl, were a boot on my wheel of self. I might outsmart my symptoms, disguise or incorporate them, frame them as eccentricity or vaudeville, but I wouldn't narcotize them, not if it meant dimming the world (or my brain – same thing) to twilight.

We survived Sarah J. Hale in our different ways. Gilbert had grown, too, and grown a scowl, and he'd learned to sneer or lurch his way through difficulties. Danny coasted elegantly on his basketball skills and sophisticated musical taste, which had evolved through "Rapper's Delight" and Funkadelic to Harold Melvin and the Bluenotes and Teddy Pendergrass. If I saw him in certain company, I knew not to bother saying hello, as he was incapable of recognizing us others from deep within his cone of self-willed blackness. Tony more or less dropped out – it was hard to be officially expelled from Sarah J., so few teachers took attendance – and spent his high-school years

on Court Street, hanging out at the arcade, milking acquaint-
anceships made through Minna for cigarettes and odd jobs and
rides on the back of Vespas, and getting lucky with a series of
Minna's ex-girlfriends, or so he said. For a six-month stint he
was behind the counter at Queen Pizzeria, shoveling slices out
of the oven and into white paper bags, taking smoking breaks
under the marquee of the triple-X theater next door. I'd stop in
and he'd batter me with cheap insults, un-Minna-worthy feints
for the amusement of the older pizza men, then guiltily slip me
a free slice, then shoo me away with more insults and maybe a
slap on the head or a too-realistic fake jab to the spleen.

Me, I became a walking joke, preposterous, improbable,
unseeable. My outbursts, utterances and tappings were white
noise or static, irritating but tolerated, and finally boring unless
they happened to provoke a response from some unsavvy adult,
a new or substitute teacher. My peers, even the most unreachable and fearsome black girls, understood instinctively what
the teachers and counselors at Sarah J., hardened into a sort
of paramilitary force by dire circumstance, were slow to get:
My behavior wasn't teenage rebellion in any sense. And so it
wasn't really of *interest* to other teenagers. I wasn't tough, pro-
vocative, stylish, self-destructive, sexy, wasn't babbling some
secret countercultural tongue, wasn't testing authority, wasn't
showing colors of any kind. I wasn't even one of the two or
three heedless, timid, green-mohawked and leather-clad punk
rockers who required constant beatings for their audacity. I was
merely crazy.

*   *   *

By the time Minna returned Gilbert and I were about to graduate – no great feat, mostly a matter of showing up, staying
awake, and, in Gilbert's case, of systematically recopying my
completed homework in his own hand. Tony had completely
stopped showing his face at Sarah J. and Danny was somewhere
in between – a presence in the yard and the gym, and in the
culture of the school, he'd skipped most of his third-year classes and was being "held back," though the concept was a bit
abstract to him, I think. You could have told him he was being

returned to kindergarten and he would have shrugged, only asked how high the hoops were placed in the yard, whether the rims could hold his weight.

Minna had Tony in the car already when he drove up outside the school. Gilbert went to the yard to pull Danny out of a three-on-three while I stood on the curb, motionless in the rush of students out of the building, briefly struck dumb. Minna got out of the car, a new Cadillac, bruise-purple. I was taller than Minna now, but that didn't lessen his sway over me, the way his presence automatically begged the question of who I was, where'd I come from, and what kind of man or freak I was turning out to be. It had everything to do with the way, five years before, I'd begun discovering myself upon Minna's jerking me out of the library and into the world, and with the way his voice had primed the pump for mine. My symptoms loved him. I reached for him – though it was May, he was wearing a trench coat – and tapped his shoulder, once, twice, let my hand fall, then raised it again and let fly a staccato burst of Tourettic caresses. Minna still hadn't spoken.

"Eatme, Minnaweed," I said under my breath.

"You're a laugh and a half, Freakshow," said Minna, his face completely grim.

Soon enough I would understand that the Minna who'd returned was not the same as the one who'd left. He'd shed his old jocularity like baby fat. He no longer saw drolleries everywhere, had lost his taste for the spectrum of human comedy. The gate of his attention was narrowed, and what came through it now was pointed and bitter. His affections were more glancing, his laugh just a wince. He was quicker to show the spur of his impatience, too, demanded less *tell your story*, more *walking*.

But at that moment his austerity seemed utterly particular: He wanted us all in the car, had something to say. It was as though he'd been away a week or two instead of two years. He's got a job for us, I felt myself think, or hope, and the years between fell instantly away.

Gilbert brought Danny. We took the backseat; Tony sat in front with Minna. Minna lit a cigarette while he steered with his elbows. We turned off Fourth Avenue, down Bergen. Toward Court Street, I thought. Minna put his lighter away and his hand came out of his trench-coat pockets with business cards.

L&L CAR SERVICE, they read. TWENTY-FOUR HOURS. And a phone number. No slogan this time, and no names.

"You mooks ever get learners' permits?" said Minna.

Nobody had.

"You know where the DMV is, up on Schermerhorn? Here." He dug out a roll, scrunched off four twenties onto the seat beside Tony, who handed them out. For Minna everything had the same price, was fixed and paid for by the quick application of twenty dollars. That hadn't changed. "I'll drop you up there. First I want you to see something."

It was a tiny storefront on Bergen, just short of Smith Street, boarded so tightly it looked like a condemned building. But I, for one, was already familiar with the inside of it. A few years earlier it had been a miniature candy store, with a single rack of comics and magazines, run by a withered Hispanic woman who'd pinioned my arm when I slipped a copy of *Heavy Metal* into my jacket and ducked for the door. Now Minna gestured at it grandly: the future home of L&L Car Service.

Minna had an arrangement with a certain Lucas, at Corvairs Driving School, on Livingston Street – we were all to receive lessons, free of charge, beginning tomorrow. The purple Caddy was the only vehicle in L&L's fleet, but others were on their way. (The car smelled poisonously new, vinyl squeaking like an Indian burn. My probing fingers investigated the backseat arm-rest ashtray – it contained ten neatly clipped fingernails.) In the meantime we'd be busy getting our licenses and rehabilitating the ruined storefront, fitting it with radios, office equipment, stationery, telephones, tape recorders, microphones (tape recorders? microphones?), a television and a small refrigerator. Minna had money to spend on these things, and he wanted us along to see him spend it. We might look for some suitable clothes while were at it – did we know we looked like rejects from *Welcome Back, Kotter*? – the only thing to do was drop out of Sarah J. immediately. The suggestion didn't ruffle any feathers. In a blink we'd fallen into formation, Pavlov's orphans. We listened to Minna's new tonalities, distrusting and harsh, as they warmed into something like the old, more generous music, the tune we'd missed but not forgotten. He rolled on: We ought to have a CB-radio setup, this was the twentieth fucking century, had we heard? Who knew how to work a CB? Dead silence, punctured by "*Radiobailey!*" Fine, said Minna, the Freak volunteers. Hello? Hello? We almond-studded cheeseballs were staring like we didn't know English – what exactly *had* we been doing for two years anyway, apart from researching how many times a day we could clean out our fish tanks? Silence. Spank our monkeys, rough up our suspects, *jerk off*, Minna meant – did he have to spell it out? More silence. Hello? Hey, had we ever seen *The Conversation*? Best fucking movie in the world, Gene Hackman. We knew Gene Hackman? Silence again. We knew him only from *Superman* – Lex Luthor. It didn't seem likely Minna meant *that* Gene Hackman. (*Lexluthor, textlover, lostbrother*, went my brain, plumbing up trouble – where was Gerard, the other L in L&L? Minna hadn't said his name.) Well, we ought to see it, learn a thing or two about *surveillance*. Talking all the while, he drove us up to Schermerhorn, to the Department of Motor Vehicles. I saw Danny's eyes dart to the Sarah J. boys playing basketball in the park across the street – but now we were with Minna, a million miles away. We ought to get limousine-operator's licenses, he went on. They only cost ten dollars more, the test is the same. Don't smile for the picture, you'll look like the Prom Date Killers. Did we have girlfriends? Of course not, who'd want a bunch of jerks from nowhere. By the way, the Old Stove was dead. Carlotta Minna had passed two weeks ago; Minna was just settling her affairs now. We wondered what affairs, didn't ask. Oh, and Minna had gotten married, he thought to mention now. He and his new wife were moving into Carlotta's old apartment, after first scouring the thirty-year-old sauce off the walls. We jarheads could meet Minna's bride if we got ourselves haircuts first. Was she from Brooklyn? Tony wanted to know. Not exactly; she grew up on an *island*. No, you jerks, not Manhattan or Long Island – a real island. We'd meet her. Apparently first we had to be drivers who operated cameras, tape recorders and CB radios, with suits and haircuts, with unsmiling license photos. First we had to become *Minna Men*, though no one had said those words.

But here, here was *the beauty part*. By Minna's own admission, he'd *buried the lead*: L&L Car Service – it wasn't really a car service. That was just a front. L&L was a *detective agency*.

* * *

The joke Minna wanted to hear in the emergency room, the joke about Irving, went like this:

A Jewish mother – Mrs. Gushman, we'll call her – walks into a travel agency. "I vant to go to Tibet," she says. "Listen lady, take my word for it, you don't want to go to Tibet. I've got a nice package tour for the Florida Keys, or maybe Hawaii—" "No," says Mrs. Gushman, "I vant to go to *Tibet*." "Lady, are you traveling alone? Tibet is no place—" "Sell me a ticket for Tibet!" shouts Mrs. Gushman. "Okay, okay." So she goes to Tibet. Gets off the plane, says to the first person she sees, "Who's the greatest holy man in Tibet?" "Why, that would be the High Lama," comes the reply. "That's who I vant to see," says Mrs. Gushman. "Take me to the High Lama." "Oh, no, you don't understand, American Lady, the High Lama lives on top of our highest mountain in total seclusion. No one can see the High Lama." "I'm Mrs. Gushman, I've come all the vay to Tibet, and I must see the High Lama!" "Oh, but you could never—" "Which mountain? How do I get there?" So Mrs. Gushman checks into a hotel at the base of the mountain and hires sherpas to take her to the monastery at the top. All the way up they're trying to explain to her, nobody sees the High Lama – his own monks have to fast and meditate for years before they're allowed to ask the High Lama a single question. She just keeps pointing her finger and saying "I'm Mrs. Gushman, take me up the mountain!" When they get to the monastery the sherpas explain to the monks – crazy American lady, wants to see the High Lama. She says, "Tell the High Lama Mrs. Gushman is here to see him." "You don't understand, we could never—" "Just tell him!" The monks go and come back and they're shaking their heads in confusion. "We don't understand, but the High Lama says he will grant you an audience. Do you understand what an honor—" "Yes, yes," she says. "Just take me!" So they lead her in to see the High Lama. The monks are

whispering and they open the door and the High Lama nods –
they can leave him alone with Mrs. Gushman. And the High
Lama looks at Mrs. Gushman and Mrs. Gushman says, "Irving,
when are you coming home? Your father's worried!"

INTERROGATION EYES

MINNA MEN WEAR SUITS. Minna Men drive cars. Minna Men listen to tapped lines. Minna Men stand behind Minna, hands in their pockets, looking menacing. Minna Men carry money. Minna Men collect money. Minna Men don't ask questions. Minna Men answer phones. Minna Men pick up packages. Minna Men are clean-shaven. Minna Men follow instructions. Minna Men try to be like Minna, but Minna is dead.

*　*　*

Gilbert and I left the hospital so quickly, and drove back in such a perfect fog of numbness, that when we walked into L&L and Tony said, "Don't say it. We already heard," it was as though I were learning myself for the first time.

"Heard from who?" said Gilbert.

"Black cop, through here a few minutes ago, looking for you," said Tony. "You just missed him."

Tony and Danny stood furiously smoking cigarettes behind L&L's counter, their foreheads pasty with sweat, eyes fogged and distant, teeth grinding behind their drawn lips. They looked like somebody had worked them over and they wanted to take it out on us.

The Bergen Street office was as we'd renovated it fifteen years before: divided in two by the Formica counter, thirty-inch color television playing constantly in the "waiting area" on this side of the counter, telephones, file cabinets and computer on the rear wall, underneath a massive laminated map of Brooklyn, Minna's heavy Magic Marker numerals scrawled across each neighborhood, showing the price of an L&L ride – five bucks to the Heights, seven to Park Slope or Fort Greene, twelve to Williamsburg or Borough Park, seventeen to Bushwick. Airports or Manhattan were twenty and up.

The ashtray on the counter was full of cigarette butts that

had been in Minna's fingers, the telephone log full of his hand-writing from earlier in the day. The sandwich on top of the fridge wore his bite marks. We were all four of us an arrange-ment around a missing centerpiece, as incoherent as a verbless sentence.

"How did they find us?" I said. "We've got Frank's wallet." I opened it up and took out the bundle of Frank's business cards and slipped them into my pocket. Then I dropped it on the counter and slapped the Formica five times to finish a six-count.

Nobody minded me except myself. This was my oldest, most jaded audience. Tony shrugged and said, "Him croaking out *L and L* as his dying words? A business card in his coat? Gilbert giving out names like a fucking idiot? You tell *me* how they found us."

"What did this cop want?" said Gilbert stoically. He would deal with one problem at a time, the plodder, even if they stacked up from here to the moon.

"He said you weren't supposed to leave the hospital, that's what he said. You gave some nurse your *name*, Gilbert."

"Fuck it," said Coney. "Fuck some fucking black cop."

"Yeah, well, you can express that sentiment in person, since he's coming back. And you might want to say, 'Fuck some fuck-ing black homicide detective,' since that's actually what you're dealing with here. Smart cop, too. You could see it in his eyes."

"Fuckicide," I thought to add.

"Who's going to tell Julia?" said Danny quietly. His mouth, his whole face, was veiled in smoke. Nobody answered.

"Well, I won't be here when he comes back," said Gilbert. "I'll be out doing his work for him, catching the motherfucker who did this. Gimme a coffin nail."

"Slow down, Sherlock," said Tony, handing him a cigarette. "I wanna know how'd it even happen in the first place? How'd the two of you even get involved? I thought you were supposed to be on a stakeout."

"Frank showed up," said Gilbert, trying to flick his deplet-ed lighter again and again, failing to make it catch. "He went inside. Fuck. Fuck." His voice was clenched like a fist. I saw the whole stupid sequence playing behind his eyes: parked car, wire, traffic light, Brainum, the chain of banalities that somehow led to the bloody Dumpster and the hospital. The chain of banalities now immortalized by our guilt.

"Inside *where*?" said Tony, handing Gilbert a book of matches. The phone rang.

"Some kinda kung-fu place," said Gilbert. "Ask Lionel, he knows all about it—"

"Not kung fu," I started. "Meditation—"

"You're trying to say they killed him with *meditation*?" said Tony. The phone rang a second time.

"No, no, we saw who killed him – *Viable Guessfrog!* – a big Polish guy – *Barnamum Pierogi!* – I mean *really* big. We only saw him from behind."

"Which one of us is going to tell Julia?" said Danny again. The phone rang a third time.

I picked it up and said, "L and L."

"Need a car at One-eighty-eight Warren, corner of—" droned a female voice.

"No cars," I said by rote.

"You don't have any cars?"

"No cars." I gulped, ticking like a time bomb.

"How soon can you get a car?"

"*Lionel Deathclam!*" I shouted into the phone. That got the caller's attention, enough that she hung up. My fellow Minna Men glanced at me, jarred only slightly from their hard-boiled despair.

* * *

A real car service, even a small one, has a fleet of no fewer than thirty cars working in rotation, and at the very least ten on the street at any given time. Elite, our nearest rival, on Court Street, has sixty cars, three dispatchers, probably twenty-five drivers on a shift. Rusty's, on Atlantic Avenue, has eighty cars. New Relámpago, a Dominican-run service out of Williamsburg, has one hundred and sixty cars, a magisterial secret economy of private transportation hidden deep in the borough. Car services are completely dependent on phone dispatches – the drivers are forbidden by law to pick up customers on the street, lest they compete with medallioned taxicabs. So the drivers and dispatchers litter the world with business cards, slip them into apartment foyers like Chinese take-out menus, leave them stacked beside potted plants in hospital waiting rooms, palm them out with the change at the end of every ride. They sticker pay phones with their phone number, writ in phosphorescent font.

L&L had five cars, one for each of us, and we were barely ever available to drive them. We never handed out cards, were never friendly to callers, and had, five years before, removed our phone number from both the Yellow Pages and the sign over the Bergen Street storefront.

Nevertheless, our number circulated, so that one of our main activities was picking up the phone to say "no cars."

* * *

As I replaced the receiver Gilbert was explaining what he knew about the stakeout, doggedly. English might have been his fourth or fifth language from the sound of it, but you couldn't question his commitment. As *Bionic Dreadlog* was my likely contribution – my mourning brain had decided renaming itself was the evening's assignment – I was in no position to criticize. I stepped outside, away from the chain-smoking confusion, into the cold, light-washed night. Smith Street was alive, F train murmuring underneath, pizzeria, Korean grocer, and the Casino all streaming with customers. It could have been any night – nothing in the Smith Street scene required that Minna have died that day. I went to the car and retrieved the notebook from the glove compartment, doing my best not to glance at the bloodstained backseat. Then I thought of Minna's final ride. There was something I'd forgotten. When I steeled myself to look in the back I saw what it was: his watch and beeper. I fished them out from under the passenger seat where they'd slid and put them in my pocket.

I locked the car and rehearsed a few imaginary options. I could go back to the Yorkville Zendo by myself and have a look around. I could also seek out the homicide detective, earn his trust, pool my knowledge with him instead of the Men. I could walk down Atlantic Avenue, sit in an Arabic storefront where they knew me and wouldn't gape, and drink a tiny cup of mudlike black coffee and eat a baklava or Crow's Nest – acid, steam and sugar to poison my grief.

Or I could go back into the office. I went back into the office. Gilbert was still fumbling with the end of his account, our race up the ambulance ramp, the confusion at the hospital. He wanted Tony and Danny to know we'd done all we could do. I laid the notebook flat on the counter and with a red ballpoint circled WOMAN, GLASSES and ULLMAN, DOWNTOWN, those crucial new players on our stage. Paper-thin and unrevealing as they might be, they had more life than Minna now.

I had other questions: The building they'd spoken of. The doorman's interference. The unnamed woman Frank lost control of, the one who missed her *Rama-lama-ding-dong*. The wiretap itself: What did Minna hope I'd hear? Why couldn't he just tell me what to listen for?

"We asked him, in the back of the car," said Gilbert. "We asked him and he wouldn't tell us. I don't know why he wouldn't tell."

"Asked him what?" said Tony.

"Asked him who killed him," said Gilbert. "I mean, before he was dead."

I remembered the name Irving, but didn't say anything.

"Somebody's definitely going to have to tell Julia," said Danny.

Gilbert grasped the significance of the notebook. He stepped over and read what I'd circled. "Who's Ullman?" said Gilbert, looking at me. "You wrote this?"

"In the car," I said. "It's the note I took in the car. 'Ullman, downtown' was where Frank was supposed to go when he got into the car. The guy in the Zendo, who sent him out – that's where he was sending him."

"Sent him where?" said Tony.

"Doesn't matter," I said. "He didn't go. The giant took him and killed him instead. What matters is who sent him – *Failey! Bakum! Flakely!* – the guy inside the place."

"I'm not telling Julia," said Danny. "I don't care what anyone says."

"Well, it ain't gonna be me," said Gilbert, noticing Danny at last.

"We ought to go back to the East Side – *TrickyZendo!* – and have a look around." I was panting to get to the point, and Julia didn't seem to me to be it.

"All right, all right," said Tony. "We're gonna put our fucking heads together here."

At the word *heads* I was blessed with a sudden vision: Lacking Minna, ours, put together, were as empty and tenuous as balloons. Untethered by his death, the only question was how quickly they would drift apart, how far – and whether they'd burst or just wither.

"Okay," said Tony. "Gilbert, we gotta get you out of here. You're the name they've got. So we'll get you out doing some hoofwork. You look for this Ullman guy."

"How am I supposed to do that?" Gilbert wasn't exactly a specialist in digging up leads.

"Why don't you let me help him?" I said.

"I need you for something else," said Tony. "Gilbert can find Ullman."

"Yeah," said Gilbert. "But how?"

"Maybe his name's in the book," said Tony. "It's not so common, Ullman. Or maybe in Frank's book – you got that? Frank's address book?"

Gilbert looked at me.

"Must still be in his coat," I said. "Back at the hospital." But this triggered a compulsive self-frisking anyway. I patted each of my pockets six times. Under my breath I said, "*Franksbook, forkspook, finksblood—*"

"Great," said Tony. "That's just great. Well, show some initiative for once and find the guy. That's your *job*, Gilbert, for chrissakes. Call your pal, the garbage cop – he's got access to police records, right? Find Ullman and size him up. Maybe he's your giant. He might of been a little impatient for his date with Frank."

"The guy upstairs set Frank up," I said. I was frustrated that Gilbert and his jerk friend from the Sanitation Police were getting the assignment to track Ullman. "They were in it together, the guy upstairs and the giant. He knew the giant was waiting downstairs."

"Okay, but the giant could still be this guy Ullman," said

Tony irritably. "And that's what Gilbert's going to find out, okay?"

I raised my hands in surrender, then snatched an imaginary fly out of the air.

"I'll go up to the East Side myself," said Tony. "Take a look around. See if I can get into this building. Danny, you mind the store."

"Check," said Danny, stubbing out his cigarette.

"That cop's gonna come back around," said Tony. "You talk to him. Cooperate, just don't give him anything. We don't want to look like we're panicking." Implicit in this assignment was the notion of Danny's superior rapport with the *fucking black cop*.

"You make it sound like we're the suspects," I said.

"That's how this cop made it sound," said Tony. "It isn't me."

"What about me?" I said. "You want me – *Criminal Fishrug!* – to go with you? I know the place."

"No," said Tony. "You go explain to Julia."

* * *

Julia Minna had come back with Frank from wherever he'd gone between the dissolution of the moving company and the founding of the detective agency. She might have been the last and greatest of the Minna girls, for all we knew – she sure looked the part: tall, plush, blond by nurture, defiant around the jaw. It was easy to imagine Minna joshing with her, untucking her shirt, taking an elbow in the stomach. But by the time we got to meet her the two had initiated their long, dry stalemate. All that remained of their original passion was a faint crackle of electricity animating their insults, their drab swipes at one another. That was all that showed anyway. Julia terrified us at first, not for anything she did, but because of her cool grip on Minna, and also how tense he was around her, how ready to punish us with his words.

If Julia and Frank had still been animated, quickened with love, we might have remained in infantile awe of her, our fasci-nation and lust still adolescent. But the chill between them was an opening. In our imaginations we became Frank and loved her, unchilled her, grew to manhood in her arms. If we were angry or disappointed with Frank Minna we felt connected to his beautiful, angry, disappointed wife, and were thrilled. She became an idol of disillusionment. Frank had shown us what girls were, and now he'd shown us a woman. And by failing to love her, he'd left a margin for our love to grow.

In our dreams we Minna Men were all Frank Minna – that wasn't news. But now we shot a little higher: If we had Julia we would do better than Frank, and make her happy.

Or so went dreams. I suppose over the years the other Minna Men conquered their fear and awe and desire of Julia, or anyway modulated it, by finding women of their own to make happy and unhappy, to enchant and disenchant and discard.

All except me, of course.

* * *

In the beginning Minna had Julia installed in the office of a Court Street lawyer, in a storefront as small as L&L's. We Men used to drop in on her there with little deliveries, messages or gifts from Frank, and watch her answering phones, reading *People*, making bad coffee. Minna seemed eager to show us off to her, more eager than he was to drop in himself. Similarly, he seemed pleased to have Julia on showcase there, under glass on Court Street. We all intuitively grasped Minna's instinct for human symbols, for moving us around to mark territory, so in this one sense Julia Minna had joined the Men, was on the team. Something went wrong, however, something soured between Julia and the lawyer, and Minna dragged her back to Carlotta Minna's old second-story apartment on Baltic Street, where she'd stayed for most of fifteen years, a sulking house-wife. I could never visit without thinking of Carlotta's plates of food being carried down the stairwell by Court Street's assorted mugs. The old stove itself was gone, though. Julia and Frank mostly ate out.

I went to that apartment now, and knocked on the door, rolling my knuckles to get the right sound.

"Hello, Lionel," Julia said after peering at me through the

peephole. She left the door unlatched and turned her back. I ducked inside. She wore a slip, her ripe arms bared, but below it she was already in stockings and heels. The apartment was dark, except for the bedroom. I shut the door behind me and followed her in, to where a dusty suitcase lay open on the bed, surrounded by heaps of clothing. It wasn't going to be my privilege to be first with the news anywhere, apparently. In a mass of lingerie already inside the suitcase I spotted something dark and shiny, half smothered there. A pistol.

Julia rummaged in her dresser, her back still turned. I propped myself in the closet doorframe, feeling awkward.

I could make out her labored breathing as she fumbled through the drawers.

"Who told you, Julia? *Eat, eat, eat*—" I ground my teeth, trying to check the impulse.

"Who do you think? I got a call from the hospital."

"*Eat, ha ha, eat*—" I revved like a motor.

"You want me to eat you, Lionel?" Her tone was grimly casual. "Just come out and say it."

"Okayeatme," I said gratefully. "You're packing? I mean, I don't mean the gun." I thought of Minna reprimanding Gilbert at the car, a few hours before. *You with no gun*, he'd said. *That's how I sleep at night.* "Packing your clothes—"

"Did they tell you to come over here and comfort me?" she said sharply. "Is that what you're doing?"

She turned. I saw the redness in her eyes and the heaviness and softness of the flesh around her mouth. She groped for a pack of cigarettes that lay on the dresser, and when she put one between her grief-swollen lips I checked myself for a lighter I knew I wasn't carrying, just to make a show of it. She lit the cigarette herself, chopping at a matchbook angrily, throwing off a little curl of spark.

The scene stirred me in about twelve different ways. Somehow Frank Minna was still alive in this room, alive in Julia in her slip with her half-packed suitcase, her cigarette, her gun. The two of them were closer at this moment than they had ever been. More truly married. But she was hurrying away. I sensed that if I let her go, that essence of him that I detected would go, too.

She looked at me and flared the end of the cigarette, then blew out smoke. "You jerks killed him," she said.

Her cigarette dangled in her fingers. I fought off a weird imagining: that she'd catch her slip on fire — it did seem flammable, practically looked aflame already — and that I'd have to put her out, drench her with a glass of water. This was an uncomfortable feature of Tourette's — my brain would throw up ugly fantasies, glimpses of pain, disasters narrowly averted. It liked to flirt with such images, the way my twitchy fingers were drawn near the blades of a spinning fan. Perhaps I also craved a crisis I could master, now, after failing Minna. I wanted to protect someone, and Julia would do.

"It wasn't us, Julia," I said. "We just didn't manage to keep him alive. He was killed by a giant, a guy the size of six guys."

"That's great," she said. "That sounds great. You've got it down, Lionel. You sound just like them. I hate the way you all talk, you know that?" She went back to stuffing clothes anarchically into the suitcase.

I mimed her striking of the match, one long motion away from my body, more or less keeping my cool. In fact, I wanted to run my hands through the clothes on the bed, snap the suitcase latches open and shut, lick the vinyl.

"Jerktalk!" I said.

She ignored me. A police siren sounded out on Smith Street and Baltic, and I shuddered. If the hospital had phoned her, the police couldn't be too far behind. But the sirens stopped half a block away. Just a traffic stop, a shakedown. Any given car on any given evening on Smith Street fit a profile, some profile. The cop's red light strobed through the margin of window under the shade, to throw a glow over the bed and Julia's glossy outline.

"You can't go, Julia."

"Watch."

"We need you."

She smirked at me. "You'll manage."

"No, really, Julia. Frank put L and L in your name. We work for you now."

"Really?" said Julia, interested now, or feigning interest

– she made me too nervous to tell. "All I see before me is mine? Is that what you're telling me?"

I gulped, jerked my head to the side, as though she were looking behind me.

"You think I should come down and oversee the day-to-day business of a *car service*, Lionel? Have a look at the *books*? You think that might be a good occupation for the widow?"

"We're – *Detectapush! Octaphone!* – we're a detective agency. We're going to catch whoever did this." Even as I spoke, I tried to order my thoughts according to this principle: detectives, clues, investigation. I should be gathering information. I wondered for a moment if Julia were the *her* Frank had lost control of, according to the insinuating voice on the wire at the Zendo.

Of course, that would mean she missed her *Rama-lama-ding-dong*. Whatever that was, I couldn't really picture Julia missing it.

"That's right," she said. "I forgot. I'm heir to a corrupt and inept detective agency. Get out of my way, Lionel." She set her cigarette on the edge of the dresser and pushed past me, into the closet.

Inupt and corrept, went the brain of Essrog the Idiotic. *You are corrept, sir!*

"God, look at these dresses," she said as she poked through the rack of hangers. Her voice was suddenly choked. "You see these?"

I nodded.

"They're worth more than the car service put together."

"Julia—"

"This isn't how I dress, really. This isn't how I look. I don't even like these dresses."

"How do you look?"

"You could never imagine. I can barely remember, myself. Before Frank dressed me up."

"Show me."

"Ha." She looked away. "I'm supposed to be the widow in black. You'd like that. I'd look really good. That's what Frank kept me around for, my big moment. No thanks. Tell Tony no thanks." She swept at the dresses, pushing them deeper into the closet. Then she abruptly pulled two out by the hangers and threw them onto the bed, where they spread over the suitcase like roosting butterflies. They weren't black.

"Tony?" I said. I was distracted, my eagle eye watching the ash burn longer, the glowing end of the abandoned cigarette inching toward the wood of the dresser.

"That's right, Tony. Fucking Frank Minna Junior. I'm sorry, Lionel, did you want to be Frank? Did I hurt your feelings? I'm afraid Tony has the inside track."

"That cigarette is going to burn the wood."

"Let it burn," she said.

"Is that a quote from a movie? 'Let it burn'? I feel like I remember that from some movie – *Burnamum Beatme!*"

She turned her back to me, moved again to the bed. Untangling the dresses from their hangers, she stuffed one into the suitcase, then held the other open and stepped into it, careful not to snag the heels of her shoes. I gripped the closet doorframe, stifling an impulse to bat like a kitten at the shimmery fabric as she slid the dress up around her hips and over her shoulders.

"Come here, Lionel," she said, without turning around. "Zip me up."

As I reached out, I was compelled to tap each of her shoulders twice, gently. She didn't seem to mind. Then I took hold of the zipper tab, eased it upward. As I did she took her hair in her hands, raised her arms above her head and turned, so that she rolled into my embrace. I kept hold of the tab, halfway up her back. Up close I saw how her eyes and lips looked like something barely rescued from drowning.

"Don't stop," she said.

She rested her elbows high on my shoulders and gazed up at my face while I tugged at the zipper. I held my breath.

"You know, when I met Frank I'd never shaved my armpits before. He made me shave." She spoke the words into my chest, her voice dopey now, absent-sounding. All the anger was gone.

I got the zipper to the nape of her neck and dropped my hands, then took a step back and exhaled. She still held her hair bunched above her head.

"Maybe I'll grow the hair back. What do you think, Lionel?"

I opened my mouth and what came out, soft but unmistakable, was "Doublebreasts."

"All breasts are double, Lionel. Didn't you know that?"

"That was just a tic," I said awkwardly, lowering my eyes.

"Give me your hands, Lionel."

I lifted my hands again, and she took them.

"God, they're big. You have such big hands, Lionel." Her voice was dreamy and singsong, like a child, or a grownup pretending to be a child. "I mean – the way you move them around so quickly, when you do that thing you do, all that grabbing, touching stuff. What's that called again?"

"That's a tic, too, Julia."

"I always think of your hands as small because they move so fast. But they're big."

She moved them to her breasts.

* * *

Sexual excitement stills my Tourette's brain, not by numbing me, dimming the world like Orap or Klonopin, those muffling medications, but instead by setting up a deeper attentiveness in me, a finer vibration, which gathers and encompasses my urgent chaos, enlists it in a greater cause, like a chorus of voices somehow drawing a shriek into harmony. I'm still myself and still in myself, a rare and precious combination. Yes, I like sex very much. I don't get it very often. When I do, I find I want to slow it down to a crawl, live in that place, get to meet my stilled self, give him a little time to look around. Instead I'm hurried along by the conventional urgencies, by those awkward, alcohol-fueled juxtapositions of persons that have so far provided my few glimpses of arousal's haven. But oh, if I could have just spent a week or so with my hands on Julia's breasts, then I could think straight!

* * *

Alas, my very first straight thought guided my hands elsewhere. I went and plucked the smoldering cigarette off the dresser, rescuing the finish, and since Julia's lips were slightly parted I stuck it there, filter end first.

"Double, see?" she said as she drew on the cigarette. She combed her hair with her fingers, then straightened her slip under her dress where I'd held her.

"What's double?"

"You know, breasts."

"You shouldn't make fun of – *Lyrical Eggdog! Logical Assnog!* – you shouldn't make fun of me, Julia."

"I'm not."

"Did something— Is there something between you and Tony?"

"I don't know. Screw Tony. I like you better, Lionel. I just never told you." She was hurt, erratic, her voice straying wildly, searching for a place to rest.

"I like you, too, Julia. There's nothing – *Screwtony! Nertscrony! Screwtsony! Tootscrewny!* – sorry. There's nothing wrong with that."

"I want you to like me, Lionel."

"You're – you're not saying there could actually be something between us?" I turned and slapped the doorframe six times, feeling my face curdle with shame, regretting the question instantly – wishing, for once, that I'd ticced instead, something obnoxious to obliterate the conversation's meaning, to smother the words I'd let myself say.

"No," she said coldly. She set the cigarette, what was left of it, back on the dresser. "You're too strange, Lionel. Much too strange. I mean, take a look in the mirror." She resumed crushing her clothes into the suitcase, more than seemed possible, like a magician stuffing a prop for a trick.

I only hoped the gun wouldn't go off. "Where are you going, Julia?" I said tiredly.

"I'm going to a place of peace, if you must know, Lionel."

"A – what?" *Prays of peach? Plays of peas? Press-e-piece?*

"You heard me. A place of peace."

Then a horn sounded outside.

"That's my car," she said. "Would you go and tell them I'll be out in a minute?"

"Okay, but – *pressure pees* – that's a strange thing to say."

"Have you ever been out of Brooklyn, Lionel?"

Breasts, underarm hair, now Brooklyn – for Julia it was all just a measure of my inexperience. "Sure," I said. "I was in Manhattan just this afternoon." I tried not to think about what I'd been doing there, or failing to do.

"New York City, Lionel. Have you ever been out of New York City?"

While I considered this question I eyed the cigarette, which had at last begun to singe the dresser top. The blackening paint stood for my defeat here. I couldn't protect anything, maybe least of all myself.

"Because if you had, you'd know that anywhere else is a place of peace. So that's where I'm going. Would you please go hold my car for me?"

* * *

The car service double-parked in front of the building was Legacy Pool, the furthest upscale of the Brooklyn competitors, with all-black luxury models, tinted windows, cell phones for the customers, and built-in tissue-box holders under the rear window. Julia was running in style. I waved at the driver from the stoop of her building, and he nodded at me and leaned his head back on the rest. I was trying out his neck motions, *nod*, *lean*, when the gravelly voice appeared behind me.

"Who's the car for?"

It was the homicide detective. He'd been waiting, staking us out, slumped to one side of the doorway, huddled in his coat against the chilly November night. I made him right away – with his 10 P.M. Styrofoam cup of coffee, worn tie, ingrown beard, and interrogation eyes, he was unmistakable – but that didn't mean he had any idea who I was.

"Lady inside," I said, and tapped him once on the shoulder.

"Watch it," he said, ducking away from my touch.

"Sorry, friend. Can't help myself." I turned from him, back into the building.

The elegance of my exit was quickly thwarted, though – Julia was just then galumphing down the stairs with her overstuffed suitcase. I rushed to help her as the door eased slowly shut on its moaning hydraulic hinge. Too slowly: The cop stuck out his foot and held the door open for us.

"Excuse me," he said with a sly, exhausted authority. "You Julia Minna?"

"I was," said Julia.

"You were?"

"Yes. Isn't that funny? I was until just about an hour ago. Lionel, put my bag in the trunk."

"In a hurry?" the detective asked Julia. I watched the two of them size one another up, as though I weren't any more a factor than the waiting limo driver. *A few minutes ago,* I wanted to say, *my hands*— Instead I hoisted Julia's luggage, and waited for her to move past me to the car.

"Sort of," said Julia. "Plane to catch."

"Plane to where?" He crushed his empty Styrofoam cup and tossed it over his shoulder, off the stoop, into the neighbor's bushes. They were already decorated with trash.

"I haven't decided yet."

"She's going to a *precipice, pleasurepolice, philanthropriest*—"

"Shut up, Lionel."

The detective looked at me like I was crazy.

* * *

My life story to this point:

The teacher looked at me like I was crazy.

The social-services worker looked at me like I was crazy.

The boy looked at me like I was crazy and then hit me.

The girl looked at me like I was crazy.

The woman looked at me like I was crazy.

The black homicide detective looked at me like I was crazy.

* * *

"I'm afraid you can't go, Julia," said the detective, shaking off his confusion at my utterances with a sigh and a grimace. He'd seen plenty in his day, could cope with a little more before needing to bust my chops over it – that was the feeling I got. "We're going to want to talk to you about Frank."

"You'll have to arrest me," said Julia.

"Why would you want to say that?" said the detective, pained.

"Just to keep things simple," said Julia. "Arrest me or I'm getting in the car. Lionel, please."

I humped the huge, unwieldy suitcase down the stoop and waved at the driver to pop the trunk. Julia followed, the detective close behind. The limo's speakers were oozing Mariah Carey, the driver still mellow on the headrest. When Julia slid into the backseat, the detective caught the door in his two meaty hands and leaned in over the top.

"Don't you care who killed your husband, Mrs. Minna?" He was plainly unnerved by Julia's blitheness.

"Let me know when you find out who killed him," she said. "Then I'll tell you if I care."

I pushed the suitcase in over the top of the spare tire. I briefly considered opening it up and confiscating Julia's pistol, then realized I probably didn't want to emerge with a gun in front of the homicide cop. He was liable to misunderstand. Instead I shut the trunk.

"That would involve us being in touch," the detective pointed out to Julia.

"I told you, I don't know where I'm going. Do you have a card?"

As he straightened to reach into his vest pocket she slammed the door, then rolled down her window to accept his card.

"We could have you stopped at the airport," he said severely, trying to remind her of his authority, or remind himself. But that *we* was weaker than he knew.

"Yes," said Julia. "But it sounds like you've decided to let me go. I appreciate it." She palmed his card into her purse.

"Where were you this afternoon when Frank was killed, Mrs. Minna?"

"Talk to Lionel," said Julia, looking back at me. "He's my alibi. We were together all day."

"*Eat me alibailey,*" I breathed, as quietly as I could. The detective frowned at me. I held my hands open and made an Art Carney face, pleading for a common understanding between us

– women, suspects, widows, whattayagonnado? Can't live with 'em, can't live without 'em, eh?

Julia powered her tinted window back up into place and the Legacy Pool limousine took off, idiot radio trickling away to silence, leaving me and the detective standing in the dark of Baltic Street by ourselves.

"Lionel."

Alibi hullabaloo gullible bellyflop smellafish, sang my brain, obliterating speech. I waved a farewell at the detective and started toward Smith Street. If Julia could leave him flat-footed, why couldn't I?

He followed. "We better talk, Lionel." He'd blown it, let her go, and now he was going to compensate with me, exercise his deductive and bullying powers.

"Can't it wait?" I managed, without turning – it took a considerable effort not to swivel my neck. But I felt him right on my heels, like a pacing man and his shadow.

"What's your full name, Lionel?"

"Lullaby Gueststar—"

"Come again?"

"Alibyebye Essmob—"

"Sounds Arabic," said the detective as he pulled even with me. "You don't look Arabic, though. Where were you and the lady this afternoon, Alibi?"

"Lionel," I forced myself to say clearly, and then blurted *"Lionel Arrestme!"*

"That's not gonna work twice in the same night," said the cop. "I don't have to arrest you. We're just taking a walk, Alibi. Only I don't know where we're going. You want to tell me?"

"Home," I said, before I recalled that he'd been to the place I called home once already this evening, and that it wasn't in my best interests to lead him there again. "Except actually I'd like to get a sandwich first. I'm starving. You want to get a sandwich with me? There's a place on Smith, called Zeod's, if that's okay, we'll get a sandwich and then maybe part ways there, since I'm kind of shy about bringing people back to my place—" As I turned to deliver my speech my shoulder-lust was activated, and I began reaching for him again.

He knocked my hand away. "Slow down, Alibi. What's the matter with you?"

"Tourette's syndrome," I said, with a grim sense of inevitability. Tourette's was my other name, and, like my name, my brain could never leave the words unmolested. Sure enough, I produced my own echo: "Tourette is the shitman!" Nodding, gulping, flinching, I tried to silence myself, walk quickly toward the sandwich shop, and keep my eyes down, so that the detective would be out of range of my shoulder-scope. No good, I was juggling too much, and when I re-ticced, it came out a bellow: "*Tourette Is the Shitman!*"

"He's the shitman, huh?" The detective apparently thought we were exchanging up-to-the-minute street jargon. "Can you take me to him?"

"No, no, there's no Tourette," I said, catching my breath. I felt mad for food, desperate to shake the detective, and choked with imminent tics.

"Don't worry," said the detective, talking down to me. "I won't tell him who gave out his name."

He thought he was grooming a stool pigeon. I could only try not to laugh or shout. Let Tourette be the suspect and maybe I'd get off the hook.

On Smith Street we veered into Zeod's Twenty-Four-Hour Market, where the odors of baloney and bad coffee mingled with those of pistachio, dates, and St. John's bread. If the cop wanted an Arab, I'd give him an Arab. Zeod himself stood on the elevated ramp behind the Plexiglas-and-plywood counter. He saw me and said, "Crazyman! How are you my friend?"

"Not so good," I admitted. The detective hovered behind me, tempting me to turn my head again. I resisted.

"Where's Frank?" said Zeod. "How I never see Frank anymore?"

Here was my chance to deliver the news at last, and my heart wasn't up to it. "He's in the hospital," I said, unable now to keep from glancing nervously at the homicide detective. "*Doctorbyebye!*" recalled my Tourette's.

"Some crazyman you are," said Zeod, smiling and arching his hedge of eyebrows knowingly at my official shadow. "You tell Frank Zeod asks, okay, partner?"

"Okay," I said. "I'll do that. How about a sandwich for now? Turkey on a kaiser, plenty of mustard."

Zeod nodded at his second, an indolent Dominican kid, who moved to the slicer. Zeod never made sandwiches himself. But he'd taught his countermen well, to slice extraordinarily thin and drape the meat as it slid off the blade so it fell in bunches, rather than stacking airlessly, to make a sandwich with that fluffy compressibility I craved. I let myself be hypnotized by the whine of the slicer, the rhythm of the kid's arm as he received the slices and dripped them onto the kaiser roll. Zeod watched me. He knew I obsessed on his sandwiches, and it pleased him. "You and your friend?" he said magnanimously.

The detective shook his head. "Pack of Marlboro Lights," he said.

"Okay. You want a soda, Crazyman? Get yourself." I went and got a Coke out of the cooler while Zeod put my sandwich and the cop's cigarettes into a brown paper bag with a plastic fork and a sheaf of napkins.

"Charge it to Frank, yes, my friend?"

I couldn't speak. I took the bag and we stepped back out onto Smith Street.

"Sleeping with the dead man's wife," said the detective. "Now you're eating on his tab. That takes some gall."

"You misunderstand," I said.

"Then maybe you better set me straight," he said. "Gimme those cigarettes."

"I work for Frank—"

"Worked. He's dead. Why didn't you tell your friend the A-rab?"

"*Arab-eye! –* I don't know. No reason." I handed the cop his Marlboros. "*Eatmebailey, repeatmebailey, repeatmobile –* could we continue this maybe another time? Because – *retreatmobile!* – because now I really urgently have to go home and – *eatbail! beatmail! –* eat this sandwich."

"You work for him where? At the car service?"

Detective agency, I silently corrected. "Uh, yeah."

"So you and his wife were, what? Driving around? Where's the car?"

"She wanted to go shopping." This lie came out so blessedly

smooth and un-tic-laden it felt like the truth. For that reason or some other, the detective didn't challenge it.

"So you'd describe yourself as, what? A friend of the deceased?"

"*Trend the decreased! Mend the retreats!* – sure, that's right."

He was learning to ignore my outbursts. "So where are we going now? Your house?" He lit a cigarette without breaking stride. "Looks like you're headed back to work."

I didn't want to tell him how little difference there was between the two.

"Let's go in here," I said, jerking my neck sideways as we crossed Bergen Street, letting my physical tic lead me – navigation by Tourette's – into the Casino.

* * *

The Casino was Minna's name for Smith Street's hole-in-the-wall newspaper shop, which had a single wall of magazines and a case of Pepsi and Snapple crammed into a space the size of a large closet. The Casino was named for the lines that stretched each morning to buy Lotto and Scratchers and Jumble 6 and Pickball, for the fortune being made on games of chance by the newsstand's immigrant Korean owners, for the hearts being quietly broken there round the clock. There was something tragic in the way they stood obediently waiting, many of them elderly, others new immigrants, illiterate except in the small language of their chosen game, deferring to anyone with real business, like the purchase of a magazine, a pack of double-A batteries, or a tube of lip gloss. That docility was heartbreaking. The games were over almost before they started, the foil scraped off tickets with a key or a dime, the contrived near-misses underneath bared. (New York is a Tourettic city, and this great communal scratching and counting and tearing is a definite symptom.) The sidewalk just outside the Casino was strewn with discarded tickets, the chaff of wasted hope.

But I was hardly in a position to criticize lost causes. I had no reason for visiting the Casino except that I associated it with Minna, with Minna alive. If I visited enough of his haunts before news of his death spread along Court and Smith Street,

I might persuade myself against the evidence of my own eyes – and against the fact of the homicide cop on my heels – that nothing had happened.

"What're we doing?" said the detective.

"I, uh, need something to read with my sandwich."

The desultory magazines were shelved two deep in the rack – there weren't more than one or two customers for *GQ* or *Wired* or *Brooklyn Bridge* per month around here. Me, I was bluffing, didn't read magazines at all. Then I spotted a familiar face, on a magazine called *Vibe*: The Artist Formerly Known as Prince. Before a blurred cream background he posed resting his head against the neck of a pink guitar, his eyes demure. The unpronounceable typographical glyph with which he had replaced his name was shaved into the hair at his temple.

"Skrubble," I said.

"What?"

"Plavshk," I said. My brain had decided to try to pronounce that unpronounceable glyph, a linguistic foray into the lands *On Beyond Zebra*. I lifted up the magazine.

"You're telling me you're gonna read *Vibe*?"

"Sure."

"You trying to make fun of me here, Alibi?"

"No, no, I'm a big fan of *Skursvshe*."

"Who?"

"The Artist Formerly Known As *Plinvstk*." I couldn't quit tackling the glyph. I plopped the magazine on the counter and Jimmy, the Korean proprietor, said, "For Frank?"

"Yeah," I gulped.

He waved my money away. "Take it, Lionel."

Back outside, the cop waited until we'd turned the corner, into the relative gloom of Bergen Street, just past the F-train entrance and a few doors from L&L's storefront, then collared me, literally, two hands bunching my jacket at my neck, and pushed me up against the tile-mosaic wall. I gripped my magazine, which was curled into a baton, and the bag from Zeod's with sandwich and soda, held them protectively in front of me like an old lady with her purse. I knew better than to push back at the cop. Anyway, I was bigger, and he didn't really frighten me, not physically.

"Enough with the double-talk," he said. "Where's this going? Why are you pretending your man Minna's still with us, Alibi? What's the game?"

"Wow," I said. "This was unexpected. You're like good cop and bad cop rolled into one."

"Yeah, used to be they could afford two different guys. Now with all the budget cuts and shit they've got us doing double shifts."

"Can we go back to – *fuckmeblackcop* – back to talking nice now?"

"What you say?"

"Nothing. Let go of my collar." I'd kept the outburst down to a mumble – and I knew to be grateful my Tourette's brain hadn't dialed up *nigger*. Despite the detective's roughhousing, or because of it, our frenzy had peaked and abated, and we'd earned a quiet moment together. He was close enough to invite intimacy. If my hands hadn't been full I would have begun stroking his pebbly jaw or clapping him on the shoulders.

"Talk to me, Alibi. Tell me things."

"Don't treat me like a suspect."

"Tell me why not."

"I worked for Frank. I miss him. I want to catch his killer as much as you."

"So let's compare notes. The names Alphonso Matricardi and Leonardo Rockaforte mean anything to you?"

* * *

I was silenced.

Matricardi and Rockaforte: The homicide cop didn't know you weren't supposed to say those names aloud. Not anywhere, but especially not out on Smith Street.

I'd never even heard their first names, Alphonso and Leonardo. They seemed wrong, but what first names wouldn't? Wrongness surrounded those names and their once-in-a-blue-moon uttering. Don't say Matricardi and Rockaforte.

Say "The Clients" if you must.

Or say "Garden State Brickface and Stucco." But not those names.

* * *

"Never heard of them," I breathed.

"Why don't I believe you?"

"Believemeblackman."

"You're fucking sick."

"I am," I said. "I'm sorry."

"You should be sorry. Your man got killed and you're not giving me anything."

"I'll catch the killer," I said. "That's what I'll give you."

He eased off me. I barked twice. He made another face, but it was clear it all would get chalked up to harmless insanity now. I was smarter than I knew leading the cop into Zeod's and letting him hear the Arab call me Crazyman.

"You might want to leave that to me, Alibi. Just make sure you're telling me all you know."

"Absolutely." I made an honorable Boy Scout face. I didn't want to point out to *good cop* that *bad cop* hadn't learned anything from me, just got tired of asking.

"You're making me sad with your sandwich and your goddamn magazine. Get out of here."

I straightened my jacket. A strange peace had come over me. The cop had caused me to think about The Clients for a minute, but I pushed them out of view. I was good at doing that. My Tourette's brain chanted *Want to catch him as much as miss him as much as a sadwich* but I didn't need to tic now, could let it live inside me, a bubbling brook, a deep well of song. I went to the L&L storefront and let myself in with my key. Danny wasn't anywhere to be seen. The phone was ringing. I let it ring. The cop stood watching me and I waved at him once, then shut the door and went into the back.

* * *

Sometimes I had trouble admitting I lived upstairs in the apartment above the L&L storefront, but I did, and had since the day so long ago when I left St. Vincent's. The stairs ran down into the back of the storefront. Apart from that inconvenient fact, I tried to keep the two places separated in my mind, decorating the apartment conventionally with forties-style furniture from the decrepit discount showrooms far down Smith Street and never inviting the other Minna Men up if I could help it, and adhering to certain arbitrary rules: drinking beer downstairs and whiskey upstairs, playing cards downstairs but setting out a board with a chess problem upstairs, Touch-Tone phones downstairs, a Bakelite dial phone upstairs, et cetera. For a while I even had a cat, but that didn't work out.

The door at the top of the stair was acned with a thousand tiny dents, from my ritual rapping of my keys before opening the door. I added six more quick key-impressions – my counting nerve was stuck on six today, ever since the fatal bag of White Castles – and then let myself in. The phone downstairs went on ringing. I left my lights off, not wanting to signal to the detective, if he was still outside watching, the connection between upstairs and down. Then I crept to my front window and peered out. The corner was empty of cop. Still, why take a chance? Enough light leaked in from the streetlamps for me to make my way around. So I left the lamps dimmed, though I had to run my hands under the shades and fondle the switches, ritual contact just to make myself feel at home.

Understand: The possibility that I might at any time have to make the rounds and touch every visible item in my apartment dictated a sort of faux-Japanese simplicity in my surroundings. Beneath my reading lamp were five unread paperbacks, which I would return to the Salvation Army on Smith Street as soon as I'd finished them. The covers of the books were already scored with dozens of minute creases, made by sliding my fingernails sideways over their surfaces. I owned a black plastic boom box with detachable speakers, and a short row of Prince/Artist Formerly Known As CDs – I wasn't lying to the homicide cop about being a fan. Beside the CDs lay a single fork, the one I'd stolen from Matricardi and Rockaforte's table full of silverware fourteen years before. I placed the *Vibe* magazine and the bag with the sandwich on my table, which was otherwise clean. I wasn't so terribly hungry anymore. A drink was more urgent. Not that I really liked alcohol, but the ritual was essential.

The phone downstairs went on ringing. L&L didn't have a machine to pick it up – callers usually gave up after nine or ten rings and tried another car service. I tuned it out I emptied my jacket pockets and rediscovered Minna's watch and beeper. I put them on the table, then poured myself a tumblerful of Walker Red and dropped in a couple of ice cubes and sat down there in the dark to try to let the day settle over me, to try to make some sense of it. The way my ice shimmered made me need to bat at it like a cat fishing in a goldfish bowl, but otherwise the scene was pretty calm. If only the phone downstairs would stop ringing. Where was Danny? For that matter, shouldn't Tony be back from the East Side by now? I didn't want to think he'd go into the Zendo without some backup, without letting us other Minna Men in on the score. I pushed the thought away, tried to forget about Tony and Danny and Gilbert for the moment, to pretend it was my case alone and weigh the variables and put them into some kind of shape that made sense, that produced answers or at least a clear question. I thought of the giant Polish killer we'd watched drive our boss away to a Dumpster – he already seemed like something I'd imagined, an impossible figure, a silhouette from a dream. The phone downstairs went on ringing. I thought about Julia, how she'd toyed with the homicide detective and then flown, how she'd almost seemed too ready for the news from the hospital, and I considered the bitterness laced into her sorrow. I tried not to think of how she'd toyed with me, and how little I knew it meant. I thought about Minna himself, the mystery of his connection in the Zendo, his caustic familiarity with his betrayer, his disastrous preference for keeping his Men in the dark and how he'd paid for it. As I gazed past the streetlight to the flickering blue-lit curtains of the bedrooms in the apartments across Bergen Street, I lingered over my paltry clues: Ullman downtown, the girl with glasses and short hair, "the building" that the sardonic voice in the Yorkville Zendo had mentioned, and Irving – if Irving really was a clue.

While I thought about these things, another track in my brain intoned brainyoctomy brainyalimony bunnymonopoly baileyoctopus brainyanimal broccopotamus. And the phone downstairs kept on ringing. Sighing, I resigned myself to my fate, went back downstairs and picked up the phone.

"No cars!" I said forcefully.

"That you, Lionel?" said Gilbert's friend Loomis, the sanitation inspector – the garbage cop.

"What is it, Loomis?" I disliked the garbage cop intensely.

"Gotta problem over here."

"Where's here?"

"Sixth Precinct house, in Manhattan."

"*Dickweed!* What are you doing at the precinct house, Loomis?"

"Well, they're saying it's too late, no way they're gonna arraign him tonight, he's gonna have to spend the night in the bullpen."

"Who?"

"Who'd you think? Gilbert! They got him up on killing some guy name Ullman."

* * *

Have you ever felt, in the course of reading a detective novel, a guilty thrill of relief at having a character murdered before he can step onto the page and burden you with his actual existence? Detective stories always have too many characters anyway. And characters mentioned early on but never sighted, just lingering offstage, take on an awful portentous quality. Better to have them gone.

I felt some version of this thrill at the news that the garbage cop delivered, of Ullman's demise. But too, I felt its opposite: a panic that the world of the case was shrinking. Ullman had been an open door, a direction, a whiff of something. I couldn't spare any grief for the death of Ullman the human being – especially not on The Day Frank Minna Died – but I mourned nonetheless: My clue had been murdered.

A few other things I felt:

Annoyed – I would have to deal with Loomis tonight. My reverie was snapped. The ice would melt in my glass of Walker Red upstairs. My sandwich from Zeod's would go uneaten.

Confused – let Gilbert glower and lurch all he wanted, but he'd never kill a man. And I'd watched him blink dumbly at the name Ullman. It had meant nothing to him. So no motive, unless it was self-defense. Or else he'd been set up. Therefore:

Frightened. Someone was hunting Minna Men.

*   *   *

I took an agency car into Manhattan and tried to see Gilbert at the precinct house, but didn't have any luck. He'd already been shifted out of the front cage, to the back, where he'd been grouped with a bunch of other fresh arrests for a night of what the cops euphemistically called "bullpen therapy" — eating baloney sandwiches, using the toilet in the open if he had to go, shrugging off petty advances on his watch and wallet, and trading cigarettes, if he had any, for a razor blade to protect himself. Industrious Loomis had already exhausted the cops' patience for Gilbert's rights and privileges: He'd had his phone call, his moment's visitation at the cell bars, and nothing more would be allowed to happen to him until the next morning at the soonest. Then he could hope to be arraigned and sent out to the Tombs to wait for someone to bail him out. So my effort was rewarded by learning nothing yet being saddled with driving Loomis back to Brooklyn. I took the opportunity to try to find out what the garbage cop had heard from Gilbert.

"He didn't want to say much without a lawyer, and I don't blame him. The walls have ears, you know? Just that Ullman was dead when he got there. The homicides picked him up coming out the place like they'd been tipped. Time I saw him, he'd mouthed a little and been roughed around, asked for a lawyer, they told him he had to wait for tomorrow. I guess he tried to call L&L but you weren't picking up, fortunately I was around-- Hey, sorry about Frank, by the way. It's a shame a thing happens. Gilbert didn't look too good about it either I can tell you. I don't know what he said or didn't but the guys weren't too happy with him by the time I showed. I tried reasoning with the guys, let them see my badge, but they treat me like I was lower than a fucking prison guard, you know? Like I couldn't make the fucking cut."

Gilbert had befriended Loomis somewhere near the end of high school, when they both were hanging around the Carroll Street park watching the old men play bocce. Loomis called to Gilbert's lazy, sloppy side, the nose-picker and cigarette-grubber, the part of him that didn't want to always have to keep up with Minna and us other Men. Loomis wasn't sharpened up the way even the most passive and recalcitrant of us orphans had to be – he was a sort of shapeless inadvertent extension of his parents' couch and television set and refrigerator, and he assumed independent life only grudgingly. At Gilbert's side he'd come slouching around L&L in the formative days and never show a glimmer of interest in either our cover-story car service or the detective agency lurking just underneath – we might have an open packet of Sno-Balls or Chocodiles sitting on the counter, though.

Loomis was nudged by his parents toward police work. He struck out twice at the civil-service qualification test to become a regular beat cop, and some kindhearted career counselor nudged him again, gently downward, to the easier test for the sanitation police, which he squeaked past. Before he was the Garbage Cop, though, Minna used to call him *Butt Trust*, a term he would apply with a measure of real tenderness.

Me and the other Boys let it go the first five or six times, thinking an explanation would be offered, before finally asking Minna what he meant.

"You got your brain trust, your most-valued," said Minna. "Then you got the rest of them. The ones you let hang around anyway. That would be the butt trust, right?"

I was never overfond of the butt trust. In fact, I hated Loomis – let me count the ways. His imprecision and laziness maddened my compulsive instincts – his patchiness, the way even his speech was riddled with drop-outs and glitches like a worn cassette, the way his leaden senses refused the world, his attention like a pinball rolling past unlit blinkers and frozen flippers into the hole again and again: *game over*. He was permanently impressed by the most irrelevant banalities and impossible to impress with real novelty, meaning, or conflict. And he was too moronic to be properly self-loathing – so it was my duty to loathe him instead.

Tonight, as we roared across the metal grating of the Brooklyn Bridge's roadway, he settled into his usual dull riff: The sanitation force gets no respect. "You think they'd know what it's like for a cop in this city, me and those guys are on the same team, but this one cop keeps saying, 'Hey, why don't you come around my block, somebody keeps stealing my garbage.' If it weren't for Gilbert I would of told him to stick it—"

"What time did Gilbert call you?" I interrupted.

"I don't know, around seven or eight, maybe nine almost," he said, succinctly demonstrating his unfitness for the force.

"It's – *Tourette is the stickman!* – only ten now, Loomis."

"Okay, it was just after eight."

"Did you find out where Ullman lived?"

"Downtown somewhere. I gave Gilbert the address."

"You don't remember where it was?"

"Nah."

Loomis wasn't going to be any help. He seemed to know this as well as I, and immediately launched into another digression, as if to say, *I'm useless, but no hard feelings, okay?* "So you heard the one about how many Catholics does it take to screw in a lightbulb?"

"I've heard that one, Loomis. No jokes, please."

"Ah, come on. What about why did the blonde stare at the carton of orange juice?"

I was silent. We came off the bridge, at Cadman Plaza. I'd be rid of him soon.

" 'Cause it said 'concentrate,' get it?"

This was another thing I hated about Loomis. Years ago he'd latched on to Minna's joke-telling contests, decided he could compete. But he favored idiot riddles, not jokes at all, no room for character or nuance. He didn't seem to know the difference.

"Got it," I admitted.

"What about how do you titillate an ocelot?"

"What?"

"Titillate an ocelot. You know, like a big cat. I think."

"It's a big cat. How do you titillate it, Loomis?"

"You *oscillate its tit a lot,* get it?"

"*Eat me Ocelot!*" I screamed as we turned onto Court Street. Loomis's crappy punning had slid right under the skin of my symptoms. "Lancelot ancillary oscillope! Octapot! Tittapocamus!"

The garbage cop laughed. "Jesus, Lionel, you crack me up. You never quit with that routine."

"It's not a – *root* – *ocelot*," I shrieked through my teeth. Here, finally, was what I hated most in Loomis: He'd always insisted, from the time we met as teenagers to this day, that I was elaborately feigning and could keep from ticcing if I wanted to. Nothing would dissuade him, no example or demonstration, no program of education. I'd once shown him the book Minna gave me; he glanced at it and laughed. I was making it up. As far as he was concerned, my Tourette's was just an odd joke, one going mostly over his head, stretched out over the course of fifteen years.

"Tossed salad!" he said. "Gotcha!" He liked to think he was playing along.

"Go touchalot!" I slapped him on the thickly padded shoulder of his coat, so suddenly the car swerved with my movement.

"Christ, look out!"

I tapped him five more times, my driving steady now.

"I can't get over you," he said. "Even at a time like this. I guess it's sentimental, like a way of saying, *if Frank were still here.* Since that routine always did keep him busted up."

We pulled up outside L&L. The lights in the storefront were on. Somebody had returned since my jaunt to the Sixth Precinct.

"I thought you were driving me home." Loomis lived on Nevins Street, near the projects.

"You can walk from here, *gofuckacop.*"

"C'mon, Lionel."

I parked in the open spot in across from the storefront. The sooner Loomis and I were out of each other's presence, the better.

"Walk," I said.

"At least lemme use the can," he whined. "Those jerks at the station wouldn't let me. I been holding it."

"If you'll do one thing for me."

"Whuzzat?"

"Ullman's address," I said. "You found it once. I need it, Loomis."

"I can get it tomorrow morning when I'm back at my desk. You want me to call you here?"

I took one of Minna's cards out of my pocket and handed it to him. "Call the beeper number. I'll be carrying it."

"Okay, all right, now will you lemme take a leak?"

I didn't speak, just clicked the car locks up and down automatically six times, then got out. Loomis followed me to the storefront, and inside.

Danny came out of the back, stubbing a cigarette in the countertop ashtray as he passed. He always dressed the prettiest of us Minna Men, but his lean black suit suddenly looked like it had been worn too many days in a row. He reminded me of an out-of-work mortician. He glanced at me and Loomis and pursed his lips but didn't speak, and I couldn't really get anything out of his eyes. I felt I didn't know him with Minna gone. Danny and I functioned as expressions of two opposed ends of Frank Minna's impulses: him a tall, silent body that attracted women and intimidated men, me a flapping inane mouth that covered the world in names and descriptions. Average us and you might have Frank Minna back, sort of. Now, without Minna for a conduit between us, Danny and I had to begin again grasping one another as entities, as though we were suddenly fourteen years old again and occupying our opposite niches at St. Vincent's Home for Boys.

In fact, I had a sudden yearning that Danny should be holding a basketball, so that I could say "Good shot!" or exhort him to dunk it. Instead we stared at one another.

" 'Scuse me," said Loomis, scooting past me and waving his hand at Danny. "Gotta use your toilet." He disappeared into the back.

"Where's Tony?" I said.

"I was hoping you could tell me."

"Well, I don't know. I hope he's doing better than Gilbert. I just left him in the lockup at the Sixth." I realized it sounded as if I'd actually seen him, but I let the implication stand. Loomis wouldn't call me on it, even if he heard from the bathroom.

Danny didn't look all that surprised. The shock of Minna's death made this new turn unimpressive by comparison, I supposed. "What's he in for?"

"*Ullmanslaughter!* – the guy Tony sent Gilbert to find, he turned up dead. They pinned it on Gilbert."

Danny only scratched at the end of his nose thoughtfully.

"So where were you?" I said. "I thought you were minding the store."

"Went for a bite."

"I was here for forty-five minutes." A lie – I doubted it was more than fifteen, but I felt like pushing him.

"Guess we missed each other."

"Any calls? See that *homosapien, homogenize, genocide, can't-decide, candyeyes,* homicide cop?"

He shook his head. He was holding something back – but then it occurred to me that I was too.

Danny and I stood pensively regarding each other, waiting for the next question to form. I felt a vibration deep inside, profounder tics lurking in me, gathering strength. Or perhaps I was only feeling my hunger at last.

Loomis popped out of the back. "Jesus, you guys look bad. What a day, huh?"

We stared at him.

"Well, I think we owe Frank a moment of silence, don't you guys?"

I wanted to point out that what Loomis had interrupted *was* a moment of silence, but I let it go.

"Little something in the way of remembrance? Bow your heads, you turkeys. The guy was like your father. Don't end the day arguing with each other, for crying out loud."

Loomis had a point, or enough of one anyway, to shame me and Danny into letting him have his way. So we stood in silence, and when I saw that Danny and Loomis had each closed their eyes I closed mine too. Together we made up some lopped-off, inadequate version of the Agency – Danny standing for himself and Tony, I for myself, and Loomis, I suppose, for Gilbert. But I was moved anyway, for a second.

Then Loomis ruined it with a clearly audible fart, which he coughed to cover, unsuccessfully. "Okay," he said suddenly. "How's about that ride home, Lionel?"

"Walk," I said.

Humbled by his own body, the garbage cop didn't argue, but headed for the door.

* * *

Danny volunteered to sit by the L&L phone. He already had a pot of coffee brewing, he pointed out, and I could see he was in a pacing mood, that he wanted the space of the office to himself. It suited me well enough to leave him there. I went upstairs, without our exchanging more than a few sentences.

Upstairs I lit a candle and stuck it in the center of my table, beside Minna's beeper and watch. Loomis's clumsy pass at ritual haunted me. I needed one of my own. But I was also hungry. I poured out the diluted drink and made myself a fresh one, set it out on the table too. Then I unwrapped the sandwich from Zeod's. I considered for a moment, fighting the urge just to sink my teeth into it, then went to the cabinet and brought back a serrated knife and small plate. I cut the sandwich into six equal pieces, taking unexpectedly deep pleasure in the texture of the kaiser roll's resistance to the knife's dull teeth, and arranged the pieces so they were equidistant on the plate. I returned the knife to my counter, then centered plate, candle and drink on the table in a way that soothed my grieving Tourette's. If I didn't stem my syndrome's needs I would never clear a space in which my own sorrow could dwell.

Then I went to my boom box and put on the saddest song in my CD collection, Prince's "How Come U Don't Call Me Anymore."

* * *

I don't know whether The Artist Formerly Known as Prince is Tourettic or obsessive-compulsive in his human life, but I know for certain he is deeply so in the life of his work. Music had never made much of an impression on me until the day in 1986 when, sitting in the passenger seat of Minna's Cadillac, I first heard the single "Kiss" squirting its manic way out of the car radio. To that point in my life I might have once or twice heard music that toyed with feelings of claustrophobic discomfort and

expulsive release, and which in so doing passingly charmed my
Tourette's, gulled it with a sense of recognition, like Art Carney
or Daffy Duck – but here was a song that lived entirely in that
territory, guitar and voice twitching and throbbing within
obsessively delineated bounds, alternately silent and plosive. It
so pulsed with Tourettic energies that I could surrender to its
tormented, squeaky beat and let my syndrome live outside my
brain for once, live in the air instead.

"Turn that shit down," said Minna.

"I like it," I said.

"That's that crap Danny listens to," said Minna. *Danny* was
code for *too black*.

I knew I had to own that song, and so the next day I sought it
out at J&R Music World – I needed the word "funk" explained
to me by the salesman. He sold me a cassette, and a Walkman to
play it on. What I ended up with was a seven-minute "extended
single" version – the song I'd heard on the radio, with a four-
minute catastrophe of chopping, grunting, hissing and slapping
sounds appended – a coda apparently designed as a private message of confirmation to my delighted Tourette's brain.

Prince's music calmed me as much as masturbation or a
cheeseburger. When I listened to him I was exempt from my
symptoms. So I began collecting his records, especially those
elaborate and frenetic remixes tucked away on the CD singles.
The way he worried forty-five minutes of variations out of a
lone musical or verbal phrase is, as far as I know, the nearest
thing in art to my condition.

"How Come U Don't Call Me Anymore" is a ballad, piano
strolling beneath an aching falsetto vocal. Slow and melancholy, it still featured the Tourettic abruptness and compulsive
precision, the sudden shrieks and silences, that made Prince's
music my brain's balm.

*   *   *

I put the song on repeat and sat in the light of my candle and
waited for the tears. Only after they came did I allow myself
to eat the six turkey-sandwich portions, in a ritual for Minna,
alternating them with sips of Walker Red. *The body and the*

blood, I couldn't keep from thinking, though I was as distant from any religious feeling as a mourning man could be. *The turkey and the booze*, I substituted. A last meal for Minna, who didn't get one. Prince moaned, finished his song, began it again. The candle guttered. I counted *three* as I finished a portion of sandwich, then *four*. That was the extent of my symptoms. I counted sandwiches and wept. At *six* I killed the music, blew out the candle and went to bed.

(TOURETTE DREAMS)

(in Tourette dreams you shed your tics)

(or your tics shed you)

(and you go with them, astonished to leave yourself behind)

BAD COOKIES

THERE ARE DAYS when I get up in the morning and stagger into the bathroom and begin running water and then I look up and I don't even recognize my own toothbrush in the mirror. I mean, the object looks strange, oddly particular in its design, strange tapered handle and slotted, miter-cut bristles, and I wonder if I've ever looked at it closely before or whether someone snuck in overnight and substituted this new toothbrush for my old one. I have this relationship to objects in general – they will sometimes become uncontrollably new and vivid to me, and I don't know whether this is a symptom of Tourette's or not. I've never seen it described in the literature. Here's the strangeness of having a Tourette's brain, then: no control in my personal experiment of self. What might be only strangeness must always be auditioned for relegation to the domain of symptom, just as symptoms always push into other domains, demanding the chance to audition for their moment of acuity or relevance, their brief shot – coulda been a contender! – at centrality. Personalityness. There's a lot of traffic in my head, and it's two-way.

This morning's strangeness was refreshing, though. More than refreshing – revelatory. I woke early, having failed to draw my curtains, the wall above my bed and the table with melted candle, tumbler quarter full of melted ice, and sandwich crumbs from my ritual snack now caught in a blaze of white sunlight, like the glare of a projector's bulb before the film is threaded. It seemed possible I was the first awake in the world, possible the world was new. I dressed in my best suit, donned Minna's watch instead of my own, and clipped his beeper to my hip. Then I made myself coffee and toast, scooped the long-shadowed crumbs off the table, sat and savored breakfast, marveling at the richness of existence with each step. The radiator whined and sneezed and I imitated its sounds out of sheer joy, rather than helplessness. Perhaps I'd been expecting that Minna's absence would snuff the world, or at least Brooklyn, out of existence.

That a sympathetic dimming would occur. Instead I'd woken into the realization that I was Minna's successor and avenger, that the city shone with clues.

It seemed possible I was a detective on a case.

I crept downstairs past Danny, who was sleeping on his arms on the countertop, black suit jacket shrugged up around his shoulders, small patch of drool on his sleeve. I switched off the coffee machine, which was roasting a quarter inch of coffee into sour perfume, and went outside. It was a quarter to seven. The Korean keeper of the Casino was just rolling up his gate, tossing his bundles of the *News* and the *Post* inside. The morning was clarifyingly cold.

I started the L&L Pontiac. Let Danny sleep, let Gilbert wait in his cell, let Tony be missing. I'd go to the Zendo. Let it be too early for the monks or mobsters hidden there – I'd have the advantage of surprise.

* * *

By the time I'd parked and made my way to the Zendo, the Upper East Side was warming into life, shopkeepers rolling fruit stands out of their shops, sidewalk vendors of stripped paperbacks unloading their boxes, women already dressed for business glancing at their watches as they hustled their dogs' waste into Baggies. The doorman at the entrance-way next door was someone new, a kid with a mustache and uniform, not my harasser from yesterday. He was probably green, without tenure, stuck working the end of the over-night shift. I figured it was worth a shot anyway. I crooked a finger at him through the glass and he came out into the cold.

"What's your name?" I said.

"Walter, sir."

"Walter sir-what?" I broadcast a cop-or-employer vibe.

"Walter is, uh, my last name. Can I help you with something?" He looked concerned, for himself and his building.

"*Helpmewalter* – I need the name of the doorman working last night, about six-thirty, seven. Older gentleman than yourself, maybe thirty-five, with an accent."

"Dirk?"

"Maybe. You tell me."

"Dirk's the regular man." He wasn't sure he should be telling me this.

I averted my gaze from his shoulder. "Good. Now tell me what you know about the Yorkville Zendo." I indicated the bronze plaque next door with a jerk of my thumb. "Dirkweed! Dirkman!"

"What?" He goggled his eyes at me.

"You see them come and go?"

"I guess."

"Walter Guessworth!" I cleared my throat deliberately. "Work with me here, Walter. You must see stuff. I want your impressions."

I could see him sorting through layers of exhaustion, boredom, and stupidity. "Are you a cop?"

"Why'd you think that?"

"You, uh, talk funny."

"I'm a guy who needs to know things, Walter, and I'm in a hurry. Anyone come and go from the Zendo lately? Anything catch your eye?"

He scanned the street to see if anyone saw us talking. I took the opportunity to cover my mouth with my hand and make a brief panting sound, like an excited dog.

"Uh, not much happens late at night," said Walter. "It's pretty quiet around here."

"A place like the Zendo must attract some weird traffic."

"You keep saying Zendo," he said.

"It's right there, etched in brass." *Itched in Ass.*

He stepped toward the street, craned his neck, and read the plaque. "Hmmm. It's like a religious school, right?"

"Right. You ever see anyone suspicious hanging around? Big Polish guy in particular?"

"How would I know he was Polish?"

"Just think about big. We're talking really, really big."

He shrugged again. "I don't think so." His numb gaze wouldn't have taken in a crane and wrecking ball going through next door, let alone an outsize human figure.

"Listen, would you keep an eye out? I'll give you a number

to call." I had a stash of L&L cards in my wallet, and I fished one out for him.

"Thanks," he said absently, glancing at the card. He wasn't afraid of me anymore. But he didn't know what to think of me if I wasn't a threat. I was interesting, but he didn't know how to be interested.

"I'd appreciate hearing from you – *Doorjerk! Doorjam! Jerkdom!* – if you see anything odd."

"You're pretty odd," he said seriously.

"Something besides me."

"Okay, but I get off in half an hour."

"Well, just keep it in mind." I was running out of patience with Walter. I freed myself to tap his shoulder farewell. The dull young man looked down at my hand, then went back inside.

* * *

I paced the block to the corner and back, flirting with the Zendo, seeking my nerve. The site aroused reverence and a kind of magical fear in me already, as though I were approaching a shrine – *the martyrdom of Saint Minna.* I wanted to rewrite their plaque to tell the story. Instead I rang the doorbell once. No answer. Then four more times, for a total of *five,* and I stopped, startled by a sense of completeness.

I'd shrugged off my tired old friend *six.*

I wondered if it was in some way commemorative – my counting tic moving down a list, subtracting a digit for Frank.

Somebody is hunting Minna Men, I thought again. But I couldn't be afraid. I wasn't game but hunter this morning. Anyway, the count was off – four Minna Men plus Frank made five. So if I was counting heads, I should be at four. I had an extra aboard, but who? Maybe it was Bailey. Or Irving.

A long minute passed before the girl with the short black hair and glasses opened the door and squinted at me against the morning sun. She wore a T-shirt, jeans, had bare feet, and held a broom. Her smile was slight, involuntary, and crooked. And sweet.

"Yes?"

"Could I ask you a few questions?"

"Questions?" She didn't seem to recognize the word.

"If it's not too early," I said gently.

"No, no. I've been up. I've been sweeping." She showed me the broom.

"They make you clean?"

"It's a privilege. Cleaning is treasured in Zen practice. It's like the highest possible act. Usually Roshi wants to do the sweeping himself."

"No vacuum cleaner?" I said.

"Too noisy," she said, and frowned as if it should be obvious. A city bus roared past in the distance, damaging her point. I let it go.

Her eyes adjusted to the brightness, and she looked past me, to the street, examining it as though astonished to discover that the door opened onto a cityscape. I wondered if she'd been out of the building since I saw her enter the evening before. I wondered if she ate and slept there, whether she was the only one who did or whether there were dozens, foot soldiers of Zen.

"I'm sorry," she said. "What were you saying?"

"Questions."

"Oh, yes."

"About the Zendo, what you do here."

She looked me over now. "Do you want to come inside? It's cold."

"I'd like that very much."

It was the truth. I didn't feel unsafe following her into the dark temple, the Deathstar. I would gather information from within the Trojan Horse of her Zen grace. And I was conscious of my ticlessness, didn't want to break the rhythm of the conversation.

The foyer and stairwell were plain, with unadorned white walls and a wooden banister, looking as if it had been clean before she began sweeping, clean forever. We bypassed a door on the ground floor and went up the stairs, she carrying the broom ahead of her, turning her back to me trustingly. Her walk had a gentle jerkiness to it, a quickness like her replies.

"Here," she said, pointing to a rack with rows of shoes on it.

"I'm fine," I said, thinking I was supposed to select from among the motley footgear.

"No, take yours off," she whispered.

I did as she told me, removed my shoes and pushed them into an orderly place at the end of one of the racks. A chill went through me when I recalled that Minna had removed his shoes the evening before, presumably at this same landing.

Now in my socks, I followed her as the banister wrapped around through a corridor, past two sealed doors and one that opened onto a bare, dark room with rows of short cloth mats laid out across a parquet floor and a smell of candles or incense, not a morning smell at all. I wanted to peer inside but she hurried us along, up another flight.

On the third landing she led me to a small kitchen where a wooden table and three chairs were arranged around a thwarted back window, through which an emaciated shaft of sunlight negotiated a maze of brick. If the massive buildings on either side had existed when this room was built they might not have bothered with a window. The table, chairs and cabinets of the kitchen were as undistinguished and homely as a museum diorama of Cree or Shaker life, but the teapot she set out was Japanese, and its hand-painted calligraphic designs were the only stretch, the only note of ostentation.

I seated myself with my back to the wall, facing the door, thinking of Minna and the conversation I'd heard through the wire. She took water off a low flame and filled the pot, then put a tiny mug without a handle in front of me and filled it with an unstrained swirling confetti of tea. I warmed my chapped hands around it gratefully.

"I'm Kimmery."

"Lionel." I felt *Kissdog* rising in me and fought it back.

"You're interested in Buddhism?"

"You could say that."

"I'm not really who you should talk to but I can tell you what they'll say. It's not about getting centered, or, you know, *stress reduction*. A lot of people – Americans, I mean – have that idea. But it's really a religious discipline, and not easy at all. Do you know about zazen?"

"Tell me."

"It'll make your back hurt a *lot*. That's one thing." She rolled her eyes at me, already commiserating.

"You mean meditation."

"*Zazen*, it's called. Or *sitting*. It sounds like nothing, but it's the heart of Zen practice. I'm not very good at it."

I recalled the Quakers who'd adopted Tony, and their brick meetinghouse across eight lanes of traffic from St. Vincent's. Sunday mornings we could look through their tall windows and see them gathered in silence on hard benches.

"What's to be good at?" I said.

"You have no idea. Breathing, for starters. And thinking, except it's not supposed to *be* thinking."

"Thinking about not thinking?"

"*Not* thinking about it. One Mind, they call it. Like realizing that everything has Buddha nature, the flag and the wind are the same thing, that sort of stuff."

I wasn't exactly following her, but *One Mind* seemed an honorable goal, albeit positively chimerical. "Could we – could I sit with you sometime? Or is it done alone?"

"Both. But here at the Zendo there's regular sessions." She lifted her cup of tea with both hands, steaming her glasses instantly. "Anyone can come. And you're really lucky if you stick around today. Some important monks from Japan are in town to see the Zendo, and one of them is going to talk this evening, after zazen."

Important monks, imported rugs, unimportant ducks – jabber was building up in the ocean of my brain like flotsam, and soon a wave would toss it ashore. "So it's run out of Japan," I said. "And now they're checking up on you – like the Pope coming in from Rome."

"Not exactly. Roshi set the Zendo up on his own. Zen isn't centralized. There are different teachers, and sometimes they move around."

"But Roshi did come here from Japan." From the name I pictured a wizened old man, a little bigger than Yoda in *Return of the Jedi*.

"No, Roshi's American. He used to have an American name."

"Which was?"

"I don't know. *Roshi* just basically means teacher, but that's the only name he has anymore."

I sipped my scalding tea. "Does anyone else use this building for anything?"

"Anything like what?"

"*Killing me!* – sorry. Just anything besides sitting."

"You can't shout like that in here," she said.

"Well, if – *kissing me!* – something strange was going on, say if Roshi were in some kind of trouble, would you know about it?" I twisted my neck – if I could I would have tied it in a knot, like the top of a plastic garbage bag. "*Eating me!*"

"I guess I don't know what you're talking about." She was oddly blasé, sipping her tea and watching me over the top of the cup. I recalled the legends of Zen masters slapping and kicking students to induce sudden realizations. Perhaps that practice was common here in the Zendo, and so she'd inured herself to outbursts, abrupt outlandish gestures.

"Forget it," I said. "Listen: Have you had any visitors lately?" I was thinking of Tony, who'd ostensibly called on the Zendo after our conference at L&L. "Anyone come sniffing around here last night?"

She only looked puzzled, and faintly annoyed. "No."

I considered pushing it, describing Tony to her, then decided he must have visited unseen, at least by Kimmery. Instead I asked, "Is there anybody in the building right now?"

"Well, Roshi lives on the top floor."

"He's up there now?" I said, startled.

"Sure. He's in *sesshin* – it's like an extended retreat – because of these monks. He took a vow of silence, so it's been a little quiet around here."

"Do you live here?"

"No. I'm cleaning up for morning zazen. The other students will show up in an hour. They're out doing work service now. That's how the Zendo can afford to pay the rent here. Wallace is downstairs already, but that's basically it."

"Wallace?" I was distracted by the tea leaves in my cup settling gradually into a mound at the bottom, like astronauts on a planet with barely any gravity.

"He's like this old hippie who hardly ever does anything but sit. I think his legs must be made of plastic or something. We went past him on the way up."

"Where? In the room with the mats?"

"Uh-huh. He's like a piece of furniture, easy to miss."

"Biggish, you mean?"

"Not so big. I meant still, he sits still." She whispered, "I always wonder if he's dead."

"But he's not a really *big* person."

"You wouldn't say that."

I plunged two fingers into my cup, needing to unsettle the floating leaves again, force them to resume their dance. If the girl saw me do it she didn't say anything.

"You haven't seen any really big people lately, have you?" Though I'd not encountered them yet, Roshi and Wallace seemed both unpromising suspects to be the Polish giant. I wondered if instead one might be the sardonic conversationalist I'd heard taunting Minna over the wire.

"Mmmmm, no," she said.

"*Pierogi monster*," I said, then coughed five times for cover. Thoughts of Minna's killers had overwhelmed the girl's calming influence – my brain sizzled with language, my body with gestures.

In reply she only refilled my cup, then moved the pot to the countertop. While her back was turned I stroked her chair, ran my palm over the warmth where she'd been sitting, played the spokes of the chair's back like a noiseless harp.

"Lionel? Is that your name?"

"Yes."

"You don't seem very calm, Lionel." She'd pivoted, almost catching my chair-molestation, and now she leaned back against the counter instead of retaking her seat.

I didn't ordinarily hesitate to reveal my syndrome, but something in me fought it now. "Do you have something to eat?" I said. Perhaps calories would restore my equilibrium.

"Um, I don't know," she said. "You want some bread or something? There might be some yogurt left."

"Because this tea is corked with caffeine. It only looks harmless. Do you drink this stuff all the time?"

"Well, it's sort of traditional."

"Is that part of the Zen thing, getting punchy so you can see God? Isn't that cheating?"

"It's more just to stay awake. Because we don't really have God in Zen Buddhism." She turned away from me and began rifling through the cabinets, but didn't quit her musings. "We just sit and try not to fall asleep, so I guess in a way staying awake *is* seeing God, sort of. So you're right."

The little triumph didn't thrill me. I was feeling trapped, with the wizened teacher a floor above me and the plastic-legged hippie a floor below. I wanted to get out of the Zendo now, but I hadn't figured a next move.

And when I left I wanted to take Kimmery with me. I wanted to protect her – the impulse surged in me, looking to affix to a suitable target. Now that I'd failed Minna, who deserved my protection? Was it Tony? Was it Julia? I wished that Frank would whisper a clue in my ear from the beyond. In the meantime, Kimmery would do.

"Here, do you want some Oreos?"

"Sure," I said distractedly. "Buddhists eat Oreos?"

"We eat anything we want, Lionel. This isn't Japan." She took a blue carton of cookies and put it on the table.

I helped myself, craving the snack, glad we weren't in Japan.

"I used to know this guy who once worked for Nabisco," she said, musing as she bit into a cookie. "You know, the company that makes Oreos? He said they had two main plants for making Oreos, in different parts of the country. Two head bakers, you know, different quality control."

"Uh—" I took a cookie and dunked it in my tea.

"And he used to swear he could tell the difference just by tasting them. This guy, when we ate Oreos, he would just go through the pack sniffing them and tasting the chocolate part and then he'd put the bad ones in a pile. And like, a really good package was one where less than a third had to go in the bad pile, because they were from the wrong bakery, you know? But sometimes there wouldn't be more than five or six good ones in a whole package."

"Wait a minute. You're saying every package of Oreos has cookies from *both* bakeries?"

"Uh-huh."

I tried to keep from thinking about it, tried to keep it in the blind spot of my obsessiveness, the way I would flinch my eyes from a tempting shoulder. But it was impossible. "What motive could they possibly have for mixing batches in the same package?"

"Well, easy. If word got out that one bakery was better than the other, they wouldn't want people, you know, *shunning* whole cartons, or maybe even whole truckloads, whole deliveries of Oreos. They'd have to keep them mixed up, so you'd buy any package knowing you'd probably get some good ones."

"So you're saying they ship batches from the two bakeries to one central boxing location just to mix them together."

"I guess that's what it would entail, isn't it?" she said brightly.

"That's stupid," I said, but it was only the sound of my crumbling resistance.

She shrugged. "All I know is we'd eat them and he'd be frantically building this pile of rejected cookies. And he'd be pushing them at me saying, 'See, see?' I could never tell the difference."

No, no, no, no.

Eatmeoreo, I mouthed inaudibly. I crinkled in the cellophane sleeve for another cookie, then nibbled off the overhang of chocolate top. I let the pulverized crumbs saturate my tongue, then reached for another, performed the same operation. They were identical. I put both nibbled cookies in the same pile. I needed to find a good one, or a bad one, before I could tell the difference.

Maybe I'd only ever eaten bad ones.

"I thought you didn't believe me," said Kimmery.

"Mushytest," I mumbled, my lips pasty with cookie mud, my eyes wild as I considered the task my brain had set for my sorry tongue. There were three sleeves in the box of Oreos. We were into just the first of them.

She nodded at my pile of discards. "What are those, good ones or bad ones?"

"I don't know." I tried sniffing the next. "Was this guy your boyfriend or something?"

"For a little while."

"Was he a Zen Buddhist too?"

She snorted lightly. I nibbled another cookie and began to despair. I would have been happy now for an ordinary interruptive tic, something to throw my bloodhoundlike obsessions off the scent. The Minna Men were in shambles, yes, but I'd get to the bottom of the Oreo conundrum.

I jumped to my feet, rattling both our teacups. I had to get out of there, quell my panic, restart my investigation, put some distance between myself and the cookies.

"*Barnamum Bakery!*" I yelped, reassuring myself.

"What?"

"Nothing." I jerked my head sideways, then turned it slowly, as if to work out a kink. "We'd better go, Kimmery."

"Go where?" She leaned forward, her pupils big and trusting. I felt a thrill at being taken so seriously. This making the rounds without Gilbert could get to be a habit. For once I was playing lead detective instead of comic – or Tourettic – relief.

"Downstairs," I said, at a loss for a better answer.

"Okay," she said, whispering conspiratorially. "But be quiet."

We crept past the half-open door on the second landing, and I retrieved my shoes from the rack. This time I got a look at Wallace. He sat with his back to us, limp blond hair tucked behind his ears and giving way to a bald spot. He wore a sweater and sweatpants and sat still as advertised, inert, asleep, or, I suppose, dead – though death was not a still thing to me at the moment, more a matter of skid marks in blood and the Brooklyn-Queens Expressway. Wallace looked harmless anyway. Kimmery's idea of a hippie, apparently, was a white man over forty-five not in a business suit. In Brooklyn we would have just said *loser*.

She opened the front door of the Zendo. "I've got to finish cleaning," she said. "You know, for the monks."

"*Im*portantmonks," I said, ticcing gently.

"Yes."

"I don't think you should be alone here." I looked up and down the block to see if anyone was watching us. My neck prickled, alert to wind and fear. The Upper East Siders had retaken their streets, and walked obliviously crinkling doggie-doo bags and the *New York Times* and the wax paper around bagels. My feeling of advantage, of beginning my investigation while the world was still asleep, was gone.

"I'm *con-worried*," I said, Tourette's mangling my speech

again. I wanted to get away from her before I shouted, barked, or ran my fingers around the neck of her T-shirt.

She smiled. "What's that – like confused and worried?"

I nodded. It was close enough.

"I'll be okay. Don't be conworried." She spoke calmly, and it calmed me. "You'll come back later, right? To sit?"

"Absolutely."

"Okay." She craned up on her toes and kissed my cheek. Startled, I couldn't move, stood instead feeling her kiss-print burning on my flesh in the cold morning air. Was it personal, or some sort of fuzzy Zen coercion? Were they that desperate to fill mats at the Zendo?

"Don't do that," I said. "You just met me. This is New York."

"Yes, but you're my friend now."

"I have to go."

"Okay," she said. "Zazen is at five o'clock."

"I'll be there."

She shut the door. I was alone on the street again, my investigation already at a standstill. Had I learned anything inside the Zendo? Now I felt dazed with loss – I'd penetrated the citadel and spent my whole time contemplating Kimmery and Oreos. My mouth was full of cocoa, my nostrils full of her scent from the unexpected kiss.

Two men took me by the elbows and hustled me into a car waiting at the curb.

* * *

The four of them wore identical blue suits with black piping on the legs, and identical black sunglasses. They looked like a band that plays at weddings. Four white guys, assortedly chunky, pinched in the face, with pimples, and indistinct. Their car was a rental. Chunky sat in the backseat waiting and when the two who'd picked me up crushed me into the back beside him, he immediately put his arm around my neck in a sort of brotherly choke hold. The two who'd picked me off the street – Pimples and Indistinct – jammed in beside me, to make four of us on the backseat. It was a bit crowded.

"Get in the front," said Chunky, the one holding my neck.

"Me?" I said.

"Shut up. Larry, get out. There's too many. Go in the front."

"Okay, okay," said the one on the end, Indistinct or Larry. He got out of the back and into the empty front passenger seat and the one driving – Pinched – took off. Chunky loosened his hold when we got into the downtown traffic on Second Avenue, but left his arm draped over my shoulders.

"Take the Drive," he said.

"What?"

"Tell him take the East Side Drive."

"Where are we going?"

"I want to be on the highway."

"Why not just drive in circles?"

"My car is parked up here," I said. "You could drop me off."

"Shut up. Why can't we just drive in circles?"

"You shut up. It should look like we're going somewhere, stupid. We're really scaring him going in circles."

"I'm listening to what you say no matter how you drive," I said, wanting to make them feel better. "There's four of you and one of me."

"We want more than listening," said Chunky. "We want you scared."

But I wasn't scared. It was eight-thirty in the morning, and we were fighting traffic on Second Avenue. There weren't even any circles to go in, just honking delivery trucks tied up by pedestrians. And the closer I looked at these guys the less I was impressed. For one thing, Chunky's hand on my neck was soft, his skin was soft, and his hold on me rather tender. And he was the toughest of the bunch. They weren't calm, they weren't good at what they were doing, and they weren't tough. None of them, as far as I could tell, was wearing a gun.

For another thing, all four of their sunglasses still bore price tags, dangling fluorescent orange ovals reading $6.99!

I reached out and batted at Pimples's price tag. He turned away, and my finger hooked the earpiece and jerked the shades off his face, into his lap. "Shit," said Pimples, and hurried the glasses back onto his face as if I might recognize him without them.

"Hey, none of that," said Chunky, and hugged me again. He reminded me of my long-ago kissing tic, the way he was crowding me close to him in the car.

"Okay," I said, though I knew it would be hard not to bat at the price tags if they came within reach. "But what's the game here, guys?"

"We're supposed to throw a scare into you," said Chunky, distracted, watching Pinched drive. "Stay away from the Zendo, that sort of thing. Hey, take the fucking Drive. Seventy-ninth Street there's an on-ramp."

"I can't get over," complained Pinched, eyeing lanes of traffic.

"What so great about the FDR?" said Indistinct. "Why can't we stay on the streets?"

"What, you want to pull over and rough him up on Park Avenue?" said Chunky.

"Maybe just a scare without the roughing-up will do," I suggested. "Get this over with, get on with the day."

"Stop him talking so much."

"Yeah, but he's got a point."

"*Eatmepointman!*"

Chunky clamped his hand over my mouth. At that moment I heard a high-pitched two-note signal. The four of them, and me, began looking around the car for the source of the noise. It was as if we were in a video game and had crossed up to the next level, were about to be destroyed by aliens we couldn't see coming. Then I realized that the beeping issued from my coat pocket: Minna's beeper going off.

"What's that?"

I twisted my head free. Chunky didn't fight me. "Barnamum Beeper," I said.

"What's that, some special kind? Get it out of his pocket. Didn't you chumps frisk him?"

"Screw you."

"Jesus."

They put their hands on me and quickly found the beeper. The digital readout showed a Brooklyn-Queens-Bronx prefix on the number. "Who's that?" said Pimples.

I frowned and shrugged: didn't know. Truly, I didn't

recognize the number. Someone who thought Minna was still alive, I guessed, and shuddered a little. That scared me more than my abductors did.

"Make him call it," said Pinched from the front.

"You want to pull over to let him call?"

"Larry, you got the phone?"

Indistinct turned in his seat and offered me a cell phone.

"Call the number."

I dialed, they waited. We inched down Second Avenue. The airspace of the car hummed with tension. The cell phone rang, *dit-dit-dit*, a miniature, a toy that effortlessly commanded our focus, our complete attention. I might have popped it in my mouth and gulped it down instead of holding it to my ear. *Dit-dit-dit*, it rang again, then somebody picked up.

Garbage Cop.

"Lionel?" said Loomis.

"Mmmmhuh," I replied, squelching an outburst.

"Get this. What's the difference between three hundred sixty-five blow jobs and a radial tire?"

"Don'tcare!" I shouted. The four in the car all jumped.

"One's a Goodyear, the other's a *great* year," said Loomis proudly. He knew he'd nailed the riddle, no faltering this time, not a word out of place.

"Where are you calling from?" I asked.

"You called me."

"You beeped me, Loomis. Where are you?"

"I don't know" – his voice dimmed – "hey, what's the name of this place? Oh, yeah? Thanks. Bee-Bee-Que? Really, just like that, three letters? Go figure. Lionel, you there?"

"Here."

"It's a diner called B-B-Q, just like barbecue, only three letters. I eat here all the time, and I never even knew that!"

"Why'd you beep me, Loomis?" *Beep and Rebeep are sitting on a fence—*

"You told me to. You wanted that address, right? Ullman, the dead guy."

"Uh, that's right," I said, shrugging at Chunky, who still held my neck, but lightly, leaving me room to place the phone.

He scowled at me, but it wasn't my fault if he was confused. I was confused, too. Confused and conworried.

"Well, I got it right here," said the Garbage Cop pridefully.

"What's the good of driving him around watching him make a phone call?" complained Pimples.

"Take it away from him," said Pinched from the driver's seat.

"Just punch him in the stomach," said Indistinct. "Make him scared."

"You got someone there with you?" said Loomis.

The four in the car had begun to chafe at seeing their faint authority slip away, devolve to the modern technology, the bit of plastic and wire in my palm. I had to find a way to calm them down. I nodded and widened my eyes to show my cooperation, and mouthed a just-wait signal to them, hoping they'd recall the protocol from crime movies: pretend they weren't there listening, and thus gather information on the sly.

I couldn't help it that they *weren't* actually listening.

"Tell me the address," I said.

"Okay, here goes," said Loomis. "Got a pen?"

"Whose address?" whispered Chunky in my other ear. He'd caught my hint. He was schooled enough in the clichés to be manipulable; his compatriots I wasn't so sure of.

"Tell me *Ullman's* address," I said for their sake. *Man-Salad-Dress* went my brain. I swallowed hard to keep it from crossing the threshold.

"Yeah, I got it," said the Garbage Cop sarcastically. "Whose else would you want?"

"Ullman?" said Chunky, not to me but to Pimples. "He's talking about *Ullman?*"

"*Whose! A! Dress!*" I shrieked.

"Aw, quit," said Loomis, jaded by now. My other audience wasn't so blasé. Pimples ripped the cell phone out of my hand, and Chunky wrestled my arm behind my back so I was wrenched forward nearly against the back of the driver's seat, and down. It was like he wanted me draped in his lap for a spanking. Meanwhile, up front, Pinched and Indistinct began arguing fiercely about parking, about whether they'd fit in some spot.

Pimples put the phone to his own ear and listened, but Loomis hung up, or maybe just got quiet and listened back, so they were silent together. Pinched managed to park, or double-park – I couldn't tell which from my strained vantage. The two up front were still muttering at one another, but Chunky was quiet, just turning my arm another degree or two, experiment-ing with actually hurting me, trying it on for size.

"You don't like hearing the name *Ullman*," I said, wincing.

"Ullman was a friend," said Chunky.

"Don't let him talk about Ullman," said Pinched.

"This is stupid," said Indistinct, with consummate disgust.

"You're stupid," said Chunky. "We're supposed to scare a guy, let's do it."

"I'm not so scared," I said. "You guys seem more scared to me. Scared of talking about Ullman."

"Yeah, well, if we're scared you don't know why," said Chunky. "And don't guess either. Don't open your trap."

"You're scared of a big Polish guy," I said.

"This is stupid," said Indistinct again. He sounded like he might cry. He got out of the car and slammed the door behind him.

Pimples finally quit listening to the silence Loomis had left behind on the cell phone, shut it down, and put it on the seat between us.

"What if we are scared of him?" said Chunky. "We ought to be, take it from us. We wouldn't be working for him if we weren't." He loosened his grip on my arm, so I was able to straighten up and look around. We were parked outside a pop-ular coffee shop on Second. The window was full of sullen kids flirting by working on tiny computers and reading magazines. They didn't notice us, carful of lugs, and why should they?

Indistinct was nowhere to be seen.

"I sympathize," I said, to keep them talking. "I'm scared of the big guy, too. It's just you can't throw a scare so good when you're scared."

I thought of Tony. If he'd come to the Zendo last night shouldn't he have triggered the same alarm I had? Shouldn't he have drawn these would-be toughs, this clown car loaded with fresh graduates from Clown College?

"What's so not scary about us?" said Pinched. He said to Chunky, "Hurt him already."

"You can hurt me but you still won't scare me," I said distractedly. One part of my brain was thinking, *Handle with scare, scandal with hair*, and so on. Another part was puzzling over the Tony question.

"Who was that on the phone?" said Pimples, still working on the problem he'd selected as his own.

"You wouldn't believe me," I said.

"Try us," said Chunky, twisting my arm.

"Just a guy doing research for me, that's all. I wanted Ullman's address. My partner got arrested for the murder."

"See, you shouldn't *have* a guy doing research," said Chunky. "That's the whole problem. Getting involved, visiting Ullman's apartment, that's the kind of thing we're supposed to scare you about."

Scare me, skullman, sang my disease. *Skullamum Bailey. Skinnyman Brainy.*

"Hurt him and scare him and let's get out of here," said Pinched. "I don't like this. Larry was right, it is stupid. I don't care about who's doing research."

"I still want to know who was on the phone," said Pimples.

"Listen," said Chunky, now trying to reason with me, as his gang's morale and focus – and actual numbers – were dwindling. "We're here on behalf of the big guy you're talking about, see? That's who sent us." He offered the morphic resonance theory: "So if he scares you you ought to be scared by us, without us having to hurt you."

"Guys like you could *kill* me and you still wouldn't scare me," I said.

"This was a bad idea," concluded Pinched, and he, too, got out of the car. The front seats were empty now, the steering wheel unmanned. "This isn't us," he said, leaning back in, addressing Pimples and Chunky. "We're no good at this." He raised his eyebrows at me. "You'll have to forgive us. This isn't what we do. We're men of peace." He shut the door. I turned my head enough to see him scooting down the block, his walk like a hectic bird's.

"*Scaredycop!*" I shouted.

"Where?" said Chunky, immediately releasing my arm. They both swiveled their heads in a panic, eyes wild behind the dark glasses, orange price tags dancing like fishing lures. Freed at last, I turned my head too, not searching for anything, of course, instead for the pleasure of aping their movements.

"Screw this," muttered Pimples.

He and Chunky both fled the rental car, hot on Pinched's heels, leaving me alone there.

*　*　*

Pinched had taken the car keys, but Indistinct's cell phone sat abandoned on the seat beside me. I put it in my pocket. Then I leaned over the seat, popped the glove compartment, and found the rental agency's registration card and receipt. The car was on a six-month lease to the Fujisaki Corporation, 1030 Park Avenue. The zip code, I was pretty sure, put it in the same zone as the Zendo. Which is where I was, as it happened. I rapped on the rental car's glove compartment door five times, but it wasn't particularly resonant or satisfying.

*　*　*

On my walk over to 1030 Park I flipped open the cell phone and rang L&L. I'd never made a street call before, and felt quite Captain Kirk-ish.

"L&L," said a voice, the one I'd hoped to hear.

"Tony, it's me," I said. "Essrog." That was how Minna always started a phone call: *Lionel, it's Minna.* You're the first name, I'm the last. In other words: You're the jerk and I'm the jerk's boss.

"Where are you?" said Tony.

Crossing Lexington at Seventy-sixth Street was the answer. But I didn't want to tell him.

Why? I wasn't sure. Anyway, I let a tic do my talking: "Kiss me, scareyman!"

"I got worried about you, Lionel. Danny said you went off with the Garbage Cop on some kind of a mission."

"Well, sort of."

"He with you now?"

"*Garbage cookie*," I said seriously.

"Why don't you head back here, Lionel? We ought to talk."

"I'm investigating a case," I said. *A guess tic eating a vest.*

"Oh, yeah? Where's it taking you?"

A well-coiffed man in a blue suit turned off Lexington ahead of me. He had a cell phone pressed to his right ear. I aligned myself behind him and imitated his walk.

"Various places," I said.

"Name one."

The harder Tony asked, the less I wanted to say. "I was hoping we could, you know, triangulate a little. Compare data."

"Give me an example, Lionel."

"Like did you – *Vesticulate! Guessticalot!* – did you get anything out of that, uh, Zendo place last night?"

"I'll tell you about it when I see you. Right now there's something important, you ought to get back here. What are you, at a pay phone?"

"*Vestphone!*" I said. "By any chance did a carful of guys try to warn you off?"

"Fuck you talking about?"

"What about the girl I saw go in before Minna? Did you find out about her?" Even as I asked I got the answer to the question I was asking, the real question.

I didn't trust Tony.

I felt the truth of it in the pause before he replied.

"I learned a few things," he said. "But at the moment we need to pool our resources, Lionel. You need to get back here. Because we got some problems coming up."

Now I could hear the bluff in his voice. It was casual, easy. He wasn't straining particularly. It was only Essrog on the line, after all.

"I know about problems," I said. "Gilbert's in jail on a murder charge."

"Well, that's just one."

"You weren't at the Zendo last night," I said. The man in the blue suit turned onto Park Avenue, still gabbing. I let him go, and stood in a crowd at the corner, waiting for the light to change.

"Maybe you ought to worry about your own fucking self

and not me, Lionel," said Tony. "Where were *you* last night?"

"I did what I was supposed to do," I said, wanting to provoke him now. "I told Julia. Actually, she already knew." I left out the part about the homicide cop.

"That's interesting. I've been sort of wondering where Julia goes off to. I hope you found out."

Alarms went off. Tony was trying to make his voice casual, but it wasn't working. "Wondering when? You means she goes out of town a lot?"

"Maybe."

"Anyway, how'd you know she went anywhere?"

"Fuck you think we do around here, Lionel? We learn things."

"Yeah, we're a leading outfit. Gilbert's in jail, Tony." My eyes were suddenly full of tears. I knew I should be trying to focus on the Julia problem, but our betrayal of Gilbert felt more immediate.

"I know. He's safer there. Come in and talk, Lionel."

I crossed with the crowd but stopped halfway, at the traffic island in the middle of Park Avenue. The thumbnail of garden was marked with a sign that read VALIANT DAFFODIL (N. AMERICA), but the ground was chewed and pocked and vacant, as if someone had just dug up a plot of dead bulbs. I sat on the wooden embankment there and let the crowd pass by, until the light turned red again and the traffic began to whiz past me. A strip of sunshine laced the avenue and warmed me on the bench. Park Avenue's giant apartment buildings were ornate with shadow in the midmorning light. I was like a castaway on my island there, in a river of orange cabs.

"Where are you, Freakshow?"

"Don't call me Freakshow," I said.

"What should I call you – Buttercup?"

"Valiant Daffodil," I blurted. "Alibi Diffident."

"Where are youu, Daffodil?" said Tony rather sweetly. "Should we come get you?"

"Goodcop, buttercup," I said, ticcing on through my tears. By calling me Freakshow – Minna's nickname – Tony had cued my Tourette's, had cut right through the layers of coping strategies and called out my giddy teenage voice. It should have been a relief to tic freely with one who knew me so well. But I didn't trust him. Minna was dead and I didn't trust Tony and I didn't know what it meant.

"Tell me where your little investigation led you," said Tony.

I looked up at Park Avenue, the monolithic walls of old money stretched out, a furrow of stone.

"I'm in Brooklyn," I lied. "*Eatmegreenpoint.*"

"Oh, yeah? What's in Greenpoint?"

"I'm looking for the – *Greenpope!* – the guy who killed Minna, the Polish guy. What do you think?"

"Just wandering around looking for him, huh?"

"*Eatmephone!*"

"Hanging out in Polish bars, that sort of thing?"

I barked and clicked my tongue. My agitated jaw jerked against the redial button and a sequence of tones played on the line. The light changed and the cabs crossing Park blared their horns, working through gridlock. Another raft of pedestrians passed over my island and back into the river.

"Doesn't sound like Greenpoint," said Tony.

"They're filming a movie out here. You should see this. They've got Greenpoint – *Greenphone! Creepycone! Phonyman!* – Greenpoint Avenue set up to look like Manhattan. All these fake buildings and cabs and extras dressed up like they're on Park Avenue or something. So that's what you're hearing."

"Who's in it?"

"What?"

"Who's in the movie?"

"Somebody said Mel – *Gisspod, Gasspoint, Pissphone—*"

"Mel Gibson."

"Yeah. But I haven't seen him, just a lot of extras."

"And they really got fake buildings out there?"

"Did you sleep with Julia, Tony?"

"Why'd you want to go and say that?"

"Did you?"

"Who you trying to protect, Daffodil? Minna's dead."

"I want to know."

"I'll tell you in person when you get in here already."

"*Dickety Daffodil! Dissident Crocophile! Laughable Chocodopolus!*"

"Ah, I heard it all before."

"Likable lunchphone, veritable spongefist, teenage mutant Zendo lungfish, penis Milhaus Nixon tuning fork."

"You fucking Tugboat."

"Good-bye, Tonybailey."

* * *

Ten-thirty Park Avenue was another stone edifice, unremarkable among its neighbors. The oak doors split the difference between magnificence and military sturdiness, tiny windows barred with iron: French Colonial Bomb Shelter. The awning showed just the numerals, no gaudy, pretentious building name like you'd see on Central Park West or in Brooklyn Heights – here nothing remained to be proved, and anonymity was a value greater than charisma. The building had a private loading zone and a subtle curb cut, though, which sang of money, payoffs to city officials, and of women's-shoe heels too fragile to tangle with the usual four-inch step, too expensive to risk miring in dog shit. A special curb man stood patrolling the front, ready to open car doors or kick dogs or turn away unwanted visitors before they even tarnished the lobby. I came down the block at a good clip and swiveled to the door at the last minute, faking him out.

The lobby was wide and dark, designed to blind an unfamiliar visitor coming in from the sunlight. A crowd of doormen in white gloves and familiar blue suits with black piping on the legs surrounded me the minute I stumbled through the doors. It was the same uniform worn by the lugs in the rental car.

So they hadn't been lugs by training – that much was obvious. They were doormen, no shame in that. But *men of peace*?

"Help you with something?"

"Help you sir?"

"Name?"

"All visitors must be announced."

"Delivery?"

"Have you got a name?"

They encircled me, five or six of them, not on special assignment but instead doing exactly what they were trained to do. Loom in the gloom. In their white gloves and their right context they were much scarier than they had been loaded into a rental car and fumbling as hoods. Their propriety was terrifying. I didn't see Pinched, Pimples, Chunky or Indistinct among them, but it was a big building. Instead I'd drawn Shadowface, Shadowface, Shadowface, Tallshadowface, and Shadowface.

"I'm here to see Fujisaki," I said. "Man, woman or corporation."

"There must be a mistake."

"Wrong building, surely."

"There is no Fujisaki."

"Name?"

"Fujisaki Management Corporation," I said.

"No."

"No. Not here. That isn't right."

"No."

"Name? Who's calling, sir?"

I took out one of Minna's cards. "Frank Minna," I said. The name came easily, and I didn't feel any need to distort it the way I would my own.

The band of doormen around me loosened at the sight of a business card. I'd shown a first glimmer of legitimacy. They were a top grade of doorman, finely tuned, factoring vigilance against hair-trigger sycophantic instincts.

"Expected?"

"Sorry?"

"Expected by the party in question? Appointment? Name? Contact?"

"Dropping in."

"Hmmm."

"No."

"No."

Another minute correction ensued. They bunched closer. Minna's card disappeared.

"There may be some confusion."

"Yes."

"Probably there is."

"Wrong building completely."

"Should there be a destination for a message, what would a message be?"

"On the chance that the destination in question is this one. You understand, sir."

"Yes."

"Yes."

"No message," I said. I tapped the nearest doorman's suit breast. He darted back, scowling. But they were penguins now. I had to touch them all. I reached for the next, the tallest, tried to high-five his shoulder and just grazed it. The circle loosened around me again as I spun. They might have thought I was staining them with invisible swatches of blacklight paint for future identification or planting electronic bugs or just plain old spreading cooties, from the way they jumped.

"No."

"Look out."

"Can't have this."

"Can't have this here."

"Out."

Then two of them had me by the elbows, and I was steered out onto the sidewalk.

* * *

I took a stroll around the block, just to glean what I could from the north face of the building. I was shadowed by the curb man, of course, but I didn't mind. The staff entrance smelled of a private dry-cleaning service, and the disposal bins showed signs of bulk food orders, perhaps an in-house grocery. I wondered if the building housed a private chef, too. I thought about poking my head in to see but the curb man was muttering tensely into a walkie-talkie, and I figured I'd probably better distance myself. I waved good-bye and he waved back involuntarily – everyone's a little ticcish that way sometimes.

* * *

Between bites of hot dog and gulps of papaya juice I dialed the Garbage Cop's office. The Papaya Czar on Eighty-sixth Street and Third Avenue is my kind of place – bright orange and yellow signs pasted on every available surface screaming, PAPAYA IS GOD'S GREATEST GIFT TO MAN'S HEALTH! OUR FRANKFURTERS ARE THE WORKING MAN'S FILET MIGNON! WE'RE POLITE NEW YORKERS, WE SUPPORT MAYOR GIULIANI! And so on. Papaya Czar's walls are so layered with language that I find myself immediately calmed inside their doors, as though I've stepped into a model interior of my own skull.

I washed down the tangy nubbin of the first dog while the phone rang. Papaya Czar's product did emulate an expensive steak's melting-in-your-mouthiness, frankfurters apparently skinless and neither bun nor dog crisped in the cooking, so they slid together into hot-dog cream on the tongue. These virtues could be taken in excess and leave one craving the greater surface tension of a Nathan's dog, but I was in the mood for the Czar's today. I had four more laid out in a neat row on the counter where I sat, each with a trim line of yellow mustard for an exclamation – *five* was still my angel.

As for papaya itself, I might as well be drinking truffula seed nectar or gryphon milk, for all I knew – I'd never encountered the fruit in any form except the Czar's chalky beverage.

"Sanitation Inspector Loomis," answered the Garbage Cop.

"Listen, Loomis. I'm working on this Gilbert thing." I knew I needed to tie it in to his friend's plight to keep him focused. In fact, Gilbert was now the furthest thing from my mind. "I need you to pull up some information for me."

"That you, Lionel?"

"Yeah. Listen. Ten-three-oh Park Avenue. Write that down. I need some records on the building, management company, head of the board, whatever you can find out. See if any names you recognize pop up."

"Recognize from where?"

"From, uh, around the neighborhood." I was thinking *Frank Minna*, but I didn't want to say it. "Oh, one in particular. Fuji-saki. It's Japanese."

"I don't know any Fujisaki from around the neighborhood."

"Just look up the records, Loomis. Call me back when you get something."

"Call you back where?"

I'd gotten the beeper and the cell phone mixed up. I was collecting other people's electronics. In fact, I didn't know the number of the phone I'd borrowed from the doorman in sunglasses. I wondered for the first time who I'd find myself talking to if I answered the incoming calls.

"Forget it," I said. "You've still got Minna's beeper number?"

"Sure."

"Use that. I'll call you."

"When do we bail out Gilbert?"

"I'm working on it. Listen, Loomis, I'd better go. Get back to me, all right?"

"Sure thing, Lionel. And, buddy?"

"What?"

"Good stature, man," said Loomis. "You're holding up great."

"Uh, thanks Loomis." I ended the call, put the cell phone back into my jacket pocket.

"Kee-rist," said a man sitting on my right. He was a guy in his forties. He wore a suit. As Minna said more than once, in New York any chucklehead can wear a suit. Satisfied he wasn't a doorman, I ignored him, worked on dog number three.

"I was in this restaurant in L.A.," he started. "Great place, million-dollar place. All the food is tall, you know what I mean? Tall food? There's this couple at a table, both of them talking on fucking cell phones, just like you got there. Two different conversations through the whole meal, yakking all over each other, what *Cindy* said, get away for the *weekend*, gotta work on my *game*, the whole nine yards. You couldn't hear yourself think over the racket."

I finished dog three in five evenly spaced bites, licked the mustard off my thumb tip, and picked up number four.

"I thought L.A., fair enough. Chalk it up. You can't expect any different. So couple months ago I'm trying to impress a client, take him to Balthazar, you know, downtown? Million-dollar place, take it from me. Tall food, *gangly* food. So what do I see but a couple of bozos at the bar talking on cell phones. My water's getting hot, but I figure, bar, fair enough, that's showing decent respect. Adjust my standards, whatever. So we get a table after waiting fifteen fucking minutes, sit down and my client's phone rings, he takes it out at the table! Guy I was with! Sits there yakking! Ten, fifteen minutes!"

I enjoyed dog four in Zen-like calm and silence, practicing for my coming *zazen*.

"Never thought I'd see it in here, though. Fucking California, Balthazar, whatever, all these guys with crap in their hair and million-dollar wristwatches like Dick Tracy. I guess I gotta adjust my standards to the modern universe but I thought at the very least I could sit here eat a fucking hot dog without listening to yak yak yak."

I'd apportioned a fifth of my papaya juice for rinsing down the last dog. Suddenly impatient to leave, I stuffed a wad of napkins in my jacket pocket and took the dog and the drink in hand and headed back out into the bright cold day.

"Fucking people talking to themselves in a public place like they got some kind of illness!"

* * *

The beeper went off just as I got to the car. I drew it out for a look: another unfamiliar number in 718. I got into the car and called from the cell phone, ready to be irritated with Loomis.

"*DickTracyphone*," I said into the mouthpiece.

"This is Matricardi and Rockaforte," went a gravelly voice. Rockaforte. Though I'd heard them speak just two or three times in fifteen years, I would have known his voice anywhere.

Through the windshield I viewed Eighty-third Street, midday, November. A couple of women in expensive coats mimed a Manhattan conversation for my benefit, trying to persuade me of their reality. On the line, though, I heard an old man's breathing, and what I saw through the windshield wasn't real at all.

I considered that I was answering Minna's beeper. Did they know he was dead? Would I have to deliver the news to The Clients? I felt my throat constrict, instantly throbbing with fear and language.

"Speak to me," rasped Rockaforte.

"Larval Pushbug," I said softly, trying to offer my name. Did The Clients even know it? "Papaya Pissbag." I was tic-gripped, helpless. "*Not*Minna," I said at last. "*Not*Frank. Frank's*dead*."

"We know, Lionel," said Rockaforte.

"Who told you?" I whispered, controlling a bark.

"Things don't escape," he said. He paused, breathed, went on. "We're very sorry for you in this time."

"You found out from Tony?"

"We found out. We find out what we need. We learn."

But do you kill? I wanted to ask. *Do you command a Polish giant?*

"We're concerned for you," he said. "The information is that you are running, going here and there, unable to sit still. We hear this, and it concerns."

"What information?"

"And that Julia has left her home in this time of mourning. That nobody knows where she has gone unless it is you."

"No*julia*, nobody, nobody*knows*."

"You still suffer. We see this and we suffer as well."

This was somewhat obscure to me, but I wasn't going to ask.

"We wish to speak with you, Lionel. Will you come and talk to us?"

"We're talking now," I breathed.

"We wish to see you standing before us. It's important in this time of pain. Come see us, Lionel."

"Where? New Jersey?" Heart racing, I allowed soothing permutations to course through my brain: *Garden state bricko and stuckface garbage face grippo and suckfast garter snake ticc-o and circus.* My lips rustled at the phone, nearly giving the words breath.

"We're in the Brooklyn house," he said. "Come."

"*Scarface! Cigarfish!*"

"What's got you running, Lionel?"

"Tony. You've been talking to Tony. He said I'm running. I'm not running."

"You sound running."

"I'm looking for the killer. Tony's trying to stop me, I think."

"You have a problem with Tony?"

"I don't trust him. He's acting – *Stuccotash!* – he's acting strangely."

"Let me speak," came a voice in the background of the call. Rockaforte's voice was replaced with Matricardi's: higher, more mellifluous, a single-malt whiskey instead of Dewar's.

"What's wrong with Tony?" said Matricardi. "You don't trust him in this matter?"

"I don't trust him," I repeated dumbly. I thought about ending the call. Again I consulted my other senses: I was in the sunshine in Manhattan in an L&L vehicle talking on a doorman's cell phone. I could discard Minna's beeper, forget about the call, go anywhere. The Clients were like players in a dream. They shouldn't have been able to touch me with their ancient, ethereal voices. But I couldn't bring myself to hang up on them.

"Come to us," said Matricardi. "We'll talk. Tony doesn't have to be there."

"Forgettaphone."

"You remember our place? Degraw Street. You know where?"

"Of course."

"Come. Honor us in this time of disappointment and regret. We'll talk without Tony. What's wrong we'll straighten."

* * *

While I considered what to do I used the doormen's phone again, called information and got the number of the *Daily News'* obituary page and bought a notice for Minna. I put it on a credit card of Minna's to which he'd added my name. He had to pay for his own notice, but I knew he'd have wanted it, considered it fifty bucks well spent. He was always an avid reader of the obituaries, studying them each morning in the L&L office like a tip sheet, a chance for him to pick up or work an angle. The woman on the line did it all by rote, and so did I: billing information, name of deceased, dates, survivors, until we got to the part where I gave out a line or two about who Minna was supposed to have been.

"Beloved something," said the woman, not unkindly. "It's usually Beloved something."

Beloved Father Figure?

"Or something about his contributions to the community," she suggested.

"Just say detective," I told her.

ONE MIND

THERE WERE ONLY and always two things Frank Minna would not discuss in the years following his return from exile and founding of the Minna Agency. The first was the nature of that exile, the circumstances surrounding his disappearance that day in May when his brother Gerard hustled him out of town. We didn't know why he left, where he went or what he did while he was gone, or why he came back when he did. We didn't know how he met and married Julia. We didn't know what happened to Gerard. There was never again any sign or mention of Gerard. The sojourn "upstate" was covered in a haze so complete it was sometimes hard to believe it had lasted three years.

The other was The Clients, though they lurked like a pulse felt here or there in the body of the Agency.

L&L wasn't a moving company anymore, and we never again saw the inside of that hollowed-out brownstone on Degraw. But we were as much errand boys as detectives, and it wasn't hard, in the early days, to sense Matricardi and Rockaforte's shadow in some percentage of our errands. Their assignments were discernible for the deep unease they provoked in Minna. Without explanation he'd alter his patterns, stop dropping in at the barbershop or the arcade for a week or so, close the L&L storefront and tell us to get lost for a few days. Even his walk changed, his whole manner of being. He'd refuse to be seated anywhere but in the corners of restaurants, his back to the wall. He'd turn his head on the street for no reason, which I of course cobbled into a lifelong tic. For cover he'd joke harder but also more discontinuously, his stream of commentary and insult turned balky and riddled with grim silences, his punch lines become non sequiturs. And the jobs we did for The Clients were discontinuous too. They were fractured stories, middles lacking a clear beginning or end. When we Minna Men tracked a wife for a husband or watched an employee suspected of pilferage or cooking the books we mastered their pathetic dramas, encompassed their small lives with our worldliness. What we gathered with our bugs and cameras and etched into our reports was true and complete. Under Minna we were secret masters, writing a sort of social history of Cobble Hill and Carroll Gardens into our duplicate files. But when the hand of Matricardi and Rockaforte moved the Minna Men we were only tools, glancing off the sides of stories bigger than we understood, discarded and left wondering at the end.

Once in the early days of the Agency we were dispatched to stand guard in broad daylight around a car, a Volvo, and we picked up a scent of The Clients in Minna's stilted, fragmentary instructions. The car was empty as far as we could tell. It was parked on Remsen Street near the Promenade, at a placid dead-end traffic circle overlooking Manhattan. Gilbert and I sat on a park bench, trying to look casual with our backs to the skyline, while Tony and Danny idled at the mouth of Remsen and Hicks, glaring at anyone who turned onto the block. We knew only that we were supposed to give way at five o'clock, when a tow truck would come for the car.

Five o'clock stretched into six, then seven, with no truck. We took pee breaks in the children's park at Montague Street, ran through cigarettes, and paced. Evening strollers appeared on the Promenade, couples, teenagers with paper-bagged bottles of beer, gays mistaking us for cruisers. We shrugged them away from our end of the walk, muttered, glanced at our watches. The Volvo couldn't have been less conspicuous if it were invisible, but for us it glowed, screamed, ticked like a bomb. Every kid on a bike or stumbling wino seemed an assassin, a disguised ninja with aims on the car.

When the sun began to set Tony and Danny started arguing.

"This is stupid," said Danny. "Let's get out of here."

"We can't," said Tony.

"You know there's a body in the trunk," said Danny.

"How am I supposed to know that?" said Tony.

"Because what else would it be?" said Danny. "Those old guys had someone killed."

"That's stupid," said Tony.

"A body?" said Gilbert, plainly unnerved. "I thought the car was full of money."

Danny shrugged. "I don't care, but it's a body. I'll tell you what else: We're being set up for it."

"That's stupid," said Tony.

"What does Frank know? He just does what they tell him." Even in rebellion Danny obeyed Minna's stricture against speaking The Clients' names.

"You really think it's a body?" said Gilbert to Danny.

"Sure."

"I don't want to stay if it's a body, Tony."

"Gilbert, you fat fuck. What if it is? What do you think we're doing here? You think you're never gonna see a body working for Minna? Go join the garbage cops, for chrissakes."

"I'm cutting out," said Danny. "I'm hungry anyway. This is stupid."

"What should I tell Minna?" said Tony, daring Danny to go.

"Tell him what you want."

It was a startling defection. Tony and Gilbert and I were all problems in our various ways, while Danny in his silence and grace was Minna's pillar, his paragon.

Tony couldn't face this mutiny directly. He was accustomed to bullying Gilbert and me, not Danny. So he reverted to form. "What about you, Freakshow?"

I shrugged, then kissed my own hand. It was an impossible question. Devotion to Minna had boiled down to this trial of hours watching over the Volvo. Now we had to envision disaster, betrayal, rotting flesh.

But what would it mean to turn from Minna?

I hated The Clients then.

The tow truck came grinding down Remsen before I could speak. It was manned by a couple of fat lugs who laughed at our jumpiness and told us nothing about the car's importance, just shooed us off and began chaining the Volvo's bumper to their rig. Less Men than Boys in suits, we felt as though this had been designed as a test of our fresh-grown nerves. And we'd failed, even if Minna and The Clients didn't know about it.

* * *

We grew tougher, though, and Minna became unflappable, and we came to take the role of The Clients in the life of the Agency more in stride. Who had to make sense of everything? It wasn't always certain when we were acting for them anyway. Seize a given piece of equipment from a given office: Was that on The Clients' behalf or not? Collect this amount from such and such a person: When we passed the take to Minna did he pass it along to The Clients? Unseal this envelope, tap this phone: Clients? Minna kept us in the dark and turned us into professionals. Matricardi and Rockaforte's presence became mostly subliminal.

The last job I felt certain was for The Clients was more than a year before Minna's murder. It bore their trademark of total inexplicability. A supermarket on Smith Street had burned and been razed earlier that summer, and the empty lot was filled with crushed brick and turned into an informal peddlers' market, where sellers of one fruit – oranges, say, or mangoes – would set up a few crates and do a summer afternoon's business, alongside the hot-dog and shaved-ice carts that began to gather there. After a month or so a Hispanic carnival took over the site, setting up a Tilt-a-Whirl and a miniature Ferris wheel, each a dollar a ride, along with a grilled-sausage stand and a couple of lame arcades: a water-gun balloon game and a grappling hook over a glass case full of pink and purple stuffed animals. The litter and smells of grease were a blight if you got too close, but the Ferris wheel was lined with white tubes of neon, and it was a glorious thing to see at night down Smith Street, a bright unexpected pinwheel almost three stories high.

We'd been so bored that summer that we'd fallen into working regularly as a car service, taking calls when they came, ferrying dates home from nightclubs, old ladies to and from hospitals, vacationers to La Guardia for the weekend flight to Miami Beach. Between rides we'd play poker in the air-conditioned storefront. It was after one-thirty on a Friday night when Minna came in. Loomis was sitting in on the game, losing hands and eating all the chips, and Minna told him to get lost, go home already.

"What's the matter, Frank?" said Tony.

"Nothing's the matter. Got something for us to do, that's all."

"Something what? For who?"

"Just a job. What do we have in here that's like a crowbar or something?" Minna smoked furiously to mask his unease.

"A crowbar?"

"Just something you can swing. Like a crowbar. I've got a bat and a lug wrench in my trunk. Stuff like that."

"Sounds like you want a gun," said Tony, raising his eyebrows.

"If I wanted a gun I'd get a gun, you diphthong. This doesn't take a gun."

"You want chains?" said Gilbert, meaning to be helpful. "There's a whole bunch of chains in the Pontiac."

"Crowbar, crowbar, crowbar. Why do I even bother with you mystic seers anymore? If I wanted my mind read I'd call Gladys Knight for chrissakes."

"Dionne Warwick," said Gilbert.

"What?"

"Psychic Hotline's Dionne Warwick, not Gladys Knight."

"*Psychicwarlock!*"

"Got some pipe downstairs," mused Danny, only now laying down the hand he'd been holding since Minna barged into the office. It was a full house, jacks and eights.

"It's gotta be swingable," said Minna. "Let's see."

The phone rang and I grabbed for it and said, "L&L."

"Tell them we don't have any cars," said Minna.

"This needs all four of us?" I said. I was courting fond notions of missing the crowbar-and-lug-wrench project, whatever it was, and driving someone out to Sheepshead Bay instead.

"Yes, Freakboy. We're going."

I got rid of the call. Twenty minutes later we were loaded up with pipes, lug wrench, car jack and a souvenir Yankee bat from Bat Day in Minna's old Impala, the least distinguished of L&L's many cars, and another bad sign if I was trying to read signs. Minna drove us down Wyckoff, past the projects, then circled around, south on Fourth Avenue down to President Street, and back toward Court. He was stalling, checking his watch.

We turned on Smith, and Minna parked us a block below

the empty supermarket lot. The carnival had shut down for the night, plywood boards up over the concessions, rides stilled, the evening's discarded beer cups and sausage wrappers glowing against the moonlit rubblescape. We crept onto the lot with our implements, following Minna wordlessly now, no longer chafing at his leadership, instead lulled into our deep obedient rhythm as his Men. He pointed at the Ferris wheel.

"Take it out."

"Eh?"

"Destroy the wheel, you candied yams."

Gilbert understood soonest, perhaps because the task suited his skills and temperament so well. He took a swing at the nearest line of neon with his chunk of pipe, smashing it easily, bringing a rain of silver dust. Tony and Danny and I followed his lead. We attacked the body of the wheel, our first swings tentative, measuring our strength, then lashing out, unloading. It was easy to damage the neon, not easy at all to impress the frame of the wheel, but we set at it, attacked any joint or vulnerable weld, prying up the electrical cable and chopping at it with the sharpest edge of the wrench until insulation and wire were bare and mangled, then frayed. Minna himself wielded the Yankee bat, splintering its wood against the gates that held riders into their seats, not breaking them but changing their shape. Gilbert and I got inside the frame of the wheel and with all our weight dragged at one of the chairs until we ruptured the hinge. Then we found the brake and released the wheel to turn so that we could apply our malicious affection to the whole of it. A couple of Dominican teenagers stood watching us from across the street. We ignored them, bore down on the Ferris wheel, hurrying but not frantic, absolutely Minna's to direct but not even needing direction. We acted as one body to destroy the amusement. This was the Agency at its mature peak: unquestioning and thorough in carrying out an action even when it bordered on sheer Dada.

* * *

"Frank loved you, Lionel," said Rockaforte.

"I, uh, I know."

"For that reason we care for you, for that reason we are concerned."

"Though we have not seen you since you were a boy," said Matricardi.

"A boy who barked," said Rockaforte. "We remember. Frank brought and you stood before us in this very room and you barked."

"And Frank spoke of your sickness many times."

"He loved you though he considered you a freak."

"He used that very word."

"You helped him build, you were one of his boys, and now you are a man and you stand before us in this hour of pain and misunderstanding."

Matricardi and Rockaforte had looked sepulchral to me as a teenager and they looked no worse now, their skin mummified, their thin hair in a kind of spider-web sheen over their reflective pates, Matricardi's ears and scarred nose dwarfing his other features, Rockaforte's face puffier and more potatolike. They were dressed as twins in black suits, whether consciously in mourning or not I couldn't know. They sat together on the tightly upholstered couch and when I stepped through the door I thought I saw their hands first joined on the cushions in the space between them, then jerking to their laps. I stood far enough back that I wasn't tempted to reach out and play pattycake, to slap at their folded hands or the place their hands had been resting.

The Degraw Street brownstone was unchanged, outside and in, apart from a dense, even layer of dust on the furniture and carpet and picture frames in the parlor. The air in the room swam with stirred dust, as though Matricardi and Rockaforte had arrived just a few moments before. They visited their Brooklyn shrine less often than in the past, I supposed. I wondered who drove them in from Jersey and whether they took any pains not to be seen coming here or whether they cared. Perhaps no one alive in Carroll Gardens knew them by sight anymore.

A neighborhood's secret lords could also be Invisible Men.

"What is between you and Tony?" said Matricardi.

"I want to find Frank's killer." I'd already heard myself say this too many times, and meaning was leaking out of the phrase. It threatened to become a sort of moral tic: *findfrank'skiller.*

"Why don't you follow Tony in this? Shouldn't you act as one, as brothers?"

"I was there. When they took Frank. Tony – *Hospitabailey!* – Tony wasn't there."

"You're saying then that he should follow you."

"He shouldn't get in my way. *Essway! Wrongway!*" I winced, hating to tic now, in front of them.

"You're upset, Lionel."

"Sure I'm upset." Why should I confess my distrust to those I distrusted? The more Matricardi and Rockaforte spoke Tony's name, the more certain I was they were tangled together in this somehow, and that Tony was far more familiar with The Clients than I'd been in the years since our first visit to this crypt, this mausoleum. I'd come away with a fork, he with something more. Why should I accuse one half of a conspiracy to the other? Instead I squinted and turned my head and pursed my lips, trying to avoid the obvious, finally acceded to The Clients' power of suggestion and barked once, loudly.

"You are afflicted and we feel for you. A man shouldn't run, and he shouldn't woof like a dog. He should find peace."

"Why doesn't Tony want me looking into Frank's murder?"

"Tony wishes this thing to be done correctly and with care. Work with him, Lionel."

"Why do you speak for Tony?" I gritted my teeth as I spoke the words. It wasn't exactly ticcing, but I'd begun to echo The Clients' verbal rhythms, the cloistered Ping-Pong of their diction.

Matricardi sighed and looked at Rockaforte. Rockaforte raised his eyebrows.

"Do you like this house?" said Matricardi.

I considered the dust-covered parlor, the load of ancient furnishing between the carpet and the ceiling's scrollwork, how it all hung suspended inside the shell of the warehouse-brownstone. I felt the presence of the past, of mothers and sons, deals and understandings, one dead hand gripping another – dead hands were nested here on Degraw Street like a series of Chinese boxes. Including Frank Minna's. There were so many ways I didn't like it I didn't know where to begin, except that I knew I shouldn't allow myself to begin at all.

"It's not a house," I said, offering the very least of my objections. "It's a room."

"He says it's a room," said Matricardi. "Lionel, this is my mother's house where we sit. Where you stand so full of fury it makes you like a cornered dog."

"Somebody killed Frank."

"Are you accusing Tony?"

"*Accusatony! Excusebaloney! Funnymonopoly!*" I squeezed my eyes shut to interrupt the seizure of language.

"We wish you to understand, Lionel. We regret Frank's passing. We miss him sorely. It is a soreness in our hearts. Nothing could please us more than to see his killer torn by birds or picked apart by insects with claws. Tony should have your help in bringing that day closer. You should stand behind him."

"What if my search brings me to Tony?" I'd let The Clients lead me to this pass in the conversation, and now there wasn't any reason to pretend.

"The dead live in our hearts, Lionel. From there Frank will never be dislodged. But now Tony has replaced Frank in the world of the living."

"What does that mean? You've replaced Frank with Tony?"

"It means you shouldn't act against Tony. Because our wishes go with him."

I understood now. It was Tony's Italian apotheosis at last. I was thrilled for him.

Unless it had been this way for years without my knowing. Maybe Tony Vermonte and The Clients ran deeper than Frank Minna and The Clients ever had.

I considered the word *replaced*. I decided it was time to go.

"I need your permission—" I began, then stopped. Who were The Clients, and what did their permission consist of? What was I thinking?

"Speak, Lionel."

"I'm going to keep looking," I said. "With or without Tony's help."

"Yes. We can see. And so we have an assignment for you. A suggestion."

"A place for you to apply your passion for justice."

"And your talent for detection. The training instilled."

"What?" Just a measure of the day's angled brightness penetrated the heavy curtains of the parlor. I glared back at a row
of thuggish midcentury faces staring out from picture frames,
wondering which was Matricardi's mom. The hot dogs I'd
eaten were rumbling in my stomach. I longed to be outside, on
the Brooklyn streets, anywhere but here.

"You spoke with Julia," said Matricardi. "You should
find her. Bring her in as we brought you. Let us speak with
her."

"She's afraid," I said. *A frayed knot.*

"Afraid of what?"

"She's like me. She doesn't trust Tony."

"Something is wrong between them."

This was exhausting. "Of course something's wrong. They
slept together."

"Making love brings people closer, Lionel."

"Maybe they feel guilty about Frank."

"Guilty, yes. Julia knows something. We called her to see us.
Instead she runs. Tony says he doesn't know where."

"You think Julia has something to do with Frank's murder?"
I let my hand trace a vague line in the dust on the marble
mantelpiece. A mistake. I tried to forget I'd done it.

"There's something on her mind, something weighing. You
want to help us, Lionel, find her."

"Learn her secrets and share them with us. Do this without
telling Tony."

Losing control somewhat, I inserted my finger into the
grooved edge of the mantel and pushed, gathering a shaggy
clot of dust.

"I don't get it," I said. "Now you want me to go behind
Tony's back?"

"We listen, Lionel. We hear. We consider. Questions occur.
If your suspicions are grounded the answers may lie with Julia.
Tony has been less than clear in this one area. However strange
and damaged, you'll be our hands and feet, our eyes and ears,
you'll learn and return to us and share."

"*Founded,*" I said. I reached the end of the mantel and thrust the accumulated dustball past the edge, following through like a one-fingered shot-putter.

"*If* they are," said Matricardi. "You don't know. That's what you'll find out."

"No, I mean founded, not grounded. Suspicions *founded.*"

"He's correcting," said Rockaforte to Matricardi, gritting his teeth.

"Find her, Essrog! Founder! Grounder! Confessrub!" I tried to wipe my finger clean on my jacket and made a gray stripe of clingy dust.

Then I belched, really, and tasted hot dogs.

"There's a little part of Frank in you," said Matricardi. "We speak to that part and it understands. The rest of you may be inhuman, a beast, a freak. Frank was right to use that word. You're a freak of nature. But the part of you that Frank Minna cared for and that cares so much for his memory is the part that will help us find Julia and bring her home."

"Go now, because you sicken us to see you playing with the dust that gathers in the home of his beloved mother, bless her sweet dishonored and tormented soul."

* * *

Conspiracies are a version of Tourette's syndrome, the making and tracing of unexpected connections a kind of touchiness, an expression of the yearning to touch the world, kiss it all over with theories, pull it close. Like Tourette's, all conspiracies are ultimately solipsistic, sufferer or conspirator or theorist overrating his centrality and forever rehearsing a traumatic delight in reaction, attachment and causality, in roads out from the Rome of self.

The second gunman on the grassy knoll wasn't part of a conspiracy – we Touretters know this to be true. He was ticcing, imitating the action that had startled and allured him, the shots fired. It was just his way of saying, Me too! I'm alive! Look here! Replay the film!

The second gunman was tugging the boat.

* * *

I'd parked in the shade of an elderly, crippled elm, trunk knotted and gnarled from surviving disease, with roots that had slowly nudged the slate sidewalk upward and apart. I didn't see Tony waiting in the Pontiac until I nearly had my key in the door. He was sitting in the driver's seat.

"Get in." He leaned over and opened the passenger door. The sidewalk was empty in both directions. I considered strolling away, ran into the usual problem of where to go.

"Get in, Freakshow."

I went to the passenger side and slid into the seat beside him, then reached out disconsolately and caressed his shoulder, leaving a smudge of dust. He raised his hand and slapped me on the side of the head.

"They lied to me," I said, flinching away.

"I'm shocked. Of course they lied. What are you, a newborn baby?"

"*Barnamum* baby," I mumbled.

"Which particular lie are you worrying about, Marlowe?"

"They warned you I was coming here, didn't they? They set me up. It was a trap."

"Fuck did you *think* was going to happen?"

"Never mind."

"You think you're smart," said Tony, his voice twangy with contempt. "You think you're Mike fucking Hammer. You're like the Hardy Boys' retarded kid brother, Lionel." He slapped my head again. "You're Hardly Boy."

My home borough had never felt so like a nightmare to me as it did on this bright sunlit day on Matricardi and Rockaforte's block of Degraw: a nightmare of repetition and enclosure. Ordinarily I savored Brooklyn's unchangeability, the bullying, Minna-like embrace of its long memory. At the moment I yearned to see this neighborhood razed, replaced by skyscrapers or multiplexes. I longed to disappear into Manhattan's amnesiac dance of renewal. Let Frank be dead, let the Men disperse. I only wanted Tony to leave me alone.

"You knew I had Frank's beeper," I said sheepishly, putting it together.

"No, the old guys have X-ray vision, like Superman. They don't know shit if I don't tell them, Lionel. You need to find a new line of work, McGruff. Shitlock Holmes."

I was familiar enough with Tony's belligerence to know it had to run awhile, play itself out. Me, I slid my hands along the top of the dashboard at the base of the windshield, smoothing away the crumbs and dust accumulated there, riffling my fingers over the plastic vents. Then I began buffing the corner of the windshield with my thumb tip. Visiting Matricardi's mother's parlor had triggered a dusting compulsion.

"You idiot freak."

"Beepmetwice."

"I'll beep you twice, all right."

He lifted his hand, and I flinched again, ducking underneath like a boxer. While I was near I licked the shoulder of his suit, trying to clean off the smudge of dust I'd left. He pushed me away disgustedly, an ancient echo of St. Vincent's hallway.

"Okay, Lionel. You're still half a fag. You got me convinced."

I didn't speak, no small achievement. Tony sighed and put both hands on the wheel. He appeared to be through buffeting me for the moment. I watched my saliva-stripe evaporate into the weave of his jacket.

"So what did they tell you?"

"The Clients?"

"Sure, The Clients," said Tony. "Matricardi and Rockaforte. Frank's dead, Lionel. I don't think he's gonna, like, spin in his grave if you say their names."

"Fork-it-hardly," I whispered, then glanced over my shoulder at their stoop. "Rocket-fuck-me."

"Good enough. So what did they tell you?"

"The same thing the – *Duckman! Dogboy! Confessdog!* – same thing the doormen told me: Stay off the case." I was mad with verbal tics now, making up for lost time, feeling at home. Tony was still a comfort to me in that way.

"What doorman?"

"Door*men*. A whole bunch of them."

"Where?"

But Tony's eyes said he knew perfectly well where, only needed to measure what I knew. He looked a little panicked, too.

"Ten-thirty Park Avenue," I said. *Energy pocket angle. Rectangle sauce!*

His hands tightened on the wheel. Instead of looking at me, he squinted into the distance. "You were there?"

"I was following a lead."

"Answer my question. *You were there?*"

"Sure."

"Who'd you see?"

"Just a lot of doormen."

"You discuss this with Matricardi and Rockaforte? Tell me you didn't, you goddamn motormouth."

"They talked, I listened."

"Oh yeah, that's likely. Fuck."

Oddly, I found myself wanting to reassure Tony. He and The Clients had drawn me back to Brooklyn and ambushed me in my car, but some old orphans' solidarity worked against my claustrophobia. Tony scared me, but The Clients scared me more. And now I knew they still scared Tony, too. Whatever deal he'd struck was incomplete.

It was cold in the car, but Tony was sweating.

"Be serious with me now, Lionel. Do they know about the building?"

"I'm always serious. That's the tragedy of my life."

"Talk to me, Freakshow."

"*Anybuilding! Nobuilding!* Nobody said anything about a building." I reached for his collar, wanting to straighten it, but he batted my hands away.

"You were in there awhile," he said. "Don't fuck with me, Lionel. What was said?"

"They want me to find Julia," I said, wondering if it was a good idea to mention her name. "They think she knows something."

Tony took a gun out from under his arm and pointed it at me.

* * *

I'd returned to Brooklyn suspecting Tony of colluding with The Clients, and now – sweet irony! – Tony suspected me of the same thing. It wasn't that much of a leap. Matricardi and Rockaforte didn't have any motive for humoring me. If they trusted Tony, they wouldn't have required him to wait and bag me outside in the car afterward. He would have been hidden inside, behind the proverbial curtain, soaking up the whole conversation.

I had to give The Clients credit. They'd played us like a Farfisa organ.

On the other hand, Tony had a secret from The Clients: the building on Park Avenue. And despite his fears his secret seemed intact. No point of this particular quadrangle had a monopoly on information. Tony knew something they didn't. I knew something Tony didn't, didn't I? I hoped so. And Julia knew something neither Tony nor The Clients knew, or else she knew something Tony didn't *want* The Clients to know. Julia, Julia, Julia, I needed to figure out the Julia angle, even if Matricardi and Rockaforte wanted me to.

Or was I outsmarting myself? I knew what Minna would have said.

Wheels within wheels.

* * *

I'd never faced Tony at gunpoint before, but at some level I'd been preparing for this moment all my life. It didn't feel at all unnatural. Rather it was a sort of culmination, the rarefied end point of our long association. Now, if I'd had a gun on him, *that* would've freaked me out.

The gun also served splendidly to concentrate my attention. I felt my ticcishness ease, and a flood of excess language instantly evaporate, like cartoon blemishes in a television commercial. Gunplay: another perfectly useless cure.

Tony didn't seem all that impressed by the situation. His eyes and mouth were tired. It was only four in the afternoon and we'd been sitting in the parked car too long already. He had questions, urgent, particular, and the gun would help move things along.

"You talk to anyone else about the building?" he asked.

"Who would I talk to?"

"Danny, say. Or Gilbert."

"I was just up there. I haven't seen Danny. And Gilbert's in jail." I left out the part about the Garbage Cop, and prayed Minna's beeper didn't go off anytime soon.

Meanwhile, with his questions Tony was telling me more than I was telling him: Danny and Gilbert weren't with him in the Park Avenue caper. Yes, this Hardly Boy was still on the case.

"So it's just you," Tony said. "You're the jerk I've gotta deal with. You're Sam Spade."

"When someone kills your partner you're supposed to do something about it," I said.

"Minna wasn't your partner. He was your sponsor, Freakshow. He was Jerry Lewis, and you were the thing in the wheelchair."

"Then why'd he call for me instead of you when he was in trouble yesterday?"

"He was an idiot bringing you up there."

A shadow strolled past the car, indifferent to our curbside melodrama. This was my second time imperiled in a parked vehicle in the space of three hours. I wondered what goonish spectacles I'd overlooked in my own career as a pavement walker.

"Tell me about Julia, Tony – *Tulip Attorney!*" The magic curative of being at gunpoint was beginning to fade.

"Shut up a little. I'm thinking."

"What about Ullman?" I said. As long as he was allowing my questions I might as well ask. "Who was Ullman? – *Doofus Allplan!*" I wanted to ask about the Fujisaki Corporation, but I figured the extent of what I knew was one of the only things I knew and he didn't. I needed to preserve that advantage, however minuscule. Besides, I didn't want to hear what hay my syndrome would make of the word *Fujisaki*.

Tony made a particularly sour face. "Ullman's a guy who didn't figure numbers right. He's one of a little group of somebodies who tried to make themselves rich. Frank was another one."

"So you and the Polish killer took him out, huh?"

"That's so wrong it's funny."

"Tell me, Tony."

"Where would I start?" he said. I heard a note of bitterness, and wondered if I could play on it. Tony likely missed Minna in his way, and missed the Agency, no matter how he'd been corrupted or what poisonous information he knew that I didn't.

"Be sentimental for a change," I said. "Make me know you didn't kill him."

"Go fuck yourself."

"That was persuasive," I said. Then I made a sour face like an uptight British butler: "*Per-shwoosh-atively!*"

"The problem with you, Lionel, is you don't know anything about how the world really works. Everything you know comes from Frank Minna or a book. I don't know which is worse."

"Gangster movies." I fought to keep the butler-face from reappearing.

"What?"

"I watched a lot of gangster movies, like you. Everything we both know comes from Frank Minna or gangster movies."

"Frank Minna was two guys," said Tony. "The one I learned from and the chucklehead who thought you were funny and got himself killed. You only knew the chucklehead."

Tony held the gun floppily between us, using it to gesture, to signal punctuation. I only hoped he understood how literally it could punctuate. None of us had ever carried guns so far as I knew, apart from Minna. He'd rarely allowed us even to see his. Now I wondered what private teaching had gone on when I wasn't around, wondered how seriously I should take Tony's notion of the two Minnas.

"I suppose it was the smart Frank Minna who taught you to wave guns around," I said. It came out a bit more sarcastic than I'd intended, then I yelled, "*Frankensmart!*" which pretty much undercut my delivery. Tony really was waving the gun, though. The only thing it never pointed at was himself.

"I'm carrying this for protection. Like I'm protecting you with it right now, by convincing you to shut up and quit asking questions. And stay in Brooklyn."

"I hope you don't have to protect me – *Protectmebailey! Detectorbaby!* – by pulling the trigger."

"Let's both hope. Too bad you weren't clever like Gilbert, to get himself put under police protection for a week or so."

"Is that the current sentence for murder? A week?"

"Don't make me laugh. Gilbert didn't kill anybody."

"You sound disappointed."

"I'm long over my disappointment that Frank liked to surround himself with a cavalcade of clowns. It was a way of life. I won't be making the same mistake."

"No, you'll think up a whole bunch of new ones."

"Enough of this. Does every conversation with you have to be the director's cut? Get out of the car."

At that moment there came a tap on the window, driver's side. It was a gun muzzle that tapped. The arm holding the gun extended from behind the trunk of the elm tree. A head poked out too: the homicide detective.

"Gentlemen," he said. "Do step out of the car – slowly."

Ambushes within ambushes.

*　*　*

He still had that threadbare, jaded, coffee-isn't-working-anymore air about him, even in daylight. It didn't look like he'd gotten out of his suit since the night before. I believed him with a gun better than I did Tony, though. He waved us over to the front of the car and had us spread our legs, to the wonderment of a couple of old ladies, then took away Tony's gun. He had Tony open his jacket and show the open holster and lift his pant legs to prove there was nothing strapped to his ankles. Then he tried to pat me down and I began to pat him back.

"Goddamn it, Alibi, cut that out." He was still fond of that nickname he'd invented for me. It made me fond of him.

"I can't help it," I said.

"What's that? A phone? Take it out."

"It's a phone." I showed him.

Tony looked at me strangely, and I just shrugged.

"Get back in the car. Give me the keys first." Tony handed over the keys and we got back into the front seat. The homicide detective opened the back doors and eased into the seat behind us, training his gun on the backs of our heads.

"Hands on the wheel and the dash, that's good. Face forward, gentlemen. Don't look at me. Smile like they're taking your picture. They will be soon enough."

"What did we do?" said Tony. "A guy can't show another guy a gun anymore?"

"Shut up and listen. This is a murder investigation. I'm the investigating officer. I don't care about your goddamn gun."

"So give it back."

"I don't think so, Mr. Vermonte. You people make me nervous. I found out a few things about this neighborhood in the last twenty-four hours."

"Mister Gobbledy Gun."

"Shut up, Alibi."

Shut up shut up shut up! I kneaded the petrified foam of the Pontiac's dashboard like a nursing kitten, just trying to keep still and shut up. Someday I'd change my name to Shut Up and save everybody a lot of time.

"I got this case because you jokers brought Frank Minna into Brooklyn Hospital. That's where he died and that's in my jurisdiction. I don't get to work this side of Flatbush Avenue that often, you get me? I don't know all that much about your neighborhood, but I'm learning, I'm learning."

"Not so many murders over here, eh, Chief?" said Tony.

"Not so many *niggers* on this side of Flatbush, that what you're trying to say?"

"Whoa, slow down," said Tony. "You're leading the witness. Isn't that against the rules?" Tony kept his hands on the steering wheel and grinned into the windshield. I don't think the homicide cop had really meant to inspire such a smile.

"Okay, Tony," said the cop, his voice a little husky. I heard him breathing heavily through his nose. I suppose unsheathing his gun had gotten him a bit worked up. I imagined I could feel its muzzle centering first on my ear, then on Tony's. "Tell me what you meant," he said. "Set me straight."

"All I meant was not so many murders – am I right?"

"Yeah, you got the lid clamped down pretty tight around here. No murders and no niggers. Nice clean streets, nothing but old guys carrying around racing forms and tiny pencils. Makes me nervous."

It was honest of him to admit it. I wondered what Mafia horror stories he'd gathered in his day-old investigation.

"Around here people watch out for each other," said Tony.

"Yeah, right up until you off each other. What's the connection between Minna and Ullman, Tony?"

"Who's Ullman?" said Tony. "I never met the guy."

That was a Minna-ism: *never met the guy.*

"Ullman kept the books for a property-management firm in Manhattan," said the homicide detective. "Until your friend Coney shot him through the skull. Looks like tit for tat to me. I'm impressed with how quick you guys get to work."

"What's your name, Officer?" said Tony. "I get to ask that, don't I?"

"I'm not an officer, Tony. I'm a detective. My name is Lucius Seminole."

"Luscious? You gotta be kidding me."

"*Lu*cius. Call me Detective Seminole."

"What is that, like an Indian name?"

"It's a Southern name," said Seminole. "Slave name. Keep laughing, Tony."

"*Detectahole!*"

"Alibi, you are not making me happy."

"*Inspectaholic!*"

"Don't kill him, Superfly," said Tony, grinning broadly. "I know it's pitiful, but he can't help himself. Think of it as a free human freak show."

"*Licorice Smellahole!*" Not turning my head was driving me crazy: I had to rename what I couldn't see.

"You a car service or a comedy team?" said Seminole.

"Lionel's just jealous because you're asking me all the questions," said Tony. "He likes to talk."

"I already heard from Alibi last night. He near about drove me crazy with his talk. Now I'm looking for answers from you, straight man."

"We're not a car service," I said. "We're a detective agency." The assertion fought its way out of me, a tic disguised as a common statement.

"Turn around, Alibi. Let's talk about the lady who ran to Boston – Mrs. Deadguy."

"Boston?" said Tony.

"*We'readetectiveagency,*" I ticced again.

"She booked the flight under her own name," said Seminole. "It's not the first time either. What's in Boston?"

"Beats me. She goes up there a lot?"

"Don't play stupid."

"It's news to me," said Tony. He scowled at me, and I made a dopey face back, stumped. Julia in Boston? I wondered if Seminole had his information straight.

"She was ready to fly," said Seminole. "Somebody tipped her."

"She got a call from the hospital," I said.

"Nope," said Seminole. "I checked that. Try another one. Maybe your boy Gilbert gave her a call. Maybe Gilbert took out Frank Minna before he took out Ullman. Maybe he and the lady are in this together."

"That's crazy," I said. "Gilbert didn't kill anybody. We're *detectives.*"

I finally got Seminole's attention. "I looked into that rumor," he said. "None of you carry investigators' credentials, according to the computer. Just limousine operators' licenses."

"We work for Frank Minna," I said, and heard my own unconcealed nostalgia, my pining. "We assist a detective. We're, uh, operatives."

"You do stooge work for a penny-ante hood, according to what I can see. A *dead* penny-ante hood. You were in the pocket of a guy in the pocket of Alphonso Matricardi and Leonardo Rockaforte, two relatively deep old dudes. Only it appears the pocket got turned inside out."

Tony winced: These clichés hurt. "We work for the clients that come in," he said, oddly sincere. For a moment Minna again came alive in Tony's voice. "We don't ask questions we shouldn't, or we wouldn't have any clients at all. The cops do the same, don't try to tell me any different."

"Cops don't have *clients*," said the homicide detective stiffly. I would have liked to see the real Frank Minna handle Seminole.

"What are you, Abraham Jefferson Jackson?" said Tony. "You running for office with that speech? Give me a break."

I snorted. Despite everything, Tony was cracking me up. I threw in a flourish of my own:

"Abracadabra Jackson!"

* * *

The gun, and Seminole's status as a law-enforcement officer, didn't matter — he was losing control of this interview. What happened was this: Tony and I, so deeply estranged, had been drawn together by the point of the detective's gun. In this post-Minna era we Men were a little panicked and raw at facing one another head on. But triangulated by Seminole we'd rediscovered the kinship that lurked in our old routines. If we couldn't trust each other, Tony and I were at least reminded we were two of a kind, especially in the eyes of a cop. And Tony, seeing chinks in the detective's confidence, was turning on him with his old orphan's savagery. A bully knows the parameters and half-life of a brandished threat — the only thing weaker than a gun so long ignored was no gun at all. The cop had had to arrest us or hurt us or turn us against each other by now, and he hadn't. Tony would cut him apart with his tongue for the mistake.

In the meantime I considered what Seminole had been saying, and tried to sift the information from his dingbat theories. If Julia didn't get a call from the hospital how did she know about Minna's death?

Again I wondered: Was it Julia who missed her *Rama-lama-ding-dong*? Did she keep it in Boston?

* * *

"Listen, you scumbags," said Seminole. He was compensating desperately for his plummeting authority. "I'd rather tangle with *homies* doing *drive-bys* all day than wade into this Italianate mobster shit. Don't get big-headed, now — I can see you're just a couple of fools. It's the wiseguys pulling your strings I'm worried about."

"Great," said Tony. "A paranoid cop. *Wiseguys pulling strings* — you read too many comic books, Cleopatra Jones."

"Clapperdapper Bailey Johnson!"

"You think I'm stupid," continued Seminole, on a real tear now. "You think a dumb black cop is going to stumble into your little nest and take it on face value. Car service, detective agency, give me a break. I'm going to push this murder bag just far enough to turn it over to the Federal Bureau of Investigation, and then I'm going to get my ass out of here for good. Might even take a vacation, sit on the beach and read about you losers in the Metro section."

Stumble, wade: Seminole's choice of words betrayed him. He really and truly feared he'd already gotten in further than was good for him. I wanted to find a way to allay his fears, I really did. I sort of liked the homicide detective. But everything out of my mouth sounded vaguely like a racial slur.

"Federal Bureau of what?" said Tony. "I never met those guys."

"Let's go upstairs and see if Uncle Alphonso and Uncle Leonardo can explain it to you," said Seminole. "Something tells me they've got a working familiarity with the FBI."

"I don't think the old guys are home anymore," said Tony.

"Oh yeah? Where'd they go?"

"They went through a tunnel in the basement," said Tony. "They had to get back to their hideout, since they've got James Bond – or Batman, I can't remember which – roasting over a slow fire."

"What are you talking about?"

"Don't worry, though. Batman always gets away. These supervillains never learn."

"Uncle Batman!" I shouted. They couldn't know how much work it was for me to keep my hands on that dashboard, my neck straight. "Unclebailey Blackman! *Barnamum Bat-a-potamus!*"

"That's enough, Alibi," said Seminole. "Get out of the car."

"What?"

"Get lost, go home. You annoy me, man. Tony and me are going to have a little talk."

"C'mon, Blacula," complained Tony. "We've been talking for hours. I've got nothing to say to you."

"Every name you call me I think up a couple more questions," said Seminole. He waved at me with his gun. "Get lost."

I gaped at Seminole, incredulous.

"I mean it. Get."

I opened the door. Then I thought to find the Pontiac's keys and hand them to Tony.

Tony glared at me. "Go back to the office and wait for me."

"Oh, sure," I said, and stepped out onto the curb.

"Close the door," said Seminole, training gun and gaze on Tony.

"Thanks, *Count Chocula*," I said, and skipped away, literally.

* * *

Have you noticed yet that I relate everything to my Tourette's? Yup, you guessed it, it's a tic. Counting is a symptom, but counting symptoms is also a symptom, a tic *plus ultra*. I've got meta-Tourette's. Thinking about ticcing, my mind racing, thoughts reaching to touch every possible symptom. Touching touching. Counting counting. Thinking thinking. Mentioning mentioning Tourette's. It's sort of like talking about telephones over the telephone, or mailing letters describing the location of various mailboxes. Or like a tugboater whose favorite anecdote concerns actual tugboats.

* * *

There is nothing Tourettic about the New York City subways.

Though at each step I felt the gaze of an army of invisible doormen on my neck, I was nevertheless exultant to be back on the Upper East Side. I hurried down Lexington from the Eighty-sixth Street station, with only ten minutes to spare before five o'clock: zazen. I didn't want to be late for my first. While I was still on the street, though, I took out the cell phone and called Loomis.

"Yeah, I was just about to call you." I could hear him chewing a sandwich or a chicken leg, and pictured his open mouth, smacking lips. Hadn't he been at lunch two hours before? "I got the goods on that building."

"Let's have it – quick."

"This guy in Records, he was going on and on about it. That's a sweet little building, Lionel. Way outta my class."

"It's Park Avenue, Loomis."

"Well, there's Park Avenue and then there's this. You gotta have a hundred million to get on the waiting list for this place, Lionel. This kind of people, their other house is an *island*."

I heard Loomis quoting someone smarter than himself. "Right, but what about Fujisaki?"

"Hold your horses, I'm getting there. This sort of place, there's a whole staff – it's like a bunch of mansions stacked together. They got secret passages, wine cellars, a laundry service, swimming pool, servants' quarters, private chef. Whole secret economy. There's only five or six buildings like this in the city – the place where Bob Dylan got killed, what's it, the *Nova Scotia*? That's a doghouse in comparison. This place is for the old-money people, they'll turn down Seinfeld, *Nixon*, doesn't matter. They don't even give a shit."

"Include me in that category," I said, unable to discern any useful information in the Garbage Cop's jabber. "I'm looking for names, Loomis."

"Your Fujisaki's the management corporation. Whole bunch of other Jap names in there – guess they own half of New York if you started digging. This is a serious money operation, Lionel. Ullman, far as I can tell, he was just Fujisaki's accountant. So clue me in: Why would Gilbert go after an accountant?"

"Ullman was the last guy Frank was supposed to see," I said. "He never got to him."

"Minna was supposed to kill Ullman?"

"I don't know."

"Or vice versa?"

"I don't know."

"Or did the same guy kill them both?"

"I don't know, Loomis."

"So you aren't learning much besides what I'm digging up for you, huh?"

"Eat me, Loomis."

* * *

"I'm so glad you're here," said Kimmery when she opened the door to me. "You're just in time. Mostly everybody's sitting already." She kissed me on the cheek again. "There's a lot of excitement about the monks."

"I'm feeling a lot of excitement myself." In fact, I felt an instant euphoria at Kimmery's alleviating presence. If this was the prospect of Zen I was ready to begin my training.

"You'll have to take a cushion right away. Just sit anywhere but up at the front of the line. We'll work on your posture some other time – for now you can sit and concentrate on your breathing."

"I'll do that." I followed her up the stairs.

"That's really everything anyway, breathing. You could work on just that for the rest of your life."

"I'll probably have to."

"Take off your shoes."

Kimmery pointed, and I added my shoes to a neat row in the hallway. It was a bit disconcerting to surrender them and with them my street-readiness, but in fact my aching dogs were grateful for the chance to breathe and stretch.

The second-floor sitting room was gloomy now, overhead track lighting still dark, the fading November daylight insufficient. I spotted the source of the heavy smell this time, a pot of smoldering incense on a high shelf beside a jade Buddha. The walls of the room were covered with undecorated paper screens, the glossy parquet floor with thin cushions. Kimmery led me to a spot near the back of the room and sat beside me, folded her legs and straightened her back, then nodded wide-eyed to suggest I imitate her moves. If only she knew. I sat and worked my big legs into position, grabbing my shins with both hands, only once jostling the sitter ahead of me, who turned and quickly glared, then resumed his posture of grace. The rows of cushions around us were mostly full with Zen practitioners, twenty-two when I counted, some in black robes, others in beatniky street clothes, corduroy or sweatpants and turtlenecks, not one in a suit like me. In the dimness I couldn't make out any faces.

So I sat and waited and wondered exactly what I was there for, though it was tough to keep my back straight as those I saw around me. I glanced at Kimmery. Her eyes were already peacefully shut. In twenty-four hours – it was only slightly more than that since Gilbert and I had parked at the curb outside the day before – my confusion at the Zendo's significance had doubled and redoubled, become veiled in successive layers. The conversation I'd heard on the wire, those sneering insinuations, now seemed impossible to fix to this place. Kimmery's voice, ingenuous, unconspiring, was all I heard now. That, of course, against a background of my own interior babble. As I sat beside Kimmery, sheltered inside her tic-canceling field, I felt all the more keenly the uneasy, half-stoppered force of my own language-generator, my Multi-Mind, that tangle of responses and mimickings, of interruptions of interruptions.

I gazed at her again. She was *sitting* sincerely, not wondering about me. So I shut my eyes and, taking my own little crack at enlightenment, tried to unify my mind and get a fix on my Buddha nature.

* * *

The first thing I heard was Minna's voice: *I dare you to shut up for a whole twenty minutes sometime, you free human freakshow.*

I pushed it away, thought *One Mind* instead.

One Mind.

Tell me one, Freakshow. One I don't already know.

I vant to go to Tibet.

One Mind. I focused on my breathing.

Come home, Irving.

One Mind. Sick Mind. Dirty Mind. Bailey Mind.

One Mind.

Oreo Man.

* * *

When I opened my eyes again, I'd adjusted to the gloom. At the front of the room was a large bronze gong, and the cushions nearest the gong were empty as if readied for celebrity sitters, perhaps the *important monks*. The rows of heads had developed features, though mostly I was looking at ears and napes, the neckline of haircuts. The crowd was a mix of sexes, the women mostly skinny, with earrings and hairstyles that cost something, the men on average more lardish and scruffy, their haircuts overdue. I spotted Wallace's ponytail and bald spot and furniture-stiff posture up near the front. And a row ahead of me, closer to the entrance, sat Pinched and Indistinct, my would-be abductors. At last I understood: They *were* men of peace. Was there a severe shortage of human beings on the Upper East Side, so the same small cast of doormen was required to pose in costume, here as goons, there as seekers after serenity? At least they'd shed their blue suits, made a greater commitment to this new identity. Garbed in black robes, their postures were admirably erect, presumably earned by extensive training, years of sacrifice. They hadn't been working all that time on their strong-arm patter, that was for sure.

So much for my breathing. I managed to check my voice, though. Pinched and Indistinct both had their eyes shut, and I'd arrived last, so I had the drop on them. They weren't exactly my idea of big trouble anyway. But I was reminded that the stolen cell phone and borrowed beeper in my jacket might shatter this ancient Eastern silence at any moment. Moving quietly as possible, I drew them out and turned off the cell phone's ringer, set Minna's beeper to "vibrate." As I slipped them back into my jacket's inner pocket an open hand slapped the back of my head and neck, hard.

Stung, I whipped around. But my attacker was already past me, marching solemnly between the mats to the front of the room, the first in a file of six bald Japanese men, all draped in robes revealing glimpses of sagging brown skin and threads of white underarm hair. Important monks. The lead monk had swerved out of his way to deliver the blow. I'd been reprimanded or perhaps offered a jolt of enlightenment – did I now know the sound of one hand clapping? Either way, I felt the heat of blood rushing to my ears and scalp.

Kimmery hadn't noticed, just placidly Zenned right through the whole sequence. Maybe she was further along on her spiritual path than she realized.

The six moved to the front and took the unoccupied mats near the gong. And a seventh entered the room, a little behind the others, also robed, also with a polished bald skull. But he wasn't small and Japanese and his body hair wasn't white and it wasn't limited to his underarms. He had silky black plumes of back and shoulder hair, rising from all sides to circle his neck with a fringe. It wasn't a look the designer of the robe had likely had in mind. He moved to the front of the room and took the last of the VIP spots before I could see his face, but I thought of Kimmery's description and decided this must be the American teacher, founder of the Zendo, the Roshi.

Irving. When are you coming home, Irving? *Your family misses you.*

The joke nagged at me, but I couldn't put it to work. Was that Roshi's original name, his American name: Irving? Was Roshi-Irving the voice on the wire?

If so, why? What linked Minna to this place?

They settled into quietude up front. I stared at the row of bald heads, the six monks and Roshi, but discerned nothing. Even Pinched and Indistinct were meditating serenely. Minutes crept past and I was the only set of open eyes. Someone coughed and I faked a cough in imitation. If I kept one eye on Kimmery I was mostly calm, though. It was like having a bag of White Castles beside me on the car seat. I wondered how deep her influence over my syndrome could run if given the chance, how much of that influence I could hope to import. How close I could get. I shut my eyes, trusting Pinched and Indistinct to stay planted obliviously on their cushions, and drifted into some pleasant thoughts about bodies, about Kimmery's body, her nervous elegant limbs. Perhaps this was the key to Zen, then. *We don't exactly have God,* she'd said. *We just sit and try to stay awake.* Well, I wasn't having any trouble staying awake. And as my penis stiffened it occurred to me I'd found my One Mind.

I was jostled from my reverie by a sound at the door. I opened my eyes and turned to see the Polish giant standing in the entrance to the sitting room, filling the doorway with his square shoulders, holding in his fist a plastic produce bag full of kumquats and gazing at the roomful of Zen practitioners with an expression of absolute and utter serenity. He wasn't in a robe, but he might have been Buddha himself for the benignity of his gaze.

* * *

Before I could figure a plan or response there came a commotion at the front of the room. A commotion by the local standards anyway: One of the Japanese monks stood and bowed to Roshi, then to the other monks in his party, then to the room at large. You still would have heard a pin drop, but the rustling of his robe was signal enough, and eyes opened everywhere. The giant stepped into the room, still clutching his kumquats like a bag of live goldfish, and took a mat – a couple actually – on the other side of Kimmery, between us and the door. I reminded myself that the giant hadn't seen me, at least not yesterday. He certainly wasn't giving me any special notice – or anyone else for that matter. Instead he settled into his spot, looking ready for the monk's lecture. Quite a gathering we made now, the various mugs and lugs attending to the wise little men from the East. Pinched and Indistinct might be real Zen students playing at thuggishness, but Pierogi Monster was undoubtedly the opposite. The kumquats, I was pretty sure, were a giveaway – weren't they a Chinese fruit, not Japanese at all? I wanted to hug Kimmery toward me, away from the killer's reach, but then I wanted to do a lot of things – I always do.

The monk bowed to us again, searched our faces briefly, then began speaking, so abruptly and casually it was as if he were resuming a talk he'd been having with himself.

"Daily life, I fly on an airplane, I take a taxicab to visit Yorkville Zendo" – this came out *Yolkville-ah* – "I feel excitement, thoughts, anticipations, what will my friend Jerry-Roshi show me? Will I go to a very good Manhattan restaurant, sleep on a very good bed in New York City hotel?" He stomped his sandaled foot as though testing out a mattress.

I vant to go to Tibet! The joke insisted itself upon me again. My calm was under pressure from all sides, the goons everywhere, my echolalia provoked by the monk's speech. But I couldn't turn and gaze and refresh my dose of Kimmery without also taking in Minna's titanic killer – he was so big that his outline framed her on all sides despite his being farther away, an optical trick I couldn't afford to find fascinating.

"All these moods, impulses, this daily life, nothing wrong

with them. But daily life, island, dinner, airplane, cocktail, daily life is not Zen. In zazen practice all that matters is the sitting, the practice. American, Japan, doesn't matter. Only sitting."

I vant to speak to the Lama! The American monk, Roshi, had half turned in his spot to better contemplate the master from across the ocean. The profile below Roshi's gleaming dome stirred me unexpectedly. I recognized some terrible force of authority and charisma in his features.

Jerry-Roshi?

Meanwhile the giant sat disrespectfully pinching the skin of a kumquat, pressing it to his monstrous lips, sucking its juice.

"It is easy practice zazen in its external form, sit on the cushion and waste time on the cushion. So many forms of nothing-Zen, meaningless Zen, only one form of true Zen: actual making contact with own Buddha-self."

The High Lama will grant you an audience.

"There is *chikusho* Zen, Zen of domesticated animals who curl up on pillows like cats in homes, waiting to be fed. They sit to kill time between meals. Domesticated animal Zen useless! Those who practice chikusho should be beaten and thrown out of the zendo."

I obsessed on Jerry-Roshi's face while the monk sputtered on.

"There is *ningen* Zen, Zen practiced for self-improvement, Ego-Zen. Make skin better, make bowel movement better, think positive thoughts and influence people. Shit! Ningen Zen is shit Zen!"

Irving, come home, went my brain. *No soap, Zendo. Tibetta-pocamus. Chickenshack Zen. High Oscillama Talkalot.* The monk's wonky syllables, the recursions of the Tibet joke, my own fear of the giant – all were conspiring to bring me to a boil. I wanted to trace Roshi's enthralling profile with my finger-tip – perhaps I'd recognize its significance by touch. Instead I practiced Essrog Zen, and stifled myself.

"Consider also *gaki* Zen: the Zen of insatiable ghosts. Those who study gaki Zen chase after enlightenment like spirits who crave food or vengeance with a hunger can never be satisfied.

These ghosts never even enter the house of Zen they are so busy howling at the windows!"

Roshi looked like Minna.

Your brother misses you, Irving.

Irving equals Lama, Roshi equals Gerard.

Roshi was Gerard Minna.

Gerard Minna was the voice on the wire.

I couldn't say which got me there first, his profile in front of me or the joke's subliminal nagging. It felt like a dead heat. Of course, the joke had been designed to get me there sooner, spare me figuring it out while in the belly of the whale. Too bad.

I tried to quit staring, failed. Up front the monk continued to enumerate false Zens, the various ways we could go wrong. I personally could think of a few he probably hadn't come across yet.

But why had Minna buried the information in a joke to begin with? I thought of a couple of reasons. One: He didn't want us to know about Gerard *unless* he died. If he survived the attack he wanted his secret to survive as well. Two: He didn't know who among his Men to trust, even down to Gilbert Coney. He could be certain I'd puzzle over the Irving clue while Gilbert would write it off as our mutual inanity.

And he felt, rightly, that no conspiracy around him could possibly include his pet Freakshow. The other Boys would never let me play. I could be flattered at the implied trust, or insulted by the dis. It didn't really matter now.

I stared at Gerard. Now I understood the charismatic force of his profile, but it inspired only bitterness. It was as though the world imagined it could take Minna away and offer this clumsy genetic substitution. A resemblance.

"California Roll Zen. This is the Zen of sushi so full of avocado and cream cheese might as well be a marshmallow for all you know. The pungent fish of zazen smothered in easy pleasures, picnics, get-togethers, Zendo becomes a dating service!"

"*Zengeance!*" I shouted.

Not every head turned. Gerard Minna's did, though. So did Pinched's, and Indistinct's. And so did the giant's. Kimmery was among those who practiced their calm by ignoring me.

"Ziggedy zendoodah," I said aloud. My erection dimmed, energy venting elsewhere. "*Pierogi Monster Zen master zealous neighbor.* Zazen zaftig Zsa Zsa go-bare." I rapped the scalp of the sitter in front of me. "Zippity go figure."

The roomful of gurus and acolytes came to agitated life but not one of them spoke a word, so my burst of verbiage sang in the silence. The lecturing monk glared at me and shook his head. Another of his posse rose from his cushion and lifted a wooden paddle I hadn't previously noticed from a hook on the wall, then started through the rows of students in my direction. Only Wallace sat immobile, eyes shut, still meditating. I began to appreciate his reputation for imperturbability.

"Pierogi kumquat sushiphone! Domestic marshmallow ghost! Insatiable Mallomar! *Smothered pierogiphone!*" The flood came with such force, I twisted my neck and nearly barked the words.

"Silence!" commanded the lecturing monk. "Very bad to make disturbance in the Zendo! Time and place for everything!" Anger wasn't good for his English. "Shouting is for outside, New York City full of shouting! Not in Zendo."

"Knock knock Zendo!" I shouted. "Monk monk goose!"

The monk with the paddle approached. He gripped it cross-handed, like Hank Aaron. The giant stood, shoved his baggie of kumquats into the pocket of his Members Only jacket and rubbed his sticky hands together, readying them for use. Gerard turned and stared at me, but if he recognized in me the twitchy teenager he'd left behind at the St. Vincent's schoolyard fence nineteen years before, he didn't show any sign. His eyebrows were delicately knit, his mouth pursed, his expression bemused. Kimmery put her hand on my knee and I put my hand on hers, reciprocity-ticcing. Even in a shitstorm such as I was in at this moment, my syndrome knew that God was in the details.

"Keisaku is more than ceremonial implement," said the monk with the paddle. He applied it to my shoulder blades so gently it was like a caress. "Unruly student can do with a blow." Now he clouted my back with the same muscular Buddhist glee his colleague had applied to my scalp.

"Ouch!" I fished behind me for the paddle, snagged it, tugged. It came out of the monk's grasp and he staggered backward. By now the giant was headed in our direction. Those between us rolled or scuttled out of his path, according to their ability to unlock their elaborately folded legs. Kimmery darted away just as he loomed over us, not wanting to be crushed. Pierogi Man hadn't checked his shoes at the door.

That was when I saw the nod.

Gerard Minna nodded ever so slightly at the giant, and the giant nodded back. That was all it took. The same team that had doomed Frank Minna was back in the saddle. I would be the sequel.

The giant wrapped me in his arms and lifted, and the paddle clattered to the floor.

*   *   *

I weigh nearly two hundred pounds, but the giant didn't strain at all moving me down the stairs and out onto the street, and when he plumped me onto the sidewalk I was more shaken and winded than he by far. I straightened my suit and confirmed the alignment of my neck with a string of jerks while he unloaded his bag of kumquats and got back to sucking out their juice and pulp, reducing their bodies to husks that looked like orange raisins in his massive hands.

The narrow street was nearly dark now, and the dog-walkers were far enough away to give us privacy.

"Want one?" he said, holding out the bag. His voice was a dull thing where it began in his throat but it resonated to grandeur in the tremendous instrument of his torso, like a mediocre singer on the stage of a superb concert hall.

"No, thanks," I said. Here was where I should grow large with anger, facing Minna's killer right at the spot of the abduction. But I was diminished, ribs aching from his squeezing, confused and worried – conworried – by my discovery of Gerard Minna inside the Zendo, and unhappy to have left Kimmery and my shoes upstairs. The pavement was cold through my socks, and my feet tingled oddly as they flushed with the blood denied them by Zen posture.

"So what's the matter with you?" he said, discarding another of the withered kumquats.

"I've got Tourette's," I said.

"Yeah, well, threats don't work with me."

"Tourette's," I said.

"Eh? My hearing's not so good. Sorry." He put the bag of fruit away again, and when his hand reemerged it was holding a gun. "Go in there," he said. He pointed with his chin at the three steps leading to the narrow channel between the Zendo and the apartment building on the right, a lane filled with garbage cans and darkness. I frowned, and he reached out and with the hand not holding the gun shoved me backward toward the steps. "Go," he said again.

I considered the giant and myself as a tableau. Here was the man I'd been hunting and wishing to go up against, howling for a chance at vengeance like an insatiable ghost or marshmallow – yet had I planned a way to take advantage of him, a method or apparatus to give me any real edge, let alone narrow the immense gap in force his size presented? No. I'd come up pathetically empty. And now he had a gun to ice the cake. He shoved me again, straight-armed my shoulder, and when I tried, ticcishly, to shove his shoulder in return I found I was held at too great a distance, couldn't brush his shoulder even with long-stretched fingertips, and it conjured some old memory of Sylvester the Cat in a boxing ring with a kangaroo. My brain whispered, *He's just a big mouse, Daddy, a vigorous louse, big as a house, a couch, a man, a plan, a canal, apocalypse.*

"Apocamouse," I mumbled, language spilling out of me unrestrained. "Unplan-a-canal. Unpluggaphone."

"I said get in there, Squeaky." Had he caught my mouse reference, even with his impaired hearing? But then, who wouldn't be squeaky to him? He was so big he only had to shrug to loom. I took a step backward. I had Tourette's, he had threats. "Go," he said again.

It was the last thing I wanted to do and I did it.

The minute I stepped down into the darkness he swung the gun at my head.

*   *   *

So many detectives have been knocked out and fallen into such strange swirling darknesses, such manifold surrealist voids ("something red wriggled like a germ under a microscope" – Philip Marlowe, *The Big Sleep*), and yet I have nothing to contribute to this painful tradition. Instead my falling and rising through obscurity was distinguished only by nothingness, by blankness, by lack and my resentment of it. Except for grains. It was a grainy nothing. A desert of grains. How fond can you be of flavorless grains in a desert? How much better than nothing at all? I'm from Brooklyn and I don't like wide-open spaces, I guess. And I don't want to die. So sue me.

Then I remembered a joke, a riddle like one the Garbage Cop would tell, and it was my lifeline, it sang like a chorus of ethereal voices beckoning me from the brink of darkness:

Why don't you starve in the desert?

Because of the *sand which is* there.

Why didn't I want to die or leave New York?

The sandwiches. I concentrated on the sandwiches. For a while that's all there was, and I was happy. The sandwiches were so much better than the desert of grains.

"Lionel?"

It was Kimmery's voice.

* * *

"Mhrrggh."

"I brought your shoes."

"Oooh."

"I think we should go. Can you stand?"

"Rrrrssp."

"Lean against the wall. Careful. I'll get a cab."

"Cabbabbab."

I flickered awake again and we were slicing through the park, East Side to West, in that taxicab channel of tree-topped stone, my head on Kimmery's bony shoulder. She was putting my shoes back on, lifting my leaden feet one after the other, then tying the laces. Her small hands and my large shoes made this an operation rather like saddling a comatose horse. I could see the cabbie's license – his name was Omar Dahl, which invited tics I couldn't muster in my state – and a view upward through the side window. For a moment I thought it was snowing and everything seemed precious and distant – Central Park in a snow globe. Then I realized it was snowing inside the cab, too. The grains again. I closed my eyes.

*   *   *

Kimmery's apartment was on Seventy-eighth Street, in an old-lady apartment building, gloriously shabby and real after the gloss of the East Side, the chilling dystopian lobby of 1030 Park Avenue especially. I got upright and into the elevator on my own steam, with only Kimmery to hold the doors for me, which was how I liked it – no doormen. We rode to the twenty-eighth floor in an empty car, and Kimmery leaned against me as if we were still in the cab. I didn't need the support to stand anymore, but I didn't stop it from happening. My head throbbed – where Pierogi Man had clubbed me, it felt as though I were trying to grow a single horn, and failing – and the contact with Kimmery was a kind of compensation. At her floor she parted from my side with that nervous quick walk I already considered her trademark, her confession of some kernel of jerkiness I could cultivate and adore, and unlocked the door to her place so frantically I wondered if she thought we'd been followed.

"Did the giant see you?" I said when we were inside.

"What?"

"The giant. Are you afraid of the giant?" I felt a body-memory, and shuddered. I was still a little *unsteady on my pins*, as Minna would have said.

She looked at me strangely. "No, I just – I'm an illegal sublet here. There are people in this building who can't mind their own business. You should sit down. Do you want some water?"

"Sure." I looked around. "Sit where?"

Her apartment consisted of a brief foyer, a minuscule kitchen – really more an astronaut's cockpit full of cooking equipment – and a large central room whose polyurethaned floor mirrored the vast moonlit city nightscape featured in its long, uncurtained window. The reflected image was uninterrupted by carpet or furniture, just a few modest boxes tucked into the corners, a tiny boom box and a stack of tapes, and a large cat that stood in the center of the floor, regarding our entrance skeptically. The walls were bare. Kimmery's bedding was a flattened mattress on the floor of the foyer where we stood now, just inside the apartment's door. We were almost on top of it.

"Go ahead and sit on the bed," she said, with a nervous half smile.

Beside the bed was a candle, a box of tissues, and a small stack of paperbacks. It was a private space, a headquarters. I wondered if she hosted much – I felt I might be the first to see past her door.

"Why don't you sleep in there?" I said, pointing at the big empty room. My words came out thickened and stupid, like those of a defeated boxer in his dressing room, or a Method actor's, while playing a defeated boxer. My Tourette's brain preferred precision, sharper edges. I felt it waking.

"People look in," said Kimmery. "I'm not comfortable."

"You could have curtains." I gestured at the big window.

"It's too big. I don't really like that room. I don't know why." Now she looked like she regretted bringing me here. "Sit. I'll bring you some water."

The room she didn't like was the whole of the apartment. She lived instead in the foyer. But I decided not to say anything more about it. There was something anyway that suited me in her use of the space, as though she'd planned to bring me here to hide, knew I'd have something to fear from the skyline, the big world of conspiracies and doormen that was Manhattan.

I took a seat on her bed, back against the wall, legs straightened to cross the mattress, so my shoes reached the floor. I felt my tailbone meet the floor through the pancake-thin mattress. Now I saw that Kimmery had double-knotted my laces. I lingered awkwardly over this detail, used it to measure my returning consciousness, allowing my obsessiveness to play over the intricacy of the knots and my stroboscopic memories of Kimmery tugging at my feet in the cab. I imagined I could feel the dented place in my skull and the damaged language flowing in a new direction through this altered inner topography and the words went *sandwiches sandwiches I scream for ice cream dust to dust* and so on.

I decided to distract myself with the books stacked near the bed. The first was called *The Wisdom of Insecurity*, by Alan Watts. Tucked into it as an oversize bookmark was a pamphlet, a glossy sheet folded in thirds. I pulled out the pamphlet. It was for Yoshii's, a Zen Buddhist retreat center and roadside Thai and Japanese restaurant on the southern coast of Maine. The phone number beneath the schematic road map on the back was circled with blue ballpoint. The heading on the front of the pamphlet said A PLACE OF PEACE.

Pleasure police.

Pressure peas.

The cat walked in from the main room and stood on my outstretched thighs and began kneading them with its front paws, half-retracted claws engaging the material to make a *pocka-pocka-pocka* sound. The cat was black and white with a Hitler mustache, and when it finally noticed I had a face it squeezed its eyes at me. I folded the pamphlet into my jacket pocket, then took off my jacket and put it on the corner of Kimmery's bed. The cat went back to working my thighs.

"You probably don't like cats," said Kimmery, returning with two glasses of water.

"*Chickencat,*" I said, ticcing stupidly. "*Cream of soup salad sandwich.*"

"Are you hungry?"

"No, no," I said, though maybe I was. "And I like cats fine." But I kept my hands away, not wanting to begin obsessing on its body – kneading back or mimicking its uneven, cackling purr.

* * *

I can't own a cat, because my behaviors drive them insane. I know because I tried. I had a cat, gray and slim, half the size of Kimmery's, named Hen for the chirping and cooing sounds she made, for the barnyard pecking motions her initial sniffing inspections of my apartment reminded me of. She enjoyed my attentions at first, my somewhat excessive fondling. She'd purr and push against my hand as I tapped her, taking her pleasure. I'd refine my impulses toward her as well as I could, stroking her neck smoothly, rubbing her cheeks sideways to stimulate her kittenish memories of being licked, or whatever it is that makes cats crave that sensation. But from the very first Hen was disconcerted by my head-jerks and utterances and especially by my barking. She'd turn her head to see what I'd jumped at, to see what I was fishing for in the air with my hand. Hen recognized those behaviors – they were supposed to be *hers*. She never felt free to relax. She'd cautiously advance to my lap, a long game of half measures and imaginary distractions before she'd settle. Then I'd issue a string of bitten-off shrieks and bat at the curtain.

Worse, her bouts of joy at my petting hands became a focal point for Tourettic games of disruption. Hen would purr and nudge at my hand, and I'd begin stroking her smooth, sharklike face. She'd lean into the pressure, and I'd push back, until she was arched into my hand and ready to topple. Then the tic – I'd withdraw my hand. Other times I'd be compelled to follow her around the apartment, reaching for her when she'd meant to be sly or invisible; I'd stalk her, though it was obvious that like any cat her preference was to come to me. Or I'd fixate on the limits of her pleasure at being touched – would she keep purring if I rubbed her fur backward? If I tickled her cheeks would I be allowed to simultaneously grasp her sacrosanct tail? Would she permit me to clean the sleep from her eyes? The answer was often yes, but there was a cost. As with a voodoo doll, I'd begun investing my own ticcishness in my smaller counterpart: Tourette's Cat. She'd been reduced to a distrustful, skittish bundle of reactions, anticipatory flinchings and lashings-out. After six months I had to find her a new home with a Dominican family in the next building. They were able to straighten her out, after some cooling-off time spent hidden behind their stove.

* * *

The big Nazi cat went on raking up thread-loops from my trousers, seemingly intent on single-handedly reinventing Velcro. Meanwhile Kimmery had placed the two glasses of water on the floor near my feet. Though the room was dim – we were lit as much by the reflected skyline in the big room behind us as by the faint bulb there in the foyer – she'd removed her eyeglasses for the first time, and her eyes looked tender and small and searching. She slid down to seat herself against the wall, so we were arranged like clock hands on the face of the floor, our shoes at the center. According to the clock of us it was four o'clock. I tried not to root for midnight.

"Have you been living here long?" I asked.

"I know, it looks like I'm camping out," she said. "It's been about a month. I just broke up with this guy. It's pretty obvious, isn't it?"

"The Oreo Man?" I pictured a weather-beaten cowboy in front of a sunset, holding a cookie to his lips like a cigarette. Then, in frantic compensation, I conjured a tormented nerd in goggle-glasses, peering at cookie crumbs through a micro-scope, trying to discern their serial numbers.

"Uh-huh," said Kimmery. "A friend was moving out and she gave me this place. I don't even like it. I'm hardly ever here."

"Where instead – the Zendo?"

She nodded. "Or the movies."

* * *

I wasn't ticcing much, for a couple of reasons. The first was Kimmery herself, still an unprecedented balm to me this late in the day. The second was the day itself, the serial tumult of unsorted clues, the catastrophe of my visit to the Zendo; that extra track in my brain had plenty of work to do threading beads together, smoothing the sequence into order: Kimmery, doormen, Matricardi and Rockaforte, Tony and Seminole, Important Monks, Gerard Minna and the killer. Minna's killer.

"Did you lock your door?" I said.

"You're really afraid," said Kimmery, widening her eyes. "Of the, uh, giant."

"You didn't see him?" I said. "The big guy who took me outside?" I didn't mention what happened next. It was shameful enough that Kimmery had had to mop it up.

"He's a *giant*?"

"Well, what do you call it?"

"Isn't gigantism a genetic condition?"

"I'd say it is. He didn't *earn* that height." I touched the delicate spot on my head with one hand, kept the other calm at my side, ignoring every impulse to return the cat's pulsing and pawing at my legs. Instead I fingered the homely, hand-stitched coverlet on Kimmery's mattress, traced its inelegant, lumpy seams.

"I guess I didn't notice," she said. "I was, you know – sitting."

"You've never seen him before?"

She shook her head. "But I never met you before today either. I guess I should have told you not to bring anyone like that to the Zendo. And not to make noise. Now I missed practically the whole lecture."

"You're not saying the lecture went on?"

"Sure, why not? After you and your friend *the giant* were gone."

"Why didn't you stay?"

"Because my concentration isn't that good," she said, bitterly philosophical now. "If you're really Zen you sit right through distractions, like Roshi did. And *Wallace*." She rolled her eyes.

I was tempted to remind her that she'd moved to avoid being trampled, but it was just one objection among thousands.

"You don't understand," I said. "I didn't bring him to the Zendo. Nobody knew I was coming there."

"Well, I guess he followed you." She shrugged, not wanting to argue. To her it was self-evident that the giant and I were dual phenomena. I'd caused his presence at the Zendo, was likely responsible for his very existence.

"Listen," I said. "I know Roshi's American name. He's not who you think he is."

"I don't think he's anyone."

"What do you mean?"

"I didn't say, like, *Roshi's really Johnny Carson* or something. I just said I didn't know."

"Okay, but he's not a Zen teacher. He's involved in a murder."

"That's silly." She made it sound like a virtue, as though I'd meant to entertain her. "Besides, anyone who teaches Zen is a Zen teacher, I think. Probably even if they were a murderer. Just like anyone who sits is a student. Even you."

"What's wrong with me?"

"Nothing's wrong with you, at least according to a Zen outlook. That's my whole point."

"Taken."

"Don't be so sour, Lionel. I'm only joking. You sure you're happy with that cat?"

"Doesn't it have a name?" Feline Hitler had settled ponderously between my thighs, was purring in broken measures, and had begun to feature tiny bubbles of drool at the corners of its mouth.

"Shelf, but I never call him that."

"*Shelf?*"

"I know, it's completely stupid. I didn't name him. I'm just cat-sitting."

"So this isn't your apartment and this isn't your cat."

"It's sort of a period of crisis for me." She reached for her glass of water, and I immediately reached for mine, grateful: The mirroring scratched a tiny mental itch. Anyway, I was thirsty. Shelf didn't budge. "That's why I got involved with Zen," Kimmery went on. "For more *detachment*."

"You mean like no apartment and no cat? How detached can you get?" My voice was irrationally bitter. Disappointment had crept over me, impossible to justify or perfectly define. I suppose I'd imagined us sheltered in Kimmery's childlike foyer, her West Side tree house, three cats hiding. But now I understood that she was rootless, alienated in this space. The Oreo Man's house was her home, or possibly the Zendo, just as L&L was mine, just as Shelf's was elsewhere, too. None of us could go to those places, so we huddled here together, avoiding the big room and the forest of skyscrapers.

Now, before Kimmery could reply, I ticced loudly, "*Detach-me-not!*" I tried to block myself, interrupt my own ticcing with the glass of water, which I moved to my lips just in time to shout into the glass, fevering the surface of the water with my breath, "*Go-shelf-a-lot!*"

"Wow," said Kimmery.

I didn't speak. I gulped down water and fondled the stitching of her coverlet again, seeking to lose my Tourette's self in texture.

"You say really weird stuff when you get angry," she said.

"I'm not—" I turned my neck, put the glass of water down on the floor. This time I jostled Shelf, who looked up at me with jaded eyes. "I'm not angry."

"What's wrong with you, then?" The question was delivered evenly, without sarcasm or fear, as though she really wanted an answer. Her eyes no longer looked small to me without the black frames around them. They felt as round and inquisitive as the cat's.

"Nothing – at least from a Zen outlook. I just shout some-times. And touch things. And count things. And think about them too much."

"I've heard of that, I think."

"You're the exception to the rule if you have."

She reached into my lap and patted Shelf's head, distracting the cat from its interrogative gaze. Instead it squeezed its eyes together and craned its neck to press back against her palm. I'd have craned as far.

"Don't you want to know Roshi's real name?" I said.

"Why should I?"

"What?"

"Unless you're really going to shock me and say he's, like, J. D. Salinger, what's the difference? I mean, it's just going to be Bob or Ed or something, right?"

"Gerard Minna," I said. I wanted it to mean as much to her as Salinger, wanted her to understand everything. "He's Frank Minna's brother."

"Okay, but who's Frank Minna?"

"He's the guy who got killed." Strangely, I had a name for him now, a name flat and terrible and true: *the guy who got killed.* When before I could never have answered that question, or if I started answering it I'd never have finished. Frank Minna is the secret king of Court Street. Frank Minna is a mover and a talker, a word and a gesture, a detective and a fool. *Frank Minna c'est moi.*

"Oh, that's terrible."

"Yes." I wondered if I could ever share with her how terrible it was.

"I mean, that's got to be one of the worst things I've ever heard, practically."

Kimmery leaned closer, comforting the cat, not me. But I felt comforted. She and I were drawn close within her dawning understanding. Perhaps this foyer had only waited for this moment, for me and my story, to become a real space instead of a provisional one. Here Minna would be properly mourned. Here I'd find surcease for my pain and the answer to the puzzle of Tony and The Clients and why Minna and Ullman had to die and where Julia was and who Bailey was, and here Kimmery's hand would move from Shelf's head to my thigh and I would never tic again.

"He sent his brother out to die," I said. "He set him up. I heard it happen. I just don't know why yet."

"I don't understand. How did you hear?"

"Frank Minna was wearing a bug when he went into the Zendo. I heard him and Gerard talking. You were there too, in the building." I recalled revising my surveillance note, trying to decide whether to declare Kimmery girl or *woman*, and my writing hand twitched, reenacting my crossing-out across the soft threads of her coverlet.

"When?"

"Yesterday," I said, though it seemed a long time ago now.

"Well, that's impossible. It must have been someone else."

"Tell me why."

"Roshi is under a vow of silence." She whispered, as if she were breaking such a vow at this moment. "He hasn't said a word for the last five days. So you couldn't have heard him talk."

I was tongue-tied for once. It was the logic of the Oreo Man, invading my moral puzzle. Or another Zen conundrum: What's the sound of a silent monk condemning his brother to death?

The quieter the monk, the gaudier the patter I thought, remembering the conversation on the wiretap.

"I can't believe you go around *bugging* people," she said, still whispering. Perhaps she imagined there was a bug in the room now. "Were you trying to frame this Frank person?"

"No, no, no. Frank wanted me to listen."

"He wanted to be caught?"

"He didn't *do* anything," I said. "Except get bumped off by his brother, the silent monk."

Though she regarded me skeptically, Kimmery went on rubbing the cat's neck and head while it nestled in my lap. I had more than the usual panicky reasons to ignore the captivating sensations, the fricative purring and chafing down there. I was suppressing two different kinds of response, two possible ways of poking back. I kept my eyes level on Kimmery's face.

"I think you've got a few things mixed up," she said gently. "Roshi's a very gentle man."

"Well, Gerard Minna's a punk from Brooklyn," I said. "And they're positively the same guy."

"Hmmm. I don't know, Lionel. Roshi once told me he'd never been to Brooklyn. He's from Vermont or Canada or something."

"Maine?" I asked, thinking of the pamphlet I'd secreted in my jacket, the retreat center by the water.

She shrugged. "I don't know. You should take my word for it, though, he isn't from *Brooklyn*. He's a very important man." She made it sound as if the two were mutually exclusive.

"Eat me Brooklyn Roshi!"

I was ticcing out of sheer frustration. In squaring her perceptions to mine I not only had a world of knowledge to build up but a preexisting one to tear down. Anyone faintly Zen was to her beyond reproach. And Gerard Minna, for the cheap act of shaving his likely-already-balding head, was secure in a pantheon of the holy.

And Gerard had a lot of damn gall to renounce the borough.

"Lionel?"

I grabbed for my glass, took another sip of water, averted my eyes from Kimmery's.

"How does it feel when you do that?" she said. "I mean, what are you thinking?"

She was close enough now, and I succumbed completely and reached for her shoulder, tapped it five times quickly with paired fingertips. Then I moved my water glass to the floor and leaned forward, forcing Shelf to make another bleary, pleasure-addled adjustment to his position in my lap, and straightened

Kimmery's collar with both hands. The material was floppy, and I tried to prop it up as if it were starched, put the collar-tips on point like a ballerina's toes. And my brain went, *How are you feeling and how are you thinking and think how you're feeling*, and that became the chorus, the soundtrack to my adamant necessary collar-play.

"Lionel?" She didn't push my hands away.

"Liable," I said softly, my gaze lowered. "Think-a-mum Feely."

"What do the words mean?"

"They're just words. They don't mean anything." The question depressed me a little, took the wind out of my sails, and this was a good thing: I was able to release her collar, still my wriggling fingers.

Kimmery touched one hand, just briefly, as I withdrew it. I was numb to her now, though. She no longer soothed my tics, and the attention she'd begun to give them was humiliating. I needed to get this interview back on an official basis. Sitting here purring and being purred at wasn't going to accomplish anything. In the city on the other side of the door a giant killer lurched around unafraid, and it was my job to find him.

"What do you know about ten-thirty Park Avenue?" I said, resuming my investigation, the legitimate inquiry.

"Is that that big apartment building?" Her hand was back riffling Shelf's fur, her body ever closer to mine.

"Big building," I said. "Yes."

"A lot of Roshi's students do their work service there," she said lightly. "Working in the kitchen, cleaning up, that kind of thing. I was telling you about it, remember?"

"Doormen? Any – doormen?" My syndrome wanted to call them dogshirts, doorsnips, diphthongs. I gritted my teeth.

She shrugged. "I think so. I never went there myself. Lionel?"

"Yes?"

"You didn't really come to the Zendo because you were interested in Buddhism, did you?"

"I guess I thought that was obvious by now."

"It is obvious."

I wasn't sure what to say. I was narrowed to a fine point,

thinking only of Frank and Gerard and the places I might have to go to finish my investigation. I'd shuttered myself against Kimmery's tenderness toward me, even shuttered away my own tenderness toward her. She was an incompetent witness, beyond that a distraction. And I was an investigator who supplied plenty of my own distractions, too many.

"You came to make trouble," she said.

"I came *because* of trouble, yes."

Kimmery rubbed the fur of Shelf's flank in the wrong direction, aggravating my senses. I put my hand on the cat for the first time, nudged Kimmery's fingers away from the chaos of up-sticking fur she'd caused, and smoothed the fur back into place.

"Well, I'm glad I met you anyway," she said.

I made a sound, half dog, half cat, something like "*Chaarff.*"

Our hands collided in Shelf's fur, Kimmery's moving to rough up the area I'd just smoothed into sense, mine preemptively slipping underneath to preserve my work. It took a big indifferent loaf of a cat like Shelf to withstand it; Hen would have been across the room reordering herself with her own tongue by now.

"You're strange to me," said Kimmery.

"Don't feel bad about it," I said.

"No, but I mean strange in a good way, too."

"Uh." She was tugging on my fingers, and I tugged systematically back, so our hands were tangling, squirming, the cat a benign mattress underneath, one vibrating like a cheap hotel's.

"You can say whatever you want," Kimmery whispered.

"What do you mean?"

"The words."

"I don't really need to when you're touching my hand like that."

"I like to."

"Touch?" Touch shoulders, touch penguins, touch Kimmery – who didn't like to touch? Why shouldn't she? But this vaguest of questions was all I could manage. I wasn't only strange to her, I was strange to myself at that moment: tugging, lulled, resistant. Conworried.

"Yes," she said. "You. Here—"

She groped at the wall behind her head and switched off the light. We were still outlined in white, Manhattan's radiation leaking in from the big room. Then she moved closer: It was a minute after twelve. Somewhere as she fit herself in beside me the cat was jostled loose and wandered ungrudgingly away.

"That's better," I said lamely, like I was reading from a script. The distance between us had narrowed, but the distance between me and me was enormous. I blinked in the half-light, looking straight ahead. Now her hand was on my thigh where the cat had been. Mirroring, I let my fingers play lightly at the parallel spot on her leg.

"Yes," she said.

"I can't seem to interest you fully in my case," I said.

"Oh, I'm interested," she said. "It's just— It's hard to talk about things that are important to you. With a new person. Everyone is so strange, don't you think?"

"I think you're right."

"So you have to trust them at first. Because everything makes sense after a while."

"So that's what you're doing with me?"

She nodded, then leaned her head against my shoulder. "But you're not asking me anything about myself."

"I'm sorry," I said, surprised. "I guess – I guess I don't know where to start."

"Well, so you see what I mean, then."

"Yes."

I didn't have to turn her face to mine to kiss her. It was already there when I turned. Her lips were small and soft and a little chapped. I'd never before kissed a woman without having had a few drinks. And I'd never kissed a woman who hadn't had a few herself. While I tasted her Kimmery drew circles on my leg with her finger, and I did the same back.

"You do everything I do," she whispered into my mouth.

"I don't really need to," I said again. "Not if we're this close." It was the truth. I was never less ticcish than this: aroused, pressing toward another's body, moving out of my own. But just as Kimmery had somehow spared me ticcing aloud in conversation, now I felt free to incorporate an element of Tourette's into our groping, as though she were negotiating a new understanding between my two disgruntled brains.

"It's okay," she said. "You need a shave, though."

We kissed then, so I couldn't reply, didn't want to. I felt her press her thumb very gently against the point of my Adam's apple, a touch I couldn't exactly return. I stroked her ear and jaw instead, urging her nearer. Then her hand fell lower, and mine too, and at that moment I felt my hand and mind lose their particularity, their pointiness, their countingness, instead become clouds of general awareness, dreamy and yielding with curiosity. My hand felt less a hand than a catcher's mitt, or Mickey Mouse's hand, something vast and blunt and soft. I didn't count her where I touched her. I conducted a general survey, took a tender sampling.

"You're excited," she breathed.

"Yes."

"It's okay."

"I know."

"I just wanted to mention it."

"Okay, yes."

She unbuttoned my pants. I fumbled with hers, with a thin sash knotted at her front for a belt. I couldn't undo it with one hand. We were breathing into one another's mouths, lips slipping together and apart, noses mashed. I found a way in around the knotted sash, untucked her shirt. I put my finger in her belly button, then found the crisp margin of her pubic hair, threaded it with a finger. She tremored and slid her knee between mine.

"You can touch me there," she said.

"I am," I said, wishing for accuracy.

"You're so excited," she said. "It's okay."

"Yes."

"It's okay. Oh, Lionel, that's okay. Don't stop, it's okay."

"Yes," I said. "It's okay." *Okay, okay:* Here was Kimmery's tic, in evidence at last. I couldn't begrudge it. I turned my whole hand, gathering her up, surrounding her. She spilled as I held her. Meanwhile she'd found the vent in my boxer shorts. I felt two fingertips contact a part of me through that window, the blind men and the elephant. I wanted and didn't want her to go on, terribly.

"You're so excited," she said again, incantatory.

"Uh." She jostled me, untangled me from my shorts and my self.

"Wow, God, Lionel you're sort of huge."

"And bent," I said, so she wouldn't have to say it.

"Is that normal?"

"I guess it's a little unusual-looking." I panted, hoping to be past this moment.

"More than a little, Lionel."

"Someone – a woman once told me it was like a beer can."

"I've heard of that," said Kimmery. "But yours is, I don't know, like a beer can that's been crushed, like for recycling."

So it was for me. In my paltry history I'd never been unveiled without hearing something about it – freak shows within freak shows. Whatever Kimmery thought, it didn't keep her from freeing me from my boxer shorts and palming me, so that I felt myself aching heavily in her cool grasp. We made a circuit: mouths, knees, hands and what they held. The sensation was okay. I tried to match the rhythm of her hand with mine, failed. Kimmery's tongue lapped my chin, found my mouth again. I made a whining sound, not a part of any word. Language was destroyed. Bailey, he left town.

"It's okay to talk," she whispered.

"Uh."

"I like, um, I like it when you talk. When you make sounds."

"Okay."

"Tell me something, Lionel."

"What?"

"I mean, say something. The way you do."

I looked at her open-mouthed. Her hand urged me toward an utterance that was anything but verbal. I tried to distract her the same way.

"Speak, Lionel."

"Ah." It really was all I could think to say.

She kissed me gaspingly and drew back, her look expectant.

"One Mind!" I said.

"Yes!" said Kimmery.
"*Fonebone!*" I shouted.

* * *

Another key contributor to my Tourette's lexicon was a cartoonist named Don Martin, first encountered in a pile of tattered *Mad* magazines in a box in the Ping-Pong room in the basement of St Vincent's when I was eleven or twelve. I used to pore over his drawings, trying to find what it was about his characters, drawn with riotously bulging eyes, noses, chins, Adam's apples and knees, elongated tongues and fingers and feet that flapped like banners, named Professor Bleent, P. Carter Franit, Mrs. Freenbeen and Mr. Fonebone, that stirred such a deep chord in me. His image of life was garish and explosive, heads being stretched and shrunk, surgeons lopping off noses and dropping brains and sewing hands on backward, falling safes and metal presses squashing men flat or into boxlike packages, children swallowing coat hangers and pogo sticks and taking on their shapes. His agonized characters moved through their panels with a geeky physicality, seeming to strain toward their catastrophic contact with fire hoses, whir-ring blades, and drawbridges, and his sophomoric punch lines mostly hinged on reversals or literalizations – "The kids are upstairs with their ears glued to the radio" – or else on outright destruction. *Mad* often held the concluding panel of a Don Martin cartoon to the following page, and part of the pleasure of his work was never knowing whether the payoff would be a visual pun or verbal riff or merely the sight of a man in a full-body cast falling out a window into the path of a steamroller. Mostly, though, I recall the distortion, the torque in the bodies he drew: These characters had met disaster in being born onto the page, and their more extreme fates were only realizations of their essential nature. This made sense to me. And Fonebone made sense, too. He had a name I could get behind. For a while he almost supplanted Bailey, and he was lastingly traceable in my tendency to append *phone* or *bone* to the end of a phrase.

When I had sex with another person and my body began to convulse and move faster, my toes to curl, my eyes to roll,

I felt like a Don Martin character, a Fonebone, all elbows and bowlegs and boomerang penis and gurgling throat in a halo of flung-off sweat drops and sound effects: *Fip, Thwat, Zwip, Sproing, Flabadab.* More than Daffy Duck, more than Art Carney, more than any other icon of my discomfort. Don Martin's drawings throbbed with the suggestion that disruptive feeling was all sexual. Though his venue denied him any overt reference his characters overflowed with lewd energies, which had to be manifested instead in tics and seizures, eruptions and deformations. His poor doomed Fonebones seemed to chart my path from twitch to orgasm, the way sex first smoothed away tics, then supplanted them with a violent double: little death, big tic. So perhaps it was Don Martin's fault that I always expected a punishment after sex, cringed in anticipation of the steamroller or plummeting anvil to follow.

Possibly Kimmery sensed it in me, this dread of a page about to be turned, revealing some ludicrous doom on the last panel of my cartoon. Another fact about Don Martin: He never used the same character twice – each was an innocent pawn with no carry-over from one episode to the next, no understanding of his role or fate. A Fonebone was a placeholder, a disposable clone or stooge. A member of the Butt Trust.

"Is something the matter?" she said, stopping what she was doing, what I was doing.

"Everything's fine. I mean, better than fine."

"You don't look fine."

"Just one thing, Kimmery. Promise me you won't go back to the Zendo. At least for a few days."

"Why?"

"Just trust me, okay?"

"Okay."

With that, her magic word, we were done talking.

* * *

Once Kimmery was asleep I dressed and tiptoed to her phone, which was on the floor in the big room. Shelf followed me in. I tapped his head five times, instantly reigniting his ragged purring, then pushed him away. The phone showed a number under its plastic window. I fed the number into the speed dial of the doormen's cell phone, wincing at the beeping tones, which echoed in the silent empty room like musical gunshots. Kimmery didn't stir on her mattress, though. She lay splayed like a child making a snow angel. I wanted to go and kneel and trace her shape with my fingertips or my breath. Instead I found her key ring and separated the five keys. The key to the apartment was easy to identify, and that was the only one I left behind – she'd have to deal with her suspicious neighbors to get into the lobby downstairs. I took the other four, figuring one would get me into the Zendo. The last two probably unlocked Oreo Man's place. Those I'd lose.

AUTO BODY

SEE ME NOW, at one in the morning, stepping out of another cab in front of the Zendo, checking the street for cars that might have followed, for giveaway cigarette-tip glows through the windows of the cars parked on the deadened street, moving with my hands in my jacket pockets clutching might-be-guns-for-all-they-know, collar up against the cold like Minna, unshaven like Minna now, too, shoes clacking on sidewalk: think of a coloring-book image of the Green Hornet, say. That's who I was supposed to be, that black outline of a man in a coat, ready suspicious eyes above his collar, shoulders hunched, moving toward conflict.

Here's who I was instead: that same coloring-book outline of a man, but crayoned by the hand of a mad or carefree or retarded child, wild slashes of idiot color, a blizzard of marks violating the boundaries that made *man* distinct from *street*, from *world*. Some of those colors were my fresh images of Kimmery, flashing me back to the West Side an hour before, crayon stripes and arrows like flares over Central Park in the night sky. Others weren't so pretty, roaring scrawls of mania, *find-a-man-kill-a-phone-fuck-a-plan* in sloppy ten-foot-high letters drawn like lightning bolts or Hot Wheels race-car flames through the space of my head. And the blackened steel-wool scribble of my guilt-deranged investigation: I pictured the voices of the two Minna brothers and Tony Vermonte and The Clients as gnarled above and around me, in a web of betrayal I had to penetrate and dissolve, an ostensible world I'd just discovered was really only a private cloud I carried everywhere, had never seen the outside of. So, crossing the street to the door of the Zendo, I might have appeared less a single Green Hornet than a whole inflamed nest of them.

* * *

My first act was to drop in next door. I found the original doorman, Dirk, asleep on his stool.

I lifted his head up with my hand and he jerked awake and away from my grasp. "Hello!" he shouted.

"You remember me, Dirk?" I said. "I was sitting in a car. You told me I had a message from my 'friend.'"

"Oh? Sure, I remember. Sorry, I was just doing what I was told."

"Sure you were. And I suppose you never saw the guy before, did you – *dirtyworker, dirketyname?*"

"I never saw the guy before." He breathed out, wide-eyed.

"He was a very big man, yes?"

"Yes!" He rolled his eyes upward to show it. Then he held his hands out, begging my patience. I backed off a little and he stood and neatened his coat. I helped him with it, especially around the collar. He was too sleepy or confused by my questions to object.

"He pay you or just scare you into giving me the bum steer?" I asked more gently. My anger was wasted on Dirk. Anyway, I felt vaguely grateful to him for confirming the giant's existence. My only other sure witness was Gilbert, in jail. Kimmery had begun to make me doubt my eyes.

"A man that big doesn't have to pay," said Dirk honestly.

* * *

One of the stolen keys got me inside. This time I held on to my shoes as I passed the sitting room and headed upstairs, past the floor where Kimmery and I had sat at tea, up to the Roshi's private quarters – a.k.a. Gerard Minna's hideout. The halls were darker the higher I climbed, until at the top I could only grope my way toward a thin margin of light squeezed out underneath a sealed door. I turned the handle and pushed the door open, impatient with my own fear.

His bedroom had the integrity of his self-reinvention. It was bare of furnishings except for a long low shelf against the wall, a board, really, propped on bricks and bearing a few candles and books, a glass of water and a small bowl of ashes, decorated with Japanese script, presumably some kind of tiny shrine. The spareness reminded me of Kimmery's empty studio apartment but I resented the echo, not wishing to see Kimmery as influenced by Gerard's Zen pretensions, not wishing to imagine her visiting his private floor, his lair, at all. Gerard sat propped on pillows on a flat mattress on the floor, his legs crossed, the book at his knees shut, his posture calm, as though he'd been waiting for me. I faced him head on for what might have been the first time – I don't know that I'd ever addressed him directly, stolen more than a glance as a teenager. In the candlelight I first made out his silhouette: He'd thickened around the jaw and neck, so that his bald head seemed to rise from his round shoulders like the line of a cobra's hood. I might have been overly influenced by that bald head but as my eyes adjusted I couldn't keep from understanding the difference between his features and Frank Minna's as the same as that between Brando's in *Apocalypse Now* and *On the Waterfront*.

"*Thehorrorthehorror*," I ticced. "*Icouldabeenacontender!*" It was like a couplet.

"You're Lionel Essrog, aren't you?"

"*Unreliable Chessgrub*," I corrected. My throat pulsed with ticcishness. I was overly conscious of the open door behind me, so my neck twitched, too, with the urge to look over my shoulder. Doormen could come through open doors, anyone knew that. "Is there anyone else in the building?" I said.

"We're alone."

"Mind if I close this?"

"Go ahead." He didn't budge from his position on the mattress, just gazed at me evenly. I closed the door and moved just far enough into the room not to be tempted to grope behind me for the door's surface. We faced each other across the candlelit gloom, each a figure out of the other's past, each signifying to the other the lost man, the man killed the day before.

"You broke your vow of silence just now," I said.

"I'm finished with my sesshin," he said. "Anyway, you brought silence to a rather conclusive finish during today's sitting."

"I think your hired killer had something to do with that."

"You're speaking without thinking," he said. "I recall your difficulties in that area."

I took a deep breath. Gerard's serenity called out of me a storm of compensatory voices, a myriad possible shrieks and insults to stanch. A part of me wanted to cajole him out from behind his Zen front, expose the Lord of Court Street lurking, make him Frank's older brother again. What came out of my mouth was the beginning of a joke, one from the deepest part of the made-Frank-Minna-laugh-once archive:

"So there's this order of nuns, right?"

"An order of nuns," Gerard repeated.

"*Ordinary nunphone!* – an order of nuns. Like the Cloisters. You know, a monastery."

"A monastery is for monks."

"Okay, a nunastery. *A plannery, a nunnetarium!* – a nunnery. And they've all, these nuns, they've all taken a vow of silence, a lifetime vow of silence, right?" I was driven, tears at the edges of my eyes, wishing for Frank to be alive to rescue me, tell me he'd heard this one already. Instead I had to go on. "Except one day a year one of the nuns gets to say something. They take turns, one nun a year. Understand?"

"I think I understand."

"So the big day comes – *Barnamum-big-nun! Domesticated ghostphone!* – the big day is here and the nuns are all sitting at the dinner table and the one who gets to talk this year opens her mouth and says 'The soup is terrible.' And the other nuns all look at each other but nobody says anything because of the vow of silence, and that's it, back to normal. Another year of silence."

"A very disciplined group," said Gerard, not without admiration.

"Right. So a year later the day comes and it's this other nun's turn. So they're sitting and the second nun turns to the first and says 'I don't know, maybe it's just me, but I don't think the soup's that bad' – and that's it, silence. Another year."

"Hmmm. Imagine the states of contemplation one could achieve in such a year."

"I never thought about it myself. Anyway, so the calendar pages flip, and the special day – *Flip-a-thon! Fuck-a-door! Flip-weed! Fujisaki! Flitcraft!* – the special day comes around again. This third nun, it's her turn – *Nun-fuck-a-phone!* – so this third nun, she looks at the first nun and the second nun and she says 'Bicker, bicker, bicker.'"

There was silence, then Gerard nodded and said, "That would be the punch line."

"I know about the building," I said, working to catch my breath. "And the Fujisaki Corporation." *Unfuckafish* whispered under my palate.

"Ah. Then you know much."

"Yeah, I know a thing. And I've met your killing machine. But you saw that, when he dragged me out, downstairs. The kumquat-eater."

I was desperate to see him flinch, to impress him with the edge I had, the things I'd learned, but Gerard wasn't ruffled. He raised his eyebrows, which got a lot of play across the empty canvas of his forehead. "You and your friends, what are their names?"

"Who? The Minna Men?"

"Yes – Minna Men. That's a very good description. My brother was very important to the four of you, wasn't he?"

I nodded, or not, but anyway he went on.

"He really taught you everything, I suppose. You sound just like him when you speak. What an odd life, really. You realize that, don't you? That Frank was a very odd man, living in a strange and anachronistic way?"

"What's *cartoonistic* about it?"

"Anachronistic," said Gerard patiently. "From another time."

"I know what it means," I said. "I mean what's so *akakonistic* about it?" I was too wound up to go back and repair the tic-pocked surface of my speech. "Anyway, *enactoplasmic* as opposed to what? A million-year-old mystical Japanese cult?"

"You wear your ignorance as aggressively as Frank," said Gerard. "I suppose you're making my point for me."

"Point being what?"

"My brother taught you only what he knew, and not even all of that. He kept you charmed and flattered but also in the dark, so your sense of even his small world was diminished, two-dimensional. Cartoonistic, if you like. What's astonishing to me is that you didn't know about the Park Avenue building until just now. It really must come as a shock."

"Enlighten me."

"Surely you've got my brother's money in your pocket even as we speak, Lionel. Do you really believe that it came from detective work, from those scuffling little assignments he contrived to keep you children busy? Or perhaps you imagine he *crapped* money. That's just as likely."

Was *crapped* a chink in Gerard's Zen façade, a bit of Brooklyn showing through? I recalled the elder monk proclaiming the worthlessness of "Bowel Movement Zen."

"Frank consorted with dangerous people," Gerard went on. "And he stole from them. The remuneration and the risk were high. The odds that he would flourish in such a life forever, low."

"Talk to me about *fool-me-softly* – Fujisaki."

"They own the building. Minna had a hand in managing it. The money involved would dazzle your senses, Lionel." He gave me an expectant look, as though this assertion ought to dazzle me in the money's stead, ought to astonish me right out of my investigation, and his bedroom.

"These people, their other home is an island," I said, quoting the Garbage Cop – not that the phrase was likely to have originated with him.

Gerard smiled at me oddly. "For every Buddhist, Japan is his other home. And yes, it is an island."

"Who's a Buddhist?" I said. "I was talking about the money."

He sighed, without losing the smile. "You are so like Frank."

"What's your role, Gerard?" I wanted to sicken him the way I was sickened. "I mean, besides sending your brother out into the Polack's arms to die."

Now he beamed munificently. The worse I attacked him, the deeper his forgiveness and grace would be – that's what the smile said. "Frank was very careful never to expose me to any danger if he could help it. I was never introduced to anyone from Fujisaki. I believe I have yet to make their acquaintance, apart from the large hit man you led here yesterday."

"Who's Ullman?"

"A bookkeeper, another New Yorker. He was Frank's partner in fleecing the Japanese."

"But you *never met the guy*."

I meant him to hear the sarcasm, or rather Frank Minna's sarcasm in quotation. But he went on obliviously. "No. I only supplied the labor, in return for consideration equal to my mortgage here on the Zendo. Buddhism is spread by what means it finds."

"Labor for what?" My brain tangled on *spread by means it finds, fed in springs by mimes, bled by mingy spies*, but I shook it off.

"My students performed the maintenance and service work for the building, as part of their training. Cleaning, cooking, the very sort of labor they'd perform in a monastery, only in a slightly different setting. The contract for those services in such a building is worth millions. My brother and Ullman tithed the difference mostly into their own pockets."

"Doormen," I said.

"Yes. Doormen, too."

"So Fujisaki sicced the giant on Frank and the bookkeeper."

"I suppose that's right."

"And he just happened to use the Zendo as his trap yesterday?" I aired out another Minna-ism: "Don't try to hand me no two-ton feather." I was dredging up Minna's usages on any excuse now, as though I could build a golem of his language, then bring it to life, a figure of vengeance to search out the killer or killers.

I was aware of myself standing in Gerard's room, planted on his floor, arms at my sides, never moving nearer to him where he sat beaming Zen pleasantness in my direction, ignoring my accusations and my tics. I was big but I was no golem or giant. I hadn't startled Gerard in deep sleep nor upended his calm with my griefy hostility. I wasn't holding a gun on him. He didn't have to answer my questions.

"I don't really believe in sophisticated killers," said Gerard. "Do you?"

"*Go-fisticate-a-killphone*," I ticced.

"The Fujisaki Corporation is ruthless and remorseless – in the manner of corporations. And yet in the manner of corporations their violence is also performed at a remove, by a force just nominally under their control. In the giant you speak of they seem to have located a sort of primal entity – one whose true nature is killing. And sicced him, as you say, on the men who they feel betrayed them. I'm not sure the killer's behavior is explicable in any real sense, Lionel. Any human sense."

Gerard's persuasiveness was a variant of the Minna style, I saw now. I felt the force of it, moving me authentically. Yet his foray against the notion of a sophisticated killer also made me think of Tony mocking Detective Seminole with jokes about Batman and James Bond supervillains. Was it a giveaway, a clue that Gerard and Tony were in league? And what about Julia? I wanted to quote Frank's conversation with Gerard the night he died: *She misses her Rama-lama-ding-dong*, find out what he meant. I wanted to ask about Boston, and I wanted to ask about Frank and Julia's marriage – had Gerard been at the ceremony? I wanted to ask him about whether he missed Brooklyn, and how he got his head so shiny. I searched for a single question that could stand for my thousands and what popped out was this:

"What's human sense?"

"In Buddhism, Lionel, we come to understand that everything on this earth is a vessel for Buddha-nature. Frank had Buddha-nature. You have Buddha-nature. I feel it."

Gerard allowed a long minute to pass while we contemplated his words. *Buddha nostril*, I nearly blurted. When he spoke again, it was with a confidence that sympathy flowed between us untrammeled by doubt or fear.

"There's another of your Minna Men, Lionel. He's pushing his way into this, and I fear he may have aroused the killer's ire. Tony, is that his name?"

"Tony Vermonte," I said, marveling – it was as if Gerard had read my mind.

"Yes. He'd like to walk in my brother's footsteps. But Fujisaki will be keeping a keener eye on their money from this point, I'd think. There's nothing to be gained and everything to be lost. Perhaps you'll have a word with him."

"Tony and I aren't exactly . . . communicating well, since yesterday."

"Ah."

I felt a surge of care in me, for Tony. He was only a heedless adventurer, with a poignant urge to imitate Frank Minna in all things. He was a member of my family – L&L, the Men. Now he was in above his head, threatened on all sides by the giant, by Detective Seminole, by The Clients. Only Gerard and I understood his danger.

I must have been silent for a minute or so – a veritable sesshin by my standards.

"You and Tony are together in your pain at the loss of my brother," said Gerard softly. "But you haven't come together in actuality. Be patient."

"There's another factor," I said, tentative now, lulled by his compassionate tones. "Someone else may be involved in this somehow. Two of them, actually – *Monstercookie and Antifriendly!* – uh, Matricardi and Rockaforte."

"You don't say."

"I do."

"You can't know how sorry I am to hear those names." *Never say those names!* warned Minna in the echo chamber of my memory. Gerard went on, "Those two are the prototype, aren't they, for my brother's tendency to dangerous associations – and his tendency to exploit those associations in dangerous ways."

"He stole from them?"

"Do you recall that he once had to leave New York for a while?"

Did I recall! Suddenly Gerard threatened to solve the deepest puzzles of my existence. I practically wanted to ask him, *So who's Bailey?*

"I'd hoped they were no longer in the picture," said Gerard reflectively. It was the nearest to thrown I'd seen him, the closest I'd come to pushing his buttons. Only now I wasn't sure I wanted to. "Avoid them, Lionel, if you can," he continued. "They're dangerous men."

He returned his gaze to my face, batted his lashes, moved his expressive eyebrows. If I'd been in striking distance I'd have tried to span his head with my hands and stroke his eyebrows with my thumb tips, just to soothe this one small worry I'd raised.

"Can I ask one more thing?" I nearly called him Roshi, so complete was my conversion. "Then I'll leave you alone."

Gerard nodded. *The High Lama will grant you an audience, Mrs. Gushman.*

"Is there anyone else – *Zonebone!* – anyone else at the Zendo who's involved in this thing? Anyone – *Kissmefaster! Killmesooner! Cookiemonster!* – anyone the killer might target? That old hippie, Wallace? Or the girl – *Kissingme!* – Kimmery?" I tried not to divulge the special freight of tenderness and hope behind this query. Whether the string of shrieks I issued in the course of its delivery made me appear more or less blasé, I couldn't say.

"No." Gerard spoke benevolently. "I compromised myself personally, but not my students or my practice as a teacher. Wallace and Kimmery should be safe. It's kind of you to be concerned."

I'm concerned about Pinched and Indistinct, too, I wanted to say. I doubted students could get any more compromised than that.

And then there was that nod of complicity I saw pass between Gerard and the giant.

The three of them – Pinched, Indistinct, and the nod – were three sour notes in a very pretty song. But I kept my tongue, feeling I'd learned what I could here, that it was time to go. I wanted to find Tony before the giant did. And I needed to step outside the candle glow of Gerard's persuasiveness to sort out the false and the real, the Zen and the chaff in our long discussion.

"I'm going now," I said awkwardly.

"Good night, Lionel." He was still watching me as I closed the door.

*   *   *

On second thought, there *is* a vaguely Tourettic aspect to the New York City subway, especially late at night – that dance of attention, of stray gazes, in which every rider must engage. And there's a lot of stuff you shouldn't touch in the subway, particularly in a certain order: this pole and then your lips, for instance. And the tunnel walls are layered, like those of my brain, with expulsive and incoherent language—

But I was in a terrible hurry, or rather two terrible hurries: to get back to Brooklyn, and to sort out my thinking about Gerard before I got there. I couldn't spare a minute to dwell in myself as a body riding the Lexington train to Nevins Street – I might as well have been teleported, or floated to Brooklyn on a magic carpet, for all that I was allured or distracted by the 4 train's sticky, graffitied immediacy.

* * *

The lights were burning in the L&L storefront. I approached from the opposite sidewalk, confident I was invisible on the darkened street to those in the office – I'd been on the other side of that plate of glass only two or three thousand nights in preparation for the act of spying on my fellow Men from the street. I didn't want to go waltzing into a trap. Detective Seminole might be there or, who knew, maybe Tony and a passel of doormen. If there was something to learn at a distance, I'd learn it.

It was almost two-thirty now, and Bergen Street was shut up tight, the night cold enough to chase the stoop-sitting drinkers indoors. Smith Street showed a bit more life, Zeod's Market lit up like a beacon, catering to the all-night cigarette cravings, to the squad-car cops in need of a bagel or LifeSaver or some other torus. Four L&L cars were scattered in parking spots near the storefront: the Minna death car, which hadn't moved since Gilbert and I returned from the hospital and parked it, the Pontiac in which Tony had shanghaied me in front of The Clients' brownstone, a Caddy that Minna had liked to drive himself, and a Tracer, an ugly modernistic bubble of a car that usually fell to me or Gilbert to pilot. I slowed my walk as I drew up even with the storefront, then turned my neck. It was pleasing to have a good solid reason behind turning my neck for once, retroactive validation for a billion tics. As I passed, I made out the shapes of two Men inside: Tony and Danny, both in a cloud of cigarette smoke, Danny seated behind the counter with a folded newspaper, radiating cool, Tony pacing, radiating cool's opposite. The television was on.

I walked past, to the corner of Smith, then swiveled and went back. This time I set up shop on the brief stoop of the big apartment building directly across from L&L. It was a safe outpost. I could duck my head and watch them through a parked car's windows if I thought they were in any danger of spotting me. Otherwise I'd sit back in the wings and study them in the limelight of the storefront until something happened or I'd decided what to do.

Danny – I gave Danny Fantl a moment of my time. He was sliding through this crisis as he'd slid through life to this point, so poised he was practically an ambient presence. Gilbert was in jail and I was hunted high and low and Danny sat in the storefront all day, refusing car calls and smoking cigarettes and reading sports. He wasn't exactly my candidate for any plot's criminal mastermind, but if Tony conspired with or even confided in anyone inside L&L's circle, it would be Danny. In the present atmosphere, I decided, there was no way I could take Danny for granted, trust him with my back.

Which meant I wasn't going inside to talk with either one of them until they were apart. If then – the image of Tony pulling his wobbly gun on me was fresh enough to give pause.

Anyway, something happened before I'd decided what to do – why was I not surprised? But it was a relatively banal something, reassuring, even. A tick of the clock of everyday life on Bergen Street, an everyday life that already felt nostalgic.

A block east, on the corner of Bergen and Hoyt, was an elegantly renovated tavern called the Boerum Hill Inn, with a gleaming antique inlaid-mirror bar, a CD jukebox weighted toward Blue Note and Stax, and a Manhattanized clientele of professional singles too good for bars with televisions, for subway rides home, or for the likes of the Men. Only Minna ever visited the Boerum Hill Inn, and he cracked that anyone who drank there was someone else's assistant: a district attorney's, an editor's, or a video artist's. The dressed-up crowd at the inn gabbled and flirted every night of the week until two in the morning, oblivious to the neighborhood's past or present reality, then slept it off in their overpriced apartments or on their desks the next day in Midtown. Typically a few parties would stagger down the block after last call and try to engage an L&L car for a ride home – sometimes it was a woman alone or a newly formed couple too drunk to throw to the fates, and we'd take the job. Mostly we claimed not to have any cars.

But the inn's bartenders were a couple of young women we adored, Siobhain and Welcome. Siobhain was properly named, while Welcome bore the stigma of her parents' hippie ideals, but both were from Brooklyn and Irish to their ancient souls – or so had declared Minna. They were roommates in Park Slope, possibly lovers (again according to Minna), and bartending their way through graduate school. Each night one or the other was stuck with closing – the owner of the inn was stingy and didn't let them double up after midnight. If we weren't actually busy on some surveillance job we'd always drive the closer home.

It was Welcome, at the door of L&L, now going inside. I saw Tony nod at Danny, then Danny stood and stubbed out a butt, checked in his pocket for the keys and nodded too. He and Welcome moved to the door and out. I lowered my head. Danny led her to the Caddy, which sat at the front of the row of parked cars, on the corner of Smith. She went around to the front passenger seat, not like the usual ride who'd sit in the back. Danny slammed his door and the interior light shut off, then he started the engine. I glanced back to see that Tony was now going through the drawers behind the L&L counter, searching for something, his desperado's energy suddenly lashed to a purpose. He used both hands, his cigarette stuck in his mouth, and unpacked papers onto the countertop hurriedly. I'd gathered a piece of vague information, I supposed: Tony didn't trust Danny with everything.

Then I saw a hulking shadow stir, in a parked car on L&L's side of the street, just a few yards from the storefront.

Unmistakable.

The Kumquat Sasquatch.

*　*　*

The car was an economy model, bright red, and he filled it like it had been cast around his body. I saw him lean sideways to watch the Cadillac with Danny and Welcome inside round the corner of Smith and disappear with a pulse of brakelights. Then he turned his attention back to the storefront; I read the movement in the disappearance of a nose from the silhouette, its replacement by an elephantine ear. The giant was doing what I was doing, staking out L&L.

He watched Tony, and I watched them both. Tony was a lot more interesting at the moment. I hadn't often seen him reading, and never this intently. He was searching for something in the sheaf of papers he'd pulled from Minna's drawers, his brow furrowed, cigarette in his lips, looking like Edward R. Murrow's punk brother. Now, unsatisfied, he dug in another drawer, and worked over a notebook I recognized even from across the street as the one containing my own stakeout jottings from the day before. I tried not to take it personally when he thrust this aside even more hastily and went back to tearing up the drawers.

The large shadow took it all in, complacent. His hand moved from somewhere below the line of the car window and briefly covered his mouth; he chewed, then leaned forward to dribble out some discarded seeds or pits. A bag of cherries or olives this time, something a giant would gobble in a handful. Or Cracker Jack, and he didn't like peanuts. He watched Tony like an operagoer who knew the libretto, was curious only to gather details of how the familiar plot would play out this time.

Tony exhausted the drawers, started in on the file cabinets.

The giant chewed. I blinked in time with his chewing, and counted chews and blinks, occupying my Tourette's brain with this nearly invisible agitation, tried to stay otherwise still as a lizard on the stoop. He had only to turn this way to spot me. My whole edge consisted of seeing without being seen; I had nothing more on the giant, had never had. If I wanted to preserve that wafer-thin edge I needed to find a better hiding place – and it wouldn't hurt to get in out of the stiff, cold wind.

The three remaining L&L cars were my best option. But the Pontiac, which I would have preferred, was up ahead of the giant's car, easily in his line of sight. I was sure I didn't want to face whatever ghosts or more tangibly olfactory traces of Minna might be trapped inside the sealed windows of the Death Car. Which left the Tracer. I felt in my pocket for my bunch of keys, found the three longest, one of which was the Tracer's door and ignition. I was preparing to duckwalk down the pavement and slip into the Tracer when the Cadillac reappeared, hurtling down Bergen, with Danny at the wheel.

He parked in the same spot at the front of the block and walked back toward L&L. I slumped on the stoop, played drunk. Danny didn't see me. He went inside, surprising Tony in his filework. They exchanged a word or two, then Tony slid the drawer closed and bummed another cigarette from Danny. The shadow in the little car went on watching, sublimely confident and peaceful. Neither Tony nor Danny had ever seen the giant, I suppose, so he had less to worry about in attracting attention than I did. But reason alone couldn't account for the giant's composure. If he wasn't a student of Gerard's, he should have been: He possessed true Buddha-nature, and would have surpassed his teacher. Three hundred and fifty-odd pounds instill a cosmic measure of gravity, I suppose. *What did the Buddhist say to the hot-dog vendor?* was the joke I remembered now, one of Loomis's measly riddles. *Make me one with everything.* I would have been happy to be one with everything at that moment.

Heck, make me one with anything.

I was pretty hungry, too, if I thought about it. A stakeout was customarily a gastronomic occasion, and I was beginning to get that itch for something between two slices of bread. Why shouldn't I be hungry? I'd missed dinner, had Kimmery instead.

With thoughts of food and sex my attention slipped, so that I was startled now to see Tony pop out of the storefront, his expression still as fierce as it had been when he was poring over the paperwork. For a moment I thought I'd been spotted. But he turned toward Smith Street, crossed Bergen, and disappeared around the corner.

The giant watched, unimpressed, unworried.

We waited.

Tony returned with a large plastic shopping bag, probably from Zeod's. The only thing I could discern was a carton of Marlboros sticking out of the top, but the bag was heavy with something. Tony opened the passenger door of the Pontiac and put the bag on the seat, glanced quickly up the street without spotting either me or the giant, then relocked the car and went back to L&L.

* * *

Figuring it was status quo for the time being, I made my way back down Bergen, up Hoyt Street, and around the block the long way, and checked into Zeod's myself.

Zeod liked to work the late hours, do the overnight, check in the newspaper deliveries at six and then sleep through the bright hours of the morning and early afternoon. He was like the Sheriff of Smith Street, eyes open while we all slept, seeing the drunks stagger home, keeping his eye on the crucial supplies, the Ding Dongs and Entenmann's cookies, the forty-ounce malt liquor and the cups of coffee "regular" with a picture of the Parthenon on the cup. Except now he had company down the street at L&L, Tony and Danny and the giant and myself enacting our strange vigil, our roundelay of surveillance. I wondered if Zeod knew about Minna yet. As I slipped up to the counter the groggy counter boy was punishing the slicer with a steaming white towel, replenishing the towel in a basin of hot suds, while Zeod stood exhorting him, telling him how he could be doing it better, squeezing some value out of him before he quit like all the others.

"Crazyman!"

"Shhh." I imagined that Tony or the giant could hear Zeod bellow through the shop window and around the corner of the block.

"You're working so late for Frank tonight? Something important eh? Tony just came."

"Important Freaks! Important Franks!"

"Ho ho ho."

"Listen, Zeod. Can you tell me what Tony bought?"

Zeod screwed up his face, finding this question sensational. "You can't ask him yourself?"

"No, I can't."

He shrugged. "Six-pack of beer, four sandwiches, carton of cigarettes, Coca-Cola – whole picnic."

"Funny picnic."

"Wasn't funny to him," said Zeod. "Couldn't make him smile. Like you, Crazyman. On a very serious case, eh?"

"What – *becausewhich, besideswhich* – what sandwiches did he buy?" It was my suddenly ravenous appetite that steered this inquiry.

"Ah!" Zeod rubbed his hands together. He was always ready to savor his own product on someone else's behalf. "Turkey with Thousand, very nice on a kaiser roll, pepperoni-and-provolone hero with peppers inside, two roast beef with horseradish on rye bread."

I had to clutch the counter to keep from falling over, this storm of enticements was so heady.

"You like what you hear, I can see that," said Zeod.

I nodded, turned my head sideways, took in the fresh-gleaming slicer, the elegant curve of the fender that sheathed the blade.

Zeod said, "You want something, Crazyman, don't you?"

I saw the counter boy's eyes roll in weary anticipation. The slicer rarely saw this much action at two or three in the morning. They'd have to sluice it down with suds again before the night was done.

"Please – *ghostradish, pepperpony, kaiserphone* – please, uh, the same as Tony?"

"You want the same? All four the same?"

"Yes," I gasped. I couldn't think past Tony's list of sandwiches. My hunger for them was absolute. I had to match Tony sandwich for sandwich, a gastronomic mirroring-tic – I'd understand him by the time I was through the fourth, I figured. We would achieve a Zeod's mind-meld, with Thousand Island dressing.

While Zeod rode his counter boy to complete the large order I hid in the back near the beverage cases, picked out a liter of Coke and a bag of chips, and reorganized and counted a disorderly shelf of cat-food cans.

"Okay, Lionel." Zeod was always most gentle with me when handing over his precious cargo – we shared that reverence for his product. "Put it on Frank's tab, right?" He gathered my soda and chips in a large bag with the paper-wrapped sandwiches.

"No, no—" I rustled in my pockets for a tight-folded twenty.

"What's the matter? Why not the boss man pick it up?"

"I want to pay you." I pushed the bill across the counter. Zeod took it and arched his eyebrows.

"Very funny business," he said, and made a *chuck-chuck-chuck* sound with his tongue in his cheek.

"What?"

"Same thing as Tony, before you," he said. "He says he wants to pay. Same thing."

"Listen, Zeod. If Tony comes back in here tonight" – I fought off a howling sound that wanted to come out of me, the cry of a sandwich predator over fresh kill he has yet to devour – "don't tell him you saw me, okay?"

Zeod winked. Somehow this made sense to him. I felt a thing that was either a nauseous wave of paranoia – perhaps Zeod was an agent of Tony's, absolutely in his pocket, and would be on the phone to him the minute I was out of the shop – or else my stomach spasming in anticipation of food. "Okay, Chief," said Zeod as I went out the door.

* * *

I came around the block the long way again, quickly confirmed that the giant and Tony were still in their places, then swerved across the street and slipped up beside the Tracer, key in hand. The giant's compact was six cars ahead, but I couldn't see his cliff-like silhouette from where I stood as I unlocked the car. I only hoped that meant he couldn't see me. I plopped Zeod's bag on the passenger seat, jumped inside, and slammed the door shut as quickly as I could, praying that the brief flash of the interior light hadn't registered in the giant's rearview. Then I slumped down in my place so I'd be invisible, on the slight chance he did turn and could make anything out through a thickness of twelve darkened windshields. Meanwhile I got my hands busy unfurling the paper around one of Zeod's roast beef and horseradish specials. Once I had it free, I gobbled the sandwich like a nature-film otter cracking an oyster on its stomach: knees up in the wiring under the dashboard, my elbows jammed against the steering wheel, my chest serving as a table, my shirt as a tablecloth.

Now it was a proper stakeout – if only I could figure what it was I was waiting to see happen. Not that I could see much from inside the Tracer. The giant's car was still in its place but I couldn't confirm his existence inside it. And at this extreme angle all I could see was a thin slice of bright L&L window. Twice Tony paced to the front of the store, just long enough for me to identify his form in shadow and a flash of an elbow, a left-behind plume of cigarette exhalation across the edge of Minna's destination map, the Queens airports at the left margin showing Minna's Magic Marker scrawl: $18. Bergen Street was a void in my rearview, Smith Street only marginally brighter ahead of me. It was a quarter to four. I felt the F train's rumble underneath Bergen, first as it slowed into the station and paused there, then a second tremor as it departed. A minute later the 67 bus rolled like a great battered appliance down Bergen, empty apart from the driver. Public transportation was the night's pulse, the beep on the monitor at the patient's bedside. In a few hours those same trains and buses would be jammed with jawing, caffeinated faces, littered with newspapers and fresh gum. Now they kept the faith. Me, I had the cold to keep me awake, that and the liter of Coca-Cola and my assignment, my will to influence the outcome of the night's strange stalemate. Those would have to slug it out with the soporific powers of the roast-beef sandwich, the dreamy pull of my fresh memories of Kimmery, the throb of my skull where the giant had clubbed me with his gun.

What was the giant waiting for?

What did Tony want to find in Minna's files?

Why were his sandwiches in the car?

Why had Julia flown to Boston?

Who was Bailey anyway?

I opened my bag of chips, took a slug of my cola, and put myself to work on those new and old questions and on staying awake.

* * *

Insomnia is a variant of Tourette's – the waking brain races, sampling the world after the world has turned away, touching it everywhere, refusing to settle, to join the collective nod. The insomniac brain is a sort of conspiracy theorist as well, believing too much in its own paranoiac importance – as though if it were to blink, then doze, the world might be overrun by some encroaching calamity, which its obsessive musings are somehow fending off.

I've spent long nights in that place. This night, though, consisted of summoning up that state I'd so often worked to banish. I was alone now, no Minna, no Men, my own boss on this stakeout with who-knew-what riding on its outcome. If I fell asleep the little world of my investigation would crumble. I needed to find my insomniac self, to agitate my problem-solving brain, if not to solve actual problems, then to worry at them for the purpose of keeping my dumb eyeballs propped open.

Avoiding becoming one with everything: that was my big challenge at the moment.

It was four-thirty. My consciousness was distended, the tics like islands in an ocean of fog.

Who needed sleep? I asked myself. *I'll sleep when I'm dead*, Minna had liked to say.

I guess he had his chance now.

I'll die when I'm dead, my brain recited in Minna's voice. Not a minute sooner, you kosher macaroons!

A diet of bread. A guy on a bed.

No, no bed. No car. No phone.

Phone.

The cell phone. I pulled it out, rang the L&L number. It rang three times before a hand picked it up.

"No cars," said Danny lazily. If I knew him, he'd been sleeping with his head on the counter, weary of pretending to listen to whatever Tony was ranting about.

I'd have given a lot, of course, to know what Tony was ranting about.

"It's me, Danny. Put Tony on."

"Yo," he said, unsurprisable. "Here you go."

"What?" said Tony.

"It's me," I said. "*Deskjob.*"

"You fucking little freak," said Tony. "I'll kill you."

I outweighed Tony only by about fifty pounds. "You had your chance," I heard myself say. Tony still brought out the romantic in me. We'd be two Bogarts to the end. "Except if you'd pulled that trigger, you might have blown a hole in your foot, or in some far-off toddler on his bike."

"Oh, I'd of straightened it out," Tony said. "I wish I had put a coupla holes in you. Leaving me with that fucking cop."

"Remember it any way you like. I'm trying to help you at the moment."

"That's a good one."

"*Eat me St. Vincent!*" I held the phone away from my face until I was sure the tic was complete. "You're in danger, Tony. Right now."

"What do you know about it?"

I wanted to say, *Going out of town? What's in the files? Since when do you like horseradish?* But I couldn't let him know I was outside and have him rush into the giant's arms. "Trust me," I said. "I really wish you would."

"Oh, I trust you – to be Bozo the Clown," he said. "The point is, what can you tell me that's worth the time to listen?"

"That hurts, Tony."

"For chrissake!" Now he held his receiver away from his mouth and swore. "I got problems, Freakshow, and you're A-number one."

"If I were you, I'd worry more about Fujisaki."

"What do you know about Fujisaki?" He was hissing. "Where are you?"

"I know – *undress-a-phone, impress-a-clown* – I know a few things."

"You better hide," he said. "You better hope I don't catch you."

"Aw, Tony. We're in the same situation."

"That's a laugh, only I'm not laughing. I'm gonna kill you."

"We're a family, Tony. Minna brought us together—" I caught myself wanting to quote the Garbage Cop, suggest another *moment of silence.*

"There's too long a tail on that kite, Freakshow. I don't have the time."

Before I could speak he hung up the phone.

It was after five, and bakery trucks had begun to roll. Soon a van would come and deliver Zeod's newspapers, with Minna's obituary notice in them.

* * *

I was in a comalike state when Tony came out of L&L and got into the Pontiac. A sentinel part of my brain had kept a watch on the storefront while the rest of me slept, and so I was startled to find that the sun was up, that traffic now filled Bergen Street. I glanced at Minna's watch: It was twenty minutes to seven. I was chilled through, my head throbbed, and my tongue felt as if it had been bound in horseradish-and-cola-soaked plaster and left out on the moon overnight. I shook my head and my neck crackled. I tried to keep my eyes on the scene even as I worked my jaw sideways to revive the mechanism of my face. Tony steered the Pontiac into Smith Street's morning flow. The giant poked his compact into the traffic a moment later, first allowing two cars to creep in behind Tony. I turned the Tracer's ignition key and the engine scuffed into life, and I followed, keeping my own safe distance behind.

Tony led us up Smith, onto Atlantic heading toward the waterfront, into a stream of commuters and delivery trucks. In that stream I lost sight of Tony pretty quickly, but held on to the giant's pretty red compact.

Tony took the Brooklyn-Queens Expressway at the foot of Atlantic. The giant and I slid onto the ramp behind him in turn. Greenpoint, that was my first guess. I shuddered at recalling the Dumpster behind Harry Brainum's, off McGuinness Boulevard, where Minna had met his finish. How had the giant contrived to lure Tony out to that spot?

But I was wrong. We passed the Greenpoint exit, heading north. I saw the black Pontiac in the distance ahead as we rounded the expressway's curve toward the airports and Long Island, but I kept dropped back, at least two cars behind the red compact. I had to trust the giant to track Tony, another exercise in Zen calm. We threaded the various exits and cloverleafs out of Brooklyn, through Queens toward the airport exits. When we turned momentarily toward JFK I generated a new theory: Someone from Fujisaki was disembarking at the Japan Air Lines terminal, some chief of executions, or a courier with a ticking package to deliver. Minna's death might be the first blow in an international wave of executions. And a flight to meet explained Tony's long, nervous overnight wait. Even as I settled on this explanation, I watched the red car peel away from the airport option, to the northbound ramp, marked for the Whitestone Bridge. I barely made it across three lanes to stay on their vehicular heels.

* * *

Four sandwiches, of course. If I weren't prone to multiple sandwiches myself I might have made more of this clue. Four sandwiches and a six-pack. We were headed out of town. Fortunately I *had* rounded up my clone version of Tony's picnic, so I was outfitted too. I wondered if the giant had anything to eat besides the bag of cherries or olives I'd seen him gobbling. Our little highway formation reminded me of a sandwich, actually, a Minna Man on either side of the giant – we were a goon-on-orphan, with wheels. As we soared over the Whitestone I took another double shot of cola. It would have to stand in for morning coffee. I only had to solve the problem of needing to pee rather badly. Hence I hurried to finish the Coke, figuring I'd go in the bottle.

* * *

Half an hour later we'd passed options for the Pelhams, White Plains, Mount Kisco, a few other names I associated with the outer margins of New York City, on into Connecticut, first on the Hutchinson River Parkway, then on something called the Merritt Parkway. I kept the little red car in my sights. The cars were thick enough to keep me easily camouflaged. Every now and again the giant would creep near enough to Tony's Pontiac that I could see we were still three, bound like secret lovers through the indifferent miles of traffic.

Highway driving was maximally soothing. The steady flow of attention and effort, the nudging of gas pedal and checking of mirrors and blind spots with a twist of the neck subsumed my ticcishness completely. I was still bleary, needing sleep, but the novelty of this odd chase and of being farther out of New York City than I'd ever been worked to keep me awake. I'd seen trees before – so far Connecticut offered nothing I didn't know from suburban Long Island, or even Staten Island. But the *idea* of Connecticut was sort of interesting.

The traffic tightened as we skirted a small city called Hartford, and for a moment we were bricked into a five-lane traffic jam. It was just before nine, and we'd caught Hartford's endearing little version of a rush hour. Tony and the giant were both in view ahead of me, the giant in the lane to my right, and as I cinched forward a wheel-turn at a time, I nearly drew even with him. The red car was a Contour, I saw now. I was a Tracer following a Contour. As though I'd taken a pencil and followed the giant's route on a road map. My lane crept forward while his stood still, and soon I'd nearly pulled up even with him. He was chewing something, his jaw and neck pulsing, his hand now moving again to his mouth. I suppose to maintain that size he had to keep it coming. The car was probably brimful with snacks – perhaps Fujisaki paid him for his hits directly in food, so he wouldn't have to bother converting cash. They should have gotten him a bigger car, though.

I braked to keep him in front of me. Tony's lane began to slide ahead of the others and the giant merged into it without signaling, as though the Contour conveyed the authority of his brutish body. I was content to let some distance open between us, and before long Hartford's miniature jam eased. *Heartfood handfoot hoofdog horseradish* went the tinny song in my brain. I took a cue from the giant's chewing and rustled in the bag of sandwiches on the passenger seat. I groped for the hero, wanting to taste the wet crush of the Zeod's marinated peppers mixed with the spicy, leathery pepperoni.

I had the hero half devoured when I spotted Tony's black Pontiac slowing into a rest area, while the giant's Contour soared blithely past.

* * *

It could mean only one thing. Having reached this point behind Tony, the giant didn't need to trail him anymore. He knew where Tony was going and in fact preferred to arrive sooner, to be waiting when Tony arrived.

It wasn't Boston. Boston might be on the way, but it wasn't

the destination. I'd finally put *men of peace* and *place of peace* together. I'm not so slow.

And appropriate to the manner of the evening's stakeout and the morning's chase, I still stood in relation to the giant as the giant stood to Tony. I knew where the giant was going – *a freakshow chasing a context* – I knew where they were both going. And I had reasons to want to get there soonest. I was still seeking my edge over the giant. Maybe I could poison his sushi.

* * *

I pulled into the next rest stop and gassed up the car, peed, and bought some ginger ale, a cup of coffee and a map of New England. Sure enough, the diagonal across Connecticut pointed through Massachusetts and a nubbin of coastal New Hampshire to the entrance of the Maine Turnpike. I fished the "Place of Peace" brochure out of my jacket and found the place where the Turnpike left off and the brochure's rudimentary map took over, a coastal village called Musconguspoint Station. The name had a chewy, unfamiliar flavor that tantalized my syndrome. I spotted others like it on the map. Whether or not Maine's wilderness impressed me more than suburban Connecticut, the road signs would provide some nourishment.

Now I had only to take the lead in this secret interstate race. I was relying on the giant's overconfidence – he was so certain he was the pursuer he'd never stopped to wonder whether he might be pursued. Of course, I hadn't spent a lot of time looking over *my* shoulder either. I twitched the notion off with a few neck-jerks and got back in my car.

* * *

She answered on the second ring, her voice a little groggy.

"Kimmery."

"Lionel?"

"*Yessrog.*"

"Where did you go?"

"I'm in – I'm almost in Massachusetts."

"What do you mean, almost? Is that like a state of mind or something, Massachusetts?"

"No, I mean almost there, literally. I'm on the highway, Kimmery. I've never been this far from New York."

She was quiet for a minute. "When you run you really run," she said.

"No, no, don't misunderstand. I had to go. This is my investigation. I'm – *invest-in-a-gun, connect-a-cop, inventachusetts*—" I mashed my tongue against the cage of my gritted teeth, trying to bottle up the flow.

Ticcing with Kimmery was especially abhorrent to me, now that I'd declared her my cure.

"You're what?"

"I'm on the giant's tail," I said, squeezing out the words. "Well, not *actually* on his tail, but I know where he's going."

"You're still looking for your giant," she said thoughtfully. "Because you feel bad about that guy Frank who got killed, is that right?"

"No. Yes."

"You make me sad, Lionel."

"Why?"

"You seem so, I don't know, guilty."

"Listen, Kimmery. I called because – *Missmebailey!* – because I missed you. I mean, I miss you."

"That's a funny thing to say. Um, Lionel?"

"Yes?"

"Did you take my keys?"

"It was part of my investigation. Forgive me."

"Okay, whatever, but I thought it was pretty creepy."

"I didn't mean anything creepy by it."

"You can't do that kind of thing. It freaks people out, you know?"

"I'm really sorry. I'll bring them back."

She was quiet again. I coursed in the fast lane with a band of other speeders, every so often slipping to the right to let an especially frantic one go by. The highway driving had begun to inspire a Tourettic fantasy, that the hoods and fenders of the cars were shoulders and collars I couldn't touch. I had to keep adequate distance so I wouldn't be tempted to try to brush up against those gleaming proxy bodies.

I hadn't seen any sign of either Tony or the giant, but I had reason to hope that Tony at least was already behind me. The giant would have to stop for gas if he hadn't, and that was when I would pass him.

"I'm going to a place you might know about," I said. "Yoshii's. A retreat."

"That's a good idea," she said grudgingly, curiosity winning over her anger. "I always wanted to go there. Roshi said it was really great."

"Maybe—"

"What?"

"Maybe sometime we'll go together."

"I should get off the phone, Lionel."

* * *

The call had made me anxious. I ate the second of the roast-beef sandwiches. Massachusetts looked the same as Connecticut.

I called her back.

"What did you mean by *guilty*?" I said. "I don't understand."

She sighed. "I don't know, Lionel. It's just, I'm not really sure about this *investigation*. It seems like you're just running around a lot trying to keep from feeling sad or guilty or what-ever about this guy Frank."

"I want to catch the killer."

"Can't you hear yourself? That's like something O. J. Simp-son would say. Regular people, when someone they know gets killed or something they don't go around trying to *catch the killer*. They go to a *funeral*."

"I'm a detective, Kimmery." I almost said, *I'm a telephone*.

"You keep saying that, but I don't know. I just can't really accept it."

"Why not?"

"I guess I thought detectives were more, uh, subtle."

"Maybe you're thinking of detectives in movies or on television." I was a fine one to be explaining this distinction.

"On TV they're all the same. Real detectives are as unalike as fingerprints, or snowflakes."

"Very funny."

"I'm trying to make you laugh," I said. "I'm glad you noticed. Do you like jokes?"

"You know what *koans* are? They're like Zen jokes, except they don't really have punch lines."

"What are you waiting for? I've got all day here." In truth the highway had grown fat with extra lanes, and complicated by options and merges. But I wasn't going to interrupt Kimmery while things were going so well, ticless on my end, bubbly with digressions on hers.

"Oh, I can never remember them, they're too vague. Lots of monks hitting each other on the head and stuff."

"That sounds hilarious. The best jokes usually have animals in them, I think."

"There's plenty of animals. Here—" I heard a rustle as she braced the phone between her shoulder and chin and paged through a book. I'd had her in the middle of the big empty room – now I adjusted the picture, envisioned her with the phone stretched to reach the bed, perhaps with Shelf on her lap. "So these two monks are arguing over a cat and this other monk cuts the cat in half— Oh, that's not very nice."

"You're killing me. I'm busting a gut over here."

"Shut up. Oh, here, this is one I like. It's about death. So this young monk comes to visit this old monk to ask about this other, older monk who's just died. Tendo, that's the dead monk. So the young monk is asking about Tendo and the old monk says stuff like 'Look at that dog over there' and 'Do you want a bath?' – all this irrelevant stuff. It goes on like that until finally the young monk is enlightened."

"Enlightened by what?"

"I guess the point is you can't really say anything about death."

"Okay, I get it. It's just like in *Only Angels Have Wings*, when Cary Grant's best friend Joe crashes his plane and dies and then Rosalind Russell asks him 'What about Joe?' and 'Aren't you going to do anything about Joe?' and Cary Grant just says, 'Who's Joe?'"

"Speaking of watching too much movies and television."

"Exactly." I liked the way the miles were flying past for me now, ticless, aloft on Kimmery's voice, the freeway traffic thinning.

The moment I observed the way our talk and my journey were racing along, though, we lapsed into silence.

"Roshi says this thing about guilt," she said after a minute. "That it's selfish, just a way to avoid taking care of yourself. Or thinking about yourself. I guess that's sort of two different things. I can't remember."

"Please don't quote Gerard Minna to me on the subject of guilt," I said. "That's a little hard to swallow under the present circumstances."

"You really think Roshi's guilty of something?"

"There's more I need to find out," I admitted. "That's what I'm doing. That's why I had to take your keys."

"And why you're going to Yoshii's?"

"Yes."

In the pause that followed I detected the sound of Kimmery believing me, believing in my case, for the first time.

"Be careful, Lionel."

"Sure. I'm always careful. Just keep your promise to me, okay?"

"What promise?"

"Don't go to the Zendo."

"Okay. I think I'm getting off the phone now, Lionel."

"You promise?"

"Sure, yeah, okay."

* * *

Suddenly I was surrounded by office buildings, carports, stacked overhead freeways clogged with cars. I realized too late I probably should have navigated around Boston instead of through it. I suffered through the slowdown, munched on chips and tried not to hold my breath, and before too long the city's grip loosened, gave way to suburban sprawl, to the undecorated endless interstate. I only hoped I hadn't let Tony and the giant get ahead of me, lost my lead, my edge. *Gotta have an edge.* I was beginning to obsess on *edge* too much: edge of car, edge of road, edge of vision and what hovered there, nagging and insubstantial. How strange it began to seem that cars have bodies that never are supposed to touch, a disaster if they do.

Don't hover in my blind spot, Fonebone!

I felt as though I would begin ticcing with the body of the car, would need to flirt with the textured shoulder of the high-way or the darting, soaring bodies all around me unless I heard her voice again.

"Kimmery."

"Lionel."

"I called you again."

"Aren't these car-phone calls kind of expensive?"

"I'm not the one paying," I burbled. I was exhilarated by the recurrent technomagic, the cell phone reaching out across space and time to connect us again.

"Who is?"

"Some Zen doormat I met yesterday in a car."

"Doormat?"

"Doorman."

"Mmmm." She was eating something. "You call too much."

"I like talking to you. Driving is . . . boring." I undersold my angst, let the one word stand in for so many others.

"Yeah, mmmm – but I don't want anything, you know, crazy in my life right now."

"What do you mean by crazy?" Her tonal swerves had caught me by surprise again. I suppose it was this strange lurch-ing dance, though, that kept my double brain enchanted.

"It's just— A lot of guys, you know, they tell you they understand about giving you space and stuff, they know how to talk about it and that you need to hear it. But they don't really have any idea what it means. I've been through a lot recently, Lionel."

"When did I say anything about giving you space?"

"I just mean this is a lot of calls in a pretty short period is all."

"Kimmery, listen. I'm not like other, ah, people you meet. My life is organized around certain compulsions. But it's differ-ent with you, I feel different."

"That's good, that's nice—"

"You have no idea."

"—but I'm just coming out of something pretty intense. I mean, you swept me off my feet, Lionel. You're kind of overwhelming, actually, if you don't already know. I mean, I like talking to you, too, but it isn't a good idea to call three times right after, you know, *spending the night.*"

I was silent, unsure how to decode this remarkable speech.

"What I mean is, this is exactly the kind of craziness I just got through with, Lionel."

"Which kind?"

"Like this," she said in a meek voice. "Like with you."

"Are you saying Oreo Man had *Tourette's syndrome?*" I felt a weird thrill of jealousy. She collected us freaks, I understood now. No wonder she took us in stride, no wonder she damped our symptoms. I was nothing special after all. Or rather my fistlike penis was my only claim.

"Who's Oreo Man?"

"Your old boyfriend."

"Oh. But what's the other thing you said?"

"Never mind."

We were silent for a while. My brain went, *Tourette's slipdrip stinkjet's blessdroop mutual-of-overwhelm's wild kissdoom*—

"All I mean is I'm not ready for anything too intense right now," said Kimmery. "I need space to figure out what I want. I can't be all overwhelmed and obsessed like the last time."

"I think I've heard enough about that for now."

"Okay."

"But—" I gathered myself, made a plunge into territory far stranger to me than Connecticut or Massachusetts. "I think I understand what you mean about space. About leaving it between things so you don't get too obsessed."

"Uh-huh."

"Or is that the kind of talk you don't want to hear? I guess I'm confused."

"No, it's okay. But we can talk about this later."

"Well, okay."

"Bye, Lionel."

* * *

Dial and redial were sitting on a fence. Dial fell off. Who was left?
   Ring.
   Ring.
   Ring.
   Click. "You've reached two-one-two, three-oh-four—"
   "HellokimmeryIknowIshouldn'tbecallingbutIjust—"
   Clunk. "Lionel?"
   "Yes."
   "Stop now."
   "Uh—"
   "Just stop calling now. It's way too much like some really bad things that have happened to me, can you understand? It's not romantic."
   "Yes."
   "Okay, bye, Lionel, for real now, okay?"
   "Yes."
   Redial.
   "You've reached—"
   "Kimmery? Kimmery? Kimmery? Are you there? Kimmery?"

* * *

I was my syndrome's dupe once again. Here I'd imagined I was enjoying a Touretteless morning, yet when the new manifestation appeared, it was hidden in plain sight, the Purloined Tic. Punching that redial I was exhibiting a calling-Kimmery-tic as compulsive as any rude syllable or swipe.
   I wanted to hurl the doorman's cell phone out onto the grassy divider. Instead, in a haze of self-loathing, I dialed another number, one etched in memory though I hadn't called it in a while.
   "Yes?" The voice was weary, encrusted with years, as I remembered it.
   "Essrog?" I said.
   "Yes." A pause. "This is the Essrog residence. This is Murray Essrog. Who's calling, please?"

I was a little while coming to my reply. "Eat me Bailey."

"Oh, Christ." The voice moved away from the phone. "Mother. Mother, come here. I want you to listen to this."

"Essrog Bailey," I said, almost whispering, but intent on being heard.

There was a shuffling in the background.

"It's him again, Mother," said Murray Essrog. "It's that god-damned Bailey kid. He's still out there. All these years."

I was still a kid to him, just as to me he'd been an old man since the first time I called him.

"I don't know why you care," came an older woman's voice, every word a sigh.

"Baileybailey," I said softly.

"Speak up, kid, do your thing," said the old man.

I heard the phone change hands, the old woman's breathing come onto the line.

"Essrog, Essrog, Essrog," I chanted, like a cricket trapped in a wall.

*   *   *

I'm tightly wound. I'm a loose cannon. Both — I'm a tightly wound loose cannon, a tight loose. My whole life exists in the space between those words, tight, loose, and there isn't any space there — they should be one word, tightloose. I'm an air bag in a dashboard, packed up layer upon layer in readi-ness for that moment when I get to explode, expand all over you, fill every available space. Unlike an airbag, though, I'm repacked the moment I've exploded, am tensed and ready again to explode — like some safety-film footage cut into a loop, all I do is compress and release, over and over, never saving or satisfying anyone, least myself. Yet the tape plays on pointlessly, obsessive air bag exploding again and again while life itself goes on elsewhere, outside the range of these antic expenditures.

*   *   *

The night before, in Kimmery's alcove, suddenly seemed very long ago, very far away.

How could phone calls – *cell-phone calls*, staticky, unlikely, free of charge – how could they alter what real bodies felt? How could ghosts touch the living?

I tried not to think about it.

*   *   *

I tossed the cell phone onto the seat beside me, into the wreckage of Zeod's sandwiches, the unfurled paper wrapping, the torn chip bag, the strewn chips and crumpled napkins gone translucent with grease stains in the midmorning sun. I wasn't eating neatly, wasn't getting anything exactly right, and now I knew it didn't matter, not today, not anymore. Having broken the disastrous flow of dialing tics, my mood had gotten hard, my attention narrow. I crossed the bridge at Portsmouth into Maine and focused everything I had left on the drive, on casting off unnecessary behaviors, thrusting exhaustion and bitterness aside and making myself into a vehicular arrow pointed at Musconguspoint Station, at the answers that lay waiting for me there. I heard Minna's voice now in place of my incessant Tourettic tongue, saying, *Floor it, Freakshow. You got something to do, do it already. Tell your story driving.*

*   *   *

Route 1 along the Maine coast was a series of touristy villages, some with boats, some with beaches, all with antiques and lobster. A large percentage of the hotels and restaurants were closed, with signs that read SEE YOU NEXT SUMMER! and HAVE A GREAT YEAR! I had trouble believing any of it was real – the turnpike had felt like a schematic, a road map, and I in my car a dot or a penpoint tracing a route. Now I felt as if I were driving through the pages of a calendar, or a collection of pictorial stamps. None of it struck me as particular or persuasive in any way. Maybe once I got out of the car.

Musconguspoint Station was one with boats. It wasn't the least of these towns, but it was close to it, a swelling on the coast distinguished more than anything by the big ferry landing, with signs for the Muscongus Island Ferry, which made the circuit twice a day. The "place of peace" wasn't hard to find. Yoshii's – MAINE'S ONLY THAI AND SUSHI OCEANFOOD EMPORIUM, according to the sign – was the largest of a neat triad of buildings on a hill just past the ferry landing and the fishing docks, all painted a queasy combination of toasted-marshmallow brown and seashell pink, smugly humble earth tones that directly violated Maine's barn-red and house-white scheme. This was one shot that wasn't making the calendar. The restaurant extended on stilts over a short cliff on the water, surf thundering below; the other two buildings, presumably the retreat center, were caged in a fussy, evenly spaced row of pine trees, all the same year and model. The sign was topped with a painted image of Yoshii, a smiling bald man with chopsticks and waves of pleasure or serenity emanating from his head like stink-lines in a Don Martin cartoon.

I put the Tracer in the restaurant lot, up on the hill over-looking the water, the fishing dock, and the ferry landing below. It was alone there except for two pickup trucks in staff spots. Yoshii's hours were painted on the door: seating for lunch began at twelve-thirty, which was twenty minutes from now. I didn't see any sign of Tony or the giant or anyone else, but I didn't want to sit in the lot and wait like a fool with a target painted on his back. An edge, that's what I was after.

Edgerog, 33, seeks Edge.

I got out of the car. First surprise: the cold. A wind that hurt my ears instantly. The air smelled like a thunderstorm but there wasn't a cloud in the sky. I went over the barrier of logs at the corner of the parking lot and clambered down the grade toward the water, under the shade of the jutting deck of the restaurant. Once I'd dipped out of sight of the road and buildings, I undid my fly and peed on the rocks, amusing my compulsiveness by staining one whole boulder a deeper gray, albeit only tempo-rarily. It was as I zipped and turned to see the ocean that the vertigo hit me. I'd found an edge, all right. Waves, sky, trees, Essrog – I was off the page now, away from the grammar of skyscrapers and pavement. I experienced it precisely as a loss of language, a great sucking-away of the word-laden walls that I needed around me, that I touched everywhere, leaned on for support, cribbed from when I ticced aloud. Those walls of language had always been in place, I understood now, audible to me until the sky in Maine deafened them with a shout of silence. I staggered, put one hand on the rocks to steady myself. I needed to reply in some new tongue, to find a way to assert a self that had become tenuous, shrunk to a shred of Brooklyn stumbling on the coastal void: Orphan meets ocean. Jerk evaporates in salt mist.

"Freakshow!" I yelled into the swirling foam. It was lost.

"Bailey!" vanished too.

"Eat me! Dickweed!"

Nothing. What did I expect – Frank Minna to come rising from the sea?

"Essrog!" I screamed. I thought of Murray Essrog and his wife. They were Brooklyn Essrogs, like me. Had they ever come to this edge to meet the sky? Or was I the first Essrog to put a footprint on the crust of Maine?

"I claim this big water for Essrog!" I shouted.

I was a *freak of nature*.

* * *

Back on the dry land of the parking lot, I straightened my jacket and peered around to see if anyone had overheard my outburst. The nearest activity was at the base of the fishing docks below, where a small boat had come in and tiny figures in Devo-style yellow jumpsuits stood handing blue plastic crates over the prow and onto a pallet on the dock. I locked the car and strolled across to the other end of the empty lot, then scooted down the scrubby hill toward the men and boats, half sliding on my pavement-walker's leather soles, wind biting at my nose and chin. The restaurant and retreat center were eclipsed by the swell of the hill as I reached the dock.

"Hey!"

I got the attention of one of the men on the dock. He turned with his crate and plopped it on the pile, then stood hands on hips waiting for me to reach him. As I got closer, I examined the boat. The blue cartons were sealed, but the boatmen hefted them as though they were heavy with something, and with enough care to make me know the something was valuable.

The deck of the boat held racks covered with diving equipment – rubber suits, flippers, and masks, and a pile of tanks for breathing underwater.

"Boy, it's cold," I said, scuffing my hands together like a sports fan. "Tough day to go boating, huh?"

The boatman's eyebrows and two-day beard were bright red, but not brighter than his sun-scrubbed flesh, everywhere it showed: cheeks, nose, ears and the corroded knuckles he rubbed under his chin now as he tried to work out a response.

I heard and felt the boat's body clunking as it bobbed against the pier. My thoughts wandered to the underwater propellers, whirring silently in the water. If I were closer to the water I'd want to reach in and touch the propeller, it was so stimulating to my kinesthetic obsessions. "*Tugboat! Forgettaboat!*" I ticced, and jerked my neck, to hurl the syllables sideways into the wind.

"You're not from around here, are you?" he said carefully. I'd expected his voice to come out like Yosemite Sam's or Popeye's, scabrous and sputtering. Instead he was so stolid and patrimonial with his New England accent – *Ya nawt from around heah, ah you?* – that I was left with no doubt which of us resembled the cartoon character.

"No, actually." I affected a bright look – *Illuminate me, sir, for I am a stranger in these exotic parts!* It seemed as likely he'd shove me off the dock into the water or simply turn away as continue the conversation. I straightened my suit again, fingered my own collar so I wouldn't be tempted to finger his fluorescent hood, to crimp its Velcro edge like the rim of a piecrust.

He examined me carefully. "Urchin season runs October through March. It's cold work. Day like today is a walk in the park."

"Urchin?" I said, feeling as I said it that I'd ticced, that the word was itself a tic by definition, it was so innately twitchy. It would have made a good pronunciation for The Artist Formerly Known As Prince's glyph.

"These are urchin waters out around the island. That's the market, so that's what's fished."

"Right," I said. "Well, that's terrific. Keep it up. You know anything about the place up the hill – Yoshii's?"

"Probably you want to talk to Mr. Foible." He nodded his

head at the fishing dock's small shack, from the smokestack of which piped a tiny plume of smoke. "He's the one does dealings with them Japanese. I'm just a bayman."

"*Eatmebayman!* – thanks for your help." I smiled and tipped an imaginary cap to him, and headed for the shack. He shrugged at me and received another carton off the boat.

* * *

"How can I help you, sir?"

Foible was red too, but in a different way. His cheeks and nose and even his brow were spiderwebbed with blossoming red veins, painful to look at. His eyes too showed veins through their yellow. As Minna used to say about the St. Mary's parish priest, Foible had *a thirsty face*. Right on the wooden counter where he sat in the shack was evidence of what the face was thirsty for: a cluster of empty long-neck beer bottles and a couple of gin quarts, one still with an inch or so to cover the bottom. A coil heater glowed under the countertop, and when I stepped inside, he nodded at the heater and the door to indicate I should shut the door behind me. Besides Foible and his heater and bottles the shack held a scarred wooden file cabinet and a few boxes of what I guessed might be hardware and fishing tackle beneath their layers of grease. In my two-day suit and stubble I was the freshest thing in the place by far.

I could see this called for the oldest investigatory technique of them all: I opened my wallet and took out a twenty. "I'd buy a guy a drink if he could tell me a few things about the Japanese," I said.

"What about 'em?" His milky eyes made intimate contact with the twenty, worked their way back up to meet mine.

"I'm interested in the restaurant up the hill. Who owns it, specifically."

"Why?"

"What if I said I wanted to buy it?" I winked and gritted through a barking tic, cut it down to a momentary "—*charp!*"

"Son, you'd never get that thing away from them. You better do your shopping elsewhere."

"What if I made them an offer they couldn't refuse?"

Foible squinted at me, suddenly suspicious. I thought of how Detective Seminole had gotten spooked by the Minna Men, our Court Street milieu. I had no idea whether such images would reverberate so far from Gotham City.

"Can I ask you something?" said Foible.

"Shoot."

"You're not one of them *Scientologists*, are you?"

"No," I said, surprised. It wasn't the impression I'd imagined I was making.

He winced deeply, as though recalling the trauma that had driven him to the bottle. "Good," he said. "Dang Scientologists bought the old hotel up the island, turned it into a funhouse for movie stars. Hell, I'll take the Japanese any day. Least they eat fish."

"*Muscongus* Island?" I'd only wanted to feel the word in my mouth at last.

"What other island would I be talking about?" He squinted at me again, then held out his hand for the twenty. "Give me that, son."

I turned it over. He laid it out on the counter and cleared his rheumy throat. "That money there says you're out of your depth here, son. Japanese yank out a roll, the smallest thing they got's a hundred. Hell, before they shut down the urchin market, this dock used to be littered with thousand-dollar bank bands from them Japanese paying off my baymen for a haul."

"Tell me about it."

"Humph."

"Eat me."

"Huh? What's that?"

"I said tell me about it. Explain about the Japanese to a guy who doesn't know."

"You know what *uni* is?"

"Forgive my ignorance."

"That's the national food of Japan, son. That's the whole story around Musconguspoint anymore, unless you count the Scientologists camped out in that damn hotel. Japanese family's got to eat uni least once a week just to maintain their self-respect. Like you'd want a steak, they want a plate of urchin eggs. Golden Week – that's like Christmas in Japan – uni's the only thing they eat. Except Japanese waters got fished out. You follow?"

"Maybe."

"The Japanese law says you can't dive for urchin anymore. All you can do is hand-rake. Means standing out on a rock at low tide with a rake in your hand. Try it sometime. Rake all day, won't get an urchin worth a damn."

If ever there was a guy who needed to *tell his story walking*, it was Foible. I stifled the urge to tell him so.

"Maine coast's got the choicest urchin on the globe, son. Clustered under the island thick as grapes. Mainers never had a taste for the stuff, lobstermen thought urchins was a pain in the ass. That Japanese law made a lot of boatmen rich up here, if they knew how to rig for a diving crew. Whole economy down Rockport way. Japanese set up processing plants, they got women down there shucking urchins day and night, fly it out the next morning. Japanese dealers come in limousines, wait for the boats to come in, bid on loads, pay in cash with wads like I said before – the money would scare you silly."

"What happened?" I gulped back tics. Foible's story was beginning to interest me.

"In Rockport? Nothing happened. Still like that. If you mean up here, we just got a couple of boats. The folks up the hill bought me out and that's that, no more cars with dark windows, no more Yakuza making deals on the dock – I don't miss it for a minute. I'm an exclusive supplier, son, and a happier man you'll never meet."

In the little shack I was surrounded by Foible's happiness, and I wasn't enthralled. I didn't mention it. "The folks up the hill," I said. "You mean Fujisaki." I figured he was deep enough in his story not to balk at my feeding him the name.

"That's correct, sir. They're a classy outfit. Got a bunch of homes on the island, redid themselves a whole restaurant, brought in a sushi cook so they could eat the way they like. Sure wish they'd outbid the Scientologists for that old hotel, though."

"Don't we all. So does Fujisaki – *Superduperist! Clientol-ogist! Fujiopolis!* – does Fujisaki live here in Musconguspoint year-round?"

"What's that?"

"*Fly-on-top-of-us!*"

"You got a touch of Tourette's syndrome there, son."

"Yes," I gasped.

"You want a drink?"

"No, no. The classy outfit, do they all live up here?"

"Nope. They come and go in a bunch, always together, Tokyo, New York, London. Got a heliport on the island, go back and forth. They just rode in on the ferry this morning."

"Ah." I blinked madly in the wake of the outburst. "You run the ferry, too?"

"Nope, wouldn't want any part of that bathtub. Just a couple of boats, couple of crews. Keep my feet up, concentrate on my hobbies."

"Your other boat's out fishing?"

"Nope. Urchin-diving's an early-morning affair, son. Go out three, four in the morning, day's over by ten o'clock."

"Right, right. So where's the boat?"

"Funny you ask. Let a couple of guys take it out an hour ago, said they had to get to the island, couldn't wait for the ferry. Rented my boat and captain. They were a lot like you, thought I'd be real impressed with twenty-dollar bills."

"One of them big?"

"Biggest I ever saw."

* * *

My detour through the middle of Boston had cost me the lead in the race to Musconguspoint. Now it seemed silly that I'd imagined anything else. I found the red Contour and the black Pontiac in a small parking area just past the ferry landing, a tree-hidden cul-de-sac lot for day-trippers to the island, with an automated coin-fed gate and one-way exit with flexible spikes pointed at an angle and signs that warned, DON'T BACK UP! SEVERE TIRE DAMAGE! There was something I found poign-ant in Tony and the giant each paying to park here, fishing in their pockets for coins before enacting whatever queer struggle had led them to hire the urchin boat. I took a closer look and saw that the Contour was locked up tight, while the Pontiac's keys were in the ignition, the doors unlocked. Tony's gun, the one he'd pointed at me the day before, lay on the floor near the gas pedal. I pushed it under the seat. Maybe Tony would need it. I hoped so. I thought of how the giant had strong-armed Minna wherever he wanted him to go and felt sorry for Tony.

On my way up the hill I felt a buzz, like a bee or hornet trapped inside my pants. It was Minna's beeper. I'd set it to "vibrate" at the Zendo. I drew it out. It showed a New Jersey number. The Clients were home from Brooklyn.

In the parking lot I got into my car and found the cell phone on the seat with the sandwich wrappings, which were beginning to mature in the sun. I rang the number.

I was very tired.

"Yes?"

"It's Lionel, Mr. Matricardi. You beeped me."

"Yes. Lionel. Have you got for us what we want?"

"I'm working on it."

"Working is wonderful, honorable, admirable. Results – now those we truly cherish."

"I'll have something for you soon."

* * *

The interior was all inlaid burnished wood to match the exterior's toasted-marshmallow color; the carpet supplied the seashell pink. The girl who met me just inside the door wore an elaborate Japanese robe and a dazed expression. I smoothed both sides of her collar with my hand and she seemed to take it well, perhaps as admiration for the silk. I nodded at the big windows overlooking the water and she led me to a small table there, then bowed and left me alone. I was the only customer for lunch, or the first anyway. I was starving. A sushi chef waved his broad knife at me and grinned from across the big, elegant dining room. The beveled-glass partition he worked behind made me think of the holdup-proof Plexiglas habitats for clerks in Smith Street liquor stores. I waved back, and he nodded, a sudden and ticcish bob, and I reciprocated happily. We had quite a thing going until he broke it off, to begin slicing with theatrical flair the whole skin off a slab of reddish fish.

The doors to the kitchen swung open, and Julia came out. She too wore a robe, and she wore it splendidly. It was her haircut that was a little jarring. She'd shaved her long blond hair down to military fuzz, exposing the black roots. Her face underneath the fuzz looked exposed and raw, her eyes a little wild to be without their veil. She picked up a menu and brought it to my table and halfway across the floor I saw her notice who she was bringing it to. She lost only a little something from her stride.

"Lionel."

"*Pisspaw*," I completed.

"I'm not going to ask you what you're doing here," she said. "I don't even want to know." She passed me the menu, the cover of which was thatched, a weave of bamboo.

"I followed Tony," I said, putting the menu gingerly aside, wary of splinters. "And the giant, the killer. We're all coming up here for a Frank Minna convention."

"That's not funny." She examined me, her mouth drawn. "You look like shit, Lionel."

"It was a long drive. I guess I should have flown into Boston and – what's your trick, rental car? Or catch a bus? This is a regular vacation spot for you, I know that much."

"Very nice, Lionel, you're very smart. Now get lost."

"*Muscongaphone! Minnabunkport!*" I gritted back a whole series of Maine-geography tics that wished to follow these two through the gate of my teeth. "We really ought to talk, Julia."

"Why don't you just talk to yourself?"

"Now we're even, since that wasn't funny either."

"Where's Tony?"

"He's – *Tugboat! Tunaphone!* – he's on a boat ride." It sounded so pleasant, I didn't want to say who with. From the vantage of Yoshii's high window I could see Muscongus Island at last, wreathed in mist on the horizon.

"He should have come here," said Julia, without a trace of sentiment. She spoke as someone whose thinking had taken a very practical turn in the past day or so. "He told me to wait here for him, but I can't wait much longer. He should have come."

"Maybe he tried. I think he wants to get to Fujisaki before

someone gets to him." I watched her as I dangled the theory, alert for any flinch or fire that might cross her expression.

It was flinch. She lowered her voice. "Don't say that name here, Lionel. Don't be an idiot." She looked around, but there was only the hostess and sushi chef. *Don't say that name* – the widow had inherited the dead man's superstitions.

"Who are you afraid of, Julia? Is it Fujisaki, really? Or Matricardi and Rockaforte?"

She looked at me and I saw her throat tighten and her nostrils flare.

"I'm not the one hiding from the Italians," she said. "I'm not the one who should be afraid."

"Who's hiding?"

It was one question too many. Her fury's crosshairs centered on me now, only because I was there and the person she wanted to kill was so very far away, working her by remote control.

"Screw you, Lionel. You fucking freak."

The ducks were on the pond, the monkeys were in a tree, the birds wired, the fish barreled, the pigs blanketed: However the players in this tragic fever dream ought to be typed zoologically, I had them placed together now. The problem wasn't one of tracing connections. I'd climbed into my Tracer and accomplished that. Now, though, I had to draw a single coherent line through the monkeys, ducks, fish, pigs, through monks and mooks – a line that accurately distinguished two opposed teams. I might be close.

"Will you take my order, Julia?"

"Why don't you go away, Lionel? Please." It was pitying and bitter and desperate at once. She wanted to spare us both. I had to know from what.

"I want to try some uni. Some – *orphan ocean ice cream!* – some urchin eggs. See what all the fuss is about."

"You wouldn't like it."

"Can it be done up as a sandwich of some kind? Like an uni–salad sandwich?"

"It's not a sandwich spread."

"Okay, well, then just bring me out a big bowl and a spoon. I'm really hungry, Julia."

She wasn't paying attention. The door had opened, pale sunlight flaring into the orange and pink cavern of the room. The hostess bowed, then led the Fujisaki Corporation to a long table in the middle of the room.

* * *

It all happened at once. There were six of them, a vision to break your heart. I was almost glad Minna was gone so he'd never have to face it, how perfectly the six middle-aged Japanese men of Fujisaki filled the image the Minna Men had always strained toward but had never reached and never would reach, in their impeccably fitted black suits and narrow ties and Wayfarer shades and upright postures, their keen, clicking shoes and shiny rings and bracelets and stoic, lipless smiles. They were all we could never be no matter how Minna pushed us: absolutely a team, a unit, their presence collective like a floating island of charisma and force. Like a floating island they nodded at the sushi chef and at Julia and even at me, then moved to their seats and folded their shades into their breast pockets and removed their beautifully creased felt hats and hooked them on the coatrack and I saw the shine of their bald heads in the orange light and I spotted the one who'd spoken of marshmallows and ghosts and bowel movements and picnics and vengeance and I knew, I knew it all, I understood everything at that moment except perhaps who Bailey was, and so of course I ticced loudly.

"*I scream for ur-chin!*"

* * *

Julia turned, startled. She'd been staring, like me, transfixed by Fujisaki's splendor. If I was right she'd never seen them before, not even in their guises as monks.

"I'll bring your order, sir," she said, recovering gracefully. I didn't bother to point out that I hadn't exactly placed an order. Her panicked eyes said she couldn't handle any banter right then. She collected the bamboo-covered menu, and I saw her hand trembling and had to restrain myself from reaching for it to comfort her and my syndrome both. She turned again and headed for the kitchen, and when she passed Fujisaki's table, she managed a brave little bow of her own.

A few members of the corporation turned and glanced at me again, ever so lightly and indifferently. I smiled and waved to embarrass them out of giving me the once-over. They went back to their conversation in Japanese, the sound of which, trickling over the carpet and polished wood in my direction, was a choral murmur, a purr.

I sat still as I could and watched as Julia reemerged to take their drink order and pass out menus. One of the suits ignored her, leaned back in his seat, and transacted directly with the sushi chef, who grunted to show comprehension. Others unfolded the spiny menu and began to grunt as well, to jabber and laugh and stab their manicured fingers at the laminated photographs of fish inside. I recalled the monks in the Zendo, the pale, saggy flesh, the scanty tufts of underarm hair that now hid behind the million-dollar tailoring. The Zendo seemed a distant and unlikely place from where I sat now. Julia went back through the kitchen doors and came out carrying a large steaming bowl and a small trivet with daubs of bright color on it. With these she threaded past Fujisaki, to my table.

"Uni," she said, nodding at the tiny block of wood. It held a thick smudge of green paste, a cluster of pink-hued shavings from a pickled beet or turnip, and a gobbet of glistening orange beads – the urchin eggs, I supposed. It wasn't three bites of food altogether. The bowl she set down was a touch more promising. The broth was milky white, its surface rippled from underneath by a thick tangle of vegetables and chunks of chicken, and decorated on top by sprigs of some sort of exotic parsley.

"I also brought you something you might actually like," she said quietly as she drew a small ceramic ladle and a pair of inlaid chopsticks out of a pouch in her robe and set them at my place. "It's Thai chicken soup. Eat it and go, Lionel. Please."

Tie-chicken-to-what? went my brain. *Tinker to Evers to Chicken.*

Julia returned to Fujisaki's table with her order pad, to contend with the corporation's contradictory barked commands, their staccato pidgin English. I sampled the uni, scraping it up in the ladle – chopsticks were not my game. The gelatinous orange beads ruptured in my mouth like capers, brackish and

sharp but not impossible to like. I tried mixing the three bright
colors on the wood, blobbing the tacky green paste and the
shreds of pickled radish together with the eggs. The combination was something else entirely: An acrid claw of vapor
sped up the back of my throat and filled my nasal cavity. Those
elements were apparently not meant to be mixed. My ears
popped, my eyes watered, and I made a sound like a cat with
a hairball.

I'd garnered Fujisaki's attention once again, and the sushi
chef's as well. I waved, face flushed bright red, and they nodded
and waved back, bobbed their heads, returned to talking. I
ladled up some of the soup, thinking at least to flush the poisons
off the sensitive surface of my tongue. Another reverse: The
broth was superb, a reply and rebuke to the toxic explosion that
had preceded it. It transmitted warmth in the other direction,
down into my gullet and through my chest and shoulders as it
passed. Levels of flavor unfolded, onion, coconut, chicken, a
piquancy I couldn't place. I scooped up another ladleful, with
a strip of chicken this time, and let the nourishing fire flow
through me again. Until placed in this soup's care I hadn't realized how chilled I was, how starved for comfort. It felt as if the
soup were literally embracing my heart.

The trouble came with the third spoonful. I'd dredged low,
come up with a tangle of unidentifiable vegetables. I drank
down more of the broth, then gnawed on the mouthful of
pungent roughage that was left in my mouth – only some of it
was rougher than I might have liked. There was some resilient,
bladelike leaf that wasn't losing the contest with my teeth, was
instead beginning to triumph in an unexpected skirmish with
my gums and the roof of my mouth. I chewed, waiting for it
to disintegrate. It wouldn't. Julia appeared just as I'd reached in
with my pinkie to clear it from my mouth.

"I think part of the menu got into the soup," I said as I
ejected the bulrushes onto the table.

"That's lemongrass," said Julia. "You're not supposed to
eat it."

"What's it doing in the soup, then?"

"Flavor. It flavors the soup."

"I can't argue with that," I said. "What's the name again?"

"Lemongrass," she hissed. She dropped a slip of paper onto the table by my hand. "Here's your check, Lionel."

I reached for her hand where it covered the slip but she pulled it away, like some version of a children's game, and all I got was the paper.

"*Lasagna ass,*" I said under my breath.

"What?"

"*Laughing Gassrog.*" This was more audible, but I hadn't disturbed Fujisaki, not yet. I looked up at her helplessly.

"Good-bye, Lionel." She hurried away from my table.

The check wasn't really a check. Julia's scrawl covered the underside:

THE FOOD IS ON THE HOUSE.

MEET ME AT FRIENDSHIP HEAD LIGHTHOUSE two-thirty.

GET OUT OF HERE!!!

* * *

I finished the soup, carefully putting the mysterious inedible lemongrass to one side. Then I rose from the table and went past Fujisaki toward the doors, hoping for Julia's sake to be invisible. One of them turned as I passed, though, and grabbed my elbow.

"You like the food?"

"Terrific," I said.

It was the one who as a monk had applied the paddle to my back. They'd been guzzling sake and his face was red, his eyes moist and merry.

"You Jerry-Roshi's unruly student," he said.

"I guess that's right."

"Retreat center a good idea," he said. "You need long sesshin. You got an *utterance* problem, I think."

"I know I do."

He clapped me on the shoulder, and I clapped his shoulder in return, feeling the shoulder pad in his suit, the tight seam at the sleeve. Then I tugged loose of his embrace, meaning to go, but it was too late. I had to make the rounds and touch the others. I started around the table, clapping each perfectly tailored shoulder. The men of Fujisaki seemed to take it as an encouragement to tap and poke me back while they joked with one another in Japanese. "Duck, duck, goose," I said, quietly at first. "Otter, otter, utterance."

"Otter-*duck*," said one of the men of Fujisaki, raising his eyebrows as though it were a significant correction, and elbowing me sharply.

"Monk, monk, stooge!" I said, circling the table faster, cavorting. "Weapongrass duckweed!"

"You go now," said the scowling paddle-wielder.

"*Eat me Fujisaki!*" I screamed, and whirled out the door.

* * *

The second boat had returned to the dock. I went back through Yoshii's parking lot and down the hill to have a closer look. Smoke still plumed from Foible's shack; otherwise the scene on the fishing pier was completely still. Perhaps the captain of the boat had joined Foible inside the shack for a drink from a new bottle of gin, on my twenty. Or maybe he'd just gone home to bed after a day's labor that had started at three in the morning, Urchin Daylight Savings time. I envied him if he had. I crept past the shack, to the other side of the pier. From what I could see the ferry landing was empty too, the boat itself out at the island, the ticket office closed until the late-afternoon landing. The wind was picking up off the ocean now and the whole coastal scene had a bleak, abandoned look, as though Maine in November really belonged to the ragged gulls who wheeled over the sun-worn pier, and the humans had just gotten the news and taken a powder.

It was farther on, in the tree-shrouded parking lot, that I saw something move, a sign of life. I went silently past the ferry landing to a place out of the harsh angled brightness so I could peer into the shadow and distinguish what the something was. The answer was the giant. He stood between his car and Tony's squinting in the wind and dappled sunlight and reading or at least staring at a bunch of papers in a manila folder, something out of the L&L files perhaps. In the minute that I watched he grew bored or dissatisfied with the papers and closed the file and ripped it in two, then two again, and walked across the lot to the edge where the pavement was divided from the sea by a wide margin of barnacled and beer-canned boulders. He hurled the torn quadrants of the folder in the direction of the rocks and water and the wind whipped them instantly back to flutter madly past him and disperse across the lot's gravel and into the trees. But he wasn't finished yet. There was something else in his hand, something black and small and shiny, and for a moment I thought he was making a call. Then I saw that it was a wallet. He rifled through it and moved some folding money into his own pants pocket and then he hurled the wallet, too, with more success than he'd had with the papers, so that it arced over the rocks and possibly reached the water – I couldn't tell from my perspective, and neither, I think, could the giant. He didn't appear particularly worried. Worry wasn't in his nature.

Then he turned and saw me: Laugh-or-cry Edgelost.

I ran the other way, across the ferry landing and the fishing dock, toward the hill, on top of which sat the restaurant, and my car.

* * *

The huff of my own exhausted breath, pounding of blood in my ears, squall of a gull and shush of the surf below – all were overtaken by the squeal of the giant's wheels: His Contour scraped into the restaurant lot just as I got my key into the ignition. His car barreled toward mine. The cliff was near enough that he might push me off. I revved into reverse and jerked my car backward out of his path and he skidded sideways to stop, nearly slamming into the nearest of the parked pickup trucks. I floored it and beat him back out of the lot, down onto Route 1, pointed south. The giant fell in right behind me. In my rearview I saw him bearing down, one hand on the wheel, the other gripping a gun.

* * *

Minna and Tony – I'd let them both be gently escorted to their quiet murderings. Mine looked to be a little noisier.

* * *

I screwed the steering wheel to the left, twitching myself off the highway toward the ferry dock. The giant wasn't fooled. He hung right on my bumper, as if the red compact were as correspondingly huge as his body and could climb over or engulf my Tracer. I veered right and left, contacting the ragged edges of the paved road to the dock in some half-symbolic finger-wagging or shooing maneuver, trying to dislodge the giant from my tail, but he matched my every vehicular gesture, Contour on Tracer now. Pavement gave way to gravel and I ground braking and sliding to the right to avoid riding straight up onto the dock and into the water. Instead I steered for the ferry's parking area, where Tony's Pontiac still sat, where the gun he hadn't gotten to use on the giant still waited under the driver's seat.

Gottagettagun, screamed my brain, and my lips moved trying to keep up with the chant: *Gottagettagun gottagettagun*.

Gun Gun Gun *Shoot!*

I'd never fired a gun.

I broke through the entrance, snapping the flimsy gate back on its post. The giant's car chewed on my bumper, the metal squeaking and sighing. Exactly how I would find breathing room enough to get out of my car and into Tony's to lay hands on the gun remained to be seen. I curled past Tony's car, to the left, opening a moment's gap between me and my pursuer, and rode for the rock barrier. Shreds of the torn file still fluttered here and there in the wind. Maybe the giant would do me the favor of plummeting into the sea. Maybe he hadn't gotten around to noticing it – since it was only the Atlantic it might not have been big enough to make an impression.

He caught me again as I turned the other way to avoid a swim myself, and veered with me around the outer perimeter of the lot. DON'T BACK UP! SEVERE TIRE DAMAGE! shouted the signs at the exit, warning of the one-way spikes meant to prevent free use of the lot. Well, I'd gotten around that one. The giant's car made contact again, rammed me so we both slid off to the left, toward the exit, away from Tony's car.

Suddenly inspired, I darted for the exit.

I hit the brake as hard as I could as I passed over the flexible spikes, came shrieking and skidding to a halt about a car's length past the grate. The giant's car smashed against my rear end so that my car was driven another couple of yards forward and I was slapped back against the seat, hard. I felt something in my neck click and tasted blood in my mouth.

The first blast was the giant's air bag inflating. In my rearview I saw a white satin blob now filling the interior of the Contour.

The second blast was the giant's gun firing as he panicked or his fingers clenched around the trigger in traumatic reflex. The glass of his windshield splintered. I don't know where the shot went, but it found some target other than my body. I shifted into reverse and floored the gas pedal.

And plowed the giant's car backward toward the spikes.

I heard his rear tires pop, then hiss. The giant's rear end slumped, his tires lanced on the spikes.

For a moment I heard only the hiss of escaping air, then a gull screamed, and I made a sound to answer it, a scream of pain in the form of a birdcall.

I shook my head, glanced in the mirror. The giant's air bag was sagging slowly, silently. Perhaps it had been pierced by the bullet. There wasn't any sign of motion underneath.

I shifted into first, swerved forward and left, then reversed into the giant's car again, crumpling the metal along the driver's-side door, deforming the contour of the Contour, wrinkling it like foil, hearing it creak and groan at being reshaped.

I might have stopped then. I believed the giant was unconscious under the air bag. He was at least silent and still, not firing his gun, not struggling to free himself.

But I felt the wild call of symmetry: His car ought to be crumpled on both sides. I needed to maul both of the Contour's shoulders. I rolled forward and into position, then backed and crashed against his car once more, wrecking it on the passenger side as I had on the driver's.

It's a Tourette's thing – you wouldn't understand.

*   *   *

I moved the map and cell phone to Tony's Pontiac. The keys were still in the ignition. I drove it out of the lot through the smashed entrance gate, and steered past the vacant ferry landing, up to Route 1. Apparently no one had heard the collisions or gunshot in the lot by the sea. Foible hadn't even poked out of his shack.

Friendship Head was an outcropping on the coast twelve miles north of Musconguspoint Station. The lighthouse was painted red and white, no atrocity of Buddhist earth tones like the restaurant. I trusted that the Scientologists hadn't gotten to it either. I parked the Pontiac as close to the water as I could and sat staring out for a while, feeling the place where I'd bitten my tongue slowly seal and testing out the damage to my neck. Free movement of my neck was crucial to my Tourettic career. I was like an athlete in that regard. But it felt like whiplash, nothing worse. I was chilled and tired, the replenishing effects of the lemongrass broth long since gone, and I could still feel my head throb in the place the giant had clubbed it twenty-four hours and a million years ago. But I was alive, and the water looked pretty good as the angle of the light grew steeper. I was half an hour early for my date with Julia.

I dialed the local police and told them about the sleeping giant they'd find back at the Muscongus Island ferry.

"He might be in bad shape but I think he's still alive," I told them. "You'll probably need the Jaws of Life to pull him out."

"Can you give us your name, sir?"

"No, I really can't," I said. They'd never know how true it was. "My name doesn't matter. You'll find the wallet of the man he killed in the water near the ferry. The body's more likely to wash up on the island."

*   *   *

Is guilt a species of Tourette's? Maybe. It has a touchy quality, I think, a hint of sweaty fingers. Guilt wants to cover all the bases, be everywhere at once, reach into the past to tweak, neaten, and repair. Guilt like Tourettic utterance flows uselessly, inelegantly from one helpless human to another, contemptuous of perimeters, doomed to be mistaken or refused on delivery.

Guilt, like Tourette's, tries again, learns nothing.

And the guilty soul, like the Tourettic, wears a kind of clown face – the Smokey Robinson kind, with tear tracks underneath.

* * *

I called the New Jersey number.

"Tony's dead," I told them.

"This is a terrible thing—" Matricardi started.

"Yeah, yeah, terrible," I said, interrupting. I was in no mood. Really no mood at all. The minute I heard Matricardi's voice, I was something worse or less than human, not simply sorrowful or angry or ticcish or lonely, certainly not moody at all, but raging with purpose. I was an arrow to pierce through years. "Listen carefully to me now," I said. "Frank and Tony are gone."

"Yes," said Matricardi, already seeming to understand.

"I've got something you want and then that's the end of it."

"Yes."

"That's the end of it, we're not bound to you any longer."

"Who is we? Who is speaking?"

"L and L."

"There's a meaning to saying L and L when Frank is depart-ed, and now Tony? What is it to speak of L and L?"

"That's our business."

"So what is this thing you have we want?"

"Gerard Minna lives on East Eighty-fourth Street, in a Zendo. Under another name. He's responsible for Frank's death."

"Zendo?"

"A Japanese church."

There was a long silence.

"This is not what we expected from you, Lionel."

I didn't speak.

"But you are correct that it is of interest to us."

I didn't speak.

"We will respect your wishes."

* * *

Guilt I knew something about. Vengeance was another story entirely.

I'd have to think about vengeance.

FORMERLY KNOWN

THERE ONCE WAS a girl from Nantucket.

No, really, that's where she was from.

Her mother and father were hippies and so she was a little hippie child. Her father wasn't always there on Nantucket with the family. When he was there he didn't stay long, and over time the visits grew both briefer and less frequent.

The girl used to listen to tapes her father would leave behind, the Alan Watts Lecture Series, an introduction to Eastern thought for Americans in the form of a series of rambling, humorous monologues. After the girl's father stopped coming at all, the girl would confuse her memories of her father with the charming man whose voice she heard on the tapes.

When the girl got older she sorted this out, but she'd listened to Alan Watts hundreds of times by then.

When the girl turned eighteen she went to college in Boston, to an art school that was part of a museum. She hated the school and the other students there, hated pretending she was an artist, and after two years she dropped out.

First she went back to Nantucket for a little while, but the girl's mother had moved in with a man the girl didn't like, and Nantucket is, after all, an island. So she went back to Boston. There she found a lousy job as a waitress in a student dive, where she had to fend off an endless series of advances from customers and co-workers. At night she'd take yoga classes and attend Zen meetings in the basement of a local YWCA, where she had to fend off an endless series of advances from instructors and other students. The girl decided she didn't hate only school, she hated Boston.

A year or so later she visited a Zen retreat center on the coast of Maine. It was a place of striking beauty and, apart from the frantic summer months when the town became a resort for wealthy Bostonians and New Yorkers, splendid isolation. It reminded her of Nantucket, the things she missed there. She quickly arranged to study at the center full-time, and to support herself she took a job waitressing at the seafood restaurant next door, which at that time was a traditional Maine lobster pound.

It was there the girl met the two brothers.

The older brother first, during a series of short visits to the retreat with his friend. The friend had some experience with Buddhism, the older brother none, but they were both a disconcerting presence there in placid Maine – vibrant with impatience and a hostile sort of urban humor, yet humble and sincere in their fledgling approach to Zen practice. The older brother was solicitous and flattering to the girl when they were introduced. He was a talker like none she'd never met, except perhaps on the Alan Watts lecture tapes, which still shaped her yearnings so powerfully – but the older brother was no Watts. His stories were of ethnic Brooklyn, of petty mobsters and comic scams, and some of them had a violent finish. With his talk he made this world seem as near and real to her as it was actually distant. In some way Brooklyn, where she'd never been, became a romantic ideal, something truer and finer than the city life she'd glimpsed in Boston.

The girl and the older brother were lovers after a while.

The older brother's visits grew both briefer and less frequent.

Then one day the older brother returned, in an Impala filled with paper shopping bags stuffed full of his clothes and with his younger brother in tow. After a sizable donation to the Zen center's petty-cash fund the two men moved into rooms in the retreat center, rooms that were out of sight of the coastal highway. The next day the older brother drove the Impala off and returned with a pickup truck, with Maine plates.

Now whenever the girl tried to visit the older brother in his room, he turned her away. This persisted for a few weeks before she began to accept the change. The lovemaking and talk of Brooklyn were over between them. It was only then that the younger brother came into focus for the girl.

The younger brother wasn't a student of Zen. He'd also never been out of New York City until his arrival in Maine, and it was a destination as mysterious and absurd to him as he was mysterious and absurd to her. To the girl the younger brother seemed an embodiment of the stories of Brooklyn the older brother had entranced her with. He was a talker, too, but rootless, chaotic in the stories he told. His talk entirely lacked the posture of distance and bemusement, the gloss of Zen perspective that characterized the older brother's tales. Instead, though they sat together on the Maine beaches, huddling together in the wind, he seemed still to inhabit the streets he described.

The older brother read Krishnamurti and Watts and Trungpa, while the younger read Spillane and Chandler and Ross MacDonald, often aloud to the girl, and it was in the MacDonald especially that the girl heard something that taught her about a part of herself not covered by Nantucket or Zen or the bit she'd learned in college.

The younger brother and the girl became lovers after a while.

And the younger brother did what the older would never have done: He explained to the girl the situation that had driven the two brothers out of Brooklyn, to come and seek refuge in the Zen center. The brothers had been acting as liaisons between two aging Brooklyn mobsters and a group of suburban Westchester and New Jersey bandits who hijacked trucks on small highways into New York City. The aging mobsters were in the business of redistributing the goods seized by the truck pirates, and it was a business that was profitable for everyone associated with it. The brothers had made it more profitable for themselves than they should have, though. They found a place to warehouse a percentage of the goods, and a fence to take the goods off their hands. When the two mobsters discovered the betrayal, they decided to kill the brothers.

Hence, Maine.

The younger brother did another thing his older brother might never have done: He fell in love with the strange angry girl from Nantucket. And one day in the flush of this love he explained to her his great dream: He was going to open a detective agency.

The older brother in the meantime had grown distant from them both, and more deeply and sincerely involved in Zen practice. In the manner of so many spiritual practitioners past and present he seemed to draw away from the world of material concerns, to grow tolerant and wry but also a little chilly in his regard for the people and things he'd left behind.

When the younger brother and the girl were away from the retreat center they'd refer to the older brother as "Rama-lama-ding-dong." Before too long they even began to call him that to his face.

One day the younger brother tried to telephone his mother and found that she'd been taken to the hospital. He conferred with his older brother; the girl overheard some of their bitter, fearful conversations. The older brother was persuaded that their mother's hospitalization had been arranged as a trap to lure them back to Brooklyn for their punishment. The younger disagreed. The next day he bought a car and loaded it with his belongings, and announced he was going back to the city. He invited the girl to join him, though he warned her of the possible danger.

She considered her life at the retreat, which had grown as close and predictable around her as an island, and she considered the younger brother and the prospect of Brooklyn, his Brooklyn, of living there by his side. She agreed to leave Maine.

On the way they were married in Albany, by a justice of the peace at the state capital. The younger brother wanted to surprise and please his mother, and perhaps also wished to offer some excuse for his long disappearance. He took the girl shopping for clothes in Manhattan before they crossed the famous bridge into Brooklyn, and then, as an afterthought, he brought her to a salon on Montague Street, where they bleached her dark hair to platinum blond. It was as though she were the one who should be in disguise here.

The mother's sickness wasn't a trap. She was dead of a stroke by the time the younger brother and his new wife reached the hospital. But it was also true that the mobsters were aware of everything that happened in the neighborhood and were watching the hospital closely. When the younger brother was spotted there, it wasn't long before he was brought in to answer for his and his brother's misdeeds.

He begged for his life. He explained that he'd just gotten married.

He also blamed his brother for the crimes they'd both committed. He claimed to have lost touch with his brother completely.

He ended by promising to spend his life in service as the gangsters' errand boy.

On that condition his apology was accepted by the gangsters. They permitted him to live, though they swore again a vow of death against the older brother, and made the younger promise that he'd turn his brother in if and when he reappeared.

The younger brother moved his new wife into his mother's old apartment and the woman from Nantucket began her adjustment to life in Brooklyn. What she encountered was first intoxicating and frightening, then disenchanting. Her husband was a small-time operator, his "agents," as he called them, a motley gang of high-school-dropout orphans. For a while he installed her as a secretary in a friend's law office, where she worked as a notary public, humiliatingly on view in a shop window out on Court Street. When she protested, he allowed her to recede into privacy in the apartment. The old gangsters paid the couple's rent anyway, and most of the younger brother's detective work was on their behalf. The woman from Nantucket didn't like what passed for detective work in Brooklyn. She wished he genuinely ran a car service. Their married life was chilly and glancing, full of unexplained absences and omissions, no walk on the beach. In time she began to understand that there were other women, too, old high-school girlfriends and distant cousins who'd never left the neighborhood and never really been very far from the younger brother's bed either.

The woman from Nantucket survived, found occasional lovers herself, and spent most of her days in the movie theaters on Court and Henry streets, shopping in Brooklyn Heights, drinking in the hotel lobbies there and then taking slow walks on the Promenade, where she fended off an endless series of advances from college boys and lunch-hour husbands, spent her days any way except musing on the serene rural life she'd left behind in Maine, the faint uncontroversial satisfactions she'd known before she'd met the two brothers and been taken to Brooklyn.

One day the younger brother told his wife a dire secret, which she had to be sure to keep from leaking to anyone in Brooklyn, lest it reach the ears of the gangsters: The older brother had returned to New York City. He'd declared himself a roshi, an elder teacher of Zen, and started a Zendo on the Upper East Side of Manhattan, in Yorkville. This Yorkville Zendo was subsidized by a powerful group of Japanese businessmen he'd met in Maine, where they'd taken over and renovated top to bottom the homely Zen center and the lobster pound next door: the Fujisaki Corporation.

The men of Fujisaki were highly spiritual, but had found themselves in disrepute in their native country, where monkhood is reserved only for those born into certain esteemed bloodlines, and where capitalistic rapaciousness and spiritual devotion are viewed as mutually exclusive. Money and power, it seemed, couldn't buy Fujisaki the precise sort of respect its members craved at home. Here, first in Maine, now in New York City, they would make themselves credible as penitents and teachers, men of wisdom and peace. In the process, as the older brother explained to the younger, the younger then to his wife, the men of Fujisaki and the older brother hoped to do a little "business." New York City: land of opportunity for monks and crooks and mooks alike.

* * *

We stood at the rail at the sea edge of the lighthouse tower, looking out. The wind was still strong, but I was used to it now. I had my collar up, the way Frank Minna would. The sky out past the island was gray and uninspiring, but there was a nice line of light where it met the water, an edge I could work with my eyes like a seam of stitching between my fingers. The birds harassed the foam below, looking for urchin, perhaps, or discarded hot-dog ends among the rocks.

I had Tony's gun in my jacket, and from this vantage we could see for miles down Route 1 in both directions should anyone approach. I had a strong urge to protect Julia, to hold her or cover her with my presence, so as to feel that I'd helped someone safely through besides myself. But I doubted that the Fujisaki Corporation cared about me or Julia directly. She and I each had been part of Gerard Minna's problem, not Fujisaki's. And Julia showed no interest in my protective urges.

"I know what happened next," I told her. "Eventually the

brothers dipped into the till again. Frank got involved in a scam to siphon money away from Fujisaki's management company." That part of what Gerard told me wasn't a lie, I understood now, just an artfully mangled version of the truth. Gerard had been leaving himself out of it, playing the Zen innocent, when in fact he was the wheel's hub. "With a bookkeeper named – *Dullbody, Allmoney, Alimony* – ah, a guy named Ullman."

"Yes," said Julia.

She'd been talking in a kind of trance, not needing me to prompt her more than once in a while. As the narrative got nearer the present day her eyes grew clearer, her gaze less transfixed on the distant island, and her voice grew heavier with resentment. I felt I was losing her to bitterness, and I wanted to draw her back. Protect her from herself if there was no other threat.

"So Frank was hiding the secret of his brother's existence from The Clients," I said. "Meanwhile the two of them are running a number on Gerard's Japanese partners. And then the deal goes – *lemongrass, sourball, fuckitall!*" I was unable to continue until I made a farting, fricative sound into the wind – "blew a raspberry," in the parlance – to satisfy the expulsive tic. Bits of saliva spattered back into my face. "Then Fujisaki figured out someone was taking their money," I said finally, wiping at myself with my sleeve.

She looked at me with disgust. I'd drawn her back, in a way. "Yes," she said.

"And Gerard fingered – *Mr. Fingerphone! Uncle Sourgrass!* – Gerard fingered Frank and Ullman to save himself."

"That's what Tony thought," she said, distant again.

"Fujisaki must have told Gerard to take care of it, as a show of good faith. So Gerard hired the killer."

Which was where I, innocent stooge, had walked into the story. Frank Minna had installed me and Gilbert there outside the Zendo two days before because he smelled a rat, didn't trust Gerard, and wanted some backup on the street. Warm bodies. If something went wrong he'd bring me and Gilbert up to speed, let us in on the scam, or so he must have thought. And if things went smoothly, it was better to keep us where we'd always been, were born to be – in the dark.

"You know more about it than me," said Julia. She grew agitated now, her storyteller's reverie dissipated, the talk turning to a killer's hiring and all that went with it unsaid. I had to turn away myself now, imitate her pensive searching of the horizon, though my fingers danced idiotically on the lighthouse tower rail, counting one-two-three-four-five, one-two-three-four-five. I'd grown more accustomed to her short new haircut, but those eyes of hers had blazed so long from behind a curtain of hair that without that curtain they blazed too hard. I was drawn and repelled at once, antic with ambivalence. Now I understood that when Frank showed her to us at the end of high school, she was only five or six years older than we were, though it seemed he'd plucked a woman off a fading movie poster. How Nantucket and Buddhism could have made her so old and fierce, I couldn't fathom. I suppose Frank himself had made her old in a hurry, in ways he'd intended, with panty hose and peroxide and sarcasm – and ways he hadn't.

"Let me work out the next part," I said. I felt as if I were trying to get through a joke without ticcing, but there wasn't a punch line in sight. "After Frank and Ullman were gone, Gerard had to make sure he eliminated any link between himself and Frank Minna. That meant you and Tony."

Gerard, I surmised, had been in a panic, afraid of Fujisaki and The Clients both. By having his brother killed he'd damaged a delicate system of controls, one that had kept him safe from Matricardi and Rockaforte for more than a decade. And Fujisaki had announced a visit to New York to inspect their holdings, to enact a little hands-on management (albeit disguised as monks), right as Gerard was frantically trying to mop up the mess. Perhaps they'd also wanted to see Gerard mop up the mess, wanted to feel him squirm a little.

Gerard had reasoned rightly that if Frank confided in anyone it would be his wife and his right-hand man, his groomed successor. Which was to say, Tony. This last part still came a little hard for me. That Tony had paid with his life for being Frank's intimate was a lousy excuse for consolation.

"It was Gerard who called to say that Frank was dead," I suggested. "Not the hospital."

She turned and looked at me with her teeth gritted, tears

making glossy tracks on her face. "Very good, Lionel," she whispered. I reached for her cheeks to blot her tears with my sleeve, but she darted back, uninterested in my care.

"But you didn't trust him, so you ran."

"Don't be an idiot, Lionel," she said, her voice vibrant with hate. "Why would I come here if I were hiding from *Gerard*?"

"*Idiot Dressfork! Alphabet Tuningfreak!*" I cleared the tic with a jerk of my stiff neck. "I don't understand," I told her.

"He arranged for me to use this as a safe house. He said the people who killed Frank were looking for the rest of us. I trusted him."

I began to see. Lucius Seminole had said that Julia's records showed a series of visits to Boston. "This was your hideaway when you got angry at Frank," I suggested. "Your retreat into the past."

"I wasn't hiding."

"Did Frank know that you and Gerard were in touch?"

"He didn't care."

"Were you and Gerard still lovers?"

"Only when his . . . *spiritual path* allowed it." She spat the words. The tears had dried on her face.

"When did you figure out the truth?"

"I called Tony. We compared notes. Gerard underestimated what Tony knew."

What Tony knew was the least of it, I thought. Tony meant to take over Frank Minna's share of the Fujisaki scam, not knowing that nothing remained to take over. He wanted that and much more. As I ached always to be a virtuous detective, Tony ached to be a corrupt one, or even to be an out-and-out wiseguy. He'd been fitting himself for the darkest shoes in Frank Minna's wardrobe from the moment he learned they existed, perhaps on that day when we unloaded the guitars and amplifiers and were introduced to Matricardi and Rock-aforte, perhaps even sooner, on some uglier errand only he and Frank knew about. Certainly he understood by the time Frank's van windows had been smashed. His special glee that day was at having his Mafioso fantasies confirmed, as well as at seeing Frank Minna's vulnerability for the first time. If Frank's fortunes could rise and fall, that episode said, then power was fluid, and so Tony might someday have a share of it himself. The moment Frank was dead Tony envisioned himself playing Frank on both stages, for The Clients in Brooklyn and for Gerard and the Fujisaki Corporation up in Yorkville, only playing the part with greater efficiency and brutality, without Frank Minna's goofy edges, those soft places that caused him to collect freaks like me or that finally led him astray.

Gerard's picture of Tony was another part of that convoluted after-hours story that hadn't been entirely a lie. I suppose Gerard couldn't be the many things he was without knowing how to x-ray a mind like Tony's at a single glance.

"You and Tony compared more than notes, Julia." I regretted it the minute I said it.

She looked at me with pity now.

"So I fucked him." She took out a cigarette and lighter from her purse. "I fucked a lot of guys, Lionel. I fucked Tony and Danny, even Gilbert once. Everyone except you. It's no big deal." She put the cigarette in her lips and cupped her hands against the wind.

"Maybe it was to Tony," I said, and regretted it even worse.

She only shrugged, worked the lighter uselessly again and again. Cars whirred past on the highway below, but nobody stopped at the lighthouse. We were alone in our torment and shame, and useless to each other.

It might not have been a big deal to Julia that she fucked the Minna Men, the Minna Boys, really, and maybe it was no big deal to Tony either – but I doubted it. *You were the original woman*, I wanted to tell her. When Minna brought you home to us we tried to learn what it meant for Frank to marry, we studied you to understand what a Minna Woman might be, and saw only rage – rage I now understood had concealed disappointment and fear, oceans of fear. We had watched women and letters soar past before, but you were the first that was addressed to us, and we tried to understand you. And we loved you.

I needed to rescue Julia now, retrieve her from this lighthouse and the bareness of her story against the Maine sky. I needed her to see that we were the same, disappointed lovers of Frank Minna, abandoned children.

"We're almost the same age, Julia," I said lamely. "I mean,

you and me, we were teenagers at pretty much the same time."

She looked at me blankly.

"I met a woman, Julia. Because of this case. She's like you in certain ways. She studies Zen, just like you did when you met Frank."

"No woman will ever want you, Lionel."

"*WantmeBailey!*"

It was a classic tic, honest and clean. Nothing about Maine or Julia Minna or my profound exhaustion could get in the way of a good, clean, throat-wrenching tic. My maker in his infinite wisdom had provided me with that.

I tried not to listen to what Julia was saying, to focus on the far-off squalling of gulls and splash of surf instead.

"That's not really true," she went on. "They might want you. I've wanted you a little bit myself. But they'll never be fair to you, Lionel. Because you're such a freak."

"This person is different," I said. "She's different from anyone I've ever met." But now I was losing my point. If I made the distinction between Julia and Kimmery plain to Julia, to myself – *she's not as mean as you, could never be so mean* – I would only be sorry I'd spoken at all.

"Well, I bet you're different for her, too. I'm sure you'll be very happy together." In her mouth the words *happy together* came out twisted and harsh.

Crappy however.

Slappy forget her.

I wanted to call Kimmery now, wanted to so badly my fingers located the cell phone in my jacket pocket and began to fondle it.

"Why was Tony coming to Maine?" I asked, running for cover back to the plot we'd begun spinning together, which suddenly seemed to have little or nothing to do with our miserable fates, our miserable lives exposed out here in the wind. "Why didn't you just get away from here? You knew Gerard might kill you."

"I heard Fujisaki was flying up here today." Again she struck with the lighter against her cigarette, as if it were going to ignite like a flint against a rock. It wasn't just the wind she was fighting now. Her hands trembled, and the cigarette trembled where she held it in her lips. "Tony and I were going to tell them about Gerard. He was going to bring some proof. Then you got in the way."

"It wasn't me that stopped Tony from keeping the date." I was distracted by the phone in my pocket, the prospect of Kimmery's soothing voice, even if it were only the outgoing message on her machine. "Gerard sent his giant after Tony," I went on. "He followed Tony up here, maybe figuring to take out two birds with one flick of his big finger."

"Gerard didn't want me killed," she said quietly. Her hands had fallen to her sides. "He wanted me back." She was trying to make it so by saying it, but the words themselves were nearly lost in the wind. Julia threatened to recede into the distance again, and this time I knew I wouldn't bother trying to bring her back.

"Is that why he had his brother killed? Jealousy?"

"Does it have to be one thing? He probably figured it was him or Frank." The cigarette still dangled in her mouth. "Fujisaki required a sacrifice. They're great believers in that."

"Did you talk to Fujisaki just now?"

"Men like that don't cut deals with waitresses, Lionel."

"It's rotten for Tony the killer found him before he found Fujisaki," I said. "But it won't save Gerard. I made sure of that." I didn't want to elaborate.

"So you say." She paced away from the railing, gripping the lighter so tightly I expected her to crush it.

"What's that supposed to mean?"

"Just that I'm not acquainted with this giant killer you keep talking about. Are you sure you're not imagining things?" She turned and handed me the lighter, plucked the cigarette from her lips and held it out. "Would you light this for me, Lionel?" I heard a weird vibration in her voice, as though she were about to cry again, but without the anger this time, maybe begin to mourn Minna at last. I took them away from her, put the cigarette in my own lips, and turned my back to the wind.

By the time I had it lit she'd taken her gun from her purse.

* * *

I put up my hands instinctively, dropping the lighter, to make a pose of surrender but also of self-protection, as though I might deflect a bullet with Frank's watch like Wonder Woman with her magic wristbands. Julia held the gun easily, its muzzle directed at my navel, and now her eyes were as gray and hard to read as the farthest reaches of the Maine horizon.

I felt jets of acid fire in the pit of my stomach. I wondered if I would ever get used to facing gunpoint, and then I wondered if that was really anything to aspire to. I wanted to tic just for the hell of it, but at the moment I couldn't think of anything.

"I just remembered something Frank once said about you, Lionel."

"What's that?" I slowly lowered one hand and offered her the lit cigarette, but she shook her head. I dropped it on the lighthouse deck and ground it under my shoe instead.

"He said the reason you were useful to him was because you were so crazy everyone thought you were stupid."

"I'm familiar with the theory."

"I think I made the same mistake," she said. "And so did Tony, and Frank before that. Everywhere you go, somebody who Gerard wants dead is made dead. I don't want to be next."

"You think I killed Frank?"

"You said we're the same age, Lionel. You ever watch *Sesame Street*?" she said.

"Sure."

"You remember the Snuffleupagus?"

"Big Bird's friend."

"Right, only nobody could see him except Big Bird. I think the giant's your Snuffleupagus, Lionel."

"*Shockadopalus! Fuckalotofus!* The giant is real, Julia. Put the gun away."

"I don't think so. Step back, Lionel."

I stepped back, but I pulled out Tony's gun as I did it. I saw Julia's fingers tighten as I raised it to her, but she didn't fire, and neither did I.

We faced one another on the lighthouse rail, the vast sky dimming everywhere and perfectly useless to us, the ocean's depths useless, too. The two guns drew us close together and rendered the rest irrelevant – we might as well have been in a dingy motel room, with an image of Maine playing on the television set. My moment had come at last. I had a gun in my hands. That it was trained not on Gerard or the giant or Tony or a doorman but on the girl from Nantucket who'd grown into Frank Minna's bruise-eyed widow, who'd chopped off her hair and tried to retreat to her waitress past and instead been cornered by that same past, by Gerard and the giant and Tony – I tried not to let it bother me. I'd been wrong, Julia and I had nothing in common. We were just any two people who happened to be pointing guns at one another now. And Tony's gun had object properties all its own, not a fork nor a toothbrush but something much weightier and more seductive. I slipped off the safety with my thumb.

"I understand your mistake, Julia, but I'm not the killer."

She had both hands on the gun, and it didn't waver. "Why should I trust you?"

"*TRUST ME BAILEY!*" I had to scream it into the sky. I turned my head, bargaining with my Tourette's that I could let the one phrase fly and then be done. I tasted salt air as I screamed.

"Don't scare me, Lionel. I might shoot you."

"We've both got that same problem, Julia." In fact my syndrome had just discovered the prospect of the gun, and I began to obsess on pulling the trigger. I suspected that if I fired a shot out into the sky in the manner of my verbal exclamation, I might not survive the experience. But I didn't want to shoot Julia. I flicked on the safety, hoped she didn't notice.

"Where do we go from here?" she said.

"We go home, Julia," I said. "I'm sorry about Frank and Tony, but the story's over. You and me, we made it through alive."

It was only a slight exaggeration. The story would be over at some secret moment in the next few hours or days when something found Gerard Minna, a bullet or blade that had been searching for him for almost twenty years.

Meanwhile, I flicked the safety back and forth, impelled, counting. At five I stopped, temporarily satisfied. That left the safety off, the gun ready to shoot. My fingers were unbearably curious about the trigger's action, its resistance and weight.

"Where's your home, Lionel? Upstairs from L and L?"

"*Saint Vengeance Home for Bailey*," I ticced.

"Is that what you call it?" said Julia.

Before my finger could pulse on the trigger the way it craved to I flung the gun out toward the ocean with all the force of my overwound-watchspring body. It sailed out past the rocks, but the tiny splash of its disappearance into the sea was lost in the wind and the ambient crash of the surf.

One, I counted.

Before Julia could calculate the meaning of my action I darted as if for an elusive shoulder and grabbed the muzzle of her gun, then twisted it out of her hand and hurled with all the strength in my legs, like a center fielder deep at the wall straining for a distant cutoff man. Julia's gun went farther than Tony's, out to where the waves that would reach the rocks were just taking shape, the sea curling, discovering its form.

That made *two*.

"Don't hurt me, Lionel." She backed away, her shocked eyes framed by the bristly halo of her crew cut, her mouth crooked with fear and fury.

"It's over, Julia. Nobody's going to hurt you." I couldn't concentrate on her fully, needing something more to throw into the sea. I pulled Minna's beeper out of my pocket. It was a tool of The Clients, evidence of their hold on Frank, and it deserved to be interred with the guns. I threw it as far as I could, but it didn't have enough heft to keep from being knocked down by the wind, and so trickled down between two wet, mossy boulders.

Three.

Next I found the cell phone. The instant it came into my hand, Kimmery's number begged for dialing. I pushed the impulse aside, substituted the gratification of flinging it off the lighthouse deck, picturing the doormen in the rental car who I'd taken it from. It flew truer than the beeper, made it out to the water.

Four.

"Give me something to throw," I told Julia.

"What?"

"I need something, one more thing."

"You're crazy."

I considered Frank's watch. I was sentimental about the watch. It had no taint of doormen or Clients.

"Give me something," I said again. "Look in your purse."

"Go to hell, Lionel."

Julia had always been the hardest-boiled of us all, it struck me now. We who were from Brooklyn, we jerks from nowhere – or from somewhere, in the case of Frank and Gerard. We couldn't hold a candle to the girl from Nantucket and I thought I might finally understand why. She was the hardest-boiled because she was the unhappiest. She was maybe the unhappiest person I'd ever met.

I suppose losing Frank Minna, hard as it was, was easier for those of us who'd actually had him, actually felt his love. The thing Julia lost she'd never possessed in the first place.

But her pain was no longer my concern.

You choose your battles, Frank Minna used to say, though the term was hardly original to him.

You also distance yourself from cruelty, if you have any brains. I was developing a few.

I took off my right shoe, felt the polished leather that had served me well, the fine stitching and the fraying lace, kissed it good-bye on the top of the tongue, then threw it high and far and watched it splash silently into the waves.

Five, I thought.

But who's counting?

"Good-bye, Julia," I said.

"Screw you, you maniac." She knelt and picked up her lighter, and this time she got her cigarette lit on the first flick.

"Barnabaileyscrewjuliaminna."

It was my final word on the subject.

So I drove with my gas-pedal-and-brake foot clad only in a dress sock, back to Brooklyn.

GOOD SANDWICHES

THEN SOMEWHERE, SOMETIME, a circuit closed. It was a secret from me, but I knew the secret existed. A man – two men? – found another man. Lifted an instrument, gun, knife? Say gun. Did a job. Took care of a job. Collected a debt of life. This was the finishing of something between two brothers, a transaction of brotherly love-hate, something playing out, a dark, wobbly melody. The notes of the melody had been other people, boys-turned-Minna Men, mobsters, monks, doormen. And women, one woman especially. We'd all been notes in the melody, but the point of the song was the brothers, and the payoff, the last note struck – a scream? a bloody beat? a bare interrupted moan? – or not even a moan, perhaps. In my guilt I'd like to think so. Let it finish in silence. Let it be, then, that Rama-lama-ding-dong died in his sleep.

* * *

We sat together in the L&L storefront at two in the morning, playing poker on the counter, listening to Boyz 2 Men, courtesy of Danny. Now that Frank and Tony were gone, Danny could play the sort of music he liked. It was one of a number of changes.

"One card," said Gilbert. I was the dealer, so I slid his discard toward me and offered him a fresh selection from the top of the deck.

"Jesus, Gil," said the ex-Garbage Cop. He was a driver now, a part of the new L&L. "You're always *one card* or *no cards* – why can't I get dealt anything but crap?"

"That's 'cause you're still in charge of garbage, Loomis," said Gilbert happily. "Even though you quit the force, doesn't matter. Someone's gotta handle it."

"*Handle with garbagecrap!*" I declared as I dealt myself three new cards.

Gilbert had been released two weeks before, after five nights in the lockup, for want of evidence in Ullman's killing. Detective Seminole had called us to apologize, excessively sheepish, I thought, as though he were still a little afraid. Gilbert's size and manner had carried him through the ordeal pretty well, though he came out short a wristwatch and had involuntarily given up smoking during his stay, having been connived out of every cigarette on his person. He was making up for it now in cigarettes, and in beer and coffee and Sno Balls and White Castles and Zeod's pastrami heroes, but no flow of indulgences could be constant enough to stem his complaints at how we'd abandoned him. Fortunately he was winning hands tonight.

Danny sat apart from the three of us, silent, eyebrows raised slightly between his poker hand and his new fedora. He sat a little farther apart and dressed a little sharper each passing night, or so it seemed to me. Leadership of L&L had fallen to him like an easy rebound, one he didn't even have to jump for, while the other players boxed and elbowed and sweated on the wrong part of the floor. What Danny knew or didn't know about Gerard and Fujisaki was never said. He took my account of the events in Maine and nodded once, and we were done speaking of it. It turned out it was that simple. Want to be the new Frank Minna? Dress the part, and shut up, and wait. Court Street will know you when it sees you. Zeod will put the tab in your name. Gilbert and Loomis and I couldn't have argued. We were Dapper and the Stooges, it was plain to the eye.

L&L was a detective agency, a clean one for the first time. So clean we didn't have any clients. So we were also a car service, a real one now, one that didn't turn away calls unless we truly were out of cars. Danny was even having flyers printed up, and new business cards, boasting of our economy and efficiency to points all over the boroughs. The Lincoln Minna had bled to death inside was clean now too, part of a small fleet of cars making regular runs between the Cobble Hill Nursing Home on Henry Street and the Promenade Diner at the end of Montague, between the Boerum Hill Inn and stylish apartment buildings along Prospect Park West and Joralemon Street.

As a matter of fact, the Boerum Hill Inn had just closed for the night, and Siobhain was at the door, her eyes dark-circled and her posture rather crushed from the effort of tossing out the tenacious flirting crowd. Gilbert put up a finger to say he'd take the job of driving her home, but first wished to lay his poker hand on the table – it appeared to be one he was particularly proud of. Seeing his recent enthusiasm for chaperoning Siobhain I suspected Gilbert had developed a little crush on her, or maybe it was an old crush he had just allowed to let show, now that Frank wasn't around to needle him constantly that she was playing for the other team.

"Come on, you suckers, I'm calling you," said Gilbert.

"Nothing," said Loomis, bugging his eyes at his hand, trying to embarrass the cards. "Load of crap."

Danny just frowned and shook his head, put his cards on the table. He didn't need poker triumphs just now, he had better things. For all we knew he was folding winning hands just to throw some glory Gilbert's way.

"*Forks and spoons,*" I said, slapping my hand down to show the card faces.

"Jacks and twos?" Gilbert inspected my cards. "That won't do it, Freakshow." He tossed down aces and eights. "Read 'em and scream, like the maniac you are."

*   *   *

Assertions are common to me, and they're also common to detectives. ("About the only part of a California house you can't put your foot through is the front door" – Marlowe, *The Big Sleep.*) And in detective stories things are always *always*, the detective casting his exhausted, caustic gaze over the corrupted permanence of everything and thrilling you with his sweetly savage generalizations. This or that runs deep or true to form, is invariable, exemplary. Oh sure. Seen it before, will see it again. Trust me on this one.

Assertions and generalizations are, of course, a version of Tourette's. A way of touching the world, handling it, covering it with confirming language.

Here's one more. As a great man once said, the more things change, the harder they are to change back.

*   *   *

Within a few days of Gerard's disappearance most of the Yorkville Zendo's students had trickled away. There was a real Zendo on the Upper East Side, twenty blocks south, and its ranks were swelled by defectors from Yorkville seeking truer essences (though, as Kimmery had pointed out, anyone who teaches Zen is a Zen teacher). Those bewildered doormen had all originally been authentic students of Gerard's, it turned out, rudderless seekers, human clay. It was their absolute susceptibility to Gerard's charismatic teachings that made them available to be exploited, first in the Park Avenue building, then as a gang of inept drivers and strong-arms when Gerard needed bodies to fill ranks alongside the Polish giant. Frank Minna had Minna Men while Gerard had only followers, Zen stooges, and that difference might have determined how the case worked out. That might have been my little edge. It pleased me to think so anyway.

The Yorkville Zendo didn't fold, though. Wallace, that stoic sitter, took over stewardship of what flock remained, though he declined to claim the title of Roshi for himself. Instead he asked to be called *sensei*, a lesser term denoting a sort of apprentice-instructor. So it was that each of the Minna organizations, Frank's and Gerard's, were gently and elegantly steered past the shoals of corruption by their quietest disciples. Of course Fujisaki and The Clients, those vast shadows, crept away unharmed, barely even ruffled. It would take more than the Minna brothers or Lionel Essrog to make a lasting impression.

I learned the fate of the Yorkville Zendo from Kimmery the only time I saw her, two weeks after my return from Maine. I'd been leaving messages on her machine, but she hadn't returned my calls until then. We arranged a rendezvous at a coffee shop on Seventy-second Street, our telephone conversation clipped and awkward. Before I left for the date I took the thoroughest shower I knew how to take, then dressed and re-dressed a dozen times, playing mirror games with myself, trying to see something that wasn't there, trying not to see the big twitchy Essrog that was. I suppose I still had a faint notion we could be together.

We talked about the Zendo for a while before she said

anything to suggest she even recalled our night together. And when she did, it was "Do you have my keys?"

I met her eyes and saw she was afraid of me. I tried not to loom or jerk, though there was a Papaya Czar franchise across the street. I was pining for their hot dogs, and it was hard to keep from turning my head.

"Oh, sure," I said. I dropped the keys on the table, glad I hadn't chosen to hurl them into the Atlantic. Instead I'd been burnishing them in my pocket, as I had The Clients' fork once upon a time, each talisman of a world I wouldn't get to visit again. I said good-bye to the keys now.

"I have to tell you something, Lionel." She delivered it with that same hectic half smile that I'd been trying to conjure in my mind's eye for most of two weeks.

"Tellmebailey," I whispered.

"I'm moving back in with Stephen," she said. "So that thing that happened with us, it was just, you know – *a thing*."

So Oreo Man was a cowboy after all, now striding back in from his sunset backdrop.

I opened my mouth and nothing came out.

"You understand, Lionel?"

"Ah." *Understand me, Bailey.*

"Okay?"

"*Okay*," I said. She didn't need to know it was just a tic, just echolalia that made me say it. I reached across the table and smoothed the two ends of her collar toward her small, bony shoulders. "Okayokayokayokayokay," I said under my breath.

* * *

I had a dream about Minna. We were in a car. He was driving.

"Was I in the Butt Trust?" I asked him.

He smiled at me, liking to be quoted, but didn't reply.

"I guess everybody needs stooges," I said, not meaning to make him feel bad.

"I don't know if I'd put you exactly in the Butt Trust category," he said. "You're a little too strange for that."

"So what am I, then?" I asked.

"I don't know, kid. I guess I'd call you King Tugboat."

I must have laughed or at least smiled.

"That's nothing to be proud of, you radish rosette."

* * *

What about vengeance?

I gave it five or ten minutes of my time once. That's a lot, a lifetime, when it comes to vengeance. I had wanted to think vengeance wasn't me, wasn't Tourettic or Essroggian at all. Like the subway, say.

Then I took the V train. I did it with a cell phone and a number in Jersey, I did it standing by a lighthouse in Maine. I did it with a handful of names and other words, strung together into something more effective than a tic. That was me, Lionel, hurtling through those subterranean tunnels, visiting the labyrinth that runs under the world, which everyone pretends is not there.

You can go back to pretending if you like. I know I will, though the Minna brothers are a part of me, deep in my grain, deeper than mere behavior, deeper even than regret, Frank because he gave me my life and Gerard because, though I hardly knew him, I took his away.

I'll pretend I never rode that train, but I did.

* * *

The next call that came in that night was a pickup on Hoyt Street for a trip out to Kennedy Airport. It was Loomis who took the call, and he grimaced exaggeratedly when he offered it to the three of us, knowing that according to L&L lore JFK was an exasperating destination. I put up my hand and said I'd take it, just to deny him the point.

For another reason, too. There was a snack I had a hankering for. At the International Terminal at Kennedy, upstairs by the El Al gates, is a single kosher-food stand called Mushy's, run by a family of Israelis, with sauce-spattered metal tins full of stewing kasha and gravy and handmade knishes, a place utterly unlike the chain restaurants elsewhere in the terminal. Anytime I took a passenger out to the airport, night or day, I'd park the car and slip up to Mushy's for a bite. Their chicken shwarma, carved fresh off the roasting pin, stuffed into a pita and slathered in grilled peppers, onions and tahini is one of the great secret sandwiches of New York, redemption for a whole soulless airport. Permit me to recommend it if you're ever out that way.

Kimmery and lemongrass broth hadn't ruined my taste for the finer things.

*   *   *

The ghosts I felt sorriest for weren't the dead ones. I'd imagined Frank and Tony were mine to protect, but I'd been wrong. I knew it now.

It was Julia I couldn't shrug off, though she was hardly more mine than the others, though she'd barely recognized my human existence. Still, my tic of guilt took the form of her shape, standing in the wind on the lighthouse rail, standing still in a mist of bullets and shoes and salt air and my saliva, like the cursed icon from a black-and-white-movie poster she'd resembled when first glimpsed so long ago, or perhaps a figure of Zen contemplation, a mark of ink brushwork on a scroll. But I didn't try to find Julia – simple as it would have been, I knew better than that. Instead I let my obsessive instinct get to work tracing that figure, waiting for it to turn abstract and disappear. Sooner or later it would.

That left who? Only Ullman. I know he haunts this story, but he never came into view, did he? The world (my brain) is too full of dull men, dead men, Ullmen. Some ghosts never even get into your house they are so busy howling at the windows. Or as Minna would say, you pick your battles – and you do, whether you subscribe to that view or not, you really do. I can't feel guilty about every last body. Ullman? Never met the guy. Just like Bailey. They were just guys I never happened to meet. To the both of them and to you I say: Put an egg in your shoe, and beat it. Make like a tree, and leave. Tell your story walking.

ACKNOWLEDGMENTS

I'm deeply indebted to the books of Lawrence Shainberg, Kosho Uchiyma, and Oliver Sacks, the words of Tuli Kupferberg, and to conversations with Blake Lethem, Cara O'Connor, David Bowman, Eliot Duhan, Matthew Burkhardt, Scott McCrossin, Janet Farrell, Diane Martel, Alice Ressner, and Maureen Linker and the Linker family.

Thanks also to Richard Parks, Bill Thomas, Walter Donohue, Zoe Rosenfeld, Tooley Cottage, the Zentrum für Kunst und Medientechnologie (ZKM) and the Corporation of Yaddo.

The name Saint Vincent's is here used fictionally and is in no way meant to impugn the venerable charitable institution nor the venerated saint of the same name.

THE FORTRESS
OF SOLITUDE

For Mara Faye

PART ONE
UNDERBERG

CHAPTER 1

LIKE A MATCH struck in a darkened room:

Two white girls in flannel nightgowns and red vinyl roller skates with white laces, tracing tentative circles on a cracked blue slate sidewalk at seven o'clock on an evening in July.

The girls murmured rhymes, *were* murmured rhymes, their gauzy, sky-pink hair streaming like it had never once been cut. The girls' parents had permitted them back onto the street after dinner, only first changing into the gowns and brushing their teeth for bed, to bask in the orange-pink summer dusk, the air and light which hung over the street, over all of Gowanus like the palm of a hand or the inner surface of a seashell. The Puerto Rican men seated on milk crates in front of the bodega on the corner grunted at the apparition, not sure of what they were seeing. They widened their lips to show one another their teeth, a display to mark patience, wordless enduring. The street strewn with bottle caps half-pushed into the softened tar, Yoo-Hoo, Rheingold, Manhattan Special.

The girls, Thea and Ana Solver, shone like a new-struck flame.

An old white woman had arrived on the block before the Solvers, to reclaim one of the abused buildings, one which had been a rooming house, replacing fifteen men with only herself and her crated belongings. She was actually the first. But Isabel Vendle only lurked like a rumor, like an apostrophe inside her brownstone, where at this moment she crept with a cane between the basement apartment and her bedroom in the old parlor on the first floor, to that room where she read and slept under the crumbled, unrestored plaster ceiling. Isabel Vendle was a knuckle, her body curled around the gristle of old injuries. Isabel Vendle remembered a day in a packet boat on Lake George, she scratched letters with a pen dipped in ink, she pushed stamps against a sponge in a dish. Her desktop was cork. Isabel Vendle had money but her basement rooms stank of rinds, damp newspaper.

The girls on wheels were the new thing, spotlit to start the show: white people were returning to Dean Street. A few.

Under the ailanthus tree in the backyard Dylan Ebdus at five accidentally killed a kitten. The Ebduses' tenants in the basement apartment had a litter of them, five, six, seven. They squirmed on the ground there, in that upright cage of brick walls, among the rubble and fresh-planted vines and the musky ailanthus sheddings, where Dylan played and explored alone while his mother turned over ground with a small trident or sat smoking while the couple downstairs sang together, one strumming a peace-sign-stickered, untuned guitar. Dylan danced with the tiny, razor-sharp, bug-eyed cats, chased them into the slug-infested brick pile, and on the second day, backpedaling from one of the cats, crushed another with his sneakered foot.

Those basement tenants took the kitten away broken but alive while Dylan, crying, was hustled off by his parents. But Dylan understood that the kitten was mercifully finished somehow, smothered or drowned. Somehow. He asked, but the subject was smothered too. The adults tipped their hand only in that instant of discovery, letting Dylan glimpse their queasy anger, then muted it away. Dylan was too young to understand what he'd done, except he wasn't; they hoped he'd forget, except he didn't. He'd later pretend to forget, protecting the adults from what he was sure they couldn't handle: his remembering entirely.

Possibly the dead kitten was the insoluble lozenge of guilt he'd swallowed.

Or possibly it was this: his mother told him someone wanted to play with him, on the sidewalk across the street. Out front. It would be his first time to go out on the block, to play *out front* instead of in the brick-moldy backyard.

"Who?"

"A little girl," said his mother. "Go see, Dylan."

Maybe it was the white girls, Ana and Thea in their nightgowns and skates. He'd seen them from the window, now they were calling to him.

Instead it was a black girl, Marilla, who waited on the sidewalk. Dylan at six recognized a setup when he saw one, felt his

mother's city craftiness, her native's knowledge. Rachel Ebdus
was working the block, matchmaking for him.

Marilla was older. Marilla had a hoop and some chalk. The
walk in front of Marilla's gate – her share of the irregular slate
path was her zone – marked. This was Dylan's first knowledge
of the system that organized the space of the block. He would
never step into Marilla's house, though he didn't know that
now. The slate was her parlor. He had his own, though he
hadn't marked it yet.

"You moved here?" said Marilla when she was sure Dylan's
mother had gone inside.

Dylan nodded.

"You live in that whole house?"

"Tenants downstairs."

"You got an apartment?"

Dylan nodded again, confused.

"You got a brother or sister?"

"No."

"What your father does?"

"He's an artist," said Dylan. "He's making a film." He
offered it with maximum gravity. It didn't make much of an
impression on Marilla.

"You got a spaldeen?" she said. "That's a ball, if you don't
understand."

"No."

"You got any money on you?"

"No."

"I want to buy some candy. I could buy you a spaldeen.
Could you ask your mother for some money?"

"I don't know."

"You know skully?"

Dylan shook his head. Was skully a person or another kind
of ball or candy? He couldn't know. He felt that Marilla might
begin to pity him.

"We could make skully caps. You could make them with
gum or wax. You got a candle in your house?"

"I don't know."

"We could buy one but you got no money."

Dylan shrugged defensively.

"Your mother told me to cross the street with you. You can't do it yourself." Her tone was philosophical.

"I'm six."

"You're a baby. What kind of a name is Dylan?"

"Like Bob Dylan."

"Who?"

"A singer. My parents like him."

"You like the Jackson Five? You know how to dance?" Marilla laced herself with her hoop, buckled her knees and elbows at once, balled her fists, gritted her teeth, angled her ass. The hoop swung. She grinned and jutted her chin at Dylan in time with her hips, as though she could have swirled another hoop around her neck.

When it was Dylan's turn the hoop clattered to the slate. He was still fat, podlike, Tweedledee. There was no edge on his shape for the hoop to lodge. He could barely span it with his arms. He couldn't duck his knees, instead scuffed sideways, stepping. He couldn't dance.

That was how they played, Dylan dropping the plastic hoop to the ground a thousand times. Marilla sang encouragement, *Oh, baby give me one more chance, I want you back.* She punched the air. And Dylan wondered guiltily why the white girls on skates hadn't called to him instead. Knowledge of this heretical wish was his second wound. It wasn't like the dead kitten: this time no one would judge whether Dylan had understood in the first place, whether he had forgotten after. Only himself. It was between Dylan and himself to consider forever whether to grasp that he'd felt a yearning preference already then, that before the years of seasons, the years of hours to come on the street, before Robert Woolfolk or Mingus Rude, before "Play That Funky Music, White Boy," before Intermediate School 293 or anything else, he'd wished, against his mother's vision, for the Solver girls to sweep him away into an ecstasy of blond-ness and matching outfits, tightened laces, their wheels barely touching the slate, or only marking it with arrows pointing elsewhere, jet trails of escape.

Marilla whirled in place, singing *When I had you to myself I didn't want you around, those pretty faces always seemed to stand out in a crowd—*

*

Isabel Vendle found the name in a tattered, leather-bound volume at the Brooklyn Historical Society: Boerum. As in the Boer War. A Dutch family, farmers, landowners. The Boerums kept their wealth in Bedford-Stuyvesant, had actually come nowhere near Gowanus, none except a wayward, probably drunken son, named Simon Boerum, who built a house on Schermerhorn Street and died in it. He'd been exiled here, perhaps, a prodigal, a black sheep sleeping off a long bender. Anyway, he'd lend his name – he wasn't about to say no! – to the band of streets laced between Park Slope and Cobble Hill, because Gowanus wouldn't do. Gowanus was a canal and a housing project. Isabel Vendle needed to distinguish her encampment from the Gowanus Houses, from Wyckoff Gardens, that other housing project which hemmed in her new paradise, distinguish it from the canal, from Red Hook, Flatbush; from downtown Brooklyn, where the Brooklyn House of Detention loomed, the monolith on Atlantic Avenue, ringed with barbed wire. She was explicating a link to the Heights, the Slope. So, *Boerum Hill*, though there wasn't any hill. Isabel Vendle wrote it and so it was made and so they would come to live in the new place which was inked into reality by her hand, her crabbed hand which scuttled from past to future, Simon Boerum and Gowanus unruly parents giving birth to Boerum Hill, a respectable child.

The houses here were sick. The Dutch-style row houses had been chopped into pieces and misused as rooming houses for men with hot plates and ashtrays and racing forms, or floor-through apartments, where sprawling families of cousins were crammed into each level, their yards and stoops teeming with uncountable children. The houses had been slathered with linoleum and pressed tin, the linoleum and tin had later been painted, the paint painted again. It was like a coating on the tongue and teeth and roof of a mouth. The lines of the rooms, the fine moldings, had been broken by slapdash walls to make hallways, the bathrooms had had Sears Roebuck shower stalls wedged into them, the closets had been turned into kitchens. The hallways had been pissed. These brownstones, these upright Dutch houses, were bodies, bodies abused, but Isabel would make them well again, she'd fill them with couples, renovators who'd replaster the ornate ceilings, refurbish the marble hearths. She'd already lured a few. The first renovators were motley, truth be told. Disappointing to her, the beatniks who came, the hippies making communes little better than rooming houses. But someone had to be first. They were Isabel's ragged first recruits, not good, only good enough.

For instance Abraham and Rachel Ebdus. The encountered reality of a marriage was always wearying to Isabel. She, Rachel, was wild-eyed, chain-smoking, too young, too *Brooklyn*, actually. Isabel had seen her talking Spanish to the men on the crates on the corner. That wasn't going to solve anything. And he, Abraham, was a painter, splendid – but need the walls of the house be filled top-to-bottom with nude portraits of his wife? Need the paintings in the front parlor sometimes be visible from the corner of Dean and Nevins, scumbled flesh beaming past half-drawn curtains?

Wife supported husband, working half days at a desk at the Department of Motor Vehicles on Schermerhorn Street. Talking Spanish to the undershirts who polished cars in front of rooming houses.

While the husband stayed home and painted.

They had a boy.

Isabel tore a thread of smoked turkey from the periphery of her dry sandwich and draped it across the orange cat's incurious nose, until the doltish thing fathomed what was offered and engaged it with clacking, machinelike teeth.

There were two worlds. In one his father paced upstairs, creaked chairs, painting at his tiny light box, making his incomprehensible progress, his mother downstairs played records, ran water over dishes, laughed on the telephone, her voice trailing up the curve of the long stair, the backyard ailanthus brushed his bedroom windows, dappling the sun into tropical, liquid blobs of light against the wallpaper which itself depicted a forest full of monkeys and tigers and giraffes, while Dylan read and reread *Scrambled Eggs Super* and *Oobleck* and *If I Ran the Zoo* or pushed his Matchbox car, #11, dreamily with one finger down its single length of orange track or exposed the inadequacy

of the Etch A Sketch and the Spirograph again, the stiffness of
the knobs, the recalcitrance of the silvery ingredient behind the
Etch A Sketch's smeared window, the untrustworthiness of
the Spirograph's pins, the way they invariably bent at perihelion when the pressure of the drawing pen grew too much, so
that every deliciously scientific orbit blooped and bent at the
crucial moment into a ragged absurdity, a head with a nose,
a pickle with a wart. If the Etch A Sketch and the Spirograph
had really worked they would probably be machines, not toys,
they would be part of the way the adult universe operated, and
be mounted onto the instrument panels of cars or worn on the
belts of policemen. Dylan understood and accepted this. These
things were broken because they were toys, and vice versa.
They required his pity and patience, like retarded children
who'd been entrusted to his care.

In his indoor world Dylan could float in one of two directions. One was upstairs, grasping at the loose, rattling banister,
sliding his small hand around a portion of its burnished smooth-
ness, then hopping his fingers over the gapped joints, to knock
on the studio door and be permitted to stand at his father's
elbow and try to watch what couldn't be watched, the incomprehensible progress of an animated film painted by single
brushstrokes directly onto celluloid. For Abraham Ebdus had
renounced painting on canvas. The canvases which filled the
halls, those lavish, painterly nudes, were his apprentice work,
the sentimental traces of his progress toward what had become
his lifework, an abstract painting unfolding in time, in the form
of painted frames of film. Abraham Ebdus had perhaps finished
two minutes of this film. There was nothing to show except
the sketches and notes pinned to the walls where the canvases
had been before. The large brushes were all stiffened and dry
in cans. They'd been replaced with brushes like those a jeweler uses to smooth away diamond dust, and in that third-story
studio where window fans whirred, pushing the yellow August
sky in to dry the paint, Abraham Ebdus hunched like a jeweler,
or a monk copying scrolls, and licked with the tiny brushes at
his celluloid frames, his work grown reverent and infinitesimal.
Dylan stood at his side and smelled the paint, the thin acrid
plume of freshly mixed pigment. He was at the height of the

light table on which his father painted, his eyes level and close, and he wondered if his tiny hands might be more suited to the work than his father's. Bored after a while, he'd sit cross-legged on the floor and draw with his father's abandoned oil crayons, carefully unpacking them from the metal tin with the French label. Or run his Matchbox car, #11, along the painted floor-boards. Or wrestle open an enormous book of reproductions, tipped-in plates, Brueghel or Goya or Manet or Di Chirico, and become lost, briefly dreaming himself into a window in the Tower of Babel or a circle of witches sitting with a goat beside a campfire at night or a line of boys with sprouted branches chasing pigs across a brook. In Brueghel and Di Chirico he found children playing with hoops like Marilla's and wondered if he might be allowed to turn her hula on its side and run it down Dean Street with a stick. But the girl with the hoop and the stick on the lonely street in Di Chirico had flowing hair like the Solver girls, so never mind.

"That looks the same," Dylan said, watching his father finish a frame, turn to the next.

"It changes very slightly."

"I can't see."

"You will in time."

Time, he'd been told, would speed up. Days would fly. They didn't fly there, on the floor of his father's studio, but they would. They'd fly, the film would speed up and run together so fast it would appear to move, summer would end, he'd be in school, he was *growing up so fast*, that was the consensus he alone couldn't consent to, mired as he felt himself to be, utterly drowning in time there on the studio floor, gazing into Brue-ghel, searching for the other children among the dogs under the banquet table at the feet of the millers and their wives. Retreat-ing from his father's studio he'd count the whining stairs.

Downstairs was another problem entirely. His mother's spaces – the parlor full of her books and records, the kitchen where she cooked food and laughed and argued on the phone, her table full of newspapers and cigarettes and wineglasses – were for Dylan full of unpredictability and unrest, like his mother herself. Mornings she was gone to Schermerhorn Street where she worked. Then Dylan could dwell in the downstairs like a ghost, curling over his own books or in a sun-dazzled nap on the couch, eating leftovers from the fridge or spoonfuls of dry cocoa powder directly from the tin so that his mouth became thick with a clay of cocoa, examining the half-finished cross-word on the table, running his Matchbox car, #11, through the ashtrays or around the rim of the pot that housed the gigantic jade plant, which with its thick, rubbery, treelike limbs was another world for Dylan's specklike self to adventure in and be lost. Then, always before he could compose himself or decide what he wanted from her, Rachel Ebdus would be home, and Dylan would discover that he did not control his mother. Dylan's solitude which his father left unbruised his mother burst like a grape. She might clutch him and with fingers kneading his skull through his hair say, "You're so beautiful, so beautiful, you're such a beautiful boy" or just as likely sit apart from him smoking a cigarette and say, "Where did you come from? Why are you here? Why am I here?" or "You know, precious child, that your father is insane." Frequently she would show him a magazine with a picture labeled CAN YOU DRAW SPARKY? and say, "That would be easy for you, if you wanted you could win this contest." When Rachel wanted to fry an egg she'd ask Dylan to stand beside her, then crack the egg on his head and hurry it into the frying pan before it spilled. He'd rub his head, half hurt, half in love. She played him Beatles records, *Sgt. Pepper*, *Let It Be*, then asked which was his favorite Beatle.

"Ringo."

"Children like Ringo," she told him. "Boys do. Girls like Paul. He's sexy. You'll understand."

She might be crying or laughing or cleaning up a broken dish or clipping the nails of the cats who lived in the backyard, the two who'd stayed from the litter downstairs and had grown and now killed birds regularly among the bricks and vines. "See," she'd say, squeezing the cat's paw to extend its claws, "you can't clip them too close, there's a blood vessel there, they'll bleed to death." She was wild with information he couldn't yet use: Nixon was a criminal, the Dodgers moved to California, Chinese food gives you a headache, Muhammad Ali resisted the war and went to jail, Hitchcock's British films were better than his American ones, circumcision was unnecessary but women

preferred it. She was too full for the house, had to vent herself constantly into the telephone, and too full for Dylan who
instead worked Rachel's margins, dodging her main force to
dip sidelong into what he could make sense of. He might creep
downstairs to slink at her shelves, in the shadows, under the
nudes. There he could pretend to consider her books – *Tropic of
Cancer, Kon-Tiki, Letting Go, Games People Play* – his eyes blur-
ring while he eavesdropped on her calls, calls, ". . . he's upstairs
. . . California never mattered . . . paying all the bills . . . said
the texture of the mushrooms reminded me of something and
he turned bright red . . . playing that Clapton record at four in
the morning . . . completely lost my French . . ." Alternately,
Dylan tiptoed close under the cover of Rachel's monologue,
thinking it was another phone call, to find someone seated at
her table instead, drinking iced tea, sharing Rachel's ashtray,
laughing, listening, detecting Dylan's footfalls which Rachel
had ignored.

"There he is," they'd say, as if Dylan were always the topic
just abandoned.

Then he was beckoned to the table to be met. Dylan would
recall the visitors only as Rachel described them later, to Abraham at dinner: the not-brilliant folksinger who'd opened for
Bobby Dylan once and wouldn't let you forget it, the horny
yippie who faced prosecution for stuffing subway turnstiles
with slugs, the rich homosexual who collected art but wouldn't
buy one of Abraham's nudes because they were women, the
radical black minister from Atlantic Avenue who had to scru-
tinize everyone new in the neighborhood, the old boyfriend
who now worked as a piano tuner at Carnegie Hall but might
join the Peace Corps to keep out of Vietnam, the Gurdjieff-
quoting English couple on their way to bicycle across Mexico,
the woman from the Brooklyn Heights consciousness-raising
group who just couldn't believe they'd bought on Dean Street.
So many of them, all reaching for Dylan's head to muss his
hair and ask why Rachel let it grow into his eyes, grow to his
shoulders. Dylan looked like a girl – that was agreed on by
pretty much everyone.

Then – and this was finally always the essential problem
with floating downstairs – Rachel would stir from her chair,

cigarette in her fingers, and usher Dylan to the front door, point out the children playing on the sidewalk, insist that he join them. Rachel had a program, a plan. She had grown up a Brooklyn street kid and so would Dylan. And so she'd eject him from the first of his two worlds, the house, into the second. The outside, the block. Dean Street.

The second world was an arrangement of zones in slate, and the peeling painted fronts of the row houses – pink, white, pale green, various tones of red and blue, always giving way to the brick underneath – those were the flags of undiscovered realms which lay behind and probably determined the system of slate zones. As far as Dylan could tell no kid ever went into another's home. They didn't talk about their parents either. Dylan knew nothing else to talk about, and so drifted silently into the group of children, who seemed to understand this, and vaguely parted their ranks to make room for him. Maybe every kid had drifted in this way.

Nevins and Bond Streets, which bracketed the block at either end, were vents into the unknown, routes to the housing projects down on Wyckoff Street. Anyway, the Puerto Rican men in front of the bodega on Nevins owned the corner. Another group, black men mostly, lingered in the doorway of a rooming house between the Ebduses' and Isabel Vendle's, and they would shoo away the ball-playing boys, yelling at them to watch out for the windshield of a car forever parked in front of the rooming house, a Stingray, which one Puerto Rican man with a waxed mustache frequently polished and rarely drove. Finally, a mean black man who glared but never spoke broomed the slate and scissored weeds in front of two houses close to Bond Street. So the children of Dean Street instinctively bunched in the middle of the block.

Henry was a black kid with a younger brother, Earl, and a front yard which was paved flat instead of a plot of ruined or halfheartedly gardened ground. The low fence dividing Henry's paved housefront from the slate of the sidewalk was stone as well, poured cement. Henry was three years older than Dylan. His stoop and yard formed the meeting point, the base of operations. Older boys from farther down the block would arrive and choose sides. Principally Davey and Alberto from across the street and near the corner, from the house which overflowed with cousins and whose stoop was for teenagers smoking. They'd arrive arms swinging, bouncing a new spaldeen. They'd buy a strawberry Yoo-Hoo and share it and give Henry or Henry's friend Lonnie the cap for skully. Dylan sat with Earl on Henry's stoop and watched. Marilla's fiefdom of black girls was across the street. Dylan never went there after the first time, but words crossed Dean Street between Marilla's yard and Henry's, and the girls sometimes crossed too. Henry's yard was the center and Henry was the center. Henry always chose the game.

Two doors from Henry's was the abandoned house. It wore cinderblock bandages over the windows and doorway like a mummy with blanked eyes and stilled howling mouth, and had a blasted yard with no fence or gate. The stoop was barren too, no rail. Possibly someone had taken the ironwork for scrap. The mummy house was a flat surface with no windows, so it made a high wall for wallball, a game where a spaldeen was bounced high against the wall by a thrower and caught by a catcher standing in the field of the street, zipping between cars to make the catch.

A spaldeen fit a hand perfectly and often seemed to be magnetized there. Henry and Davey in particular seemed only to have to lope a step or two and raise their hand to have a ball appear in their palms. A shot winged off the third floor of the abandoned house flew out the farthest, and one which cleared the gates on the opposite side of the street was a home run. Henry seemed able to do this at will and the fact that he didn't each time was mysterious. Henry could err too, throw too high and roof a spaldeen, and then the groan would go out to buy another, and pocket change was collected. "That's how many up there by now?" mused Alberto one day. "If I could get up there I'd be throwing them down all day."

Dylan and Earl would be sent to visit the bodega and say the pregnant word, *spaldeen*, and Old Ramirez would supply another one suspiciously, resenting the business. Dylan would fondle the newborn pink spaldeen but surrender it instantly to Henry, and likely not touch it again until it was scuffed and enervated, bounced out from a thousand angled hurls. That was if Dylan touched it again at all. His chance came between games, the airy transitions when all arms unexplainedly dropped and someone asked for a suck of someone else's Yoo-Hoo and someone else turned their T-shirt inside out stretched over their elbows, to the laughter of the girls. The spaldeen would roll inert to the gutter and Dylan could retrieve it and marvel at its destruction. Now it deserved roofing. Maybe Henry had a system, like an umpire taking baseballs out of circulation.

The stoop of the abandoned house was also a proscenium stage for secrets, hidden in plain sight in the middle of the block. The broken slate in front of the abandoned house was thirty feet of no-man's-land. Dean Street's trees bunched, like the kids, in the center of the block. They seemed particularly inclined to cover the abandoned house in dappled shade, blobs of light like those thrown by the backyard ailanthus into Dylan's bedroom, and to muffle the sound of parents calling kids' names in for dinner into distant phenomena, like birds' cries. Dylan walked his side of Dean with his head lowered and memorized the slate, could say when he was in front of Henry's or the abandoned house without glancing up, just by the shapes at his feet, the long tilted slabs or the one sticking-up moonlike shape or the patch of concrete or the shattered pothole which always filled with water after those summer thunderstorms which came and instantly broke the humid afternoons into dark, electrified pieces.

Wallball, stickball, stoopball, touch. Henry and Lonnie played Alberto and Davey most afternoons, touch in the street, Puerto Rican against black, two-man football, screaming for a long catch in the stolen time between passing cars and the Dean Street bus. The bus stopped the game the longest, the players pressed impatiently against the doors of parked cars to make room, waving the bus on, faster, faster, go. Don't be afraid of hitting us, they waved at the drivers. Just go, damn, don't watch us, we watch ourselves.

One day Henry slapped the side of the bus hard with his palms, then lay flat in the street as though hit. The big bus ground to a halt and stood pulsing in the middle of the block, passengers craning heads to peer open-mouthed through the windows while the driver stepped out to see. Then Henry stood and laughed and ran, freakily fast, feet kicking back like a cartoon, and disappeared around the corner. Lonnie and Alberto laughed at the driver and then pointed down the block. "It wasn't me, man," said Lonnie, still laughing, spreading his hands wide in innocence. "Fuck you want me to do? I don't even know the guy, he's a crazy kid from the projects." This lie was told in the street in front of Henry's yard, his home. But *the projects* explained pretty much anything, so the driver shook his head and got back in the bus. Dylan watched.

The girls might play tag. There was something faintly regrettable and unmanly about tag but if the girls played Henry and Lonnie played too, and then Dylan and Earl were slipped into the circle of tapped feet – Eeny, meeny, miney, Moe, my-mother-says-to-pick-the-very-next-one. You might be *It*. As *It* Dylan floundered madly and sometimes heard himself yell. *It* made him a little yellish, he couldn't say why. Nobody cared, everybody yelled sometimes seemed to be the verdict. Games dissolved mysteriously, groups bunched, *It* split into two, a boy chased a girl to the corner and out of the game. Subjects of focus changed like the angle of light. A kid might have a bunch of baseball cards one day, there was no explanation. Potential skully caps were collected, the need for wax discussed, but skully was never played. Maybe nobody knew how. Isabel Vendle looked out her window. The men on the corner arranged clacking dominoes, the fish store on Nevins Street was full of sawdust, a kid would come up from the projects and pierce the privacy of the Dean Street kids and everyone would be mysteriously jangled. Whole days were mysterious, and then the sun went down.

Dylan didn't recall giving out his name but everyone knew it and nobody cared what it meant. They might sometimes bother to mention that he looked like a girl but it wasn't apparently his fault. He couldn't throw or catch but that was just too bad. Not everyone could was the general drift. So Dylan communed with the spaldeen in distaff moments, when it went dribbling to the curb or was punched down the street by the fender of a passing car. Dylan was pleased to fetch it then for the older boys who stood aggrieved, shaking their heads. The ball might be swept nearly to Nevins Street, to the bodega, it might be stopped by one of the grizzled domino players on the crates who'd peruse it briefly before turning it over. The spaldeen was always scarred from its encounter. "Roof it, Henry," Dylan would whisper as he ran it back, whisper it to himself, but to the ball too, an incantation. Sometimes roofing it was the very next thing Henry would do. Then instead of calling for a new spaldeen the older boys would abruptly slink off, to hang on Alberto's gate at the other end of the block and bathe in innuendoes and flicked cigarette butts from the teenagers on the stoop there. The teenagers were waiting for night. Dylan stuck to Henry's concrete fence, the white kid. He could hear Rachel call from there, beyond he wasn't so sure. From Henry's and the abandoned house to his own Dylan knew the slate precisely.

The boy lingered in the study and paged through Isabel's photo albums while the mother sat on the back terrace, smoking. Isabel watched a squirrel ribbon the telephone pole, begin to scurry across the fence top. The squirrel moved as an oscillating sequence of humps, tail and spine bunching in counterpoint. Some humped things are elegant, Isabel mused, thinking of her own shape.

Inside, an Italian plasterer reshaped a florette on the parlor ceiling, sweating atop a ladder in the corner by the high front window. The boy at Isabel's table flapped the laden pages, absorbed as if he were reading.

The boy was humped too, over the book. More a hedgehog than a squirrel, Isabel decided.

"Can you get any flavor out of this?" said Isabel to the young mother, frowning.

"Sure," said Rachel. She hadn't extinguished her cigarette to accept the beaded glass of ice and soda. The smoke drifted into the August air unstirred.

"For all of me that's dying my tongue is dying soonest."

"Maybe put lemon in it," Rachel suggested.

"I put lemon in my soup. I can't also put it in my soda. Take the bottle with you when you go. I should drink formaldehyde."

Rachel Ebdus ignored the remark. She was unshockable, a bad sign if Isabel was looking. The young mother leaned back in her chair perilously, cigarette between fingers on a hand propped over her shoulder. Her black unbrushed hair was madness. Isabel pictured it on fire on her patio in the deafened afternoon.

The man on the ladder gathered excess with his blade and allowed it to drip heavily to the butcher paper on the parlor floor, which crackled as it accepted the weight.

The boy's intensity, his gaze, might be wearing the gloss off her old photographs. He hadn't turned a page for a whole minute. He remained curled around the album as Isabel was curled involuntarily around her whole self.

Isabel saw that Rachel Ebdus watched the plasterer. "The old art lives in him," she told the younger woman. "He drinks beer on his breaks and talks like John Garfield, but look at the ceiling."

"It's beautiful."

"He says his father taught him. He's only bringing out the beauty which was hiding. He's an instrument of the ceiling. He doesn't need to understand."

Isabel felt irritation with herself or Rachel Ebdus, she wasn't sure which. She hadn't brought the image entirely into the light: that though mute, the house conveyed a language of itself, as the plasterer carried forward his father's trade.

"He's got a great ass," said Rachel.

Outside, the squirrel shrieked.

Isabel sighed. She actually craved one of the woman's cigarettes. Was it possible to begin smoking at seventy-three? Isabel thought she might like to try. Or perhaps she was only impatient with her own inability to fathom anything about Rachel Ebdus besides the woman's insatiability. And the cigarettes lay on the ironwork grille of Isabel's patio table within a hand's reach, whereas the plasterer's ass was in every sense less accessible.

"If it's in any way a question of money—" Isabel began, surprising herself by getting to the point.

"No, it isn't," said Rachel Ebdus, smiling.

"I don't want to embarrass you. Both Packer and the Friends School have scholarship possibilities. I don't know about Saint Ann's. But I would also be glad to help."

"It isn't about money. I believe in public school. I went to public school."

"That's idealistic indeed. I do think you'll find that all his friends will be at one or another of the private schools."

"Dylan has friends on the block. I doubt they're going to Brooklyn Friends or Packer."

Days were not always like this. There were days like white pages, when no squirrels screamed in the trees and no boys leafed through her albums and no plasterer sweated at her ceiling and a neighbor stinking of radicalism and a tenuous marriage did not sit grinding cigarettes into Isabel's china tea-cups and enjoying the ginger ale Isabel could no longer taste while offering as conversational checkmate a neat implication of racism, days when the only discord in the tall Dutch house was the orange cat clawing newspaper bundles in the basement apartment into frayed, piss-smelling bales, days when Isabel sat upstairs at her table, scraping the nib of her pen across the signature line of a check to some moderately worthy cause, or to her favorite and completely unworthy one, her nephew Croft who'd hidden himself at a commune in Bloomington, Indiana, after impregnating a black cook at the house in Silver Bay and who, she'd been assured, divided Isabel's monthly donation neatly neatly in half, sending one portion to the distant cook and her child and donating the other to the commune's petty-cash reserves for food and marijuana. To hell with Rachel Ebdus. Isabel subsidized feral hippies and the mulatto offspring of her criminal relations and Rachel Ebdus could certainly send Dylan, God help him, to Public School 38 to show his sole white face among that ocean of brown, to air his waterfall of girlish hair among the Afros, if that was what suited her principles. Isabel could wish now for this day to be unsquirreled entirely, for it to be one spent not even at her desk but rather one in which she lay in bed still, ignoring the orange cat's cries, rereading Maugham or De Maupassant.

She wondered if Rachel Ebdus would also have admired Croft's ass. Likely so.

The boy put the big photo album on the cast-iron patio table and pointed. "That's your name," he said inquiringly. Isabel turned, surprised.

The long-ago photographer had in the darkroom burned a row of small white letters at the bottom corner of each of the black-and-white shots of the boats, the harbor, the parties on the lawn: VENDLE'S HARD, SILVER BAY, LAKE GEORGE, NY. The boy pressed his nubby fingertip to Isabel's family name, and waited for an answer.

Vendle's Hard. Cranberries soaked in cognac. Emptied bottles rolling in the belly of a skiff. The famous oar, fouled in aquatic vines, that shattered and speared her side, puncturing her lung nearly to the spine. The old injury around which she was so rigidly curled.

"He reads," said Isabel, allowing herself to be mildly impressed.

"Mmmmh hmm," said Rachel Ebdus, humming the syllables through the ignition of another cigarette. "He sure does. He reads Abraham's *New York Times*."

"He'll be with children who'll never learn," said Isabel, feeling impulsive and a little cruel. The fact was undeniable. Let Rachel squirm now.

"Maybe he'll teach them," Dylan's mother said easily, then laughed. "It's a problem for him to solve, school. I did it, so can he." Cigarette between her fingers pointed to the sky and leaking smoke, she put her hand in Dylan's hair.

CHAPTER 2

SKULLY DID EXIST. It was a science more closely related to the Spirograph and the Etch A Sketch than to the spaldeen and Dylan fell on it with gratitude. In fact when it was actually played he lost the game more often than he won but skully was an art that involved the conveyance of a body of knowledge, like the methods of a guild, and by his second summer on the block Dylan had mastered all its peripheral notions and was widely recognized for this mastery. For instance drawing the skully board. The first step involved finding the ideal square of slate and so Dylan's long communion with the Dean Street sidewalk was rewarded. The slate shouldn't be flawed by a crack or vein, or tilted, or bowed. Dylan favored a square in front of the blue-painted brownstone, midway between the home of the woman his mother sometimes, laughingly, called *Vendlemachine* and Henry called *the olelady*, and Henry's own house. It was Dylan's secret that other squares of slate farther down the block were as good or better but that he preferred this one for being nearer his own house and close also to Henry's, where the kids gathered, and for the way it was shaded by a particular tree – the dynamics of space and sound, the quality of privacy and access, for a whole series of subtle aesthetical distinctions and that he could still hear his mother if she called for him from the stoop of their house – it would have been impossible to express all that went into his selection and so Dylan instead declared it the best square for skully, on the whole. And he was believed. The kids might scratch a skully board into another square from time to time, testing the principle, but after Dylan's declaration the principle was in place.

Then the chalking of the skully board on the slate. Dylan could draw, though he came to understand this only by the inability of the others to match him. They'd drop their chalk at the sight of his skully boards, and he'd be enlisted by Marilla to draw hopscotch diagrams for the girls who'd otherwise scoffed at his shoes and pants – he wore what they called *roachsteppers* and *highwaters*. His skully boards were straight and clean, the four corners numbered elegantly, one, two, three, four, the winner's zone in the center embellished with a double circle, his own innovation. This, like his choice of slate, became institutional, so much that one day Lonnie and Marilla scoffingly insisted it had always been done that way, and Dylan's authorship of the double-ringed winner's circle was permanently obscured.

Other innovations were resisted outright. Dylan one day designed a star-shaped skully board, where players would be expected to shoot their caps from triangular corners into center stage, as in Chinese checkers, a game which Dylan had been taught in his kindergarten class. Nobody understood, nobody played – it wasn't skully. Dylan wiped the board away but the six heavily chalked points of the star remained etched lightly on the slate to haunt him until the next hard rain.

Then there was the making of the skully caps. Metal bottle tops from soda or beer were the standard, and the slightly heavier tops lined with cork were best, though from time to time a kid would experiment with a plastic cap, or a wide metal one from some other type of jar or bottle, ketchup, even pickles or applesauce. The notion of a monster cap, one which would drive opponents off the board with crushing blows, haunted the institution of skully. But in practice the bigger caps were unwieldy, tended to hang across the boundary lines, and were painful to shoot hard across the board with flicked fingers. You could fool with a big cap before it was filled with wax but then it would skid and slide right off the board too easily, and anyway a cap not filled with wax wasn't really *skully*. You wanted wax. Candles could be bought or "boosted" – shoplifted – from Mr. Ramirez's bodega, or volunteered by Dylan from his mother's bedside supply. And Dylan became an expert at melting the candles, an operation always performed on the stoop of the abandoned house in the cause of not freaking out either parents or "little kids" – though Dylan and Earl were still the littlest kids around, apart from a couple of mute girls in severe cornrows – with lit matches. Then damping the wax into the cap, so it hardened into a smooth whole without seams or bumps, one which wouldn't pop out when struck by an opponent's cap. Like a tiny factory Dylan made rows of perfect skully caps and lined them up along the stoop: vanilla Yoo-Hoo with pink wax, Coke with green, Coco Rico, the cork of the cap still stinking of sugar, with white.

Strangely, after Dylan's rapid rise to chief alchemist and philosopher of skully, nobody seemed to want to play the game anymore. Dylan presided over an ideal slate which was persistently shirked, deserted in favor of just about anything including standing around Henry's front yard with hands in pockets, kicking at one another's ankles and saying, "Fuck you, motherfucker." Perhaps the Dean Street kids had never really been able to keep their attention on skully but only on the attendant crafts, on puzzling out the tradition. So much easier to tell a younger boy that he didn't know to play skully than to have to play him to take his caps away, and what good were the caps anyway? Everybody lost their caps or even perversely threw them at the passing bus to watch them ding harmlessly and go wheeling into the gutter. Maybe skully sucked. Maybe to perfect a thing was to destroy it.

The Solver girls moved away. That was the first surprise. One day they were gone. Isabel Vendle peered out her window and saw the van, the movers tramping down the stoop with liquor-store boxes loaded with books and glassware, the girls on the sidewalk in the skates that seemed to grow from their ankles, whirling untouchable as ever, one final taunting pirouette. The girls' parents hadn't paid Isabel the courtesy of saying a word, hadn't apparently known they were lines in a blueprint drawn by Isabel, founding participants in her Boerum Hill. So at the very start the circle shrank.

It didn't matter much to Dylan, though. The Solver girls had gone to Saint Ann's for school that first year, had vanished into Brooklyn Heights. They didn't live on Dean Street, they floated above it. Dylan had gone to first grade at Public School 38 on the next block, real school, according to Rachel, public school. "He's one of three white children in the whole school," he'd overheard her boasting on the phone. "Not his class, not his grade – the whole school."

She made it sound important. Dylan didn't want to disillusion Rachel, but in fact each day his time in the classroom at

P.S. 38 was only a prelude to affairs on the block. Kids in school didn't look at each other, they looked at the teacher. Nobody Dylan knew from the street was in his class except Earl and one of the silent girls from Marilla's yard. Henry and Alberto and the others were older and though they were presumably at the same school might as well have been in some other galaxy during the hours Dylan spent listening to Miss Poobner teach the alphabet or how to tell time or what were the major holidays, hours Dylan spent reading the classroom's small collection of tattered picture books over and over until he'd memorized them, hours spent abstracted, scribbling his pencil, drawing utopian skully boards with ten, twenty, fifty corners, drawing rectangles like frames of his father's painted film and filling them in until they were entirely black. The alphabet Miss Poobner taught was represented on the wall above her head by a series of personified cartoonlike letters – Mr. A, Eating an Apple; Mrs. B, Buying a Broom; and so on – and something insipid about the parade of grinning letters defeated Dylan's will utterly. He sensed that no narrative could be constructed that would make Mr. A and Mrs. B do anything other than Eat an Apple or Buy a Broom and he couldn't bear to drag his eyes along the row of letters atop the chalkboard to discover what it was that Mr. L or Mrs. T were doomed to do. Miss Poobner read stories, so slowly it was agony. Miss Poobner played records, songs about crossing the street and how different men had different jobs. Was someone trying to entertain him? Dylan had never learned less in his life. He glanced from side to side but the other kids sat blank-eyed in invisible cages at his left and right, legs tangled in the chair-desks, fingers up their noses. Some of them might be learning the alphabet, you couldn't say from their faces. Some were from the projects. One girl was Chinese, which was strange if you thought about it. Whatever, they were helpless to assist or communicate with one another. Older kids picked up the first graders after class and led them away as though retarded, shaking their heads. What had the first graders done all day in class? Nobody could really say. The teacher talked to them like they were a dog all day and by three o'clock it was like leading a dog home.

The kids in your first-grade class might be in your

second-grade class or you might never see them again. It might not matter. Even the ones you knew from the block you didn't know in school. Dylan tried to touch his nose with his tongue until someone told him to stop. One or two kids didn't ask to go to the bathroom until it was too late and they'd peed in their chair. One kid scratched his ear until it started bleeding. Sometimes Dylan could barely recall first grade seconds after bursting out onto Dean Street again.

The strange and unfortunate Abraham Ebdus might actually be on to something, she admitted privately. Time was indeed a series of days, and the film of the block's changing was as static as a series of hand-painted frames, considered singly. *The New York Times* had put her new name for the neighborhood into print, *Boerum Hill* – that was something. But Isabel Vendle wished to see the film in motion now, the frames run together, trees hurrying in the wind instead of dying in the humid stillness, the abandoned house unbricked and rescued. Growth, process, renovation. The only thing that moved on the block were the boys in the traffic, like insects skating on the surface of a still pond, the one white skimming among the black. The incinerator at the Wyckoff Houses housing project was on fire every other day, or so it seemed, a plume rose which the air refused to dissolve. A single man had bought the house with the terrible blue siding and threatened to renovate so slowly that it might as well be never. He lived in one room near the back and renovated from the inside out so that no one could tell the house wasn't a ruin. It *was* a ruin, the block was hopeless, and Pacific Street was progressing more quickly than Dean. Isabel wished she could tear away the blue siding with her own hands, an idiotic thought, but nevertheless: she wished she could paste money over the blue siding which stung her eyes like ointment, wished she could slather money over Dean Street entirely, could bribe the man with the car with the painted flames to polish it on Pacific or Nevins instead or just to drive it into the Gowanus Canal. She didn't actually have so much money as that. She had white paper and envelopes and stamps and days which refused to end – a thunderstorm might break the heat and an hour afterward the humidity clamped itself over the block again as though no thunder had struck. She wrote to Croft, who'd gotten another woman on the commune pregnant, *I'm running out of days, Croft, or maybe not. I can't tell if I'm any older than I was forty-seven years ago when as a mere girl the oar pierced my side* and *Croft you're a fool.* Croft to her was becoming a character in Graham Greene, *The Heart of the Matter* or *The Comedians*, Croft ought to be made to swelter on some imperial island, he ought to be brought up on charges by outraged local authorities.

It was hard to say when Robert Woolfolk began hanging around. He was from somewhere down Nevins Street, maybe the projects, maybe not. One day he was there on the stoop of the abandoned house, another day he sat on Henry's low wall and looked at the girls. Then he got into a game or two, though he wasn't really a game player. Robert Woolfolk was taller than Henry and could fling a ball as far but there was something disorganizing in him as a presence that broke games apart, some slangy way of moving his arms and head that could only throw football interceptions or roof a spaldeen. Once he stood a few feet from the implacable surface of the abandoned house, while a catcher waited in the street, and somehow hurled a spaldeen in such a way that it flew directly sideways to smash a parlor window in the house next door. Woolfolk could run, they agreed after that. He'd danced around the corner of Nevins, like Henry after pretending to be hit by the bus, seemingly before the glass rained out of its frame to the garden below, while the ball itself actually penetrated the window to be lost inside the house, an unheard-of accomplishment. The other kids stood gazing in a mixture of astonishment and defiance. They hadn't been the ones to throw it, after all. Robert Woolfolk didn't appear again for two weeks after his miraculous aberrant throw, during which time the landlord next door to the abandoned house had replaced the pane with a cardboard patch, then stood every day on his stoop for a week glaring at the afternoon players, who dispersed guiltily into football or tag or just pushing one another off Henry's low concrete wall, glancing back at the landlord and muttering softly, too softly for the landlord to hear, "Damn, man. What are you looking at?" until the landlord wearied of his symbolic protest and hired a glazier to replace the patch with a new pane. Once the Dean Street kids felt it safe to wield a spaldeen again they spent an afternoon or two trying to reproduce something like the perverse and famous throw but couldn't, the angle was sheerly impossible. When Robert Woolfolk came peering back around the corner they tried to involve him in the experiment but he refused for days, sulking around the edges of the game. When, finally made curious by their egging, Robert Woolfolk consented to touch a spaldeen again, it had an abrupt dampening effect. The kids scattered before he could approach the wall, traumatized by the possibility that his arm would shoot out again in its hectic way, and Robert Woolfolk was left to pocket their new spaldeen and go home, wherever that was.

Nobody seemed to know where Robert Woolfolk lived.

Robert Woolfolk might live in the projects and just not say.

Likely he did live in the projects.

"He's got a fucked-up name," said Henry one day, to nobody in particular.

"Who?"

"Will Fuck."

"*Mother*fuck," added Alberto, sort of generically inspired. No one else spoke.

That was the whole conversation. The words floated away, or so you would have thought. But two days later Robert Woolfolk lurked on Henry's stoop and everyone sensed the unsavory weight of his vigil there. You could read it in the noncommittal language of the kids staked out at various distances, nobody playing anything specific in the claylike, immovable afternoon. Henry stood especially proud and oblivious, slanting handball shots from inside his yard into the joint of the pavement at his low wall, not looking at Robert Woolfolk.

"Why don't you come here for a minute?" said Robert. He was leaned back, one knee up, other leg sprawled with toe pointing inward, elbows braced on the stoop, shoulders up around his ears, hands dangling dangerously. He resembled a puppet with live eyes, his strings limp just for a moment.

"I'm right here," said Henry.

"Why don't you say my name again?"

The question was what alliance ran invisibly around the

corner to Nevins Street, whose voice had found Robert Woolfolk's ear, and where, and when. Each kid wondered and had
to consider the possibility that he alone didn't know, that the
lines of force were visible to the others. The Dean Street kids
were widened in that instant, a gasp of breath went in and out
of the lung of summer just then. It made you dizzy to taste the
new air.

"I never said your name."

"So say it now."

"Go home."

When Robert Woolfolk undraped from the steps and bid at
Henry it was like his famous spaldeen throw. You could never
have predicted his one bony arm would wrap around Henry's
waist so that they crumpled, knees folding together like spooning lovers, Robert on top, to the pavement of Henry's yard.
Robert didn't punch until they were on the ground, and then he
kneed and punched maniacally, his eyes and mouth and whole
face squeezed shut as if he were underwater, boxing a shark.
Henry wriggled into a ball. For a moment the combatants were
both viewed distantly, through a haze of watery interference.
Then the silence broke with a rush, the fight bobbed up from
its oceanic depths and the kids pushed in close to watch. How
else would they have heard the strange whining sounds, the
almost animal keening which came out of both of the bodies in
Henry's yard? You were learning something. That kids fought
was understood but your chances to see it were still rare. The
same sound might come out of your own body one of these
days. It was worth a look, worth holding back a moment from
breaking it up no matter what your sympathies, which anyway
weren't so clear. Then you broke it up, shouting "Breakitup!
Breakitup!" – words that emerged by fluent instinct though
you'd never spoken them before. In this case, Alberto dashed
into Henry's yard and pulled Robert off by his shoulders.

"See, see, see," said Robert Woolfolk, breathing like a bellows, pointing his finger. Captured by Alberto, arms wrapped,
he still raged toward Henry, and his and Alberto's legs trembled
like those of an animal bucking and cringing in its stall. He'd
scraped the top of his hand to bleeding on the pavement or
perhaps on Henry's teeth. "See, that's what you get, see, that's

what you get." Robert Woolfolk elbowed out of Alberto's embrace and stalked back to the corner of Nevins. He turned just once at the corner to scream, "See!" Almost as if it was someone's name he was calling. Then he vanished.

Nevins Street was a river of unhappiness running through the land of Dean Street.

Who cleaned Robert Woolfolk's clothes, for instance?

He probably wouldn't come back for a while. He'd probably come back after a while.

Maybe he had a brother or a sister.

Nobody could say.

There wasn't any way to think about it. No one was accountable. The traffic of cars and the bus rolled past under the shade of Dean Street's trees, whirring through blobs of light and shadow. The drivers were blinded by the flicker. The men in the doorway of the rooming house advertised disregard in the way they wore their little felt hats even in this weather. They drank discreetly from a sack. Anything they thought to say they said in Spanish or kept to themselves. Probably everybody's mother was in the kitchen making dinner now – assuming they had a mother. Nobody looked at the kids in Henry's yard. The old white lady didn't even look out her window so much these days.

Sometimes the kids didn't even look at each other. You could argue for hours about who said what or who was really there when something important happened. Pretty often it turned out that someone hadn't been there in the first place. The girls never confirmed anything for anyone, though you'd supposed they were right there, watching. Marilla might know a given kid's sister and you'd never hear a word about it. Days were full of gaps, probably because they were too alike. And when something big happened it was impossible to hold it clear. The gaps rushed in even there.

Henry, for his part, revived instantly and disdained any injury, though he had a shiny stripe of blood under his nose. He sucked it back and wiped it away, swallowed. He ran his tongue around his teeth and straightened his limbs, which were on the whole a lot straighter than Robert Woolfolk's. The fat lip was more an attitude than anything else, an earned sneer.

"Stupid motherfucking shitty bastard."

"Huh."

"Bet you he won't come back."

"Huh."

It was suddenly conceivable Henry had been pummeling Robert Woolfolk and not the other way around – from the way he shrugged the fight off and threw several arching stoop-ball home runs right afterward you had to consider whether you'd misjudged from appearances. You couldn't always tell the winner by who was on top. They'd all seen how Robert Woolfolk ran off after Alberto pulled the fighters apart, or at least walked quickly in his loping manner, and alone.

Here was the thing about the fight between Henry and Robert Woolfolk: Dylan Ebdus never was able to sort out whether he'd been there and watched it himself or only heard every detail, burnished into legend by the other kids. He just couldn't work it out, and after a while quit trying.

The film was changing. In the early frames, the first four thousand or so, abstracted cartoonish figures had cavorted against a sort of lakeside, a shore and sky which might also be a desert-scape sprouted with weeds. The figures he'd painted with his needle-thin brushes could be cactus or fungus or gas station pumps or gunfighters or charioteers or florid reefs – sometimes in his mind he named them as figures from mythology, though he knew the mythological allusions were a vestige, a literary impulse he should have already purified from his work. Yet without confessing it completely he had scrubbed a tiny golden fleece over the shoulder of one of the figures as it darted and wiggled through two or three hundred frames. He saw the figures dart and wiggle, of course, in his mind's eye, as though the film were running on its sprockets through a projector. In fact the endless painted film was still, had never been shown. He didn't want to run it until the end, whenever that would be. He'd been offered a hand-cranked editing device for viewing short sequences of celluloid and refused it. The stillness of the film was part of the project. Each frame bore the weight of this cumulative discretion. Together the frames made a diary of painter's days, one which would confess its life only at the finish.

Now the figures, the airy dancers, were expunged from the frames. They'd melted into blobs of light. He'd shelved the thinnest brushes, the jeweler's tools, let them stiffen. The bright forms he painted now, the simpler and more luminous blobs and rectangles of color, hovered against a horizon which had evolved from the reedy, brushy lakeshore of the early frames into a distant blurred horizon, a sunset or storm over a vast and gently reflective plain. The hued forms in the foreground which he painted again and again until he knew them like language, until they moved like words through meaning into nonsense and again into purer meaning – these were beginning to merge with the horizon, to flow in and out of the depths of the tiny celluloid frames. He allowed this. In time, over many days, the forms would become what they wished. By painting them again and again with the minutest variation he would purify them and the story of their purification would be the plot of the film he was painting.

He'd begun looking out the window. One day he loaded a large brush with paint and outlined the Williamsburg Savings Bank tower on the glass pane itself, then filled in the outline so that the painted tower blotted out the tower in the distance.

As in the newer frames of his film, the painted glass flattened distance into proximity.

Each time the boy visited the studio he looked different.

His wife joked that she should have the phone company put a new line into his studio so she could call from the kitchen downstairs. When they fought now he'd forget halfway through what the point was. He knew she could easily spot that moment of surrender, when abstraction washed through his eyes, erasing language. In his mind he'd be painting a frame. His fingers twitched for the brush.

His old teacher called from the Art Students League, to ask why he wasn't painting anymore. He said, "I paint every day."

Second grade was first grade with math. Third grade was second grade with a period in the schoolyard to play kickball, a version of baseball with a giant blubbery ball, dull red and pebbled like a rubber bath mat, which was pitched along the ground toward home plate and that a better kick could get aloft. A fly ball was almost uncatchable, it was bigger than a kid when it was flying through the air. Positioning yourself under a fly was just stupid, and if you reasoned out what happened after the outfielder invariably stepped aside pretty much anything in the air was a home run. You just ran, you didn't look to see if they were throwing it in. More often, though, you didn't get it in the air. A mistimed kick scudded back idiotically to the pitcher and you were thrown out at first base.

Still, a home run. If you put the bloated thing in the air half the time everyone on the field fell down. There'd be a kid on his ass at every base as you went by.

Anything you painted, however slapdash, got hung on the wall. The brushes at school, though, were like painting with your elbows if you had any point of comparison. The school paint dried like scabs.

Nobody peed in their chair anymore.

A book report told the story of a book.

Second grade had two Chinese kids, and third grade had three, a soothing presence since they always had their hands up. Where they went after school was a mystery. They weren't white and they weren't not, so that was a plus. It prevented things from getting too black and white and Puerto Rican. At the current rate you'd all be Chinese by high school, which come to think of it might solve a few problems.

It wasn't their fault they were Chinese, and if you asked them about it they'd shrug – they *knew* it wasn't their fault. Everyone knew. In third grade you were still only just settling into your skin and couldn't be expected to answer for it. After that was anyone's guess.

CHAPTER 3

VENDLEMACHINE LAY ON her high bed in the parlor. The gray-yellow October light which filtered through the tall curtains swarmed with motes, with writhing flecks that made the slanted light appear as solid as the polished oak spindles of the bed frame and the third-full glasses of water and cognac on the bedside table and the cane leaned against the table and more solid than the faintly stirring limbs of the tiny woman curled on the bed, now groping slowly for the cane without yet turning her light-haloed head from the pillow in which it was buried.

"I fell asleep," she said distantly.

Dylan Ebdus didn't speak, but stood not crossing the line into the room filled with the haze and piquancy of the old woman.

"You were long."

Dylan found his voice. "There was a line." He'd ferried another clutch of her hand-scratched letters on cream stationery to the post office on Atlantic Avenue and stood waiting for his turn at the Plexiglas window, studying the wanted signs and the posters promoting stamp collecting and literacy, scuffing his sneaker toes at the scraps of paper, the yellow slips and torn government envelopes that layered the floor.

Dylan worked for Isabel Vendle for a dollar an hour each Saturday morning the year of his tenth birthday, the year of fourth grade. *Vendlemachine*, *Vendlemachine*, Dylan sang in his head, though he'd never said it aloud once beyond his own doorstep, not even whispered it alone in Isabel Vendle's house on those days when she was away visiting family at Lake George and he used her key and let himself in through the basement door to gather her mail and pour dry food into a dish for the orange cat.

Vendlemachine was Rachel's word. Rachel Ebdus awarded secret nicknames to her visitors and to people who lived on Dean Street and Dylan understood they couldn't be leaked from the house, from Rachel's kitchen. His mother had instilled this doubleness: there were things Rachel and Dylan could say to one another and then there was the official language of the world, which, though narrowed and artificial, had to be mastered in the cause of the world's manipulation. Rachel made Dylan know that the world shouldn't know everything he thought about it. And it certainly shouldn't know her words – *asshole*, *pothead*, *gay*, *pretentious*, *sexy*, *grass* – nor should the bearers of nicknames know the nicknames: *Mr. Memory*, *Pepe le Pew*, *Susie Cube*, *Captain Vague*, *Vendlemachine*.

His father's nickname was *The Collector*.

Vendlemachine stayed upstairs each Saturday morning while Dylan took out the foul, liquefied garbage in the tall pail in the basement kitchen and lined the pail with a new bag. Isabel couldn't lift a bag of garbage herself and so the smell massed for seven days, waiting for Dylan to uncork it. Then the silent and massive orange cat would creep downstairs to watch. It had a skull like a Gila monster. Dylan couldn't know whether the orange cat loathed him or Isabel or was indifferent, couldn't know what it understood about Dylan's situation, so it was useless as a witness. It might not even know that Isabel wasn't meant to be bent the way she was, might instead regard Isabel as a standard for the human form and therefore find Dylan's shape objectionable. Nevertheless the orange cat was the only witness. It seemed to live for the moment each week when the garbage was transferred and the room inflated with the stink of coffee grinds and orange peels and stale milk.

"I don't want to work for you anymore," Dylan Ebdus said to Isabel Vendle now as she swam in the coverings of her bed, in the mustiness and shadow. The orange cat sat in a solitary pool of clean sunlight near the parlor windows, ducking its reptile head rhythmically against its paw.

Isabel moaned softly into the silence.

Dylan waited.

Outside the Dean Street bus breathed down the block, took the pothole which served as home plate with a clunk, then shuddered on.

"I need you to go to the store," Isabel said at last. "Not Ramirez. Go to Mrs. Bugge's on Bergen." Isabel Vendle pronounced the name of the Norwegian immigrant woman *Byu-gah*. Everyone else on the block called the shop on the corner of Bergen and Bond, the bodega that wasn't a bodega because instead of Puerto Ricans it was run by a fat white woman with tiny eyes, Buggy's.

Ho, snap — you lifted some cakes from Buggy's? I heard Buggy's German shepherd once bit a kid's ass off.

Isabel raised her arm from the bed and let her fingertips fall on the side table. Her nails rapped lightly. Dylan came close, crossing the invisible line into the aquarium light of Isabel's parlor bedroom, to gather the bills which lay there.

"Kraft American slices, Thomas' muffins, and a quart of milk." The old woman spoke as if describing a recurrent dream. "Five dollars should be enough."

Dylan crumpled Isabel's money into his pocket, wondering now if he'd spoken aloud. "I, don't, want, to, work—" he began again, softly, carefully, spacing the words.

"*Skim* milk," said Isabel.

"Idon'twanttoworkforyou," Dylan said quickly.

The orange cat blinked up.

"It tastes like water," Isabel mused. "White water."

The block was empty except for a couple of teenagers on Alberto's stoop near the corner. Dylan didn't know where the kids were. It was October, getting colder, everyone was wearing jackets and ranging away from the block. Henry left to play football in the schoolyard near Smith Street and Earl just didn't come out. Somebody had left a bottle in a bag on the stoop of the abandoned house. Days before there'd been a guy sleeping on the stoop, one of those drinkers who just nested for a while. A stained paper bag was like a pissed pair of green pants, it was only a matter of where the leak showed. That's why they called it a leak.

Dylan cornered Bond Street, feeling how irrational a block was, one face so familiar, the housefronts and slate walk a surfaced iceberg, one with Dylan's own flag planted on it, his chalk skully boards, the ghostly traces of his chasing down a ball or being tagged *It*. The rest of the block was under water. Dylan for years had clung to this one face, bent over the slates as though they were sheets of Spirograph paper on the floor of his room, not noticing until too late that they were part of an edifice which curled past Bond and Nevins Street, into the unknown. He'd sooner take Isabel's letters all the way to Atlantic Avenue to the post office than walk around the corner to Buggy's. He didn't trust Bergen Street. He could feel the sidewalk tilt there.

Robert Woolfolk sat draped on the stoop beside Buggy's, leaned back just as he had been on Henry's the day of the fight, the knuckles of his knees seeming higher than his shoulders though they rested two steps lower. Dylan stopped there before the store, commanded. The sun of the day made a desert of light all around them, and the traffic was still and distant. Dylan could see the bus up near Smith Street, where it seemed to rest at a tilt, fatigued. Dylan heard church bells.

"You work for that old lady?"

Dylan tried to shake his head for a thousand reasons. He thought of Isabel swimming in her bed, the nearest authority for miles. Or there was Buggy and her dog, a pane of glass away, but they were entombed inside a cave of products, rice, bicarbonate, Nestlé's Quik. The store was so dark inside Dylan imagined Buggy would wilt if she ever stepped out into the sun.

"You got her money in your pocket?"

Dylan was certain he'd said nothing.

"How much you got?"

"I have to buy milk," Dylan said dumbly.

"How much she pay you for doing her errands, a dollar? You got it on you now?"

"She gives it to my mother," Dylan lied spontaneously, amazing himself.

Robert only turned his head quizzically, lazily, and swung his hand where it dangled from the step, as though just then discovering his wrist's capacity for motion. His slung weight didn't cleave from the stoop.

The two of them were in a rehearsal for something, Dylan sensed. How much of something, and whether it was personal to him and Robert or larger than that, he couldn't yet say.

So he stood frozen while Robert continued to examine him.

"Go buy milk," Robert said at last.

Dylan moved for Buggy's door.

"But if you come around here with that old lady's money next time I might have to take it off you."

Dylan recognized this as a sort of philosophical musing. He was grateful for the implied sense of pooled information. He and Robert could move forward together from this point into whatever was required.

"Tell Henry fuck you," added Robert in a meaningless flourish.

Dylan ducked his head inside the dark, cheese-acrid storefront. Buggy's German shepherd snapped up to the limit of its chain behind the counter, whining into a single pointed bark, and Buggy floated out of the back like a pale bloated pickle in a jar to hover at the register. When Dylan emerged with the brown sack of groceries Robert was gone.

It was a whole week and Sunday morning again before Dylan found his voice. Abraham was in his high room, Rachel in her garden, Dylan stewing alone in his room as he dressed at noon, the ritual time. Downstairs he paused in the kitchen calculating his defection, then went down the backyard stair. He approached his mother where she knelt on the cold ground beneath the bare ailanthus, hacking with a trident at a network of unwanted roots, cigarette smoldering from between her lips. The cigarette's filter was smudged with mud. Rachel wore jeans and an orange denim jacket and a Dodgers cap. Rejected blooms lay heaped in a pile of green and brown that bleached and shrank in the air as Dylan stood watching.

When he opened his mouth Robert Woolfolk was left out of the story.

"Poor old Vendlemachine. So don't work for her, kiddo."

"I tried to tell her, though."

"What do you mean you tried?"

"I said it two times."

"You're kidding me, Dylan."

"She pretended not to listen."

"Just ignored you?"

Dylan nodded.

"Come on," she said. She stood and brushed the dirt from her thighs. "We'll go together."

Dylan absorbed the thrill of Rachel's indignation, his breath short. "Maybe you should just call her," he said as they went into the kitchen.

Rachel scrubbed under her nails at the sink, and slurped from her cooled coffee.

"Let's see what she has to say," she said, and Dylan was silent, understanding that his fate was to cross Isabel's threshold at least once again.

In the yard of the abandoned house the boys who would never be invited to work for Isabel Vendle played running bases: two basemen tossing a spaldeen between two squares designated as bases and four or five base stealers – Earl, Alberto, Lonnie, some other Puerto Rican kid. The runners bunched in between, bobbing and colliding like cartoon mice, while Henry gripped the ball and faked a throw once, twice, three times, wagging the spaldeen, showing it to them like a stuck-out tongue as he threatened the chase with a stomped footfall in their direction, until his bluff became irresistible and in glee and exhaustion the congregated runners surged, loping toward his base as though his hand was empty, and were tagged out one after the other in quick sequence. The base runners lolled their heads, drunk on being fooled, on Henry's mastery.

Robert Woolfolk wasn't among them.

Maybe nobody saw Dylan looking. Often a kid was invisible walking with his mother halfway down the block. You didn't look, you didn't want to get mixed up in that space between a kid and his parents.

Then Earl waved, but he could have been pointing out a bird or a cloud in the sky. Instead of returning the wave Dylan looked up at the sky himself, pretended he'd seen something move there, a body dart across the cornices, or leap from one side of Dean Street to the other.

"I'm Croft," said the man who opened Isabel Vendle's door, amused with himself already. "You're the kid that works for Isabel, I guess." He shook Dylan's hand comically before looking up at Rachel. His cropped black hair was astonishingly equal in length everywhere on his head, including his eyebrows. "You got a girlfriend, huh? Come on in, Isabel's upstairs. Me and her are drinking Coca-Cola, and there's plenty."

It was as if Vendlemachine had calculated the coming affront and defended herself with the visitor. She was supposed to be alone on Sunday mornings, adrift in bed or curled at her desk, moaning, trembling to moisten a stamp with her tongue. She had always waited for Dylan by herself and now she'd cheated him, denied him the chance to show his mother the deathly house he'd been forced to enter. The darkened street-level front room was opened now, the corners only Dylan and the orange cat knew exposed to light, the dusty chairs rearranged to make room for a green plaid sleeping bag and a hiker's backpack spilling with clothes, T-shirts balled like used tissues, and a stack of paperbacks: *God Bless You, Mr. Rosewater; In Watermelon Sugar; Sexus.* Even the garbage smell was mysteriously gone.

Vendlemachine sat at her patio table, scowling, her grip crackling the real estate section of the Sunday *Times.* The table was littered with sections of newspaper and the promised Coca-Cola and a scattering of violently colorful comic books. "Isabel's Sunday paper was stolen this morning," began Croft, as though he felt generally destined to explain everything and accepted the assignment with good humor. He might next start explaining that he was young and Isabel Vendle was old, or that they sat in a backyard in Brooklyn.

"Again," said Isabel Vendle.

"I had to walk all the way up to Flatbush Avenue and Atlantic to buy a replacement," Croft said. "I found that newsstand on the traffic island. There were all these great comics, you never know where you're going to find them. The Fantastic Four, Doctor Doom, Doctor Strange, you know."

Dylan wasn't clear whom Croft was talking to until Rachel Ebdus grabbed one of the comic books and looked at the cover. "Jack Kirby's a god," she said.

"Oh, yeah, you're into this stuff? You know the Silver Surfer?"

"Everyone's got Peter Max posters but I think Jack Kirby's about ten times more psychedelic."

A Rachel word.

"Yeah, sure," said Croft. "But who do you like? Silver Surfer? Thor? What about Kirby's DC stuff? You know *Kamandi: The Last Boy on Earth*?"

Dylan's gaze scattered against the comic-book covers. A man of stone, a man of fire, a man of rubber, a man of iron, a brown dog the size of a hippopotamus, wearing a mask. That was all Dylan saw before his sight blurred in the sun and shadow and the figures were liquefied into blobs like Abraham Ebdus's abstractions.

"Black Bolt," said Rachel, tapping to point out a figure on the cover of one of the comic books. "You know, the Inhumans. The leader of the Inhumans." Rachel seemed tangled in herself, seemed bewildered as Dylan to find herself in this conversation. The force of Dylan and his mother's arrival at Isabel Vendle's, the arrow of Rachel's intention flying down the block, had been captured and utterly redirected by Croft and his comic books.

"Sure, the strong silent type," said Croft, grinning. "I get it."

"Croft, you are an irresponsible man," said Isabel Vendle with weary affection.

"Sweet Aunt Petunia," said Croft obscurely.

"Yes you are," Isabel went on. "And now an irresponsible boy has brought his mother here to tell me he doesn't want to visit me anymore on Saturdays. We know this because the boy isn't interested in your comic books, Croft. He's staring at me, isn't he?" She flapped her newspaper so it bowed over her hands, then glared over the tented top. "Do you find me evil, Dylan? Or boring?"

I find you *psychedelic*, Dylan wanted to say.

"You know there probably isn't any difference, Aunt Isabel. Not to the kid."

"You knew he wanted to quit, Isabel," said Rachel, faintly recalling her purpose. "He tried to tell you." She half stood in her chair to work her cigarettes out of her front pocket, then offered one to Croft, who shook his head.

"Oh, I felt him working up to it," said Isabel. "I'd imagined I might get another few weeks out of him."

"It's a coming-of-age thing," said Croft. "Running away from scary old ladies. I had to do it myself."

"Shut up, Croft."

That was the end of the discussion and the end of Dylan's

working for Vendlemachine. Croft went into the kitchen and returned with more glasses and they sat in the mottled sunlight squeezing lemon into Coca-Cola and turning the pages of his comic books, Dylan and Rachel and Croft, while Isabel Vendle stained her fingertips nearly to black with the ink of the *Times*. The Human Torch was the Invisible Girl's younger brother, and the Invisible Girl was married to Mr. Fantastic, and Ben Grimm was The Thing and Alicia was his blind girlfriend, a sculptress who could honestly appreciate his hideous but monumental body, and the Silver Surfer was Galactus's emissary and Galactus ate planets but the Silver Surfer had helped the Fantastic Four protect Earth, and Black Bolt couldn't open his mouth because a single syllable of his speech was so powerful it might crack the world apart – Croft and his mother explained it all to Dylan, word balloons in the bright panels on the pale yellow paper, while Vendlemachine moved her lips silently and eventually dozed in her chair, and the late-October Sunday afternoon collapsed to evening, Abraham in his studio darkening squares of celluloid with brushstrokes, the nudes in the parlor below with no light to make them glow, the backyard window boxes and fire escapes black against the ruddy streaked sky, the street too dark to judge a throw properly so the spaldeen hit a kid in the face and anyway it was time for dinner. Dylan fell asleep in his chair for just a minute and for that minute he and Isabel had the *exact same dream* but when they awoke neither of them remembered.

"Let me see it for a minute."

Let me see it: you *saw* a basketball or a pack of baseball cards or a plastic water gun by taking it into your hands, and what happened after that was in doubt. Ownership depended on mostly not letting anyone see anything. If you let a kid *see* a bottle of Yoo-Hoo for a minute he'd drink what was left in it.

"Let me see it, let me check it out. I only want to take it for a ride."

Dylan gripped the handlebars. Abraham had pried off the training wheels the day before, and Dylan still wobbled, still scuffed with his sneakers groping away from the pedals to steady and brake against the sidewalk. "Only if you stay on the block," Dylan said, miserably.

"You afraid I'm gonna take it? I just want a ride. You get it back after that, you got it all day, man. Just let me go around the block."

It was a trap or puzzle, the way Robert Woolfolk already knew to work Dylan's guiltiness. And the empty block conspired to leave Dylan alone to solve it. Robert Woolfolk carried a vacuum around with him, or revealed by his presence the vacuum on Dean Street, the expanse of moments when no one saw and no one knew what happened in plain sight, when all of the block was shrouded in daylight like the abandoned house was shrouded in leaf shade.

Old Ramirez stood in front of his store and sipped a Manhattan Special and squinted at them from under his fisherman's hat. He was beyond appeal, watching them like television.

Robert Woolfolk added his hands to the bars beside Dylan's and tugged gently at the bike.

"Stay on the block."

"Around once, that's all."

"No, I mean stay in front of the house."

"What, you think I'm not coming back? Just around the block."

What came out of Robert Woolfolk's mouth was petition and chant, irresistible in its illogic. His eyes, meanwhile, were hard, a little bored.

"Just once around."

Robert Woolfolk's legs were too long to unfold in the span between seat and pedals, so he rode with his knees doubled and knobbing up near the handlebars, like a clown on a tricycle. Then he changed his approach, elevated his hips above the seat to stand on the pedals and pump side to side, elbows flaring. The bike teetered, annexed to Robert Woolfolk's stretching limbs. Like that, a vanishing pile of elbows, he took the bike around Nevins.

When Dylan used the word *block* he didn't mean Bergen Street, the other side.

How long did it take to go around the block?

How long was twice as long as that?

The tonguelike latch of Dylan's black ironwork gate rattled with the vibration of the bus going by. Though there were no trees on the Nevins end of Dean Street red fallen leaves had blown into the gutter from somewhere. The plastic milk cartons in front of the bodega claimed you could be fined or go to jail for not returning them to May Creek Farm, Incorporated, a fairly unlikely destination if you gave it any thought.

The afternoon withered like a balloon around Dylan on his stoop, waiting for Robert Woolfolk to return. Old Ramirez wasn't watching, there was nothing to watch. Dylan stood naked in the minutes as they accumulated, as they stacked up indifferently on the distant face of the Williamsburg Savings Bank tower clock. The day was like an unanswered telephone, the mute slate ringing. The call of Dylan's arm-swinging vigil went unreplied.

Nevins Street might as well have been a canyon into which Robert Woolfolk had vanished like a cartoon coyote, wordlessly, trailing puffs of dust. When Lonnie wandered up bouncing a Super Ball and asked what Dylan was doing Dylan said he wasn't doing anything. It was pretty much as if there had never been a bike.

Abraham Ebdus lost a day to finding the boy's bicycle. He stalked Wyckoff and Bergen and Nevins, thinking unavoidably that Rachel would have found it herself in the first half hour. She knew Brooklyn in ways he didn't. He walked the periphery of Wyckoff Gardens, not crossing into the grounds, the maze of walkways and hedge and low Cyclone fence, not knowing where to start if he did. Light soured in the shade of the graffitied white brick of the projects. They seemed designed as future ruins. He put his head into a Puerto Rican social club on Bond Street, a small hangar full of cardplayers. Before he ducked out he registered a tiny pool table, blue carpeted walls, the tang of malt-stale cork. Nobody spoke to him.

But by the end of the afternoon word was out, somehow. A woman with a baby stepped out of her door, seemingly angry at him for wandering. Abraham's family was possibly famous for being white, fools. She passed the child back inside and led Abraham around to a vacant lot on Baltic, a fenced yard

filled with debris shot through with ailanthus sprouts, the
mongrel trees which grew as fast as a crack in a windshield
spread under pressure of a fingertip. The heap of crushed baby
carriages and rotted lath with clinging bits of plaster and torn
tin ceiling made a pattern with which Abraham Ebdus refused
to permit his eye to become fascinated. The bicycle was on top
of the pile, above his head, flung there who-knew-how, its blue
curved fender twisted like a splintered wing. Give it another
day and the ailanthus might have shot through the spokes. He
had to climb the fence and ended up tossing the bike to the
ground to free his hands. No one was inclined to help, though
some watched. He wasn't sure it mattered to rescue the bicycle.
If it had been stolen for use by another child, maybe. But this,
this gratuitous trashing, was just the street's incomprehension,
its resistance. That shadows stood sipping from paper bags as he
struggled down to join the bicycle on the pavement was only
appropriate, matched his mood. The bicycle was defeated, and
Abraham Ebdus wondered why he'd taught the boy a useless
skill. He knew Rachel required he bring the bicycle home for
repair but suspected the boy would never choose to ride it outside of the dirt of their backyard.

Marilla and another girl were waiting, playing jacks at the base
of Dylan Ebdus's stoop.

Marilla sang in crazy falsetto *The prob-lem is you ain't been
loved like you sho-huh-hood, what I got will sure-nuff do you good—*

The other girl – Dylan recalled that Marilla called her
La-La, wondered if that could really be her name – scooped
jacks between ball bounces, counting with a slurred inrush
of breath *whoosies, whreesies, whorsies, whivesies*. The game was
splayed beneath his bottom step so he couldn't pass. He sat on
the third step from the bottom and watched.

"Robert Woolfolk says he didn't take your bike and if you say
he did he's gonna mess you up," Marilla announced suddenly.

"What?"

"Robert said don't go saying he took your bike since he
didn't even."

"He said he'd fuck you up," clarified La-La. Her hand darted
in distraction to fumble *eightsies*, the jacks scattering.

"I didn't say—" he began, thinking he hadn't, hadn't said a thing.

The bicycle was in Abraham Ebdus's studio, its fender straightened and decorated now with Dylan's name in his father's brushwork hand. Soon it would be downstairs again, leaning in the hallway like a stuffed animal, a blind chrome elk loaded with his parents' expectation and Dylan's dread.

Marilla shrugged. "I'm just saying." Squatted like she was peeing, her ass an inch above the slate, she seized the tiny red ball and swept the jacks up, and sang *You refuse to put anything before your pri-hi-hide — what I got will knock all that — uh — pride aside!*

"Robert told you to say it?"

"Nobody told me nothing, I'm just saying what I heard. You got a dollar for some candy, Dylan?"

Who was on the block? Was Henry in his yard? Was Robert Woolfolk there?

Dylan Ebdus's head twitched, trying not to look. His fingers clenched the two quarters in his pocket. He'd meant to buy a spaldeen, a fresh ticket of entry in pink rubber. Maybe practice taking shots off the face of the abandoned house until a game built up around him. Dylan had a knack for making catches only when no one was looking, in private rehearsal, but any day now that knack might translate into Henry's genius. Though come to think of it you couldn't say when the last time was anyone played wallball, it might be another lost art. Forgotten games stacked up like the grievances of the losers of wars, unrecorded in the street's history.

You didn't think of who got money from where. Every kid kept the change when their mom sent them to buy milk. Alberto bought Schlitz for his cousin. Old Ramirez knew who it was for, so he let a kid buy beer, also cigarettes.

Word had gone around that on Halloween the kids from the projects threw, no, hurled with bruising force, eggs. It was a holiday but you still had to go to school, a bad deal, a bad situation, every kid for himself, scattering once the bell rang at three o'clock, and more likely to be hit if he bunched with another kid, let alone tried to protect him. You couldn't protect anyone from a thrown egg or much else.

What if everything changed? Probably it had. It had before.
You and *what army*?

You and *your so-called friends*.

Yo *mama*.

From his bedroom Dylan Ebdus heard like a dog's inaudible whistle the lonely call of the Spirograph: the pins, the toothed cogs, the skipping red pens. "No," he said to Marilla, terrified. "I don't have any money."

"You scared of Robert?" Marilla dashed the jacks across the slate in a crazily wide swath, and frowned at the result.

"I don't know."

"He got a razor."

"*Tell me something good!*" screamed La-La, then Marilla dropped the red ball which dribbled under Rachel's forsythia and the two girls stood away from the array of paint-chipped jacks and danced, knees bowed, eyes slitted, cheeks blowing out as they chanted *Ooh ah, ooh-ooh ah, ooh ah, ooh-ooh ah*—

The elongated rectangular grid of these streets, these rows of narrow houses, seen from above, at dusk in late October: imagine the perspective of a flying man. What sense would he make of the figures below, a white woman with her black hair whirling as she struck with the flat of her hand at the shoulders and back of a black teenager on the corner of Nevins and Bergen? Is this a *mugging*? Should he *swoop down, intervene*?

Who does this flying man think he is anyway – Batman? *Black*man?

These streets always make room for two or three figures alone in struggle, as in a forest, unheard. The stoops lean away from the street, the distance between row houses widens to a mute canyon. Our lone figure above flies on, needing a drink more than anything, and the woman's beating of the boy continues.

The day after Halloween the pavement outside school was stained with egg, bombs that had missed their targets, streaks of browning yolk studded with grains of shell, so distended by velocity they seemed to speak of the Earth's rotation on its axis, as though not gravity but centrifugal force had smeared them lengthwise across the planet. The ones who'd worn home an omelet drying in their corduroys, borne a throbbing red oval punched onto their thigh, they'd deny it until you saw tears mass in the edges of their eyes. Any kid honest with himself was sobered, though, by the glimpse of whatever raged inside the bullies from Intermediate School 293, the berserkers just a grade or two ahead. The egg throwers had worn cartoon-smooth, store-bought masks – Casper, Frankenstein, Spider-Man – so they resembled Symbionese bank robbers or chainsaw killers, figures from nightmares fueled by stolen looks at television news and *The Late Movie*.

Everyone moved at a fixed rate toward the same undiscussable destinations.

No one could push the concept of a razor blade or a heroin-filled hypodermic stuck into an apple completely out of their heads.

There were days when no kid came out of his house without looking around. The week after Halloween had a quality both hungover and ominous, the light pitched, the sky smashed against the rooftops.

No Vember.

"Go deep," Henry commanded. Now he wagged a football, the latest enticement. Four kids were like yo-yos strung to his hand, running to jump in a cluster when he finally spiraled the football half the length of the block. No matter what happened, whichever hands the ball came down in or eluded, Henry's expression was sour. There was something inelegant or compromised in the ball's descent from the air where he'd placed it.

Dylan Ebdus waited on Henry's stoop in a bubble of silence, seeing he made *six*, wondering if they'd call him into the street to even the sides for a game. He'd detected in himself a certain translucency today, a talent for being ignored. Rachel had flushed him from a four-day hide in his room, from a retrenchment into the secret power of his books and pencils, into the mysteries of eavesdropping on Abraham's footfalls and Rachel's clangor on the telephone, into the dreary conundrums of the Etch A Sketch and the Spirograph, and something in his conjured solitude had followed him out onto the street, then reversed itself to drape all over him anywhere he sat still.

Gaze long enough into Dean Street and Dean Street will gaze into you.

Hands in pockets, Dylan went into the street and leaned against a car. Then, as if tide-swept from a beach, he began to sway with the others toward the place the ball descended, making no show of trying to catch it, just drawn to the site, taking air through his mouth, silently emulating play.

"You seen Robert Woolfolk?" said Alberto casually.

Dylan wasn't surprised. He felt the irresistible relevance of Robert's name. He shook his head.

They stopped playing. Henry tried to dribble the football. Two or three times it actually came back to him instead of twisting away across their shoe tops. The ball was scarred with grease where it had lodged under a car and been scraped down the block.

"He got beat up," said Alberto reverently.

Lonnie nodded his head, Alberto nodded, Earl and Carlton nodded. They gathered wide-eyed as though warming at a campfire of their own awe. Dylan waited. Henry slapped the football against the ground and Alberto and the others stared as though it was Dylan who should explain Robert Woolfolk's beating to them. Then Henry flicked them away, as easily as flicking a drop of water from his hand, by muttering "End zone," and dropping back, the ball hidden behind his knee, to roll his eyes at the sky. The four scuttled to the place where Henry's glance promised to deliver the ball, each yearning to be the kid made pure by the perfect catch. Henry turned away the instant the ball was aloft, uninterested. He gestured to Dylan and the two of them crossed to the abandoned house. The bus thumped past, giving cover.

"Your mother kicked his ass, right out on Bergen Street," Henry said. "He was crying and everything."

Dylan was silent.

"I guess nobody told you," said Henry.

Could there be a distant island or hidden room where your life took place without your knowing? Dylan tried to picture the incident on Bergen Street, the lunatic collision between Rachel Ebdus and Robert Woolfolk, but the spotlight of his wondering slipped to the invisible floating room in the dark of the house at night where through the walls as he lay awake in bed he heard his mother's rhythmic whimpering or his father's urgent, angry whisper. *I guess nobody told you*, Henry said, and Dylan began to drown in the stuff he dammed with silence at the brink of sleep.

Did Abraham beat Rachel, to bring those moans?

Who was kicking whose ass?

Of course that fury would slip out of the house to hammer some kid on the street. At least it was Robert Woolfolk who'd taken it.

It suddenly seemed that Henry and every kid on the block might know the sound of Abraham and Rachel fucking and fighting at night, that only Dylan was protected and blind.

"Your mother's crazy," said Henry. He didn't say it as a snap, like *Yo mama's so ugly bigfoot takes her picture*, but instead with admiration and goofy horror in his voice.

Dylan saw now that it wasn't strict invisibility that had cloaked his presence on the street, had kept him wavering like a mummy on the sidelines, but instead his mother's hidden act hovering over him, a force field, a pale blur of shame. Who told Rachel about Robert Woolfolk? Had he betrayed himself, wept and murmured in his sleep about a razor?

Dylan wanted to tell Henry he'd already known, but couldn't voice the lie. Alberto reappeared with the football, rushing ahead of the others, and flipped it into the air. The ball rose out of the canopy of leaf-bare twigs between the frame of cornices and found a backdrop of low clouds against which it was illuminated like a bomb. Henry stretched back and snared it with his fingertips, then in his downward motion plumped it to Dylan, a sneak play. Dylan hugged the ball to his shoulder like a pledge of allegiance. The thing ticked with cold, its skin impossibly tight.

CHAPTER 4

NIXON QUIT, and NIXON QUITS read the full front page of the *Daily News*, a guilty pleasure tacked to the wall of her study. The block words suited her that summer, her seventy-eighth, fifty-second since the oar, and she imagined her own headline: VENDLE QUITS. She felt her coming *quit* like the stone of a sour plum in her mouth, felt it graze her teeth as it nestled there but couldn't tell whether it wanted to be spit out or swallowed: quit, quit, quit. Swallowing hurt. Her hand hurt where it met the cane, her grip slipping, wrist crimping. Her eyes hurt where they met the page of a book. The words hurt. One day she thrilled, almost drunkenly, to scratch with a ballpoint pen in the pages of Anthony Powell's *Casanova's Chinese Restaurant*, breaking a taboo of seventy-eight years: she heard her father's voice then, a shred of memory, commanding her reverence for the leather-lined vault of his library. There might be nothing worse than defacing a book, but now she felt the urge to drop them, half read, from her deck into her overgrown garden. She would only need to turn her wrist, let her grip slip once more. She knew she'd quit, one way or another, drop the book or simply die, before finishing the twelve volumes of Powell's novel, his *Dance to the Goddamn Music of Time*. Powell had written too much, taken too much of her time already, and she punished him by scribbling in his book, a wavering row of lines, like some hieroglyphic tide. Was it Lake George she wished to return to? Was it waves she'd miss, at the end? The rocking and thump of waves against the swollen planks, a kiss in a skiff in the minutes just before her spearing by the oar?

Grips slipped. Hers had from every surface. She'd shaped nothing after all, only been crushed and reshaped. No wonder she felt for the brownstones, the cripples, now filling chaotically with no regard for her plan. Take for example the black singer who'd taken the house between hers and the Ebduses'. Was that progress? He had money but looked stoned. The singer's mulatto son stood each afternoon that August in the middle of the weedy backyard next door, dressed in a full Boy Scout uniform, gazing up boldly at Isabel on her deck, saluting her as though she were his troop master. Dean Street had produced its own weird spore, and she couldn't track or account for what bloomed now. Homosexuals colonized Pacific Street; a collective of naïve communists spilled from a row house on Hoyt Street, pasted signs on streetlamps announcing a slide show on Red China or a fund-raiser for squatters in Loisada. She'd founded a Bohemian grove. *They won't have Isabel Vendle to kick around anymore.* But then they wouldn't even know it was she who'd gathered them here.

They walked together to Pintchik on Flatbush Avenue at Bergen, a complex of interconnected shops selling paint and furnishings and hardware and plumbing, a business likely once a single storefront, now infiltrated through a block of fronts, and lodged below row houses painted schoolbus yellow with PINTCHIK emblazoned in red, brownstones turned into a street-long billboard, brownstones wearing clown makeup. Something in Pintchik's unmistakable age and specificity, its indifference, made Dylan ache. Apparently Brooklyn needn't always push itself to be something else, something conscious and anxious, something pointed toward Manhattan, as on Dean Street, on Bergen, on Pacific. Brooklyn might sometimes also be pleased, as here on Flatbush, to be its grubby, enduring self. Pintchik pointed only into Pintchik for provenance. It was a lair, a warren, and the hairy men selling dust-layered shower-curtain rings and glass doorknobs, the tangible stuff of renovation instead of the *idea* of renovation, from behind cash registers thick with newspaper clippings, they were rabbits like Bugs Bunny or the March Hare, snug into their hole and only amused or impatient that you might tumble in. Pintchik was a white Brooklyn unimagined by Isabel Vendle.

On the walk to Pintchik Rachel had taught him the word *gentrification*. This was a Nixon word, uncool. "If someone asks you say you live in *Gowanus*," she said. "Don't be ashamed. Boerum Hill is pretentious bullshit." Today Rachel was talking and Dylan was listening, listening. She sprayed language as the hydrant opened by the Puerto Rican kids around the corner on Nevins on the hottest days that year sprayed water, unstoppered, gushing. You might scrape the bottom of a tin can until it was open at both ends, then use the can to direct the water momentarily through the window of a passing car, but the force of the spray would win in the end. When Dylan had tried it the pillar of water captured the can from his hands and sent it spinning across the street to clatter under a parked car. His mother's flow he wouldn't dare try to direct. "Never let me hear you say the word *nigger*," she said, whispering it heavily, lusciously. "That's the only word you can't ever say, not even to yourself. In Brooklyn Heights they call them *animals*, they call the projects a zoo. Those uptight reactionaries deserve the break-ins. They ought to lose their quadraphonic stereos. We're here to live. Gowanus Canal, Gowanus Houses, Gowanus people. The Creature from the Gowanus Lagoon!" She inflated her cheeks and curled her fingers and attacked him at the entrance to Pintchik.

What would Dylan find if he walked across Flatbush, past its shops selling dashikis, and T-shirts which read I'M PROUD OF MY AFRICAN HERITAGE, past Triangle Sports, past Arthur Treacher's Fish and Chips, past Pintchik itself? Who knew. His world found its limit there, under the narrowed shoulders of the Williamsburg Savings Bank tower. Dylan knew Manhattan, knew David Copperfield's London, knew even Narnia better than he'd ever know Brooklyn north of Flatbush Avenue.

"We don't live in a box, we don't live in a little square box, I don't care what anyone says we don't live in a sixteen-millimeter frame!" She flew like the Red Queen in *Through the Looking-Glass* through Pintchik, whispering madly to him. "He can't put us inside, we'll break out, we'll bust out of the frame. He can't paint us in a little celluloid box. We'll run out in the streets! We'll paper him into his studio!"

Inside, Rachel led him to a room full of wallpaper rolls. He was meant to choose a replacement for the jungle animals hiding in palm leaves, that children's-book design, too young for him now. The samples in the room were furred with velvet, decorated with orange Day-Glo peace symbols and Peter Max sunsets and silver-foil-stripes and lime paisley – Pintchik might be implacable and timeless but it hosted wallpaper that looked like the newest candy wrappers, Wacky Wafers or Big Buddy. Dylan felt embarrassed for the wallpaper. It had the bad taste to be passing through and not know it. Dylan preferred Pintchik itself, its yellow-and-red painted-brick scheme, its cigar-glazed walls.

"I'll pry him out of his studio the way I drive you out to play, let him get a job instead of living on his mountaintop like Meher Baba—"

Now Dylan was startled to find a roll of his jungle among the Pintchik swatches. Here it was no better than paisley or Day-Glo. The jungle he gazed into while falling asleep had no age at all, was flat and empty, corrupt as advertising. Abraham would never have had wallpaper in his studio.

Dylan wanted wallpaper as old as slate, profound and murky as his father's painted frames. He wanted to scratch a skully board on his wall, wanted to live in the abandoned house. Or Pintchik.

Brooklyn was simple compared to his mother.

"A gang from the Gowanus Houses picked up a fifth grader after school and took him into the park and they had a knife and they were daring each other and they *cut off his balls.* He didn't fight or scream or anything. It's not too soon for you to know, my profound child, the world is nuttier than a fruitcake. Run if you can't fight, run and scream *fire* or *rape,* be wilder than they are, wear flames in your hair, that's my recommendation."

They walked home from Pintchik along Bergen, Rachel filling his ear. His mother never mentioned Robert Woolfolk, never once, but as they passed the corner of Nevins and Bergen, the site where she'd *kicked Robert's ass right out on the street* Dylan felt the shaming thrill of it again, felt it in her as well as in himself. Rachel wasn't responsible for what she said, he knew. She was afraid too. Dylan's role was to unravel what Rachel said and ignore ninety percent of it, to solve her.

"That beautiful black man who moved in next to Isabel Vendle is Barrett Rude Junior, he's a singer, he was in the Distinctions, he's got this amazing voice, he sounds just like Sam Cooke. I actually saw them once, opening for the Stones. His son is your age. He's going to be your new best friend, that's my prediction."

It was Rachel's last setup.

"You don't want any kind of wallpaper, we'll tear it off and paint, whatever. It's your room. I love you, Dylan, you know that. Come on, race me home."

Dylan put his confusion into his running, tried to put his mother somewhere behind him.

"Okay, can it, your mother's out of breath. You run too fast."

His sneaker-slapping footfalls petered at the corner of Nevins and Dean, where he waited for Rachel to catch up, and crooked his head up to gulp air. In that instant Dylan was sure he'd seen it again: the ragged figure arching from the roof of Public School 38 to the tops of the ramshackle storefronts on Nevins, to disappear then under the sky. The impossible leaper. He looked like a bum.

Dylan didn't ask his mother if she'd seen. She was lighting a cigarette.

"You're not only beautiful and a genius but you've got a pair of legs. I wouldn't say it if it wasn't true. You're growing up, kid."

Merit badges were cryptograms, blips of unlikely information from another planet of boyhood, and Mingus Rude, though in principle *showing off*, seemed to regard them with an anthropological detachment not so different from Dylan's. "Swimming, fire, tying, compass," he mouth-breathed as he ran his thumbs over them, talismanic evidence of the Philadelphia suburbs, flotsam from a dead world.

Mingus Rude made Dylan wait in the empty, weedy backyard while he dressed himself in the full Scout uniform, then stood before Dylan and they both considered the non sequitur of it, sleeves and legs already too short, yellow scarf stained with a slug trail of snot. He went inside again and came out in a green-and-white hockey uniform with his name pressed across the shoulders in glossy, slightly crooked iron-on letters. He held a splintered stick with black electrical tape wound around the handle. Dylan absorbed it silently. Then Mingus again vanished, to return in a crimson football uniform, with helmet reading MANAYUNK MOHAWKS. Together they peeled back the ventilated nylon jersey to examine the foam-and-plastic shoulder pads that gave Mingus Rude the outline of a superhero. The pads smelled of sweat and rot, of dizzy, inaccessible afternoons. *But can you catch a spaldeen? Can you roof one?* Dylan wondered bitterly. Mingus Rude would soon know that Dylan Ebdus could not.

Dylan was torn between wanting to claim to possess merit badges in *skully, Etch A Sketch, sneaking down creaky stairs,* and *drawing "Skippy"* and a desire to protect Mingus Rude from mockery, theft, incomprehension. He could already hear *Yo, let me see it, let me check it out, what — you don't trust me?* He wished to protect them both by commanding the new boy never to bring any of these madly fertile and irrelevant possessions out onto the block for any other kid to see.

Dylan tangled in silence. There in the high-fenced sanctuary of the backyard he wanted to heap the various uniforms in a bonfire, like the one Henry and Alberto had once set on the stoop of the abandoned house, igniting smoldering newspapers and dried dog shit and the stinky green late-summer ailanthus branches which had fallen to litter the street everywhere. Dylan wanted Mingus Rude and himself to build a fire and smother the uniforms in damp smoke until the plastic blackened and melted, until the numbers and names, the evidence, was destroyed. A Dean Street fire, no merit badges involved. Instead he watched as Mingus Rude somberly packed the uniforms into the bottom of his closet.

"You like comics?" said Mingus Rude.

"Sure," said Dylan unsure. *My mother likes them,* he almost said.

Mingus Rude excavated four comic books from the closet floor: *Daredevil #77, Black Panther #4, Doctor Strange #12, The Incredible Hulk #115.* They'd been tenderly handled to death, corners rounded, paper browned by hot attentive breath, pages chewed by eyes. MINGUS RUDE was written in slanted ballpoint capitals on each first interior page. Mingus read certain panels aloud, incanting them, shaping Dylan's attention, shaping his own. Dylan felt himself permeated by some ray of attention, moved so that he felt an uncanny warmth in the half of his chest that was turned toward Mingus. He wanted to put his hand in Mingus Rude's crispy-looking hair.

"You know what they say now? Doctor Strange could take the Incredible Hulk by making some kind of mystical cage but he couldn't take Thor because Thor's a godlike figure, as long as he doesn't lose his hammer. If he loses his hammer dude's nothing better than a cripple."

"Who's Thor?"

"You'll see. You know where to buy comics?"

"Uh, yeah." Dylan thought of Croft, that afternoon on Isabel Vendle's deck, the newsstand on the traffic island at Flatbush Avenue and Atlantic. The Fantastic Four.

Could Doctor Strange "take" the Fantastic Four? he wondered. "Ever steal comics?"

"No."

"It's no big thing. You go to camp this year?"

"No." No *year*, Dylan almost said. He'd found an artifact on Mingus's dresser, a sort of tuning fork.

"That's a pick," said Mingus.

"Oh."

"Like a comb, for black hair. It ain't nothing. Want to see a gold record?"

Dylan nodded mutely, dropped the pick. Mingus Rude was a world, an exploding bomb of possibilities.

Dylan wondered how long he'd be able to keep him to himself.

They crept upstairs. His father had abandoned to Mingus Rude the spectacular gift of the entire basement level: two rooms to himself, and possession of the magically blank backyard. Mingus Rude's father lived on the parlor floor. Like Isabel Vendle, Barrett Rude Junior slept in a bed opposite the heavily ornate marble mantelpiece, behind the shaded light of the tall windows, the showpiece windows meant for front parlors filled with pianos and upholstery, eighteenth-century Bibles on stands, who knew what else. But unlike Isabel Vendle's, Barrett Rude Junior's bed, which lay on the floor there under the scrolled Dutch ceiling, was a wide flat bag filled, as Mingus Rude demonstrated in passing with a neat two-palmed

shove, with actual *water*, an undulating sea trapped in slick
sheets. The two gold records were, oddly, just what their name
promised, gold records, 45s, glued to white matting and framed
in stained aluminum, not up on the bare walls but propped
on the crowded mantel beside balled dollar bills and half-filled
glasses and empty packs of Kools. "(NO WAY TO HELP YOU) EASE
YOUR MIND" (B. RUDE, A. DEEHORN, M. BROWN), THE SUBTLE
DISTINCTIONS, ATCO, CERTIFIED GOLD MAY 28, 1970, was the
legend on one, and "BOTHERED BLUE" (B. RUDE), THE SUBTLE
DISTINCTIONS, ATCO, CERTIFIED GOLD FEBRUARY 19, 1972, the
other.

"Downstairs," said Mingus Rude. They left the gold records
behind. Dylan walked ahead on the stairs, feeling strangely
formal as he gripped the banister, imagining Mingus Rude's
gaze on his back.

In the backyard they winged rocks into the sky, let them plop
into the Puerto Ricans' yard. Mostly Mingus, Dylan watching.
It was August 29, 1974. The air smelled like somebody's arm
up close. You could hear the steady ding of a Mister Softee
truck on Bergen Street, probably with a string of the usual kids
hanging on it.

"My grandpop's a preacher," said Mingus Rude.

"Really?"

"Barrett Rude Senior. That's where my daddy started singing, in his church. But he doesn't have a church anymore."

"Why not?"

"He's in jail."

"Oh."

"I guess you know my mother's white," said Mingus Rude.

"Sure."

"White women like black men, you heard that, right?"

"Uh, sure."

"My father don't talk to that lying bitch no more." He followed this with a sharp laugh of self-surprise.

Dylan didn't say anything.

"He paid a million dollars for me. That's what he had to pay
to get me back, a million *cold*. You can ask him if you think
I'm lying."

"I believe you."

"I don't *care* if you believe me, it's true."

Dylan looked at Mingus Rude's lips and eyes, his exact brownness, took it in. Dylan wanted to read Mingus Rude like a language, wanted to know if the new kid had changed Dean Street or only changed Dylan himself by arriving here. Mingus Rude breathed through his mouth and his tongue curled out of one side of his mouth with the effort of a throw. Mingus was black but lighter, a combination. The palms of his hands were as white as Dylan's. He wore corduroys. Anything was possible, really.

A million-dollar kid doesn't belong on Dean Street, Dylan wanted to say. The word *million*, even.

Mingus Rude might be insane, Dylan didn't mind.

Two days later he was already playing, standing in the street, a catcher in stoopball, taking a lean on a parked car to let the bus go by. Like he'd been there all along. He caught laconically, perfectly. He might be the Henry of his own block, now transported here – he might be a Henry of the mind, recognizable anywhere. Dylan crept up and sat on Henry's wall and watched, with Earl and a couple girls, younger kids. Mingus Rude was viable, apparently. He'd been folded into the ongoing game while Dylan wasn't looking.

Robert Woolfolk wasn't around. Otherwise the last splendid day had shucked every verifiable kid out onto Dean Street. Two girls turned a rope with three others inside, their knees shining like a bunch of grapes. The empty, blue-tiled school, Public School 38, hummed, just down the block. Nobody looked at it, nobody cared.

"D-Man."

"John Dillinger."

"D-Lone. Lonely D."

Dylan didn't know what Mingus Rude was yelling about, didn't recognize himself in the nicknames.

"Yo, Dylan, you deaf?"

Captaincy was an essence lurking in Henry above all. But one captain needed another, even if inferior, a stooge. Someone had to step up. Dylan had seen Alberto assume it, Lonnie too, once even Robert Woolfolk, to make a lopsided game of punchball, fast dissolved in scowls and a faked limp. Now, at the bright weary end of summer, Henry and Mingus Rude were stickball captains, unexplained.

Mingus chose Dylan first, over Alberto, Lonnie, Earl, anyone.

"He can't hit," said Henry. It was a reasonably sympathetic diagnosis. Dylan was any captain's problem, a communal drag.

"I got Dillinger," said Mingus Rude coolly. He wrapped and rewrapped the wrist fastener of a Philadelphia Phillies batting glove, teasing reminder of the motherlode of outfits buried in his closet. "Take your man."

That last August afternoon before school began was something like those heartbreaking, dazzling glimpses of the opening credits for *Star Trek* or *Mission Impossible*, before you were commanded to switch the television off and go to bed: it was going to haunt you, play inside your eyelids, after the door was closed, the light extinguished, your pounding rib cage calmed. A summer was unfinished, broken off at the end, a bad splice. Now, Mingus Rude's arrival promised the possibility of *another summer*, hinged to this one like a door you couldn't look beyond.

The palm-sweaty broomstick was wrapped with new black tape, like the hockey-stick handle.

"Lead off, Dill."

The names, Dylan began to understand, conveyed that he and Mingus were to be one thing to each other indoors, off the street, and entirely another outside. On the block.

Inside, outside, a distinction Dylan understood. Could work with.

Henry pitched. Dylan waved at something barely seen, like a bee overhead. "Ball one," said Mingus Rude, captain, umpire, announcer.

"Ball one?" scoffed Henry. "Dude chased it."

"Doesn't matter," said Mingus. "Too high." To Dylan he said: "Don't swing at that shit." To Henry: "Strike zone." Then back to Dylan, he whispered. "Don't close your eyes."

You evolved in full view and secretly at once, grew bony and hairy, twisted out a baby tooth and spat blood and kept playing, claimed to know certain words the first time you heard them. A day came when you made contact, stung it somewhere not foul, rounded first before the bat clattered to stillness in the street. It was no big thing, you weren't looking for congratulations. Dylan danced off on the manhole cover, second base, daring the throw, the next order of business. Reward for trickling the ball between Alberto's feet. Leading off, batting *one thousand*.

Any private thrill was like peeing your pants. Dylan knew to be ashamed of the relief.

He scored on Mingus Rude's own home run. Struck out hyperventilating his next time up. But. Five kids in a batting order and no defense to speak of, you'd get up a hundred times on a night like this. Strike out ninety. Lace it off a lamppost and call it a triple, didn't matter – you could *bunt* a triple in the dark. The close of this day you'd resist like sleep, like sickness. One kid's mom yelled for half an hour and even then nobody else paid attention, nobody went inside.

Rachel Ebdus didn't call from the stoop. Dylan Ebdus wondered if Rachel and Abraham were taking the opportunity to kick each other's ass in one form or another.

Given that he was *outside* at this particular moment, Dylan didn't care.

Didn't *give a shit*.

Fuck you know about it, anyway?

If. Mingus Rude was a scant four months older than Dylan Ebdus, but those four months hit the calendar such that Mingus was a grade ahead, had finished fifth grade in Manayunk, Pennsylvania. Like Henry and Alberto, Mingus Rude would start sixth this year, at the Intermediate School 293 annex, on Butler Street between Smith and Hoyt, in the turf of the Gowanus Houses. No-man's-land.

"Dill-*icious*," Mingus called him once as he stood at the plate.

I.S. 293 was a hidden sun drawing kids screaming out of Dean Street's orbit, one by one. If Mingus Rude was four months younger, if Mingus Rude and Dylan Ebdus had been headed to grade five together, if. Then Dylan could have watched out for him, maybe. Kept an eye.

A grade of school was a bridge in mist. No way to picture where it touched land again, or who you'd be when it did.

One stickball game was your whole career, your whole life to this point.

These weren't innings, they were dreams of innings. You couldn't remember who got the last out, you could barely recall the batting order until it was just two guys, Mingus and Dylan. Gus and D-Man. Another kid quit and Henry had to pitch from the outfield. You could do just so much, trap a grounder with your body like a grenade, fish it from behind a tire and lash it toward home base, maybe hit the ass of the guy who'd scored. The pink spaldeen turned black, like a piece of night. Some Puerto Rican guy reparked third base, pissed off at fingerprints. The spaces between outs were like summers themselves.

Public School 38 was on fire. No it wasn't.

If. If Mingus Rude could be kept in this place, kept somehow in Dylan's pocket, in his stinging, smudgy hands, then summer wouldn't give way to whatever came after. If. If. Fat chance. Summer on Dean Street had lasted one day and that day was over, it was dark out, had been for hours. The Williamsburg Savings Bank tower clock read nine-thirty in red-and-blue neon. Final score, a million to nothing. The million-dollar kid.

Your school wasn't on fire, you were.

—and now Major Amberson was engaged in the profoundest thinking of his life she found herself quoting in her hospital bed at Long Island College Hospital on Henry Street, where the television bolted to the ceiling showing *Ryan's Hope* and *The Gong Show* had to stand for a hearth, brutally angry and brutally fat Jamaican nurses for her lonely company, her vigil. She'd die in Brooklyn Heights instead of Boerum Hill because Boerum Hill had a jail instead of a hospital – *and Major Amberson realized that everything which had worried or delighted him during this lifetime, all this buying and building* – and not in her bed beneath her parlor ceiling because the oar had dented her, crushed her, folded her like a letter into the envelope of herself, unread for fifty-two years. Unreadable medically now, at the end: she'd watched the interns puzzling at her X rays – how can *this* be nestled beside *this*? How can old Vendle fit into herself, how'd she do it, all these years? Her body was Boerum Hill, just as King Arthur's body had been England. She was all of Boerum

Hill's contradictions crushed together: she was the Schlitz can in the brown paper sack sitting in the plaster-and-marble nook for turning coffins in the curve of stairwell in the nineteenth-century town house. She was a jail in the shadow of which boys frolicked. *Everything which had delighted him, all this buying and building, that it was all trifling and wasted, for the Major knew—*

Two visitors had come. Croft, of course, who'd stayed a week in her basement room and visited the hospital every day, plaguing her with small packages of inedible curative food, ferrying in *Temporary Kings* and *Hearing Secret Harmonies*, the last volumes of the Powell, drawing glares from the furious Jamaicans for rinsing her bedpan in the bathroom and for his earnest, pointless questions regarding her care. Then, at her request, he'd taken the orange cat with him to Indiana. She wished the orange cat luck. It might perhaps serve as conscience for the rural commune, its missing moral center. Croft had shaven or grown a beard – Isabel couldn't focus except on her own irritation, centering somewhere around his mouth. Croft would get the house. He'd sell it, she didn't want to conjecture to whom. Isabel found she couldn't read the Powell now, couldn't make it work, couldn't operate the sentences. She watched *The Gong Show* instead. There was an act, a comic with a paper bag on his head, whom she rather liked: Take that, Anthony Powell!

Isabel's second visitor, Rachel Ebdus, had also brought a book, which Isabel regarded in astonishment: *Woman on the Edge of Time*. Really, imagine calling oneself "Marge Piercy"! Isabel had smiled and turned her wrist as she was learning to do – that small slackening, that relinquishing, rehearsal for the deeper operation – turned her wrist and let the book drop to the floor, then whispered more faintly than was required that Rachel should put it on the bedside table. She enjoyed playing at dying while she was dying. *You fool*, she'd wanted to say, *I don't read women authors*.

Rachel Ebdus had been crying. She and her recluse filmmaker were surely fighting again. The woman had something she wanted to say but Isabel Vendle decided to invoke the petty majesty of the near-dead and prevent her saying it. *It's enough that you'll inherit my Dean Street, beatnik child. Don't come here to inter your woes in my dying heart.*

Rachel Ebdus was talking but it was as distant to Isabel Vendle as footprints on the moon.

"I might go," she heard the young woman say.

"Yes," Isabel said. "That's best. Go." If Rachel Ebdus were on television singing this song of woe Isabel would have long since "gonged" her – *the Major knew that now he had to plan how to enter an unknown country, one where he was not even sure of being recognized as an Amberson*—

Then she was alone, Rachel Ebdus discouraged, Croft scooted back to Indiana. Boerum Hill was what it was – partial, recalcitrant, corrupt – and whatever it would next become it could manage without Isabel Vendle's help. Let it be carved up, let it be forgotten, let it be forgiven. *We must be of the sun*, she thought, irritated at herself for continuing to quote, so late in the game, *there wasn't anything here but the sun in the first place, the earth came out of the sun, we came out of the earth* – in her last dream Simon Boerum, the old drunk, came to her and rowed her to the shore of Vendle's Hard, both oars secure in his hand, *so whatever we are, we must come from the sun*—

Gong!

Fifth grade was fourth grade with something wrong. Nothing changed outright. Instead it teetered. You'd pushed futility at Public School 38 so long by then you expected the building itself would be embarrassed and quit. The ones who couldn't read still couldn't, the teachers were teaching the same thing for the fifth time now and refusing to meet your eyes, some kids had been left back twice and were the size of janitors. The place was a cage for growing, nothing else. School lunch turned out to be the five-year plan, the going concern. You couldn't be left back from fish sticks and sloppy joes. You'd retain at the least two thousand half-pint containers of vitamin D-enriched chocolate milk.

Two black guys from the projects, twins, were actually named Ronald and Donald MacDonald. The twins themselves only shrugged, couldn't be made to agree it was incredible.

Chinese kids wouldn't go to the bathroom all day, they lived that much in their own world.

At home, Rachel Ebdus's telephone was ringing unanswered.

You met zones everywhere. The schoolyard was neighbor-hoods: black, black girl, Puerto Rican, basketball, handball, left behind. Through the Cyclone fence someone had brushed the word FLAMBOYAN in white paint on the stone wall, along with a square box for a strike zone.

Bruce Lee was famous now that he was dead.

A game of tap-it-in took place above the ground, in moments. Between jumps you weren't playing. You were inert, copping an attitude.

Black girls had a language of partial words, chants harder to learn than anything in class. There was a general noise at the edges you'd begun to detect, akin to indecipherable ballpoint desktop-gougings. A scribbled voice.

The first few times someone said *Hey, white boy* it sounded like a mistake. You had to be guided into the new relation by the girls, the boys were actually a little shy about it.

Wrong sneakers, wrong shoes, wrong length of pants. *Highwaters.*

Where's the flood?

What you laughin' at, fool?

Dang. Boy's laughin' at his own self.

From I.S. 293 or from nowhere, from the projects, older kids bunched at the school entrances and in corners of the yard. Previous fifth graders had been a layer between. Now you were the layer. Robert Woolfolk was among one of those regular bunches, the precocious paper-bag drinkers. Even standing in one place Robert Woolfolk moved like a sprained knee, like he was forever angling a too-small bike around the corner of Nevins. He flashed a smile like a torn photograph, his voice crept around corners in the air. Dylan Ebdus saw in Robert Woolfolk's eyes that same scribbled quality.

Red Hook, Fort Greene, Atlantic Terminals.

You built up associations, which would pass for understand-ing. Nobody was explaining anything. Fifth grade was an abstract art, painted one frame at a time.

Dylan could still hear the telephone ring from the kitchen while he sat on his stoop, waiting, watching, afternoons sliding to twilight, air chilling so the bodega sitters left their milk crates, shaking their heads, pinching their cold noses, leaving

Old Ramirez alone. Dylan and Ramirez were paired in their two doorways, keeping watch, ignoring each other. Dylan watched the traffic trickle down Nevins, watched the mothers walking kindergartners home from the YWCA, counted the buses which drifted like humming loaves to the stoplight, waited, drifted on. Henry's yard was empty, Marilla's yard was empty, somebody saw a rat in the yard of the abandoned house. Bruce Lee and Isabel Vendle were dead and Nixon was strolling on a beach. Nobody moved, nobody played, strange kids walked the block in groups. It was a season of vanishing, of a silence like raw stupidity, like the unbearable ticking silence of a teacher expecting an answer from a kid everyone knew couldn't even say his own name right.

Let Abraham answer the phone, if he could even hear it. Let Abraham say she's not here.

Most days Dylan waited alone until Abraham called him in for dinner. Mingus Rude had other places to go, sixth-grader places, I.S. 293 places – other friends, Dylan guessed, then kept his own guessing hidden from himself. One or two afternoons a week Mingus would lope down the block and raise his hand. His coat was brown corduroy with a sheepskin collar, not the shiny plastic-stuffed bubblecoats every other kid wore. Mingus Rude carried his notebook and textbooks loose under his arm, no bag, and he'd clatter them on the stoop carelessly, expressing something less than utter disdain and more than total mastery.

The comic books Mingus Rude treated as a presence delicately alive, some piece of still-beating flesh he and Dylan might be capable of healing by their absolute fixity of attention, by their reverence. The overlapping storylines were a field of expertise, skully again, all fine print and ritual. Dylan was really horrified to learn he'd let so much time slip past, so much essential cultural history. Forget what you thought you knew. The Silver Surfer, for example, was a situation you couldn't really understand if you came in too late. Mingus only shook his head. You didn't want to try to explain something so tragic and mystical.

New comics arrived at newsstands on Tuesdays. Mingus Rude would have an armload, bought or stolen, Dylan didn't ask. Some were bimonthly, some monthly, you learned by reading the letters page, you built up anticipation for special issues, too, oversized *Annuals* and one-time special events like the *Avengers-Defenders Wars* or *Origins*. In *Origins* you learned how superheroes got started, the answer generally being: radiation. In the *Annuals* and *Wars* you satisfied, at least provisionally, questions of *who could take who*. Hulk and Iron Man would face off for a page or two, always vowing to settle it for good another time.

Spider-Man's girlfriend, Gwen, had been killed by the Goblin, it wasn't funny in the least. That's why Spider-Man was so depressed all the time.

Captain Marvel wasn't Shazam, it was confusing. He'd been revived to assert a copyright on the name, and nobody could say whether he really fit into the Marvel Universe all that well. DC Comics, Marvel Comics' antithesis, presented a laughable, flattened reality – Superman and Batman were jokes, ruined by television.

In truth, Superman in his Fortress of Solitude reminded you all too much of Abraham in his high studio, brooding over nothing.

Swamp Thing was a rip-off of *Man-Thing*, or vice versa.

An uneasiness hung over certain titles. Different artists drew the same characters different ways – you could hurt your eyes trying to account for it, to grant continuity to these hobbled stories. Weaker superheroes were propped up with guest appearances by Spider-Man or the Hulk, confusing chronology terribly. An Einstein could lose his mind trying to explain how the Fantastic Four had helped the Inhumans fight the Mole Men when by clear testimony of their own magazine they were trapped in the Negative Zone the whole time.

The Incredible Hulk, if you followed him closely over time, lost the use of pronouns.

Two afternoons a week, sitting in the dimming light on Dylan's stoop, never discussing fifth or sixth grade, stuff too basic and mysterious to mention. Instead just paging through, shoulders hunched to protect the flimsy covers from the wind, puzzling out the last dram, the last square inch of information, the credits, the letters page, the copyright, the Sea-Monkeys ads, *the insult that made a man out of Mac*. Then, just when you thought you were alone, Dean Street came back to life, Mingus Rude knowing everyone, saying *Yo* to a million different kids coming out of Ramirez's store with a Yoo-Hoo or a Pixy Stix, to Alberto fetching Schlitz and Marlboros for his older brother and his older brother's girlfriend. The block an island of time, school a million miles away, mothers calling kids inside, the bus lit inside now, fat ladies coming home from offices at the Board of Education on Livingston Street, their weary shapes like black teeth inside the glowing mouth of the bus, Marilla strolling by a million times singing *It's true, hah, sometimes you rilly do abuse me, you get me in a crowd of high-class pee-pul, then you act real rude to me,* the light fading anxiously, streetlights buzzing as they lit, their arched poles decorated with boomeranged-up sneakers, and Mingus Rude saying, one dying afternoon, eyes never ungluing from a panel in *Marvel's Greatest Comics* in which Mr. Fantastic had balled himself into an orb the size of a baseball, his tiny face including signature gray temple hair still visible in incredible wrinkled detail, in order to be shot from a bazooka into the vulnerable mouth of an otherwise impervious fifty-foot-tall robot named *Toomazooma, the Living Totem,* "Your moms is still gone?"

"Yeah."

"Dang, man. That's fucked up."

CHAPTER 5

AFTER FIVE WEEKS he was ready to sell the nudes. They nagged at his mind, they spoke to each other from opposite walls in distorted whispers, they reflected him back to himself like fun-house mirrors, they, along with the ringing telephone, the abandoned kitchen counter, the stale unemptied ashtrays, made the parlor floor of the brownstone seem a skull lacking a brain, an empty skull decorated with memories, déjà vu. She wasn't coming back, and his knowledge of it throbbed from the canvases like heat traces.

Erlan Hagopian, an Armenian collector who lived on the Upper East Side, had looked at the paintings two years before. He'd asked to see them after one had been hung in a group show on Prince Street, at Abraham Ebdus's old teacher's request – a request Abraham should have refused, a vanity, a mistake. Hagopian and the Prince Street dealer had come around to Dean Street wanting to see the paintings and also wanting to see the studio. Abraham had refused them that, protecting the film, protecting his secret work, and inadvertently extending the confusion that the nudes were recent, or that his work on canvas continued. It didn't. His larger brushes rotted, not even properly cleaned the last time he'd touched them. That day Erlan Hagopian had made a production of asking the price of the whole roomful, of wanting to be told the number which would need to be written on a check to rob the parlor of its fleshy insulation in one grand gesture. Confident, surely, that it would be denied – the Armenian had read Abraham Ebdus's diffidence at least that well. Perhaps not so well, though, that he'd expected what he got: being refused even one of the paintings. Abraham Ebdus's reward was the sorry, grumbling shake of the Prince Street dealer's sunglass-bearing, golden-maned head. That look was worth any number on a check.

Now, two years later, Ebdus phoned Hagopian directly, knowing that to circumvent the dealer – a secret that wouldn't keep for a so-called New York minute if Hagopian actually purchased any art – was to burn a bridge to his old career, a bridge to SoHo, to Manhattan. Abraham Ebdus would be perfectly glad if the bridge was gone. He'd turned his back on the city which lay across that river and was stalking off in the opposite direction, into a desert of his own making, a desert of celluloid.

Erlan Hagopian, for his own purring reasons, didn't hesitate. He seemed to recognize the logic of Abraham Ebdus's capitulation: Having asked you to set your price for a roomful of paintings you refuse to sell me even one – and in that overcompensating gesture, that childish underestimation of money's force, is the seed of the moment to come, when you will inevitably come begging to sell me the roomful. Naturally.

Perhaps Erlan Hagopian had always wanted to buy a whole roomful of nudes, and now would be able to say he had. Perhaps he bought roomfuls of nudes every week. Perhaps he'd intuited the death of Abraham's career in painting and knew he was collecting a luminous mass tombstone, perhaps Rachel Ebdus was now his mistress, captive in luxury in a Park Avenue penthouse, and the paintings were only the seal on an invisible deal Abraham Ebdus couldn't sense he was making. Anyway, Erlan Hagopian didn't ask to see the paintings a second time. He sent a check, and a truck.

Dylan Ebdus's friendship with Mingus Rude lived in brief windows of time, punctuation to the unspoken sentences of their days. There was no single story: for all he knew Mingus might be off fighting the Mole Men at the I.S. 293 annex, where sixth graders went, while Dylan, in fifth grade, was still trapped in the Negative Zone – it didn't matter, didn't contradict, they weren't the Fantastic Four, after all, just a couple of kids. By the time Dylan saw Mingus again what had happened in between was too much to explain, for either of them. For Dylan sensed that Mingus had his own secret burden, his own changed world beating away under the silence. There was nothing to do but pick up where they'd left off, pool what they still had in common. What was new in the other you pretended to take for granted, a bargain instinctively struck to ensure your own coping on the other end.

In between anything could happen and was beginning to. One example: the day Robert Woolfolk effortlessly corralled Dylan in the schoolyard, by gesturing with his slanted shoulders and saying, "Yo, Dylan, man, let me see you for a minute." *See you*, like Dylan himself was now a bottle of Yoo-Hoo to be gulped or a bicycle to steer around the block forever. Dylan had stepped once, twice in Robert Woolfolk's direction, not understanding how to refuse, and found himself alone with him.

Robert said, sleepily, "I saw them take yo mama outside the house *naked*."

Dylan said, "What?"

"In the truck. They wrapped her all in blankets but they fell off. I saw her hanging out all over the street like a *ho*."

Dylan calculated distances between the spot where they stood and the four exits from the schoolyard, despairing at the emptiness of a November afternoon that had succumbed to the Woolfolk Principle of human desertion. "That wasn't my mother," was what came out of his mouth. It wasn't half an answer to Robert's craziness.

"Came out of your house, man, naked like a witch. Don't lie. They put her in a police truck and took her away."

Now Dylan was baffled. Had Robert Woolfolk seen something Dylan hadn't? He couldn't really be confusing paintings with a person, art handlers with police.

At the same time a glow of fear rose in him, knowing that however muddled, Robert Woolfolk grasped that Rachel was no longer around to *kick his ass*.

Robert went on, in a reasonable tone of commiseration. "Threw her in jail, I expeck. Locked her up for being too motherfuckin' loud and crazy."

"She wasn't naked," Dylan defended, laps behind. "Those were paintings."

"She weren't wearing no paintings when I saw her. She was hanging out all over the street for anyone to see. Ask somebody if you think I'm a lion."

"A liar?" In dizziness Dylan wanted to lead Robert Woolfolk back to his home, to show him the trails of dust and shadows of faded housepaint on the parlor walls marking where the nudes had hung, missing pictures of a missing woman, ghosts of ghosts.

"Don't call me no fuckin' lion, man. I'll *fuck up* your white ass before I'm done. Show me your hand."

"What?"

"Your hand. Right here. Let me show you something." Robert encircled Dylan's wrist with his long fingers and turned it downward – Dylan watching in fascination as though from a vast distance – then curled it in one sharp motion toward Dylan's shoulder blade, so Dylan doubled at the waist, following the line of force. Dylan's knapsack tumbled over his head, notebook pages spilling to the concrete in view between his knees. His face flooded with blood and breath.

"See, don't *let* nobody get you like that," said Robert. "You do anything they want, they get you arm twisted back. I'm just telling you for your own good. Pick up your shit and clear out of here now."

None of this was tellable. As they sat in the winter-squeezed light of Mingus Rude's backyard window, Barrett Rude Junior upstairs, strains of the Average White Band and his slippered footfalls trickling through the hardwood, Dylan and Mingus downstairs with their two heads bent together, leafing through the new issues of *Luke Cage, Hero for Hire* and *Warlock*, Dylan couldn't ask Mingus whether he'd also seen the art handlers loading their truck or whether he'd instead somehow witnessed Robert Woolfolk's imaginary police. It was outside speech. To begin with, Rachel's disappearance didn't want to be given a name, a form to etch it in Dean Street history. And if Mingus had seen that parade of fleshy canvases, Dylan didn't want to know. Too, he couldn't describe how the balance of terror Rachel had struck in Robert Woolfolk was now tipped, because he felt a queasy instinct that Mingus and Robert should be kept ignorant of each other. If they were destined to meet Dylan didn't want to be the one who introduced them, and if they were already familiar it was another thing Dylan was in no hurry to learn. Finally, Dylan couldn't ask Mingus Rude if black people called liars *lions* because Mingus Rude was black. Sort of.

So silence and comic-book word balloons and the bass thump of the stereo upstairs.

One December afternoon Mingus tossed down his loose-leaf binder, bowed cardboard pressed with blue fabric, fraying at the corners, and Dylan saw that on every surface surrounding Mingus's old Philadelphia Flyers sticker the binder was laced with ballpoint scrawlings, lines dug in repetition like Spirograph ovals, gestures toward some perfect, elusive form. Here was the scribble from schoolyard walls, now carried home to Dean Street and plopped on Dylan's stoop.

"That's my tag," said Mingus when he caught Dylan studying the cloud of visual noise. "Here." He tore out a page and, holding his pen with fingers close to the point, tongue curling against his cheek in concentration, wrote DOSE in angled block letters. Then he drew it again in a clumsy balloon font, the D and O barely distinguishable, the E swollen so its three digits overlapped – faint mimicry, it seemed to Dylan, of a Marvel Comics sound-effect panel.

"What's it mean?"

"It's my tag, Dose. It's what I write."

It was a new given. Anyone might have a tag. Dylan might have one himself any day now. Further explanations were or weren't coming. The narrowed hours of winter light were a form of patience themselves, a stoic reply to no question. Rachel had vacated a certain hysteria from the house, replaced it with the telephone and assorted other ringing tones. A day had a hum like a seashell. Dylan watched television, watched the mails, watched his father trudge upstairs to his studio. He listened to his mother's abandoned records at low volume, Carly Simon, Miriam Makeba, Delaney & Bonnie. From the barred window of his second-floor classroom he watched janitors trudge through a thin carpet of snow to Dumpsters, which were covered with the newly visible scribble. Dylan had begun to pick out names, layers in the mess. Most things had happened some time before Dylan came along, that's why taking them for granted was so crucial. You could dial up any example in reruns, *Room 222*, *The Courtship of Eddie's Father*, *The Mod Squad*. All was exemplary of daily life, the undertow of the normal.

Things occurred in one another's company that Dylan Ebdus and Mingus Rude might never discuss. They watched the Super Bowl in Mingus Rude's parlor, first sealing a five-dollar bet in whispers in the basement room, Mingus taking the Pittsburgh Steelers, Dylan, on helmet aesthetics, the Minnesota Vikings. Then they'd tiptoed upstairs, under the eye of the gold records. The parlor was rearranged, the water bed hidden, the couch and a tremendous Barcalounger arrayed around a mammoth color television. Barrett Rude Junior sat enthroned before the screen in blue satin pants and an unsashed silk robe, his thick arms fallen to either side, palms open, legs sprawled halfway to the television. Coils of black-and-white hair were like false starts, unfinished cursives on the flat brown page of his chest. He cinched his head halfway from the pregame show to consider Dylan, squinted through his granny glasses, his goatee warping wryly as he pursed immense lips.

"This your friend, huh?"

Mingus ignored the question, sat on the couch.

"What's your name?"

"Dylan."

"Dylan? I *met* that cat, man. Who you like in the game, Little Dylan?"

"Huh?"

"Who you like in the game?"

"He likes the Vikings," said Mingus, distantly, fallen into some trancelike state induced by his father and the immense, pulsing screen.

"Vikings lose," said Barrett Rude Junior, so flatly that Dylan was momentarily confused – weren't they all here to find out who won? The game wasn't a rerun.

"You know the Dolphins?" said Barrett Rude.

Dylan lied *yes*.

"I worked out with them, summer of '71. Get the picture, Gus."

Mingus rose from the couch and slid into his father's carpeted bedroom, returned with a framed color photograph, worm's-eye, showing Barrett Rude Junior in a football uniform, ball curled to his chest, dreaming eyes fixed worlds beyond the lens.

"Mercury Morris said I'd make the cut as a second-string

wideout, never got the chance, though. Damn record company put the kibosh, thought I couldn't protect myself. Cost me a Super Bowl ring, man."

Barrett Rude Junior wound down, his voice purring to nobody in particular. The game itself, when it began, turned out to be a long green flattening: of huffing, robotic men, and of Dylan's interest. Football was an arrangement of failures, a proving how unlikely most things were. Mingus kept his betting stake private, just rooted maniacally for anyone to put it in the air. Dylan chanted silently along with the commercials, *I'd like to buy the world a Coke. Indigestion.* Barrett Rude Junior twitched his fingers, beating some tune on the Barcalounger's arm.

"Gus, get me a Colt from the fridge, man."

The yellow forty-ounce bottle sweated beads in the radiator-dry apartment. Barrett Rude wiped his fingers on his blue silk knee after each sip, dark wipes which evaporated but left puckered signatures, trails.

"Halftime y'all take ten dollars, get us some sandwich makings. Go round to Buggy's, get me some of that Swedish cheese I like. I hate that Puerto Rican cheese they got at Ramirez, man." Barrett Rude Junior said *Buggy's* like the rest of the block, it didn't matter that he never went out. Names were known indoors. The block was one thing, whole, it was proven again. The brownstones had ears, minds ticking away.

Y'all was a couple of *yos* walking together.

Dylan and Mingus wrapped themselves in their coats and jammed their hats to their eyes. Wind ripped around the corner of Bond Street, flaying their bony legs, whistling in the vents of their Keds. Fists balled in pockets, palms sweaty, knuckles frozen. Prying Buggy's door against the wind. She and her German shepherd loomed as apparitions, creatures from Mars peering through glass. A black kid and a white kid buying cheese and mustard. Buggy might not know it was the Super Bowl, might even think the word was toilet-related, a blue dusty item lining her top shelf, which nobody bought.

Mingus and Dylan assembled sandwiches and the three of them ate, Barrett Rude Junior raving about the taste of the hot mustard, licking his fingers, muttering, punishing a second bottle of malt liquor. The third quarter was a floodlit desert, men piled in disarray, time desolately stretched. Somewhere ice-laden planes might be crashing, Manhattan might have snapped in two and drifted out to sea. Brooklyn was the winter island. Outside it was black as night. You'd never have guessed the Super Bowl was so grim and insistent. A shot from a drifting blimp alleviated nothing. Mingus kept his vigil, closed into himself, father-struck, father-stilled. Dylan scooted on his knees and picked through Barrett Rude Junior's record collection, which filled the far corner beneath the mantel. Dylan flipped them forward and back, the Main Ingredient's *Afrodisiac*, Esther Phillips's *Black-Eyed Blues*, Rahsaan Roland Kirk's *The Inflated Tear*, the Young Holt Trio's *Wack Wack*, the names and cover art windows to some distant world as embedded with irretrievable meaning as any single issue of Marvel Comics.

"You don't need to be looking at that stuff now," said Barrett Rude Junior, distantly annoyed. "Sit up and watch the game." He squinted, seemed to consider Dylan's entirety for the first time.

The whiteness of the boy in the black man's house.

"Your mother know you're here?" Barrett Rude Junior asked.

"Dylan's mother's gone," volunteered Mingus from the couch.

"Your mother's gone?"

Dylan nodded.

Barrett Rude Junior weighed it. Dylan's presence in his room was explained, that might have been his first conclusion. Then, in slow motion, something else dawned. Dylan sensed in Barrett Rude's heavy-lidded gaze a flare of tenderness, felt it like a headlight's beam turning to enclose him.

"Mother's gone, but the boy is keeping it together." Barrett Rude Junior spoke the sentence twice. In the first rendition the words emerged thick, deliberate, tongue-mashed. The second was a lilting echo of the first, the line now a song of admonition, a beguilement. *"Mu-tha's gone, but the boy is keeping it together."*

Dylan nodded again, dumb.

Mingus Rude's father still gripped the blunt yellow bottle at its base. He waved it in a circle, toasting an invisible table.

"That's cool. You're cool. Now, check out the long-players another time, Little Dylan. Sit and watch the game."

Did Barrett Rude Junior remind him of Rachel? Or was this only the longest the word *mother* had been strung in the air since Rachel's vanishing? Dylan felt that she'd drifted into the room, a mist or cloud, a formation. Mingus Rude squirmed on the couch, wouldn't meet Dylan's eye – seemingly he felt her too, Rachel Ebdus or some other mother, pressing on him like a force from above, like weather. Then she drifted out of sight, the camera angle switched to the struggle of inches, runners writhing on shredded ground, a helmet hugged like a baby on the sidelines, the long wait for a measuring chain to come upfield.

When at the end Mingus Rude put a fist in the air and said, "I won," his father said, "What you win?"

"Me and Dylan had a bet."

"How much?"

"Five dollars."

"Don't play your friend like that. Any fool knows the Vikings can't win no Super Bowl. Come here. Come *here*." When Mingus stood near enough Barrett Rude reached out with his wide hand, robe spilling forward, exposing a nipple weirdly soft and large, and cuffed his son on the cheek with his palm. It might have been affectionate if Barrett Rude's voice, the theatrical summoning, hadn't marked it as something else. Dylan watched Mingus rock delicately on his sneaker heels in expectation of another, stronger blow. But Barrett Rude grew absent, examined his own hand front and back, as though for something written there. Then he said, "Want money, don't steal from your friend." He extended an arm to the mantel and peeled off a twenty from the roll which lay there, shoved it at Mingus. "Put your hat back on and walk Little Dylan home now. And when you get back take a pick to your nappy-ass head, don't make me keep telling you."

Winter days were static glimpsed between channel flips. Rotting snow like black diseased gums in the street. The projects were sealed up, the kids didn't come out. Henry could be seen slinging a football into the sky, basket-catching it himself.

Alberto had abandoned him, shifted into new, more Puerto Rican friendships. It was shocking how Henry was diminished, how much his stature had depended on Alberto after all. Mingus appeared on the block before nightfall or was elusive for weeks. Comics got weird, were thrown down in disgust. *Warlock* was canceled, they'd never know how his battle with Thanatos turned out. Jack "King" Kirby's return to Marvel, from his exile at DC, was still building steam. Dylan pictured Kirby in a laboratory leaching the Superman toxins from his body, recovering from kryptonite poisoning.

A guy jumped from the fifth floor of the halfway house on Nevins and impaled himself on the spiked iron gate, which had to be cut out in a section and moved with him to the Brooklyn Hospital surgery room. Kids took trips to see the fence, until the telltale spikes were capped by a new steel bar running along their tops. You hadn't known it was a halfway house until someone jumped out, then it turned out everybody knew. As with the Brooklyn House of Detention on Atlantic, you'd avoided that block on communal instinct, knowledge you couldn't have guessed you already had.

Dylan and Abraham stayed up late to see *Saturday Night Live* but after ten minutes Abraham declared he didn't get it, and rummaged angrily for a misplaced Lenny Bruce record. Time was running backward, said Abraham. Things used to matter and be funny. Dylan took it on faith. One day Dylan found Earl slamming a spaldeen high off the face of the abandoned house, his teeth gritted as he said, over and over, *"I'm Chevy Chase and you're not!"* Earl was furious, disconsolate, nobody's friend at the moment. For anybody, ballplaying was now explicitly nostalgic. If a few kids formed a game they were like the Puerto Ricans at the corner on milk crates, recounting the past, grumbling in ritual. Ball games broke like false fevers, passed like moods. Marilla and La-La sang, nearly screaming, *Got my sunroof down, got my diamond in the back, put on your shaggy wig woman, if you don't I ain't comin' back, oh, shame, shame, shame, sha-ay-ame, shame on you! If you can't dance too!*

One thawing Saturday in March Dylan met Mingus at noon to walk up Court Street, through the scrap-strewn park that stretched beyond Borough Hall, on a solemn mission Dylan didn't understand. In the park they bought hot dogs and knish-es in greasy wax paper from a steaming cart, Mingus producing a balled-up five from his coat pocket. Mingus rewrapped half his knish and put it where the money had been, stash for the unknown destination. Just past the war monument the park tilted toward Brooklyn's edge, the crumpled waterfront: park-ing lots, garbage scows, city scrap yards. The Brooklyn-Queens Expressway was a vibrating shadow, beneath it the streets still showed cobblestone in places, elsewhere old trolley tracks lay half buried in the new tar.

Mingus showed the way. They circled under the on-ramp to find stone stairs up into the sunlight of the bridge's walk-way, then started across, over the river, traffic howling in cages at their feet, the gray clotted sky clinging to the bridge's veins, Manhattan's dinosaur spine rotating into view as they mounted the great curve above the river. The walkway's slats were uneven, some rotten. Just an armature of bolted wire lay between Mingus's and Dylan's sneaker tips and the pulsing, glit-tering water. The bridge was an argument or plea with space.

They halted two-thirds across. On the vast tower planted at Manhattan's mouth were two lavish word-paintings, red and white and green and yellow sprayed fantastically high on the rough stone, edges bled in geological texture. The first read MONO, the second LEE, syllables drained of meaning, like Min-gus's DOSE.

Dylan understood what Mingus wanted him to see. The painted names had conquered the bridge, pinned it to the secret street, claimed it for Brooklyn. The distance between Mono's and Lee's blaring, blurry, timeless ten-foot letters and the binder-scribble and wall-scribble, the gnomic marks every-where, might be traceable, step by step. Tags and their invisible authors were the next skully or Marvel superheroes, the hidden lore. Mingus Rude pulled out his half-eaten knish and nibbled it and the two of them stood in awe, apes at a monolith, glimps-ing if not understanding their future. The cars rushing below knew nothing. People in cars weren't New Yorkers anyway, they'd suffered some basic misunderstanding. The two boys on the walkway, apparently standing still: they were moving faster than the cars.

Nineteen seventy-five.

Dylan Ebdus and Mingus Rude in the spring of 1975, walking home along Dean Street studying marker tags in black and purple ink, on mailboxes and lampposts, DMD and FMD, DINE 11 and SCAR 56, trying to break the code, mouthing syllables to themselves. Dylan and Mingus together and alone, in windows of time, punctuation. One crossing Nevins to dodge a clump of kids from the projects, keeping his white face hidden in a jacket hood; one hanging in loose gangs of black kids after school, then walking alone to Dean Street. The two of them, a fifth and a sixth grader, stranded in zones, in selves. White kid, black kid, Captain America and Falcon, Iron Fist and Luke Cage. In windows of time, returning from different schools to the same block, two brownstones, two fathers, Abraham Ebdus and Barrett Rude Junior each wrinkling back foil edges on TV dinners to discover peas and carrots that had invaded the mashed potatoes and Salisbury steak, setting them on the table in dour silence. Dinner in silence or to the sound of the television drowned by the baying of sirens, Nevins Street a fire lane, a path of destruction, the projects flaring up again, an apartment on the eighteenth floor with a smoldering mattress pushed halfway out the window, stuck. The grid of zones, the huddled brownstone streets between prison and projects, Wyckoff Gardens, Gowanus Houses. The whores on Nevins and Pacific. The high-school kids pouring out of Sarah J. Hale all afternoon, black girls already bigger than *yo mama*, Third Avenue another no-man's-land, the empty lot where *they raped that girl*. The halfway house. It was all halfway, you walked out of your halfway school and tried to chart a course through your halfway neighborhood to make it back to your own halfway house, your half-empty house. Dylan Ebdus and Mingus Rude like figures stepping through mists of silence every few weeks to read a comic book or fool around with tags in ballpoint, dry runs, rehearsals for something else.

His old teacher's office was unchanged, so it might all be a dream, a mistake. He might be cutting out on a City College lecture at 135th Street to visit the Art Students League on 57th Street in 1961, might be again the Columbus Avenue kid gawking like he wasn't even a New Yorker, like he was some hick loosed in hipsters' paradise, positive he saw de Kooning around every corner, airing his fresh goatee and praying nobody would call him on the bluff, banish him back uptown. Back then Brooklyn had been unknown to him, apart from Coney Island, that distant faded Wonderland where, at seventeen and high on Coca-Cola, under the squeaking boardwalk, in bands of sun and shadow, he'd unclasped his first brassiere, Sasha Koster's, and, balls aching, jetted spontaneously into his binding underwear. He should have known that by spilling seed there, in the cold littered sand of Brooklyn, he'd doomed himself. That though MacDougal and Bleecker Streets seemed his future he would instead marry a life-drawing model from Williamsburg, a Hunter dropout, a chain-smoker and pot-smoker, a hippie before there were hippies, and end up raising their child alone in a row house five blocks from the Gowanus Canal. By venting Sasha Koster's breasts to the salt air he'd sworn himself to the borough.

His office was unchanged and Perry Kandel was unchanged, still genially shabby in an elbow-patched sweater, teeth and skin still gray as an erased charcoal sketch, hair wild like a *New Yorker* cartoon of a shrink. Kandel tipped his stolid middle over his desk to shake hands and wave at a chair, then sat back and spoke as if resuming pursuit of a conversational point to which he'd been building for half his life but wouldn't reach if he lived twice.

"Thinkers aren't thinking, Abraham, teachers aren't teaching. The writers don't write, they stand onstage and play with themselves instead, emulating Mailer and Ginsberg. We've lost a generation. Young men walk into my office and declare their intention to live in a geodesic dome and tend bees, or compose choral music in Esperanto. To do *happenings*. Tradition's kaput. Nothing's good enough, not since Warhol, that schmuck with earlaps. It isn't interesting enough to be merely a man or a woman, even. I went to see a so-called film at the Quad and in three hours learned only that David Bowie is without a penis. Him, he can't even play with himself. Me, I have a smaller ambition, to keep painters painting, a few, anyway. You, Abe, you're a grave disappointment."

"You said a job, Perry. Don't torture me."

"I regard it as an act of despair. You weren't selling when you sold to Hagopian, you were burying the evidence like a guilty animal. You're ashamed of paint, it embarrasses you. What, you're surprised? You think word doesn't reach me?"

"Has word of my wrecked marriage reached you?" Abraham Ebdus spoke the words he hadn't to this point, and looked his old teacher in the eye, wanting to shock and silence him. In fact, he'd shocked only himself. Perry Kandel didn't even pause for breath.

"There's a problem nobody's solved. A painter leaves a trail of wrecked marriages should he be so lucky to get laid in the first place, but, but, but – essentially he persists in covering canvas with rabbit-skin glue and pigment. That's how he earns the right to go on wrecking them."

Abraham wasn't going to descend to mentioning *son*, or *mortgage*. "If what you told me on the telephone was just to get me here for a lecture—"

"Listen, it's a job. Whether it's for you, you'll decide. It would involve the application of paint with a brush, but only for purely tasteless and reprehensible ends, so relax. Your renunciation of your talent should remain uncompromised."

"I appreciate the concern."

"It's nothing. An editor acquaintance, a clever man to whom I frequently lose sums at the poker table, he asked if I knew any young painters with both a figurative and an abstract bent, and with a sense of color. I said sure, a couple. He presides over a line of science-fiction paperbacks, which he wants to market with an eye on adults for a change, *the college crowd*, god knows what he imagines that is. For this he wants someone outside the usual hack commercial painters. He used the word *upscale*. Personally, I hear that word, I tremble. I wouldn't want it applied to myself."

Though certain to resume his galactic harangue before long, Perry Kandel paused now to savor his own last rhetorical flourish like he was sucking on an invisible cigar. Then, price extracted – Abraham Ebdus was more than usually conscious this day that every single thing in the world had its price – his

old teacher scribbled a name and a phone number on the pink
duplicate copy of a student evaluation form and pushed it across
the desk.

CHAPTER 6

RABBIT-FURRED PARKA HOOD laced tight around his neck, tunnel vision further reduced by his bowed head, the boy's narrowed view consists only of his own ribbed Converse sneaker toes shooting forward in alternation through a fur-lined oval window of rushing-past pavement. He walks this way along Atlantic Avenue to Flatbush and Fourth, hands plunged in pockets, winter giving a certain minimal cover, a chance to mask hands, face, all whiteness. Crossing Fourth he's forced to lift the furred viewfinder, turn it right and left, searching for the right moment to cross the lanes of heavy traffic to the newsstand on the triangular island. Seen through the windshields of the steaming cars at the red light on Fourth, or through the dusty windows of the Doray Tavern or the Triangle Pawn Shop, the boy might resemble a mole or rat on two legs, gray hood tugged into a shape that resembles a darting, questing nose, one which sniffs air for danger.

The mole-figure now scurries across the intersection to the shelter of the newsstand. There he looks up again, turns the nose anxiously full circle, perhaps suspecting he's been followed. Finally, satisfied, the mole crouches, under the indifferent eyes of the newsstand's proprietor, a bearded Arab who warms his hands over the portable heater wedged at his feet in the narrow cubicle lined with *People*, *El Diario*, *The Amsterdam News*. The mole kneels, peels up his pants leg, wrinkles down his orange-striped tube sock. Tucked moistly against his ankle is a paper dollar and three twenty-five-cent coins. It's Tuesday. The mole-boy pushes the dollar and one of the quarters forward on the smooth-worn wooden lip of the newsstand, then gently works the freshly arrived comic books out of the cold metal racks. One each of *The Avengers #138* and *Marvel Team-Up #43*, featuring Spider-Man and Doctor Doom, and three copies of the debut issue of *Omega the Unknown*, an instant collector's item, as promised by months of buildup in the "Marvel Bullpen Bulletins" columns in other titles. The proprietor glances, nods glazed consent. The mole-boy's parka is opened for a dangerous instant, the comics slid ever so carefully into the waistline of his pants. The mole-boy closes his coat, relaxes his arms, tests to see that he's walking normally, that the presence of the comics is concealed, but also that the precious #1s are uncrumpled. The remaining two quarters are now shifted to the coat pocket. They're to travel with him, gripped in a clenched, sweaty fist, for offering up at the first opportunity, the slightest confrontation. Mugging money. Walk these streets with pockets empty, you're an idiot, asking for it.

This creature of pure fear waddles home, tiny steps to be sure the comics don't slip.

Once indoors the mole-boy sheds his protective cover. *The Avengers* and *Team-Up* are put aside, afterthoughts. Two copies of *Omega the Unknown* are tucked in sober plastic, the plastic is taped shut, the sealed bags moved to a high shelf, archived. The last copy, that's for reading.

The heralded Omega? He turns out to be a mute superhero from another planet, pretty much Black Bolt mated with Superman, if you allowed the comparison. The comic is weird, worse than unsatisfying. Omega, it turns out, isn't the main point of the thing. The majority of pages are given over to another character, a twelve-year-old kid with an unexplained psychic connection to Omega, a bullied, orphaned kid who's going to a public junior high in Hell's Kitchen.

Hey, maybe even the geniuses up at Marvel Comics knew you were in hell. Didn't matter, didn't help, because you weren't allowed to know it yourself, not really. There wasn't any connection between you and the poor, helpless kid in *Omega the Unknown*, not that you could permit yourself to see.

That kid? He just didn't have any *street smarts*.

Sixth grade. The year of the headlock, the year of the *yoke*, Dylan's heat-flushed cheeks wedged into one or another black kid's elbow, book bag skidding to the gutter, pockets rapidly, easily frisked for lunch money or a bus pass. On Hoyt Street, on Bergen, on Wyckoff if he was stupid enough to walk on Wyckoff. On Dean Street, even, one block from home, before the dead eyes of the brownstones, in the shadow of the humming, implacable hospital. Adults, teachers, they were as remote as Manhattan was to Brooklyn, blind indifferent towers. Dylan, he was a bug on a grid of slate, white boy walking.

"Yoke him, man," they'd say, exhorting. He was the object, the occasion, it was irrelevant what he overheard. "Yoke the white boy. *Do* it, nigger."

He might be yoked low, bent over, hugged to someone's hip then spun on release like a human top, legs buckling, crossing at the ankles. Or from behind, never sure by whom once the headlock popped loose and three or four guys stood around, witnesses with hard eyes, shaking their heads at the sheer dumb luck of being white. It was routine as laughter. Yoking erupted spontaneously, a joke of fear, a piece of kidding.

He was dismissed from it as from an episode of light street theater. "Nobody hurt you, man. It ain't for real. You know we was just fooling with you, right?" They'd spring away, leave him tottering, hyperventilating, while they high-fived, more like amazed spectators than perpetrators. If Dylan choked or whined they were perplexed and slightly disappointed at the white boy's too-ready hysteria. Dylan didn't quite get it, hadn't learned his role. On those occasions they'd pick up his books or hat and press them on him, tuck him back together. A ghost of fondness lived in a headlock's shadow. Yoker and yokee had forged a funny compact.

You regularly promised your enemies that what you did together had no name.

Dylan leaked saliva, tears. On a cold day a nostril path of snot. Once, pee. He'd bite his tongue and taste the seepage, the tang of humiliation swallowed back. They made faces, rolled eyes. Dylan was hopeless, stained with shame. They'd try to overlook it.

"Boy bleeds you touch him, dang."

"Nah, man, he all right. Let him alone, man."

"You ain't gonna say nothin', right? Cuz you know we just messin' around. We wouldn't never *do* nothin' to you, man."

He'd nod, collect himself, not open his mouth. Wait to be congratulated for gulping back a clog of tears, for exhibiting silence.

"See? You pretty cool, for a white boy. Get outta here now."

White boy was his name. He'd grown into it, crossed a line, become visible. He shined like free money. The price of the name was whatever was in his pockets at the time, fifty cents or a dollar.

"White boy, lemme talk to you for a minute." Head tipped sideways, too lazy to take hands from pockets to summon him. One black kid, two, three. One near a bunch, maybe, you couldn't say who was with who. Eyes rolled, laughing. The whole event a quotation of itself, a little boring, nearly an indignity to perform.

If he ignored it, tried to keep walking: "Yo, *white boy*! I'm *talking* to you, man."

"What's the matter, you can't *hear*?"

No. Yes.

"You don't like me, man?"

Helpless.

The fact of it: he'd cross the street to have his pockets emptied. The outcome was obvious anyway. He'd cross magnetized in disgrace, under the sway of an implicit yoking, so no one was forced to say *See now I got to fuck you up, cuz you don't listen, man.* It was a dance, steps traced in yokes gone by. *Call me white boy and I'll hand you a dollar spontaneously, I'm good at this now.*

"Just come here for a minute, man, I ain't gonna hurt you. What you gotta be afraid for? *Dang*, man. You think I'm gonna hurt you?"

No. Yes.

The logic was insane, except as a polyrhythm of fear and reassurance, a seduction. "What you afraid of? You a *racist*, man?"

Me?

We yoke you for thinking that we might: in your eyes we see that you come pre-yoked.

Your fear makes it our duty to prove you right.

He was caged on street corners, stranded anywhere. A pair of kids made a human jail, a box of disaster waiting on the innocent sunlit pavement, as though he'd climbed into the legendary abandoned refrigerator.

Two voices made paradoxical, unanswerable music. Their

performance for one another's sakes, not his. The pleasure was in counterpoint, no place for a third voice.

"Who you looking for? Ain't nobody gonna help you, man."

"Nah, man, chill out. This white boy's all right, he's cool. You don't got to fuck with him."

"Fuck he starin' at me for, then? Yo, man, you a racist motherfucker? I might have to fuck up your stupid ass, just for that."

"Nah, man, shut up, he's cool. You cool, right man? Hey, you got a dollar you could loan me?"

The distillation, the question at the core of the puzzle, asked a million times, a million ways:

"What you lookin' at?"

"*Fuck* you lookin' at, man?"

"Don't look at me, white boy. I'll slap you, motherfucker."

Here was what Robert Woolfolk had prepared him for. He'd awarded Dylan the gift of his own shame, his mummy's silence, for use on a daily basis. Each encounter bore Robert's signature – glancing pain and tilted logic, interrogations spinning nowhere. Ritual assurance that nothing had actually happened. And the guilt of Dylan's whiteness excusing everything, covering it all.

What
the
fuck
am
I
looking
at?

If mole-boy ever lifted his darty eyes from the pavement he might have been casting around for a grownup, or maybe some older kid he knew, someone to bail him out. Mingus Rude, say, not that he was clear he'd want Mingus to see him this way, cowering at the prospect of a yoke, white boy with cheeks hate-red. *Hey, I'm not racist, my best friend is black!* This wasn't halfway sayable. Nobody had ever said who was whose best friend. Mingus Rude likely had a million of them, seventh graders, black, white, who knew. And the mole-boy could have said *black* aloud about as easily as *Fucking looking at motherfucking*

YOU, man! Anyway, Mingus Rude was nowhere near. The seventh and eighth graders were housed in the main building on Court Street, while Dylan was alone in the annex, one block and a million years, a million terrified footsteps, and one million-dollar kid away.

Abraham Ebdus handled the stack of postcards just as he had the slices of burned toast, loosely, nearly dropping them, and frowning as though they had ruined something or were ruined themselves. He stared at his fingers after he'd scattered them on the breakfast table. Perhaps the postcards had left a scent or a smudge of something on his fingertips. Maybe they'd be improved by being scraped clean, or smeared with butter and orange jelly. Really they wanted to be tossed out. He let the kid have them instead.

"Someone you know in Indiana?"

The boy had come to breakfast with his backpack on, running late, as always. They were like old men at the YMCA, the two of them waking to their two alarm clocks in their two bedrooms and meeting for breakfast. Dylan's a clock radio tuned to an all-news station which leaked through Abraham's wall a blaring theme of trumpets and teletype sound effects, a voice boasting "The newswatch never stops," like being driven out of sleep by a newsreel headache. The kid lived in an anxious world. His nervous system seemed tuned like a robot's. Now he edged up to the table with the backpack humped up onto the back of his chair and blinked at the postcards while he gulped orange juice.

"The first one came a month ago," said Abraham. "The one with the crab."

Abraham Ebdus saw the kid needed new shoes. Dylan crushed his shoe backs by cramming into them with the laces tied, and carved away the inner rim of the heels with his pigeon-toed walk which corrective soles left uncorrected. He wanted to wear sneakers every day, certain sneakers which every kid desired. He'd spoken angrily and Abraham had understood that at stake was less status than a certain bottom line of humiliation, the survival of the kid's willingness to even keep braving school every day. He'd bought him the sneakers but still insisted on the brown corrective shoes which looked like 1950s boaters. Sneakers two days out of five was the rule.

The boy fingered the postcards but didn't comment. "Toast is burned," he said instead, head ducked down. He turned the postcard with the picture of the crab over twice, reading the lines, then scowling again at the Technicolor-hued photograph of the red crab on tan sand. His glasses slipped downward and he shoved them back quickly with his thumb, an occult gesture performed with a fugitive's deftness. The kid was a hider.

"Give me your glasses," said Abraham.

Dylan didn't speak, just handed them over. Abraham fished out of a kitchen drawer a tiny screwdriver and cinched the hinge screws on the kid's plastic frames. The glasses were shit, made of shit, part of the contemporary ocean of plastic. Abraham frowned at them and did what he could, tightened the screws, doing his miniaturist's work. This was the level at which things could be improved. He wished now he'd taken the strange, inadequate postcards to his studio and altered them, forged the typist's Courier font with his delicate brushes, fixed the stupid, enigmatic words to make them mean something more than they did, repainted the fire-engine-red crabshell a natural green and brown. As though crabs were bright red before you cooked them, idiots.

Abraham Ebdus had studied the crab postcard for an hour the day it arrived, five weeks ago, in fact. Dylan's name was typed in full on the back, the address was typed, the message too, all with a manual typewriter that had a misaligned ribbon which ornamented each of the wobbly-struck letters with a faint under-halo of red. Close inspection revealed too a miniature trail of oily gear marks made by the grinding of the postcard along the type-writer barrel's right edge. The postage stamp was a reproduction of *LOVE* by Robert Indiana – that charlatan – and the message, which included no capitals or punctuation, read:

this crab runs sideways west
out of the pot
but not out of potluck
pacific ocean mermaid dreams
be good d and you'll see one

Unsigned. Postmarked Bloomington, Indiana, which to Abraham could hardly mean less. Three more postcards came in the following weeks. The second showed the same Indiana postmark, followed by two boasting an erratic trail west, Cheyenne, Wyoming, and Phoenix, Arizona. All stamped with *LOVE* and all equally gnomic, only now the typist had given attribution, still in type, at the foot of the flighty poems, capitalized to show it was the author's name: *Running Crab*. Abraham Ebdus had read Running Crab's subsequent messages with a fury that blurred the dopey words so they swam in his vision. Anyhow, they weren't addressed to him.

Now he again asked his son, "Got a friend in Indiana?" He was fishing, couldn't help himself.

Dylan didn't reply, just scooped the postcards together like a deck of cards and shoved them into his backpack without reading them. Saving them for later. He seemed quite unsurprised.

"I should have given them to you when they came," said Abraham. "I will from now on. If more come."

Dylan stared up at him for an instant, adjusting the placement of his tightened frames on his nose.

"I already got two," Dylan said. "They came on Saturday."

Now Abraham was silenced.

Outside, at the bottom step of his stoop, the boy looked back to be sure Abraham wasn't watching through the parlor window, then slung his knapsack off his shoulders and unsnapped the top. Inside were his sneakers, Pro Ked 69ers in navy blue canvas, with the red-and-blue rubber stripes on the sole as thick and satisfying badges of legitimacy. Under the prodding of a fingernail the rubber stripes had the chewy, resistant texture of a fresh spaldeen. Today nobody would hound him singing *Rejects, they make your feet feel fine, rejects, they cost a dollar ninety-nine*, because these sneakers indisputably weren't rejects. Few things were as clear. While the knapsack was open the boy stashed his glasses, pushing them into the corner beside the six Running Crab postcards, the two he'd retrieved from the mail himself, the four new ones, three unread, which he'd study later. His interest in the postcards was clinical. The missives from Running Crab were amusing but had nothing to do with his life, like a dated and essentially forgettable television show you watched a lot anyway, but disdainfully, priding yourself on how seldom you laughed or even cracked a smile, *Gilligan's Island* or *Mister Ed*.

He changed his brown corrective shoes for the Pro Keds, but the shoes didn't go in the knapsack. They didn't go anywhere near school, not anymore. The shoes had a place under Rachel Ebdus's overgrown forsythia plot in the yard to the left of the stoop, a cranny the boy had scooped out where they could nest with the earth and the bugs and the twigs until the boy came home from school and retrieved them. The shoes were an artifact from the fitful past, fossil shoes, and they belonged in the ground. Everyone knew to call them roachstompers because they associated them, properly, with their ancient cousins. That their survival into the present was uncanny didn't make it any less embarrassing. The shoes ought to adapt, grow wings and disguise themselves as present-day birds, like the dinosaurs had. Or return to the ocean, become turtles. Until they burrowed back into the past where they belonged they could live in the earth, nestled in the cool forsythia roots which would never again be thinned or trimmed, and there they would be denied the sunlight which embarrassed them. It was for their own good. If Running Crab sent a postcard with a return address maybe he'd send her the shoes in the mail. Crab and shoes could run together, could scuttle into the sea. Dylan, he'd stick with Pro Keds.

Near the finish of that desultory sixth-grade spring they found each other again, like it was the most normal thing in the world, like they hadn't missed half a year of afternoons. Mingus wore a military-green jacket though it was too warm for a jacket, and the jacket clanked, full of some metallic something which had been pushed through torn pockets to nestle in the lining. The jacket's back panel bore Mingus's tag, DOSE, elaborately surrounded by asterisklike stars and swooping punctuation. All went unremarked. Dylan pushed his schoolbag just inside Mingus's basement door and they slouched their way together down Dean Street, the block which had become so useless now, no skully, no ball games, any kid you could think of off in some cluster or gang, like survivalist cells. Just Marilla and La-La, but they didn't even seem to recognize you now as they sang to each other *I'm eightee-een with a bullet, got my finger on the trigger, I'm gonna pull it, yeah—*

They crept wordlessly into Brooklyn Heights, away from Dean Street, putting the Gowanus Houses and the Wyckoff Gardens at their backs, leaving Court Street and I.S. 293 skirted entirely. By way of Schermerhorn Street they slipped past the shadow of the Brooklyn House of Detention into the preserve of the Heights. There they fell with relief to perfect invisibility on the silent, shady streets – Remsen and Henry and Joralemon – ancient brownstone blocks like placid opening shots, scenes never to be disturbed by any action. Remsen in particular resembled an arboretum, a diorama of perfect row houses beneath a canopy of trees, their underlit parlor ceilings glowing through curtains like sculpted butter, brass doorknockers and doorknobs like the features of gleaming masks, street numbers etched in silver and gold leaf on beveled-glass transoms. Here was *Brooklyn prime*, the condition to which Boerum Hill lamely aspired. Here, stoops were castle stairs. No one went in or out that Dylan saw.

They were pretty much invisible too in the throngs on Montague Street, the three o'clock flood of private-school kids from Packer Institute and Saint Ann's and Brooklyn Friends. The Heights kids clustered around the Burger King and the Baskin-Robbins in giddy crowds, boys mixed with girls, all in Lacoste shirts and corduroys, suede jacket sleeves knotted at their waists, flutes and clarinets in leather cases heaped carelessly with backpacks at their feet, senses so bound up in a private cosmos of flirtation that Dylan and Mingus passed through them like an X ray.

Then a blond girl with an intricate mouthful of braces stepped out of her gaggle of look-alikes and called them over. Eyes wild with her own daring, she showed a cigarette.

"Got a light?"

Her friends busted up at the self-conscious comedy of it, but apparently Mingus didn't care, could live inside the quote, make it real. He dug in his jacket lining and pulled out a bright blue lighter, like a PEZ container that blurted a curl of fire.

How she'd known he'd have it Dylan couldn't fathom. The tone of the scene switched again, the girl leaned in, eyes narrowed ferally now, thrilled and wary, tilted her head, scooped her hair around her ear to protect it from the flame. She turned her back the moment the cigarette was lit and Dylan and Mingus moved on, dismissed.

The Heights kids were rich most of all with each other.

The Heights Promenade was a rim of park cantilevered over the Brooklyn-Queens Expressway and the shipyards, Brooklyn's sulky lip. Old men and women pecked forward like pigeons on cobblestone, or sat arrayed, frozen with clutched newspapers on benches in the face of Manhattan's tedious spires, the skyline a channel no one watched that played anyway, like an anthem, like famous static. Beyond it spilled the garbagey bay, yellow Jersey smoke clung over inching ferries, over the trinketlike Statue. Dylan and Mingus were detectives, not really here. They followed clues. The trail was legible in gushy, streaked font on lamppost bases and mail deposit boxes, fire-alarm poles, garage doors, finger-traced in dust on the panels of trucks.

ROTO I, BEL I, DEAL, BUSTER NSA, SUPER STRUT, FMD.

"Non-Stop Action," translated Mingus. He was hushed by the knowledge, his eyes unfocused. "Flow Master Dancers." Tags were no different from anything else: codes in layers, ready to be peeled away or overwritten.

Roto and Bel and Deal were in DMD Crew, a new outfit, jokers from Atlantic Terminals, a housing project across Flat-bush Avenue.

Super Strut was old school, he went way back. The style might look funny now, but you wouldn't disrespect it.

The syllable TOY was written in mockery over certain tags, disrespect for a writer who was a toy.

Write TOY on a DMD tag, get your *ass kicked*.

Mingus fished in his lining for his El Marko, a Magic Marker consisting of a puglike glass bottle stoppered with a fat wick of felt. Purple ink sloshed inside the tiny screw-top bottle, staining the glass in curtains of color. Mingus drew out a safety pin and stuck the felt in a dozen places, *pinning it out* he called it, until the ink bled so freely it stained the light skin at his palm, then the green cuff of his oversize jacket. Dylan felt a quiver of the pleasure he associated with his father's tiny brushes, with Spirograph cogs and skully caps.

DOSE went up on a lamppost, Mingus's hand moving in studied arcs.

A tag was a reply, a call to those who heard, like a dog's bark understood across fences. A reply in moist purple. The letters dripped and stunk thrillingly. Every time they went up Mingus hustled Dylan away, the El Marko clanking back in his jacket lining against the blue lighter and whatever else. Mingus pushing at Dylan's elbow, the two boys crossed the street diagonally, ducking pursuers who weren't necessarily real. Their path was a zigzag sentence consisting of a single word, DOSE, written in blank spots found everywhere.

Under oblivious eyes, the invisible autographed the world.

The long path of the Promenade curled at the end in a small abandoned playground, two swings, a slide. Mingus took a minute to tag DOSE on the heel-dented mercury sheen of the slide, a particularly juicy rendition with a dripping halo.

He offered Dylan the El Marko. The purple-fingerprinted bottle rolled like something ripe in Mingus's stained palm, a plum.

"Go ahead," he said. "Tag up. Hurry."

"How do I know what to write?"

"Don't you got a tag yet? Make one up."

Vendlemachine, *Will-Fuck*, *Dose*. Marvel Comics had it right, the world was all secret names, you only needed to uncover your own.

White Boy?

Omega the Unknown?

"Dillinger," Dylan said. He stared, not quite reaching for the El Marko.

"Too long, man. Something like Dill Three, D-Lone."

A Filipino babysitter creaked a stroller into the playground. Mingus slipped the marker into his jacket, tilted his head.

"Let's go."

You could flee a woman who was four feet tall and a baby lashed into a stroller, scramble away giddy and hysterical. It was only real threat that froze you where you stood, your feet like

bricks, to dig in your pocket and offer up your bills and change.
Go figure.

Mingus hoisted onto the fence surrounding the playground,
swung a leg, dropped. Dylan, trying to follow, doubled himself
on the fence. Mingus braced under Dylan's arms while Dylan
scrabbled with his foot. They fell together like cartoon cats in
a sack on the other side.

"Dang, son, get off me!"

Dylan found his glasses where they'd tumbled in the grass.
Mingus brushed at his pants, his jacket, like James Brown
checking his suit for imaginary lint. He was grinning, lit up. A
shard of leaf in the coils of his hair.

"Get up, son, you're on the ground!" Mingus at his happiest
called Dylan *son* in a booming voice, another quotation, half
Redd Foxx, half Foghorn Leghorn.

He offered his hand, yanked Dylan to his feet.

There was something about a physical collision, a moment
when fond irritation found an outlet. It wasn't sexual, more just
the routine annoyance of what you were supposed to be doing
with your time being answered by the occasional pratfall.

You felt its use. The Italian kids on Court Street knocked
each other down at regular intervals.

Dylan wanted to clear the leaf from Mingus's hair but left
it alone.

They trudged down a grade to a hidden patch of land, a tilted
triangle of desolate ailanthus and weeds, choked in exhaust at
the edge of the Brooklyn-Queens Expressway, cars whirring
indifferently below. The patch was littered with cigarette butts,
forty-ounce bottles, shreds of tires. It formed another oasis of
neglect, with all the secret authority of the abandoned house.
Even the Heights was shored with wreckage, the characteristic
crap that underpinned everything.

Again they'd traveled in famous traces, like pilgrims. The
stone wall that rose up to the Promenade was covered with
six-foot letters, patient graffiti masterpieces to be viewed by
the passing drivers. They backed toward the traffic to view the
art, Dylan adjusting his glasses on his nose. MONO and LEE: the
Dynamic Duo had struck here too.

In Dylan's mind Mono was black and Lee was white.

Mingus leaned against the painted wall, shaded by a canopy of ailanthus, and thumbed the blue lighter, held it sideways to the tip of a small, faucetlike chrome pipe, another surprise product of the green jacket's lining. Head tilted, eyes squeezed in concentration, Mingus sipped at smoke, held it in with thin-pressed lips. Fumes leaked from his nose. He nodded his chin at Dylan, finally exhaled.

"You want some weed?"

"Nah." Dylan tried to keep it breezy, an incidental turn-down that could have gone either way.

Below, trucks roared past, a wall in motion. They bore their own graffiti markings from other parts of the city, alien communication spread by an indifferent carrier, like a virus.

"I took it from Barrett. He keeps it in the freezer."

These days Mingus called his father Barrett. To Dylan it was probably the key to everything, a crucial stance. Alone, he'd rehearse the possibility under his breath: *Abraham, Abraham, Abraham.*

"Does he know?" Dylan asked.

Mingus shook his head. "He got so much, he won't even notice." He flicked the lighter again, the bowl of the pipe flaring orange, crackling faintly. Dylan worked not to tip his fascination.

"You ever smoke weed?"

"Sure," Dylan lied.

"It's no big thing."

"I know."

"Everybody gets theyselves high on something – that's what Barrett says." *Every-body gets they-selves high on some-thing* carried like musical DNA a trace of *Mu-tha's gone but the boy is keeping it together.*

"It's okay, I did it before, I just don't want to right now."

"Before?" Mingus tested him gently.

"Sure," said Dylan. "My *mom's* a pothead." As it came from his mouth Dylan knew he'd betrayed Rachel, tossed her out like a skully cap you played indifferently, didn't mind losing.

Shrugging around in your own language, falsely casual, you discovered what you already knew. The stories embedded in the words like puns, waiting.

Running Crab *not out of potluck*.

"Yeah, well, speaking of which, my moms kicked Barrett out for smoking drugs," said Mingus. He was compelled to chip in his own disaster, then went mute. Possibly mentioning anyone's moms out loud, even your own, was miscalculation enough to blow an afternoon.

You were never ineligible for a screwup like that – say the unsayable word and watch it foul the sky. Dodging any mention of Intermediate School 293 or the terms *white* or *black* you might think you were in the clear, but you'd be wrong.

There ought to be a whole other language. As it was, talk of Rachel pointed like a sundial shadow to situations like Robert Woolfolk, stuff you'd worked to leave obscure. Then you were right back where you didn't want to be. Pinned to the grid.

A white boy in sixth grade, squirming in the glare.

Yoked.

Yo mama.

Mingus made the pipe disappear into his jacket. The two of them clambered up the grade, scaled the fence easily, and in silence stalked back along Pierrepont, putting the Promenade behind them. Though Dylan was ready now to be offered the El Marko, ready to uncap the pinned-out, purple-soaked felt and feel it flow under his own hand, to discover his own graffiti name and to plop it dripping on the sides of lampposts beside Mingus's DOSE, they tagged nothing. Mingus's hands remained buried in the pockets of the jacket, fists pushed into the lining to grip the lighter and the pipe and the El Marko so they didn't clank together as they bounced against his thighs.

Mingus stalking ahead. Leaf still in his hair.

Dylan wasn't even a *toy*, not yet.

Probably Mingus was high too, his brain in some other quadrant, the Negative Zone maybe. That part was too much to factor. Just *another revoltin' development*, to quote Ben Grimm, more commonly known as the Thing.

He'd learned to let the mail sit until the boy came home from school, to let the boy toss down his knapsack and sort whatever had been pushed through the mailslot and palm away the Running Crab postcard, when one had come, hide it among his *private stuff*, a category of the boy's that was ever-expanding. Only after Dylan had slid the mail around with his foot, spreading it on the hallway floor and abandoning it there did Abraham Ebdus retrieve the bills, letters, exhibition announcements, whatever else might have come. So the day's mail sat all afternoon just inside the door, and Abraham on his journeys downstairs from studio to kitchen for coffee or sandwiches did his honest best not to notice whether there might be a postcard sticking out of the pile. He didn't want to know.

Tonight, after Dylan had passed through the hallway and moved to the kitchen to unpack his homework on the table, Abraham found a thin package pushed through the slot, return-addressed with the name of his new employer. Though he guessed its contents instantly, he held the package in his gaze for a long minute, darkness massing behind his eyes, a sort of headache of pride and rage. When he finally tore it open a shudder of self-loathing went through him, and he nearly ripped the package in half down the center, destroying the thin mass-market paperback book before it was unveiled.

Neural Circus by R. Fred Vundane, the first in a series called the New Belmont Specials, heralded as "Mind-Warping Speculative Fiction for the Rock Age." Jacket art by Abraham Ebdus: a third-rate surrealist landscape or moonscape or mindscape of brightly colored yet somehow ominous biomorphic forms, indebted to Miró, indebted to Tanguy, indebted to Ernst, indebted even to Peter Max, and repaying none of those debts in the least. The art department of Belmont Books had overlaid his gouache-on-pasteboard with an electric-yellow sans serif font meant to resemble computer-screen lettering. Abraham wished now he'd denied them the use of his real name, substituted a pseudonym instead, as the author apparently had: A. Fried Mothball or J.R.R. Foolkiller. The colors he'd applied with his own brushes hurt his eyes.

Abraham carried the book into the kitchen, thinking he'd drop it casually onto the table in the middle of Dylan's homework. Pique compelled his wrist and he flipped the book to the floor instead. It skidded, spinning to a spot under the table near Dylan's feet. Dylan raised his eyebrows, looked under the table.

"What's that?" said Dylan.

"My first published book," said Abraham, unable to modulate the bitterness in his tone.

Dylan scooped the book up from the floor and took it into the parlor, wordlessly. Abraham moved a package of defrosted lamb chops from the refrigerator to the sink, ran the tap. Set onions on the counter, considered them. He could only bear the silence for a few minutes before peering in to see Dylan screwed into the corner of the couch, his whole body curled around *Neural Circus*. Dylan didn't look up as Abraham entered. The kid read books like he was engaged in some sort of scavenger procedure, scowling in concentration, turning pages at improbable speed while he flayed away the inessential flesh of prose and inspected the skeleton of story, the bare facts or crucial nonsense. Dylan Ebdus didn't read, he *filleted*.

Abraham returned to the kitchen. He sliced onions, tossed the chops in a pan. By the time he'd gotten dinner on the table and was about to summon Dylan, the boy trotted back in with the garish little book.

"Not bad," said Abraham Ebdus's son. His tone suggested he'd read plenty that were worse. And then, in an act of almost unbearably dry wit, the boy returned the book carefully to the spot on the floor where Abraham had thrown it, covered his mouth with his fist and mimicked a slight cough, and turned to his dinner.

The book lay there through dinner, at sea between their feet. Later, after the television was on, Dylan safely established at his pew in the church of *The Six Million Dollar Man*, Abraham retrieved the book and slipped it into his back pocket, carried it upstairs to his studio. There he cleared a row of ink bottles from a shelf just above eye level, at the desk where he painted film. *Neural Circus* would have company soon enough: he'd already painted three more jacket designs for the New Belmont Specials, and a fourth lay in rough form on a table across the room. He couldn't consider it now.

He dipped his brush, and focused his hot, onion-stinging eyes on the small celluloid frame where he'd left off work. His film's plot had lately turned to the banishment or purgation, by degrees, of color. By infinitesimal movements, small blottings and eclipses, black and gray were coming to dominate the zone

above the horizon line at the center of the frame, and white and
gray the zone below. What colors remained were muted, fading
rapidly as though disheartened by the trend, their obvious death
sentence. They'd seen the writing on the wall. *First they came
for the crimsons and I didn't speak up, then they came for the ochres—*
The New Belmont Specials were purgatory for the banished
colors, Abraham decided now. By expelling onto the jacket
designs his corruptest impulses – the need to entertain or distract with his paints, the urge to do anything with his paints
apart from *seeing through them* to the absolute truth – he'd further
purify his film. The published paperback art, he saw now, with
a thrill that felt almost vindictive, would be a Day-Glo zombie
standing in for his painting career, a corpse that walked. Meanwhile, thriving in seclusion, like a *Portrait of Dorian Gray* in
reverse, would be the austere perfection of the unpublished,
unseen film.

Mole-boy ventures out in springtime unprotected. Takes his
chances. He folds a dollar into sixteenths and works it into a
slot on the inside of his belt buckle, arms himself with a double
bluff: two quarters in his pocket, and another fifty cents he's
willing to cough up tucked into his sock. Whatever it takes.
This operation is routine. In his front pocket, though, the scrabbling furtive creature has a stash he's nervous about, his hands
eager, prickly. His own El Marko, jet-black, seal unbroken. At
Pearl Paint on Canal Street the Saturday before, on a run for art
supplies, the mole-child had gathered it up with a sketch pad
and a long tin box of colored pencils. Abraham Ebdus paid for
the lot, no questions asked.

It's Saturday, not quite ten in the morning the fifth day of
June. Sixth grade is nearly shed now, the I.S. 293 Annex a one-
year carapace, like a gross bodily phase, a mistake. What's the
point of a one-year school? You couldn't grow into any useful
stature. Next year was what mattered now, always had been,
if you'd only known. You were readying for seventh grade.
The main building on Court Street, with Mingus Rude in
the grade ahead. There you'd stand some chance. Maybe.
Seventh grade: concentrate, bring it into being. Looking anywhere beyond that, to high school, the guilty muffled fantasy

of girls, blond girls like the lost-not-forgotten Solvers, is likely unwise for a mole-creature looking to avoid getting yoked. Take it one step at a time, o creature of the depths.

Meantime, prepare to enter Mingus's ranks. Earn your stripes, locate your name. Saturday morning you could dare to hope the kids in the projects were all still in their Jockey underwear, five to a couch, watching *Merrie Melodies* on black-and-white screens. The stink of the solvent factory on Bergen is the only thing loud today, the Puerto Ricans not yet assembled in front of Ramirez's store, the vacant bus floating like a chubby mote in new-summer light toward Third Avenue. A morning like this one might be a safe time to bring your name into being, throw it up on a wall. Nevertheless, mole-boy moves with nothing short of usual caution. Day, night, doesn't matter. Who knows how he'll explain if he's cornered and forced to empty his pockets, show the El Marko. The thing's a stolen passport, a charm he hasn't earned the right to carry.

Glancing behind, he moves up Nevins.

On the block of Pacific Street between Nevins and Third a couple of side-by-side empty lots had been converted into what was called a vest-pocket park. Really just a dent in the block's façade of brownstones, a square of ungreen public space, full of an oddly deep sandpit and some modernistic climbing furniture made of heavily lacquered wooden beams, plus the convention-al slide and swings. The vest-pocket's floor was black rubber matting in squares, joined by jigsaw-puzzle hinges, and strewn everywhere with broken glass and stubbed cigarettes and evap-orated puddles of urine that marked the site's true life. The slide and swings and the bolted-down garbage bins and the brick of the walls that made the vest-pocket's three sides were thick-layered with tags in spray paint and marker. A kid was widely regarded as an idiot for setting foot in that sand even in sneakers, forget barefoot. That's if you entered the Venus Flytrap of the park at all. Mole-boy regards it as a zone he sees the less of the better, and it takes courage for him to enter it now, though a quick glance confirms he's alone.

He fumbles the El Marko free of his pocket and looks for a clean spot.

The last square of untagged surface in the vest-pocket is low on the underside of the slide, the angle awkward-to-impossible. Knees bent, he duckwalks into the slide's shadow and uncaps. Smells the fresh reek of the black ink. He's got a name ready, a secret with himself, practiced a thousand times the past two weeks, ballpoint on school desk, Sharpie marker on loose-leaf binder, bare fingertip in the air.

But this isn't going to happen today.

Because today is the day the flying man falls from the roof.

First a shadow flashing at the corner of the boy's eyes as he crouches under the slide, an immense bird- or bat-like stretch of black against the brick wall. Flight, reversed. Then a collapsing thud, someone thrown, and the wheezing sigh, the exhale thrown from a body by force of impact. The long sigh resolving into a moan. The boy starts, grazing his head on the slide's underside, drops the marker. Caged in the slide's shadow, he wonders if he could somehow hide there from the whatever.

Answer's nope, he can't.

"Little white boy," groans the voice. "Whatchoo doin'?"

The flying man is huge, up close. He's seated on the rubber matting and against the wall, a few feet away, knees up, two hands at his right ankle, rubbing. The skin of his knobby, flinty hands and at his ankle, at each of his ankles, bare above ratty red sneakers – *rejects*, in point of fact – is scaly, psoriatic, white tracing on alligator black. He's dressed in jeans oiled gray with filth and a formerly white shirt, cuffs shredded, a button dangling by a thread. And over his shoulder, crumpled between his wide back and the brick wall, a bedsheet cape, knotted at the neck just like the kid in *Where the Wild Things Are*, only stained yellow. Unavoidably the boy thinks: *pee*-stained. And the flying man smells like pee, even worse than the park does.

The flying man grumbles again, looks up even as he goes on rubbing his ankle. His jaw is stubbled and pitted, curls of white boiled in dark acne. His nose points sideways. And where the flying man's eyes ought to be white they're that same pee-stain color, as though he's somehow urinated even into his own eyeballs.

Dylan Ebdus doesn't speak, he stares.

The flying man nods at the fallen El Marko. "Scrawling up some nassyshit on the walls, I seen you."

"You fell down," says Dylan Ebdus.

"Nah, man, I *flew* down," says the flying man. "Fucked up my motherfucking leg, though. Can't land right no more."

"How – how can you fly?"

"Hah. Ain't 'cause of this fucking thing, that's for damn sure." The flying man pulls now at the sheet around his neck, sticks his blunt fingers in the knot and jerks it loose, surprisingly easily. He balls the soiled cape and tosses it to the side, into a pile of broken glass. "Tangle me up, hurt my leg, dang," he mutters. "Got to be fallin' all the time."

Dylan Ebdus takes a cautious step toward the uncapped El Marko where it lies on the rubber floor of the park.

"Gohead, pick it up. I don't give a shit 'bout no fucking *graffiti*, man. Least of my problems, shit."

Dylan grabs the marker, caps it, and puts it away. The flying man seems to be talking to himself now, anyway.

"Hey, man, you got a dollar, man?"

Dylan Ebdus stares again. The flying man shows his teeth, which are small and too spacious. His gum a flare of brown and pink.

"You can't talk, man? I axed if you got a dollar."

The mole-boy is almost relieved to shift to such familiar turf. On automatic, he digs in his pocket. Another part of him, though, still calculates trajectories, replays that flash and thud of descent a minute before. His eyes flicker to the rooftop, three stories high. From *there* to *here*?

Elsewhere this day's unstarted. The park an empty bracket, no one walking Pacific Street's sidewalk to confirm or triangulate any goings-on.

The flying man reaches up and Dylan Ebdus hands him fifty cents, stepping into the aura of stink to do it. He steps quickly back.

The flying man palms the quarters, turns a silver ring on his pinky finger, his eyes locked on Dylan's. There's a rime of white crusted in the fine lines of the flying man's neck, as though he's been beached, baked in evaporating salt.

"I used to fly good," says the flying man.

"I've seen you," says Dylan, nearly whispering, the knowledge appearing with the words.

"Can't no more," says the flying man angrily, then licks his lips. "Muthafucking" – here he works to find a word – "*air waves* always got to be knocking me down."

"Air waves?"

"Hah. Hah. I can't stay in the *air* no more. That's the *problem*, man." The flying man suddenly spots the quarters shining in his cracked palm, like shards of mirror sun-caught in a muddy curb. "That's all you got, man? That's all you got for me?"

Dylan nods mutely, then undoes his belt and surrenders the tiny, wadded dollar, not unfolding it but dropping it like a Chiclet into the cup of the flying man's vast fissured hand.

"Hah. You really seen me flyin'?"

The flying man lifts his chin to point at the distant rooftops above Pacific and Nevins, the roof of P.S. 38 and beyond, to the Wyckoff Houses. Seagulls wheel in the pale sky, strayed from Coney Island or Red Hook.

Dylan Ebdus nods again, then flees the park.

CHAPTER 7

A POSTCARD FROM Running Crab, postmarked Bloomington, Indiana, August 16, 1976. The front a black-and-white photograph of Henry Miller on the beach at Big Sur, naked apart from a loincloth so big it's like a baby's diaper, wrinkled chest sagging below caustic grin and sunburned brow. A statuesque, black-haired woman stands aloof behind him, in a bikini and a filmy wrap, ankles in surf, ignoring the camera.

> *don't let hank fool you d*
> *a brooklyn street kid never quits*
> *dreaming of stickball triples*
> *egg creams and the funnies*
> *in his mind he's dick tracy*
> *she's brenda starr*
> *not venus on the half shell*
> *love beachcomber crab*

He stared at the tickets so long his eyeball vibes might have scoured off the ink bearing that blind coon's name and replaced it with his own. Some fool up at Artists and Repertory had sent him two tickets to see *Ray motherfucking Charles* at Radio City Music Hall, as though he was likely to sit pondering a mile of the spangled white pussy known as the Rockettes – from the goddamn balcony! – just to see that haughty jive-ass banging on a grand piano hollering "God Bless America." Never wished to *play* Radio City, why would he be found in the *balcony*?

He'd propped his parlor windows open high. Outside, Dean Street moaned in an ailment of humidity. The heat was granular, undissolved. The sunlight on the strewn mirror blobby, swimmy. Nothing rippled the curtains, the air didn't move. Just a steady distant Puerto Rican beat from the square in front of Ramirez's store, might be the same song for the last two hours, the whole afternoon. Cars moved like jellyfish, barely distinguishable from their medium, a ripple where the tar met the air.

Four black kids dancing like startled spiders in the flow of a wrenched-open hydrant on Nevins and Bergen.

He tossed the tickets on the mirror, then carved out a line, taking care to point his toes outward, ten and two on the face of an imaginary clock. He'd recently developed a technique of widening his hips and knees and keeping his back arched as he leaned forward, so that breathing a line became more natural, the blow raining into his open lungs, flushing him through with cool air. Too many cats snorted while balled up, imbibing the drug ragefully, their bodies fistlike.

It was like singing, a matter of what distant quadrants in your belly and chest you could find to offer up.

Commitment on a deeper level.

From the low angle he puzzled the tickets with his eyes, exploring how they lay twinned on the mirror, dark writing inaccessibly sandwiched in shadow between the two pairs, the real and the reflected. Maybe Crowell Desmond, his so-called manager, had engineered this affront. A widely unknown historical fact was that Ray Charles had personally bounced a reel of Subtle Distinctions' demos when he was running Tangerine, saying, reputedly, *Don't come around here with this Motown-sounding doo-wop horseshit*. But could Desmond, who'd crept onto the scene only a year ago, be savvy to that fact? Not likely. Anyway, Crowell Desmond lacked initiative for such a cryptic put-down.

Barrett Rude Junior picked up a rolled dollar bill and drew a line clear into his lower gut, into his balls and dick. Felt the chill there shudder outward everywhere through his clammy, sweat-boiled carcass.

Nigger, he thought. Nig-*guh*, major falling to minor, an interval of sevenths.

Fugitive melodies lurked in the space between syllables, niggers themselves crouching in the dark.

No, the bestowal of the Ray Charles tickets was A&R working on its own, twitches from a corporate body which had never walked, only groveled. The resemblance to sentient life purely accidental. Someone in the offices had the wholly asinine and improbable notion they'd sweet-talk him up to Montreal to record some discofied bullshit with the German producer of the Silver Convention, wanting to turn him into Johnnie Taylor, maybe, or the Miracles after Smokey split, soul men in mirror-studded spandex bodysuits singing for horny Valley of the Dingbat housewives.

Move it up, move it down, move it in, move it out, Disco Lady! Then take me out behind the house and shoot my lame black ass.

Nihhh-*gahhh*, like breathing.

Could turn into a Curtis Mayfield falsetto thing, maybe.

In the same cause the sycophantic flacks had one month earlier dragged to his doorstep a slick new four-track tape recorder with a note on cream-colored gold-embossed stationery reading *Barry, never forget you wrote Bothered to get me off your back, I'm still on it, Ahmet.* As if that white-goateed upper-management hipster had likely even noticed the tune until the Mantovani Strings version had floated into his private fur-lined elevator.

Atlantic had ripped him off in his incarnation as the lead voice of the Servile Distinctions, siphoned royalties from his account like draining a pool. Then as final insult brought in Andre Deehorn and some no-name scab singers and built tracks around unfinished vocals, for release as a bogus final album – *The Subtle Distinctions Love You More!* – after he'd quit. Now they wheedled and cajoled for the chance to resume ripping him off as a solo act. Only heartfelt emotion they'd ever know, like hungry cousins ringing your phone: *Come back and spread green on us again, brother!* He'd stashed the four-track below, in Mingus's apartment, its magnetic virginity intact. Now he turned the same way with the tickets, shouted down the stairwell.

"Gus, man, get up here. Got something for you."

Mingus came upstairs in a T-shirt and his Jockey shorts, looking sleepy-eyed at one in the afternoon. He cocked his head at the drift of cocaine on the sun-mottled mirror, the smeary ghosts of inhaled lines that trailed out of it.

Kid stared at the blow like he'd never seen it before.

"What?" said Barrett Rude Junior. "You want to get high?" He waved his hand at the mirror from his big chair where he sat, felt the weight of his arm, a banner of flesh moving in the damp air.

Nihhh-gahhh, nihh-gahh, got you-self an itchy tri-ggahhh fin-gahhh. Could be a theme song for some movie about a pimp. Maybe he ought to fish that four-track recorder upstairs, shock their minds with a new track, number-one hit single on the R&B charts, first time the word *nigger*'s ever been on the radio. *Go fuck yourself, Omlet!*

It seemed to take a thousand years for Mingus to quit staring and shake his head.

Barrett Rude Junior just laughed. "Don't tell me you ain't hittin' it when I'm not around. Nothing to be ashamed of."

"Lay off."

"I know what's wrong with you. You're saying, Barry best get this cleaned up before Senior comes up here. Read your eyes, man."

"I didn't say nothing."

"Whatever. I got these tickets for you if you want them. Brother Ray Charles, up at Ray-*dee*-oh City. *Drinkin' wine spo-de-o-dee, drinkin' wine.*"

"You don't want to go?"

"Nah, not tonight. Why don't you call up a friend, hop up there on the F train."

Mingus took the tickets. Barrett Rude Junior rubbed his nose and upper lip with his knuckle, waiting. Him and Mingus both fine-beaded in the day's wet heat.

"Ray Charles is the man, Gus. Big part of your cultural heritage right there, my man. You'll be telling your kids you were there, *Never fo-get the time I saw Bruth-a Ray.*" He couldn't say why he wanted the boy to go. "Plus they got some fine air-conditioning up there in that balcony, man. Go cool out with a friend, get out the heat. Take Dylan. Or that raisin-looking ghetto child you been bringing around, what's his name? Robert. Radio City likely blow that boy's mind."

The talk came out of him in one breath and was strangely taxing. He closed his eyes and when he opened them Mingus stood there still looking at the tickets as though Barrett hadn't spoken.

"You gonna go, or what?"

"You got other plans?" asked Mingus.

"What's that got to do with it?" In truth, Barry had his eye on a double feature at the Duffield Theater up on Fulton Street, *The Bingo Long Traveling All-Stars & Motor Kings* and *Car Wash*. Leverage his own ass out of the day's heat, into some dark windowless auditorium with best-be-working air-conditioning. Just not to contemplate Ray Charles in a tuxedo. "You want the tickets?"

Mingus shrugged. Scratching himself in his underwear, eyeballing his father, trying to figure the angle.

"Take them, think it over, give Dylan a call."

"You don't care if I sell them?"

Barrett Rude Junior eyeballed his son in return. "Nah, man, I don't care." His disappointment was irrational, huge. "But once you're all the way up there, why not check it out? It's bread you want, I'll *give* you bread, Gus."

His pushing only stoked Mingus's own resistance, he saw now. If your old man doesn't want to go see Ray Charles why should you want to go? Too much effort all around, this day especially. Brooklyn was a tropical place, faint marimba notes suspended in the yellow air, now a Mister Softee truck's incessant, circular tune, rising and falling like an ambulance whine as it positioned itself on Bergen, Bond, Dean, Pacific, drawing sluggish kids like ants to a soda spill. Manhattan seemed a thousand miles away, another city.

Barrett Rude Junior could have done with a soft-dipped cone himself come to think of it.

Getting one was another whole story altogether.

Didn't see himself standing at no ice-cream truck.

Under the marimba and the Mister Softee jingle he breath-chanted *nihhh-gahhhh, nihhh-gahhh*, the tune, let's admit it now, going nowhere, unfolding into nothing but itself. *Nigger* would be a song unsung, more dust blown away. Besides, the four-track recorder was impossibly distant, a rumor as farfetched and unlikely as the ice-cream cone, as Manhattan.

You don't *fetch* what's too *far*. Hence the phrase.

Now, how was it that blow always make him want to close his eyes? Made no sense at all.

And why couldn't Mingus answer one simple goddamn question?

When Barrett Rude Junior opened his eyes again hours

had passed. He'd been wallowing there all afternoon and into the dusk hour, Mingus long gone *wherever* with the tickets. He awoke entombed in the dark, heat-glazed to the leather chair, the folds of his chin and neck chafed with sweat. The curtain flapped lightly in a useless breeze which had quietly worn the knoll of cocaine and chased grains to the edges of the mirror. Probably on the carpet as well.

He'd already spilled it on the water bed the night before, a new layer of sheen between his body and the sheets. Let it cover the whole house in a layer – it would be there when he'd need it, he'd run his fingers over the walls, snort the carpet. He'd bring a woman home and use her like a sponge to pick it up and get high cleaning it off her body.

True enough, he'd need to get this part of his life stashed away before Barrett Rude Senior got sprung and came up north.

Now haul your ass up splash water on your neck get out the damn house already, it's nighttime.

The Duffield was a grand ruin of an Art Deco movie palace, an experiment in what happened if you never cleaned a place for fifty years, just sold tickets and stale candy to stick to the floor and flat cola to erode the hinges of the sprung upholstered chairs when it spilled. One chair in four was upright enough to sit in. Others looked like they might have been attacked, stabbed by angry gangs. The walls were panels of torn crimson felt between gold-painted cherubs and rosettes, now blackened and nose-chipped into dingy gargoyles. The place was unnaturally dark. Red exit signs hovered in the murk, cigarette haze floated up through the projector beam to nest in the massive wrecked chandelier, below the peeling vault of the ceiling, the misaligned film played over the edges of the heavy rotting curtain at both sides of the screen. The screen itself showed bullet holes and was prominently tagged by Strike and Bel II.

Barrett Rude Junior paid for his ticket and went inside, found a seat under the balcony. *Bingo Long* was started already, maybe half over. The air was cold and rank. The place was two-thirds full, heads clustered in groups to the distant reaches of the giant room, all smoking and laughing and talking back to the movie. Squeals and moans in the darkest corners. A woman could be giving birth to twins in the balcony, nobody'd know. Barrett

Rude leaned back, tested his springs, settled in. He'd had the foresight to ferry in a brown sack with a forty-ounce Colt, not troubling to hide it from the indifferent ticket ripper. Now he eased the cap off. It voiced a quick *shuffff* of freed carbonation, answered by an envious murmur from those in the Duffield near enough to have heard: *Wish I'd thought of that, damn.*

Bingo Long was no good. It stunk, in fact, full of cloying Dixieland jazz and Billy Dee Williams in a three-piece suit like he thought he was Redford in *The Black Sting.* Plus too little Richard Pryor, too much James Earl Jones making like Paul Robeson, that tired nobility jive. Didn't matter. It was half over and soon *Car Wash* would start and the crowd was good and the air was cold and the liquor was cold. He only had to stretch it out, not drink it up before the second feature. Everyone was here to see *Car Wash* in the first place. Not that they'd be any quieter then.

It was at the break when the lights rose that he saw them, the nappy dark head and the straight and nearly blond-haired head beside it, the two of them slumped twenty rows closer, at the front where the screen surely loomed like a sky they couldn't see to the edges of, their identical blue Pro Keds thrown up across the seats in front of them. Mingus had rounded up Dylan, sure – probably dragged him uptown to Radio City to scalp the tickets too. Unloaded them on some white folks in evening dress, no doubt. Then hauled ass back to Brooklyn, like he'd read Barrett Rude Junior's mind, for the double feature. Shit, it didn't take a mind reader. Anyone in their right mind for a mile around was at the Duffield tonight, and if you'd delivered free Ray Charles tickets to their mailboxes that morning it wouldn't be any different. Who wouldn't want to be here jeering through *Bingo Long* in the dark, anticipation just making things better, waiting for *Car Wash*, all that Norman Whitfield-Rose Royce pizzazz on the soundtrack? Only proved the boy had sense.

It was entirely possible that one song could destroy your life. Yes, musical doom could fall on a lone human form and crush it like a bug. The song, *that song*, was sent from somewhere else to find you, to pick the scab of your whole existence. The song was your personal shitty fate, manifest as a throb of pop floating out of radios everywhere.

At the very least the song was the soundtrack to your destruction, the *theme*. Your days reduced to a montage cut to its cowbell beat, inexorable doubled bass line and raunch vocal, a sort of chanted sneer, surrounded by groans of pleasure. The stutter and blurt of what – a *tuba*? French horn? Rhythm guitar and trumpet, pitched to mockery. The singer might as well have held a gun to your head. How it could have been allowed to happen, how it could have been allowed on the *radio*? That song ought to be illegal. It wasn't racist – you'll never sort that one out, don't even start – so much as anti-*you*.

Yes they were dancing, and singing, and movin' to the groovin', and just when it hit me, somebody turned around and shouted—

Every time your sneakers met the street, the end of that summer, somebody was hurling it at your head, *that song*.

Forget what happens when you start haunting the green-tiled halls of Intermediate School 293.

September 7, 1976, the week Dylan Ebdus began seventh grade in the main building on Court Street and Butler, Wild Cherry's "Play That Funky Music" was the top song on the rhythm and blues charts. Fourteen days later it topped *Billboard*'s pop charts. Your misery's anthem, number-one song in the nation.

Sing it through gritted teeth: *WHITE BOY!*

Lay down the boogie and play that funky music 'til you die.

When Dylan Ebdus first spotted Arthur Lomb the other boy was feigning pain in the far corner of the schoolyard. At some distance Dylan heard the cries and turned from the entrance of the school to look. Catching sight of Arthur Lomb was like noticing the flight and fall of a bird across a distance of leaf-blurred sky, that flicker at the corner of vision, the abrupt plummeting. Like the flying man too, something Dylan did and didn't wish to have noticed. It occurred at that moment of slippage after the bell had rung and the gym teachers who patrolled the yard had returned inside, ahead of the flood of students, so the yard became a lawless zone, that terrible sudden reframing of space which could happen anywhere, even inside the corridors of the school. Nevertheless it was a clumsy mistake for the boy now cringing on the ground to be caught so far from the yard's entrance, a mistake Dylan felt he couldn't forgive. He wouldn't have forgiven it in himself.

Arthur Lomb fell to his knees and clutched his chest and keened. His words were briefly audible across the depopulating yard.

"I can't breathe!"

Then, each syllable riding a sharp insuck of air, *"I!"* Pause. *"Can't!"* Pause. *"Breathe!"*

Arthur Lomb was pretending asthma or some other weakness. It was an identifiable method: preemptive suffering. Nobody could do much with a kid who was already crying. He'd become useless, untillable soil. He had no spirit to crush and it was faintly disgusting, in poor taste. Anyway, this weirdly gasping kid might not know the rules and talk, tattle to some distant cloddish figure of authority what he imagined had been done to him. He might even be truly sick, fucked up, in pain, who knew? Your only option was to say *Dang, white boy, what's your problem? I didn't even touch you.* And move on.

Dylan admired the strategy, feeling at once a cool quiver of recognition and a hot bolt of shame. He felt that he was seeing his double, his stand-in. It was at least true that any punishment Arthur Lomb endured was likely otherwise Dylan's, or anyway that a gang of black kids couldn't knock Dylan to the pavement or put him in a yoke at the exact moment they were busy doing it to Arthur Lomb.

From that point on Arthur Lomb's reddish hair and hunched shoulders were easy to spot, though he and Dylan had different homerooms, and schedules which kept them from overlapping anywhere except the schoolyard at lunch hour. Arthur Lomb dressed in conspicuous striped polo shirts and wore soft brown shoes. His pants were often highwaters. Dylan once heard a couple of black girls serenading Arthur Lomb with a couplet he hadn't himself elicited since fourth grade, snapping their fingers and harmonizing high and low like a doo-wop group: *The flood is over, the land is dry, so why do you wear your pants so high?*

Arthur Lomb carried an enormous and bright blue backpack, an additional blight. All his schoolbooks must be inside, or maybe a couple of stone tablets. The bag itself would have tugged Arthur Lomb to the ground if he'd stood up straight. As it was the bag glowed as a target, begged to be jerked downward to crumple Arthur Lomb to the corridor floor to enact his shortness-of-breath routine. Dylan had seen it done five times already before he and Arthur Lomb ever spoke. Dylan had even heard kids chanting *the song* at Arthur Lomb as they slapped at his reddened neck or the top of his head while he squirmed on the floor. Play that *fucking* music, white boy! Stretching the last two words to a groaning, derisive, Bugs-Bunnyesque *whyyyyyyyyboy!*

There were just three other white kids in the school, all girls, with their own girl factors to work out. One shared Dylan's homeroom, an Italian girl, black-haired and sullen and tiny, dwarfed by the girls all around them who exploded with hormonal authority. The black and Puerto Rican girls had risen to some other place where they were rightly furious at anything in view, jostling at one another and at the teachers in a rage of sex. However, their very size offered an approach: it was feasible to pass unseen below. Homeroom was a place for honing silence in a theater of noise and so the Italian girl and Dylan never spoke. As for Arthur Lomb, Dylan supposed he and the other boy had been kept apart intentionally by some unseen pitying intelligence, to avoid making both more conspicuous in their resemblance. This was a policy Dylan endorsed heartily, whether it existed outside of his own brain or not. Even at that remove, Arthur Lomb bore the mingled stink of Dylan's oppression mixed with his own, so that it was hard to tell where one began and the other left off. Dylan wasn't in any hurry to get closer. Really, he wanted no part of Arthur Lomb.

It was the library where they finally spoke. Dylan and Arthur Lomb's two homerooms had been deposited there together for a period, the school librarian covering some unexplained absence of teachers for an afternoon, a blip in the routine nobody cared about anyway. Most kids sent to the library never arrived there, ended up outside the building instead, taking the word as a euphemism for *class dismissed*. So the I.S. 293 library was drab but peaceful, an eddy of calm. Below a poster advertising *A Hero Ain't Nothin' But a Sandwich*, a book the library didn't actually offer, Dylan placed himself against a wall and flipped open issue number two of the Marvel Comics adaptation of *Logan's Run*. As the period ticked away glacially, Arthur Lomb buzzed him twice, squinting to see the title of the comic, then pursing lips in false concentration as he mimed browsing the half-empty shelves nearby, before stepping close enough for Dylan to hear him speak in an angry, clenched whisper.

"That guy George Perez can't draw Farrah Fawcett to save his life."

This was a startling allusion to several bodies of knowledge simultaneously. Dylan could only glare, his curiosity mingled with the certainty that he and Arthur Lomb were more objectionable, more unpardonable, together than apart. Up close Arthur Lomb had a blinky agitated quality to his features which made Dylan himself want to knock him down. His face seemed to reach for something, his features like a grasping hand. Dylan wondered if there might be a pair of glasses tucked in the background somewhere, perhaps in a side pocket of the monumental blue backpack.

Dylan hurried the comic book into his binder. He'd bought it on Court Street at lunchtime and debated allowing it to be seen inside the school, a breach of general good sense. It was a lousy comic, though, stiff with fidelity to the movie, and Dylan had decided he wouldn't care anymore than he'd be surprised if it was taken away. This, a conversation with his homely double, wasn't the price he'd expected to pay. But Arthur Lomb seemed to sense the dent he'd made in Dylan's attention and pressed on.

He smirked again at the comic book where it had vanished into the binder.

"Seen it?"

"What?"

"*Logan's Run*."

Fuck you looking at? Dylan wanted to shriek at Arthur Lomb, before it was too late, before Dylan succumbed to his loneliness and allowed himself to meet Arthur, the other white boy.

"Not yet," Dylan said instead.

"Farrah Fawcett is a *fox*."

Dylan didn't answer. He couldn't know, and was only chagrined that he even knew what Arthur Lomb was talking about.

"Don't feel bad. I bought ten copies of *Logan's Run #1*." Arthur Lomb spoke in a hurried whisper, showing some awareness of his surroundings, but compelled to spill what he had, to force Dylan to know him. "You *have* to buy number ones, it's an investment. I've got ten of *Eternals*, ten of *2001*, ten of *Omega*, ten of *Ragman*, ten of *Kobra*. And all those comics stink. You know the comics shop on Seventh Avenue? The buildings on that corner are all brand-new because a plane crashed there, you heard about it? A 747 tried to crash-land in Prospect Park and missed, no kidding. Big disaster. Anyway, guy runs that shop is an a-hole. I stole a copy of *Blue Beetle #1* from him once. It was pathetically easy. Blue Beetle is Charlton, you ever hear of *Charlton* Comics? Went out of business. Number one's a number one, doesn't matter. You know *Fantastic Four #1* goes for four hundred dollars? The Blue Beetle might be an all-time record for the stupidest character ever. He was drawn by Ditko, guy who created Spider-Man. Ditko can't really draw, that's the weird thing. Makes everything look like a cartoon. Doesn't matter, it's a number one. Put it in plastic and put it on the shelf, that's what I say. You use plastic, don't you?"

"Of course," said Dylan resentfully.

He understood every word Arthur Lomb said. Worse, he felt his sensibility colonized by Arthur's, his future interests co-opted.

They were doomed to friendship.

CHAPTER 8

THREE WEEKS EARLIER, Dylan Ebdus had stood on the slate in front of Mingus Rude's stoop, waiting.

Women trudged little kids to kindergarten at the Y or moved alone up Nevins to the subway. Two gays from Pacific Street tugged leashed dachshunds, in another world. A bunch of black girls swept up from the projects to gather Marilla, who was in high school now, at Sarah J. Hale, down on Third Avenue. They shared a cigarette for breakfast, rumbled around the corner in a ball of smoke and laughter. All under the angled morning light, distant Jersey haze, merry solvent-factory stink getting you mildly high, the pillar of the Williamsburg Savings Bank clock tower organizing the sky, time different on its two visible faces but either way it was time to go, today the first day of school everywhere in the world, possibly. This day when summer ended was as hot as summer, even at eight in the morning.

Only one thing wrong with this picture, as the block cleared, the bus breathed past, a dog barked in a cycle like code. Dylan standing in long pants and with his backpack full of unruined binder pages and dumb pencils and hidden glasses and still-virgin El Marko. He felt like an apple skinned for inspection at the new school, already souring in the sun. Those dogs could tell and probably anybody else too, he stank of panic.

If Mingus Rude would walk with him up Dean Street to Smith or Court, walk through the doors of the school with him, side by side, it might be different.

Dylan went to the shuttered basement window and rapped. Mingus's own entrance under the stairs had no doorbell.

Dylan should have planned it with him in advance, he saw now.

Up the stoop, he rang the bell.

He rang it again, shifting in his Keds, anxious, time ticking away, the day and the prospect of seventh grade rapidly spoiling with him in the sun.

Then, like an irrational puppet, panicked, he leaned on the doorbell and let it ring in a continuous trill.

He was still ringing it when the door opened.

It wasn't Mingus, but Barrett Rude Junior in a white bathrobe, naked underneath, unhidden to the street, arms braced in the door, looking down. Face clotted with sleep, he blinked in the slanted, scouring light. He lifted his arm to cover his eyes with shade, looking like he wanted to wave the day off as a bad idea, a passing mistake.

"Hell you doing, Little Dylan?"

Dylan took a step back from the door, to the first step down.

"Don't *never* be ringing my doorbell seven in the morning, man."

"Mingus—"

"You'll see Mingus at the *got-damn* school." Barrett Rude was waking into his anger, his voice like a cloud of hammers. "Get out of here now."

Seventh grade was where it turned out when you finally joined Mingus Rude in the main building Mingus Rude was never there. As if Mingus walked another Dean Street to school, another Court Street, had actually all this time gone to another I.S. 293 entirely. The only evidence in the opposite direction was the proliferation of DOSE tags on lampposts and mailboxes and on trucks which moved wearily through the neighborhood, Mingus's handiwork spread in a nimbus with the school building at the center. Every few days, it seemed, produced a fresh supply. Dylan would covertly push a forefinger against the metal, wondering if he could measure in the tackiness of the ink the tag's vintage. If his finger stuck slightly Dylan imagined he'd followed Mingus by minutes to the spot, barely missed catching him in the act.

For three weeks Mingus Rude was like the flying man, a rumor with himself Dylan couldn't confirm. Mingus's vacancy from his own schooldays, and from Dylan's, was the secret premise of an existence which was otherwise unchanged except by being worse every possible way. Seventh grade was sixth grade desublimated, uncorked. It was the *Lord of the Rings* trilogy to sixth grade's *The Hobbit*, the real story at last, all the ominous foreshadowed stuff flushed from the margins and into view. It wasn't for children, seventh grade. You could read the stress of even entering the building in the postures of the teachers, the security guards. Nobody could relax in such a racial and hormonal disaster area.

Bodies ranged like ugly cartoons, as though someone without talent was scribbling in flesh.

The biggest shapes were the angriest. That's what they were, shapes – between hiding your glasses and averting your gaze you were Mr. Magoo now. The less you met anyone's eyes the less chance you'd ever risk doing it, a self-fulfilling program.

Chinese kids had apparently gotten some warning well in advance, and had thoroughly disappeared.

Puerto Rican or Dominican kids seemed to be tiptoeing away from the scene of everything. They decorated themselves differently and spoke more Spanish each passing hour. The way they occupied space in homeroom or gym class they were there and not there, an operation of mass adjacency.

The scariest fights were between two black girls.

On Court Street and Smith Street it wasn't even clear who was and wasn't in your school. Other bodies floated around, loose elements. A couple of black kids might corner you and ask, "You Italian or a white boy?" and all you'd know for sure was not to point out that the Italian kids *were* white. A black kid might be scared of something, might be watching his back on Court like an Italian kid watched his on Smith, but whatever they were scared of it was never going to be you. Anyway, no Italian kid would've answered *I'm Italian.* He'd have said *Fuck you* think *I am?* Or just grabbed his dick through his pants and sucked his teeth, flared his nostrils.

You, you were a million miles from any such procedure.

More in the market for a case of fake asthma.

The day after Dylan Ebdus and Arthur Lomb spoke of the Blue Beetle in the library, Mingus Rude resurfaced. At three o'clock, the hour when the doors were thrown open and the school exploded onto the October-bright pavement, when Court Street shopkeepers stood arms-crossed in doorways, their jaws chewing gum or nothing at all, just chewing under narrowed eyes. Dylan used the Butler Street entrance, looking to be lost in the flow of anonymous faces as he left the building, hoping to be carried a distance down Court Street disguised in a clot of anybodies before exposing himself as a solitary white boy. Today he stopped. Mingus sat cross-legged on the rise of a mailbox on the corner of Court and Butler, regarding the manic outflow of kids with a Buddha's calm, as though from an even greater height than the mailbox, another planet maybe. He might have been sitting there placidly for hours, unnoticed by the school security guards or the older Italian teenagers who roamed Court, that's how it felt. Dylan understood at once that not only hadn't Mingus been inside the school today, he'd never crossed its doors since summer, since the start of his eighth-grade year.

"Yo, Dill-man!" said Mingus, laughing. "I was looking for you, man. Where you been?"

Mingus unfolded his legs and slid off the mailbox, pulled Dylan sideways out of the crowd, like there was never a question they left school together, like they'd done it every day for three weeks. They crossed Court, into Cobble Hill, Dylan hitching his backpack high on his shoulders and trotting to keep up. Mingus led him up Clinton Street to Atlantic Avenue, kids from I.S. 293 all left instantly behind. There the neighborhood opened out, the shipyards visible under the Brooklyn-Queens Expressway, the avenue tilting down to the yellow-glinting water. It was as though Mingus knew paths from the school Dylan in his stupefaction couldn't have plotted for himself.

"I haven't seen you—" Dylan began.

"*Whenever you call me, I'll be there,*" Mingus sang. "*Whenever you need me, I'll be there – I been a-round!* Here." He crumpled a couple of dollars into Dylan's hands and nodded him to the Arab newsstand on the corner of Clinton. "Get me a pack of Kools, Super-D." He tipped his head again. "I'll be over here."

"I can't buy cigarettes."

"Say it's for your mom, say she always comes in there. He'll sell it to you, don't worry. Better let me hold your backpack."

Dylan tried not to turn his head at the rack of comics as he stepped into the narrow, darkened corridor of a shop.

"Uh, pack of Kools. It's for my mother."

The operation unfolded precisely as scripted. The guy raised an eyebrow at the word *mother*, then slid the Kools across the linoleum counter with nothing besides a grunt.

Back outside, Mingus stashed both cigarettes and change in his jacket-of-mystery, then led Dylan back along Clinton, toward the park on Amity Street.

"Dill-Man, D-Lone, Dillinger," Mingus chanted. "Diggity Dog, Deputy Dog, *Dillimatic*."

"I haven't seen you anywhere," Dylan said, unable to check the plaint in his voice.

"You all right, man?" Mingus asked. "Everything cool with you?"

Dylan knew precisely what *everything* Mingus meant – all of seventh grade, whatever went on or didn't inside the building which was apparently no longer Mingus's problem.

According to Mr. Winegar, science teacher, the universe was reportedly exploding in slow motion, everything falling away from everything else at a fixed rate. It was a good enough explanation for now.

"Everything cool?" Mingus demanded.

They were together and not together, Dylan saw now. Mingus Rude was unreachable, blurred, maybe high. There wasn't going to be any communing with his core, that vivid happy sadness which called out to Dylan's own.

Dylan shrugged, said, "Sure."

"That's all I want to know, man. You know you're my main man, Dillinger. D-Train."

It was a rehearsal and now Dylan learned what for. As they slipped into the park Mingus exaggerated his ordinary lope, raised a hand in dreamy salute. Arrayed at the concrete chess-board tables were three black teenagers in assorted slung poses. One more chaotically slung than the others, a signature geo-metry of limbs which caused Dylan's heart to guiltily, madly lurch. Nevertheless he strolled beside Mingus into the thick of it, accepted whatever was meant to unfold in the park from within his own sleepwalker's daze, which, perfected at the new school, covered even the resurrection of Robert Woolfolk as a presence in his life.

"Yo," said Mingus Rude, lazily slapping at hands, humming swallowed syllables which might be names.

"What's goin' on, G?" said Robert Woolfolk.

Robert Woolfolk called Mingus G, for Gus, Dylan supposed. Did it mean he'd also met Barrett Rude Junior?

Then Robert Woolfolk recognized Dylan. He flinched with his whole face, his sour-lemon features hiding nothing, yet didn't alter the arrangement of his limbs an inch.

The park was full of little white kids with bowl haircuts, maybe second or third graders from Packer Institute or Saint Ann's. They ran and screamed past the chessboard tables, dressed in Garanimals, arms loaded with plastic toys, G.I. Joes, water pistols, Wiffle balls. For all they inhabited the same world as Dylan and Mingus and Robert Woolfolk they might as well have been animated Disney bluebirds, twittering harmlessly around the head of the Wicked Witch as she coated an apple with poison.

"Shit," said Robert Woolfolk and now he smiled. "You know this dude, G?"

"This my man *D-Lone*," said Mingus. "He's cool. We go back, he's my boy from around the block."

Robert looked at Dylan a long while before he spoke.

"I know your boy," he said. "I seen him from before you were even around, G." He flicked his eyes at Dylan. "What up, Dylan man? Don't say you don't remember me because I know you do."

"Sure," said Dylan.

"Shit, I even know this dude's *mother*," said Robert Woolfolk.

"Oh, yeah?" said Mingus, carefully blasé, downplaying any further speculations. "So you down, right? You cool with my man Dylan."

Robert Woolfolk laughed. "What you need me to say, man? You can hang with your white boy, don't mean shit to me."

At that the thin, worthless pretense of Robert Woolfolk's fondness for Dylan was shattered in hilarity. The other two black teenagers snorted, slapped each other five for the words *white boy*, as ever a transport to hear said aloud. "Ho, *snap*," said one, shaking his head in wonderment like he'd just seen a good stunt in a movie, a car flipped over or a body crumpled in a hail of blood-spurting bullet thwips.

Dylan stood frozen in his stupid backpack and unpersuasive

Pro Keds in the innocent afternoon, his arms numb, blinking his eyes at Mingus.

Weebles wobble but they don't fall down.

"We going down to bomb some trains or we sit here all day talking 'bout this and that?" said Robert Woolfolk.

"Let's go," said Mingus Rude softly.

"You bringing your homeboy here?"

Suddenly a woman stepped into the thick of them. Out of nowhere she made herself present where they sat and stood around the tables. It was a shock, as though she'd ruptured a bubble, disturbed a force field Dylan hadn't thought was permeable, one where their talk, no matter how many times the word *fuck* was included, was sealed in a glaze of distant car horns and bird tweets and the younger kids' sweet yells.

The woman was a mom, surely, one of the running kids had to be hers. She was maybe twenty-five or thirty, with blond hair, matching blue-jean jacket and bell-bottoms, and granny glasses – she might have been familiar from one of Rachel's parties. Dylan could see her now, waving a joint around, making some passionate digression about Altman or Szechuan, aggravating men accustomed to holding the floor. Or Dylan might have been kidding himself. There were probably a million like her, false Rachels who'd never known his.

"You okay, kid?"

She spoke to Dylan alone, there was no mistaking. The rest of them, Mingus included, were one thing in her eyes, Dylan another. Dylan felt Robert Woolfolk had somehow called the nearest thing to Rachel into being, as though white women everywhere were charged with bearing Rachel's one crucial intervention however far into the future it needed to go.

Of all times, it would have to be now. Dylan had wished what felt like a million times for an adult to step up, for a teacher or a friend of his mom's to turn a corner on Bergen or Hoyt and collide with one of his unnameable disasters, to break it open with a simple question like *You okay, kid?* But not now. This disaster sealed his status as *white boy* with Robert Woolfolk forever, precisely when Mingus had been working to change it.

Mingus, it was clear, had been communicating a message to Dylan by his three-week vanishing act, his elusiveness: that at the new school Dylan was on his own. Nobody *had his back*. It simply wasn't possible. It had taken every day of those three weeks for Dylan to abandon the fantasy that Mingus would float him through seventh and eighth grades. Mingus cannily showed himself only after the message was sunk in: *I can't carry you, son, it's beyond my power.* Then, in a compensatory statement of equal clarity, he'd guided Dylan into Cobble Hill to the park on Amity Street to meet and make a pact of *being down* with Robert Woolfolk in order to say, *Where I can help, I will. I'm not actually blind or indifferent here, Dylan. I'm* looking out.

"Hey, kid? Something wrong?"

Dylan had turned to her, helpless, gaping. There was no way to tell her how right and wrong she was at once, no way to make her evaporate. All the worse that she was beautiful, gleaming like the cover of one of Rachel's *MS.* magazines which stacked up scorned by Abraham in the living room for Dylan's eventual guilty perusal of illustrated features on braless-ness. Dylan wanted to protect the blond woman from Robert Woolfolk's eyes. She shouldn't have popped out of the other world, the Cobble Hill world of private-school kids and their caretakers, it was a misunderstanding. He wanted to send her home to entice Abraham from his studio, that was where she might have done some good.

Of course, Robert Woolfolk didn't really matter. He was only an enemy, finally. The worst thing the woman had done was humiliate him with Mingus.

"They're my friends," Dylan said feebly. As it was out of his mouth it occurred to him he'd failed another test, another where the correct answer was *Fuck you lookin' at?* That phrase, robustly applied, might have actually transported them all back in time to a moment before Robert Woolfolk had said the words *white boy.* Dylan might have then been invited to trail the others to a transit yard or wherever else they were going in order to *bomb some trains*, a richly terrifying prospect. Dylan craved to bomb some trains as fiercely as if he'd heard that phrase for years instead of just once, moments ago. And he had the El Marko in his backpack to bomb them with, if he'd only get a chance to produce it.

No one else piped up to say *Lady, mind your own fuckin'*

business and Dylan saw that Robert Woolfolk and his two companions, Robert's laugh track, were missing. Gone. Dylan had slipped a gear in staring perplexedly at the blond woman, lost a moment in dreaming, and in that moment Robert Woolfolk had shunted away, out of the blithe park which seemed intended to contain anything but him. As though making a silent confession of whatever it was the woman suspected was going on. Only Mingus remained, and he stood apart from the table where the others had sat, and from Dylan.

"Do you want me to walk you home?" asked the woman. "Where do you live?"

"Yo, Dylan man, I'll check you later," said Mingus. He wasn't fearful, only uninterested in contending with the blond woman and anything she thought she knew. Dylan felt her irrelevance to Mingus. Mingus's own mother having been cleanly bought off with a million-dollar payment, he was immune to echoes. "Be cool," Mingus said. He held out his hand, waiting for Dylan to tap it with his fingertips. "I'll check you on the block, D."

With that Mingus hunched his arms around his jacket pockets as though leaning into a strong wind and ambled into the sun-blobbed trees in the far corner of the park, toward Henry Street, the BQE, the shipyards, wherever he was going where Dylan wasn't going to be swept along now. His gait was mock-infirm, a quotation of something amusing and profound you'd seen somewhere but couldn't place, Mickey Rivers or Weird Harold or Meadowlark Lemon. He seemed a figure cut out of one kind of day and plopped into another, a cartoon squiggle or bass line come to life.

That's my best friend, Dylan wanted to tell the blond woman, who the longer he didn't reply to her offer was more and more squinting at Dylan like she might have miscalculated, like he might be a thing spoiled by the company she'd found him in, a misfit, not a kid worth her rescue in the first place.

And that's what he wanted to be to her, spoiled, stained with blackness.

Racist bitch.

Where do I live? In his fantasy Dylan replied, *I live in the Wyckoff Gardens, the housing projects on Nevins and Third, that's where. You know the ones, they're always on fire. If you want to walk me home, lady, let's go.*

Arthur Lomb and his mother lived on Pacific Street between Hoyt and Bond, the far side of the hospital. Arthur's block was eerie, kidless, no bus, the hospital's laundry stack cascading silent white steam to the sky, the bodega on the corner another sidewalk congregation of old men on milk crates but graver, less amused, less musical than Old Ramirez's bunch. On Pacific the men grumbled in some middle distance, leathery fingers shifting dominoes across felt. Everything on Pacific including a gray cat darting across the street seemed farther away and more pensive. The block might have been the Bermuda Triangle of Boerum Hill, a space arranged the precise distance from the Gowanus Houses, the Brooklyn House of Detention, and Intermediate School 293 to fall under no domain whatsoever. Not a long-term solution to anything, Arthur Lomb's stoop nevertheless formed a kind of oasis on certain October afternoons when he and Dylan would tiptoe there unharassed and set out a chessboard under the furling shadow of the hospital's steam.

"You're in Winegar's science class, huh? I feel sorry for you. He's a worm. You see the way he toys with his mustache when he's talking to the Puerto Rican girls with developed breasts? It makes me want to vomit. Doesn't matter, pretend you like him. Science teacher's your ticket out of here, that's my view. Don't move that bishop, it's the only thing keeping me from crushing you. I told you a thousand times, link your pawns."

Arthur Lomb sat with one leg folded under his body like a kindergartner. His monologues were all brow-furrowed and lip-pursed, craven machinations cut with philosophical asides and vice versa. His jabber had a glottal, chanted quality, seemingly designed to guide you past the territory where you might wish to tell him to shut up already or even to strike him, into a realm of baffled wonderment as you considered the white noise of a nerd's id in full song. Arthur Lomb had been at Saint Ann's until the day his parents divorced and his mother could no longer afford the private school. Now he was intent on getting into one of the specialized public high schools, one of those with academic requirements, entrance exams. Arthur Lomb never pined for the lost school behind him, for the company of other white children whom Dylan could only surmise had loathed him in their way as acutely as the black kids at 293. He was all grim necessity, a soldier in open ground casting for his next foxhole.

"Only thing that matters is the test for Stuyvesant. Just math and science. Flunk English, who gives? The whole report card thing's a joke, always was. I haven't gone to gym class once. You know Jesus Maldonado? He said he'd break my arm like a Pixy Stix if he caught me alone in the locker room. Gym's suicide, frankly. I'm not stripping down to my underwear any-where inside the four walls of this school, I'm just not. If I have to BM, I hold it until after school."

Arthur Lomb and his mother lived in an apartment on the top floor of a brownstone and Arthur Lomb had the back bed-room. His comics were stacked on low shelves in neat piles, all in plastic. He handled them with somber disdain, and radiated disapproval when Dylan turned pages too quickly to have read certain essential thought balloons. Though carefully archived, his comics bore faint marks where Arthur Lomb had placed thin paper over the pages and traced the breasts of the Wasp and Valkyrie with a ballpoint pen. The resultant page of blue parenthetical breasts was stashed like secret Chinese writing in Arthur Lomb's desk drawer. There Dylan found it one day while Arthur Lomb prepared a plate of graham crackers.

"Just pass that test. Your life depends on it. You think this is bad, wait until high school. If you don't get into Stuyvesant or at least Bronx Science you're dead. That's how the test works, highest scores get into Stuyvesant, next highest Bronx Science, Brooklyn Tech's a last resort. Sarah J. Hale or John Jay, those places are practically like prison. A teacher got shot at Sarah J. Hale, it was on TV. Algebra, geometry, biology. Get Winegar to give you a practice test, I'm telling you out of kindness. Make him think you like him. Say you want to enter some kind of project in the science fair. You don't really have to do it. If he knows you want to go to Stuyvesant maybe he'll call someone. Do whatever it takes."

On the same shelves as his comics Arthur Lomb kept mass-market paperback editions of Al Jaffe's *Snappy Answers to Stupid*

Questions and Dave Berg's *The Lighter Side*. The snippy irony of the *Mad Magazine* cartoonists seemed perfectly matched to Arthur's bitter views, everything funny in a not-funny-at-all kind of way. Sarcasm as something you practiced like karate. Later concealing your mute fury when nobody fed you the opening lines.

Arthur Lomb's bedroom windows faced the rear entrances and neglected, ailanthus-choked backyards of the stores on Atlantic Avenue, the rear windows of apartments above the stores, the Brooklyn House of Detention above the rooftops, the municipal buildings and courts of downtown Brooklyn behind the jail, the trace of Manhattan's high teeth visible past downtown Brooklyn. Arthur Lomb gazed out of his bedroom with a pair of binoculars. Fading evenings after their inevitable chess Arthur and Dylan would gaze through the binoculars in turn, spying on nothing in particular, in silence for once, until Arthur snapped on his radio, which was tuned to an AM station permanently playing "Dream Weaver" or "Fly Like an Eagle."

Mostly, though, they sat on the stoop, studying Pacific Street's failure to acknowledge its connection to Bond or Hoyt. On certain summer days they might have made up the contents of a diorama in the Museum of Natural History on the Upper West Side, creatures shot by Theodore Roosevelt, then stuffed and mounted in a case: Dylan Ebdus, Arthur Lomb, Homo sapiens, Pacific Street, Brooklyn, 1976. Days were falsely still, gelled in slow motion, Dylan not thinking of Mingus Rude or Dean Street at all, just studying the gray cat as it skittered under a car, the hypnotic tumbling cloud of hospital steam, the mailman reading magazines on another stoop halfway down the block, wondering how long weird detachment could cover losing a thousand chess games in a row to Arthur Lomb's blunt but remorseless rook play.

Arthur Lomb using both hands to knead sensation back into his folded-under leg, brain whirring behind consternated gerbil eyes as he dialed up another digression.

"It makes no sense to be a Mets fan, not when you look at the facts. Few people our age have actually considered the record, but the Yankees are simply the greatest team in the history of baseball based on sheer championships, players in the Hall of Fame, etcetera. The whole Mets things is a very recent development. But so many kids like you have fallen for it hook, line, and sinker. I maintain you can't argue with the Yankee legacy."

"Hmm."

"You've probably wondered why I always wear shoes. I had a pair of Pro Keds and some kids took them from me, made me walk home in my socks if you can believe it. My mother bought me another pair but I keep them at home. My sources tell me Pumas are actually what's coming next. If you go in for that sort of thing: wearing what everyone's wearing just because they're wearing it. I don't, really."

"Hmm."

"Mel Brooks's funniest film is *The Producers*, then *Young Frankenstein* or *Blazing Saddles*. Terri Garr is hot. I feel sorry for any kid who hasn't seen *The Producers*. My dad took me to all the humor movies. The best Panther is probably *Return*. The best Woody is *Everything You Always Wanted to Know About Sex*."

Positioning, positioning, Arthur Lomb was forever positioning himself, making his views known, aligning on some index no one would ever consult. Here was Dylan's burden, his cross: the accumulated knowledge of Arthur Lomb's smug policies on every possible question. The cross was Dylan's to bear, he knew, because his own brain boiled with pedantry, with too-eager trivia ready to burst loose at any moment. So in enduring Arthur Lomb Dylan had been punished in advance for the possibility of being a bore.

"Develop your pawns or Hulk Will Smash."

Now and again Dylan saw a shutter wink open, a glimpse into the furnace of anger inside Arthur Lomb. Dylan didn't mind. He regarded himself as deserving, according to the same principle of similars which had dictated their friendship in the first place. Just as Dylan should absorb the ennui of Arthur's poseurdom because of that kernel which thrived inside himself, so again with those glimpsed coals of rage.

"I couldn't help but notice the other day you were talking to that Mingus Rude kid after school. Ahem, keep your eye on the board, you're going to be shocked again. It's going to be bad for your health until you learn to start castling. As I was saying, I noticed you talking to Mingus Rude, he's an eighth grader, how'd you get to know him? Not that he's in school much, huh. Still, it must be advantageous to be friends with, hurrh, that sort of person."

Arthur Lomb's speech bore like a small puckered scar a characteristic hitch of intaken breath in that place where he'd omitted the word *black* from a sentence but not from the thought which had given rise to the sentence. And that hitch of breath, it seemed to Dylan, was Arthur in a nutshell, making such show of a card unplayed that he tipped his whole hand.

"How'd you know Mingus's name?" Dylan heard himself say. He'd been concentrating on the game for once, waiting for Arthur to castle as he always ostentatiously castled, but ready this time, with something in store. Distracted, he'd blurted a question which confessed his possessiveness of Mingus, his jealousy. Listen to Arthur Lomb for a month of afternoons and your own talk would be stripped of disguises, that was the price you'd pay.

"Oh, various kids talk about him," said Arthur airily.

Dylan couldn't imagine which various kids would ever be seen speaking to Arthur Lomb in school, as opposed to browsing his pants pockets for loose change. Dylan himself shunned Arthur inside the school building, only met up with him afterward for their mutual creeping to the safety of Pacific Street. He understood Arthur's acceptance of the humiliation of Dylan's silent treatment at school as a clear measure of Arthur's desperation and loneliness. So, which various kids?

"Yeah, well, I knew him before," said Dylan, shutting up before it was too late. Let Arthur fish. Dylan advanced his knight in reply to Arthur's castling. He made the move lackadaisically, but his heart pounded. Arthur was blind to knights, it had only taken the first thousand games to see it.

"Before what?" said Arthur with thin sarcasm. He pushed a pawn absently, scowling past Dylan and the chessboard, toward Hoyt Street, perhaps mentally groping for a suitable Snappy Answer.

"Check," said Dylan.

Now Arthur frowned at the board, his eyes racing hectically to consider this unanticipated turn.

"Is this pawn *here* or *here*?" he asked.

"What?"

Arthur pointed, Dylan leaned in. Suddenly the board rattled, jarred at the corner. Then the ripple among the chessmen became an explosion, and the board was lost, pieces tipping, rolling, Arthur's doomed king clattering atonally down the stoop toward the street, revealed as plastic.

"Look what you made me do," said Arthur Lomb.

"You knocked it over."

Arthur opened his palms: sue me.

"I was going to beat you."

"Now we'll never know."

"You win every time and you couldn't stand letting me beat you once!"

Arthur Lomb stroked his chin thoughtfully. "Actually, I do think we were headed for a stalemate. You shouldn't get overexcited, Dylan, it may be a while before you beat me. But your game is improving. I congratulate you. You've definitely picked up a few things. Speaking of which, har har, would you pick up that king? My leg seems to have fallen asleep."

Two men, two fathers. Two fathers expelled from their lairs, headed to Manhattan for a change, dressed for a day threatening rain, having shaved their chins to make some nominal impression at their target destinations, tightened scarves with momentary vain glances at hallway mirrors before flushing themselves out of hiding, onto the street. Two fathers each sighing as they plunge down stairwells to underground trains, to endure the shoulder-jostling crowds which mill on platforms and pass through the jerky opening doors, then hang wearily from straps or clutch poles in the blinking, grinding trains. One carrying evidence, a black pebbled-cardboard portfolio with lace ties, the other empty-handed, his instrument his throat and lungs, carried in the valise of his chest. Two fathers ride a while on two separate trains, then, stations attained, Times Square for one, West Fourth for the other, two fathers again put shoe leather to pavement, out on the big island now, two fathers negotiating Abe Beame's crumbling, deranged infra-structure in the year of the Tall Ships. Two fathers blinking in confusion, each startled how reclusive they've become, drifted into their Dean Street solitudes, Brooklyn a mind-state peeling further from Manhattan each day, like continental drift. Two fathers briefly and involuntarily recalling other less morbid and sensitized selves as they move dazed through strobing faces in the late-October streets, two fathers each realizing he alone is distracted by a slide-show sequence of false recognitions – *You! Didn't you go to City College? Ain't you Charles What'sisname?* – among dulled millions trudging Manhattan daily, millions jaded out of such free-associated overstimulation. Two fathers shake it off, forcibly raise the thresholds of their own naïveté, get back to their twin metropolitan missions in the chill-now-beginning-to-rain. Two fathers bearing down, recalling their work-selves, their places in the world. Two fathers here after all for a reason, to do some business, no fooling around.

One father stops abruptly, ducks beneath an umbrella to trade fifty cents for a hot dog from a street vendor, another lost ritual unavailable in his part of Brooklyn, his circumscribed rounds. He juggles the portfolio full of painted boards to one arm, then frees both hands, crumples wax paper back and con-sumes the mustardy dog in four chunks more swallowed than chewed. The snack glowing nicely in stomach's pit but, breath possibly fouled, conscious again of the impression he'll make, the hot-dog-gobbling father halts again at a newsstand for mint chewing gum. Forty-one blocks south, the other father's got similar pangs and is tempted to stop by the siren odors, suspend-ed in misty cold, of a similar cart with hot dogs in boiling water and greasy knishes on the grill, in fact pats his stomach at the smell but pushes on, relying in anticipation on the spread he's been promised waits at the recording studio, corn bread and barbecued brisket and red beans and rice trucked down from *Sylvia's*, that's the word.

Two fathers come to their respective thresholds, pause. Rain's falling sideways now, borne on wind, hastening them to curtail reflection. Two fathers exhale deeply. One steps inside the elevator in the lobby of the Forty-ninth Street office tower and pushes the button for the eighteenth floor. The other

squints through a porthole window, then rings the buzzer at the
door of the squat recording studio on West Eighth Street, the
place known as Electric Lady.

To be in this place is to admit you exist.

To be in this place is to admit you want something.

Or maybe tell yourself you're doing it for the kid.

One father paces at the reception desk, stands rather than
sits waiting for the art director of the second-largest publisher
of science fiction in mass-market paperback in the city, no fly-
by-night Belmont Books offices now, Belmont Books with its
three-months-late checks and Fashion District office of six guys
in Chinese-food-stained shirts, no, this is publishing proper,
dour receptionist with butterscotch sucking candy in a jar and
a phone with three blinking lines. Other father, downtown,
is welcomed off the street of leather outlets and white teenage vagabonds into the odd brick fortress of a building by the
soundboard man, apologetic, telling him the others are late, no
sweat though, come in. Guy knows your name and is *a big fan
of your work*, actually says it, rare for one of these guys not to
disguise any awe, hoarding their technician's seen-it-all cool.
Fine, fine. Downtown father nods coolly, taking it out on the
guy, feeling like an ass for being early, for being first.

So, two fathers each given more time for stewing than
they'd banked on. Then the art director emerges to pump
the hand of the one father uptown, guy in a sweater-vest and
chewing an unlit pipe, well-fed corporate hipster head-to-toe,
while downtown at that same moment the doors to Electric
Lady burst open and piling in from a white limo parked at the
curb is the whole gang in their Elton John glasses and pimp
hats and boas, the bassist in his spaceman outfit of puffy satin
shoulder pads and belt, dressed this way just because that's the
way they're dressed, not for stage or a photo session but because
they're a bunch of freaks who think they're Jimi Hendrix and
Sly Stone and Marvin the Martian rolled into one – and the
father reminds himself he knows these guys, they like him and
that's why he's here, they come from the same place. Shit, they
all – every one of these jokers and himself – were signed to
Motown back in the day.

Taking his elbow and steering him inside, saying, *Really good*

*to meet you, Ebdus. I have the feeling we're both going to be glad you
called.*

Slapping his hands high and low, insisting on the whole circuit of bullshit, saying, *Hey, man, we just couldn't get out of bed this
morning! But we're here now! You're gonna luuuv this motherfuckin'
track, man.*

*You outgrew Belmont before you started working for them, Ebdus.
Don't think everyone didn't notice your work the minute it appeared.
This isn't a big industry, not once you're in it. It's like high school,
everybody knows who the cool kids are. I frankly don't understand why
you didn't come to us in the first place.*

*Forget the legal bullshit, man. We'll put some other name on the
sleeve, call you, huh, Pee-Brain Rooster. You like that? Anyone with
ears is gonna know it's you the minute you open your mouth, man.
Minute you let out that motherfucker of a voice. We'll sort out the legal
shit some other time, can't let that trouble us.*

What one father doesn't say is that being here means
admitting that what he's engaged in is some sort of *career*. The
arrangement with Belmont, he'd always told himself, with
admittedly perverse logic, was a sort of favor to Perry Kandel:
permitting his old teacher to imagine he'd welcomed him back
into the world. It was a lark. Plus the notion of the New Belmont
Specials suggested a sort of limited engagement, a run to some
conclusion. But to make this call and keep this appointment
was to grant that he's a paperback painter now, a commercial
artist. And being welcomed so eagerly here meant despite the
contempt dripping from his brush he'd done acceptable work.
The seduction of craft had led here, to the seduction of praise.
In the elevator he'd sworn he'd heard Perry's bitter wheezing
laughter.

What the other father doesn't say is that though he envies
these men dressed as cartoon pimps and superheroes their freedom, that though a part of him thinks *Shit, why didn't I haul
out the overt freak shit myself, why did I always stay so buttoned down
in the goddamn Philly system*, another part just doesn't think the
singing and playing on the backing track is any good. Funk is
soul on acid, for better and for worse; today worse. This track
sprawls to no purpose, slack, in its way, as disco. Pornographic
disco, that's really what it is. He's expected to doodle over a

harmonizing backdrop but the harmonizing isn't any good, and for the first time since leaving the Subtle Distinctions he misses their sweet uptight voices, the way they provided him such a smooth clean cushion of sound from which to launch his rhapsodies, his flights.

You want a cup of coffee? It's not too bad, actually.

Hey man, food's gonna get here. Need a little blow?

Something the matter?

Just say what you need, man.

Fathers, fathers, why so grim? Today you emerged from your houses, your hiding, and were warmly welcomed. Smile, fathers. Relax. Today this world wants you in it.

CHAPTER 9

AT THE END OF another winter, lion giving way to lamb, he comes to lie there one day in the long sun and shadows and stays for good, curled into a ball at the corner of Atlantic and Nevins, at a spot on the pavement just short of the street, in front of the never-closed liquor store and the never-open lock-smith. Fouled in himself, baked in vomit and urine and sweat, his pants black with it, he lies still as a bog man or mummy pre-served in a glass case, eyes shut and mouth rigid, arms wrapped around his middle, fighting the chill of one week before, when he first took the position. He's huddled as if against time itself, enduring the winter that's already passed, his pose a record of pain, a full-body grimace frozen in sunlight. Over his shoul-ders and tucked under his ass is a child's thin synthetic sleeping bag, feeble cover though if he's alive it must have gotten him through. The sleeping bag's two corners are peeled away in torn strips, exposing cottonoid filler stained gray with street filth, and the two strips meet in a knot under his white-grizzled chin, so the thing weirdly resembles a superhero's cape.

The flying man, grounded for the foreseeable future.

Guy looks dead if you ask me.

How? Why's it allowed? Isabel Vendle's Boerum Hill was declared "The City's Best-Kept Secret," *New York Magazine*, September 12, 1971. Gentrification – say the word, nothing to be ashamed of, only what's this alcoholic coma victim doing here in plain sight? How likely no one expresses concern or touches his shoulder to see if he still moves, still lives, how likely no one even calls the cops?

Is it because he's black?

Maybe Atlantic Avenue between Nevins and Third isn't quite Boerum Hill. Maybe it's Gowanus or some other thing without a name. Anyway this gentrification is strange and slow and not at all as coherent as Isabel Vendle might have hoped. There's a cluster of antique shops now on Atlantic between Hoyt and Bond, new families on Pacific and Dean, Bergen too. Not

Wyckoff, Wyckoff's too close to the projects, no point hoping. Then there's the communes. Assuming no one stashes Patty Hearst in a Dean Street basement they're harmless enough, an acceptable placeholder. Some eager beaver's opened a French restaurant on Bergen and Hoyt, jumping the gun perhaps but worth a shot. Even State Street, so close to Schermerhorn and the House of Detention and the eye-agonizing blight of downtown Brooklyn, even State's got a tender little boomlet of brownstone renovation.

Yet it exists under a spell, a pall. The white families appear continuously these days, now too many to count, but collectively they're still a dream, a projection conjured up by Isabel's will. The renovators – that's a politer word for them – they're a set of ghosts from the future haunting this ghetto present. They're a proposition, a sketch. Blink and they might be gone.

Ghetto? Is that the name for it? Depends which block in this patchwork you have in mind. Rise up, the way the flying man no longer can. Look. Here Fourth Avenue's a wide trench of light-industrial ruin, oil-stained auto-body shops and forlorn, graffitied warehouses, sidewalks marked with sprays of broken glass which trace the shape of nighttime incidents in front of Chinese take-out places, liquor stores, bodegas, all of them serving their customers through slots or sliding drawers in shields of Plexiglas. At the opposite end, Court Street's an old Italian preserve, the side streets south of Carroll hushed in the grip of Mafia whispers, old ways enforced with baseball bats and slashed tires, down to where the looming, curling Brooklyn-Queens Expressway forms a steel curtain severing what used to be Red Hook. South, the Gowanus Canal is a wasteland of buried or sunk toxins and smoldering strips of rubber, while Ulano, the solvent factory, is a block-long engine, its windows like slit eyes, pumping out fresh invisible toxins and accompanying legends of nerve damage and brain tumors. The projects, Wyckoff Gardens and Gowanus Houses – well, they're projects, their own law, like meteors of crime landed in the city's midst, still unapproachably hot. The jail's called a House of Detention, a thin euphemism nonetheless worth clinging to. So, the brownstone streets which span these margins – Wyckoff, Bergen, Dean, Pacific – a ghetto?

Call it "The City's Best-Kept Secret."

Nevins has unique properties, venting at the top to Flatbush Avenue and running south smack into the Wyckoff Gardens, on the way threading the halfway house, the Department of Motor Vehicles, Schermerhorn Park, and the Nevins Day Care Center, on the steps of which drunks gather to greet welfare moms as they pass in and out of the center, yanking bawling kids' arms like yo-yo strings. And widely known but rarely spoken of is this: Pacific Street at Nevins is a place where prostitution's tolerated. Some default in authority has chased it to this corner, where after eleven o'clock a lone streetwalker or sometimes a pair can be spotted in the shadow of Public School 38, heard cooing enticements to lone strollers on a quiet night. Outraged calls to local officials gain promises and nothing more. At that inexplicable level where such civic deals are struck this one's irrevocable, even as the neighborhood on all sides is gentrifying fast. So the police are revealed as skeptics, insensible to the concerns of Realtors. This zone's on their official map – never displayed to the public – of Hopeless.

So, perhaps it's by this same principle that the no-longer-flying man has been allowed to rest undisturbed for weeks in his fetal curl on the corner of Nevins and Atlantic. He's still there the last Saturday of March, when the black kid and the white kid go by. Yes, they're together again, that uncanny sporadic pair, their solidarity a befuddlement to passersby, a shred perhaps of utopian symbolism, sure, something Norman Rockwell might have chosen as a subject, but not outweighing the fact that the two look furtive, maybe stoned, unmistakably headed for if not already deep into all kinds of black-white-combo trouble. Even those who don't happen to spot them slipping blunt felt-tipped markers sopped with purple ink in and out of their jackets sense the likelihood that something's not right. This is Brooklyn, nothing integrates innocently. Who's fooling who? If the cops were on the ball they'd likely split up this pair just on general principles.

The white kid and the black kid take turns playing lookout while the other tags up. Things are radically simplified: the white kid's stopped looking for his own moniker, been encouraged by the black kid to throw up his perfect replication of the black kid's tag instead. DOSE, DOSE, DOSE. It's a happy solution for both. The black kid gets to see his tag spread farther, in search of bragging points for ubiquity, that bottom-line stand-ard for a graffiti writer's success. The King of the C Line, for instance, is just a lousy tagger with too much time on his hands who's thrown up the unimaginative tag CE on every window of every car of the trains that run that line. A success of this type is as impossible to dispute as it is mechanical, crude. Graffiti writers compete like viruses, by raw proliferation.

What's in it for the white kid? Well, he's been allowed to merge his identity in this way with the black kid's, to lose his funkymusicwhiteboy geekdom in the illusion that he and his friend Mingus Rude are both Dose, no more and no less. A team, a united front, a brand name, an idea. The white kid's control of line, honed in a thousand Spirograph spirals, and his gift for mimicry – Can You Draw Tippy? – both have served him well. His rendition of the DOSE icon is clarified, perfected, automatic – in fact cleaner and more sure in its lines than the black kid's. Just a trick of the hand, nothing anyone couldn't learn if they practiced it a gazillion times waiting for this moment.

The marker's in the black kid's hands now. The white kid's the lookout. The black kid puts DOSE on the base of the traffic light at the corner of Atlantic and Nevins, and on the locked-up locksmith's rolling metal gate. Then he turns and considers the curled figure near the curb. They both consider the figure. The bum – the word they'd find if they bothered to find a word – has been sleeping or dead on this corner for long enough now that they've both noticed him at different times. This is the first time together, though, and being together forces them to acknowledge the figure in a way they wouldn't apart.

The white kid has one set of feelings, the black kid another. The white kid's seen this particular bum on better days, seen him *in the sky*, idiotic as that sounds. He's got no idea whether his friend Mingus has this information, and no idea where he'd begin explaining it if he wanted to try. He's just locked into a permanent state of stupid wonder here, along with a slug of fear.

The black kid's curling his lip, suffering a ripple of sudden shame: of course it's a *black* guy who'd be lying here in the street, goes without saying. Not a Latin guy. No matter how many Hispanic drunkards might spill out of Dean Street's rooming houses, they always wobble home, sleep in beds, change clothes, cash government checks, and begin again. And he's no white guy, no need to even think about it.

"Watch this," says the black kid.

"What?" says the white kid.

The black kid dashes forward with splendid daring, taking the white kid's breath away. He's got the marker uncapped. The plasticky sleeping bag stretched across the bum's back has a sheen despite the grime, a slickness to welcome the marker's slide. The black kid kneels at the stinky form and tags up, managing despite the drag of the felt on the blackened synthetic: in a moment the thing is done and they both spring away, amazed.

The bum's back reads DOSE.

"Run!"

"He's not moving. Ho, shit! Look at that!"

"Come on!"

That's it, they're done tagging for the day, nothing could top this anyway. The two of them scramble down Nevins, gasping with laughter, drunk on the atrocious prank, on the demonstration of their dangerous new ability to reach out and plop a logo on the maybe-dead of this world.

They arrived late and had to take single seats a distance apart. Dylan sat near the front, in the second row. His father had insisted Dylan take the nearer seat, had himself taken one farther back and at the far left side of the lecture hall. Dylan understood he was meant to appreciate this up-close glimpse of the experimental filmmaker Stan Brakhage, whom Abraham regarded soberly as *a great man, a beautiful man*. The topic, generally, was paint on film. Dylan hadn't known before this moment that painted film existed, apart from Abraham's. Let alone that the topic could draw a crowd to fill a hall full of uncomfortable metal folding chairs.

In fact, Dylan found Brakhage, when he spoke, enthralling, though he understood zip of what he said. Brakhage was charismatic and orotund and evoked Orson Welles on television. Like Welles he suggested a greatness both distant from itself and fully at rest, in this case scarcely bothering to taste the air of adulation in the room. The problem with the presentation was that Brakhage rarely spoke. He sat sipping water and blinking rapidly, examining the audience, remaining largely silent in favor of a panel of younger men who in laborious turns pronounced on the significance of Brakhage's films. Their spiky, resentful tones failed at concealing (or were perhaps not designed to conceal) the implication that they alone understood the filmmaker's work. Dylan was bored, as Rachel would have said, *shitless*.

"I would rather see my work as an attempt to clear aesthetic areas, to free film from previous arts and ideologies," said Brakhage when he was permitted. His words rippled through the room, resonating in minds so straining toward their speaker that they practically boiled. Dylan felt it himself. He looked back at his father, who sat straining too, in love and anger toward the stage. "Perhaps to leave it clear to be of use to men and women of various kinds which might help evolve human sensibility."

The fluorescent-lit, plaster-crumbled lecture hall in the Cooper Union basement was full to capacity now, to standing room only. Dylan twitched, but he wasn't alone. The man in the seat beside him was tearing a Styrofoam cup into a thousand dandrufflike shreds which floated down to form a drift between his tapping feet. The Styrofoam-tearing man might have been in an agony of suppressing some question he wanted to cry out to the men on the stage. Perhaps he thought he belonged on the stage. Everywhere chairs creaked.

"I believe in song," said Brakhage. "That's what I want to do and I do it quite selfishly, out of my own need to come through to a voice that is comparable with song and related to all animal life on earth. I am moved at the whole range of songs that the wolf makes to the moon, or neighborhood dogs make, and I in great humility wish to join this."

When the tension in the room was at its height and the Styrofoam cup had been wholly processed the shredder beside Dylan jumped up and shouted into the panel's droning, "What about Oskar Fischinger? None of you are acknowledging Fischinger!"

Having thrown this gauntlet he stood trembling, perhaps expecting to find the crowd at his back, enraged, ready to rush the dais.

"I don't think anyone's denying Fischinger," said one of the men on the panel, in a tone of draining sarcasm. "I don't think that's really the point at all."

"Never mind Fischinger," came another voice. It was Abraham Ebdus. He spoke from the corner of the room without rising from his chair, and more quietly than the shredder, who still stood. "Maybe at this point someone should mention Walther Ruttman."

Silence on the podium, marked only by Brakhage's slight and unsurprised nod, which seemed to say, *Ruttman, yes, Ruttman.* The shredder took his seat, humbled.

Then, from the back of the hall another cry pierced the breath-inheld tension: "Fuck Ruttman! What about *Disney*?"

This brought a roar of relief, since no one actually relished the burden of understanding how little they knew of the careers of Fischinger and Ruttman. The moment was now lost in a calamity of babble and laughter. Then Brakhage smoothed everything, began taking questions from the crowd. Hostility slowly dissipated as the panelists were rendered equal to the audience by Brakhage's authority. Silent, the younger men could be more-or-less forgiven for being onstage.

Forgiven perhaps by all but Abraham.

Afterward Brakhage was mobbed at the foot of the stage. Abraham found Dylan in the swirling mass of bodies, took his hand, and together they pushed to the exit. Dylan felt his father's smoldering inarticulate fury, felt enclosed in it as in a cocoon as they descended the subway stairwell at Astor Place and as they waited on the platform, then boarded the 6 train, felt it shut them out against the other night riders, whose heads lolled with the train's movements on the weary sticks of their bodies, felt it shut them against the whole city everywhere around them.

Dylan breathed his father's embarrassment. Something had gone wrong in Abraham's demonstration to his son of Brakhage's greatness, and of his, Abraham's, kinship with the great filmmaker, this man who was Abraham's secret tutor, his North

THE FORTRESS OF SOLITUDE 433

Star. Perhaps the hall had been too full. Perhaps it would have been too full if there had been even one other soul there apart from Brakhage and Abraham Ebdus and his son. The evening was essentially ruined as soon as it was obvious Brakhage wasn't only not as lonely for recognition as Ebdus but wasn't lonely for recognition in the least.

Or maybe it was just that asshole shouting *Disney* for an easy laugh.

The mood lasted as they waited at Brooklyn Bridge for the 4 train, that extra indignity of the 6's refusal to bother entering Brooklyn, lasted as they emerged at Nevins to walk in silence toward Dean Street, toward their beds, oblivion for their demolished evening. It might have gotten them home, Abraham's bubble of muted rage, if it hadn't been for the tagged bum still in his self-clench on the corner of Atlantic.

Dylan glanced as they passed. The once-flying man's mummified pose was unchanged, though he seemed nearer to the gutter now. DOSE gleamed on the billboard of his back, spotlit by the streetlamp.

Abraham Ebdus raised his eyes from his dark contemplation of the pavement at his feet and followed Dylan's gaze to the bum's back. He halted in his steps.

"What's that?"

"What?" blurted Dylan.

"*That.*" Abraham pointed, unmistakably, horribly, at the spotlit DOSE on the bum's sleeping bag.

"Nothing."

"What's it say?"

"I don't know," said Dylan, hopelessly.

"You do," said Abraham. "You write it on your notebook." Certainty rose in Abraham's voice, his fog of anger given shape. "I've seen it. That's the word you and Mingus write on everything. You think I don't *notice*? You think I'm *stupid*?"

Dylan couldn't speak.

"Let me see your sneakers."

Abraham Ebdus took Dylan's shoulder, his hand clawlike, a startling assertion of force between them. Abraham's disapproval or affection were usually aspects of a floating arrangement of father-notions, largely sonic: footsteps pacing overhead, a voice descending stairs. Abraham was a collection of sounds bound in human form by gloom.

Now they stood in the cool night on the corner of Atlantic Avenue, connected by Abraham's grip. The streetlamp's nimbus on the shape at their feet, a stinky outcropping of the gutter ignored for weeks and improbably come to human attention at last. Abraham turned Dylan by the shoulder and squinted to examine his son's sneakers like evidence in a murder.

Eyes behind passing windshields could care less.

A block away, a whore paced to the corner of Pacific. She called to some old man walking a dog, no illusions, just out of boredom.

Spring was coming, though, a general thaw, she could feel it.

"What's that?" Abraham said, his grip fierce. "It's the same, isn't it?"

There was no way to hide. The fat white margin at the sole of each of Dylan's Pro Keds was crammed with miniature tags. The mushy rubber took a blue ballpoint like butter under pressure of a fork's tine, a discovery which had enraptured Dylan's attention during a crushingly dull math class. Though technically he was destroying his prize 69ers, Dylan couldn't stop himself. At least it rendered them not worth stealing.

"Mingus wrote it," Dylan heard himself say.

Abraham freed Dylan's shoulder and they sprang apart, a physical renouncing as sharp as the contact itself.

"Look at us!" Abraham said, squeezing his eyes and forehead with one hand. It wasn't clear that he was speaking to Dylan.

Dylan waited frozen.

"What could this possibly mean?" said Abraham, his voice erupting from him now. "Is this what I raised you for? This disrespect for a human life? What do you and Mingus do out on the streets, Dylan? Just run like feral animals? Who *taught* you this?"

"I didn't—" But Dylan couldn't offer Mingus's name again.

"Maybe this is just a terrible place. Maybe in these streets right and wrong are confused, so you and your friends run insane like animals that would do this to a human person." Rachel went omitted, unnamed, but both knew that to speak of this place was to speak of her, however little they wished to. Possibly Dylan and Abraham only remained in Gowanus for Rachel, holding down her spot. Now they'd tiptoed together to the brink of an implication that Rachel had outlawed. Some shadow lurked in the word *animals* that shamed Abraham deeply.

"It's this time in the world," said Abraham, groping for some epic sentiment to blur the thought that had come over them both. "We're in hell, that's the only explanation." The body on the street with DOSE on his back could be ascribed to Gerald Ford or Abe Beame, perhaps the Shah of Iran.

In a city commanded to *drop dead* it wouldn't be improbable for a few of its citizens to do so literally and in full view. Especially on Nevins Street.

"This neighborhood is killing us, it's my fault, Dylan, I'm sorry. These choices I've made." At last and almost mechanically, Abraham was turning on himself, with every resource of disappointment and loathing. He might have farmed humiliation from the Cooper Union lecture hall and beyond, from who knew where. From Rachel. It was no relief to Dylan. "Look at us, God," Abraham moaned. Previously he'd covered his eyes; now he widened them.

Absolution lay in one direction only. At their feet.

"Is this man even *alive*?"

"I don't know," said Dylan.

Abraham knelt and embraced the form's shoulder through the wrapped sleeping bag. Nudged, then rolled the body slightly. Dylan watched, horrified. "Are you—" began Abraham, stupidly. What question was appropriate? Did you ask a corpse if it was okay, comfortable? Abraham resorted to "Hello?"

Incredibly, the man on the ground unkinked, rustled his limbs. Then spoke, in a snorelike groan: "*Fuckin'!*"

The man on the ground twisted his neck, beat at the air with wrists and elbows doubled, resembling a T. rex scrabbling with tiny forelegs. However long his nap, the man woke into resumed conflict, warding something or someone away. The movement stirred his odor, made his size apparent. Abraham jerked his hand back, startled.

They'd thought he was dead, really. Dylan and his father

blinked, appalled to see they'd been talking over a live body. The fallen man might even have been listening.

"Hold on, man," said Abraham, his voice hollow, rushed. To Dylan it sounded as if Abraham thought the man on the pavement had been fine a moment before, had only fainted, as though this spell on the street corner didn't define a man's life but was only an interruption, a hiccup. "We'll get an ambulance."

The whore, pacing uncommonly far in her boredom, reached the avenue. Atlantic was quiet, no cars at the lights which changed red-to-green with a *chunk-chunk* just audible above the insect hum of the streetlamps. She teetered halfway across the intersection and called out to the three, the small man and the thin tall one and the thick black one on the ground:

"Any y'all need a date?"

The best colors all have the best names: Pastel Aqua, Plum, John Deere Yellow, Popsicle Orange, Federal Safety Purple. A blind guy could steal the right paint just hearing the monikers. These colors are the necessities for *throwing up a burner*, a top-to-bottom masterpiece of flaming 3-D letters studded with rivets or bleeding from gashes, surrounded by clouds of stars, lightning bolts, and a Vaughn Bode wizard or Felix the Cat character standing to one side like a master of ceremonies. A burner comes into life either on the panels of a stilled subway car or on a handball court or schoolyard wall, an unsimple matter of five or six hours in the dead of night, two guys spraying paint, the more talented one handling outlines and fade effects, the lesser doing flat fill-ins, usually two more guys looking out at the end of the block or the entrance to the train yard. Plus ruining a set of clothes, coming home pore-and-tear-duct-clogged with pigment. Plenty more obvious than drugs, to a vigilant parent; the potheads have it easy.

First, though, you've got to assemble the paint.

That means *racking at McCrory's*.

Today it's the Dean Street Crew: a temporary, maybe one-time agglomeration, led by Mingus Rude. The crew consists of Lonnie, Alberto, Dylan, and Mingus. Mingus the oldest. The four have a scheme, a plan of attack, which, like the expedition itself, is Mingus's original conception – or if Mingus learned it from another kid he's not giving credit. The scheme feels brilliantly original to the Dean Street Crew, feels fine. In fact they're high on it, jangled, dancing.

McCrory's is the feebler of Fulton Street's two department stores. The other, a block away, is A&S – Abraham and Straus – an eight-story Art Deco monolith, a gilded time machine into some glorious shopping Utopia. It's also intimidating and Manhattanesque, with its uniformed elevator operators and old ex-cop guards. On floor six of A&S there's a gourmet shop with rows of hand-dipped chocolates, on the eighth there's toys, puzzles, a counter selling collectible coins and stamps. Also an enclosed record store, four walls within four walls, out of which no kid's yet claimed to succeed in boosting records. Gangs roam clear of A&S, perhaps embarrassed by memories of parent-guided expeditions to sit on Santa's lap. That place, it's just a little too dreamy.

McCrory's is the department store they understand and deserve, McCrory's is a tad more approachable. It's a Wool-worth's knockoff, really, with butter-sour popcorn smells and costume jewelry in Plexiglas cases and a photo booth and a desolate sandwich counter where a sharp-eyed kid can order a milk shake and pay for it with tips he's slid away from other placings on the counter, if he drinks the shake slowly enough. The main floor's acres of underwear and baby clothes and brandless reject sneakers in bins. Back-to-school specials give way to orange crepe-paper pumpkins that give way to half-dim strings of Christmas lights that give way to Valentines and Easter crap and summer bargains, all flacked by a recorded drone from unseen speakers. Downstairs is the hardware department. That's their destination today, the Dean Street Crew. They've cased the joint the afternoon before. They're ready.

According to the scheme Dylan Ebdus now stands waiting alone, a still figure in the passing crowds, mostly black ladies with young kids in tow, on Fulton Street. He's wearing his glasses for once, plus a green-and-white striped Izod shirt – ironically not his but Mingus Rude's – buttoned up to his neck, to complete the picture of harmless private-school nerd. He's also wearing a backpack, empty but fluffed out from inside with a bent wire hanger to appear, they all hope, heavy with schoolbooks.

Lonnie, Alberto, and Mingus, they're already inside McCrory's basement, shifting cans of spray paint from one aisle to another, secreting them in less closely watched sections, behind IF YOU DON'T SEE WHAT YOU WANT, ASK signs and vinyl wood-grain photo albums. The three of them, two black kids and one Puerto Rican, are drawing attention from McCrory's security staff, plenty. That's fine: their very presence is a silent alarm going off in the store, meant to be. They're happy to be spotted picking up Krylon and wandering with it into the other aisles, more careful to be undetected stashing the cans here and there. A few times they even enact an empty-handed pantomime of stuffing paint into their baggy coats, sniggering. This crimeless crime, this game of baiting racist expectation that they're robbing the place blind, is good value entertainment.

Now comes Dylan, trailing into the basement five minutes later, and doing nothing to acknowledge any connection to the two black kids and the one Puerto Rican. Eyes slitty, he orients himself on the field of play, the bright-lit confusion of aisles, shoppers, guards, plus his homeboys. Inhales the popcorn perfume, gulps. The security staff, mostly enormous Jamaican women, are in their predicted tizzy, trailing Mingus and Lonnie and Alberto deeper into the hardware section, to a high aisle of garbage pails and brooms and rakes, preselected for low visibility. Suck-ahs! Dylan scowls, adjusts his glasses, wanders innocuously into aisles designated the day before. Here's the scheme's payoff. Dylan's the collector. His breath clicking in his throat, he gathers the Krylon from the various stashes in the innocent aisles and, electric fear in his fingertips, plops them into his backpack: Tangerine, Chrome, Surf Blue.

Today you're a white boy for a reason.

Leave it to Mingus Rude to recuperate their differences for his own purposes, for Robin Hooditry in art's cause.

Dylan goes for the exit. The cans of Krylon clunk and ping seductively in his knapsack, treasure for sure. Spreading gratuitous confusion now, the other three chart divergent paths through the aisles, leave separately. Mingus, the broadest performer, is halted and frisked by a couple of guards. Alberto screams into the doorway behind him, "*Fuck you!*" No reason, just because he can.

Back on Fulton they regather in the shade of the parking garage, all out of breath before they've even begun their run, hearts thrilled. The paint is quickly weighed, shaken to reveal the shuttle's promising clatter, then parceled out to coat pockets, stuffed in sleeves. Let some superhuman guard chase them, he'll never catch all four. They scramble down Hoyt Street, pretending to be pursued, laughing and shouting: "Oh, shit! Book, man! Can't you run? Something wrong with your legs?"

Animals, Abraham? We can give you animals.

They shared a long walk in silence across Flatbush, up St. Felix, to the red brick hospital wedged against one side of Fort Greene Park. A Saturday afternoon in early April, first blush of heat in the air, the rutting birds and sun-stoned children in the dizzying, near-vertical park screaming in unison, bombarding the hospital windows with a shrill hail of sound. The flung-open windows couldn't decant the detox ward's deep linoleum-urine rot, an air of body poisons overlaid with disinfectant and sharp wafting farts from the recently destarved. No fear a bird would fly into the hospital. They'd be knocked back by a wall of odor as though butting a glass pane.

Dylan hung in the doorway. A Jamaican nurse stood beside him, one eyebrow cocked. Abraham went to the bed. The man was a draped hulk, wrists buckled into cloth restraints to the aluminum bed frame, hands hanging below, pitiful and large. One scabby foot was flung past the bed's lip, the other curled inward like a dancer's, tucked beneath the sheeted bulk of knee. His left cheek and brow were knit in a petrified wink. An intravenous line dripped something green-yellow into his arm, something that had also made a green-yellow stain on the sheet. Spills were his nature, even here. Hard to fathom he'd negotiated the sky.

Abraham frowned at the bound wrists, the crust at the IV's point of connection, the unsavory smell. This care wasn't good, not good enough. Perhaps Abraham was compensating: nothing could be good enough for the man in the bed. He needed to be treated like a human being, not a bum or a scoundrel, for by still breathing when he should have been dead he'd become a symbol of possible atonement. The Jamaican nurse stood in the corner and watched. She frowned too, showing her disagreement with Abraham Ebdus's implication that the hospital wasn't doing its job with this drunk fool, who was killing himself like many thousands of others and deserved no particular special notice for having happened to be checked into this ward by a white man.

"Does he eat?" asked Abraham finally.

The nurse rolled her eyes. "He eat if he want to. He spit in da meal at breakfast. We can no make anybody eat you know."

"I want to speak to a doctor," Abraham concluded peremptorily.

"Doctor come at four o'clock, no here now." She budged Abraham aside to fuss with the dial regulating the IV's drip, showing her command. "Is no need of a doctor here."

"Your supervisor, then."

The nurse clucked, said nothing. She and Abraham Ebdus went together into the hall, the nurse's white sneakers shrieking on the tile. Dylan was left alone with the man in the bed.

Abraham might be this man's champion, but he'd never done more than groan a curse or two at Abraham. Dylan he knew, and seemed to sense now; they'd spoken before. His bruised lids fluttered open.

"Little white boy."

Was Dylan going to be asked to surrender his spare change? What use could the captive flying man have for fifty cents or a dollar here in the hospital, strapped to a bed frame? Instinctively Dylan felt in his pockets, didn't find anything.

"Get up here. Cain't see."

Dylan obeyed.

"You seen me."

No question, but Dylan nodded.

"Hah. Hah. Go in that drawer." Not unscrewing his screwed-up eye, he nodded at the small cabinet beside the bed, where flowers would be set if anyone were setting flowers. "Yass, that drawer, get *in* it!"

Dylan tugged at the drawer, fearing to find some hellish hypodermic the flying man would want stuck in his arm.

Only a corroded plastic wallet, thin like a bus-pass holder. Driver's license, issued in Columbus, Ohio, 1952, to Aaron X. Doily.

And the silver ring the flying man had worn on his pinky.

"Thassit, thassit."

"The ring?"

"I'm done, I'm *through*, man. Cain't fight the *air waves*."

"You want—?"

"Take it, man."

By the time Abraham Ebdus and the nurse ran back to the room the man in the bed was deep into his screaming throes of withdrawal or D.T.'s or whatever, sweat broken everywhere on his body, contortions wrenching the bed frame. The bounds held, so that body and bed became one shape rattling, shivering in agony. He found the IV pole and knocked it to the floor, bag bursting yellow spill everywhere. The kid was pressed to the far wall, but not panicked, watching coolly. Nurse harrumphed to broadcast her unsurprise: this only went to show and was all in a day's etcetera. Abraham, having achieved no satisfaction from the higher-ups at the nurses' station in the corridor, gathers the poor kid, who's been punished enough by now you'd have to think, gets him out of there. The man's bellowing is insane. It's frankly hard to take.

Dylan Ebdus with a ring gripped in his fist, the fist buried deep in his pants pocket, the ring itself pulsing in his sweaty fingers as though it were a token, a tiny fragment of the mad paroxysm of the man in the hospital bed, now borne covertly away into the breezy Fort Greene afternoon.

"What was he saying?" Abraham asked his son gently, once they'd gone a few blocks, the yellow insanity of the hospital receding into dream.

Dylan Ebdus just shrugged. The flying man, he'd said a lot of things.

The last — it couldn't actually have been "*Fight evil!*" could it?

CHAPTER 10

SUMMER'S START, 1977: various persons are sprung, various terms and sentences completed. For instance here's Barrett Rude Senior, six years served on a ten-to-fifteen, now paroled on good behavior, dressed in the green sharkskin suit and worn wingtips he'd been tried in, at a Greyhound's window seat as it courses a circular ramp into the guts of Port Authority, midtown towers doubled in the smoked glass's reflections and dancing with the engine's vibration. His only baggage, a hard leather briefcase tucked upright between his ankles, contains legal papers, a certificate of ministry in the Church of the Parlor of God, and a pair of photographs – teenage Barrett Junior and his then-thirtyish, now-late mother in one, fifth-grade school head shot of Mingus grinning in a mortarboard and tassel the other – in a frame constructed of ingeniously woven cigarette packages, Parliament emblem alternated with Marlboro. Plus mother-of-pearl cufflinks, rolled tie, and gilt-leather Bible. Mingus Rude's been sent to meet this bus, to guide his grandfather to a cab, and by cab to Dean Street. He'll offer to carry the briefcase and be refused. No offense, little man, but Reverend Barrett Rude Senior can handle his own stuff.

Cut to Aaron X. Doily, passing through this same bus station a week later. He's got a bus ticket for Syracuse pinned into the breast pocket of one of Abraham Ebdus's old herringbone jackets, one Abraham wore to Franz Kline's last one-man show during Kline's lifetime, as it happens, and this jacket is stretched tight as a canvas and near to splitting across Aaron Doily's shoulders. In Syracuse he'll be met by the local Salvation Army and installed in a shelter, given three squares and a bunk on the guarantee of his attendance at the local Alcoholics Anonymous, where among the hard-bitten, laid-off-lathe-operator types he'll be the sole black face. That's if he gets aboard the Syracuse bus; see him now, eyeing the ticket counter, knowing he could probably cash the ticket. Bottle of Colt's in five minutes' reach, easy. But let's not truck in false suspense: Aaron Doily finds strength to bypass this possibility, boards the bus. Sits blinking atop the humming engines in the dark garage, absently twisting with his right thumb and forefinger a phantom ring on his left pinky. He's uncertain how and when he lost the ring but figures it might be just as well gone. Let's leave him, he's no mysterious flying man anymore, just an incomprehensibly lonely alcoholic with a funny name, risen from pavement in spring to find himself restored to the daily world, sponge-bathed clean and tagged with a plastic wristband, now pointed out of town.

Peek ahead further, another two weeks: there's Dylan Ebdus himself climbing aboard a bus, destination sign reading SAINT JOHNSBURY, VERMONT. Abraham Ebdus nodding goodbye through the tinted pane. Abraham's got a grudge against the city these days, and a new penchant for exiling those he wishes to protect, first the detoxified Doily and now his own son, to the north, to New England's countryside. Dylan's signed up to be a Fresh Air Fund kid this summer. What was good enough for Rachel, a Fund-ee back in the fifties, ought to be good enough for Dylan. This scheme she would have approved; father and son both sense it, impossible not to. Abraham's hunch will seem brilliant after the July blackout, the subsequent looting and mayhem which comes as near as Ramirez's bodega, whose sprays of smashed shopwindow will be kicked up and down Dean's slate for days after, and the spree and capture of Berkowitz. These give that season an air of disaster, and Dylan, safe in his idyll, will miss it.

But wait, Dylan's not bound for Vermont, not yet. He's not even thinking about it. Today's the first morning after the last afternoon of seventh grade. Spring is sprung, and so is he. I.S. 293 is behind Dylan Ebdus for now, he can go three months not crossing Smith Street if he likes. Eighth grade's a distant rumor, a tabled issue, and Dylan knows from experience that the summer between might change anything, everything. He and Mingus Rude too and even Arthur Lomb for that matter are released from the paint-by-numbers page of their schooldays, from their preformatted roles as truant or victim, freed to an unspoiled summer, that inviting medium for doodling in self-transformation. Who knows how it'll come out, what they'll resemble by the end of it? All Dylan knows is he's giddy, loosed, flying.

It's *flying how far* that remains to be seen.

Today, first day of freedom, he's keeping a date with himself. Abraham's out so Dylan's free to climb the ladder out of the painting studio, unhook the hatch to their roof and push it aside, crawl out across the mushy tar paper into the new summer's morning.

Dylan wouldn't have said he feared heights, but the brownstone's roof has always made him dizzy, not so much the view to the ground as the view across rooftops, out to Coney Island and beyond. Easier if you gaze on Manhattan's towers. Those place you, fix you in a firm relation of puniness and awe. Easier still to kneel at the roof's edge, hands gripping the ankle-high rim of masonry, and stare down at the contents of your own yard: ailanthus, brick pile, shoots of weed, a dirty spaldeen you can just make out like a speck of flesh. The grainy reality is reassuring.

What's unsettling is to put Manhattan at your back and face the borough. Up from the canyon floor, out of the deep well of streets, gazing out into the Brooklyn Beyond is like standing in a Kansas prairie contemplating distance. Every rooftop for miles in every direction is level with that where you stand. The rooftops form a flotilla of rafts, a potential chessboard for your knight-hops, interrupted only by the promontory of the Wyck-off housing projects, the skeletal Eagle Clothing sign, the rise of the F-train platform where it elevates past the Gowanus Canal. Manhattan's topped, but Brooklyn's an open-face sandwich in the light, bare parts picked over by pigeons and gulls.

A sky full of pigeons and gulls and you standing there with a flying man's ring on your finger.

Dylan stands at the front edge, as close as he's stood, then closer. Shifts a toe onto the cornice, bends his knee like George Washington in the prow. He can just see down into the pit of Dean Street, the tops of new-planted trees, the roof grilles of the passing bus, but the feeling's vertiginous. He steps back. No good staring and daring yourself: the will to fly sours, leaks away. That may have been Aaron Doily's mistake. It needs a running start, a glorious oblivious leap to the opposite rooftop, not the dying quail of a fall that would surely result from long and woozy contemplation.

Close your eyes, reach out and feel the *air waves*, if there are any. Use the force, Luke.

Okay, okay. Dylan charts with backward steps an invisible runway he'll retrace. Five steps ought to be enough. He's retreated to the center of the roof. Anyone watching would think he was cowering, but it's just the opposite – he's spring-loaded, expecting to fly. Then, as though smacked by a vast hand from the sky, he crumbles to his knees in terror of the thing he's proposed for himself. Fingers balled in one doubled fist around the ring, Dylan Ebdus huddles, shivers, and slowly and without resistance pees his pants. The urine runs inside his jeans leg to his ankle, drips into his sock and sneaker and onto the gummy, sun-warmed tar.

Here might be the ring's only spell, to induce self-pissing.

Got to give it up to the flying man: it's not that easy to throw yourself off a roof.

The Dean Street bus, unable to slip past the white stretch limousine double-parked in front of Barrett Rude's place, nestled at its bumper instead, humming like a refrigerator, traffic behind stacking to Bond Street. The bus carried just two passengers, one intermittently asleep, but the thing still had its dumb round to make, its loop. The driver kneaded his horn, bleats cutting the drowsy, humid afternoon. The chauffeur had abandoned the limo, snuck to Ramirez's for a bottle of Miller and a ham-and-cheese.

So anyone on the block not already eyeballing the limo through parlor or upstairs windows was alerted to the anomaly, the bright unlikely event plopped into their June's last afternoon. Nobody saw it come, but they'd be damned if they weren't going to see it go, to learn who'd climb inside. Men on stoops wrinkled new bags open just to the lips of bottles, no farther. Women leaned clubby arms on sills, watching for something to unfold. Behind a basement window grille La-La knit Marilla's hair in cornrows, jerking her head back with increasing force until Marilla said, "Dang! You got a problem?"

A white man with a rake scraped a day's new crop of

wrappers and bottle caps out of his forsythia, muttering under his Red Sox cap.

Abraham Ebdus daubed gray on a frame of celluloid, totally unaware.

Dylan missed the limousine too. He sat sequestered in ailanthus shade in his backyard, speedily turning the pages of *The Pod Thickens*, a New Belmont Special written by Semi Chellas, cover art by A. Ebdus.

The chauffeur popped out of Old Ramirez's, sandwich already half-unwrapped, then took in the sight of the clogged-up bus and nearly dropped his beer, performed a corny double take with his elbows, sensing his audience. The line of backed-up drivers horn-serenaded him as he fumbled key into ignition, muttering, "Hold up, baby, hold up." The limo cornered Nevins, loosing the clog.

The street grew calm. For a moment it was as though the watchers had dreamed it, they might be returned to their lives, only mystified. Then the white car rounded Bond, sharklike, and resettled at Barrett Rude's address. The driver stuck at the wheel now, gnawed his sandwich there, a lazy hand dropping balled butcher paper to the asphalt, then rising to adjust the rearview for a spell of tooth-picking.

Blobs of yellow-green sun refracted through trees grew elliptical, spanned the white hood, moved on.

The chauffeur was asleep, what a life.

When the door at the top of Barrett Rude's stoop opened it was like a Sunday newspaper flipped open to the funny pages. The figures poured out one after another, cartoon pimps, Batman villains, outsize mercurial goofs impossible to fix in vision. The Funk Mob, singers, players, and what passed for an entourage, a couple of freakazoid chicks. They'd dropped in to visit Barrett Rude Junior, en route to a promotional appearance at the Fulton Mall and in utmost regalia: mauve feathers, star-frame glasses, padded silver-foil shoulder pads, lightning-bolt headgear, spaceman boots, six-inch heels, King Tut beards, the works.

They burst out of the house loud and happy and moving with zany grace, a Ralph Bakshi cel in the open air, high on Barrett Rude's hospitality and cocaine, both powdered and cooked into base. To Dean Street they resembled nothing so much as a slice of human graffiti, a masterpiece in motion like a train car gone before you could check it out. This vision, too, quickly evaporated, each band member hand-slapping Barrett Rude farewell where he stood in his boxing robe and satin pants at his door, then piling into the back of that clown-car-in-reverse. The smooth white container swallowed the whole chaos of glints and textures and jiving walks behind tinted windows. The chauffeur rubbed his eyes, turned the key, revved the engine. The limo coursed down the block, gone.

Barrett Rude Junior stood in his robe on the top of the stoop, chuckling, shaking his head, kneading at his coke-frozen nose and lips with the back of his hand. He might have basked for a second or two in Dean Street's eyes on him: Shouldn't they know he was a star? Damn, time they learned. Problem with being in a group, no one ever knew your name, just the group, the Distinctions, like White Castle or Oldsmobile.

White and Puerto Rican motherfuckers around here probably never even heard his million-selling songs, probably thought he was a pimp or gangster coming in buying up a house on renovator's row, right in their faces.

He stood, hands on hips, for a long assertive minute, grinding his jaw, staring at nothing, taking the pulse of the block before he turned and went inside.

It was after his door had shut, Dean Street at last absented of limousine and costumes and singers in satin robes, that eyes might have found the figure below, in the well of the basement entrance under the stoop, one foot and knee propped out in late sunlight, the rest of him in shadow, watching. An old man with coiled salt-and-pepper beard on grave-lined cheeks, arms ropy in a sleeveless white T-shirt, gold Star of David on a chain hung to his sternum: Barrett Rude Senior. It had been hearsay up until now that a third generation was arrived in the Rude house. This was the first sighting. Only, Senior had been watching the whole time, watching for days already, peering through the half-sunken basement windows, seated in a low chair beside the paint-chipped radiator, eyes level with the knees of passersby on Dean's slate. He'd been watching Marilla and La-La across the street, watching the new wave of ballplayers who'd inherited Henry's stoop, watching dog walkers furtively toe piles of shit to the gutter. He'd watched the Funk Mob come and go, heard their hoots of laughter through the ceiling. Now he watched Dean Street watching him, fine with it, as willing to be seen, in his half-seen way, as his son.

The ring wasn't helping him win chess games with Arthur Lomb, that much was for certain. He toppled his king in surrender three times an hour, the two of them hunched on the stoop in sunlight, lizards on a rock. Dylan prayed for Arthur to ferry down the red juice and turkey sandwiches and raisin cookies his mother wrapped in wax paper and packed into the refrigerator each day before leaving for work. Their lunch break, which was the only relief from Arthur's bearing down with his phalanx of pawns, and behind them his thuggish rooks ready to surge and crush Dylan's limp knights, dozy bishops, naked king, spirit. Arthur's mother figured on Dylan's presence, made double sets of sandwiches now. It was pitiably easy to fall into a routine with a kid when you were his only friend and his mother knew it. Dylan suspected the sandwiches and cookies were a bribe. Perhaps Arthur suspected it too, perhaps that was why he chewed them with a morbid gnashing intensity which resembled his chess. As if Arthur were trying to pulverize the mornings and afternoons of the new summer into crumbs, defeated pawns to be swept away.

The problem was he never actually did sweep the pawns away, only set them up again as quickly as he'd crushed them, flogging Dylan to the next match, and the next. Arthur, as ever both slavish and sadistic, always reorganized both their chessmen. If the Yankees or Mets had a day game afternoons were more tolerable, Arthur's transistor tuned to Lindsey Nelson or Phil Rizzuto, the Mets going nowhere, the Yankees stacked with hired guns and bound for glory. Otherwise it was another tight rotation of "Afternoon Delight" and "Right Back Where We Started From" on one of the Top 40 AM stations which were Arthur's fixation.

"This is really quite an interesting song," said Arthur whenever "Convoy" played. He never explained. The ritual comment was intended as self-evident.

Dylan didn't ask, didn't fall for it, just fiddled with the ring on his hand. He was immune, off elsewhere in his mind, in diving flight.

Arthur began saying *breast* for *check*. "Breast. Breast. Breast-*mate*."

For relief they scored the latest *Fantastic Four* and *Defenders* and *Ghost Rider* from the newsstand on the traffic island on Flatbush. They read them in five minutes, then Arthur put them in plastic and began setting up the pieces again.

The day Dylan began to hallucinate that Arthur's furrowed, sweat-beaded brow was actually ticking like a bomb, he toppled his king and said, "Let's go see if Mingus is home."

Arthur stared up from the board. "Did I hear you correctly?"

"Sure."

"You'll introduce me to Mingus Rude?"

Arthur's expression mingled astonishment and gloat. It was as if the entire dull ten-day stand of chess demolitions had been intended to produce this one specific result.

"Why not?" said Dylan.

"You won't hear any objection from me," said Arthur.

Dylan shrugged, not wanting to suggest in his response that he'd given anything valuable away. In fact he'd vowed never to bring Arthur Lomb around to Dean Street, at least never when any of the Dean Street kids, such as remained hanging around the block, would possibly see. Hell, it was only another promise to himself broken, nobody else would ever know. If the Dean Street kids confused Dylan with Arthur Lomb at this late date it was hopeless anyway. Arthur's whiteness couldn't rub off on Dylan, couldn't make him any whiter than he was. The taboo was pointless.

Anything, anyway, not to see his decimated pawns clapped back on their squares.

Mingus was home. In fact he was sitting on his own stoop, halfway up to catch the shade thrown by the house, staring dazedly at what he held between his two hands like a treasure, or perhaps a small live thing which required his protection: a fresh spaldeen, its pink flesh unscuffed, as though it had never had contact with the street, as though every latent bounce remained sealed inside it, pure potential.

He looked up when Dylan and Arthur approached and Dylan understood instantly that Mingus had been into Barrett Rude Junior's freezer pot stash, had gotten deeply stoned, a solo afternoon jaunt. His eyes were dewy with it.

"I *found* it," he pronounced, raising up the spaldeen.

"This is Arthur," said Dylan lightly, making the introduction he'd never meant to make, but tossing it off. "From Pacific."

Mingus snapped to exaggerated attention, reached to shake Arthur Lomb's hand. "Yo, Arthur, how you doin'?"

"Okay," said Arthur sheepishly.

"Pa-*cif*-ic," said Mingus, measuring it with his dope-thickened tongue, tasting the syllables. "You got your own homeboys up around *Pacific*, Arthur?"

"There, uh, aren't any other kids my age on my block."

"Oh yeah?" Mingus looked impressed. "All right, I think I know what you mean, yeah. So, what you think – some little kid lost this ball, man?"

"I guess that's most likely," said Arthur. He looked stymied to be interviewed by Mingus Rude, pushed out of his ordinary range of operation. He might fear himself on the verge of a *stupid answer* to *a snappy question*, that was what his eyes seemed to say.

"You think we ought to play stoopball?"

Arthur made a helpless face, looked at Dylan.

"What you think, D-Man?"

"If you even remember *how*," said Dylan. He savored a certain hard-boiled flavor in his reply, pleased to assert before Arthur Lomb the deep and weary history between himself and Mingus Rude, a history extensive in ways Arthur couldn't begin to imagine.

"I'll throw a home run on your ass, boy."

"Let's see you," said Dylan.

Maybe the summer was only waiting for them to resume their places, the light and heat waiting to gel around them. The block was like an open-air museum of their former days, the slate cracked and skewed in all the usual places, the abandoned house still theirs any time they wanted to reclaim it. It had taken Arthur Lomb's presence, though, to rouse the effort. They'd silently partnered to show him what Dean Street meant, the old essential traces. If it had been only Dylan and Mingus they would have been off tagging DOSE on lampposts, away from headquarters on some undercover operation.

Arthur Lomb, and the beacon of the fresh spaldeen. It had something to do as well with the pink ball which appeared in Mingus's hands like a problem unsolved, an old itch.

There were only the three of them at first. Mingus at the abandoned stoop, turned sideways as he wound up to slam the ball high off the steps. Dylan on the opposite sidewalk, beyond the parked cars, playing the outfield. Arthur Lomb placed between, in the street, under the canopy of trees, to play infield and flatten himself to one side to make way for the rare car.

"Mother*fucker!*" Mingus shouted when Dylan made a perfect catch. Consoling himself, he rattled a double up the middle, chattering too-late encouragement: "Block it with your body, Artie, Arthur Fonzarelli, Fonzie, *A-Boy.*"

Dean Street's kids were drawn out-of-doors, or back to the block from some other place by magnetism, a weird call. Nobody knew they were nostalgic until they saw Dylan Ebdus and Mingus Rude in the golden leaf-light that covered the middle of the block, a dream of a summer ago, ripened into history while nobody noticed. Plus here's this new gawky grim-faced white boy in the street, knees tangling as he tried to stop the screaming rifle-shot grounders and line drives Mingus kept winging off the stoop.

Irresistible not to look. And then to wander over.

"King Arthur, man, you done fell down!"

"Sorry."

"Don't *sorry* me, son! Sorry is for snakes. *Catch* the damn ball!"

Mingus arched one high over the parked cars, destined for number 233 Dean's sunken concrete yard, the shallow where a stoop had been demolished. Dylan leaped to intercept, found the spaldeen cool in his palm, transmitted from Mingus's hand to his by way of the stoop and the air. He tossed it back casually, over Arthur. Mingus shook his head, medium-impressed, unwilling to exaggerate.

Alberto drifted up, hands in pockets. He quickly sussed the situation, then set himself behind Arthur to gather what dribbled or zinged through, just wanting to put his hands on the ball. Next came Lonnie, then a couple of young Spanish kids whose names nobody could stop forgetting. Mingus waved them into place, the infield turned into a mob. He kept throwing.

Marilla and La-La arrived, elbow-perched themselves on Henry's stoop, trying not to look like they cared.

Henry himself had gone off to Aviation High School in Queens, was never around. Just a ball-game ghost, the name given a particular stoop.

In theory five catches got a kid up to bat, in practice today who knew? Mingus was writing the rules. Arthur and the little kids, they didn't know any better. Alberto was deferential, easy. Dylan, Mingus's conspirator, was camped in the outfield, not saying. He knew Mingus's druggy adamancy, had seen him go into a zone, tagging, or just making some point aloud, talking in circles. He'd stay at the stoop until he threw a home run.

Arthur Lomb shot Dylan paranoid eye-bolts from within the crowd of kids jostling in the street for up-the-middle position.

Dylan if he bothered to notice was one of the older kids around Dean Street now.

He was more aware of his feet leaving the ground as he reached for another line shot, robbed another long bomb out of 213's yard. Perfect catch numero tres.

Marilla sang, high falsetto, *I used to go out to parti-i-ies, and stand around—*

He'd hung in the air just as long as it took, matched the flight of the spaldeen exactly. Then came down soft, unjarred.

White boy was some kind of catching machine today.

You were *flying.*

'Cuz I was too nerv-uh-us, to really get down—

Arthur Lomb kicked a grounder down the street sideways and they all stood head-lolled watching him corral it.

"Yo, Mingus," said Lonnie, falsely breezy. "I seen all of the Funk Mob visited your pops the other day."

"I don't know what you're talking about," Mingus deadpanned.

"You must of seen it, Mingus, man. They had a big white limo all in the street. They looked like superheroes, man."

"What drug you on, Lon?"

"Don't say you don't know what he's talkin' about," said Marilla.

Dylan had heard Earl and a couple of kids mention it the day before – the limousine, the wild-costumed musicians that had poured out of it.

"I saw nothing," said Mingus, increasingly pleased with himself, thriving on the absurdity of denying it.

"That boy's *lying*," said La-La, shaking her head.

Mingus reared, the spaldeen shot into the sky. A dark smudge wobbled to describe the pink ball's torque against the background of sun-stained leaves.

"Take *that*!" taunted Mingus.

Dylan flew and found it in his hand again.

The ring and the ball in some kind of partnership of magical objects.

You between them: the beneficiary, airborne.

"Dang! My man can *jump*!"

Dylan flipped the ball back past gapes of astonishment in the street.

"Watch your boy D-Lone, King Arthur man. Learn a thing."

"I'm taking notes," said Arthur Lomb sourly.

Marilla flopped her head and rolled her eyes, resumed singing, syllables stretched in petulance, *But my bod-dee-ee, yearned to be – freee—*

By the time Robert Woolfolk arrived Dylan had robbed nine of Mingus's sure home runs, was perhaps assembling a legend, some kind of miraculous stand patrolling the far sidewalk, the air above. The game had become nominal, just an elaborate contest of wills between the stoned Mingus, the flying Dylan. The others were stranded, monkeys-in-the-middle, feeding off scraps.

Marilla and La-La chose not to note Robert Woolfolk's saunter past their place on the stoop, his bid for their eyes. Robert couldn't bring Dean Street crumbling to attention just rounding the corner anymore, that's what their taunting voices claimed. *I got up on the flo-oo-or board, somebody can – choose – me—*

Inspired, street-flippant, Dylan decided not to fear Robert Woolfolk today, not on his own block, not wearing Aaron Doily's ring. Besides, Arthur Lomb was here, official weakest link. You could practically feel Robert measuring Arthur's neck for a yoke, like Wile E. Coyote replacing the Roadrunner with a roast chicken in his mind's eye.

It seemed to Dylan now that Robert Woolfolk's argument was with Rachel. Who was gone from their lives, even if Robert Woolfolk hadn't grasped it. That wasn't Dylan's problem. There were days he hardly thought of Rachel once.

Today, for one.

"Yo, Gus, man, let me see the ball for a minute," said Robert. He tilted his head, moved his eyes sideways, checking his back. "I'll give it back, man, you know I will." Another kid could ask to join a ball game: Robert Woolfolk had to *hustle* in. His basic premise was criminal. It wasn't something he could leave behind when it happened to be unnecessary.

Mingus cocked his head, stared at Robert Woolfolk like Robert was speaking Martian. The younger kids wandered off, half-intimidated, half-bored, never touching the ball. Arthur Lomb frowned at Dylan, his trademark glare-of-despair. He might be calling up an asthma attack any minute now.

"Aight," said Mingus suddenly, and bounced the spaldeen to Robert Woolfolk, home run forgotten, stakes evaporated. Mingus could do that, flip like a switch. "You can find me in the outfield," he announced. "Me and my man *Dee*."

Dylan shifted to his left and Mingus joined him, two center fielders in rivalry for anything in the air. Robert's first throw, slung underhand, knuckles nearly grazing pavement, produced a line drive at eye level which banked off the car between infield and outfield, nearly taking Arthur Lomb's head off coming and going. Robert Woolfolk remained a source of bizarre ricochets, like a busted pinball machine left for years in the arcade and still eating your quarters.

"My mother said I have to go home, Dylan," said Arthur Lomb glumly. The non sequitur betrayed his discomfort. Who'd said anything about *mothers*?

"Okay," said Dylan, uninterested.

"All right then, I've got to go." Arthur seemed to think Dylan ought to walk him home, or at least break off playing to acknowledge the fact of his departure.

"See ya."

"Hey, King Arthur," said Mingus, picking up the thread. "Catch you on the rebound."

"Nice to meet you."

"Give my regards to Pacific Street, man – and your mother."

Alberto and Robert Woolfolk busted an instantaneous gut. Mingus and Dylan deadpanned, pretended nothing was unusual. It was hilarious in a way you couldn't pin down, Mingus essentially saying *yo mama* without saying it.

Mutual assured deniability.

Arthur Lomb just slumped and moved down the block, a crushed pawn.

And Marilla sang *No more stand-di-ing beside the wall—*

Robert wound and unwound himself again and the ball struck high on the stoop and flew the farthest yet.

Albert leaned on a car, not imagining for a moment this was his to catch. He turned to watch Dylan and Mingus jostle elbows together, preparing to leap.

I done got myself togeth-a, baby—

As he rose, Dylan saw the block complete. He nestled easily in the air, under the branches, above the cars. He was aware of Mingus beside him, rising not quite so high. The pink ball found Dylan's left hand, his catching hand, ring hand, met palm of its own volition. Dylan simply there to keep the appointment. He had time to glance around, Marilla's song slowed, *to, geth, a, ba, by*, from above Dylan saw that Robert Woolfolk had what couldn't actually be a bald spot, but a bare place, an off-center patch of scuff or mange on the top of his head. The ball compressed in Dylan's palm as if sighing. At the corner of Dylan's vision Arthur Lomb sagged home along the slate. *The boy can't catch, ain't nothin' you can do about it.* Dylan noticed La-La's nice tits, was amazed he had the term *nice tits* ready the first time he'd noticed any. In truth he probably owed it to Arthur Lomb, the availability of that concept, not that he'd ever give Arthur the credit. So who needed the Solver girls, anyway? Maybe your life wasn't bereft, your fortune robbed before it could be spent. Maybe life, sex, everything that mattered, was right here, on Dean, not gone elsewhere. At his side, Dylan felt Mingus Rude nestled slightly below him, their bodies clunking sweetly as Mingus tried to match Dylan's leap and fell short, minus the advantage of the flying man's ring. Mingus rising not quite so high as Dylan.

At perihelion Dylan felt himself to be a note of music, one delayed, now floating upward. They might all be notes in a song, the Dean Street kids. Mingus was Dose. Though Dylan had been tagging the name it belonged to Mingus wholly. Mingus had his drug thing, his access to Barrett's stash, and it was okay, it was cool. Robert Woolfolk, his part was to be skulky and scary. Robert was criminal-minded, Dylan couldn't begrudge it. You allowed for the kid from the projects, steered a berth. Arthur Lomb, he was the white boy, slotted into place. Even Arthur was okay, he just didn't know it yet.

As for Dylan, he had the ring. Befuddled witnesses were only part wrong, Dean Street possessed superheroes: not musicians in a limousine but Dylan, the flying kid. He'd sew a costume and take to the rooftops, begin *bounding down on crime* and they'd know then what they couldn't be allowed to know yet. Today it had to be disguised: the Discovery of Flight, right under their noses. On his maiden bound, though, he already felt love and sympathy for all as he swam in the air, his view rearranged.

Then Marilla completed the line, hands waving for syncopation, the beat only she heard, *I done got myself togeth-a, baby – now I'm havin' a ball!* Dylan landed, Keds squeaking softly, a millisecond after Mingus, though they'd jumped in tandem. The ball in Dylan's cool palm. Elsewhere sweat had broken everywhere on his thrilled body while aloft.

"Kangaroo boy!" barked Mingus. "Been takin' his *vitamins*, dang!"

La-La answered Marilla's falsetto call with a jeering response: *Got to give it up, baby!*
Oh, yeah: Got to give it up!

It would be the throwdown of the summer of '77 though it was still just the start of July: Grandmaster DJ Flowers is coming with his crew from Flatbush to spin discs in the schoolyard of P.S. 38 after the block party on Bergen. Word's gone out. Hottest day of summer so far only nobody complains, nobody's tired, the sun plummets on Manhattan and the harbor, making orange light, but the day hadn't started yet, not if you knew what was about to go down. You couldn't drink enough beer to cool off or get sleepy. The block party itself is just preliminary, the white renovators grilling chops in their front yards, trying to get to know their neighbors, couple of Spanish guys playing steel drums, nothing special. The little kids run wild, girl and boy, Spanish, black and white mixed the way they did at that age. They spend themselves in the sun, winning and losing shitty prizes, Super Balls, green-haired gremlins, sucking sweet juice through shaved ice in paper cones, getting face-painted by a clown who's really somebody's mom roasting in a Day-Glo Afro wig. The young ones shriek and run, are pooped and whining by four o'clock. The older kids are stalling for night. They kill the afternoon stoop-sitting, eyeing that balloon-filler's huge canister of helium, eating dollar-fifty plates of paella.

By six o'clock the first kids have begun to group in 38's yard, though Flowers won't show until nightfall. The local crews are here in the meantime, setting up a minor skirmish to whet the appetite. P.S. 38 is the domain of the Flamboyan Crew, since their celebrated DJ Stone operates out of the basement of the Colony South Brooklyn youth center next door. Indeed, it was Flamboyan Crew's invitation to Flowers which resulted in tonight's plans. That doesn't mean nobody disputes Flamboyan's primacy here, though. Geography dictates the 38 schoolyard's really a nexus between different forces, the Atlantic Terminals kids crossing down from Fort Greene, the Wyckoff Houses element coming up Nevins. Plus the tough Sarah J. Hale High School kids, drawn to the neighboring block of Pacific from all over.

So, up from Red Hook are the Disco Enforcers – they've heard about Flowers's visit and demanded a turn in the proceedings. Flamboyan's found itself backed into a battle of the jams when all they'd intended was to host Flowers with themselves as the warm-up. No sweat, though, Stone's up to it. He's so sharp on the cross-fader he might be Brooklyn's king if not for Flowers. The rival crews work together to set up, to steal juice out of the nearest streetlight base and run it down to the far end of the yard for their turntables and amps. At the same time trying to conceal from one another their crates of twelve-inches, thinking to maintain some edge of surprise. The secrecy's a bit of a joke, though: they're all, including Flowers when he gets there, certain to be spinning the same fifteen or twenty cuts.

The Enforcers go first. They're an all-black crew, *Enforcers* compensating easily for any faggy associations in the first part of their name. Similarly, their partisans dance on roller skates – *uprocking*, that's what they call it – and nobody's laughing. They balance kneebends and one-heel spins against a series of crotch-grabbing and fist-clenched poses, an in-your-face aspect. One mimes feeding you an endless firehose of dick. The Red Hook DJ leans on "Fatbackin" by the Fatback Band and Babe Ruth's "The Mexican" but also stumps the crowd with Alvin Cash and the Registers' "Stone Thing (Part 1)," an unfamiliar jam. On the drum breaks the line of roller-skated dancers freaks for the crowd, a storm of limbs, skates striking sparks on the cement.

If you managed to meet the eyes of the dancers, though, you'd find them flinching, shy. To actually get out there and uprock isn't easy. Far easier to stand pouting with arms crossed, head perhaps bobbing slightly as you stake out your chosen proximity and consider what unfolds.

The beat's a sonic clatter resounding down Pacific, down Nevins and Third Avenue, a clarion to any who might have missed word: *Something's happening up at thirty-eights, yo.*

Flamboyan takes over next. Those who recalled anything beyond Flowers's appearance that night would later grant DJ Stone blew the Disco Enforcers *out the yard*. Stone not only finds the break, he wears it out. Plus, where the Enforcers' DJs provided their own exhortations to the crowd – a scant few *Evveybody git down!*'s – Stone's got a boy on a vocal mic calling out to the crowd, one who must imagine he's Flowers's kid brother. The scrawny boy, who calls himself MC Ruff, just won't quit with the chants and rhymes.

Flamboyan Crew doesn't provide its own dancers – Stone's breaks and Ruff's shouts merely turn the whole yard into *Soul Train*. No big surprises, just "Paradise Is Very Nice" and "Love Is the Message" sliced a hundred different ways. Those are the grooves get people off the wall. "Love Is the Message" in particular. It's by MFSB, house band of the Philly Groove. Their name ostensibly stands for "Mother, Father, Sister, Brother," though those hip know it really means "Motherfuckin' Sons of Bitches." No DJ is without three or four copies of the precious twelve-inch, it's the staple of any set and nobody complains.

Two hours later they hear "Love Is the Message" again from Flowers. In his hands it sounds just as good, better. Flowers in person casts a spell, he's some kind of heavy Jamaican or West Indian dude, beyond affiliation or strife, like Kung Fu. Flowers is one of the discoverers – *the isolators* – of the break, one of those who proved how furiously people could be made to dance to a section of song unencumbered by vocals or melody. And proving it again tonight.

By this time the card tables and crepe paper back on Bergen have long been cleared. Here is the only place you'd want to be. Maybe three hundred kids spilled around the turntables and amps, dancers at the front, hard-asses clustered according to faction: Atlantic Terminals, Wyckoff Gardens, Spanish dudes from Fifth Avenue. Nobody wants to be the fool who starts a ruckus, though pride requires vigilance against anyone gazing too long at you or your lady. Rivals form Apache lines and dance their aggression, throwing moves. Sure, there's a scuffle or two. But this gathering's peaceful, hardly calls for the cops to come shutting it down just before midnight, stripping one group of kids of sock-hidden steak knives, one cop snapping a pair of nunchucks over his knees, everyone sent streaming out of the schoolyard still buzzing, barely gotten started.

Nevertheless, Flowers's set runs long enough to carve the night into legend. The Jam of '77, just before the blackout. The dark yard lit by the glow of the DJ's flashlights as they cued up grooves, ran breaks together: it merges in memory with that night of flares and candles a week later. In memory, that is, of all but the white kid, the one white face in the whole yard, brought there by, and hewing close to the side of, his homeboy Dose. No blackout for whiteboy. He's lost his last chess game, eaten his last of Mrs. Lomb's turkey sandwiches, tomorrow he's boarding a Greyhound for Vermont. The Fresh Air kid.

Dylan's gone unhassled tonight. Who knows why unless it's evidence of the jam's benignity. He's stood all night soaking it up, one in the mob of flickering bodies and animated faces, even shouting out *Ho-o!* and *Ow!* when Flowers called for it, though this does garner stern looks from some bruthas standing nearby. Still, he skates through. Maybe this night's just lucky, maybe he's passed through some flame and come out the other side. Maybe it's the ring. Maybe the ring has made him invisible. Maybe the ring has made him *black*. Who can say?

A black-and-white photograph of Fidel Castro in a baseball uniform, standing on a pitcher's mound:

> if the mets had to trade seaver
> for a red
> they should have shipped him
> to cuba for this guy
> better fit for che stadium
> so saith commissioner crab

The postcard slipped from between the gallery flyers and Chinese takeout menus stuffed through the mail slot and landed on the hallway carpet, message side up. Abraham Ebdus didn't raise an eyebrow, only dropped it onto the small pile accumulating on the parlor's side table. He trusted there was no urgency to the Running Crab postcards by this point, nothing in any way timely. The boy could wait to read them when he returned. Abraham himself never even glanced at the things anymore.

CHAPTER 11

FISH MOUTHED THE pond's surface, seeming to sip air. Mist clung to the long grass curling from the banks and in the tops of the trees beyond the grass. The short, rotten dock where the boy from the city sat floated inside a gray-green smear, like a corroded photograph of a cloud. Easier to see through the pond's lens to the baublelike sunfish and the broccoli-bright fronds growing underwater than through air to the opposite bank.

"Fish in the rain," Buzz, the delinquent teenage son of the city kid's host family, the Windles, had said that morning. "I'll set you up. You can't miss." Buzz had begun sloughing off the boy from the city with bogus rural assignments, stuff he likely wouldn't touch himself if you paid him. Buzz at sixteen had a small mustache and was hot to rejoin his Vietnam-vet pals chain-smoking over the open hood of a theoretically souped-up, in truth inert, Mustang. The city kid had trailed along for an afternoon and an evening before Buzz cut him loose. In an oil-stained, weedy driveway Buzz's grown friends flicked glowing butts at a lame golden retriever, urinated into empty bottles of Pabst Blue Ribbon, and joked in a language the boy from the city couldn't understand.

It was only malicious to wrench fish through that lens to drown on mushy planks. The boy had no interest in reenacting Buzz's hasty demonstration. The pole rested in the curved grass at the dock's base, hidden like a comb in hair. The boy hunched in borrowed yellow slicker, back turned from the path up to the fields behind the house, painting a figure of solitude for anyone approaching, for his own mental eye: Brooklyn-bereft in Vermont, 1977.

Anyway, he might have an audience for ostentatious kindness to fish. Heather, the Windles' daughter, thirteen to his twelve. He'd felt her trailing him with her eyes. The bookish way the boy talked to their parents and his long, bowl-cut bangs, turnoffs to Buzz, had aroused her curiosity.

She was blond like a Solver.

She darted on her bicycle in quick silence like a figure in Brueghel or Di Chirico.

You might murmur to a girl on a dock in the summer, what you'd never dream of trying in school.

You might be one lucky motherfucker.

Heather Windle picked her way down the path. Her legs had outgrown her own yellow raincoat so it rode high, giving her a Morton Saltish aspect. She hopped side to side on the wet rocks, and slapped, fingers splayed, at a cloud of gnats.

So the kid from the city had completed the transfer, brother to sister.

"Hi, Dylan."

"Hi."

"What are you doing?"

"Nothing."

She stood at the top of the dock, glanced at the pole in the grass.

"Are you sad?"

"Why would I be sad?"

"I don't know, you just look sad."

Maybe he was. Not, though, if the rest of July could be theirs, on the dock, in the field, in the mist, anywhere but out in the oily, pull-tab-strewn driveway, the 7-Eleven lot full of pickups. Dylan Ebdus was ready to vanish out of Buzz's Vermont into a girly world, into Heather's hair. He wanted to ask her if he could simply breathe the oxygen of her blondness, nose the wisps at her cheek.

"I was waiting for you," he heard himself say.

She didn't speak, just clambered to sit beside him at the rain-puckered window of the pond.

"Are you sad because you have no mom?" she said eventually.

"I said I wasn't sad."

"That's why you came to stay here, though, right?"

Dylan shrugged. "Plenty of Fresh Air kids have moms," he said. He'd been justifying the Fund to a stoned man with an eye patch the night before, and the spiel came easily. "The whole point is for city kids to, you know, spend the summer in the country. For variety's sake. I guess your parents thought it was a good idea."

"I know," she said. "We had one last year, but he was black."

"My best friend is black," said Dylan.

Heather thought for a minute and then leaned into him. Raincoat elbows squeaked together. "I've never been to New York City."

"No?"

"Not yet."

"You have no idea." A glow in Dylan replied to the pressure of her body. He felt her curiosity as a kind of enclosing radiance, a field.

Sure, he'd be sad, accept pity, work with whatever came his way.

At that moment he decided to tell his secret, show her the costume he'd brought hidden in his knapsack, the ring, his secret powers.

"You know what graffiti is?" he asked.

"Uh-uh."

"Motion-tagging?"

"What's *that*?" she said, delighted.

"You do graffiti on a moving train," he said. "Instead of in the yard."

"But what's graffiti?"

Yes, he'd reveal the costume, he'd wear it for her. First, though, they sat inside a cloud and he told her about Brooklyn.

When after dinner Heather's mother called to where they played and whispered in the sharply pitched attic Dylan felt a bolt of guilt, as though accused of what hadn't yet happened, as though his yearnings were films projected on the walls downstairs. He'd anticipated Buzz's scorning gaze all afternoon, but when Buzz missed dinner no one even spoke his name. Dylan had felt himself and Heather to be invisible under the Windles' eyes, attic mice, dust balls. Now at her mother's voice he and Heather shared one luscious gaze of complicity, then moved in silence to the stairs.

"You'll want to call your dad, if the phones are getting through," said Heather's father from his recliner, in the room lit by the television's glow. He spoke without turning his head from the spectacle. In shades of blue, New York was in the dark and on fire.

The phone rang four times before his father answered.

"I wouldn't care to be on Fulton Street," said Abraham Ebdus. "There's no sign here, though, just fools yelling. Ramirez parked his station wagon on the sidewalk blocking his shop window. He's standing with a bat, I can see him. I suspect he'll be disappointed."

Dylan nearly asked about Mingus, didn't.

"It's been so hot, it's really a blessing. I'm in my studio, I'll paint the stars, you never see them. Or I'll paint Ramirez. I'll be fine, don't worry."

"Okay."

"Everything well with you, Dylan?"

"Sure."

"Put Mrs. Windle on."

Dylan handed over the phone and turned to Heather. To show provenance over the distant riot he said, "It's no big deal." Then, a bit wildly: "This actually happens all the time, it just doesn't usually get on the news." This drew a look of perplexity from Heather's mother, who'd just replaced the receiver.

The television never returned to the blackout. Still, those rapid-flashed shots of spilled glass and running figures trumped his father's report. Dylan lay dreaming awake of the city on fire.

While Mrs. Windle shopped, the three wandered together to the magazine rack in the broad, white-lit aisle of the super-market. There Buzz marked his indifference to the new order. Dylan and Heather knelt at the comics rack and murmured in low tones, Dylan patiently explaining the mysteries of Marvel's *Inhumans* while Buzz leafed at hot-rod magazines and *High Times*, then wandered away.

As he did, Dylan saw Buzz was trailed by a middle-aged woman with a dirty blue apron and a sticker-gun dangling in one hand like Dirty Harry's Luger. She leaned on her hip to follow Buzz's progress around the aisle's corner, then strolled after him. Dylan smiled to himself, returned to the comics. Heather was oblivious.

Followed in a shop like a black kid.

Dawdling through checkout behind Mrs. Windle, Buzz labored at innocence, shrugging, poking at a rack of gum, making small talk, doomed. The woman with the gun and a bald, stern manager hung near at a closed register, biding time until it was official, until Buzz moved for the exit without plopping whatever he had in his pants and sleeves onto the scudding rubber belt. Only Mrs. Windle and Heather were surprised when the manager corralled them just through the automatic doors.

"I'm sorry, Mrs. Windle." The manager squinted in the pounding sunlight, his tone full of sorrowful inevitability. "We gotta ask Buzz here to step into the back, please."

"Oh, *Buzz*," moaned Mrs. Windle.

Buzz stood pouting sarcastically, shifting from leg to leg, player in a script he was too dull to resist.

"Why don't you younger kids come along. This lesson couldn't hurt you to learn."

In a narrow, windowless office they watched as Buzz dutifully produced *Hot Rod*, *Penthouse*, and a box of shotgun shells from the hunting and fishing aisle.

"Last time we said next time we'd call the sheriff, Buzz."

"Say something," Buzz's mother commanded.

"*I* should've called the sheriff, after how Leonard treated me last time," mumbled Buzz. "Shit, I shouldn't even come in here anymore."

"Afraid that's right, Buzz, you shouldn't. Leonard's got nothing to do with it."

"Well, I don't know about that," said Buzz, locating his rallying cause. "You need to have a word to him about getting off my back, man."

"What did Leonard say to you?" said the manager, his face instantly growing red.

"You kids go wait at the car," said Mrs. Windle, nodding at Heather and Dylan.

They drove in silence, Buzz in the Rambler's passenger seat, forlornly leveraging elbow, head, and neck, as much of himself as possible out the window, his mother rigid with fury at the wheel. Heather and Dylan slumped low and traded grimaces beneath the horizon of the long front seat. Dylan lifted his shirt as in a striptease and flashed the copy of *Inhumans* #7 and the two Nestlé's Crunches tucked at his waist. Heather widened her eyes obligingly, put her hand to her mouth. Home, they ate both bars of chocolate together in the attic while downstairs Buzz reckoned with his father.

Vermont was permeable to Brooklyn ways. Nothing simpler, really, than racking the chocolate and the comic book with Buzz in the role of the black kid, drawing heat.

Buzz had *set a pick* for Dylan – that's what Mingus would have called it.

Afternoons had a dazing slackness. You dropped a bicycle in the grass or on the gravel, wherever you were sick of it, stripped off your T-shirt and kicked away flip-flops and resumed swimming, since you'd been cycling in your drying trunks in the first place. Heather's tits were plums in the armholes of her tank tops and there was always the possibility of an angle, another take on that subject. You compiled views until the postulated form burned in mind's eye, gathering obsessive force like an advertisement you'd passed over forever until the day you just had to know, Sea-Monkeys or X-Ray Specs.

Blackflies and boners, each were solved by immersion.

Dylan mentioned he'd turn thirteen in August at least twice a day.

It was natural enough in those humid, bug-drunk afternoons, the house, pond, field, gravel front yard all Dylan's and Heather's alone, that they'd find themselves sprawled in their suits making wet ass-prints on the sofa one minute, side by side, panting heavily and laughing hysterically in rapid alternation, and then a moment later kneeling barekneed on chairs at the counter, stirring up a Tupperware quart of lemonade crystals and cold tap water. Equally likely to next be ferrying ice-filled beading glasses to the attic, which in daylight boiled with a psychedelic swarm of dust swimming in angled light.

Half naked on the checkered bedcover they again lay side by side, sucking ice.

"I can't feel my lips."

"Me neither."

"Feel this."

"Cold!"

"You now."

The country-city premise freed them to pretend anything was a surprise. Maybe ice didn't work the same in New York City.

"Kiss where I kissed."

A pause, then the attempt.

"I can't feel anything."

"Kiss my lips."

Though they'd been mashing iced lips to wrists, the first was a graze, a bird's peck.

"I'm numb – *dumb*." They cracked up.

"Okay, again."

"Ah."

She'd closed her eyes.

They rolled away. Dylan flopped onto his stomach, quashing a throb in his trunks. "You ever suck laughing gas from whipped cream?" he asked to keep up the stream of distractions, a permitting air of larkiness.

"Noooo," she said. "*Buzz* did though."

Buzz, code for all things crude, contemptible, townish. Dylan and Heather were beings of the pond and the distant-recalled city, nothing between. Forget laughing gas.

"You want a back rub?"

"Sure."

"Turn over."

She obeyed, keeping their deal: nothing was related to any other thing. They were sprites who'd banished taboo and were also a bit stupid, willingly dim. The kiss was on one planet, the back rub another.

He kneaded and pinched, gave her spine a noogie, whatever seemed artful.

Inside the arrangement of her flung arms on the bedspread her tits bulged, third-moons. He earned a grope through extensive rib work, lingered just enough to find them disappointingly lozenge-like, hamburger-hard. Her eyes fluttered inside their lids.

When his fingers curved slightly inside the tight band of elastic at her hips she twisted away, sat up.

"I can't breathe in here."

They tumbled out and onto the bicycles and raced down the gravel shoulder, just two local kids killing time as far as dozing passersby in any passenger windows might care, Heather ratcheting ahead madly, knees flashing in and out of bronze shadow, Dylan chasing, relieved, mouth wide gobbling the moist air, the infinite Vermont afternoon.

Mr. Windle parked the Rambler at the rear of the drive-in lot to shorten his walk across Route 9 to the Blind Buck Inn. There, Buzz predicted, he'd not stir from the bar through the entire double feature – *Star Wars*, *The Late Show* – and emerge so crocked he'd pass the keys Buzz's way for the three-mile drive home. The lot was two-thirds empty, maybe fifty cars hooked as if on life support to units thrusting at angles from weed-cracked pavement.

Space in the city, like time, moved upward. Here the direction was sideways, into the trees.

At blue twilight figures browsed car to car, leaning through windows for a light, making mock of an overfull backseat, a social moment before hunkering down.

"I'm taking a pass on the first feature," Buzz said, not looking at Dylan. With the ten Mr. Windle had floated their way and Buzz confiscated, Heather's brother had magnanimously bought Cokes for Dylan to convey back to the car, then pocketed the change. He was humped over the *Evel Kneivel* pinball machine in the concessions hut, intent on making it tilt a hundred or a thousand times. Or possibly there was an agenda beyond pinball, say a four-foot bong in a trunk. Likely accomplices milled nearby.

Always there was a pond or quarry rumored through the fields, where the real action went on.

Buzz tipped his chin at the distant screen. That scuffed blank billboard was the least interesting place to rest your eyes in the whole sky, which was full of what looked like feathers the color of bruises. "You can stay in the backseat with my sister if you want."

Dylan stood dumbly clenching the paper frame full of Cokes. A week kissing Heather every stolen moment had made him faint and dreamy, incapable of reading either sincerity or scoffing in Buzz. This might actually be some rough blessing.

He nodded and Buzz grinned.

"Bet about now you're thinking the Avoid Nigger Fund's the best deal you ever had in your life, huh?"

They did watch from the backseat. Dylan steered Heather's attention to crucial details, though *Star Wars* didn't carry the same impact here, flashing like a View-Master slide in the pinpricked bowl of night, as it did at the Loews Astor Plaza on Forty-fifth Street. Dylan had seen it four times there, the last two alone, a dwarfed figure growing amazed as the frames pulsed in his eyes, feeling in his subvocal anticipation of certain lines, his sense-memory of certain actorly gestures, the possibility of floating up and intercepting the light halfway, of being a human projector secretly responsible for the existence of the images.

"Parsecs measure *space*, not time," he droned, unable to quit though the point felt unworkable, Arthurish. "Some claim it's a mistake but I'm sure it's intentional, Han Solo's pretending—"

"Dylan," Heather whispered.

"What?"

She closed her eyes. Dylan completed the sentence silently, groping for a relation between speech and the passage of breath in two mouths, the miasmic world created at the junction of two faces. As in the dusky cool of the attic, as at the noon-blazed pond, there was nothing between, the rupture was total, bliss speechless.

'Nuff said.

It was only hard to believe it wasn't illegal. But shut up already and kiss her.

Then he opened his eyes.

The Windles' car was rocking.

Four sets of ass cheeks like blond lunar pancakes pushed the Rambler's windows in gentle alternation, side to side.

Their hair flash-dried in horns and Superman spit curls as they swam and kissed. The sun-dazzled heads were calm, bobbing like floes while an eye-level dragonfly described chess problems on the table of the water. Just below, animal bodies thrashed in green cold. The boy had grabbed the girl everywhere by now, his demented hands inventorying shapes there in the Negative Zone, where nothing counted. Twice he'd felt her fingers graze his pond-numbed prong and practically drowned.

He was returning to Brooklyn tomorrow.

"Your dad might send you to private school," said Heather, breath rippling pond between them. She ducked lower, water past her nose, blue eyes floating doubled in reflection, pupils near invisible.

"What are you talking about?"

"Buzz heard him talking to my mom. Buzz says you're *struggling with a black influence*." She'd plainly rehearsed the phrase, dared herself to speak it.

"Buzz is struggling with a *moron* influence," said Dylan. "I think he's losing the struggle."

"He said you got beat up."

Dylan dove, plunged fully into the silt and shadows of the Negative Zone. He'd taught himself to open his eyes underwater these past weeks. The pond didn't punish eyeballs like the chlorine-poisoned Douglas Pool, down behind the Gowanus Houses, where he'd gone swimming with Mingus a couple of times. You also didn't need to wear sneakers underwater for fear of broken glass. He'd have liked to see Buzz contend with that.

Now he rushed in echoless slow motion at Heather's seal-like body, her red one-piece, limbs glowing like milk in the bent emerald-yellow light. She cycled afloat, not fending him off. Wrapping one arm around her middle, he mashed his mouth into her stomach. A fugitive hand found a tit. She didn't thrash, or even pull away. Anything underwater was between him and her body, apparently.

When he'd come up for air and they lay panting and dripping on the dock, gaze squinted through fingers to protect their eyes from the sun, Dylan said, "I've got something to show you."

"What?"

"Surprise." He'd meant to reveal the costume today anyway. Now it seemed a correction too, to Buzz's garbage.

"Where is it?" she said.

"Go on your bike. Get some Mountain Dews. Meet back here."

She nodded, spellbound, guileless.

In the Windles' guest room he slipped the ring onto his finger, then bundled the costume under his arm. Paranoid he'd be seen, he moved sideways through the kitchen and out, then slipped through the fields.

On the dock he spread the costume out and looked at the thing for the first time since riding the Greyhound bus out of the city.

He'd had his father teach him the simple stitches he'd used to sew it together, though he hadn't said what for. The cape, cut out of a worn Dr. Seuss bedsheet featuring *A Lion Licking A Lemon Lollipop*, was attached at two corners of the neck of the sky-blue T-shirt which formed the costume's body. He'd centered the lion, a suitably enigmatic logo, as nearly as possible in the middle of the cape. The sleeves of the T he'd extended with brightly striped bell-bottom legs scissored off a pair of his mother's abandoned pants, scavenged from the heap at the bottom of her closet where only Dylan ever visited. They hung imperially, his hands extending through a fringe of threads like the clapper in a bell. Impractical, but this was only a prototype. A showpiece. The shirt's chest he'd stretched flat over cardboard and decorated using the Spirograph, the rusty pins, the balky cogs, a clumsy labor with imperfect results. The emblem was an oscillated circle, the widening path of an atom traced a thousand times through space to form *bands of power*. At any distance, though, it blurred to a fat zero.

The boy from the city wriggled into the elaborate top and stood on the yawning dock in a veil of tiny insects, waiting.

A moment later the girl appeared at the top of the path, two green bottles clanking where she had them cradled at her belly, head bowed as she placed bare feet on rocks.

At the foot of the dock she set the bottles of soda in the grass and stood considering.

"Well?"

"What is it?"

"What does it *look* like?"

She didn't seem to know.

He fluffed the cape with his elbows, wishing for a wind. The weight of it dragged the neck of the shirt back so it rode against his throat, a design flaw. He'd attach the next cape at the shoulders, maybe.

"This is who I really am," he said.

She still didn't say anything, just stood.

"Aeroman."

"Who's that?"

"It means *flying man*. Dylan Ebdus is my secret identity."

Forehead knit, she said: "Well, I don't like it."

"What do you mean?"

"It looks weird."

"When it's done it'll cover my legs. This is just the top half."

"Where did it come from?"

"I made it." He said nothing about the ring, about Aaron X. Doily.

She nudged the Mountain Dews, her bare toes cast in green shade by the sunstruck bottles. "It doesn't seem like you."

"Well, it *is* me," he said, adamant. He realized now he wanted Heather to tell her brother, so Buzz would understand he could presume nothing about Dylan or Brooklyn.

She sat, folded her legs in the grass. He stood, still looking for the sign she comprehended the importance of what he'd shown her.

"Dylan?"

"What?"

"If you stayed here you wouldn't have to go to private school."

He was stupefied. The remark was so irrelevant and appalling, he didn't even know where to start.

"I'm not staying here," he said simply, perhaps cruelly.

Heather abruptly stood, her face red and shocked, as if he'd slapped her.

"Take it off," she said. "I don't like it."

"No."

She moved to the path, abandoning the bottles which lay in the grass.

"What about the surprise?" he said. There was a breeze

suddenly, and he felt the cape flutter and snap perfectly at his back, like a stadium flag.

"I don't care," she said without turning.

"*I haven't even shown it to you yet*," he yelled, but she was gone.

After a moment he moved, anyway, to the end of the dock, there bent his knees, pointed his hands straight from his body, preparing what he'd planned for weeks. Heather might be watching from high in the grass at the field's edge; it was possible. Or not, didn't matter now. He didn't need to be known in Vermont, this null area that was only measured in its distance from the city, its use as a restorative, a place to get your act together before returning to the real world. In his case, to prepare to be thirteen in the city, to kiss city girls, to be the flying boy who fights city crime, shit incomprehensible to anyone from Vermont.

He dove in air. The mirrorlike surface dazzled his eyes as he executed a pinball circuit, like one of those dragonflies, inches above. He trained on the far bank to keep from dizziness, flew near and turned, brushing the high grass there, springing an explosion of waterstriders snoozing deep in roots.

He toured the water twice around. When he landed running on the dock he took a splinter in his heel: never fly without proper footgear. And the corner tips of the cape had dangled and were soaked. That's how close he'd been. So: 1. Wear sneakers. 2. Hem cape. One way or another, you were always learning something.

CHAPTER 12

THE CHURCH WAS a garage, set back on Dekalb Avenue behind a low white picket fence that fooled no one, being flush to the busted slate sidewalk and wedged between an ironworks and a plumber's shop. On a Saturday the ironworks was in full operation, oblivious to the services next door, rolling gate up to reveal a man in a welder's mask dipping an acetylene torch against a window grille, sparks spilling on the concrete floor. The block also included an auto body shop, its windows showing a 1967 pinup calendar; a "record" store, glass papered with empty album jackets to conceal the interior from the street, protecting sellers of something likely not records; and two boarded lunch counters with thirties vintage Coca-Cola signs intact, emblazoning forgotten names. The church, whitewashed cinder-block exterior decorated with a handpainted tin sign reading PARLOR OF GOD, "IN HIS BOSOM WE ARE REVEALED," REV. PAULETTA GIB, PASTOR and decorated with a golden Star of David was absolutely a garage, plywood doors open to expose five rows of backs and nodding heads of sitters in folding chairs facing the woman with the microphone at the front of the room. August sun blazed down, baking the churchgoers. Ties were tugged loose at necks, knees eagled to ventilate genitals, cuffs hitched. The pastor's floral dress was soaked at the belly and where the wattles of her upper arms pressed against her ribs. As she paced at the front she expertly flipped the mic's cord across the floor at her feet, keeping it looped far from her high, thick-heeled shoes, which bore a print to match the dress.

The two men, father and son, each boiling in a suit and tie in the midmorning heat, moved through the gate of the picket fence and took seats at the back, just inside the shade of the garage.

"We had better *strive* to emulate the five virgin brides," the woman said at the pitch of her talk. "Keeping our wicks cropped close, keeping our oil clean, preserving the flame, oh yes."

"Oh yes," came the murmured and shouted reply.

"Keeping that *light* in the window so when the robber bride-
groom arrives he can see us waiting faithfully in the window,
oh yes, all in our *fine* things, in our finery all untouched, not
one fingertip soiling our garments, not one."

"Not one, not one."

At the end, as the tiny congregation milled through the
picket fence and onto the sidewalk, the pastor found her way
to the strangers who'd arrived late and seated themselves in
the rear, Barrett Rude Senior and Junior. They stood as she
approached.

"Welcome," she said, holding out her hand. "Pauletta Gib."

"That's a fine service, Sister Gib," said Senior, bowing
deeply. His tie was still knotted tightly at his neck, despite the
heat.

She nodded at him, then opened her hands, and they stepped
out together into the glare. Pauletta Gib turned to the son.
"You're that singer with the Distinctions," she said.

"Barrett Rude Junior, ma'am. No longer with the group."

"I'd heard word you were raised within the Parlor."

"Raised by my father in the church, yes." The singer softened his voice, spoke as humbly as he could. The pilgrimage to
the garage-front church today was for Senior, not a concession
but a gift.

But Pauletta Gib had eyes for the tall man who wished today
only to stand in his father's shadow. "Your singing's given a lot
of easement to folks," she said.

Barrett Rude Junior lowered his head as his father said: "My
son is not a worshipful man, Sister."

Pauletta Gib arched an eyebrow. "I'm sure I don't have to
tell you, Mr. Rude, that a worshipful man is measured one Sabbathday at a time. Today I find your son here within my walls."

"I have only just joined him here in the city. He had no idea
of the existence of your temple." His choice of words conveyed
hesitation over the setting, the dressed congregation lingering
on the sidewalk where men from the ironworks now misted a
section of grille with black Krylon. The paint settled to form a
blurred negative of the grille on the pavement.

"Yet you found us today, praise be to God."

The father at last found voice for what he wanted her badly to know: "I once had a ministry of the Parlor of my own in Raleigh, North Carolina."

Her frown seemed to go through the older man, to pass over his tight-knotted tie, his fresh shave, his keen and defiant expression, to ask *How long ago was that? And what transpired in between?*

What she said, though, revealed nothing of her conclusions at the going-over her eyes had conducted: "Love sets up a Parlor wherever it wanders."

To that Barrett Rude Senior could only add, grumpily, "Praise God."

The woman took the son's hands in hers, gazed deep in his flinching eyes. "Would you sing in our church next Sabbathday?" The tone suggested it was a kindness she offered the singer, not the request for a freebie it should seem to be.

But it was the father, now shifting his weight from squeaking shoe to squeaking shoe, who ached to be at Pauletta Gib's microphone.

"I don't know," said Barrett Rude Junior sincerely, not certain what his father would prefer to hear, mostly wishing he could cause the question to be unasked.

"Don't speak to it at present," said Pauletta Gib, patting the singer's hand. "Your heart will clarify the question in your sleep." Then she turned to the father, her tone slipping an octave. "I trust I'll see *you* next week, Mr. Rude. Unless you've already set up a temple of your own."

"Hrrph."

Barrett Rude Senior turned and pouted, squinting into the sun. He checked his cuffs, picked a nonexistent thread off the breast of his jacket and examined it briefly before tossing it toward the curb, elaborate dandyish mime.

Inevitably, Pauletta Gib had begun to remind Senior and Junior of their deceased wife and mother.

Like the woman they both remembered, she disfavored the father for the son.

Now two of Pauletta Gib's flock who'd hovered at the edge of the talk came forward with an envelope and a ballpoint pen and pressed them into the hands of Barrett Rude Junior. A girl in a print dress, bare dusky arms with a trace of talcum powder, her young brother a twig in a pale peach suit. The boy stood shy at his sister's hip, so the girl had to make the request. They wanted nothing much, though it was a thing the singer hadn't given in nearly two years: just an autograph.

"Yo."

"Yo, man."

"What up?"

"Nothin', man. What you doin'?"

"What you think, man? Same as you – gettin' some ink."

"Cool, cool."

Samuel J. Underberg's, Inc. Food Store Outfitters is a boxy, pale-green five-story building on the other side of Flatbush, beyond the newsstand on the traffic island, in the region of flattened lots and stilled warehouses in the shadow of the Williamsburg Savings Bank tower. The area is a big zero in most senses, a region of lack. Past the Brooklyn Academy of Music, the Long Island Rail Road terminal, there's nothing doing, nobody home. In fact, though no one seems to know it, this is the site once slated for Ebbets Field's relocation, before the Dodgers defected. They got as far as knocking down a lot of old brick and putting nothing up in its place. Nobody smells beer and peanut ghosts here because the ballpark never arrived. The flattened region is a sort of brick-dotted outline tracing a phantom limb. As far as a wandering crowd of kids would care, housing projects-wise, it's beyond the safety zone of Wyckoff Gardens, well into the turf of Atlantic Terminals.

Strange groups on the bare sidewalk give uneasy props all around, heads bobbing and nodding, eyes averted.

All gaze is deferred to the warehouse wall, the splendid explosion of graffiti there.

At the center of this dead land Samuel J. Underberg's is a site of mysterious life, one to which the family-owned business is oblivious. It's nothing to do with their real profitability, which is mainly in supplying new shopping carts, replacements for those stolen by the homeless or wrecked in parking lot collisions. Every day Underberg's trucks dozens of carts out of their warehouse to supermarkets all over Brooklyn. From the warehouse they also shift big-ticket items like registers and rubber matting and display carousels. Call it a niche. At least it keeps a number of men employed, cousins, many of them.

None of this remotely explains the special magnetism of Underberg's for the kids who congregate there. The secret's inside the dinky showroom, practically an afterthought, which features the trimmings a supermarket needs to dress itself as a stage set for the play of shopping: fake parsley-sprig barriers to lay between different cuts of meat inside coolers, fake plastic salamis and gourds of cheese to bulk up displays of real goods, vinyl and laminate signage cut in shapes of fish and pigs to stick in the fronts of delicatessen trays, hot-pink and orange fluorescent signs blaring SPECIAL!

"Yo, man, check it out, that's Strike, man."

"Strike? Really?" This a whisper of disbelief that *the King of the Broadway Line* would materialize in human form.

"Check it out man, he's tagging up."

"Ho, snap, man. *Strike*."

"I'm gonna get him to sign my book."

The Underberg's showroom is the sole place in Brooklyn where a walk-in customer can buy, no questions asked, an eight-ounce bottle of Garvey Formula XT-70 Violet, an industrial ink comprised of ethanol, butyl ether, and polyamid resin, formulated specifically for stamping prices on frozen cellophane and plastic-wrapped packages of slimy meat. Garvey Violet's unique grabability extends also to grime-covered windowpanes – the panes in question being those of subway cars. For use in the homemade markers of graffiti artists Garvey Violet is an irreplaceable elixir, and that, in turn, makes lowly, oblivious Underberg's a destination. It also ensures that the sides of the building form a constantly updated museum of tags from every corner of the borough, a showcase for rival tribes in temporary collaboration.

The skull-capped men at the showroom counter have sussed out this much: Garvey Violet is stacked well behind the counter, so it can only be purchased, never shoplifted. And the counter it hides behind is a glass case filled with cutlery, boning knifes, fat cleavers. At $5.99 a bottle Garvey Violet's enough of a bargain the writers pony up – the only other option, anyway, would be to storm the place with shotguns. Their acting out inside the showroom is more covert: stealing fake fruit and scribbling tiny tags here and there on the cardboard displays.

But apart from this the writers tend to shift in and out glumly, one at a time plunking cash on the counter and mumbling the request, their braggadocio damped until back on the street.

"Yo, man, you hear that? He said *Jew want a bag for that?*"

"Ah, shut up, man."

"I swear man, he said it. I'm not making it up."

These wary groups pass around drawing books bound in pebbly black board, full of their own and others' tags, as well as full-color felt-tip blueprints for top-to-bottom burners they hope someday to dare to reproduce on a train. Underberg's is a place for displaying books, for gathering autographs from all over, though the risk is always abasement or mockery if a group of older, stronger writers decides to bully some younger faction.

From up Flatbush Avenue, off the D train, from up Fourth Avenue off the N and the R at Pacific Street, wandering up from the projects, small groups arrive in waves and mingle jostling on the sidewalk there, blocking the Underberg's men from loading their truck. They come and go noisily, the groups themselves like a form of human scribbling,

This day two white kids stand hoping to be inconspicuous in the gabble of activity that's suddenly all around them, a simple run to Underberg's not so simple after all. One's frozen in the act of tagging up.

"Check out the white boys, man, think they bad."

"What you write, white boy?"

The white kid with the marker is silent, shoulders bunched against his harassers, but with a certain plodding integrity he finishes marking his tag on Underberg's wall, in the small space he's found between larger, spray-painted throw-ups.

"Whazzat say? Art? A-R-T?"

"Dude's tag is *Art*, man. That's wack."

"Your name *Arturo*, dude? You don't look Puerto Rican to me."

"Shut up, man, leave the guy alone."

"He's a toy."

"Leave him alone, man."

"I'm not messin' with the dude, yo, I just want to see what he's writin'. You with a crew, *Art*?"

Question's rhetorical: What white kid could be with a crew? For that matter, what self-respecting crew could contain a white dude, let alone a small, ferrety white dude like this one, let alone *two* white dudes? Not to mention two like these, beginning to cower instinctively against Underberg's wall in the manner in which negotiating the halls and schoolyard and adjacent streets of Intermediate School 293 has tutored them.

Ritualized cringes buried millimeter-deep in the psyches of the two white kids, mock-asthmatic seizures and other forms of beseeching, are ready to surface when the nearest thing to *a crew* these guys could ever hope for pops back out of the showroom with a fresh-purchased bottle of Garvey Violet: Mingus Rude.

Mingus's assessment of the situation is so instantaneous and smooth his remark seems to emerge from his mouth even as he himself emerges from Underberg's, while at the same time he slips the bottle of ink into the fat thigh pocket of his military-surplus pants. He doesn't address the four black kids who are tightening the lasso of themselves around Arthur Lomb and Dylan Ebdus, instead speaks as if all but Arthur and Dylan are invisible, his tone one of annoyance.

"Fuck you doin', Art man? I tole you them other dudes are waiting for us. Ain't time to be foolin' around here, man, we got to *go*."

A reference to *other dudes* is magic. The lasso slackens. Arthur and Dylan nod obediently to Mingus, duck their heads, eyes cast down on the sidewalk as they follow him.

The three escape together, leaving the Underberg's pavement to other confrontations.

Across Flatbush, Arthur Lomb skips up excitedly beside Mingus, while Dylan lags behind. Arthur's eager mimicry produces a twee, mechanical version of Mingus's hunched lope. He really is, in this sense, a *toy*: he's turning himself into a Mingus-puppet. "Yo, them dudes were talking about Strike, man, they said he was there tagging up; but I didn't see him. Could be wishful thinking, just like everybody claims they saw Son of Sam. Anyway, Strike's okay, but I prefer Zephyr, I think he's really got the most original tag, yo, man, you know what I mean?" Mingus only grunts and stalks on, but that's encouragement enough for Arthur. "Man, that one guy was trying to act real scary, but I could see his face, he looked like a baby, his lips were all blubbery. Yo, I probly could of taken him if you hadn't come out just then. Lucky for him I'd say, yo." Arthur's careful slurring of certain words, in contrast to his sharply nerdish pronunciation elsewhere, is wincingly obvious to Dylan, who wonders why Mingus doesn't just smack him upside the head and command him to stop. But Mingus tolerates Arthur's parroting talk, accepts this transformation Arthur's accomplished, somehow, in the month Dylan's been away. Arthur Lomb, it appears, contains multitudes: he's managed this utter self-reformatting with the same sleazy facility with which he earlier dumped the Mets for the Yankees. "Couple white boys could of taken their paints and shit off them, I bet, that is if they had anything worth taking, which I doubt, yo, judging from the poor condition of their sneakers."

"Be cool," says Mingus now, as without glancing sideways he throws out an arm to slow Arthur's pogo-ing gait. There may be no stopping the flow of Arthur's talk, not once he's on this kind of roll. At least, though, he might quit hopping.

Arthur does slow. He allows Mingus to move ahead, giving him some room to glower in his own irritated headspace, often a necessity when Mingus hasn't smoked a joint in a while. Arthur turns to Dylan instead. "What you think, we could of taken them, yo?"

"Don't yo me," said Dylan.

He crouched in darkness at the top of the abandoned house's stoop, hearing distant sirens. Nearer by, voices at Bond Street, a laugh knifing through the humidity, floated to the sky. Though the night was hot he wore a sweatshirt. Underneath was the costume, the cape crammed up into the back like a soft turtle's shell, bell-bottom sleeves doubled around his wrists. He sweat furiously, it couldn't be helped. The ring he kept like a folded dollar, hidden in his sock: the possibility of being yoked while still on the ground was very much with him. Perhaps he should have begun on rooftops, but access to his own was through Abraham's studio, and Abraham was painting frames of film tonight. Dylan had opened the studio door to find his father planted under a single clip-on floodlamp, fingers crabbed around a tiny brush, transistor radio tuned low to goose-like jazz, the barely audible squonks of Rollins or Dolphy.

"I'm going out."

"Tonight?"

"Just for an hour."

"Shouldn't you sleep?"

"Just an hour."

It was the evening of the day before eighth grade.

It was somewhat unclear how to begin.

Mingus Rude and Arthur Lomb were off painting a burner on the side panel of an abandoned police truck in the city salvage yard at the foot of the Brooklyn Bridge. The expedition had been planned for days, a wake for summer's death, a last fling. Dylan involved himself in preparations, including the harvesting of Krylon from McCrory's and the assembling of a sheaf of marker sketches in full color, then bowed out of the jaunt itself at the last second. This ensured that tonight he wouldn't bump into Mingus or Arthur. Anyway, Dylan was exhausted with the whole Mingus-Arthur situation. He'd begun to wonder if he was encouraging it by his own presence. Let them be alone together, let Mingus endure the raw, grasping force of Arthur's sycophancy without Dylan around as a buffer, and see how he liked it.

Besides, the two would be painting Dylan's design on the police truck, Dylan's hand was inherent in the sketches. Mingus might be Dose, but Dylan was Dose's auteur.

Teenagerdom was a secret identity in the first place.

At thirteen you'd begun to leave traces, occult names and signs proliferating, sheets you fiercely insisted on laundering yourself.

Like a Spirograph cog your wobbling path made messes.

Aeroman was a bolder route, only he was proving hard to bring out of his sweatshirt shell.

Where in Gowanus did a fresh-minted superhero go to find the sort of crime in which he could meaningfully intervene? Dylan huddled on the abandoned stoop, ear cocked to the damp howl of the late-summer wind as it bore voices through the night. The gays walked their dog, otherwise the block was empty. Dean Street wouldn't cut it. Nevins, that was too much, the prostitutes, the old men on Ramirez's corner, the chance of Wyckoff kids ranging up from the projects. Smith Street, same problem. He needed an isolated nightscape, an alley, a woman yelling for return of her stolen pocketbook, the classical Spider-Man mugging scenario: exactly what he'd never seen in his life. A superhero spliced criminals from victims. In Gowanus things tended to be more mixed up.

He needed height, perhaps. To rise above.

He roused himself from the stoop and walked to the corner, then up Bond Street, to the subway, the Hoyt-Schermerhorn station, knowing it was a place he'd never go at this time of night if conditions weren't changed, and they were barely changed. He resembled himself, not Aeroman, until he shed the sweatshirt. And Aeroman didn't walk, he flew. Until he brought himself to fly down from a rooftop he wasn't Aeroman, he was a kid in a costume in a sweatshirt, walking. The ring was in his sock – he reached down and confirmed it. A white boy on the corner of Bond and Schermerhorn at eleven at night. The place was desolate enough, barren parking lots and basketball courts, darkened municipal buildings, the street's wide lanes silent. Too desolate, maybe. Places you feared most were empty, your fear of them theoretical. You wouldn't be caught dead there, so you didn't go, so no one went because what was the point?

In truth the action was below, in the long urine-stinking subway tunnel beneath Schermerhorn. The token booth there was buried deep in the block, the path to it a terrifying gauntlet, a home for beggars who slumped against the dimmed windows of subterranean displays, relics from a time before Abraham and Straus figured there was no one worth advertising to in the stations underground, and no way to protect the merchandise displayed there. The tunnel was a famous danger.

He caught himself, though: *What use was a flying man in the subway?* A novice mistake, barely outsmarted. He felt a degree of accomplishment in avoiding it. Aeroman's first triumph, a prudent hesitation. It was a relief not to enter the tunnel.

Maybe Smith Street was a better bet after all.

Tomorrow eighth grade began.

Aeroman wanted to emerge before it was too late, but he needed crime to call him out.

Beneath his feet the pavement rumbled as the A or GG slowed at the underground platform, then a handful of lonely figures leaked from the station into the night. He stood beneath the lamppost across Schermerhorn, watching. One white woman glanced in his direction, eyes darting, surveying the empty street. She turned down Bond, then onto State Street.

Sweating, hunchbacked, Aeroman followed.

Maybe something would happen. He was magnetized by her fear, a thing he understood. Seeing it reflected in the woman was acutely thrilling. Here was precisely what Aeroman meant to combat, the hectic, accelerating heel steps in darkness, on a block where the canopy of limbs masked the streetlights. He reached down, not breaking stride, and palmed the ring up from his ankle, slipped it onto his left forefinger. The voices of hidden paper-bag drinkers drifted from the recessed stoops, idle jaded watchers who'd never help a woman in danger.

She was underdressed, rape-able, regretting she'd ever heard the word *Brooklyn*, let alone nibbled the bait of the reputed astonishing rents here, the hardwood floors.

Just one catch: the scene sorely lacked a villain. No one followed the girl apart from him.

He was chasing her down the block. It was his footsteps she fled.

It was a mugging like an egg on a roosterless farm, unfertilized, incomplete.

When she began actually running he stood still in the middle of State Street and let her go, made dumb with chagrin. Should he fly ahead, somersault over and intercept her, perhaps, to apologize? But he'd only scare the shit out of her worse than he already had.

Aeroman had met the enemy, and it was Aeroman.

Now he trudged to Smith Street.

He went unnoticed here in his humped shirt, his hands bunched at his waist, right covering left, the finger with the ring. Happy enough for the moment to be scaring no one, to be a part of the crowd. The summer night was alive, Puerto Ricans spilling from social clubs in groups of four at sidewalk domino games, younger men in Yankee shirts tuned to the game. The entrance to the Bergen subway station was clotted with Gowanus Houses kids, teenage boys in stocking caps, angry girls he might or might not recognize from school. School, ready to resume, ready to pin him in place. He felt urgently again the need to find a meaningful crime, something he could handle. He slunk past the crowd of Gowanus kids at the subway, certain there was less than nothing for him there.

He was hungry. Looking both ways, he fished in his other sock for the dollar tucked inside. It was soaked. He transferred the dollar to his pocket and rubbed it against the cloth at his thigh to dry it. At Bergen and Smith was a pizzeria, also thronged with older teenagers, a place he and Arthur Lomb had braved one afternoon on the way from school to Pacific, to Arthur's stoop, in the early days of their friendship. It seemed possible now his friendship with Arthur Lomb had peaked in the first month of that summer, during the deplorable chess marathon, that he would never taste Arthur's mom's red juice or turkey sandwiches again. He couldn't permit himself to be nostalgic. Arthur was a phony, and Mingus would know soon enough. He imagined Arthur saying, *Yo, Mister Machine sucks, Jack Kirby can't draw anymore, dang, but a number one's a number one, yo, seal it in airtight plastic and put it on the shelf, that's my policy, yo.* He went into the pizzeria and ordered a slice, spread his moist dollar on the counter.

A hand clapped over the two quarters change as they appeared in place of the dollar. Dylan looked up. Robert Woolfolk scooped the coins into his pocket. The men at the pizza counter were uninterested: the event occurred at the teenage stratum, which they filtered at a preconscious level. Dylan or Aeroman was a little uninterested himself. He kinked the slice of pizza at the crust, folding it so it supported the floppy weight of its own tip, fluffed the sheet of translucent paper underneath, then shook garlic salt onto the pizza's surface, tan grains which saturated instantly in pooled oil. With the slice he stepped into the populated street. Robert Woolfolk followed. Robert had a companion along, a small version of himself, dark and rangy, whom Dylan had never seen before.

"Don't bite that, man," said Robert.

"Why not?"

"Take it off him," Robert told the other boy, who was small-er than Dylan.

"What you talkin' about?" said the younger boy, disbeliev-ing the obvious.

"Take his slice."

Among yokings, this was a familiar format to Dylan: the master instructing apprentice, commanding *Take it off him* or *Check his pockets, man*. Call it the Batman-and-Robin.

Never for a slice, though. That was fairly original.

"C'mon, man," implored the protégé, not looking at Dylan.

"Take it, man. Do it."

Dylan bit the pizza's tip. Chewing open-mouthed to venti-late molten cheese, he sought out the younger kid's eyes. He felt a peculiar cheer at the animal bewilderment he inspired there. Yes, I am your first *whiteboy*. Gaze on me. You'll know many before you're through. Some you'll be large enough to handle, some you'll even terrify.

He took a second bite.

"Don't eat it, I told you," said Robert, his voice rising. "Take the slice," he directed again.

"Awww, he's bitin' on it," said Robert's trainee, misery in his voice.

Robert pointed at the pizza. "Quit now, man, or I'll fuck you up!"

Dylan swallowed, sank his teeth in again. Robert Woolfolk was hamstrung by his intractable sidekick – if he reached for the pizza himself it was an admission of failure. The slice was dwin-dling anyway, so the principle was all that remained, if there'd been anything apart from principle in the first place. Dylan understood he functioned as a passing occasion here, object in an obscure ritual which had for once nothing to do with Dylan himself. The young black kid would take the brunt tonight, be bullied through a series of low-end quasi-criminal stunts.

The kid knew it too. He sulked in the background as Dylan's bites made the slice irretrievable. Robert Woolfolk turned to

Dylan now, but was jangled, distracted, with only a minute more to spare, seemingly a bit out of his skin.

Last day before school could get to practically anyone.

"I'm still gonna kill you one day," Robert Woolfolk said.

Dylan chewed, facing Robert with a dope-eyed, cowlike aspect.

"Don't pretend you don't know."

Dylan shrugged, only certain Robert wasn't killing him tonight.

"Fuck's the matter with *yo back*, man?"

"Nothing," said Dylan between bites.

Robert looked harder. "Lemme see that ring for a minute."

"It's a present," said Dylan. "From my mother."

"*Fuck* your mother, *motherfucker*." Now Robert Woolfolk danced as though attacked by invisible insects. The ring, anyway, was clearly off-limits, tainted with Rachel-magic. Robert twitched like a bot moving in circles, his circuits blown.

"Think Gus be gonna proteck you forever?"

No, Aeroman be gonna proteck me forever, thought Dylan, swallowing unchewed chunks of pizza defiantly.

But Aeroman hadn't flown tonight, there was no pretending.

Dylan had now gnawed all the way to the ragged crust, which he held at his mouth like a jack-o'-lantern smile.

Robert herky-jerked his arm out and slapped the crust from Dylan's hand. Like hilltop observers musing on a distant nova they watched it tumble to the gutter, officially ruined. Robert's worst excess of tension was spent in the act. He could return to his protégé who stood abjectly to one side.

Robert Woolfolk pointed a finger at Dylan as they parted, but his voice was lost, his menace dispelled by the conundrum of this encounter.

On Smith Street alone, ignored by the Puerto Rican social club members in their floral shirts and straw porkpies, the humpbacked, overdressed, and sweating thirteen-year-old turned onto Dean and strolled home along the shadowed slate, weirdly satisfied.

Aeroman had not flown, had remained tucked into Dylan's sleeves and waistband, in chrysalid form.

Nevertheless, two happenings, incomplete in themselves,

somehow clicked puzzle-ishly together to form a whole, the phantom image of a mugging averted, Gotham's streets made safer.

The running woman on State Street had been the one afraid tonight, not Dylan. That was something, a crack of daylight in the night. Aeroman would slip through that crack, he just wasn't ready yet.

Eighth grade, right, you could almost grasp the shape now. A given day was a model of the grade in miniature, something to get through. Just perfect one single day and you'd have a method to apply to the whole.

Abraham did his part scraping toast while Dylan worked math problems at the table, a take-home test due in fifteen minutes, first period.

Barrett Rude Senior might be lighting a breakfast cigarette in the well of his basement entrance, stroking white stubble, patrolling the morning.

Ramirez rolling up his gate, moms tugging first graders to P.S. 38.

Henry was in his second year at Aviation in Queens, he'd grown a foot and a half and was the man you saw sometimes on the block who'd high-five with younger kids. Recalling he'd been in a fistfight with Robert Woolfolk was useless. There was no history of kids on a block, such facts you couldn't impart in a way to make anyone care.

Whacking off was a new organizing principle, the rare thing completely under your own command. You might get hard on the way home from school, clutch it in your pocket, anticipating an afternoon session.

Aeroman's new outfit-in-progress was simpler, cape lighter and shorter and secured at the shoulders, sleeves tight at the wrists.

It progressed slowly, stitch by stitch, no hurry this time.

When the weather cooled Dylan and Arthur took the A to Canal Street. They browsed bins full of Lucite knobs, drank egg creams at Dave's Famous, then made their way to the army surplus store. With money for coats they'd cadged off Arthur's mom and Abraham they purchased green fatigues like Mingus

Rude's, jackets with heavy vented pockets, strange loops for military knives or rounds of ammunition, who knew. Maybe dudes in Nam had died in the jackets, you couldn't exclude it, though they lacked telling bullet holes.

Returning to the subway they paused to flip through some worn Beatles LPs for sale on the sidewalk, *Let It Be, Abbey Road*. Dylan found a name he recognized. The name was superimposed on a photograph of five grinning, beardless black men in peach suits and ruffled shirts seated on stools of various heights, backlit in blue and arranged like a bouquet in a photographer's studio: *The Deceptively Simple Sounds of the Subtle Distinctions*.

Dylan showed it to Arthur. "That's Gus's dad."

Arthur looked unimpressed. Dylan bought the record and took it home, but it was scratched, unplayable.

For a week Dylan and Arthur wore the jackets to school pristine. Then one day Arthur appeared with his jacket glamorously ruined with gold and silver paint, sleeves laminated in Krylon, burner scars, evidence. Arthur smirked, Dylan said nothing. That night he retired his virginal jacket before Mingus caught him in it.

Mingus himself was a random factor, a shade or rumor now, only glimpsed. He'd vanish for weeks, then you'd meet up, get high in his basement, and go to the Rex on Court Street to take in a Charles Bronson double feature, sit in darkness for hours not speaking a word apart from *dang* and *ho snap*.

Mingus was flush erratically, blew cash in a hurry. Later you'd catch him fluffing cushions for change, palming pennies from the dish Abraham kept at the front door, scraping up enough for a nickel bag.

Nobody took fifty cents or a dollar from Dylan that he didn't see coming a mile off. One day in the basement Dylan applied Abraham's hacksaw to a couple of quarters, then strolled with fragments jingling, waiting for the inevitable frisk. When with a dumb grin Dylan offered the sawed half-quarters and quarter-quarters the Gowanus kids who'd cornered him walked off shaking heads, pained, as if he'd spoken Chinese or wriggled an antenna.

You knew this game of days like the back of your hand, if the back of your hand was changing like a werewolf's.

One day Dylan came home to find Abraham with a package on the kitchen table, an upright bundle wrapped in layers of butcher paper and twine. Abraham shredded at it with a steak knife, freeing the hidden object, unpeeling onion layers of newspaper insulation like Humphrey Bogart unpacking the Maltese Falcon. Dylan imagined it might be something from Rachel, perhaps a statuette depicting *A Crab, Running.* Then Abraham exposed the top of the prize inside: the gleaming golden nose of a 1950s-style rocketship.

"Don't worry, I won it fair and square," said Abraham. "Sidney accepted on my behalf."

Words on the gilded rocket's base explained, at least partly. HUGO AWARD, BEST NEW ARTIST, 1976, ABRAHAM EBDUS.

"Recognition creeps up on one," said Abraham darkly.

Dylan hefted the thing, scowled.

"You want it for a doorstop?"

Dylan considered, nodded.

"Just don't say I never gave you anything."

CHAPTER 13

THE SONG COULD be heard on New York radio for a week or
two, mid-February 1978, not yet charting high but *picked to
click*, scored on the R&B chart at number eighty-four with a
bullet – it was asserted to be *with a bullet* each time that discouraging number was mentioned aloud – and slipped into rotation
between Earth, Wind and Fire's "Serpentine Fire" and Con
Funk Shun's "Ffun": "(Did You Press Your) Bump Suit" by
Doofus Funkstrong, a three-minute, forty-second single edited
out of the sprawling eighteen-minute jam that covered side two
of the band's Warner Brothers debut, *Double-Breasted Rump*. DJs
solicited phone calls weighing in – bold or cold, smash or trash,
funk or junk? A few dozen requests could still tip a song up
regional charts and push it toward a national breakout. Anyone
trusting their ears knew Doofus Funkstrong was a disguise for
the legally hamstrung, hence recording-under-pseudonyms
Funk Mob – for those less sure, a look at the psychedelic Pedro
Bell jacket art did the trick. Fewer ears would place the name
of the vocalist whose melismas decorated just the last thirty-
eight seconds of the single edit, credited on the album jacket, as
according to plan, as Pee-Brain Rooster: under his own name
Barrett Rude Junior was a voice from radio's middle distance,
years out of rotation, not yet an oldie. If a few formed the
question *Ain't that the singer from the Distinctions?* it was only a
passing thought – how likely, anyway, that the tenor voice of
the smooth and mellow Distinctions should show up riding the
crest of that distorted synth bass line?

Then the song died. No explanation was called for – certainly none was given. Songs die, this one did. Figure it freakish that
it charted at all, with refrains like *Up jumped the globster, caught
her with a mobster!* and *Goof a wedgie up your rump pocket!* There
are limits. So it died; call Doofus Funkstrong an *album-oriented
act*, euphemism for *Who cares?* Performance royalties trickled
through a legal maze, never enough to fight over should Pee-
Brain Rooster choose to consult a lawyer. For a few weeks you

heard the song or you didn't, while nerd connoisseurs were left to savor it later, to champion or slag it in their endless tinny dialogue. History, basically, wasn't made. Marilla and La-La would never be heard chanting this song in their front yard, not skipping rope nor braiding hair nor teasing boys with their fresh-grown hips. That test it couldn't pass: the song, musicianship aside, lacked a hook.

When Mr. Winegar asked him to remain after class he sat imagining that he'd somehow become known, that the science teacher had taken it upon himself as gravity's local spokesman to pronounce on the matter: *Young man, human flight is sheerly impossible! Renounce it at once!* Instead Mr. Winegar took a letter from his drawer and handed it across his desk, sat twisting the end of his mustache as he watched Dylan Ebdus absorb its contents: test scores permitting entrance to Stuyvesant.

Outside it snowed, jigsaw chunks which piled on the ledge, clotted the grate which covered the window. The school had poured out into the white-muffled afternoon. Staying late Dylan had lost his chance to sneak across Smith in a protective mob of bodies in motion, would instead be snowball target prime for anyone prowling near the school.

"Only kid in the school to make it," said Winegar. "But then only six even tried the test. I requested the chance to tell you in person, don't mind saying I'm proud of how you've applied yourself."

Winegar's mustache-torturing and puzzled gaze contradicted this potted speech: he'd retained the letter in order to glimpse the freak, the reverse-retard who'd surfaced unexpectedly in the ocean of screaming, proto-criminal souls that made up Dylan's classmates, made up for that matter all five periods of science teaching in his day's schedule – made up, come to think of it, his entire blighted career. *If I'd known you'd pull this I'd have flattered myself by noticing you sooner.*

But caretaking Winegar's astonishment wasn't one of Dylan's priorities.

"What about my friend Arthur Lomb?"

Winegar frowned. "I shouldn't discuss anyone else's results with you."

It could only mean one thing. Dylan found himself pained for Arthur, felt an unexpected throb of empathy.

"He must of gotten into Bronx Science, though," he suggested to the teacher.

Winegar looked hurt. "Certain persons—" he began, and broke off. Dylan understood: not Bronx Science, not even Brooklyn Tech. Arthur Lomb, chess demolitionist, whiz mimic, master strategist of escape, hadn't honored his own advice and studied for the test. Perhaps he thought a last-minute asthmatic seizure would carry the day, perhaps proudly held a bowel movement through the test period, perhaps thrown a few *yos* their way. All useless in the teeth of algebra. Houdini had drowned inside his padlocked cabinet.

From Winegar's tone it was plain Arthur had bragged to the teacher in advance, worked up expectations with a series of snappy answers and arch asides.

"Well, Sarah Hale is right by my house," said Dylan, impulsively sadistic. He adopted a moronic, grating monotone, tribute to Arthur Lomb, fallen soldier. "I mean, it does seem like all my friends are going there."

"I'm sorry?"

"I only took the test to see how I'd do. I might not go."

Winegar looked traumatized. Sarah J. Hale High School was the next grim repository, following Intermediate School 293 by rote. You could cut class for two years straight, as in the case of Mingus Rude, and they'd eventually palm you off to Sarah J. just to free up the chair in your homeroom for someone else. Dylan might as well have said *I think I'll just go straight to the Brooklyn House of Detention.* "I'd hate to see you neglect an opportunity—"

You're white! Winegar wanted to scream.

Man can fly! Dylan wanted to scream.

"I'll think it over," said Dylan.

"You've shown an aptitude—"

You should see my altitude.

"I have to talk to Abraham. My dad."

The mustache might dissolve in Winegar's fingers if Dylan didn't show a little mercy. "Certainly. Please let your father know I'd be glad to answer any questions—"

"Okay." He glanced outside. Brooklyn was captured in a net of false calm, the school drowned. Dylan was bored with Winegar now, prepared to meet his ice-ball fate.

Snow-thick roofs could be a fine place to study cornice-hopping, leave inexplicable footprint trails, jumpings-off to nowhere.

Aeroman, you understand, works locally, like his predecessor.

Marijuana was Rachel Ebdus's totem fume. To inhale it was communion, a forgiving and being embraced by her smoke-form. Dylan Ebdus learned slowly, first faking when Mingus Rude handed him a joint, making sucky sounds around the damp tip as wisps wreathed his head. Then not faking but getting nothing for his trouble apart from a raw impression that his throat was an overpicked nostril. It was only later, the sixth or seventh time he sincerely inhaled, that Mingus's room slowly widened outward from pinprick size, the thing Dylan had pretended to feel all along.

At that moment Rachel joined him there, in Mingus's room with the towel stuffed at the bottom of the door and the back windows vented to the icy air. Whether in the drug or in Dylan, she'd seemingly lurked in one to be catalyzed by the other. Or perhaps it was simpler: as while listening to her records, the Modern Jazz Quartet and Nina Simone and Three Dog Night, Dylan could still be just getting acquainted with Rachel, through her appetites, her puns, her drugs.

Dylan stored the Running Crab postcards, maybe thirty-five or forty now, in order by postmark, pinned upright between Heinlein's *Stranger in a Strange Land* and the New Belmont Specials numbers one through sixteen – a run halted when Abraham had quit painting their covers – on a shelf bookended by the Hugo Award statuette. Dylan archived the postcards alongside Abraham's commercial art not only to ensure Abraham's irritation, should father sniff into son's Batcave while son was at school, but also because it felt deeply right: the objects made a voodoo poem of Abraham-and-Rachelhood, of his parents' DNA, their semivoluntary sheddings like fingernails or hair, mixed on a shelf.

Dylan determined now to reread the whole sequence of

postcards stoned, to start at the beginning again and with the assistance of the drug decode Rachel's vanishing.

"Check this out," said Mingus Rude, after he'd fanned the smoke into his backyard and shut the windows. The cold didn't matter, Mingus always wore his stained army jacket indoors. He was always just passing through, ready for action even when he never stirred from the room for hours.

Now he slipped Rhythm Heritage's "Theme from S.W.A.T." extended-mix seven-inch from its sleeve and smoothly to the turntable, moved the needle to the groove.

As crackle gave way to the opening break, Mingus began shifting the record back and forth under the needle, isolating the beat. Under his breath he rapped calls to an imaginary schoolyard audience in a rubbery voice of cartoon affront, the Bugs Bunny of the ghetto.

Dylan nodded appreciatively.

"That's bad, right?" said Mingus.

"It's *fly*," Dylan ventured.

"All the cuts them DJs can't even find, I just snuck upstairs and stole out of Junior's collection. Wanna hear some more?"

"Yeah."

"That's *right* my boy wants to hear more, you *bet* he does."

This time Mingus set the needle on Dennis Coffey and the Detroit Guitar Band's "Scorpio." Again he scratched it back and forth, again he mumble-rapped along with the song, shy eyes slanted downward.

Mingus might not be ready to take it to the schoolyard, but he had the tracks. They might be the only two kids in Brooklyn with a collection of vinyl beamed direct from Planet Superfly.

Mingus's room had changed. The Philadelphia Flyers' Dave Schultz and the Miami Dolphins' Mercury Morris were gone, the Jackson Five was gone. All three posters had been auto-graphed in real ink, gifts to Barrett Rude Junior. No matter: they'd been ripped from the wall, leaving only shreds under tacks. Just one poster remained, one permanently creased in sixths from its life as a giveaway inside a double gatefold LP: Bootsy Collins and his Rubber Band, in chrome tuxes, plat-forms, pink smoke. It was autographed too. On a visit upstairs to see Barrett Rude Junior Bootsy himself had been directed to the basement apartment, had stood in Mingus's room to sign the poster in dripping Garvey Violet, a messy slogan that half-covered his spangled, star-shaped guitar: *Love Ya, Bootsy!* More recently the poster had been half-covered in silver spray. Mingus had begun tagging inside his room. Too lazy or stoned to go out and put it in the public eye, the tags still flowed from him, DOSE, DOSE, DOSE. Silver loops sprawled over the walls, across molding, touching the ceiling, silver mist even touching the glass of the back windows. The radiator was tagged, a puzzle in three dimensions. If you stood sideways so the radiator's grille formed a single surface you could read the tag: ART. From other angles it dissolved into stripes, empty code.

Farrah Fawcett-Majors was gone too, the red one-piece and erect nipple and blond tilted grin which had been pinned at telling eye level to Mingus's single bed. Instead, a clutch of Barrett Rude Junior's hand-me-down *Playboy* and *Penthouse* magazines were inadequately hidden beneath the bed, tattered centerfolds torn from their staples and flapped out like the tongues of exhausted dogs. A white bloom of balled Kleenex failed to conceal a jar of Vaseline.

"You never told me about the girl in Vermont, man."

"What girl?" Dylan was turning the pages of *Defenders #48*, ogling Valkyrie in her blue sleeveless armor, her chain-mail brassiere. Mingus's comics were in tatters, he'd tagged their slick covers with black El Marko.

"King Arthur said you were bragging about it, man, so don't even try to lie."

"I didn't tell Arthur anything. He's full of it."

"Look at my boy, trying to cover up! Arthur said you done *got over*. You can't hide from me, D-Man, you *know* you'll be telling me in a minute."

Dylan thought for less than a minute and said, "Her name's Heather."

"There you go."

"We went swimming."

"I heard more than swimming."

Despite cutting class for two years, Mingus had graduated to Sarah J. Hale. Like a sundial shadow he'd crept into the next time zone, the next phase. His room had changed, his body had changed, he'd grown gruffer and larger, when he loped down Dean Street he chanted rhymes under his breath, disc jockey patter. He had his own stereo. He scored his own pot, nickel bags through a slot in the door of a tenement on Bergen, no longer raiding Barrett Rude Junior's freezer stash. His room was a sanctum. Though Barrett Rude Senior had moved into the front of the basement apartment Mingus's room seemed remote from any authority beyond his own. The rooms of the duplex had become fortresses, the three generations of Rudes barricaded into their dominions in an unspoken war. Mingus called his grandfather Senior and never stepped into his front room, which when it was seen through a half-open door looked barren, as though Senior had forgotten how a large room might be filled. Senior sat by the radiator and stared through the bars of the basement windows onto Dean Street as through the bars of a cell. Sometimes he burned candles. Mingus called him Senior, and he called his own father Junior. Mingus's room smelled of Vaseline and something else. The jacket of the Ohio Players' *Fire*, which depicted a girl's impossibly hot torso with a firehose snaking obscenely between her legs, was sticky with something, resin maybe, and seeds and stems from rolling joints on the jacket were stuck in the something. It was a bit disgusting, but also fascinating, like a leaf stuck in hair or a smear of food on chin you didn't want to point out.

Junior's rooms upstairs smelled of something else, something wicked, heated foil, singed crystal grains. Senior melted candles and chain-smoked Pall Malls, frequently igniting the next with the stub of the last, Mingus and Dylan, sealed into the sanctum with the towel at the door, puffed pot, while upstairs in the parlor which nobody entered Junior burned freebase cocaine in a glass pipe.

Barrett Rude Junior and the Famous Flames.

"Don't think I forgot you was telling me about Heather, man."

"You wish."

"How old is she?"

"Thirteen."

"Older woman – always said that's the way to go."

"I gave her a back rub."

"Oh yeah. There you go. I *know* you didn't stop at no back rub."

"We kissed, in the attic." Saying the words Dylan smelled the place, recalled groaning wooden stairs, blond light. "All she had on was her swimsuit."

"Get serious now. She a *old* thirteen or a *young* thirteen?" Mingus's open hands described fullness in the air.

Dylan thought *oranges*, said, "Grapefruits."

"*Damn!*" Mingus's pleasure was so great he scowled. "Hold on a minute." He pushed himself up and put Sly's *Fresh* on the stereo, cranked the volume. Then he slumped back on his bed, fingers spread wide on thighs. Between thighs and spread fingers, tenting his corduroys, a boner.

"You were saying."

Something moving in the brain of a doer sang Sly in a lubricious, dozy drawl.

"I'll show you," said Dylan. "Turn over."

Mingus nodded, and obeyed.

Dylan was the storyteller here, he understood now that Mingus had no way to contradict him, was only waiting for the story to continue.

Mingus waiting facedown on his bed as though it had only been a matter of time until Dylan understood how to make him quiet.

Dylan's palms on Mingus's shoulders through his green jacket.

"So, you're the girl, right?"

"Uh huh."

"They're bulging out on the sides and I'm going crazy."

"Uh huh."

"But I go slow."

"Uh huh."

"Then I'm grabbing around the sides."

"Shit."

"She doesn't say anything or try to stop me."

"Uh."

"Then I try to get inside her pants."

The world was unnamed, you wore disguises, were Inhumans. Mingus's room was another Negative Zone, under water, under the house, detached from Dean Street and whirling away to another place. It had been from the day Mingus stood in his Scout uniform and ran his fingers over merit badges, passport stamps from distant realms.

You built fires, marked bridges and trains, jerked into tissues and socks.

A hand molding Mingus's ass through his pants didn't need explaining, it wasn't a faggot thing, just a story you were telling: the pile of *Playboys* under the bed, the massing thunderhead of tits everywhere, of wanting women's bodies in your life, the horizon breaking into shared view.

Anyway, if you caressed Mingus after all this time you'd only want to *take a pick to his nappy-ass 'Fro*, you've always yearned to know what it would feel like to cradle his head and pluck at it with that mysterious fork.

But tuck weird tenderness away, this is boy time.

"Just touching her ass I was hard like a rock."

"No shit."

"She didn't let me get inside, though."

"You must of been dying!"

"Uh huh."

"I'd a said: *Yo!* Wait a minute!"

"Well, that's what I did," said Dylan, inventing with abandon, unmoored. "I told her look at the condition I was in, what was she going to do about it?"

"Don't *say* what I think you about to say."

They were side by side now, as Dylan and Heather had been side by side in the sun-smashed attic then, stretched on the bedspread, draining lemonade from sweaty glasses, icing their forearms. Only Dylan and Mingus lay stoned, sprawled head-propped on Mingus's drooly pillows, each grappling through pockets and pretending not to notice. Their breath lengthened, Mingus's sigh rattling like a small snore.

Mingus reached to the stereo and turned the music up another notch so they were swarmed in funk, stupefied deeper.

"Tell me."

"We didn't have a rubber so she had to give me a blow job."

"Damn!"

They were silent awhile. When Mingus spoke his voice was quiet and intent:

"You shoot white or clear?"

"White. It use to come out clear."

"Yeah."

Then, after further silence:

"How's it feel in a girl's mouth, man?"

"Best feeling in the world," Dylan lied with certainty.

"I heard *that*."

"I wish I had a girl sucking on me right now."

Another pause, then Dylan said: "You can take it out if you want."

Mingus's penis was hued dun-to-rose, like his palms. He trembled in his own hand.

"Close your eyes," said Dylan.

"No shit?"

"Hands behind your head."

Dylan let himself get in whispering range before chickening out, close enough to smell the air of Mingus's legs, the pubic tangle in his jockey fly.

"Do it with your hand," said Mingus.

When the door flew open Dylan and Mingus were caught Vaseline-fisted, their pants irretrievably down, bunched like mufflers over their Pumas. There wasn't remotely time to do anything but stare back at Mingus's father as he stood in the doorway barefoot in his blue satin bell-bottoms and a white designer T cut wide on his shoulders like a girl's blouse. Barrett Rude Junior dressed more and more like a man who never left the house, his whole parlor floor a sort of self-harem, a region of pajamas. Mingus and Dylan might have been termites or mole-men who'd burrowed underneath the Playboy mansion and now were caught, a spade breaking into their burrow, filling it with daylight. Pants down, they were still more dressed than Junior, Mingus in his jacket, Dylan in his sweater, both in their street shoes. They'd only have to jerk the pants back over their bared thighs and be out on the street again, in motion, rats scurrying, street beings. They pulled them up. Dylan looked at the floor.

"Turn that music down, Gus, man."

Mingus rolled the dial until it was tinny, faint like Junior's own music now heard arguing through the ceiling.

Mingus's father regarded them with narrow, sleepy eyes, smacked lips in slow motion, scratched goatee with one blunt finger's untrimmed nail. His nostrils flared, perhaps sniffing the medicinal goo on their hands and dicks. He lingered, seeming to wait for the right beat to come in on, not from the stereo but instead following his own inner music. When he spoke again it was low, tossed-off, melodic.

"I don't really care what you motherfuckers get up to down here, but you got to keep it down, man."

His weary delivery implied encompassing knowledge of anything they might bother to think they'd invented for themselves, along with a smidgen of affectionate distaste for their clumsy disarray, their poorly upholstered love nest. Maybe Dylan and Mingus ought to have lit incense and worn purple dressing gowns – whatever, it was none of his business. He took the door handle.

"You best know you one lucky soul, Gus, it was me not someone else walked in here. Get a lock for this goddamn door, man."

Then he was gone.

His few sentences might have been the kindest words Dylan had heard spoken in his life.

"Shit," said Mingus softly to the closed door, mildly disgusted with his father's presumption once he could afford to be.

Dylan only watched Mingus and waited. Perhaps he bugged his eyes a little.

"Don't worry, Junior won't say anything to your pops. I walked in on him doing way more wack shit than this and he knows it."

"Really?"

"Don't *even* ask."

That was the end of it, it was as if they'd never been discovered. Mingus flipped the record over, defiantly tweaked the volume upward.

Ten minutes later, sputtering into one another's fists while Sly's whole band groaned *Que sera, sera, the future's not ours to see,* Dylan was flushed with new understanding: he and Mingus were restored. They had secrets again, ones shored by risked accusations of faggotry, secrets from Arthur Lomb and Robert Woolfolk, absolute secrets from anyone. Even Barrett Rude Junior's complicity was consoling, they were sealed by it as a lump of wax seals an envelope. Not faggots, of course: best friends, discoverers. Dylan could trust Mingus, they were again sole and extraordinary. Dylan had kept a secret and been poisoned by that secret, he now understood. But it was safe, it was okay: he could tell Mingus about the ring. He could show him the costume.

A lone figure on the pavement, a white kid, makes nervous tracks along the block of Atlantic Avenue between Court Street and Boerum Place. It's a chilly April Tuesday night, just past twelve. In isolation and seeming undersized, a puppet on a human stage, the boy casts shrinking and again lengthening shadows as he moves through streetlight pools. The natural question: What's he doing there? This block's bounded on the Court side by Atlantic's Arabic shops, at Boerum by St. Vincent's Home for Boys. Across Boerum looms the glass-brick monolith of the Brooklyn House of Detention. The block where he walks is a nullity, though: only a parking garage, a concrete embankment of ramps four levels high. On the other side of the street a Mobil station, closed.

The boy strolls to the garage's one corner, then the other, as though penned, a gerbil in an invisible Habitrail. What he's doing there's really inexplicable, the longer you consider it, which no one does. The block's a lousy choice for a midnight stroll, something bad is bound to happen.

Exactly the point.

To the corner and back again: hurry up and happen already.

Now it does. Attackers come in their expected fashion, two black teenagers, one tall and one stubby, each wearing a net of stocking wrapped on their thin-shaved skulls – a *doo-rag*, that's the term – a pair out of central casting for their part in this tableau. They're roaming down Boerum Place after who-knows-what diversion up in the Fulton Mall, maybe a late movie at the Duffield or the Albee, or maybe they've just scored a nickel bag at one of the pot stores on Myrtle-otherwise-known-as-Murder

Avenue. Anyway, their whiteboy radar's operative tonight. Tonight's dish is served up a bit too rare to be believed: under the shadow of the vast garage they can afford to take their time, have some fun. There's really no one around for miles. White boy this stupid deserves whatever comes, only hope he's not some retard who starts crying too quick.

"Yo, let me talk to you for a minute."

The white boy only blinks. The two are strangers, unknown to him from school. This is a first encounter. It ought to be one they'll remember.

"What, you don't hear him talkin' to you, man?"

"Nigger's deaf or some shit."

"Maybe he don't like the color of your skin, man, maybe that's the problem."

Then's when it comes out of the night sky, the blur in cape and mask. The leap begins three stories above, on the roof of the garage, and for the first moment looks to be nothing better than a headfirst plummet, a suicidal drop. The black teenager wearing the home-stitched outfit and with the ring on his finger has been practicing for weeks, in backyards and on roofs – this is the first time, though, he's taken it to the street.

No problem, he's a natural. Whatever it is flying requires – balance, poise, unhesitation, an organ for sensing *air waves* – he's apparently got. His swoop begins just below the garage's second story, two balled fists leading the charge as he curves from the expected collision with the pavement, first falling aslant, then unmistakably horizontal. By the time he collides with the white boy's would-be yokers he's rocketing upward, back toward the sky. The flying boy batters at shoulders and doo-ragged crowns with his fist and again with his knees and lastly with his sneaker toes as he soars over – a perfect and bewildering assault from the sky. The two victims stumble cowering to the ground, incredulous, swearing, caressing their bruised noggins.

"Fuck was *that*?"

"Shit, man, you clocked me!"

"I didn't touch you, man, fuck you talkin' 'bout?"

The flying boy rolls in air, soars down again, leading with his knuckles. His white cape flutters and flaps dramatically at the elbows of his Spirograph-decorated long-sleeve T. He's wearing a sewn white mask too, one tied behind his ears and open at the top to vent his Afro to the air, like Marvel's *Black Goliath*.

"Book, man, let's get out of here!"

"Go!"

Seconds later they've vanished, fled down Boerum Place, toward Bergen, home to the Gowanus Houses most likely. The costumed boy lands beside the white boy on the pavement and yells at the departing shadows: "Run, motherfuckers! That's right! You don't mess with Arrowman!"

"*Aer*-o-man," corrects the white boy.

"That's what I said – Arrowman."

CHAPTER 14

SOMEONE HAD PAINTED the interior walls here a lush medical pink in semigloss, a shade like Kaopectate, or the representation of a suffering brain before its relief by a headache pill. On this dirty, leak-warped surface was pinned bank-giveaway calendar, mimeographed schedule, yellowed fifties-vintage Alcoholics Anonymous recruitment flyer, not much else – nothing, say, like a placard reading YOU DON'T HAVE TO BE CRAZY TO WORK HERE BUT IT HELPS, certainly no snapshots of wives or pets or children. The wooden desk on either side of which the two men sat showed coffee-steam rings, paperclip scars, thirty years of gouges in its cherry-blond veneer: it had been reassigned from a nearby public school for its use here. On the side of the desk which faced the door of the pink office the desk bore a few nervous tags, graffiti or scratchiti accomplished with ballpoint or key tip or pocketknife at discreet knee level, where resentful hands could be hidden from their questioner's view while an earnest listening expression was maintained on the face above.

A folder lay open on the desk between the two men.

It was July 1978. Each wore a tie: the thirtyish white man over a white, short-sleeve shirt with no jacket, the tie a fat powder-blue number, color like an inflamed nerve in the pink brain of the office. The elderly black man wore an unfashionably thin black tie, clipped neatly inside the vest of his newly thrift-store-purchased gray pinstripe three-piece, a banker's suit except for clownishly wide lapels. The vest's five buttons were done up, sealing thin torso like a sausage in casing. No air-conditioning here, so a lace-embroidered handkerchief got some use blotting brow, nose tip, and corded well of throat, visible just above the firm knot of the tie.

"I tell you, there's goings-on in that house," said Barrett Rude Senior.

"Why make it your business?"

"A man of God is duty bound."

"This man of God ought to make three years clear of the

girls on Pacific before he gets on anyone else's ass," said the man behind the desk. "Just because some rookie took pity and didn't book you doesn't mean the write-up didn't find its way to my desk. Don't play like you're getting over, Barry, don't think for a minute I don't know what goes down."

The man behind the desk might have seemed young to speak this way to the elder Rude, or to anyone: his hard-boiled tone a tad unearned, street dialect feigned. If so, explanation for his arrogance wasn't in the pistol holstered on his ankle, evident as he hitched his pants to cross one leg over the other, nor in the handcuffs which dangled from his belt; really, these were all symptoms of one thing, all indicative of a type of person likely to fall to this particular line of work. An incarcerated man would call the type a *cowboy*. Like bail-bounty hunters or prison guards, cowboys were the type of men too sadistic or willful to make the conventional police force. Among parole officers the scattering of do-gooding Serpico types are a tiny minority; cowboys are the norm. To them busting your balls is daily static, nothing remarkable.

If the halfway house and rehab center and DMV weren't sufficient to explain a certain thuggish vibe on Nevins between Flatbush and State, here's the secret: a parole office carefully unadvertised on the second floor of a building on the corner of Schermerhorn Street, six offices off a waiting room, kitchen converted to a lab for on-the-spot urinalysis, windows of one back room heavily barred for use as an impromptu holding cell. Barrett Rude Senior had been making his weekly trudge to this place since the morning he first reported, the day after getting off the Greyhound at Port Authority, never less than impeccably decked out. His officer didn't return the favor, dressing with his shirt untucked, beard stubble unshaved, with redolent sandwich wrappings unfurled on his desk.

"You misunderestimate an old man," said Barrett Rude Senior. "I was attempting to bring those girls the blessings of Jesus."

"You and Jesus keep your blessings off Pacific Street at one A.M., that's my advice. You got a signature for me?"

Barrett Rude Senior was made to produce an autographed sheet, certifying hours of community service under supervision of Pastor Gib at the Myrtle Avenue Parlor of God Ministry. In lieu of employment a parolee needed some clock to punch; this was his, personally selected. He nonetheless felt it as a humiliation. Each week a bolt of rage split his countenance as he fished with skeletal fingers in his breast pocket for the required proof.

"I go out walking," he said, rigid with damaged pride, not letting the point go. "Spend too much time in that house I got to air out my mind."

"Take afternoon walks, not midnight. Feed the ducks."

"Sounds come through the ceiling nobody should hear because nobody should be making."

"What am I supposed to say, Barry? Wear earmuffs." The parole officer glanced at the page and handed it back.

"I got to be relocated out of that house because the devil is making trouble in my mind. Knowing that boy's getting warped up and not doing anything."

"Terms of your transfer up from Carolina were habitation in your son's apartment." He spoke as though reciting some dull recipe: two parts water to one part rice. "We can talk about sending your file back to the Raleigh office and you with it, if that's what you want. Your being in New York City where miniskirts walk the streets all night depends on maintaining current residence and you know it."

"I'm going on the record as it's not good for my rehabilitation to be around hard narcotics and funk music. Write it down."

"C'mon, Barry. Be straight with me."

"I regret to say my only son is courting Satan. Put it in your report. He and I will come to blows or worse. I'm asking a relocation for the good of everyone involved and you're responsible. I'd take the child with me but he's already half a man himself and will have to fight through it on his own. I pray nightly, when I can hear myself over the bellows and groans and the crackle of the pipe."

"We're concerned here with you keeping together what you need to keep together and you're not talking to me. I've heard this stuff before, it's old tunes. I'm not going to have your son arrested and I'm not a religious man, so far as I can hear you haven't said a word yet."

"I want to get a room in the Times Plaza and take the pressure off."

"Who's paying?"

"I believe the devil will pay to have me out of his hair."

"That old fleabag hotel's no better than a jail. Half the rooms are filled with cons killing time between bids."

Barrett Rude Senior stiffened again as though he'd been misunderstood. "From the church I know a man there, a fine saintly man. He gazes out his window and he doesn't see filth all around him."

"The Birdman of Alcatraz, eh?"

Senior only returned a look of unshrouded disdain. In his glare he summoned for one moment the mummified eloquence of a legacy of chanting men in cotton fields, sweat-bathed parishioners, masked riders, galley ships from Africa, all the parole officer with his Dion and the Belmonts Bronx accent couldn't pretend to fathom. For one moment it was as if Senior had ridden into this meeting on a mule, as if the baying of beagles as they crashed through swampland had leaked into the room.

Whatever grain of tenderhearted Serpico resided in the parole officer's cowboy psyche was touched for just that moment. "It's really shitty between you and your son, huh, Barry? I have to figure you're not kidding me to want to move into that dive the Times Plaza."

"I seen women on women and other counternatural things."

"Enough already, you're giving me hives. Let me see what I can do."

"Born in Arizona, moved to Babylonia—"

"We are the knights who say *Ni!*"

"Get all excited and go to a yawning festival."

"You – must – bring – us – a – shrubbery!"

"Hey, let's go get Blimpies, I'm so hungry I could beat a dead horse. Ow, shit, what's that for?"

"I said I'd punch you the next time you said *Blimpie*."

"You bloody bastard!"

In ragged, rasping voice: "It's the blimp, it's the blimp, it's the mothership!"

"C'mon."

Falsetto, as they crossed the street from school: *"Basketball Jones, I got a basketball Jones—"*

Gabriel Stern and Timothy Vandertooth ranted in a vocal graffiti of impersonations: Steve Martin and Marty Feldman and George Carlin, Devo, Python, Zappa, Spock, *The Prisoner.* Gabe Stern had memorized the songs of Tom Lehrer, Tim Vandertooth could do Liverpool, Wild and Crazy Guy, Peter Sellers–Swami. Induction into the company of Gabe Stern and Tim Vandertooth had begun the second week of school, Monday, just after three o'clock. Gabe and Tim surrounded Dylan before he reached the subway station on Fourteenth Street and bought him a slice of Original Ray's, extra cheese. Then they went to Crazy Eddie's showroom and played the demonstration model of Pong, writhing in fake agony at each loss, oblivious to customers or staff.

"You bastard!"

"Revenge, I swear revenge."

"I fart in your general direction."

Gabe, broad-shouldered, dark, and curly-haired, had blistered nuclei of acne on each cheek, as though acid had been dripped there and was eating through. Tim was sandy, angular, walked hippily, seemingly steering his lean, high body like a kite in wind. Beside them Dylan was smaller. He'd grown, had private developments, weird fists of hair, but with Gabe and Tim felt childlike and possibly invisible. Anyway everyone's body betrayed them in different ways, it was all forgiven and never discussed.

Dylan folded into the unit of Gabe and Tim as a redundant third: arbiter, audience, appendix. One day Gabe and Tim might seem to be playing to Dylan, wooing him, as though he'd be capable of adjudicating a conflict they'd been trying all their lives to resolve: Which of us is funnier, louder, more irresistible? Those days Dylan felt that it was essential he balance the two in their mania, that if he chose or even slightly favored either Tim or Gabe the other would die sizzling on the pavement like the Wicked Witch of the West. Other days their energies were exclusive, circuit complete between themselves, Dylan might as well have been watching a Tom and

Jerry cartoon on television, head propped in his hands, antics reflected in his glasses.

Gabe and Tim would abruptly fall to wrestling on the sidewalk in front of school, knapsacks skidding to the curb as if attacked, yoked. This was different, though, from real hostilities, which drew instantaneous crowds. Anyone besides Dylan knew not to pay attention. When either Tim or Gabe got the other subdued, knees on chest, head clamped in elbow, arm wrenched high behind back, he'd demand some idiot password.

"Say Fanta."

"No. Ow! Dr Pepper!"

"Not Dr Pepper, *Fanta*."

"Tab!"

"*Fanta*."

"Mr. Pibb! No. Shit, stop! Bastard, bloody bastard!"

"You know what I want."

"Okay, ow, okay, okay – Fanta!"

"Now Sprite!"

"No! Never that! Let go!"

Stuyvesant drew high-scorers from all five boroughs, a migration hidden under the skin of rush hour, subway floods of Lacoste-clad Upper West Siders who'd known each other since kindergarten, dazed black math geniuses from the South Bronx who slumped in the hallways wondering if they'd ever recover from the shock, studious Puerto Rican nerds from Stuyvesant Town who'd only crossed the street to attend school and were still in thrall to local bullies from their pre-high-school lives, diligent Chinese achievers from assorted immigrant neighborhoods, Greenpoint, Sunnyside, usually in sequences of siblings, an older sister in an upper grade nearby to grab an ear if a younger began to trickle toward the mass of kids who cut class almost from day one, smoking joints and playing Frisbee in Stuyvesant Park down the block. The lemmings gathered from every corner of the city, some unlucky souls coming from Staten Island on the ferry every morning had to set their alarms for five or six or some wilder hour.

Gabriel Stern and Timothy Vandertooth lived on Roosevelt Island, had met three years before when their families moved to the new housing there. Roosevelt Island was an enigma, carless and dogless, haunted by the ruins of a tuberculosis sanitarium on the southern shore. Residence there was like cult member-ship. The science-fiction tram on pulleys which dangled beside the span of the Fifty-ninth Street Bridge and which Tim and Gabe rode to school and home together every day stood nicely for their resolute and impenetrable best-frienditude: they were freaks beamed daily to the island of Manhattan from their own subordinate, moonlike isle, no wonder they spoke a private language, nanu-nanu, live long and prosper.

Stuyvesant was Jewish white, Wasp white, hippie white, Chinese, black, Puerto Rican, and much else but crucially it was nerd, nerd, nerd, nerd, the great family of those able to ace the entrance test. Pencil chewers, teacher's pets in glasses, the Arthur Lomb in everyone unbound now, no longer having to cower. It was pathetic to think of Arthur himself, on course for this natural destination all those years at Saint Ann's, then derailed by Dean Street only six months or so short of his goal. The mystery was how so many who'd toed the line, favored studies over socialization in order to pass the test, then within a few weeks of freshman orientation broke out Jim Morrison-and Led Zeppelin-painted jean jackets and began loafing all day in the park, immaculate scholastic careers ruined overnight.

Timothy Vandertooth and Gabriel Stern didn't drift into stoner affiliation, not exactly. The sole class they cut was gym, and though they did spend that period and lunch hour and some after-school hours in the park they were inept with Frisbees and retained their short haircuts and were uninterested in Hen-drix or Morrison or Zeppelin, music too blunt and earnest to be swallowed straight. The languorous, slack-haired park girls paid Tim and Gabe no attention at all, seemed unable to parse jokes in any register.

"I swear she almost looked at you when your voice cracked. You ought to talk like that all the time, get a tank of helium." Tim and Gabe discussed matters in full voice as if girls were deaf, lame payback for the silent treatment they themselves received.

"I think she was distracted staring at your pants, actually. Check your fly, maybe there's a spot of chocolate milk or scum or something."

"It's because of the zucchini I'm concealing in my underwear, my new method which I highly recommend. I offer it free, you don't owe any royalties. The cold wears off eventually."

Tim and Gabe would smoke pot or not. Either way they didn't fit, were tourists, comic relief to the longhairs in the park who were comic relief to them in turn, never clear who ought to be laughing at who, only that Tim and Gabe were moving at a faster clip, their movements and thoughts hectic, jerky. Those first months of high school Tim and Gabe waited for something else to complete them, or the reverse, something waited to complete them. They were stalled like robots, incanting their encoded frustration.

"Open the pod bay doors, Hal. Open the pod bay doors, Hal. Open the pod bay doors, Hal. Open the pod bay doors, Hal."

"I am not a number. *I am a free man!*"

You waited too, feeling it.

Another sensibility agitated in periphery, one located in the conjunction of the midnight movies at the Eighth Street Playhouse and the Waverly, on Sixth Avenue: *Clockwork Orange, Pink Flamingos, Rocky Horror, Eraserhead.* Within six weeks you'd seen all but *Eraserhead*, the prospect of which was too terrifying, though you'd never admit it, just fumbled out an excuse about being grounded that night. In fact you'd never been grounded in your life, wondered where you'd even picked up the word.

One guy came to class in Tim Curry pancake whiteface and black-varnished nails every day, the focus of scoffing laughter and secret awe.

Each morning you passed Max's Kansas City on your way from the Fourteenth Street subway to school, talismanic site of what exactly you weren't sure.

The band Devo might have to do with the new something in the air, lyrics about *mongoloids* and *swelling itching brains* offering some ironic back door into animal nature, a way to evade the appalling, head-on Jim Morrison route.

The main problem any kid faced if he could have found the word was how to find himself in any way *sexy*. Forget girls themselves for the time being, the problem was between you and the mirror.

Manhattan thankfully didn't give a shit about you.

What about Mingus and Aeroman, though?

Dylan crept as he reapproached Dean Street in the perishing light of afternoons spent with Gabe and Tim bouncing in and out of Crazy Eddie's and Ray's Famous and Blimpies and J&R Music World and Washington Square Park, crept in his mind, furtive like an escapee returning nightly for meals in his old cell. The block was dead as far as he could tell. He'd killed it by graduating from I.S. 293 and leaving for Stuyvesant. It wasn't only Mingus. Henry, Alberto, Lonnie, Earl, Marilla, and La-La had all fled the scene or been so transformed they might not be recognizable. Some days you passed in silence some kid you'd known, they had a mustache or tits and they were black and you were white and you didn't say a word.

There was no new crop of kids unless you counted the scruffy batch, mostly Puerto Rican, who didn't even know you were meant to gather in Henry's yard or at the abandoned house, they didn't even know Henry's name, they squatted like bugs on the sidewalk and were as little able to carry forward the block's work as bugs would have been. One day Dylan saw one scratching some primitive botched skully board, not on a slate but on a pebbly square of poured concrete, hopeless, like a fallout survivor dim with radiation sickness sketching a blue-print for reinvention of the wheel. One day Dylan passed the buglike kids and one called out "Honky" in a voice so tentative Dylan died laughing at the sweetness of it. The abandoned house wasn't even abandoned anymore. It wore a sign reading CINDERELLA #3, A PROJECT OF BROOKLYN UNION GAS, and one day they punched through the cement blocks and replaced them with dull aluminum-frame windows, dumb eyes. The site of mystery was destroyed. For a few months bums resolute-ly drank and passed out on the stoop anyway, then moved on.

Maybe every other week, though, Dylan would find Mingus seated on his own stoop, like a bum, with a forty-ounce in a bag. Mingus ruled his own yard again, now that Barrett Rude Senior had shifted into the welfare hotel on Atlantic Avenue, several blocks away. He'd greet Dylan in the old manner, as though they'd been interrupted a minute before.

"That Parlet record I was telling you about? I just scored it."

"Oh yeah?"

"That shit is serious, I'm telling you, Dillinger, you need to check it out *now*."

Dylan and Mingus met according to no plan or reason, might have been darts hitting a calendar, a roulette of days. He and Mingus would go into the basement apartment and get high and Tim and Gabe, Dylan's whole Stuyvesant world, would evaporate, Manhattan unlikely as Neptune or Vulcan, restored to its status as an unexplored planet, the future.

Hallway and bathroom were tagged now, the whole basement a subway tunnel. Senior's room was still off-limits, though, an abandoned shrine which stank of dust-rotting candles.

Mingus chugged beer now, Colt and Cobra, a regular thing.

Dylan didn't, only got high.

Dylan knew Mingus still hooked up with Arthur Lomb too, saw Arthur's practice tags in ballpoint on scattered pages around Mingus's room, sometimes saw Arthur himself. Arthur Lomb had the curse of puniness: he still looked eleven or twelve, no number of *what-ups* and *yos*, no degree of street slaunch in his walk, no green suede Pumas could compensate. After flunking the Stuyvesant test Arthur's mother had falsified their residence to get him transferred to Edward R. Murrow, a white high school deep in the Irish Italian heart of the borough. It was too late, though, he might as well have been at Sarah J. Hale from the look of things. Arthur had become yucky, his sleeves always crusted with Krylon, his red hair slack and ratty, jeans black. Arthur was a pothead now, often looked red-eyed, glazed with an afternoon's doping. His street credibility was all he had and it was direly thin.

Arthur's being seen with Mingus was a gift Dylan wouldn't begrudge him now: it was a thing Arthur needed much worse than Dylan ever had. Let Arthur imagine a parity. In fact, Dylan knew, their two friendships with Mingus, his and Arthur's, were vastly different. Dylan and Mingus lived in a motherless realm, full of secrets. Aeroman, for one thing. Certain other things, for another. Dylan doubted Arthur even had pubic hair yet. Plus Dylan and Mingus knew each other's dads, and Mingus went into Dylan's house. Dylan was certain Arthur wouldn't ever want Mingus to see inside his own mommified sanctuary of Hi-C juice and Hydrox cookies.

When Mingus was a dollar short of a nickel bag he and Dylan might scrape for loose change in Dylan's kitchen or even climb the stairs to Abraham's studio. There Mingus waited at the door, dim transistor jazz seeping through, while Dylan cadged folding money. Abraham, always sensing the lurker in the corridor, would ask:

"Is that Mingus?"

"Yeah."

"He doesn't need to hide. Tell him to come say hello."

In Abraham's presence Mingus Rude grew courtly, called Abraham *Mr. Ebdus*, asked about the progress of his film. Abraham would sigh and produce some opaque riddle.

"As well ask Sisyphus, my dear Mingus."

"*Cookypuss?*" Mingus would be quick with a free-associated reply. He and Abraham had hatched some running joke of mishearing one another. They couldn't get enough of it.

"Ah, Cookypuss. Maybe Cookypuss for one is showing some progress. I'd like to think so."

On the other hand, the two no longer went upstairs to Barrett Rude Junior. The stairway between basement and parlor floors might as well have been sealed now. Dylan saw evidence Mingus avoided the upstairs kitchen, cans of Chef Boyardee heated on Senior's hot plate, Slim Jim wrappers in the bathroom garbage pail. When they cranked Mingus's stereo, though, Dylan felt himself expecting, even yearning for Junior at the door singing *Fuck you doin' Gus?*, his sweet disapproval a fragment of melody you pined to hear whole.

But no amount of volume drew Junior to the door, in Mingus's apartment they were mole-men now for sure, on their own deep exploration.

Foxy's "Get Off" they played fifteen times in a row, louder each time, trying to destroy the distance between that rubbery, fleshlike bass line and themselves, as if the song was a photograph, a *Playboy* centerfold they enlarged by degrees until they could enter the frame, walk into the picture.

They also stared at certain photographs until they might have left sheddings from their blistered eyeballs strewn on the pages, then exchanged relieving hand jobs without making a particularly big deal of it.

Mingus kept the ring and the costume, Aeroman was officially him. Both were stashed on a shelf high above the door, with a hockey trophy and Mingus's old football helmet, ring out of sight above eye level, costume balled behind the helmet, nothing any random visitor to the room, Arthur Lomb, say, would bother remarking on. Whether Mingus ever donned them out of Dylan's company went undiscussed. Afternoons passed when Aeroman wasn't mentioned, the ring wasn't handled or even seen, Dylan sat on Mingus's bed and glanced at the shelf between joint tokes but nothing happened, they'd hit the street or catch a Kung Fu flick or Dylan would only go home stoned to whatever supper Abraham had prepared. Then Aeroman might as well have been the lead in a quickly canceled Marvel title like *Omega* or *Warlock*, or a murdered sidekick, quickly avenged then forgotten, or a name from the Golden Age, perhaps, like Doll Man or the Human Bomb: in other words, no superhero at all, not really, not one anyone remembered.

Other days he'd have told Abraham he was having dinner at Mingus's house, or slipped out after wolfing dinner at Abraham's table to return to the basement apartment, and then after a certain hour Mingus would glance at the shelf too, and say:

"Fight crime?"

"Yeah."

"You sure?"

"Uh huh."

Mingus would grin and say, "Look at you, you're like, *I thought you would never ask.*"

Aeroman flew six or seven times that fall, was perhaps involved in eight or nine incidents, could claim maybe three bona fide rescues, legible crimes authentically flown down on and busted up. On State Street near Hoyt they halted a six-foot Puerto Rican showing a steak knife to a small Chinese guy, who was busy pulling balled wadded dollars from his pockets, magicianlike, in terrified surrender. Mingus-Aeroman swooped from a fire escape and scissored legs around the knife-wielder's neck, torque twisting them both to the pavement, Dylan scooted from an apartment building's entrance to pounce on the knife, plucking it from the ground and surrounding it with his body as though it might detonate. Puerto Rican and Chinese both fled in shock. Though Dylan waved the fluffy bills and called after the victim, he didn't turn. Breathless and amazed at confiscated weapon and money, Dylan and Mingus stuffed Aeroman's outfit and mask into a paper sack and walked to Steve's Restaurant on Third Avenue, celebrated with midnight cheeseburgers and chocolate shakes, adrenaline and marijuana buzz given way to a ravenous appetite, adolescent cells howling for lipids. Waiters gave the hairy eyeball all through the meal, suspecting a scarf-and-run, but Dylan and Mingus didn't care. They had the dough, even left an ostentatious *fuck-you* tip.

On Smith Street, howling an unrehearsed cowboys-and-indians *woo-woo-woo* as he descended, Aeroman spooked drunks boxing at the door of a social club, sole duty at the tail end of a long night's stalking around, prowling for gigs, killing time tagging on metal doors. On Third Avenue in a cold mid-October rain he foiled a holdup attempt at one of the Plexiglas-barrier Chinese joints, leaving a spilled mound of orange fried rice trampled to pudding at the entrance. At the far end of the Heights Promenade, under cover of darkness, he was cooed at in his costume by men rendezvousing on park benches, men who didn't need his protection. On Pacific Street near Court, Dylan and Aeroman found roof access to a tenement and lay on their bellies, in costume and street clothes, peering over the cornice, memorizing the life of the unfamiliar block, every girl screaming *"Mira, mira!"* at someone who wouldn't reply, every boy slapping a spaldeen into the joint of a wall, every grandmother window-perched on Buddha arms, watching just as Mingus and Dylan watched, absorbed, doing nothing.

The bridge crossing after dark was a sure spot, a famous mistake to walk there at night, so they took it to the bridge: Dylan standing as bait by the massive shoring tower still bearing Mono's and Lee's fabulously weathered autographs, Mingus in costume flown to a perch on the high, swaying cable. Below, on the streets, it was late summer, but here above the city winter was arriving, swept off the ocean. Dylan was mugged in minutes, it was comically predictable, almost corny when two homeboys lurched out of the gloom beyond the tower and said: "Hey, whiteboy, lemme borrow a dollar off you, man."

Dylan gladly played at reaching into his pockets for money, his attackers fish in a barrel. Only Mingus didn't shoot the fish, he didn't swoop.

"What you checkin' around for, man?"

Dylan had made them nervous. They smelled setup in his hesitation and followed his gaze to the bridge, the sky-harp of spun lines. So all three saw the caped figure struggling in the gust which had torn it from the cable, saw Mingus cycling in air, trying to reclaim a footing, nearly doing so before being wind-wrested into the breach between the bridge and the water, the wild void. All three watching lost sight of him below the line of the bridge's roadway. He was just a twinkle, mask, cape, Puma soles maybe, then nothing at all.

He'd been blown from the bridge.

Dylan turned on the walkway's planks and bolted for the Brooklyn end, abandoned the scene exactly as Rachel had always told him to do – *Just run, kiddo, use those pogo sticks, they can't catch up with you!* – and which he'd never done once in a thousand yokings. For Mingus he found his legs, he ran. He nearly tumbled dodging a beat cop staked at the foot of the stairs, waved a quick hello-I-must-be-going to the cop's dull glower, then panted on, limbs wheeling. Cabs curled off the bridge, faceless, cornering through Cadman Plaza to Henry Street, Clinton Street, to placid brownstones with mock gas-light fixtures. There wasn't anybody to appeal to for help, Dylan was alone, Mingus, Aeroman, ring all drowned, smashed on the water. Dylan veered to the dark paths below the bridge, seeking the edge of the river, the junk-strewn wasteland where the city hid crashed police cars and looted parking meters and other evidence of helplessness.

Mingus sat hunched and dripping at the base of the anchor-age, twisting water from the tips of his cape, stain spreading on the concrete embankment like a snow angel. Dylan arrived gasping, hot-faced, couldn't speak before Mingus said: "Ho, *shit*, man."

"You're okay?"

"I was swimming, man. I don't even know how to swim."

He spoke with quiet amazement, nodding his head at the water.

"What do you mean?"

"Like a fish, D-Man."

"You're saying the ring *gave you the power of swimming*?"

"Or flying underwater, don't ask me. I was up to some serious Aquaman shit, though."

They slunk to Dean. The staged rescue left unfinished on the walkway and the plummet from the wires, both were put behind them, though Dylan and Mingus and Aeroman skirted the bridge after that. Aeroman, having been laid flat to dry, mellowed on the shelf for weeks, regathering his wits and bravado, perhaps, shaking off effects of the fall. Mingus didn't reach for the costume and Dylan didn't push. Dylan instead became briefly obsessed with clandestine powers in the ring. Why imagine Aaron X. Doily had plumbed them all? Possibly Aeroman was named prematurely, had more to offer. Dylan wore the ring and immersed his head in Mingus's filled tub, hoping to breathe underwater. He snorted a flood into his lungs, came up hacking, nearly puked, bathwater scalding his nostrils.

The ring also conferred no X-ray vision, though they spent one thrilled night persuading themselves, scowling hard at dresses, black hos working Pacific and Nevins, white Saint Ann's girls massed at the Baskin-Robbins on Montague.

"Wait, wait, I see something."

"My turn now."

"Oh – sweet – Jesus. She's wearing no panties."

Aeroman's last venture that first season of high school was in a light, freak-early midnight snowfall two weeks past Thanksgiving, Dylan walking State Street, Mingus hopping the rooftops above, keeping pace. Ever since the Chinese victim who'd dropped his money, State between Hoyt and Bond was their lucky mugging strip, safe distance from anyone they'd know on Dean or Bergen, dark with a smashed streetlamp, close enough to the Hoyt-Schermerhorn subway stop that dumb junkies frightened of venturing into the Heights considered it safe prowling for renovators' wives, trembling whiteboys, geezers. Tonight, though, a snowball was all Dylan drew. A lone, tall

Puerto Rican kid leaning on a car scooped a windshield-mass of fresh stuff and flung an unerring bull's-eye in Dylan's back. When Dylan whirled he said: "Try it, motherfucker, I dare you throw one."

At that moment Mingus descended with a cradled armload, shoveled it into the tall kid's collar.

Then Mingus landed softly beside Dylan and they ran together hooting, Mingus stripping the costume and cape off over his head, momentarily bare-chested in the snowfalling night.

Mingus afternoons, Aeroman nights, they were untellable the next day at Stuyvesant, if he'd even wanted to try, if he'd somehow corralled Tim Vandertooth's and Gabriel Stern's ears for the attempt. Dylan had no interest in telling. Mornings after, he felt himself an orbiter on reentry, his hidden knowledge sealed in flame. Mingus and Aeroman were a million miles away, another realm, Brooklyn. Besides, the thing coming for Tim and Gabe had found them.

Once it arrived it was obvious, had a common name already known: punk. Or new wave. They were related strands: Sex Pistols, Talking Heads, Cheap Trick. Discerning their difference, articulating your precise relation, that was part of the point, a continuum of the now it was suddenly clear anyone could be placed on. Even the longhaired stoners in their refusal were anti-punk, defining something.

Tim came to school one day with a point-studded dog collar. He showed them how it worked, a simple snap. Gabe taunted him uneasily for a week, then went out and bought a Ramones-ian leather jacket loaded with zippers and buckles, smelling of preservatives and sizing, almost like one of Abraham's canvases. Gabe slapped the jacket against a rock in the park, trying to age it. They studied the results. The jacket looked new as licorice. Or the problem was themselves, their bangs, hair curled over their ears. The next week Tim and Gabe returned from Roosevelt Island having fucked up their hair with children's scissors. The jacket looked slightly improved.

Tim smoked cigarettes now.

Gabe etched a tiny swastika on his forearm with a razor blade. *"You know what my parents would do to me if they saw this?"*

he whispered darkly, like he'd been kidnapped by Satanists and forced to recite a pledge.

The girls with short black-dyed hair were suddenly visible. Sarcastic, pale, and titless, they were a different flavor, previously overlooked.

A few even *had* tits, which might violate punk aesthetics but you'd consider making an exception.

Dylan shunted knapsack-loads of Rachel's Blind Faith and Creedence Clearwater Revival records to Bleecker Bob's record exchange, embarrassed to see them in the house, returned with the Clash's *Give 'Em Enough Rope*.

Steve Martin was for children.

There wasn't much terror. Fourteenth Street, First Avenue, they were scungy but populated, jostling with drug traffic but not a lot of yoking. Maybe you'd outgrown victim size, though it was hard to imagine there could be universal consensus on that point, you had to stay alert. A girl your age was pushed from a subway platform on her way to Music and Art, a cellist who lost her arm under the train and had it reattached in a miracle surgery. The incident made a brief noise of panic among white kids on subways and their parents, but that was 135th Street, Harlem. Poor kid but what did she expect? Thank God you hadn't gone to Music and Art. To escape the outer boroughs only to soar on the subway past Manhattan's safe zones all the way into Harlem was ironic, one crazy mistake you'd at least avoided.

It was the leather jacket which caused the only piece of trouble. For once it wasn't Dylan's trouble. A Puerto Rican perhaps eighteen or nineteen – mustached and tall and particularly thick around the middle, pearish, apparently self-appointed one-man gang patrolling Fourteenth Street between Second and Third – isolated Gabe in his new leather from among the hundreds of other streaming Stuyvesant kids and stepped up to block his path on the sidewalk. Something affronted him and he demanded reciprocal understanding from Gabe.

"You wanna fight me?"

"*What?*" Gabe squinted in fierce incredulity.

"Think you're tough, you wanna fight me?" He poked

Gabe's shoulder. Gabe looked to Tim and Dylan, who both stepped back.

Gabe enunciated with Maxwell Smart precision. "I actually *don't* think I'm tough, no."

"You in a *crew*?"

This was a problem of codes, the self-loathing ironies of punkism not sufficiently conveyed yet to the Puerto Rican-gang quadrant of the universe. The guy himself wore just a jean jacket, wasn't particularly fitted out or flamboyant. A red hand-kerchief knotted on his belt loop was maybe significant. Again Gabe's glance sought Tim or Dylan but they'd melted away. Throngs parted around Gabe and his confronter, uninterested.

When Gabe spoke again sarcasm curdled to a whine. "I'm just *wearing* it, it doesn't *mean* anything." Dylan detected scars in Gabe's cringe-readiness, schoolyard mortifications they'd never have discussed. His tone wasn't so far from Arthur Lomb pleading *I can't breathe*.

"Don't come around here wearin' that, man, or I have to take it off you."

The fact of their being lost in a crowd was no help, only added a lunatic degree of humiliation. So despite Tim's mockery, Gabe diligently obeyed the Puerto Rican. He required Tim and Dylan to accompany him the long way around that block every day for weeks. Even taking that precaution he was spooked, now hustled through subway stations and down certain blocks peeking over his shoulder, wore his jacket with doomy fear – not a bad accouterment, actually, to his punk aura.

Incredibly, the one day they defied the edict, again in what should have been a protective swarm, the guy's radar guided him from nowhere to square against Gabe. He chest-bumped him out of Tim and Dylan's company and to the curb.

"I tole you. Now we gotta fight."

Gabe's face was hot red and he spoke quietly under a strain of absurdity. "I'm not *fighting* you."

It wasn't Dylan or Aeroman who rescued Gabe, but Tim, in a delicate maneuver Dylan barely understood. Stepping out to where Gabe and the guy stood in the street he reached into the vest pocket of his own jean jacket and showed his Marlboros.

"Smoke?" He inserted a cigarette in his own mouth and held out the pack. As the Puerto Rican stared, weighing the offering, Tim said:

"Give him a break, man. He doesn't mean anything, he can't help it."

Seemingly the Puerto Rican had only needed Gabe's deep objectionability confirmed by an outside source. He accepted a cigarette. "Tell him not to come around here," he said, ignoring Gabe, all violence leached from his tone.

"Sure, sure."

For the first time Dylan and perhaps Gabe really noticed how Tim was taller, cooler, maybe really *cool*, in fact. He'd quit wearing the dog collar. His hair took the choppy haircut well, unlike Gabe's curls. He triumphed each time those two wrestled, when you thought of it – only Gabe ever had to cry out *Sprite* or *clitoris*. But anyway, they hadn't wrestled for months. Tim now cut all classes, was flunking madly, while Gabe like Dylan clung to respectability. One day in the park Tim appeared wearing sloppy eyeliner, and a James Dean slouch that dared you to mention the eyeliner. You didn't. Tim smoked pot with the hippies at eight in the morning before class, while Gabe stood angrily aside in his useless jacket, the jacket he couldn't defend without Tim's help.

Maybe Gabe and Tim didn't even like each other, you realized now. They barely spoke and never joked, didn't necessarily arrive or leave school together, rode separate trams. In algebra Mr. Kaplan gestured at Tim's empty seat and said, "Mr. Stern – any notion as to the whereabouts of our friend Mr. Vandertooth?" and Gabe said "Why ask me?" – summing it up pretty well. By Christmas vacation Gabe and Dylan played demonstration Pong at Crazy Eddie's in rageful silence and you'd never even picture Tim Vandertooth being there. It wasn't his kind of thing.

Mingus Rude, Arthur Lomb, Gabriel Stern and Tim Vandertooth, even Aaron X. Doily: Dylan never met anyone who wasn't about to change immediately into someone else. His was a special talent for encountering persons about to shed one identity or disguise for another. He took it in stride by now. Maybe Rachel-Running-Crab had taught him that art.

4/3/79
viewed from space radioactive
nostrils want a kleenex
if sneezy they might blow
brooklyn to merrie england
however bad molten core might itch
don't pick down there too deep
or you'll toast your shell
infrared like mine
meltdown crab

CHAPTER 15

TWO SONS MIGHT think two fathers never budged from their hiding places apart from runs to Ramirez's or Buggy's for bare necessities – toilet paper, Tropicana, cold cuts at gouging prices, whatever.

Two sons might think fathers utterly unschooled in the craft of stoop-sitting – might suppose them ignorant equally of their neighbors and of the delirious nature of sunshine spilled into the chasm of brownstones.

Two sons might be wrong all over. Abraham Ebdus and Barrett Rude Junior had their own Dean Street, the eleven A.M. weekday edition.

Abraham Ebdus was up for hours by then, having packed off to school a mute and bleary Dylan, half-eaten toast in his fist, then ferried a thermos of coffee upstairs for a session painting celluloid frames under natural light. Abraham made film early mornings and late nights, his best hours, reserving lunch-dulled afternoons for painting outer spacescapes and electrical gremlins from the fourth dimension, whatever the latest art director required. Book jackets took care of themselves; he could be half asleep. Drowsiness dulled rage and good taste, unnecessary functions. The film required his sleep-purified, caffeine-honed eyes and mind. From eight-thirty he might accomplish five or six seconds of footage and by eleven be ready to unkink his limbs, rinse the thermos, wander briefly from the house. Dean Street at that hour was pensive, transitive, those with jobs and school all scurried away, idlers just rousing. The first of Ramirez's corner-men would have found a milk carton, or not. Half a block away a landlord might be brooming his portion of slate. And Barrett Rude Junior would have woken, tucked feet in slippers, moved to his stoop for a gander at the day, a first gulp of air and light.

Junior, on waking, often staggered first to the stereo whose red lights still glowed, to re-drop needle on whichever long-player had lullabyed him the night before, so when in robe or pajamas he took possession of his stoop it was with strains of Donny Hathaway's *Extension of a Man* or Shuggie Otis's *Inspiration Information* at his back. If the volume was sufficient and the Dean Street bus nowhere near, Abraham Ebdus, five doors away, could hear the music, faintly. Junior came sound-tracked, wore a halo of music like a wafting smell, literal funk. No actual bodily odors reached Abraham at that distance, but it wasn't much of a leap to suppose they clung to those frayed silks in concentrated form.

Seeing Mingus Rude's father at eleven cheered Abraham. He couldn't have said why. It happened every few mornings: no pattern but an accumulation, or a long polyrhythm. They lorded from the height of respective stoops, the block's true kings. On warmer mornings they'd each sit, in cold or rain they might be outdoors less than a minute. Either way, Abraham made an effort to keep the appointment and imagined Barrett Rude Junior doing the same. No way to know, since they only nodded, chins tipping upward, sometimes waved.

Abraham never saw the old man anymore and wondered slightly.

Bus purring through leaf-blotched shadow.

Run-on sentence of cracked slate.

Cornices a horizon, lintels slag in a canyon or quarry wall.

Dean Street of course infiltrated the work, it couldn't not. Abraham painted row-house façades, then blacked them over, presences drowned in abstraction. The film was among other things a record of methods disguised, a graveyard of strategies. He startled himself one day brushing in a figure, a stoop-wanderer, an armless pylon limned in gray rays. The anomalous form, Barrett Rude Junior taking the morning air, jiggled and danced in place through two weeks' work, a minute of film, before censure. Abraham didn't blot the figure retroactively, though. He let it stand. The sprite simply inhabited space for a minute, then *turned and went inside*. Gone like that.

The film devoured days and years and Abraham let them be devoured. He'd optical-printed earlier sections and now and then ran them in his hand-cranked splicer, not editing so much as dwelling in his own work in progress. At sea. He could no longer relate the motifs in earlier sequences to raw dates, facts in his life. Watergate, Erlan Hagopian, Rachel's leaving. The film floated above his routine, coffee cups, newspapers, the kid growing. The rest was trivia, moods, implementation. A body moving through days, serving higher purposes.

Abraham Ebdus was reasonably certain he was demolishing the concept of time.

For that reason, and not because of any fetish for death, he savored obituaries. They might be the only news that mattered, quiet closings on forgotten accounts, revealing lives lived decades past their ostensible peaks, their nodes of fame. He turned to them over breakfast and quoted with exaggerated relish, a touch of hammy gusto. "Lived in Mexico as one of Trotsky's bodyguards and later edited *Popular Mechanics* – isn't that *amazing*, Dylan? These lives, so full and crazy, so *contradictory*, and you never learn this stuff until they happen to die. You might not even know they'd *existed*!" The more Dylan met these ravings with silence the more his father hectored: "Jean Renoir, his father was the painter Renoir, you know," or "Listen: Al Hodge, he played the Green Hornet and Captain Video – incredible." Charles Seeger, Jean Stafford, Sid Vicious, the names stacked up, a breakfast litany. If nothing else it was a way to chase the boy from the house and onto the IRT. Dylan owed a sterling attendance record to the obituary page, probably. "The best-written part of the newspaper, these guys are *geniuses*, listen—"

So it was dumb luck the kid was still at the breakfast table that particular morning: nobody good died. The page was a rare bore. Abraham survived this slight disappointment and turned to the Metro section, and there it was, a photograph of Mingus Rude in a weird shirt, surplus cloth bunched around the collar.

"Huh, huh. Wow. Dylan, you'll want to see this."

The kid ignored him, mouth-breathing through a cud of Cheerios, par for the course.

Abraham quarter-folded the section and handed the article to Dylan so he couldn't miss it. The item was smart-alecky, sloppily reported, and full of holes and questions begged, no obituary by a long shot, but it contained its own amazements.

DRUG STING NETS CAPED CRUSADER

BY HUMBOLT ROOS

BROOKLYN, MAY 16. An undercover operation at the Walt Whitman Houses in Fort Greene was tripped up by the efforts of a teenage vigilante dressed as a superhero late Monday night, according to police at the 78th Precinct.

The costumed do-gooder, later identified as Mingus Rude, 16, was apparently concealed in a tree on housing complex grounds when he assaulted an undercover detective conducting a drug transaction with known dealers, presumably mistaking the officer for a criminal. The attempted citizen's arrest resulted in a literal headache for plainclothesman Morris, who was treated for minor injuries on the scene, and a paperwork headache for officers filing reports. The surveillance operation, a complex sting in preparation for several weeks, was unsuccessful, and no arrests were made.

All narcotics detectives got for their trouble was the consolation prize of Mr. Rude, later released into his parents' custody with a warning, but no charges. Dressed in a hand-decorated mask and cape, and giving his name as "Aeroman," Mr. Rude initially refused to answer questions without the presence of an attorney. Detectives confirmed that several local incidents had been reported recently involving the would-be hero—

And so on.

Dylan had turned bright red. "Can I take this?"

"Sure, sure." Abraham spread his hands. "Why not?"

The kid hustled the folded newspaper into his knapsack and swept in a mad rush from the table, nearly upsetting his abandoned glass of OJ and his unfinished Cheerios floating in a half-bowl of milk, with face averted, ears blazing like taillights.

"Bye!" he shouted from the hall.

And was out the door.

Questions? Sure, Abraham had questions. *Do you know something about this, son? Is there anything you might like to share with me? Just where do you and Mingus Rude go all day and all night, anyway?*

For that matter, is Brooklyn itself a geographical form of insanity?

Are we, do you happen perhaps to know, my darling boy, cursed by God?

But who in this day and age got answers to his questions?

He did what he never did: cut school. And a thing he hadn't done for years: searched Mingus out instead of relying on chance to bring them together. First, though, he squirmed through morning classes, knowing Mingus wouldn't necessarily even be out of bed before ten, unwilling to risk waking Barrett Rude Junior, and not wanting policemen, truant officers, security guards, gangs, *whomever*, to draw an absolute bead on him as he imagined they would if he went straight to Mingus's school, whiteboy with a knapsack on the curb outside Sarah J. Hale after morning bell, nine in the morning. So he rode the train to Stuyvesant and agonized in his seat, swallowed anxiety through French and physics and history, slid the folded newspaper out of his binder for horrified reconfirmation, *yes, it happened, Aeroman was arrested*, perhaps a hundred, perhaps a thousand times. At least they'd gotten the name right! At lunch period he split, took the IRT back to Brooklyn and prowled the blasted land of Sarah J. Hale's sidewalk and schoolyard seeking after Mingus Rude. His reward was about what his guilty, panicked heart might have felt it deserved: Robert Woolfolk.

Robert and a couple of his homies occupied a Pacific Street stoop across from Sarah J. Hale. All three had tallboys of beer concealed in their sleeves for furtive slugs when the coast was clear – just another Wednesday afternoon in late-spring glare, life was sweet. The block was vacant, no guards, cops, gangs, no vibrations from within the building, Robert Woolfolk still the human neutron bomb of Gowanus. Dylan got a blissful crooked smile out of Robert as he approached. The scene was the opposite of what Dylan had imagined, Sarah J.'s sidewalks teeming with cutters like the park across from Stuyvesant. Instead Pacific Street was like a cartoon desert, Dylan crawling across the expanse with cartoon buzzards overhead, Robert and his crew like a batch of cartoon banditos you met on your knees.

We don't need no stinking badges.

Dylan halted on the sidewalk, but Robert didn't move. Nobody seemed much impressed at what had bumbled into their laps. This crew might find motivation another time to resume careers as criminals or at least harassers, menaces, inspirers of fear: this day they'd got a thirty-year head start on the men who sat on rooming-house stoops or in the entranceway of the Colony South Brooklyn Daycare Center on Nevins, mellow lackadaisical observers of life's passing streams, Thoreaus at Walden. They were drunk off their asses.

Life's passing streams might be urine trails from doorways to the curb, but never mind.

"Hey, Robert?" said Dylan.

"Yo," said Robert Woolfolk, his eyes glazed. He didn't object to being addressed by Dylan, not today: *We're on the same planet, might as well admit I know you.*

"Have you seen Mingus?"

Robert tilted his head back and to the side, Ali ducking a jab. Or possibly he mimed a braying laugh, but no laugh came out.

One of his homeboys extended a hand to slap and Robert Woolfolk slapped it. Dylan had stepped into some slow sculpture, a frieze in motion. Though he'd penetrated the frieze's reality, barely, he nonetheless couldn't hurry it along.

"Have you seen him?" he asked again, helpless, his morning's panic only mounting.

"You lookin' for *Arrowman?*" said Robert Woolfolk.

He made it sound like *errorman.*

Dylan didn't offer a correction.

Now came braying laughter, in triplicate. Robert's cohorts squirmed in their spots as though brutally tickled, immediately gasping for air, begging for release from the excess of hilarity. Hands were again slapped, Robert accepting congratulations for his rapier wit.

"Ho, *shit,*" said one of Robert's homeboys, shaking his head as he recovered.

"Nah, man, G ain't come around here today," said Robert. "You want me to tell him something for you?"

"That's okay."

"I'll tell him a message, man. What, you don't trust me?"

"Just that I came around looking for him, I guess."

"Aight. You was lookin' for him, cool."

Dylan mumbled thanks.

"Yo, Dylan, wait up man. You got a dollar you could lend me?" No one budged from slanted attitudes on the stoop. Someone drained a bag-sheathed tallboy, tossed it aside. Robert Woolfolk might have been addressing the sky, Dylan wasn't worth settling eyes on. "Because you know I'm good with you, man. These dudes don't know you, I had to stop them coming down throw a yoke on you. I told them you were my man, we practilly grew up together, you's like my little brother."

The logic was airtight. Certainly Robert's homeboys weren't saying otherwise, though neither looked inclined at this moment to yoke anything larger than a cat. Dylan emptied his pockets, his despair absolute, the dollars negligible for passage out of here.

One thing transfer of funds always did accomplish was a turning of the page.

He walked to the Heights, knowing he couldn't risk being seen on Dean Street before three, figuring no authority would doubt the legitimacy of a white kid with a knapsack in Brooklyn Heights being home early from school. There he took up station on a bench at the south end of the Promenade, sat chin-propped, pancaked between sky and the truck traffic roaring underfoot, the exhaust-flooded Brooklyn-Queens Expressway. He abandoned himself gazing into the bay, ferries slugging across to Staten Island and the Statue, garbage scows loaded up for Fresh Kills, the whole watery mouth of the city. Every reeling gull was Mingus Rude tumbling from the bridge again, white wings like cape ends tipped to the water, Dylan's eye fooled a thousand times.

The sky was full of Aeroman, except it wasn't.

Dylan had never flown in Brooklyn, if the ring was gone. They'd meant to swap it back and forth, the changing from black to white one of Aeroman's mystifying aspects, another level of secret identity, but it had always been Mingus in the costume, always Dylan crouched behind a parked car or dangled as bait while Mingus flew. Now this, Mingus heroing into the projects on the far side of Flatbush Avenue, where Dylan would never go. Dylan had sewn Rachel's scraps together and told a story and then clothed in those tatters Mingus had launched himself onto a cop in a drug deal. If the newspaper was to be believed. Of course it had to be understood before it could be believed.

There was something in the story not to understand.

Or maybe something you didn't want to know.

What did Aeroman care about a *drug deal*?

Two black kids found Dylan there at the end of the bench faced out to the island and the water and the sky. Lodge in any one place long enough and they'd find you, drawn like flies. These were just about as problematic as flies, too small to yoke him, fifth or sixth graders probably, a couple of mugging Robins lacking a Batman to back them up. If they'd roamed to the Heights from wherever, I.S. 293 probably, it had to be after three, school out.

They circled as if Dylan were a beehive, daring themselves to prod.

"What's the matter, whiteboy?"

"Your friends leave you all alone?"

"What, you can't go home? You lost?"

"You crying, whiteboy?"

"He ain't talkin'."

"Boy's stupid or retarded."

"Check his pockets."

"You do it, man."

Dylan looked up and they danced back. There was really no chance they'd touch him. He wasn't Aeroman, but he'd gained in gravity, was something middle-sized, neither gull nor mole.

"Ooh, ooh, he's mad now."

"He's gonna grab you, man, you better book!"

"Nah, he's going back to his crying."

"He a stupid whiteboy."

"He stoopid."

"*Stoo*-pid."

"Nigger's a faggot."

It was enough to make you miss Robert Woolfolk. The situation minus fear was only idiotic. Dylan was sick of it, the racial rehearsal. He'd been identified as whiteboy a thousand times and there was nothing more to learn. Another option,

Manhattan, was so prominent it was nearly sticking in his eye. If Aaron X. Doily's ring was gone Dylan might be done with Brooklyn for a while, be done vindicating fifth grade, be through with Mingus's fucked-up mysteries and ready to complete his escape.

The two black kids grew bored of him and wandered, maybe to find some Packer or Saint Ann's kid and work off steam, pick up a dollar or two.

A barge grunted from the docks with a three-color throw-up by *Strike* on its side, a strong piece of work.

He sat and sat, chanting Clash songs in his head, "I'm So Bored with the USA," "Julie's in the Drug Squad," records he'd never played for Mingus Rude because they embarrassed him on Dean Street, because he didn't know how. Then the Talking Heads, *Find myself, find myself a city to live in.* He sat and measured skyscrapers through bars and when he was done sitting the sun had fallen, squinting its narrowed orange beams through towers and bridges, the honey light flared and grew dull, and Dylan had missed Abraham's dinner, he'd sat all day.

In darkness he returned to the block and tried Mingus's door.

Mingus Rude appeared at the gate of the basement entrance, himself, intact, dope-eyed. He showed no particular objection to Dylan being there.

"D-Man. What up?"

"Where's the ring?"

"I got it, it's cool, don't worry."

"Where?" Dylan looked up and down the block, fearing surveillance of some kind. There was nothing, his paranoia wasn't even mirrored in Mingus. Two nights later nobody cared, Aeroman or Errorman was a joke, a name passed along stoops before fading from memory.

"I hid it away."

"Did the police see you fly?"

"The cops, man? They think I sprung out a *tree*."

"What—"

Mingus put up his hand to say *Enough, not now.* "You wanna come in? I got King Arthur here."

The shelf was empty, no costume, no ring, just the football helmet, Manayunk Mohawks, its bowling-ball curve now tagged in soppy marker by Art and Dose. "Get Off" was on the stereo, the needle hadn't actually plowed the music off the vinyl yet though it sounded like it was getting close. Arthur Lomb lay on his side on the bed, his cruddy Pumas on the bedspread, sifting seeds from a nickel bag in the gatefold crotch of the Spinners' *Pick of the Litter*. Crumpled rolling paper lay balled in a loose circle around him, failed tries, like some ring of dubious enchantment. He grinned at seeing Dylan: *Welcome to my chamber, bluh-hah-hah!*

Arthur Lomb had become a foul gnome. He seemed smaller. That was likely an optical illusion, a matter of losing himself inside titanic hooded sweatshirts and droopy military pants which could have held dozens of his pipe-cleaner legs. Arthur's clothes were growing though he wasn't. He completed a joint at last, repulsively swooping it through his mouth to cauterize the paper with saliva. He only spoke after it was lit, in order to demonstrate expertise in speaking through gagged breath, his voice helium-dwindled with effort:

"You heard Gus got arrested?"

"*Shut up*, Arthur."

Arthur handed the joint to Dylan, his own held toke exploding in a gust from his lips. "He went to the Myrtle Avenue projects at midnight and jumped out of a tree in his underwear. I suppose if you're tripping on LSD or heroin it might strike you as a good idea. I saw something like that on *The FBI* once. A girl ate the bark off a tree in a vacant lot. She was pretty hot, too."

"I'm right about to kick your ass."

"Do it, superhero."

"When I do you'll be weeping."

"I'll look forward to that day, it'll be worth seeing you dress up in your homo suit, *Arrow Man*."

Arthur needled like he moved rooks, unashamed of the obvious. He was monotonous and punishing, easy to tune out. Mingus had seemingly acquired the skill.

"What's your power going to be, Dylan? Because we all need powers now, we're Superfriends. I was thinking maybe

I'd be able to undress people with my mind, I mean like their clothes would really actually *vanish*, criminals would be humiliated and surrender on the spot. I'll call myself *Fig Leaf Man*."

Mingus didn't meet Dylan's eyes when they handed off the joint. Questions remained simpler to leave unanswered, Mingus flying solo, Aeroman's agenda at the Walt Whitman Houses. If he'd wanted to bust up a drug deal he only had to go as far as Bergen, or Atlantic, the foyer of the prostitute hotel. Or upstairs, for that matter, to Junior's apartment, where deals occurred on a daily if not an hourly basis.

But maybe that was the dilemma which had spun Aeroman off his usual orbit – the risk of meeting someone familiar in a local deal. Up to and including Barrett Rude Junior or Senior.

"Yo, D-Man, you *got* to hear this record 'King Tim Personality Jock' by Fatback—" Mingus began. He moved to the stereo, marking the conclusion of his two-nights-ago adventure as a topic, announcing the resumption of the real story: they lived in a famous era where heroic advances in musical styles, the discovery of a new *break* previously unheard, could happen at any moment. "Shit is seriously *dope*, check it out."

Mingus only turned away briefly to punch Arthur Lomb on the arm. Arthur shouted "Mother*fucker!*" and stroked the punched spot, but didn't shift from where he lay sprawled, a cackling, smoke-numbed dwarf on the bedspread.

Aeroman was dead or at least on hiatus, a serious layoff. He'd likely never appear in the same form again. Dylan was certain the costume was lost or destroyed. The costume was irrelevant anyway. With its bedsheet stripes and wobbly Spirograph emblem it had been too personal, too tender for the street, Dylan understood that now. Aaron X. Doily was right to renounce his cape, Dylan had missed the hint. Now Doily's ring was hidden and it should be. The ring was an enigma to contemplate, a subject for further review. The costume was likely just as *stoopid* as Arthur Lomb made it sound but the ring wasn't a part of Arthur's story, or for that matter the cops', or *The New York Times*'s.

They got stoneder and stoneder and quit talking.

The three together might have been a normal occasion if

you didn't think about it too hard. From one perspective it was odd it hadn't happened before.

But Dylan Ebdus and Mingus Rude still had secrets, even if those were on ice, hidden somewhere unspecified behind Mingus's thousand-yard stare.

Dylan Ebdus told stories and drew pictures, Arthur Lomb carped and needled, but Mingus Rude possessed a greater force, moods which prevailed, moods like laws. He cold-shouldered whole unwished regions of existence, his scowl chopping down fathers, grandfathers, schools. It wasn't an argument. For now, Aeroman was vanished, painted out.

Three white high schoolers cavort along West Fourth Street, returning from J&R's Music World to an apartment on Hudson where a certain divorced mom's not home, where they've got keys and the regular afternoon run of the place. All three are armored against late-fall weather in black motorcycle jackets, the Brando-Elvis-Ramones variety, leather skins studded with chrome stars and skulls, buckles dangling loose and fronts unzipped against the chill. The three grab-ass, swing incompetently from lampposts, talk in private tongues, nerd-punk argot.

November 1979: "Rapper's Delight" has just cracked the top forty. It's also cracked the attention spans of the white kids at Stuyvesant, including this bunch. The song is on the radio and on the street, leaking from stores and passing shoulder-hoisted boom boxes, a different sound, and impossible to miss.

But to really hear it for yourself someone's got to lay down cash and bring the thing home.

The Sugar Hill Records twelve-inch in its generic sleeve is bagged with their other purchases, Eno, Tom Robinson, Voidoids, *Quadrophenia* soundtrack. "Rapper's Delight"'s place on the pop charts is as a novelty single, late entry in the lineage of "The Streak," "Convoy," and "Kung Fu Fighting," and it's in this spirit these white boys have made their purchase: the record strikes them as inconceivably stupid and killingly funny, two concepts lately the opposite of mutually exclusive, Gabba Gabba Hey.

Self-loathing worn inside out as a punk's moron pride.

If one of these three knows more, he's not telling.

But put it this way: if one of those shops on St. Marks Place retailing punk fashion sold T-shirts reading PLEASE YOKE ME you'd buy one in a minute.

Then zip your jacket wearing it home from Manhattan.

Now, in the safety of the apartment, the other records are put aside while the twelve-inch is plopped on mom's turntable for instant-gratification hilarity. The needle is stopped and shifted backward a dozen times for incredulous confirmation of some sequence of chanted rhymes, *I don't care what these people think, I'm just sittin' here makin' myself nauseous with this ugly food that stinks.* The three white boys bust up, barely able to breathe for laughing.

"The – chicken – tastes – like – wood!" one gasps.

Jackets are shed. Divorced mom's boyfriend left a six of Heinekens in the fridge, the fool, and these are swiftly drained. A box of Nilla Wafers is demolished, down to the crumbs at the bottom of the wax liner, which are shaken out and inhaled. "Rapper's Delight" is played again, the punks doing an antic dance, pogoing on the couch, playing at break dancing, striking poses.

The record includes among others a passage mocking Superman, the rapper calling himself Big Hank mock-wooing Lois Lane with boasting couplets. *He may be able to fly all through the night, but can he rock a party 'til the early light?* An excellent question for Superman or any other flying personage, really.

That's if flying wasn't the last thing on your mind.

Now the three begin quoting favorite lines, trying to mimic the rappers' inflection while keeping straight faces. *"I understand about the food,"* says one, nearly weeping with pleasure. *"Hey, but bubba, we're still friends!"*

Two of these harmless, pink-cheeked punks are Manhattan-born, were privately schooled until the year they switched to Stuyvesant to spare their parents the expense. For all they know this record might have been cut specifically for their private anthropological enjoyment, and they hear it with detachment suitable for an artifact fallen from the moon. They've never heard anyone *rap* before, anymore than they've met Fat Albert or Sanford & Son walking down the street. Consensus might be that what makes "Rapper's Delight" and black people in general so criminally funny is their supreme lack of *irony*. Hey, it's not racist to find blacks earnest as hippies, broad and embarrassing as a comic book. These boys is punks, and punks sneer. That's what they do, deal with it.

Lack of irony's scarcely a problem for the third in the room, the punk from Gowanus.

Tied in splendid baroque knots, that's him. Ready to pass any and all litmus tests for self-partitioning. But hey, if standing in your Converse All Star high-tops on the couch cushions rotating hips in awkward parody you recall Marilla's curbside hula-hoop instruction a million years ago, recall too your disappointment Marilla wasn't a blond Solver, your guilt at this disappointment, your shame at your body's inexpressiveness, its unfunky failings – *so what?* Laughing at "Rapper's Delight"'s no revenge, and anyway it wasn't your idea, and anyway it's *funny*. Dean Street's another story, a realm of knowledge inapplicable here.

You've just about finished leaving Dean Street, and Aeroman, behind.

If this means avoiding the one who protected your ass all through junior high, the one you once ached to emulate, the one whose orbit you were happy just to swing in – if it means leaving the million-dollar kid's regular phone messages in Abraham's precise handwriting unreturned – that's a small price to pay for growing up, isn't it?

This ain't no party, this ain't no disco, this ain't no foolin' around.

It's the end, the end of the seventies.

CHAPTER 16

THOUGH BARRETT RUDE JUNIOR had it in mind all along, grist for his own heart's musing, the evening's theme was kept a mystery to those in attendance. That hadn't slowed them delving into the spread, the sliced meats and cheese and olives and egg bread and rye and cherry cheesecake he'd dialed in from Junior's, the Seagram's, the dope. This posse of freaks, Horatio, Crowell Desmond, the three girls, they never needed an excuse to party. When finally he made the announcement he got only a faint echo back, most of the crowd already too wasted by then to do more than nod sweetly and spacily, raise a glass with ice if they held one. *Barry's hyped about something, Whose birthday? Whatever, that's cool.* But the one girl, whose name he'd forgotten, said:

"How old?"

She'd given him a shy smile when she came in, one of three numbers on Horatio's arm, all jingling earrings and Egyptian eyelashes, tan skintight slip-sheer dress to her pumps, nearly fifty buttons on one side, ankle to armpit; bottom dozen undone. Prime Horatio specimen, but new and unfamiliar. Picture her answering the phone, Horatio saying, *Wanna meet Barrett Rude? Singer from the Distinctions? Wear something nice, baby.* Standing at a mirror counting how many buttons up from the floor to undo, nothing's accidental.

It talks without talking.

Brother, it sings if you listen.

Right through the door she'd started fussing, dimming the overheads digging in his drawers looking for candles, until he told her there weren't any. Then she'd thrown her shawl on his lamp, made a web of shadow that stretched across the ceiling like a groaning mouth with tassel teeth.

"You down with some Fleetwood Mac gypsy type of thing there, girl?"

Again she'd smiled without speaking, then gone and sucked up a line Horatio had laid out on the kitchen counter.

All elegance, one nail-painted finger pressed aside a nostril. Pinky high like she was sipping Earl Grey.

He ignored her, slipped something mellow on the turntable, Little Stevie Wonder's *Journey Through the Secret Life of Plants*. Then got to sampling Horatio's product himself, did a line while waiting for the base to get cooked for the pipe. One of the other girls asked him about the gold records on the mantel and he told her there ought to be four more up there, if the truth be known. He didn't even get angry, it was just a story now. While he told it he kept half an eye on the quiet girl, as she watched and pretended not to, the usual game. No hurry, the quiet ones always came around. Like a timer going off. Now she showed some curiosity about his having a son, the procreational instinct.

Fine, girl, we can work with that. That'd be a direction we could definitely explore. He said: "Seventeen, you believe that shit? I'm an old man, damn."

Barrett Rude Junior sat in his butterfly chair, arms flung behind his head, spread open to the air the way he preferred, not caring if the girls on the rug were seeing up his gym shorts. Exhibit A, help yourselves. Y'all *came* here to see me, make sure I'm real.

"Well, if it's his birthday, where is he?" Her voice was girlish, purring, porny.

He lifted his eyes to the door to the basement apartment. "Why don't you call him up here? Name's Mingus."

Outside a thunderstorm had eased the June night, a tide of cool coming through the parlor windows, flapping the curtains.

Night the kid was born it was raining too, 1963.

The girl glanced at the door, surprised, like he was keeping some damn prisoner. "Whole downstairs to himself," he said in defense. "I called him before but he was out doing his own thing. Motherfucker lives for the street. Storm likely blew him home, though. Or it will." He shut his eyes and sang in falsetto, tonguing his palate for an Al Green lisp, "*I can't stand the rain – against my window – bringing back sweet memories – hey windowpane—*"

Taking the dare, she went to the basement door and called the name, tentative, like she didn't believe it. A minute later the birthday boy arrived, was suddenly in their midst like a dog on the carpet in his stained fatigues and napped hair, his proto-dreadlock nubbins. The girls all looked him over as if on cue, went *mm mm*, vamping for the sake of the grown men.

"What?" said Mingus.

"Hey, Gustopher, man, how you *doin'*?" said Crowell Desmond, leaning over the counter and sticking out his palm for a slap Mingus gave half-willingly. "How come I never *see* you, man?"

"Gus only come upstairs steal my records and the dope out my freezer," said Barry. "He don't *deign* to hang with us no more."

"You father said it's your birthday," said the gypsy-looking girl, still skeptical.

Mingus nodded.

"You looked stoned, boy. You asleep? Intro*duce* yourself to the woman."

She held his hand. "Yolanda."

"Yo. Mingus."

"Yolanda, *Yomingus*," said Barry. "Y'all a couple of twins."

Desmond Crowell, standing over by the sink where Horatio was cooking up some base in a glass tube, laughed like a horse.

"Yeah, that's funny, Barrett," said Mingus softly.

"Don't go calling me Barrett, boy. Look at you, all in your hippie Vietnam shit. You ought to be stealing my *clothes*."

Yolanda returned to the couch where the girls were arrayed and Mingus was stranded on the long fringe of the rug. The album side was finished, needle crackling to the label, hollow clunk of the tone arm's return, silence. Now all in the room grew attentive, the birthday concept perhaps penetrating dim brains at last. Or else they'd sensed a crackle in the air, summer lightning. Barry felt rebuked and scorned, though he'd hardly alerted Mingus to his plans. But such feelings lay beyond sense.

You commune with a boy in genetic vibrations and no one but you knows the full history, not even the boy himself who wasn't born when vibes originated.

The mother half of vibes being an uncontrolled factor.

Under his grubby clothes Mingus was a hunch-shouldered man. Lean, coiled, his eyes slanting to the street where he'd likely rather be. When had Barry last looked him over? Couldn't say. Not looking was a reciprocal deal, struck who-knew-when. He didn't want to picture himself in his son's eyes – or for that matter in the eyes of the girl Yolanda – him with his fingernails grown horny, pudding thighs, thickened neck veiled in mutton-chop whiskers. Only cocaine kept him from bloating up entirely, turning into some fleshy Isaac Hayes cartoon.

He should be dancing around the room, instead he felt weighed to the chair, a thousand pounds of ballast.

It was that *world-feeling* coming over him again. That was the only way he'd ever been able to describe it.

"Only fooling on you, Gus, lighten up. Take a seat. We're here to toast a man's birthday, people. Desmond, put on a damn record."

Mingus twisted on his sneaker soles in the middle of the rug.

"You got one of your friends hiding downstairs? Don't be all furtive now, bring 'em up."

"Nope, just—"

"See, Yolanda, Mingus digs white boys."

He just said it, no big thing, let it mean what it wanted to mean. Silence, though, had crept over everything, bugging him. The room was full of ions, thunderstorm stuff, and Barrett Rude Junior felt himself to be a massive leaden presence. He ought to dance but there was no music, and as his world-feeling increased his forearms and thighs seemed to grow mountainous. If the girl Yolanda came to him she'd be like a mewling kitten, crawling on the landscape of him. On a television nature show a kangaroo's pink larva had squirmed from birth to pouch, the parent a planetary form. That was his proportion now. The longer he didn't get off his ass the bigger he grew.

Mingus just stood, playing at being eerie like the kid in *The Shining*, mooning at his father.

Meantime something good was happening over at the sink, a sizzled stink, a smell with promise. It buoyed him immediately, made him want to sing.

"Don't immolate yourself in some Richard Pryor deal, now, Horatio. Get that pipe loaded up and bring it here. And pick some music, Desmond, you good-for-nothing flunky. Gonna write you a theme song, *Good-fo-nuthin' flunky man, he can't book me a gig I bet somebody else can—*"

Perhaps motivated to stop Barrett's improvisation Desmond at last picked a new record. Prince's *For You*, nothing too grating.

If Barry wasn't looming in size like a bloated planet, Horatio and Desmond and Mingus and the girls all tiny and floating in orbit around him, everything would be fine.

"Desmond, I ever tell you about how this feeling comes on me, like I'm getting bigger while everyone else is getting small?"

"Nah, man." Desmond sounded baffled.

"We all gonna be gettin' *small*," said Horatio. "Nothin' wrong with that."

"My former wife the mother of this boy here used to tell me I was getting *grandiose*, but there's nothin' grand about it. Just at times I feel like my fingertips is a thousand miles away."

"*Crazy*, man," said Desmond, afraid of saying anything specific or controversial.

"Yeah, crazy," said Barrett Rude Junior, seeing the futility in trying to explain. "It's some crazy shit all right. Yo, give the kid his present, 'Ratio."

"What?"

"Don't play like you don't remember." His voice crept from within the tomb of his chest and made its way into space, where the curvature of his own ears retrieved and confirmed it. He trusted that he'd actually spoken.

Eyes widened, Horatio came from behind the kitchen counter and reached in his inner vest pocket for the slip of folded foil, the gift he might have been unsure Barrett Rude Junior wasn't joking about. He'd prepared it anyway: never could have too much product on you, partying with Barry.

"They you go. A gram of your own. You don't have to go jumping out no trees now."

Mingus only stared.

"That's for you, take it. You want a line now Horatio cut you up some of his."

Mingus slipped the packet into his baggy thigh pocket and shook his head.

"Happy Birthday. You a man now."

Then Barrett Rude Junior, swimming back inside himself, his voice and mind more and more a speck within the sea of his body, saw the gift was incomplete. Sure Mingus was ungrateful, he should be. The gram wasn't enough. His father had to give him the girl, Yolanda. Barry had no use for her himself, not tonight with these brick-heavy limbs. The girl would be crushed if he somehow mounted her. And if she offered him head she'd be undetectable, miles off, beneath the horizon of the real. Tonight was the boy's turn.

"Horatio, you done already? Bring me the pipe because I swear like Old King Cole I'm too damn *lazy* get out this chair. Hey, Yolanda?"

"Yes?" she said, surprised to be named by him now, a bit prim.

"How'd you like to go downstairs and check out Gus's crib?"

He'd spoken easily, like she'd know his thinking, one thing flowing from the next. But nobody else saw the essential grace of the handoff, father to son. They all got on him at once.

Yolanda said, "What's *that* supposed to mean?" She didn't leave the couch, but crossed her legs, guarding the prize, and angled her body resentfully to the door.

"That's fucked up, Barrett," said Mingus in a low and pitying tone.

"Barry, be cool," added Horatio, like he had any say in this house.

"I don't *mean* anything, relax y'all. Damn. What if I make you a bet, though? How old are you, little Yo-*landa*? If you're closer to his age than mine, what about you go downstairs? Do a few lines of birthday blow with my son, it's only fair."

"She can't," said Mingus flatly.

"Wait up, Gus, let's hear from the girl. What about it, baby? Year of the Dragon or Rat or what?"

"You're a sweet-looking man, Mingus," said Yolanda defiantly, refusing to look at Barrett. Her voice was layered with sex, mothering, other mystical woman shit meant to shame Barry and let him know what he'd missed. For he'd missed it, blown it, she was gone. "Don't let your father ruin your birthday for you. I'll come see your room if you want."

But Mingus ignored her. "She can't come downstairs," he said again.

"Why is that?" said Barry.

"Senior's in the front. I heard him in there."

"He snuck back in?"

"What you expect? You didn't take his key."

Barry was resigned to the world-feeling now. This was how it felt: he'd become a planet and his population swarmed like gnats, flitting in and out of sight. So his old man was back, the skulker! Senior'd done something to get himself in bad with the pimps and dealers running the Times Plaza Hotel, talked some girl into his room and tried to baptize her, or maybe just fulminated too long in the lobby – anyhow, got himself unwelcomed, then crept back here to the basement. Mingus and Senior were two of a kind, creatures ungrateful by nature and grown as remote from him as his own distant hands. Horatio, Desmond, son, father, pussy, gold records, all flew in a cloud, godforsaken and tinny.

What he needed was a hit on the pipe. A line or two lines or a dozen wasn't going to do it tonight, wasn't going to shrink his unendurable weight or expand the other inhabitants of the room from irritant size.

Outside, rain misting on the day-baked tar.

Pipe, bowl, and be *damn* sure the Fiddlers Three don't weasel themselves a co-writer's credit.

It was the fact that the venue was the New School, a name he associated with pinkish causes and the hiring of scantily credentialed professors, which had beguiled him to committing this mistake. That and the Dutch collector of original paperback art who'd enthused through his telephone a half-dozen times until Abraham relented. Perhaps also some morbid curiosity to encounter his colleagues: one Howard Zingerman and one Paul Pflug, incredible as the names might seem. Likely his own name *Ebdus* struck others the same way and it was the oddness of their monikers which had caused them to drift into this enterprise. Perhaps Abraham had accepted out of vanity. Certainly vanity. The term *pop culture*, thrown around so freely by the Dutchman. He was pop culture now. So let him go and see what that meant and let him meet Zingerman and Pflug. What harm to sit on a panel?

Well, he'd learned what harm, what cost to be baited out of hiding. The New School auditorium was no insurance against humiliation. The small crowd, fewer than fifty, nearly all of them lurching males with complex facial hair, had come expressly to meet Pflug. Pflug was himself perhaps thirty, had a long ponytail like many of his admirers, and appeared to be a weight lifter, though he also wore the wispy beard of an old man, or possibly a wizard.

Pflug worked in the style which had succeeded Abraham's in time and overwhelmed it in popularity. That was, if Abraham's style had in fact ever enjoyed any real popularity except with art directors, who had for a few years vied to hire Abraham himself and, when he proved unavailable, commissioned bald imitations of his work. This no longer happened. Though Abraham still worked, the vogue for arty psychedelia was done. Pflug was typical of what replaced it. He painted dragons and strongmen in the fashion of the posters of certain recently popular films, his skies full of billowy Maxfield Parrish clouds, his barbarians and gladiatrixes and even his dragons rendered with a uniform photorealist gloss, down to each feather and scale, down to each blond, blow-dried strand of their anachronistic haircuts.

In fact, it became clear it *was* Pflug who'd created the poster for one of the recently popular films. This explained the resemblance, and also the existence of his fans. They'd barely concealed their impatience through the brief panel, waiting for the chance to mob Pflug with posters, now reverently uncurled from cardboard tubes, which they hoped he'd autograph. No one here cared about paperback cover art, and why should they? It wasn't a thing to care about.

The exception was the Dutchman who'd single-handedly organized this event, God help him, coming from Amsterdam to do so. And it was Zingerman he cared about, exclusively. The Dutchman, younger than Pflug even, was clean-cut and shaven. He'd sounded older on the phone, but in person was soft-spoken, dumbstruck with reverence. Zingerman was his hero. He'd been buying Zingerman originals from the warehouses of defunct paperback houses, from thieving art directors, from catalogues which circulated among aficionados like himself. The Dutchman was authoring a monograph, a catalogue raisoné, and sought Zingerman's blessing. His Atlantic crossing should have been a direct pilgrimage to the feet of his master but he'd been shy, it now seemed, and so had arranged this whole sham panel, Zingerman-Pflug-Ebdus, "The Hidden World of Paperback Art," as a blind.

Zingerman the painter had a certain integrity, a kind of Ashcan school realism. He was painterly in the mood of the Soyer brothers, or, if you were generous, even the earliest Philip Guston. Zingerman's milieu was urban gothic, characters caught at heights of expressive torment, men tearing shirts from women and vice versa, but also moments of tenderness or even pensiveness. Small dogs and rusted cans lay in the gloom of Faulknerian porches. The women were only always a tad beautiful, Playboy bunnies in disarray, slumming. Hands, faces, and cleavages were all in clean focus, while much else was lost in chiaroscuro, a signature style which also saved man-hours and was surely far less wearing than Pflug's autistic micro-detail in the long run.

The examples on hand, books sealed in protective plastic sleeves and two of the paintings themselves, were all from the Dutchman's collection. The titles spanned four decades, from the forties, Paul Bowles and Hortense Calisher beside outright pornography – Zingerman's treatment was consistent. He'd conceded to the seventies only his sfumato palette of grays and browns, brightening his tones and adding *Laugh-In*-style paisley bikinis and unbuttoned print shirts to his girls' wardrobes, fluffy sideburns to his protagonists' clenched jaws.

Zingerman the human? He was toxic. Maybe seventy, he stooped from a basketballer's height, his enormous frame draped in a dust-colored suit and folded awkwardly behind the table they shared. Hair sprouted from his French-cuffed sleeves like he wore an ape suit beneath, but the skin of his hands and face was papery, drained of vitality. Against the auditorium's posted prohibitions he chain-smoked cigars thick as his clubby fingers. He coughed frequently around the cigars. Hard to picture those fingers with a brush – but then so many things were hard to picture and yet *were*, like this evening's occasion.

Zingerman wanted no part of Pflug, and barely seemed to tolerate the Dutchman, his Boswell. Perhaps they lay beyond some
age requisite for Zingerman's attention. As Pflug autographed
posters – another artistic task he handled in excruciating detail,
lavishing each with cartoons and inscriptions – Zingerman
stretched in his chair, offered Abraham a cigar, and wholesaled
his life's philosophy.

"Lay the girls."

"Sorry?"

Zingerman's voice was graveled and abrupt and possibly
Abraham had mistaken a baroque cough for speech.

"Lay the girls, every one of them." Zingerman gestured
at the paperbacks on the table before them, then back at the
large originals hung on the curtain. "The models. That was my
only consolation for staying in this dirty stinking business, and
that's why I can't fathom a guy like you goes on painting these
whatever-you-calls, geodesic forms. What are you, going to lay
a geodesic form? That's a lonely road."

"Your models? You took them to bed?"

"To the bed, to the couch, right in the middle of the room
with a leopard-skin outfit, in a mermaid costume, with fake
fangs, with a toy gun in their hands, with paint all over my
fingers, lay them, lay them, lay them. Strict policy. Hire the
boy, hire the girl, arrange the pose, snap Polaroids, send the
boy home, give with an excuse to start touching the outfit, fix
the collar, hand on the ass, lay the girl, lay the girl, lay the girl,
thirty-five years."

"Like Picasso," was all Abraham could think to say.

"You bet your ass. I couldn't bear to paint those pictures
any other way, I'd put my head in the stove. I tried telling my
friend Schrooder, he thinks I'm joking. I'm not joking. You a
married man?"

"I was."

"We all were. These kids have no idea. That one there? You
think he lays them? He's too busy painting hair, painting feathers, painting the shine on bubbles. If I got one of those girls
with the swords and the hair in my room I'd know what to do.
Him, see those arms? I think he's looking harder at the boys."

"Or the dragons."

"Or the dragons. So you, what? You screw forms? At least Picasso started real. After he laid them both eyes were on one side. He made them walk funny. You, it's like looking in a microscope. You're not lonely, just you and your germs?"

Abraham thought: ladies and germs. Which was pretty much Zingerman's vintage. So this was what it came to, Ebdus the bridge between Ashcan school schlock and photorealist dragons, a momentary interlude. Just him and his germs.

No, the film would not be discussed here, the film would not be considered, not be thought of.

"I'm lonely," he said honestly.

"Of course you are, you stink of it."

"A big career mistake, biomorphism."

"Now you're talking. Take a leaf from my book," said Zingerman. "Live. Lay the girls."

"I will."

Here Zingerman lowered his voice, to conclude the lesson, to share what he'd earned, what he really knew. "Look," he said. "Don't tell Schrooder."

"Yes?"

"*Riddled.*" He passed his cigar magically over the length of his body.

"Sorry?"

"Started lung, so they cut lung. Doesn't matter where it started. Gone lymph, gone brain, gone bloodstream."

"Oh."

"I *shit* cancer. Doesn't matter, don't pity me. You know why don't pity me? One guess."

"Lay the girls?"

"Give the man a cigar."

> bad december
> no joke kid
> i haven't slept a wink
> put a rose at the door
> of the dakota for me
> i am the walrus crab

"Horatio, fuck you been, man?"

Pause.

"Oh, hey, what up, Barry?"

"You got so much action you can't even respect a nigger's phone calls?"

"I'm sorry, baby, I was gonna ring you. Ain't no thing. What's goin' on?"

"I need you to set me up with a piece."

Pause.

"You *talkin'* 'bout, Barry?"

"You watch television, Horatio?"

"Sure, I watch television, black man, what's with you?"

"You know what a Beatle is?"

"What? Oh, yeah, yeah."

"I got to pack some weight. Simple matter, Horatio. Now can you come through for me? *That's* the question."

"Man, you crazy? That shit got nothing to do with you."

"I *seen* that Chapman-ass motherfucker walking around on Dean Street staring at my house just last week. Wasn't him it was his cousin. White motherfucker had a *list*."

"You *serious*?"

"You know how many forces want me out the picture, get they hands on some four-track tapes? I don't even trust *Desmond*, shit. Must be five or ten smash number-one records on them tapes, you think people don't *know* that? I've got enemies, 'Ratio, on the streets, in the executive boardrooms, no shit, even under my *floor*boards. The question is can you help a brother out or do I have to go elsewhere? Whatever you say to me, be for real."

Pause.

"No sweat, Barry. That what you want I got you covered."

"Now you're speaking words I can understand."

CHAPTER 17

STATELY WAYNE MANOR is scheduled to go on between Miller Miller Miller & Sloane and the Speedies, the whole lineup a battle of high-school bands, the members all from Music and Art and Stuyvesant and City-As-School and Bronx Science or Dewey, wherever it is the Speedies go to school or had dropped out of. The Bowery sidewalk is thronged, nobody checks IDs, there are twelve-year-olds, junior high schoolers around. The girls are incredible, sensational, they teem outside CBGB in print dresses and fifties lipstick shades and teased hair, zits sunk in foundation, cupping cigarettes against light wind, bare arms goose-pimpled. They light up the night, birds of paradise to induce trembling in grown men but there are no grown men here apart from a few flophouse dwellers suffering already from delirium tremens. 1981, sixteen-year-olds could rule the Manhattan night, puff joints openly, and inside the hole-in-the-wall club order beer in plastic cups. Twos or threes of boys in leather and jeans mutter around the mobs of girls, faking hand stamps with ballpoint pen and pushing inside toward the stage, or stalling outside, passing bagged bottles of something harder, occasionally shoving one another to the curb in a hail of shouts, bluffed hostility. Somebody arrives and stickered amps and guitars come out of a trunk. Everyone admires the guitarist's bandaged fingers, he'd punched a car window and broken three knuckles, just raging at something some girl had gotten away saying unanswered. He's playing tonight anyhow, with mitts for hands, a showbiz hero.

In a nearby lobby a man enters a cage elevator, returning to a single room he's lived in since 1953.

A black-and-white curbed on Rivington jiggles slightly, a cop getting blown in the cage while his partner on the Bowery's corner looks out and waits his turn. Likely there's some code for this operation, *a stroller*, or an *O-five-O*.

Walls here show punk graffiti, another type entirely, the letter A circled for anarchy, jerky uppercase remembrances of bands like the Mice and Steaming Vomit perhaps the one lasting impression they'll make.

Tonight's a bigger than usual deal in the Stuyvesant crowd, with somebody's apartment parent-vacated for the weekend and mass plans to drop acid there. Weekend, it all happens on the weekend, as if school isn't twenty-four hours away, as if your life has changed one iota. You could fight the structure, on a Tuesday or Wednesday night go to shows or to Bowl-Mor, the all-night alley on University Place which advertised "Rock-'n'-Roll Bowling!" – but down that road lay too much cutting, failing out, the rock-bottom destinations of City-As-School or your local high. Like Tim Vandertooth you might never be seen again.

So dress up and pretend you won't all see each other in gym outfits Monday morning, hungover and sheepish as shit.

Inside, Miller Miller Miller & Sloane conclude their set. Their famous encore is a comic cameo, drummer emerging from behind traps to sing Aretha Franklin's "Respect," which can be safely adored inside the ironical brackets of Upper West Side whiteboys playing the most famous punk club in the world.

Admittedly it's a pretty great song, which everyone will be humming the next day if LSD doesn't brainwipe all recollection.

Stately Wayne Manor is on in fifteen minutes.

Dylan Ebdus mills in the crowd at the base of the riser, though he's only heard this band play about a hundred times already, between small gigs and practices at the rehearsal space on Delancey. His friend Gabe Stern plays bass in Stately Wayne Manor – he taught himself onstage, like Sid Vicious. Dylan, he's like Manor's fifth member, he knows their tiny set by heart, hand-letters their posters, listens in confidence to their girlfriends' grievances.

Sometimes makes out with their girlfriends.

Might one day get laid by their girlfriends.

Girlfriends present and future make a sizeable portion of the crowd which packs the bar like the soda counter in an Archie comic. The three bands lack a sole fan over eighteen. Every kid here would surely claim they'd seen Talking Heads on CB's tiny stage and be lying, since they were twelve or thirteen last time that happened. You could grow up in the city where history was made and still miss it all. Talking Heads nowadays play the tennis stadium in Forest Hills: buy a seat at Ticketron in the basement of Abraham and Straus and take the subway to Queens like any other schmuck.

The key to mostly anything is pretending your first time *isn't*.

Tripping on acid tonight's just the nearest example.

Now Dylan's friend Linus Millberg appears out of the crowd with a cup of beer and shouts, "Dorothy is John Lennon, the Scarecrow is Paul McCartney, the Tin Woodman is George Harrison, the Lion's Ringo."

"*Star Trek*," commands Dylan over the lousy twangy country CB's is playing between sets.

"Easy," Linus shouts back. "Kirk's John, Spock's Paul, Bones is George, Scotty is Ringo. Or Chekov, after the first season. Doesn't matter, it's like a Scotty-Chekov-combination Ringo. Spare parts are always surplus Georges or Ringos."

"But isn't Spock-lacks-a-heart and McCoy-lacks-a-brain like Woodman and Scarecrow? So Dorothy's Kirk?"

"You don't get it. That's just a superficial coincidence. The Beatle thing is an *archetype*, it's like the basic human formation. Everything naturally forms into a Beatles, people can't help it."

"Say the types again."

"Responsible-parent genius-parent genius-child clown-child."

"Okay, do *Star Wars*."

"Luke *Paul*, Han Solo *John*, Chewbacca *George*, the robots *Ringo*."

"*Tonight Show*."

"Uh, Johnny Carson *Paul*, the guest *John*, Ed McMahon *Ringo*, whatshisname *George*."

"Doc Severinson."

"Yeah, right. See, everything revolves around John, *even Paul*. That's why John's the guest."

"And Severinson's quiet but talented, like a Wookiee."

"You begin to understand."

Dylan's the bagman for tonight's LSD run, holding everyone's folding money, a hundred and ninety bucks which from habit he clutches tightly, hand within his pocket. Pride resists deeper habit's call to transfer the roll to his sock. The task of copping acid has fallen to Dylan and Linus Millberg for two reasons: 1. They're regular customers of the dealer, a gay on Ninth Street who sells Stuyvesant kids nickels from his apartment. 2. They're not in the band.

Linus Millberg is a freak math prodigy, a sophomore running with juniors, formerly shy.

"If we go now we can catch the Speedies' set," says Linus.

"Okay but wait a minute."

"We should have gone an hour ago."

"Okay I know but wait a minute. Go get me a beer."

Linus nods and dips back toward the bar.

Dylan is absently gratified by Linus's puppy-dog servility, perhaps because in the Stately Wayne Manor crowd it serves to mask his own. There's plenty that might be considered cool about being to one side instead of in the band itself. Mostly, though, it sucks. That's the self-loathing root of his dawdling: Stately Wayne Manor has never played CB's before, and Dylan's reluctant to surrender the borrowed glamour of their debut.

You could not be on the stage and still be on the stage.

It's not unrelated to standing beside Henry while he roofed a spaldeen you'd fetched from the street.

There's drama too: whether Josh, the singer, will show up drunk or if Giuseppe, the guitarist, can play with bandaged hands. Though Manor's chords are such that you might shape them on a Stratocaster's neck with an elbow or foot.

"There's the *Gawce*, she's looking great."

Linus has returned with the beers.

"The Gawcester's here, Ebdus," he said again. "You better do something this time."

Linus has a valid point: another factor in dawdling is Liza Gawcet. Liza's a new freshman Dylan Ebdus maybe-likes. She had a well-publicized curfew, so she wouldn't be along afterward tripping or bowling: this was his only chance. Dylan had leaked acknowledgment of the spell cast by her blond, mute, new-developed, fishnet-bound cuteness through a network of go-betweens, amazed and appalled that this system of proxy flirtation worked for him as it did for so many he held in contempt. But the system, oblivious to his superiority, *had* worked.

She maybe-liked Dylan in return – that was the message Liza's girl squad leaked back.

He'll talk to her tonight if he can split her from the gaggle, a dicey operation.

The way Liza's fishnets show through knee- and ass-torn OshKosh B'Gosh's is killingly childish and hot, like she's slipped the punky leggings on beneath outfits unchanged since fifth-grade hopscotch spills.

You could be sixteen and still suspect yourself of pederastic lusts.

The whole band's lately sniggering about Liza, infuriating their junior-year girlfriends, but Dylan's got an inside track.

Linus says, "You're good-looking in the face and Josh has a body and Gabe's in the band and I can start a conversation with anyone – if we were combined in one person we could fuck any girl in the school."

"Shut up."

"Yeah, but do something."

"Go see if she wants to meet a drug dealer."

The miracle of Linus is he tends to oblige. This isn't a matter of daring, just Gumby pliancy. For instance, at Gabe's command he'd grabbed a boxed pizza cooling on the counter of Famous Ray's and scrambled all the way to Washington Square. Now Dylan watches as Liza Gawcet and her friends listen to Linus's exuberant proposal. Linus points at the door, then at his hand stamp, explaining how they'll be readmitted, no problem.

And Liza Gawcet is *nodding*.

Stately Wayne Manor's amps are set up and the band's in the back room, smoking pot, acting like a band, making the crowd wait. Fuck them. Dylan hears the opening chords, the false starts and in-jokey banter, in his head. Gabe will play and not see Dylan at the stage and later ask and Dylan will say, *Didn't see Gawcet either, did you?* Let him wonder.

Hey, maybe he'd really luck out. Maybe they'd get high at the dealer's and Liza would break curfew.

He's glad, anyway, to shield her from Manor's moment of glory. No shock finding jealousy of the band roiling in his heart, he's got every shit feeling catalogued there if he glances.

On the sidewalk they fall to a boy-boy, girl-girl-girl

formation, Dylan having yet uttered zip to Liza directly. But he and Linus are leading the freshmen away from CB's, up across St. Marks Place, holy shit.

Through the city's night they move in a giddy bubble. Older teens, men with shopping carts, taxicabs, all of it recedes to the margins, invisible.

"Mary *John*, Lou *Paul*, Murray *George*, Ted Baxter *Ringo*."

Linus will do this until he's told to stop, but Dylan doesn't wish him to, it's serving a nice purpose of keeping their mouths moving. "Good one."

"I didn't make this shit up," says Linus. "It's like some essential human grouping pattern."

"So you're saying that's why Stately Wayne Manor's doomed – bad *Beatle dynamics*."

"Oh yeah, it's painfully obvious."

"Andrew thinks he's John, nobody wants to be Paul."

"They *all* think they're John. They're four wannabe Johns. They're like four *Georges*. With no Ringo to lighten things up."

"Not *one* real John?"

"Maybe Giuseppe. Doesn't matter. Without Paul to play peacemaker, John's just as bad as George."

"I thought George wasn't bothering anybody, he just wants to, you know, write one song per album and play his sitar."

"No, no, George is evil, he wants to usurp John, that's his nature."

Chewbacca wants to usurp Han Solo? But never mind. Dylan says: "They have to break up, then."

"Indubitably."

"We'll go back and tell them."

The girls become attentive. "Stately Wayne Manor's breaking up?" asks Liza Gawcet.

"Tonight," jokes Dylan, and the amazing thing is he's honestly never thought it before. Not for a minute had he doubted the band would be signed, famous, an exclusive quadrangle for life. Now realizing that's unlikely, his jealousy eases into generosity: Stately Wayne Manor's going nowhere; so let them play CBGB tonight. Hell, let them last a month more and get that Halloween gig opening for Johnny Thunders's Heartbreakers at the Roxy.

Meanwhile Linus attempts to explain Beatle dynamics to the girls, using his ungainliest example yet. "—the reason they'll never get off the island is Skipper's such a weak Paul and Gilligan's a John who'd rather be a Ringo. He's like, practically fighting Mr. Howell for Ringo status. Plus Professor's such an overbearing George, they're completely screwed up—"

When one of Liza's friends says, "What about the girls?" Linus impatiently replies "*The girls don't matter*" before he can stop himself.

Dylan decides to step into this breach. "A rock band requires a certain alchemy," he says ominously. "You saw *Quadrophenia*?"

"Sure."

"Like that, you know – the four faces of the Who."

Liza stares blankly, as if she might have regarded *Quadrophenia* more along the lines of *that movie with Sting in it*. Dylan feels despair rising. Fishnet tights do not a cultural vocabulary make. To the ironized, reference-peppered palaver which comprises Dylan's only easy mode of talk former prep-school girls have frequently proved deaf as cats.

"I think I mostly like bands with one strong personality," she says. "Like the Doors."

Dylan's triply whiplashed. Liza's found the gist of Linus's conceit through the smokescreen of the *Gilligan's Island* example, then just as quickly dismissed it, which is nimble as hell. Alternately, and fully depressing, she's into the Doors. Worse, though – if he's grasped the implication – does she think someone in Stately Wayne Manor has *a strong personality*?

But they're at Ninth Street and Second Avenue now, nearly to the connection's stoop, and Dylan means to shift focus to his own status as criminal savant. *She said she wanted to meet a drug dealer.* "I can't take this many people up, it's not so cool," he says. As though it's an arbitrary selection he adds, "Uh, Liza, you come up with me. Linus can stay downstairs with you other girls."

Linus gets it, and, hunching his shoulders and slanting his eyes, adds, "We'll keep a *lookout*."

"A lookout for what?" says one of Liza's pals, instantly spooked.

"Nothing," says Dylan, with quick exasperation.

"Why can't we stay together?" whines the spooked girl.

"Don't worry." Dylan's always found the notion of street-wisefulness in Manhattan a joke, has trouble not sneering at his West Side- or Chelsea-born friends who cross streets to duck clusters of homies, as though shit *ever* happens here. The East Village is too full and frenzied to be dangerous, and, truthfully, cops are everywhere. His friends don't know fear, they've got no idea. Though, go figure, now here's a black kid in a drawn sweatshirt hood sitting legs-wide on the gay's top step and look-ing not at all intimidated to be stranded from his usual turf.

Then a glance down Ninth reveals two in eyebrow-low Kangol caps and baggy pants walking with deliberate slowness across the street and the vibe's not great but this is getting *stupid*: Dylan's spooking himself. And now's no time for hesitation.

"We'll be down in five. You can go around to St. Marks and get a slice but come back."

"Uh, Dylan?" says Liza, once they're buzzed inside. At the second-floor landing they wait for the dealer to unbolt his door.

"Yeah?"

"I don't think the door downstairs closed all the way."

"What do you mean?"

"Like someone put their foot in it."

"*Relax*. Linus is just hysterical, it's catching."

Dylan's screwy secret is he likes visiting Tom's apartment, despite the pervasive odor of unfresh kitty litter. The gay dealer recalls someone Dylan might have found sitting in Rachel's breakfast nook on afternoons when he returned from P.S. 38. Like Rachel, Tom smokes not in the hammily clandestine manner of adolescents, that huffing and crouching and voice-squeezing which Dylan privately despises, but grandly, legs crossed, waving a joint and talking uninterruptedly through inhalations, unmindful of conserving the smoke. The satin shorts Tom sports year-round show too much hairy thigh, but Tom's okay. Two or three times Dylan's loafed around his place listening to albums and even meeting other buyers, and Tom's never bartered to suck anyone's cock, contrary to legend.

Tonight's different: all's appalling here, and Dylan can't think of why on earth he's brought Liza upstairs. He sees only the filthy pile carpet and chintzy decor, Coca-Cola glasses, framed *Streamers* poster. And Tom looks like a boiled lobster, all red for some reason. Dylan only wants to score and leave, but Tom can't be rushed.

"You know this record?" Tom asks. *And the colored girls go doo, doo-doo, doo, doo-doo-doo, doo, doo-doo, doo, doo-doo-doo, doo, doo-doo* is what's coming out of the stereo and certainly Dylan's heard it before, but at the moment, distracted partly by strobe visions of Marilla and La-La, he can only imagine that's the song's *title*: "The Colored Girls Go Doo-Doo-Doo," etc. Which can't be right. So he gives out a gruff nod which Tom translates easily: *I've got no idea.*

"Lou Reed, how soon they forget."

"Sure," says Dylan. In Dylan's mind Lou Reed dwells with Mott the Hoople and the New York Dolls in a hazy Bermuda Triangle between sixties rock, disco, and the punk which has supposedly demolished both. The music's brazen sophistication irritates category. The simple solution, particularly from the vantage of Tom's pad, is to call the phantom genre *gay*. This is gay music. Pretty catchy, though.

"You and girlfriend aren't planning to gulp all this blotter by yourselves, I hope."

"No."

Tom's gray Maine coon cat has crept into Liza's overalled lap, and now she's curled around it, head ducked, cooing. She's less than present, off communing with things female and feline.

"Oh gee, I shouldn't have said *girlfriend*. I'm always opening my yap. Just a minute, I'll get the door."

Don't, Dylan wants to say, but fails.

The door's chain snaps and Tom stumbles backward into the living room.

It's the two in the Kangols and the one in the hooded sweatshirt, and they're in Tom's apartment immediately, yelling, "Sit down, motherfucker! *Sit the fuck down!*" Tom stumbles to the couch and plops there between Dylan and Liza, his bare thighs touching them both.

"Shit, shit, shit," Tom moans.

"*Shutup*," says one of the Kangols.

A few things are simultaneously notable about the man–boy

in the hood, the lurker Dylan and Liza passed coming up the stoop:

He's holding a pistol. Waving it. The pistol's small, dark, unshiny, totally persuasive. All three on the couch watch it and the three black teens watch it too, even the one who holds it. Even the cat. The optics of the room seemingly distort toward the dull fist-like object, as though it were sucking light.

He's the obvious leader.

He's tall and moves with weird angularity.

He's not just any random black guy with an Adam's apple big as an elbow, he's one in particular.

"*Robert?*" says Dylan incredulously.

"Ho, shit," says one of the Kangols softly.

Robert Woolfolk stares from under the hood, as stunned as Dylan. There's no plan, that's apparent. This is some godless universe's dumb notion of a joke.

"You *know* him?" says Tom.

"Who this whiteboy, nigga?" wonders a Kangol.

Liza's hugged around the ball of fur, trembling.

Robert Woolfolk just shakes his head. He has instantaneously processed the surprise. What's left is just lip-sucking disappointment, spiked with pure rage. "You one lucky motherfucker," he says quietly.

"Get out of my house, all of you."

"*Shutup*, faggit, I ain't *even* talkin' to you. Come over here, Dylan, what you got for me, man?"

Robert explores Dylan's jeans with ancient and tender familiarity, seeming to find the wad of twenties, tens, and fives unremarkable, his due. These pockets and Robert's fingers have journeyed on parallel tracks from Brooklyn for this unlikely rendezvous: Why shouldn't something extraordinary come of it?

Then, sparing Dylan any violence or even the mildest of jibes about Rachel, Robert Woolfolk disappears the gun into his waistband, deep-muffled beneath a sweatshirt that's nearly to his knees, and waves his homeboys to the door and out into the hall. Perhaps Robert's forgotten the origins of the prohibition against his harming Dylan. Perhaps as in *Chariots of the*

Gods he goes on obeying a deity he can no longer name or even properly recall.

All that's heard is a last: "*Who the whiteboy, Robert?*" and the reply: "*Shutup, nigger.*" And they're gone.

Dylan stares at Tom in bewildered silence.

"Get out of my house."

"But—"

"You brought this here, now *get out.*"

Dylan touches Liza's shoulder and she slaps him away, expelling the cat in the same motion. Is it possible for a cat to have peed in fear at the sight of a gun? For the ammoniac stink seems nearer than the bathroom now, and Liza's got a wet patch on her OshKosh B'Goshes.

Oh.

On the stoop comes the fear that Robert Woolfolk's still around, that the episode's not over. As the outer door clicks shut behind them Dylan's vibrant with this possibility, a plucked string. But no, here's Linus, just walking up nibbling the tip of a wax-papered slice and saying, "Hey, what's the problem?" Dylan wants to turn to Liza and plead *don't tell* but she floods past Linus, crying now, hands cupping pants seat where urine pooled, seeking the consolation of her gaggle – she never should have left their side, never should have come on this expedition, probably never should have graduated Dalton's eighth grade and allowed her parents to talk her into taking the Stuyvesant test, the cheapskates. Dylan's searching, almost hopeful, but Robert Woolfolk's gone, there's no trace, no proof, nothing but the tale he dreads to tell, the implausible, unworkable, unlikely confession.

Brooklyn's stranded thirty punks in an apartment unpsychedelicized and they'll be needing an account of why.

Brooklyn's chased you to the ground and nobody's going to comprehend except that you're marked, cursed, best avoided.

Brooklyn's bepissed your blond destiny.

You'd strain pee from fishnets with your teeth to make it up to her but fat chance.

Maybe Liza Gawcet and Linus Millberg can be enlisted in the cause of explaining it to the others in Beatle-dynamic terms: how Dean Street's George Harrison tonight spared the

life of Dean Street's Paul McCartney. If you're willing to tell
it all – Mingus Rude, Arthur, Robert, Aeroman – it might be
enough, one hell of a story, worth two hundred bucks, an acid
trip of its own. But that's an awful lot of telling, and it opens
to realms you've diligently left gray to yourself. Be real: *it ain't
gonna happen.*

The four-track recorder was secure at the pawnshop on Fourth
and Atlantic Avenues, not in the window but deep in the
back, on the shelves behind the counter. It would wait for him
there: Who's got use for a four-track hereabouts? The tapes
themselves were stashed beneath the loose floorboard under the
water bed, along with pipe, silk rope and handcuffs, gun, and
assorted drug detritus, though nothing left to smoke or snort
or he would've smoked and snorted it. At times he was unsure
whether the tapes weren't actually blank, whether he'd demoed
any of those compositions floating through his mind. Elsetimes
he was positive he slept above a McDuck vault of riches, future
sonic gold.

Either way, nobody pillaging the basement closet was gonna
find shit, whether pillager came through a window or door
or was already there, an inside man, a mole. They'd have to
storm his citadel upstairs. If someone were to force him to reach
inside his stash hole it wouldn't be magnetic tapes he'd come up
with in his hand, it'd be the forty-five.

And he didn't mean no seven-inch record. Damn straight.

The Times Plaza Hotel was on the way back from the pawnshop and that was where he stopped on his way home, figuring
to buy himself a treat out of the fresh money. There was always
some deal cooking in the lobby there. He'd only had to stop by
twice, looking for Senior, to suss the general atmosphere.

"Hey, honey, I know you."

"Nah, you're mistaken. You don't know me. But we can
change that."

"I know you because I know your daddy and your little boy.
I just never seen you around here before, but I *know* you."

"Baby, I come 'round here all the time, you just missed me."

"You a *singer.*"

"That's right."

"See, I would of seen you if you come around before, because I know your daddy. He a *religious* man. He tole me all *about* you."

"That so?"

"Mmm hmm. I don't even want to *tell* you what he said though."

"Maybe he told me about you too."

"See, now you just talkin' shit."

"Listen, baby, you know these Trinidadian dudes come around here sometimes?"

"Maybe I *do*."

He made it songlike and seductive, dropped register: "I know you know everybody, that's the reason I ask."

It's 1981: nobody's heard the term *crack*. They won't for two or three years, at least. What's slipped lately onto the street from Jamaica, Trinidad, from the Leeward and Windward Islands, is called variously *base-rock*, *gravel*, *baking-soda base*, and *roxanne*. The stuff's not pure as home-cooked, and in a few years its erratic Columbia-Hollywood-New York-Caribbean-Miami-and-back genealogy will be neatly concealed by the new name. Crack will be eligible then to be taken for a deadly meteorite from an unknown planet, ghetto Kryptonite. In this current epoch of transition, though, confusion reigns. Some folks will tell you base-rock and freebase aren't the same thing at all, and Barrett Rude Junior, who feels a certain proprietary interest – *Shit, man, I was there at the birth, me and them Philly cats might of practically* invented *freebasing!* – is half inclined to agree with them.

But the point wasn't to debate chemistry or semantics or authorship. It would hardly be the first of his inventions for which he'd received no credit or royalties. The point now is to figure out what this woman calls the stuff and whether she can lay hands on any now.

"You gonna bring me to party along with you, girl?"

Party: the word was like *Open Sesame*. "Of course I am, baby. I just need you to show me where the party is at."

Sometimes when you walked around the neighborhood now it was like you were already a visitor from the future.

The pavement, the slate's not changed, but though you'd never flown higher than one precocious spaldeen catch you might be drifting now, a released balloon, too far off to discern distinctive cracks formerly memorized, let alone rain-rinsed skully ghosts.

Three college applications were in the mail, Yale an unlikely joke, UC Berkeley a safety net at Abraham's urging but he'd never go, Camden the only one he cared about, with its weird disreputability and allure of pure dollars. If a kid from Gowanus goes to the most expensive college in America maybe he's from Boerum Hill after all. If not Brooklyn Heights.

Running Crab with her romance of poverty can go fuck herself.

Last postcard came you-can't-remember-when, anyhow.

It only meant working after school every day senior year of high school and all the summer before college to blunt the cost – loans and scholarships and work-study and your own pathetic savings, all these would be required to meet that famous $13,000 tuition, the number like a crazy carrot dangling in the sky. Abraham almost shit his pants when he heard, he had to sit down and breathe slowly.

The big breakout costs big.

So Dylan Ebdus in a red apron scooped ice cream at the Häagen-Dazs on Montague for the girls from Saint Ann's he'll soon be at college with, a twelve-year wait to be a private schooler at last. Don't spit in their cones if they're not glancing your way – it's always darkest before blond dawn.

Winter months no one came in but moms needing hand-packed quarts for birthday parties. Dylan daily made himself ill on tasting spoons of double chocolate, cranked his Specials cassette to the limit during cleanup, afterward glowered home along Henry Street all the way to Amity, only cut across Court and Smith at the last possible minute. Dean Street's nothing but a route now, no life in it, and Dylan kept his head bowed against the risk of recognizing a kid from before.

It did happen occasionally, some lanky mustached Puerto Rican calling out "Hey, Dylan!" who turned out to be Alberto or Davey. Certain persons never left the block, maybe never would.

Impossible to explain they shouldn't greet you because you're not really there, you're gone. Easier just to say *Hey, Alberto, what's up, man?*, fake a smile or hand slap. Then realize maybe that's all anyone does – fake it. Maybe there were pavement zombies like you all over the place.

Given how often he bumped into Mingus Rude, he might as well have been *teleporting* back to Abraham's house. Dylan's choice of hours returning to the neighborhood or streets chosen for walking, a system formulated at deep needful levels, thwarted all encounters.

One morning at breakfast Abraham said:

"I saw your friend Mingus."

"Mmmh."

"He always asks where you've been, why he never sees you anymore."

What Dylan couldn't say was that Mingus's needs scared him now. Mingus's black-man's drugs, Mingus's dark filthy room, these were impossible realms, quarantined in the past. When Dylan felt guilty for assiduously avoiding his best friend – which was only every single day of his life – he just had to recall that Mingus had the ring.

Aaron X. Doily's Cracker Jack prize was a sort of buyout, a seal on what Dylan Ebdus couldn't risk contemplating anymore.

"He didn't look so well to me," said Abraham. "When I asked he laughed it off, only suggested I give him a dollar."

"Did you do it?"

"Of course."

"You got yoked, Dad."

"Sorry?"

"Never mind."

Mondays, on his way to Montague, Dylan stopped to deposit last week's minimum-wage Häagen-Dazs check at Independence Savings on the corner of Court and Atlantic. There was a couple thousand marked in the passbook, representing one season plopping flavors on cones with a blunt instrument. He'd double that sum by the end of the summer, then turn it over in a lump, to Abraham. So that particular February day, Dylan, Brando-collar flipped against the wind, perversely unhatted, ears red, trudged past blackened curb-rinds of snow along Atlantic.

As Dylan passed Smith Street, a guy putting gas in his car at the Shell station pointed with a finger at the jail, the Brooklyn House of Detention, his mouth hung open in some kind of *look, up in the sky, it's a bird, it's a plane* posture of astonishment.

Doesn't he know there *ain't no such thing as a Superman*?

Maybe Buddy Jacobsen, the girlfriend-murdering horse trainer from Long Island had broken out again, bedsheeting from a high window. News of that escape had put the House of D on the map for a week two years ago, the neighborhood's blight suddenly plastered all over the five o'clock news. It might have been Isabel Vendle's worst nightmare, a decade of public relations undone in a stroke.

So Dylan glanced at the jail tower.

There on the vast glass-brick and concrete face, maybe ten stories above the street and three stories tall, was a brazen impossibility, the biggest tag in the history of tagging. The lines were broken and wobbling as they'd have to be, spray-painted from the open window of a hovering helicopter, which was the only way the tag could have got there in the first place, right? *Right?* Still, however ragged, the thing was a master-piece, dwarfing Mono's and Lee's old bridge stunt, and meant to shock the viewer's brain with the obvious question: *How the fuck DID it get up there?*

Four letters: D, O, S, E.

The tag was a cry, a claim, an undeniable thing. The looming jail which no one mentioned or looked at and the trail of dripping paint that covered the city's every public surface and which no one mentioned or looked at: two invisible things had rendered one another visible, at least for one day.

(In fact it would be ten days before it was gone. Who knew how to clean the exterior of a twenty-six-story jail? And after, a phantom DOSE remained etched in scrubbed concrete.)

Dylan stared up in stupid guilty wonder, trying to figure it out, wondering what now ensued in the world he'd abandoned. Puzzling the message in the four letters. Puzzling whether it *was* a message.

Or just a tag.
Someone's betrayed someone but you can't say who.
Someone's flying and it isn't you.

CHAPTER 18

ONE HOT JULY afternoon, six weeks before he departed the city for college, Dylan Ebdus looked up from Hesse's *Steppenwolf* to find Arthur Lomb leaning on the Häagen-Dazs counter, pinching a sweat-drenched white T away from his body, sighing and puffing his cheeks at the chill of the air-conditioning. The little shop was empty, just the two of them, Dylan leaning over the book in his glasses, his chocolate-smeared smock over a polo shirt, his *Remain in Light* tape just audible over the hum of the coolers. Arthur Lomb had gained his height at last. In fact he swayed, a beanpole with jeans loose like banners from his legs, in maroon suede Pumas, a cigarette behind his ear. His eyes were red and small and wrinkled like those of some fetal animal, a blind mole rat or cauled calf. It shouldn't have been such a shock to see him there: a Gowanus kid could stroll into Brooklyn Heights any time he cared to, they'd all proved it a million times.

Dylan sat up, removed his glasses, flopped the book over on its cracked spine.

"Yo, D, lemme get a taste of that, um, macadamia."

He gave Arthur a spoon.

Arthur tipped his chin at the paperback. "What are you reading *that* for?"

"What's wrong with it?"

"Those guys *suck*. Yo, I hear you're going to college."

"From who?"

"Oh, you know, around. I think your dad told Barry."

"Yeah. Vermont."

"Cool, cool. I'm going to Brooklyn College. I'm just doing some summer school to make up a few credits at Murrow."

So even Arthur had trudged through high school, the nerd in him a flame Dean Street couldn't entirely extinguish. Probably his mother had ridden his back.

"Nice setup here," said Arthur. "Hot days you must rake it in, huh?"

THE FORTRESS OF SOLITUDE

"It's not like a taxi. I get paid the same if no one comes in."

"You're socking it away for college, I guess."

Dylan's mental fingers tightened around his mental passbook.

"I only mention it because I've got a proposition I thought you might be interested in," said Arthur slyly, lapsing into his old routine, boy huckster. "I just thought I'd give you first crack before I haul it over to the comics shop on West Third Street. Because I'm liquidating the collection. All those number ones. I figured you might still be interested in that kind of stuff."

"Why?"

"Oh, I don't know, I remember you always said you were going to buy *X-Men* forever, unless Chris Claremont quit writing. I always thought of you as like the ultimate collector."

Demoralizing how Arthur owned him, like a stink you couldn't wash off. True enough, Dylan still picked up the new *X-Men*. Not every month, but sometimes. Other months' issues he didn't take home, just skim-read beside the spinning rack at the cigar shop on Fourteenth. Like making out with an ex-girlfriend at a party, grudgingly, a chip on your shoulder that you had nothing better to do. Which was exactly what Dylan and Amy Saffrich had been doing all summer, clinching in hallways and bathrooms in the desultory wake of their term's-end breakup. The months between high school and college were a time of glum derangement, everyone half-spun to new destinies and arrived nowhere yet, living at home, infantile. It only followed that Arthur Lomb would wander into this breach to assert his thin claim.

"No," Dylan said now. "I mean, why sell."

"Oh. Heh. I'm just trying to raise some – funds." Arthur spoke airily. "Now seemed like a good time to get out."

"Right, right," said Dylan, pretending to mull.

"I'm sure it's pretty valuable by now. Everything's still in fine or near-fine condition."

"Uh huh."

Dylan's plan dawned in curiosity, no notion it would lead to Mingus and the ring, no inkling it was born in the betrayal and rebuke of seeing DOSE on the prison. It began merely as an impulse to see inside Arthur Lomb's house one last time, to see inside his room, to see Arthur's mom again, maybe. Nothing more. Dylan was safe already, he was gone, scot-free to Vermont. Why not tour what he'd left behind?

"When can I stop by and take a look?" he said lightly.

"Tonight?"

Arthur looked like he couldn't believe his luck. His proposition had been a potshot, a lark.

So, like all the best deals, each would believe they were gypping the other. "I'm off at eleven," Dylan said. "Be at home."

The apartment was the same, a time capsule: carpet, piano, addled tortoiseshell cats. Arthur Lomb's mom braless in a batik T, listening to WBAI. She greeted Dylan with gushy gratitude, seemingly awed to find him still associating with her son. Dylan was generous, her manner seemed to say, just allowing her to consider Dylan Ebdus and Arthur Lomb still some version of two-of-a-kind. Arthur, meanwhile, had already sneered into his room and shut the door.

"Off to college?"

"Camden."

"That's wonderful, Dylan. I'm so happy for you. God, you're so grown up."

Disgusting to realize he was flirting with Arthur's mom, to realize, now that he grokked girls, he'd *always* been flirting with Arthur's mom. Worse, she was fuckable.

"I, um, I've got to look at some stuff Arthur's got for me."

"It's good to *see* you, Dylan."

"Yeah."

The collection was buried in Arthur's closet beneath balled underwear and a heap of brand-x porn mags, mostly *Players* and *Hustler*. Arthur seemed unembarrassed at the spill of black centerfolds, their purple-backlit Afros and cocoa aureolae. Was he practicing being black? Dylan didn't want to know. Arthur tugged the plastic dairy crates full of Mylar-sealed comics into the center of the room and sprawled back on his bed, lit a Kool.

"Good as gold."

Dylan knelt self-consciously on the carpet, which was full of pot seeds and blackened matchheads, and browsed the crates. He felt he'd been reduced to something, propelled back in time to bug juice and chess disgrace, but pushed it from his head.

The collection looked mostly status quo. Arthur had massed a surprisingly strong war chest of mint number ones: five or ten each of *Peter Parker*, *The Eternals*, *Kobra*, *Ragman*, *Mister Machine*, *Nova*. For what it was worth.

"You want to sell the whole thing?"

"Yup."

"What, uh, what number did you have in mind?"

"Five hundred."

"You're insane."

"Four."

"I'm not even making an offer unless you put back the *Howard the Ducks* and *Omegas*. Plus *X-Men #97*. I assume that's what's under your bed." Dylan had spotted the plastic sleeves glinting there.

Arthur was impossible to shame. "Sure. Four for everything, *Howard*, *Omega*, whatever."

"I'll give you a hundred bucks."

"You must think I'm a chump."

"One-fifty."

"You shitface. When can you get it?"

"I've got it with me. But you have to help me carry them home."

They fished the hidden cache from under the bed, then each hoisted up a crate. They slipped downstairs, to Arthur's stoop. In the glow of money Arthur would be incautious, boastful. Now would be safe for Dylan to confirm what he suspected, that the trail of funds led to Mingus. As he counted out twenties he said:

"So – funds for what?"

"Gus and Robert and me are gonna buy a quarter kee and cut it up and make some real money. From Barry's connection."

"Cocaine?"

Arthur pounced. "No, we thought we'd go into your line – chocolate sprinkles."

"So you guys are pooling cash."

"Uh huh."

"Do you think Mingus would be interested in selling his comics, too?" Dylan asked.

"You've got to be kidding," said Arthur. "Those comics

are *ruined*." As if the interior pages of his own didn't feature breast-tracings and Sea-Monkey ads adorned with oversize cock-and-balls. But Dylan let it go.

"Yeah, I know they're in bad shape but he's got some titles I'm interested in." Let Arthur think him crazy, suspect what he liked, he'd never grasp Dylan's real angle here, behind the blind of the comics. No worry, anyway: dollar signs served in place of Arthur Lomb's eyes and, behind them, his brain.

"I suppose he'd listen to a reasonable offer."

Dylan milked it. "I'd have to get some more cash from the bank."

"That's an excellent idea, so you can finish the transaction right there."

"But mention it to him."

"I'll do that."

Only six weeks. Arthur Lomb's two crates of number ones relocated to his own closet's depths, Dylan Ebdus in his loft bed stewed in self-contempt, and the only solace was the escape so near he could hear it like a distant throb, a summer boom box on a Puerto Rican patio or a DJ in the Wyckoff Gardens court-yard. He might seem momentarily to have been drawn back into Arthur and Mingus's morass but it was only to conclude some old business, the thing left undone to earn his vanishing from Dean Street. Six weeks: he could scheme, be craven as Arthur, didn't matter. He was waving goodbye.

He jerked himself to sleep to thoughts of Arthur's mom, a tribute he'd owed for years.

Arthur, playing liaison now, set it up for the following night, a Friday. He was pretentiously vague and spooky on the phone, as though Dylan and Mingus couldn't manage an encounter without his help.

"We'll meet you on the stoop and let you in. Don't knock, you'll wake up Senior."

"I know Mingus's grandfather, Arthur."

"You haven't seen him lately."

"No, not lately."

"Just take my word for it."

Arthur and Mingus were on the stoop at the appointed time.

Mingus greeted Dylan with a hug, butted his head into Dylan's shoulder, phantom-boxed him. "Dillinger, where you *been*, man? My boy's done got all grown, *damn!*"

Dylan told himself he'd have returned the hug if he and Mingus were alone. Under Arthur Lomb's gaze he felt brittle, iced over. Whatever punkish stature Dylan had assembled in Manhattan didn't register in Arthur's eyes: reflected there Dylan saw a cone scooper, a *whiteboy*. So in defensiveness he shrugged Mingus off, was all business. Best for now to emphasize the transaction. Anyhow, Dylan had conceived a plan in which this was only a dry run: buy comics now, buy something else later.

Any sentiment could be reserved for the return visit Dylan had projected, one where Arthur would be absent.

"I hear you're trying to put together some cash," Dylan said.

"Yeah, yeah, D-Man, you want in on this deal we got going?" Mingus seemed immune to any slight.

"I might take those comics off your hands."

The room was a cave, kept dark. Whatever damage the comics had suffered surely wouldn't include sun-faded inks, but rot was a possibility. Dylan raised his eyes enough to see the shelf over the door had been tugged down, its hardware scarring the plaster. No football helmet or anything else. He averted from the rest, the sprayed walls and ceiling, didn't care to take it in. Then someone in the shadows moved, shifted, hitched trousers from knees and tugged at crotch in sitting up straight. Robert Woolfolk. *The party of the third part*, it only figured. Robert nodded, barely. Dylan back. Mingus recranked the volume once the door was shut, some pulsing funk. Arthur scraped and tapped with a razor blade at a jagged chunk of mirror, its sharp edges rimmed in black electrical tape. He sniffed a line and offered the rolled dollar to Dylan.

Dylan shook his head.

"Good stuff."

"No thanks."

Arthur handed the dollar to Robert, who tipped his upper half out of shadow and over the mirror.

"You know Robert, right?" said Arthur coolly, tauntingly.

"Sure," said Dylan. "He stole my bike once." He'd grant nothing after: no Rachel, no pizza slice, no East Village ambush.

Let Arthur and Mingus each muse on the allusion to the block's prehistory. Robert wouldn't contradict him. Dylan was certain of the bargain of silence they'd struck locking eyes in the gay dealer's apartment or even earlier, the lifelong misunderstanding they'd forged in the P.S. 38 schoolyard. Robert Woolfolk wouldn't contradict Dylan because whatever he might be he wasn't a liar, or a lion.

"But that was a long time ago," Dylan added with munificent sarcasm. "How's it going, Robert?"

"Yo," said Robert Woolfolk murkily, as he sucked a slush of coke down the back of his throat.

Mingus had quarried the comics from his closet, scooting them into hasty piles. He'd likely not laid eyes on them for years. "I never did get these in no plastic bags," he said apologetically, dazedly. He flipped open an issue of *Fantastic Four* and grew transfixed in nostalgia. "Dang, I even wrote my *name* in all these, check it out."

Mingus was talking to himself. His nostalgia was a non sequitur, no one was interested in the comics.

"I'll give you a hundred and fifty." Dylan spoke not looking at Mingus but staring bullets at Arthur, who made himself busy with the razor blade.

Robert Woolfolk only reclined in the low chair, grew hooded in shadow.

Mingus frowned in mock deliberation, a performance dying in the thin air of the bullshit transaction. "Well, I guess that would be fair."

Dylan tossed the money on the mirror. He relied on their understanding how puny the sum was to him. This was a demonstration to all three of them, as representatives of Gowanus, that Dylan was no longer of this place.

In reply, Robert Woolfolk only scooped up the cash, produced a thick-curled roll and layered Dylan's bills to the outside of it.

"I brought a knapsack," Dylan said. "I don't need any help."

Mingus nodded and blinked, defeated by Dylan's efficiency. "Okay, then, that's chill."

Turning his back to the three of them, Dylan shoveled the marker-tagged, fingerprint-worn comics into the sack. He was tangled in rage, to be there on the floor on his knees. In an irrational gesture he scooped up one of Mingus's Afro picks too, and pushed it into the mouth of the sack, on top of the comics. Then he remembered his cool, how he'd thrown down the money. He had a larger purpose here, his plan. The comics were only a joke. Dylan was like the garbage man of their entire youth, come at last. He might have been acquiring a collection of roofed spaldeens, or old cum-gummed socks.

"Walk me out," he said when he'd stood.

"Yeah, yeah, sure."

Again they tiptoed past Senior's crypt. At the apartment's gate Dylan whispered:

"Call me tomorrow. When Lomb and Woolfolk aren't around."

Lomb and Woolfolk, like Abraham and Straus or Jekyll and Hyde, an old association. Dylan almost laughed.

Mingus widened his red eyes, but Dylan left him hanging. Two could play at spurious mystery, or three, or four: anyone could be spooky, bogus street rap was no commodity in Gowanus. Dylan had survived Dean Street when Mingus Rude was a Philadelphia Boy Scout, Arthur Lomb a private-school dork. Only Robert Woolfolk held any real fear, and Rachel Ebdus had taken care of that, Dylan was untouchable. The other two were newcomers and comic-book collectors forever, and if they wanted to play at being players Dylan could play too. He assumed his demonstration was adequate to show it was the one with the fat passbook who held the cards.

Eleven in the morning, heat already gripping the day like a vise, it nearly went wrong right at the start, Abraham walking in as Dylan counted money. "Goodness," Abraham said.

Dylan shuffled it into the pocket of his yellow-checked shorts, *Ska*-wear for the concrete jungle.

"How much have you got there?" said Abraham.

"Three hundred," Dylan lied.

"Doesn't it belong in the bank?"

"It's none of your business."

Abraham grew consternated, and tried to formulate a stern reply, an effort Dylan always pitied.

"I'd say it is my business, Dylan. What's the money for?"

"I need to lend it to Mingus," said Dylan lamely, landing too near the truth.

"Why does Mingus need three hundred dollars?"

"I don't know." Dylan moved to the door.

"Dylan?"

"Treat me like a grown-up, Abraham," said Dylan coldly. "I told you how much I'd contribute at the end of the summer, and it's not the end of the summer yet."

Not summer's end, no: summer's *crotch*. Yoo-Hoo, Rheingold, Manhattan Special, everywhere bottle caps were massaged irretrievably into caramel tar by inching cars with gauges in red. Coming up Nevins passenger-siders jerked windows to block tin-can vented streams: some vigilante had again wrenched a hydrant open to belch the city's supply, and nobody rallied heatstruck brains to summon cops or firemen. By noon every house, every window was jammed open to suck air from the street. Pointless, though. The air was dead.

With five hundred in his pocket, his final offer determined in advance, Dylan Ebdus strolled to Mingus Rude's, casual as shit, sweating bullets.

Arthur Lomb and Robert Woolfolk weren't among the creatures slugging at minimal speeds along the heat-watery sidewalk. Dylan recognized nobody, his eyes walled.

Sunday, Senior was at the Parlor of God Ministry on Myrtle Avenue, so Mingus had the basement to himself, doors all flung open.

Dylan followed the music inside.

Mingus lay tumbled in baggy shorts and a grayed undershirt on his bed, sheets kicked to the foot, pillow doubled under his neck, dozing in daylight and loud funk. Possibly he'd started his day two or three times and lagged back, nothing on the agenda until Dylan arrived, sleeping off a night or series of nights, still sleeping off high school. The mirror was stowed somewhere, the room in midday light unmysterious, just a room. The walls and ceiling had been rolled black, maybe the only shade which would cover silver Krylon and Garvey Violet.

Mingus rubbed his eyes with balled fists like a newborn.

"Yo, D."

Dylan replied self-consciously, "Yo."

"So, my boy wants in the deal after all."

"Maybe."

Mingus swung his feet from the bed, gestured Dylan to sit down, kneaded his muzzle and smacked his lips.

"Master Dillinger has concerns," Mingus said, mock-pompous. "Things he *needs to know*. He's operating on a *need-to-know* basis."

Dylan didn't speak.

"I keep trying to make you bust a smile, D-Man. What? You afraid Robert wants to mess with you? Because you know I'm looking out."

"I'm not afraid of Robert."

"Aight, cool. I didn't mean to say you were."

Dylan wanted to get to business. "How much are you short for the deal?"

"We could be short nothing. The question is how much you want to come in?"

"Two hundred."

"Two hundred." Mingus ruminated. "Right. I see no problem with that." Antenna up now, he waited for the kicker. "We can cut you in for two bills, that's not that big a deal one way the other."

"But I want something else."

"Ah, something else."

"The ring."

"Ho, shit." Mingus covered his face with his fingers, laughed grimacing behind them, shaking his head. "Dude come round here talking about *this* and *that*, whole time he wants the ring back."

"You still have it?"

"So we on *that* basis. You had me thinking this was about, I don't know, *comic books*, or a *drug* deal, or some shit."

Mingus's laughter was bitter. It was as if Dylan had asked to buy their friendship back, all their secrets with it, Aeroman and the bridge and things which had no right name. As if on six or seven summers he'd put a price tag of two hundred dollars, ten twenties, the wage of a week spent shaving pistachio and butter pecan curls out of frosted tubs. Perhaps he had.

Pushing off with hands on bare knees Mingus stood, stumbled out into the hallway without a word. Through open doors pee bombed into porcelain.

"I still got it, yeah," he said when he returned. "You know, you only had to ask me for it back."

"Okay, give it back."

"What, now you ain't gonna pay me?"

There was a terrifying satisfaction in hearing Mingus's anger, at last. "No, I appreciate your keeping it for me," said Dylan, voice still cold, face growing hot. "I'm glad to pay."

"Damn straight."

"Who knows about the ring?" asked Dylan. He'd only waited all of high school to ask it. Now he'd paid for the right.

Mingus turned away.

"You told Arthur?"

"Nah."

Of course not, who would? "Robert?"

Silence.

"Motherfucker, you told Robert."

"He was with me when I jumped the cop at Walt Whitman," said Mingus. "I had to give it to him to get it off me when they took me in."

"Did he ever – try?"

Mingus shrugged. "He was like you."

"What's that mean?"

"Means he *tried*."

Of course. The ring was not a neutral tool. It judged its wearer: Aaron Doily flew drunkenly, and Dylan flew like a coward, only when it didn't matter, at the Windles' pond. So it had attuned to Robert Woolfolk's chaos.

"Don't tell me," said Dylan. "He flew sideways."

Mingus left it vague. He'd always made it his habit to protect their honor against one another – Dylan, Arthur, Robert. To say nothing.

Dylan stood and placed two hundred dollars on the stained sheet. Mingus frowned at it.

"Looks light to me," he said coldly.

It was a moment before Dylan understood.

"What do you want?" he asked, his voice a husk.

Mingus almost smiled. "Let me see what you got on you."
The phrase was a cue from a yoking script – *let me see it, let me
hold it for a minute, I'll give it back, man, you know I wouldn't take
nothing from you* – the stony authority over whiteboys Mingus
never exercised. Mingus had let him hear it: their difference,
finally.

For the first time Dylan considered all Mingus might have
spared him. His cheeks flushed as he felt for the remaining three
hundred in a pocket which might as well have been made of
glass. Just because the ring never bestowed X-ray vision that
didn't disprove X-ray vision's existence.

Sweat had broken everywhere on Dylan's body. Now it
trickled into his eyes.

"All right." Mingus yanked a dresser drawer and added
Dylan's bills to a heap of money there. Perhaps it was Robert
Woolfolk's roll, perhaps another supply, impossible to say.
Mingus left the drawer open, expressing indifference, perhaps
daring Dylan to risk pilfering his college funds back.

All through Gowanus fortunes were being massed by enter-
prising young men, who knew?

Isabel Vendle would have been proud. She'd always told
Dylan to put every dollar into a drawer and see what grew.

"I have to get it from upstairs," said Mingus.

"Upstairs?"

"It's hid in Barrett's stash," said Mingus. "Don't bug out,
it's safe. Anyway, Barrett wants to see you, I told him you
were coming around. He's always asking why you never come
around." Then, unable to keep from twisting the knife, he
added: "You see anything else 'round here you want? But then
I guess you out of folding money."

They went upstairs.

The gold records were gone from the wall, leaving faded
rectangles topped with nail holes. Little else had changed, only
been worn, neglected. Barrett Rude Junior stood behind the
counter pouring Tropicana into a wide tumbler and the lip of
the tumbler was chipped in three places and the tiles of the
counter were loose in crumbled grout, crunching where he
set the carton. His silk robe was thready, wide sweat stains
under each arm. It hung on him too loosely. He'd shrunk, his

bulk gone. His beard was still trimmed into boxy chops but they were asymmetrical, gray-coiled. His fingernails and toe-nails were thick and yellow as claws. The skin below his eyes had retreated, sunk in.

A fan whirred in the bedroom. There was no music apart from what leaked with the dead air from the street.

"Little Dylan, damn."

Dylan was stunned, dumb.

If Abraham was going to grow this old he didn't want to know.

"Been too long, man. I don't even recognize you, big man. Look at you."

"Hey, Barry," Dylan managed.

"Good to see your skinny ass, boy. I see your father all the time, I *never* see your ass. Day's shaping up hot like a mother-fucker, ain't it? Y'all want some cold juice?"

"Nah, I'm good," said Mingus.

"No thanks," said Dylan.

"Need to drink OJ, Gus, restore your *vitamins*. See you don't get all depleted, boy. Sit down, you both making me nervous. Look like a couple of cats on a *mission*."

"I need something from your room," said Mingus.

"Get it then, what's the problem? Dylan, sit down. Take some juice with ice, don't say that don't sound good in this heat. Check out the Yankee game? Five minutes, Ron Guidry, man. Best pitcher in the world."

Mingus went into the back. Dylan sat on the couch, behind the coffee table. Barrett Rude Junior's mirror was maybe the only unbroken surface in the room, powder splayed like a galaxy. A plastic straw lay to one side.

Barrett Rude Junior caught him staring at this pinwheel of dust, said, "Don't be shy."

"Oh, no, thanks."

"Don't be *thanking* me, baby, help yourself."

"Go ahead," said Mingus, emerging from the bedroom. "Do a line, D."

"It's all right."

"What, you never got high before, man?"

"Leave him alone, Gus. Little Dylan can do what he wants.

He's my boy, he's going to college, *damn*, I can't believe how the time goes, can you *believe* it, Gus? Little Dylan's taking off to college, the boy can't get high because he's *keeping his shit together.*"

While Barrett Rude Junior improved this lyric, a variation on the old song – call it "Little Dylan Is the Man, Part 2" – Mingus Rude plopped beside Dylan on the couch, knees touching as they sank together to the middle, and without saying a word opened his hand, so that Aaron X. Doily's ring clanked gently into a clear spot on the cokey mirror.

Barrett Rude Junior set down two tumblers of orange juice, with half-moon ice drifting like bellied fish.

"What's that?" Junior asked.

"Just something I was keeping for Dylan in your floorboard. He's taking it with him to Ver-*mont*, where the girls go swimming without any clothes and niggers work in gas stations."

"Oh." This was lost on Junior. He arranged himself in the butterfly chair, his robe curtaining to show boxing trunks and wasted chest, his sternum like a tent pole.

A mansion of a man had been scooped out, done in as if by termites.

Dylan palmed the ring, got it into his pocket. Half thinking, he lifted his fingers to his nose, sniffed where they'd skimmed the glass.

"There you go," said Junior. "Cool you right out."

"See, he wants it," said Mingus, "he just doesn't know he wants it."

Ring safe in his pocket, Dylan suddenly heard his own song, the one he'd been humming to himself all summer, "Little Dylan's Almost Gone." He recalled his basic condition: Not In Jail, Just Visiting. Let Mingus lead him one more new place before he ejection-seated to Camden College, Camden, Vermont. He'd dropped acid, popped a quaalude in a bowling alley, mushroomed at Jones Beach, so what's this hesitation? Arthur wasn't here to witness, to call him on the bluff. He'd get away with taking a sniff of the cocaine. Only recall the routine, pretend it wasn't your first time.

Dylan moved the straw from the mirror to his nose and sucked like he'd seen.

And Mingus Rude did a line.

And Barrett Rude Junior did a line.

And they all did another line and Dylan Ebdus was doing coke with Gus and Junior, just another summer afternoon on Dean Street, no biggie. It was like a visit to an alternate life, one where he'd never abandoned the block, never quit visiting this house. The drug rained through Dylan and streamlined the illusion, scoured away doubt.

Your body could be cooled from inside, sweating like an iced glass.

A bass line never sounded so profound as when Barrett Rude Junior dropped a needle on Bunny Sigler's *Let Me Party with You*, and orange juice loosened the slushy trickle in the back of the throat surprisingly well.

"You like that?" said Junior. His bearded skull spread in a smile. Dylan might be getting used to it.

"Yeah," said Dylan honestly, his eyes open.

"That's nice stuff, right?" said Mingus. His tone softened, as though he'd only wanted Dylan to join him all this time, only wanted his oldest and best friend to ratify him in the medium of cocaine.

"Yeah," said Dylan again.

Maybe it was possible to be forgiven. Maybe you'd misunderstood and everything was actually completely cool. The ring was in your pocket now. You were hanging out with Mingus and Junior and you were also just weeks, days away from leaving for the most expensive college in the world. The two weren't mutually exclusive, your fear was wrong.

Maybe everything was perfect but even as you thought it Barrett Rude Senior came up the stairs and popped into the room, astonishing them all, no one more than himself.

Despite the day he was in his black suit, his gold tie clip and cufflinks, white handkerchief.

He smelled heavily of flowers, of roses.

Mingus was the one caught with his face to the mirror. He dropped the straw and smoothed at his nose with a finger.

"This what goes on any chance I'm out the door," said Senior, his voice quavering. "Corrupting the morals of another neighbor child."

"Get downstairs, old man," said Junior simply, not looking at his father.

"Messing with the white folks' child you'll bring down cataclysm on this house."

Dylan failed to recognize himself or anything he knew about Gowanus or the world in this. It was suddenly so funny he almost guffawed. Mingus elbowed him.

"Why you home early on a Sunday anyway?" said Junior. "Sister Pauletta finally kick you out for taking a pinch on one of her flower girls?"

"Lord forgive the twisted soul who was formerly my little boy."

Barrett Rude Junior rose, pulled his robe tight, went past his father to the sink. "I *came* twisted, old man. The twist got handed down. So why don't you take a load off, baby. Loosen your tie, day's too hot. You want some blow, help yourself."

"I praise God every day your mother never lived to see it."

Barrett Rude Junior turned and said softly, "You praise God, is that right? Over the name of my *mother*?"

"I do."

"And what's God say back to you, old man? When that name comes up?"

Mingus said quietly, "Go to your room and pray, Granddaddy."

"Each day and night I pray beneath the feet of sinners," said Senior. "One fine morning I'm coming out of my hiding to say what I've seen."

"Go now," said Mingus, pleading.

"I'll cry it to the hills."

Dylan didn't know how it was possible for Barrett Rude Junior to cross the room as quickly as he did, and gather his father's suit lapels in his two fists to slam him back against the stairwell's wall. A sigh came out of them both, Junior and Senior, seemingly one sound. Then Senior was gone, down the stairs, and Junior had again turned his back to the couch, was running water at the sink.

Dylan bowed in guilty silence at seeing it. Mingus just shook his head and returned to the straw and the mirror.

Dylan felt his pulse beating everywhere in his skin: the drug, probably.

The music went on playing and for a moment it was as if nothing had happened. One moment, then the room refilled with the scent of roses, Senior was at the top of the stairs again and it was instead as if he'd never gone and the moment of peace had been an eye blink. Except Senior had made a trip to the basement apartment: proof was in what he'd retrieved there and now displayed in his two hands. The left gripped a bouquet of twenties, which he immediately flung before him so they twirled to the carpet. The right was filled with a gun.

From the speakers Bunny Sigler sang on, oblivious.

"You don't lay hands on your father," said Barrett Rude Senior to his son. "It says so in the book. Now I got the evidence you been using children for your dealing ways. The boy's room is full of your dirty money. You got no shame, I got to teach it to you, boy."

"Mingus has his own money," said Junior quietly, watching the gun waver in his father's hand.

"You teach sinning ways and you got to pay for laying a hand on your own father."

"Lay down the gun, old man."

"Call me father, now. The gun's to put some fear in you."

"*You got to ad-mit, you an old man.*" It was another of Barry's impromptu melodies, the last Dylan would hear.

Mingus hurdled from the couch, and ran to his father's doorway. He turned, before vanishing into the back, and shouted, "Go *home*, Dylan!" Protecting him still.

Dylan Ebdus never would remember getting from the couch to the door, from door to stoop, stoop to gate, to the sidewalk. A part of him was still inside, beating like a pulse behind eyes staring at the faces, at the gun, at Mingus framed for an instant in the doorway before turning away, moving inside his father's bedroom. Dylan Ebdus still heard the music and felt the scuff in his nostril, still puzzled at the missing gold records on the wall, the missing flesh in Barrett Rude Junior's face. So the blazing day into which he'd been ejected made no impression. Still, he was outside. Mingus shouted at him to go and he'd gone and he was intact, ring in pocket, five hundred college dollars scattered from Barrett Rude Senior's fist to the floor, mission accomplished. He wasn't inside. He was on Dean Street, teetering on a square of slate, when he heard the shot.

PART TWO
LINER NOTE

BOTHERED BLUE ONCE MORE:

The Barrett Rude Jr. and the Distinctions Story

NOTES BY D. EBDUS

The singer's role is deceptive; in identifying and exploring disintegration and other potentially destructive aspects of black American life he or she is performing an integrative function . . . the sense of identity is built not only into the performer-audience relationship . . . but into the very relationships between the sounds he or she makes — the musical techniques themselves.

—CHRISTOPHER SMALL, *MUSIC OF THE COMMON TONGUE*

People don't recognize the importance of call-and-response. This is because most songs are now written by the people who plan to sing them, and for them the picture is normally complete when they're in it. But a listener likes more than this. The backing vocals, the response, are the voices of society: whether gossiping (as in "Is she really going out with him?") or affirming (as in "Amen!" and "Yeah, yeah, yeah") . . . I would like to do a systematic study of hit songs over the last 30 years. I am sure that at least 80% of them have second vocals in some form or another. But I would bet that not 30% of all recorded songs use backing vocals . . .

—BRIAN ENO, *A YEAR WITH SWOLLEN APPENDICES*

VOICES IN MEMORY you can't name, rich with unresolved yearning: a song you once leaned toward for an instant on the radio before finding it mawkish, embarrassing, overlush. Maybe the song knew something you didn't yet, something you weren't necessarily ready to learn from the radio. So, for you at least, the song is lost. By chance it goes unheard for fifteen years, until the day when your own heartbreak unexpectedly finds its due date. This happens the moment the song takes you by surprise, trickling from some car radio, to retie the frayed laces of your years. Beguiled, you permit yourself to hear. But the disc jockey flubs the call list, never names the singer. Or maybe it happens in a movie theater, over a montage that relies on the old song. Afterward you scan the credits, but a dozen licensing permissions go by in a blur, hopeless.

So you forget the song again. Or recall just the hook, a dumb central phrase which sours in memory. How could it ever have seemed bittersweet as your own lost youth? Of course, what's missing in your recollection is the cushion of vocal harmony the lead voice floated in on, and the wash of strings, the fuzzy mumble of bass guitar, the *groove*, all so dated, so perfect. What's missing as well is the story, the context, the space the song lived in. Not to mention any chance for you to make it your own, a chance to spend, say, $34.99 on a two-CD set. That's okay. No one's harmed if you never follow the trail. In an uncertain world it's a reasonable certainty this forgotten song needs you even less than you need it.

Right?

Behind the uppermost pantheon of male soul vocalists – Sam Cooke, Otis Redding, Marvin Gaye, and Al Green (you add your names to those four, I'll add mine) – lies another pantheon, a shadow pantheon, of those singers who fell just short. They gather, more or less, in two categories. The first are those denied by the vagaries of luck or temperament – Howard Tate and James Carr, say, maybe O. V. Wright. The singers who record for a few different labels, cut a classic side or two, then bag out, drift away. In the "great man" theory of soul, these are the also-rans. The second category is the singer disguised within the fame and achievement of a group. Ben E. King of the Drifters, David Ruffin of the Temptations, Levi Stubbs of the Four Tops, Philippe Wynne of the Spinners: all known by their peers as among the finest vocalists ever to step to the mic. The world knows them only by ear.

Barrett Rude Jr. is one of the most elusive and singular figures in pop-music history. Though none with ears needs telling – if you're reading the booklet, play the damn CDs already! – I'll say it anyway: he's also one of the greatest soul singers who ever lived, not merely one of the best who never got his due. Born in Raleigh, North Carolina, in 1938, Rude was the only child of a troubled marriage, his father an itinerant Pentecostalist preacher (and eventual convict), his mother dying in her late twenties ("of a broken heart," Rude told *Cash Box* magazine in 1972). His musical experience is frequently exaggerated: he sang in his father's church, yes – but Rude's father had his pastorship stripped from him before the future singer was 11 years old, and a year later was in prison. Raised by his aunt, Rude dropped out of high school and migrated from Raleigh to Memphis, where he worked as a janitor, a school-bus driver, then, briefly, as a night-owl disc jockey, specializing in blues and jazz, at a Memphis radio station. There he met Junie Kwarsh, the daughter of the station's white owner, who'd been working as a secretary in her father's offices. Rude and Kwarsh quickly married and had a child – unless it was the other way around.

In 1967, at age 29, Rude recorded a pair of singles at Willie Mitchell's Hi Records studio. No one recalls how he came to the studio's attention – Rude always denied his father-in-law had arranged the opportunity. In 1967 Hi was still treading water with instrumentals and novelty cuts, while producer Mitchell, with singer O. V. Wright, had begun exploring the deep-bottomed groove he'd soon exploit so masterfully with Al Green. Maybe Rude could have stepped into Al Green's shoes in advance, and altered pop history – the evidence is here in four cuts, including the horn-driven proto-funk of **"Set a Place at Your Table,"** which briefly touched the R&B charts in February of 1967, and the slowed-down, eerily sexy Hank Williams cover **"I Saw the Light."** But it wasn't to be. Gaining a reputation as a brooding eccentric, Rude was dismissed as intractable by the even-tempered Mitchell before his career had even begun.

So Rude was seemingly on his way to the first kind of story – the handful of cult singles – until the day in February 1968, in a Philadelphia rehearsal studio, when a session guitarist named Marv Brown, who'd played at Hi Records a year before, suggested his name to a road-worn, journeyman vocal group known then as the Four Distinctions. The group had signed a management deal and were rehearsing under the hand of a young producer named Andre Deehorn. Deehorn had a sheaf of songs he imagined could be hits for a harmony-and-lead group. What he had in the Distinctions was harmony without the lead.

Brown thought he knew the singer they were looking for, a fellow who'd bottomed out in Memphis and was driving a bus in Raleigh, North Carolina – where, with his young wife and child, Rude had retreated to live with his aunt. No matter that there might be a dozen unemployed singers in Philadelphia; they took Brown's recommendation and made a call. Rude bought a Greyhound ticket and came in for an audition. Unknown at thirty, Rude might have seemed a dark horse for pop immortality. Indeed, demons were never far at bay in a career vexed by rages, whims, and disappearances from studio and stage dates. Safe guess that among his woes an unhappy interracial marriage was a formidable cross to bear in '60s America. His recording career spans just a decade; Rude was silenced by drug abuse and domestic tragedy at the end of the '70s.

Nevertheless, from the moment he walked into the Philadelphia studio, Barrett Rude Jr. was destined to be a singer of the second type: the secret, soaring voice contained within a famous harmony group. Rude had in the Distinctions found the context within which he could tell the story he had to tell, a place to do the one thing a human being can hope to do – matter for a while. If he regarded it as something like a prison, we can only respectfully disagree, and be grateful that his was an art built on dramas of confinement and escape.

But who were these four men that I'm selling to you here as *a context and a containment* for Barrett Rude Jr.? The Distinctions began as friends, working-class black teenagers in the era of

Johnny Ace and Jackie Robinson, growing up in the industrial suburb of Inkster, Michigan (also home to the Marvelettes). James Macy, Dennis Longham, Rudolph Bicycle, and Alfred Maddox were a quartet before they were a singing group, forming the all-black infield of the Dearborn-Inkster Chryslers, an early integrated high-school baseball team which won a controversial state championship in 1958. That after they switched from ball to doo-wop it was the shortstop, Jimmy Macy, who sang bass and the first baseman, Rudy Bicycle, who handled the tenor leads, stands only as further evidence pop truth is stranger than fiction. Baritones Fred Maddox and Denny Langham ranged between Macy's lows and Bicycle's highs. The Chrystones, as they were first known, were a resolutely secular group, and it was only a year later that Langham pointed out to the others the misleading resonance of their name, and suggested an alternative: The Four Distinctions. Under that name the teenage group would go on to play school dances, state fairs, and, yes, baseball games.

In May 1961 the Four Distinctions paid a fifty-dollar entrance fee for the privilege of winning a sing-off sponsored by Jerry Baltwood's notorious Tallhat label. Their prize was a pair of sessions. Who penned the four numbers cut in Tallhat's storefront studio that June? It's likely the Distinctions walked in with the songs, but Baltwood took the songwriter credit. Included here are **"Hello"** and **"Baby on the Moon,"** the first a lovely doo-wop plaint, the latter a Five Royales-style vamp. Neither charted, on this world or the moon.

In 1965 Tallhat's stable was bought out by Motown, but at the bigger company the group met with only frustration. Fourth or fifth in line for songs behind the Four Tops, the Temptations, and a host of other aspirants, the Distinctions found themselves singing backup and running errands, answering telephones, and fetching star acts from the airport. Denny Longham learned to cut and process hair; he was said by Martha Reeves to give "the best conk in town." They did, however, come as near to glory as **"Ain't Too Proud to Beg,"** the same Norman Whitfield production the Temptations would soon ride to the Top 10. Rudy Bicycle's lighter-than-air falsetto version was suppressed in favor of the senior group, but not before a B side was prepared.

"Rolling Downhill" might have seemed to describe the group's plight in Berry Gordy's organization; in fact it's a lost gem of a Holland–Dozier–Holland ballad. It would be three more years before career rescue, and before Andre Deehorn added "Subtle" to their moniker. But the Motown tracks are all the proof needed that the Distinctions before Rude *were* subtle, and polished, with a habit of making the hard plays look easy.

From Gerald Early's *One Nation Under a Groove: Motown and American Culture*: "The three major early groups of the company – the Supremes, the Temptations, and the Miracles – were put together and rehearsed at their high schools. They were not church groups . . . and in various autobiographies there is little talk about the influence of the black church in their music . . ." This is a useful correction, but stops a little short. The sound which defines soul is epitomized by the configuration the Subtle Distinctions fell into once Barrett Rude Jr. signed on: a Detroit- or "Northern"-style high-school harmony group fronted by a rougher, churchified, "Southern"-style lead. This collision of grit and elegance, of raw R&B lust and repentance with polished, crossover-seeking pop is also the crossroads where sufferation and exile briefly joins hands with new-glimpsed possibilities of middle-class striving and conformity.

Take for example the Drifters' 1959 "There Goes My Baby," seen by some as the definitive moment when R&B turned to the possibility of another music called *soul*. Lead singer Ben E. King's strangled, despairing vocal is pinned between a vaguely Latin beat and mock-classical strings. The results at the time not only horrified the record label, which nearly refused to release it, but puzzled the song's producer, Jerry Leiber, who said, "I'd be listening to the radio sometimes and hear it and I was convinced it sounded like two stations playing one thing." This drama was reenacted in James Brown's strings-and-shrieks ballads like "Bewildered" and "It's a Man's Man's Man's World," as well as in the treacly arrangements which dogged the recording careers of moaner-shouters like Jackie Wilson and Solomon Burke.

What's remarkable isn't that '50s song structures were inadequate to those unfettered soul voices just then locating their force. What's remarkable is how '60s soul produced at black-run companies like Motown, Vee-Jay, and Stax created an entire language based on the confinement of such voices in inadequate or mock-inadequate vessels. This drama took its purest form in the vocal interplay developed in groups like the Soul Stirrers and the Five Royales, as well as in a thousand doo-wop stairwells – voices rattling in a cage of echoes, or shaking off a straitjacket of rhyme, or outrunning billows of harmony that threatened to engulf it.

That's where the Distinctions come in. The Philadelphia production style within which they cut their great records revived the smoothest of doo-wop harmonizing styles to suit a new sophistication of recording technique. Producers like Thom Bell and the team of Gamble and Huff raised this game of confinement to the next level, so testifyin' singers like the Bluenotes' Teddy Pendergrass and the O'Jays' Eddie Levert had to find every possible way not only to shout, grunt, and plead their way out of the traps devised but to chortle and whisper in falsetto as well.

In this game no one set traps like Deehorn and the Distinctions, and no one slipped them like Rude. Hear it first in the spring 1968 demo recordings which secured the Distinctions' deal with Philly Grove: a sketch of their first chart hit, **"Step Up and Love Me."** With Deehorn's production scheme still incomplete, the nearly a cappella voices weave a nest for Rude's whispery intro, then push it out into soaring flight. From the same sessions comes the previously unreleased debut of Rude's songcraft, **"So-Called Friends."**

The new group was installed at Sigma Sound studios to record a full album. Rude, who'd been sleeping on Marv Brown's couch, bought a house and sent for his wife and child, who'd been waiting in North Carolina. On the debut, the strings-drenched *Have You Heard The Distinctions?*, Deehorn's warm, appealing love songs and his lush, aching productions dominate proceedings – here was the group worthy of his sure-fire hits. His arrangement of "Step Up and Love Me," complete with flügelhorn and glockenspiel, established the group's chart viability, smashing through to #1 on the R&B charts while attaining #8 pop. Rude was given a co-credit on the wrenching

"Heart and Five Fingers," though it's hard to imagine his cajoling, sobbing outro was ever actually written down. When tour promoters at last began ringing the phone, the group was ready; they'd only been practicing their footwork for a decade.

Apprenticeship was past. Atlantic Records purchased the smaller label's contract and returned the team to Sigma to cut their first masterpiece, *The Deceptively Simple Sounds of the Subtle Distinctions*. The classic **"(No Way to Help You) Ease Your Mind"** inaugurated a brief songwriting partnership between Deehorn, Rude, and Brown. With **"Happy Talk"** and **"Raining on a Sunny Day"** also reaching the charts, if you owned a radio, Rude's aching falsetto and the Distinctions' rich, percolating harmonies dominated the summer of '70. The album was a banquet of elegant contemporary moods, the group at the summit of their early form, best described by Dave Marsh in his *Heart of Rock and Soul*: "Pure déjà vu, seeming to call up nostalgia for a doo-wop soul that had never actually existed." Though it may seem inevitable that the tone would darken, at the time it was easy to wish for summer to last forever – or for a hundred albums as lovely as *Deceptively Simple Sounds*. Instead we have just one.

Taking a cue from Curtis Mayfield in "Move on Up" and Marvin Gaye in "What's Going On," the Subtle Distinctions recorded their socially conscious *In Your Neighborhood* in the fall of 1971. With a cover photo of the group in a vacant lot warming their hands over an oil-drum fire the album was rushed into stores before Christmas by an A&R office fearful the appetite for conscience might peter out. No fear – *Superfly* was right around the corner – but the look didn't fit the group, and *Neighborhood* was no Christmas record. Rude delivered coruscating vocals on his own **"Sucker Punches"** (which reached #18 R&B while failing to dent the pop charts), **"Jane on Tuesday,"** and **"Bricks in the Yard,"** but the album bombed. In the dubious tradition of 100-Proof (Aged in Soul)'s "I'd Rather Fight Than Switch," Marvin Gaye and Tammi Terrell's "Ain't Nothing Like the Real Thing" and other Madison Avenue-inspired tunes, Deehorn's **"Silly Girl (Love Is for Kids)"** nudged to #11 R&B, #16 pop, providing some tonal – and chart – relief.

Redemption was sweet indeed: *Nobody and His Brother* was less a retreat than a recasting of the darkness of *Neighborhood* in deeper, more personal terms, made possible by Rude's assertion of songwriting leadership. **"Bothered Blue"** was an immediate #1, topping both charts in October 1972, and if it's the only song you were certain you knew when you purchased this set, you're forgiven. Listen again. The song is better, more heartrending and true with each passing year, one of the most *grown-up* testaments of ambivalence and ennui ever to be made the backdrop for a Volkswagen commercial. Album tracks like **"The Lisa Story," "If You Held the Key,"** and **"So Stupid Minded"** form a war for the band's allegiance with co-writer Deehorn – Rude's voice and lyrics raging against the tame formats Deehorn throws in his path, while Maddox, Longham, Macy, and Bicycle try to play peacemakers, to give harmonic soothing to the voice burning in the foreground. When Rude flies they offer a landing pad, when he stumbles they pull him to his feet, when at last he needs to sleep they tuck him in. Only "Bothered Blue" charted, but that was all it took for the album to find its place, and become their number-one seller.

Rude quit the group with the song still on the charts. The Distinctions' last album, *Love You More!*, is a retroactive shambles, Deehorn's weaving together of rehearsal tapes Rude left in his wake. The catchy, understated **"Painting of a Fool"** was a brief R&B hit in June 1973, but the album fooled no one. The Distinctions were dropped from Atlantic, and quickly parted ways with Deehorn, who had some disco fish to fry. The group slipped quickly and easily into an afterlife on the dinner-club oldies circuit, seemingly as reluctant to completely retire the name as they were to sully it by recording without Rude up front. Few retire as gracefully.

As for the departure of the irreplaceable, erratic, and beloved Rude, no one was surprised. His studio battles with Deehorn were a legend, and for good reason. Black pop was headed in another direction, "Bothered Blue" notwithstanding. Deehorn would produce many hits in the next years, but the place of a Barrett Rude Jr. was far from certain. For every soul-shouter like Johnny Taylor, who, with "Disco Lady," found career revival, were dozens who'd come to the end of the road. But if the slick rhythm of the up-tempo Philly numbers anticipated (and helped create) disco, that only adds a poignance to what became – in the sound of the Spinners, Manhattans, Bluenotes, Delphonics, Stylistics, and Subtle Distinctions – classic soul's last burst.

It's hard to describe what changed in Stevie Wonder's records once he began playing all the instruments, except that it doesn't *feel* like soul – more like the most humane pop-funk ever recorded. By bringing the music into full accord, Wonder outgrew the paradoxes. Similarly, Al Green's late-'70s gospel is fine stuff, but once he abandoned Willie Mitchell and the house band at Hi, the music no longer teetered between worlds. The counterexample is Marvin Gaye, who, when he began arranging his own material, waded even deeper into the unresolvable mire. Gaye is soul's paradigmatic figure, carrying his confinements anywhere, embedded in voice itself.

Could Barrett Rude Jr. have carried on with something like Gaye's force through the '70s? Maybe. He tried. He failed. Rude was never a confident songwriter – all but two of his Distinctions songs carry Deehorn's or Brown's name as collaborator. Record buyers and radio programmers knew his voice but not his name: he might sing "Bothered Blue" on stage until he was bothered gray, but he couldn't record it again. At 34, he was starting over. *On His Own* (1972) shouldn't have been a bad start: with Marv Brown in tow as arranger, Rude recorded a dreamy suite of love songs as intimate as notebook jottings. Unbilled, the Distinctions sang backup on two numbers, **"This Eagle's Flown"** and the sole hit, **"As I Quietly Walk,"** which lodged comfortably at #12 on the R&B charts but couldn't rescue the album from public indifference.

Our hearts tend to turn away when ballplayers sign with new teams, when child actors grow older, when groups break up and go solo. Still, in Rude's view the Distinctions represented a kind of infancy, and the solo career his long-delayed adulthood. The non-reception of *On His Own* was bitter. Increasingly isolated from the advice of friends, Rude divorced Junie Kwarsh and moved to New York. His last album, *Take It,*

Baby, treats the split with agonized specificity – the million-dollar contract he'd negotiated on leaving the Distinctions had been turned over in a settlement. Eschewing Atlantic's resources, and leaving behind even Marv Brown, Rude recorded at the New Jersey studios of Sylvia Robinson, later the godmother of the Sugarhill Gang. The result is a tour de force of unleashed resentment, and nearly unlistenable by the standards the Distinctions' audience had come to expect. **"Lover of Women"** and **"Careless"** briefly visited the R&B charts. **"A Boy Is Crying"** alludes to a custody battle, but from the sound might be a battle between Rude's two or three selves, among which there are only losers.

Rude's last, stray single, **"Who's Callin' Me?"**, recorded and released in 1975, is a confession of paranoiac retreat. It takes the form of a string of guesses at the identity of a caller; a ringing telephone is audible through the seething funk. "*A bill collector?*" Rude wonders. "*Can't be my brother, my brother never calls.*" After considering "*A wrong number/Some unwed mother/my last producer/a slick seducer/a mob enforcer*" and others, just barely heard on the fadeout is a last, anguished possibility: "*Is it my mean old father, callin' me?*" In light of later events the coincidence is jarring.

Rude's last visit to the recording studio was in 1978 as a guest vocalist on Doofus Funkstrong's **"(Did You Press Your) Bump Suit"** (single edit), a twenty-minute funk workout boiled down for release as a single. It touched the charts, but didn't stick. Rude's vocal aeronautics never sounded better and – unmoored from sense by goonish lyrics – never meant less. An even odder epilogue is provided by two examples of privately recorded four-track demos, circa 1977–79. **"Smile Around Your Cigarette"** and **"It's Raining Teeth"** are each haunting and disjointed compositions, and each beautifully if lazily sung, suggesting the influence of Sly Stone. Rude was smashed on cocaine at the time.

I promised a story, and stories have endings. Andre Deehorn produced a variety of acts in Philadelphia and later in Los Angeles, scoring on the dance charts with Sophistifunction and Fool's Gold, among others. He now works as a personal manager in Los Angeles. Rudy Bicycle and Alfred Maddox remain lifelong friends, each living with their families in Dearborn, Michigan, and working in the industry which has supported them all their lives, Bicycle booking musical acts at casinos in nearby Windsor, Ontario, and Maddox as a publicist for the Motown museum. Denny Longham never lost his interest in hair; after the Distinctions disbanded in 1977 he opened King's Hair Throne, a clip shop in South Philly, and was a neighborhood fixture until his death from pneumonia in 1985. He was 44. In 1977 James Macy followed Andre Deehorn to Los Angeles, and struggled for years to find a hit on a variety of distaff labels. He and two companions were killed by shotgun blasts by unknown assailants while sitting in a car at a traffic light in Culver City on September 25, 1988. He was 47. Marv Brown never again found a musical partnership as satisfying as that which began at the Hi Studio in 1967. He worked with the house band at Sigma for a year, then vanished, and later took his own life by hanging in a Patterson, New Jersey, flophouse in 1994. He was 56.

After winning custody of his son, Barrett Rude Jr. moved to Brooklyn, and there sank gradually into a cocaine-fueled desolation. Rude's father joined the household after his release from prison in 1977; his relationship with Rude was uneasy at best. The atmosphere was volatile, a bad blend of Rude's hedonism and his father's quirky brand of Pentecostalism, with its moral fervor, its love-hate fascination with music and sensuality, its arcane Sabbath-days. (It's odd to consider that Marvin Gaye, Philippe Wynne, and Barrett Rude Jr. were all, by choice or upbringing, *weird black jews*.) On August 16, 1981, during a family dispute, Barrett Rude Senior aimed a pistol at his son and grandson. Whether he intended to use it can't be known. Another gun appeared, and grandson shot grandfather to death. Rude's son, who'd turned eighteen two months earlier, was convicted as an adult, of involuntary manslaughter. Though Rude was uninjured, the gunshot ended what remained of his public life. His silence since that time is complete. For what it's worth, the man is still alive.

That's the story. But what matters is a story in song. The music in this collection tells a tale – of beauty, inspiration, and pain – in voices out of the ghetto and the suburb, the church and the schoolyard, voices of celebration and mourning, sometimes voices of pensiveness and heartache so profound they feel unsustainable in the medium of pop. The voices may propel you to warble along, or to dance, they may inspire you to seduction or insurrection or introspection or merely to watching a little less television. The voices of Barrett Rude Jr. and the Subtle Distinctions lead nowhere, though, if not back to your own neighborhood. To the street where you live. To things you left behind.

And *that's* what you need, what you needed all along. Like the song says: sometimes we all must get bothered blue.

Disc 1: 1-2: The Four Distinctions, **singles on Tallhat** 1961, "Hello," "Baby on the Moon." 3-4: The Four Distinctions, **canceled Tamla single**, 1965, "Ain't Too Proud to Beg" b/w "Rolling Downhill." 5-8: **BRJ singles on Hi**, 1967: "Set a Place at Your Table" (R&B #49), "Love in Time," "Rule of Three," "I Saw the Light." 9-10 **Unreleased demos**, 1968: "Step Up and Love Me," "So-Called Friends." 11-14: From *Have You Heard the Distinctions?*, Philly Groove, 1969: "Step Up and Love Me" (R&B #1, pop #8), "Eye of the Beholder," "Heart and Five Fingers," "Lonely and Alone." 15-19: From *The Deceptively Simple Sounds of the Subtle Distinctions*, Atco, 1970: "(No Way to Help You) Ease Your Mind" (R&B #1, pop #2), "Far More the Man," "Raining on a Sunny Day" (R&B #7, pop #88), "Happy Talk" (R&B #20, pop #34), "Just in Case (You Turn Around)." Disc 2: 1-4: From *The Distinctions in Your Neighborhood*, Atco, 1971: "Sucker Punches" (R&B #18, pop, did not chart), "Silly Girl (Love Is for Kids)" (R&B #11, pop #16), "Jane on Tuesday," "Bricks in the Yard." 5-9: From *Nobody and His Brother*, Atco 1972: "Bothered Blue" (R&B #1, pop #1), "Finding It Out," "So Stupid Minded," "If You Held the Key," "The Lisa Story." 10: From *The Subtle Distinctions Love You More!*, Atco, 1973: "Painting of a Fool" (R&B #18). 11-13: from *On His Own* (**BRJ solo**), Atco, 1972: "As I Quietly Walk" (R&B #12, pop #48), "It Matters More," "This Eagle's Flown." 14-16: From *Take It, Baby* (**BRJ solo**), Atco, 1973: "Careless" (R&B #24), "Lover of Women," "A Boy Is Crying." 17-18: **BRJ solo single**, Fantasy 1975: "Who's

Callin' Me?" (R&B #63) b/w **"Crib Jam."** 19: Casablanca, 1978: **BRJ guest appearance** on Doofus Funkstrong's "(Did You Press Your) Bump Suit" (R&B #84, pop #100). 20–21: **Unreleased BRJ demos**: "Smile Around Your Cigarette," "It's Raining Teeth."

PART THREE
PRISONAIRES

CHAPTER 1

IN THE ATTIC ROOM I called my office sat a daybed that was usually spread with paper, the press packets which accompanied promotional copies of CDs and the torn bubble wrap and padded mailers the CDs arrived in. This morning, though, the bedspread, bathed in sideways seven A.M. September light, Indian summer light, was clear of packaging husks, clear of publicity. Instead the daybed held two things: a CD wallet, with plastic sleeves to hold twenty-four discs, and Abigale Ponders, in threadbare Meat Puppets T-shirt (mine) and Calvin Klein men's underwear (not mine, she bought her own), her limbs bent in sleepily elegant disarray. Only one of the two would be joining me on the nine-thirty flight to Los Angeles. Discman and headphones were already packed, along with a single change of clothes, in a small overnight satchel waiting at the door downstairs.

It wasn't usual to see Abby in my attic office. In truth, I was peevish to have her there. I'd been hoping to slip from the house while she was still asleep in the room below. Instead she'd trotted upstairs after me. There, in slanted light, her white shorts glowing against her skin and the maroon bedspread, she made a picture – one suitable, if you discounted the Meat Puppets emblem on the thin-stretched white shirt, for the jacket art on an old Blue Note jazz LP. She resembled a brown puppet herself, akimbo, head propped angled, mouth parted, lids druggy. I would have had to be a scowling Miles Davis to feel worthy of stepping into the frame. Or, at least, Chet Baker. Abby's whole being was a reproach to me. I loved having a black girlfriend, and I loved Abby, but I was no trumpet player.

Shopping at my wall of CDs, I opened a jewel case and dropped Ron Sexsmith's *Whereabouts* onto the spread beside the wallet.

She yawned. "Why are you staying overnight, anyway?" Abby counted on groggy insouciance to break the stalemate of the night before. We'd been in a silent war, worse than ever. This was worth a try – I rooted for her, even if I couldn't cooperate.

"I told you I've got a friend to see."

"Are you going on a *date?*"

I mumbled the lie out. "An old friend, Abby." Bill Withers's *Still Bill* was my next choice. I flipped the disc to the bedspread without looking away from the shelves.

"Right, old friend, dinner, I forgot. Oops." The CD clattered to the floor. "I kicked it." She laughed for an instant.

I caught the disc still spinning, and slid it into the wallet, near her toes.

"I'm trying to make you talk to me."

"I'll miss my plane."

"They leave on the hour, I've heard."

"Right, and I'm expected at Dreamworks at one. Don't fuck this up."

"Don't worry, Dylan, I won't fuck anyone. Is that what you said?"

"Abby." I tried scowling.

"Not even you. So don't be jealous of yourself, because you're not getting any."

"Go back to bed," I suggested.

She yawned and stretched. Hands on her bare thighs, elbows dipping toward her middle as if seeking to meet. "If we *were* fucking anymore, Dylan, maybe that would help."

"Help who?"

"The nature of fucking is it involves both people."

I tossed Brian Eno's *Another Green World* onto the bed and envisioned a row to myself at sixty thousand feet.

She ran thumbs under elastic. "I made myself come last night after you were asleep."

"Telling someone else about masturbation involves two people, Abby, but that doesn't make it fucking." This sort of stuff passed easily between myself and Abby. The tang of déjà vu to the banter made it a simple task to carry on browsing my record collection.

"Do you want to know who I was thinking about when I came? It's gross."

"Could you see the whites of his eyes?"

"What?"

"Never mind. I'm interrupting."

"I'll tell you if you tell me the name of your secret date in L.A."

"We're swapping a real person for an imaginary one? That's supposed to be a good deal?"

"Oh, he's real."

I didn't answer, but made another couple of quick CD selections – Swamp Dogg, Edith Frost.

"I was half dreaming, really. Guy d'Seur was putting his froggy little hands all over me. Isn't that *stupid*, Dylan? I've never thought of him that way, not for a minute. When he took out his dick it was *enormous*."

"I'm not surprised."

I wasn't. Not at d'Seur's appearance in Abby's fantasy or at the size she'd granted his apparatus. Guy d'Seur was more than Abigale Ponders's thesis advisor, he was a Berkeley celebrity. Forget being a rock critic – forget even being a rock musician. The professors of the various graduate departments were the stars that wowed this burg. To walk into a Berkeley café and find seated before a latte and scone one of the Rhetoric or English faculties' roster of black-clad theorists – Avital Rampart, Stavros Petz, Kookie Grossman, and Guy d'Seur formed the current pantheon – was to have your stomach leap up into your throat. In Berkeley these were the people who hushed a room. Their unreadable tomes filled front tables at bookstores.

Abigale Ponders was the sole child of a pair of black dentists from Palo Alto, honorable strivers through the middle classes who'd only wanted to see her attain a graduate degree and then been completely bewildered at the result. Abby's thesis, "The Figuration of the Black Chanteuse in Parisian Representations of Afro-American Culture, from Josephine Baker to Grace Jones," had led her, two years earlier, to come calling on the one working journalist in Berkeley who'd interviewed Nina Simone. I'd made my humbling pilgrimage to Simone on behalf of *Musician Magazine* in 1989, and Abby had proved she could research a bibliographic index with the best of them. That day, I'd charmed Abby out of interview mode by playing rare Simone records, until it was late enough to suggest a bottle of wine.

We'd moved her into my little Berkeley house three months later.

"Now you owe me one," she said. "Who are you seeing in L.A.? What's worth a hotel room you can't afford?"

"The hotel room is in Anaheim, and it isn't costing me anything," I said. "I guess that's a clue." I'd resigned myself to giving up the secret.

"You're being *paid for sex*? With a *Disney character*?"

"Try harder, Abby. Who in life, when you visit them, insists on paying for everything?"

She fell silent, just slightly shamed.

I took my advantage. "You're dreaming about d'Seur because you owe his froggy little hands a chapter draft, you know."

"Fuck off."

"Okay, but why not use this as a chance to get back to work?"

"I've *been* working."

"Okay. Sorry I said anything."

She sat up and crossed her legs. "Why is your father going to Anaheim, Dylan?"

"He's got business there."

"What kind of business?"

"Abraham is the guest of honor – the *artist* guest of honor – at ForbiddenCon."

"What's ForbiddenCon?"

"I guess I'm about to find out."

A pause. "Something to do with his film?" She spoke this softly, as she ought to have. Abraham Ebdus's unfinished life's work was no laughing matter.

I shook my head. "It's some science-fiction thing. He's winning an award."

"I thought he didn't care about that stuff."

"I guess Francesca convinced him." My father's new girl-friend, Francesca Cassini, had a gift for getting him out of the house.

"Why didn't you tell me he was coming?"

"He *isn't* coming. I'm meeting him there." Our tone was rote and flat, a comedown from Abby's sexual provocations. Those now drifted off as easily as fumes from a solitary cigarette.

I took Esther Phillips's *Black-Eyed Blues* from its jewel case and slid it into the wallet. The light outside was altered. An airport shuttle van would come in half an hour.

Abby tugged at one of the short dreadlocks at her forehead, twisting it gently between her knuckles. I recalled a baby goat scratching tender, nubby horns against a gate, something I'd witnessed in Vermont a hundred or a thousand years ago. When she felt my gaze Abby looked down, stared at her own bare knees. Her mouth worked slightly but formed nothing. I thought I could smell that she had made herself a little excited hectoring me.

"You seem a bit down," I said.

"What?"

"A little depressed again, lately."

She looked up sharply. "Don't use that word."

"I meant it sympathetically."

"You have no right."

With that she suddenly took herself out of the room, peeling the Meat Puppets shirt off over her head as she descended the stairs and moved out of sight. I only got a flash of back. A minute later I heard the shower. Abby had a seminar today, the second of the new semester. She ought to have spent the summer months writing a segment of her dissertation – as I likely should have been drafting my screenplay. Instead we'd fought and fucked and, increasingly, lapsed into separate glowering silences in our two rooms. Now, just as Abby was going in to face her mentors more or less empty-handed, I'd be winging down to Los Angeles to talk out a hot notion for which I'd not scribbled even the first hot scrap of note.

My sometimes-editor at *LA Weekly* had arranged the pitch meeting, my first. Over the last two years I'd slowly ground myself into $30,000 of credit card debt as a freelancer, my recent livelihood consisting mainly of the work I'd been doing for a Marin-based reissue label, Remnant Records. My dealings with Remnant's owner, a graying beatnik entrepreneur named Rhodes Blemner, vexed me. So today's pitch was a bid for freedom.

I must have lapsed into some kind of fugue, because the next thing I knew Abby was dressed and back at the top of my stairs. She wore jeans and a black sleeveless top and knee-high boots which raised her above my height. The boots still needed to be laced through their elaborate upper eyelets. She stood rubbing moisturizer into her palms and elbows and regarding me with steely fury.

"I don't talk about the hardest parts of my life only to have you throw them back at me," she said. "If I've ever been depressed at least I've had the nerve to admit it. I don't want you to ever use that word with me again, do you understand?"

"Sure you've got a nerve. Apparently I touched it. That's called letting someone know you intimately, Abby."

"Oh, yeah? What's it called when you don't know *yourself* intimately?"

"What do you mean?"

"Why didn't you tell me your father was coming, Dylan? How could you let me twist like that?"

I stared.

"*You're* depressed, Dylan. That's your secret from yourself. You don't let it inside. You surround yourself with it instead, so you don't have to admit you're the source. Take a look."

"It's an interesting theory," I mumbled.

"Fuck you, Dylan, it's not *interesting*, it's not a *theory*. You're so busy feeling sorry for me and *whoever*, Sam Cooke, you conveniently ignore yourself."

"What exactly do you want, Abby?"

"To be let inside, Dylan. You hide from me, in plain sight."

"I suppose that's another way of describing one person sparing another their violent shifts of mood."

"Is that what we're talking about here? *Moods*?"

"One minute you're jerking off on the carpet, now this outburst. I can't take it, Abby."

"You think you've spared me your *moods*? What do you think it's like for me, living under your cockpit of misery, here?" She gestured at the wall I'd been contemplating, covered with fourteen hundred compact discs: two units each holding seven hundred apiece. "This is a *wall* of moods, a wall of *depression*,

Mr. Objective Correlative." She slapped the shelves. They rattled.

"Wow, you've really drawn up an indictment." I was fumbling for breathing room, nothing more.

"That's what you call it when I won't play *depressed* for you? You switch to your little Kafka fantasies? I don't have the power of *indictment*, Dylan. I'm just the official mascot for all the shit you won't allow yourself to feel. A featured exhibit in the Ebdus collection of *sad black folks*."

"That's unfair."

"Let's see, Curtis Mayfield, 'We People Who Are Darker Than Blue' – sounds like depression to me." She chucked the CD to the floor. "Gladys Knight, misery, depression. Johnny Adams, depression. Van Morrison, total fucking depression. Lucinda Williams, give her Prozac. Marvin Gaye, dead. Johnny Ace, dead, tragic." As she dismissed the titles she jerked them from the shelf, the jewel cases splitting as they clattered down. "Little Willie John, dead. Little Esther and Little Jimmy Scott, sad – all the Littles are sad. What's this, *Dump*? You actually listen to something called Dump? Is that real? Syl Johnson, *Is It Because I'm Black?* Maybe you're just a *loser*, Syl. Gillian Welch, please, momma. The Go-Betweens? Five Blind Boys of Alabama, no comment. Al Green, I used to think Al Green was *happy music* until you explained to me how fucking *tragic* it all was, how he got burned with a pot of hot grits and then his woman *shot* herself because she was so very *depressed*. Brian Wilson, crazy. Tom Verlaine, *very* depressed. Even *you* don't play that record. Ann Peebles, *I Can't Stand the Rain*. Harold Melvin and the Blue Notes, blecch. 'Drowning in the Sea of Love,' is that a good thing or a bad thing? David Ruffin, I know he's a drug addict. Donny Hathaway – dead?"

"Dead," I said.

"The Bar-Kays, it *sounds* happy, but I get a bad feeling, I get a bad vibe from this disc. What's going on with the Bar-Kays?"

"Uh, they were on Otis Redding's plane."

"*The Death-Kays!*" She overhanded it to shatter against the far wall and rain onto the pillow.

"Okay, Abby." I held out my palms, pleading. "Peace. Uncle." My spinning brain added, *Sprite! Mr. Pibb! Clitoris!*

She stopped, and we both stared at the crystalline junk around her feet.

"I have some happy music," I said, dumbly adopting her terms.

"Like what?"

"'You Sexy Thing' is probably my favorite single song. There's a lot of disco-era music I like."

"Terrible example."

"Why?"

"A million whining moaning singers, ten million depressed songs, and five or six happy songs – which remind you of being beaten up when you were thirteen years old. You live in the past, Dylan. I'm sick of your secrets. Did your father even ask if I was coming down with you?"

My face was hot and no speech emerged.

"And all *this* shit. What *is* this shit, anyway?" Alongside the box sets on the shelf above the CD cases were arrayed a scattering of objects I'd never shown off or named: Aaron X. Doily's ring, Mingus's pick, a pair of Rachel's earrings, and a tiny, handmade, handsewn book of black-and-white photographs titled "For D. from E." Abby's unlaced boots crackled in the broken plastic cases as she walked. "Whose little shrine is this? Emily? Elizabeth? Come on, Dylan, you put it there so I could see it, you owe me an explanation already."

"Don't."

"Were you once married? I wouldn't even know."

I took the ring from the shelf and put it in my pocket. "This is all stuff from when I was a kid." It was a slight oversimplification: E. was the wife of a friend from college, the gift of the book commemoration of an *almost* which was really a *just-as-well-not*.

Mingus's comic books were in a box in my closet, mingled with mine.

She grabbed the Afro pick. "You were already taking souvenirs from black girls when you were a kid? I don't think so, Dylan."

"That's not a girl's."

"Not a girl's." She tossed the pick onto the bed. "Is that your way of telling me something I don't *even* want to know? Or did you buy this off eBay? Is this Otis Redding's pick, stolen from the wreckage? Maybe it belonged to one of the Bar-Kays. I guess the truly *haunting* thing is you'll never know for sure."

I lashed out. "I guess I have to listen to this shit because you don't feel black enough, Abby. Because you grew up riding ponies in the suburbs."

"No, you have to listen to it because you think this is all about where you grew up and where I grew up. Listen to yourself for a minute, Dylan. What *happened* to you? Your childhood is some privileged sanctuary you live in all the time, instead of here with me. You think I don't *know* that?"

"Nothing happened to me."

"Right," she said with heavy sarcasm. "So why are you so obsessed with your childhood?"

"Because—" I truly wanted to answer, not only to appease her. I wanted to know it myself.

"Because?"

"My childhood—" I spoke carefully, finding each word. "My childhood is the only part of my life that wasn't, uh, overwhelmed by my childhood."

Overwhelmed – or did I mean *ruined*?

"Right," she said. And we stared at one another for a long moment. "Thank you," she said.

"Thank you?"

"You just told me where I stand, Dylan." She spoke sadly, no longer concerned to prove anything. "You know, when I first spent a night in this house, you don't think I didn't walk up here and check out your shit? You think I didn't see that pick on your shelf?"

"It's just a pick. I like the form."

She ignored me. "I said to myself, Abby, this man is collecting you for the color of your skin. That was okay, I was willing to be collected. I liked being your nigger, Dylan."

The word throbbed between us, permitting no reply from me. I could visualize it in cartoonish or graffiti-style font, glowing with garish decorations, lightning, stars, halos. As with the pick, I could appreciate the *form*. Most such words devaluate, when thrown around every day on the streets by schoolboys of all colors, or whispered by lovers such as myself and Abigale

Ponders. Though it had been more than once around the block of our relationship, *nigger* was that rarity, an anti-entropic agent, self-renewing. The deep ugliness in the word always sat up alert again when it was needed.

"But I never was willing to be collected for my *moods*, man. You collected my depression, you cultivated it like a cactus, like a sulky cat you wanted around to feel sorry for. I never expected that. I never did."

Abby was talking to herself. When she noticed, a moment after I did, her expression curdled. "Clean up your room," she said, and went downstairs.

The airport shuttle's horn had been sounding for some time now, I realized. My room would have to wait to be cleaned, and the five or six CDs I'd selected would have to be enough. The Syl Johnson record, *Is It Because I'm Black*, had skated to the top of the small heap of discs and plastic left behind where Abby had been. I fished it up and added it to the wallet.

At the kitchen table Abby stood, one boot up on a chair, cinching the endless laces. She'd already refreshed the Africanoid jewelry in her piercings. It would seem an absurd costume for a student in a classroom, if I hadn't known how hard her fellow students dressed for the same occasion. The boots were only a little obstacle to the art of dramatic exitry – she'd surely meant to be out the door before me, meant her last words upstairs to be conclusive.

I grabbed the bag at the door. Her face, when she looked up, was raw, shocked, unmade. The van honked again.

"Good luck today," she said awkwardly.

"Thanks. I'll call—"

"I'll be out."

"Okay. And Abby?"

"Yes?"

"Good luck, too." I didn't know if I meant it, or what it was meant to apply to if I did. Was I wishing her good luck in leaving me? But there it was, our absurd coda completed, *good luck* on all sides. Then I was gone.

CHAPTER 2

IT WAS SEPTEMBER 1999, a season of fear – in three months
the collapse of the worldwide computer grid was going to
bring the century's long party to a finish. Meanwhile, as the
party waned, the hottest new format in radio was a thing
called Jammin' Oldies. Los Angeles's MEGA 100, recently
reformatted (or in radio parlance, "flipped") to the new trend,
was playing in my cab – the song was War's "Why Can't
We Be Friends?" – as I instructed the driver to take me to
the Universal Studios lot and we swung away from the LAX
curbside, into palm-lined gray traffic. The trees looked thirsty
to me.

San Francisco had a Jammin' Oldies station too. All cities
did, a tidal turning of my generation's readiness to sentimen-
talize the chart toppers of its youth. Old divisions had been
blurred in favor of the admission that disco hadn't sucked so
bad as all that, even the pretense that we'd adored it all along.
The Kool & the Gang and Gap Band dance hits we'd struggled
against as teens, trying to deny their pulse in our bodies, were
now staples of weddings and lunch hours in all the land; the
O'Jays and Manhattans and Barry White ballads we'd loathed
were now, with well-mixed martinis or a good zinfandel, foundation elements in any reasonably competent seduction. From
the evidence of the radio I might have come of age in a race-
blind utopia. That on the other end of the dial hip-hop stations
thumped away in dire quarantine, a sort of pre-incarceration,
no matter. Not today, anyway, not for one borne in the backseat of a taxicab helmed by one Nicholas M. Brawley, through
sun-blanched smog, toward a meeting with a Dreamworks
development executive, nope.

"You like this song?" I asked Nicholas Brawley's fortyish
gray-coiled neck.

"It's all right."

"You know the Subtle Distinctions?"

"Now see that's some real fine music."

At the guard-post gates of the Universal lot was proof I was expected, so Brawley's cab could be waved through, to wend past the curbed Jeeps and the long windowless hangars and the brick huts which appeared to have been thrown up just that morning. Dreamworks' building resided what felt to be a mile or so inside the compound, behind a tree-sheltered parking lot requiring a special pass for entrance. None had been issued, so Brawley dropped me at the inner gate.

"You have a card?" I asked him. "I'll need a ride out of here in, I don't know – maybe an hour?"

He jotted a number on the back of the company's card. "Call my cell phone."

As I crossed the shade-spangled lot to the entrance a well-dressed lackey was just crossing it in the other direction, moving for a break in the eucalyptus trees. He carried an Oscar. Palms cupping the statuette's base and shoulders, he appeared to be looking for someone to bestow it on. I wondered if his whole job was to cross this lot all day with the golden prize, back and forth, reminding any visitor of the local stakes.

Inside, I was directed upstairs, where I gave my name to a pretty girl with a headset. She fetched me a bottled water before abandoning me to a flotilla of couches and magazines. There I plopped my sad little overnight bag, hitched up my pants to cross my legs and tried not to look too demoralized beneath the smirk of framed posters. Time passed, phones rang, carpets sighed, someone whispered around a corner.

"Dylan?"

"Yes?"

I dropped *Men's Journal* and a boy in a sharp-creased suit took my hand. "You're the music guy – right?"

"Right."

"I'm Mike. Great to see you. Jared's just ending a call."

We moved to Mike's little office, an intermediate space, a staging area, apparently, for encounters with Jared. You had to meet Cats-in-the-Hat-A-through-Z before you got to the One True Cat. At least we were all on a first-name basis.

"Mike?" said an intercom voice.

"Yes."

"I'm ready for Dylan."

Mike gave me a thumbs-up endorsement to cross Jared's threshold, and a wink for luck.

The room had earth tones to spare. No posters here, nothing jarring – it was like a shrink's office. Sunlight sliced through a couple of potted rubber trees, to ornament the carpet. Jared launched from behind his desk. He was jacketless, blond, thick and soft and relaxed in his body, a gym junkie, I guessed. I'd have kicked his ass at stoopball, though.

A conclave with Jared Orthman was meant to be the next best thing to an audience with Geffenberg himself. A thousand or a million writers hungered for what I had today. I hoped not to blow it, not so much on their behalf as on that of my own shriveled prospects and swollen debt.

"Here, let's sit here." He guided me away from the desk, to a pair of facing love seats across the room, the pitch zone. I dropped my bag, which sagged like a Claes Oldenburg sculpture, seeming to stand for an artist's impotence in corporate surroundings. I wished I'd packed my Discman and change of underwear in something more like a briefcase. We sat, smiled, crossed legs.

Jared frowned. "Did you get water? Did they give you water?" he asked anxiously.

"I left it outside."

"Do you want something? Water?" He looked ready to provide the vital essence if he had to wring it from stones.

"I'm fine, thanks."

"So." He smiled, frowned, widened his hands. We studied one another and tried to remain friendly. Jared and I were probably the same age but otherwise had traveled from opposite ends of the universe to this meeting. My black jeans were like a smudge of ash or daub of vomit in this cream-and-peach world.

"I'm a friend of Randolph's," I reminded him. "From the *Weekly*."

"Riiight." He nodded, considering it. "Just . . . who is Randolph?"

"Randolph Treadwell? The *Weekly*?"

He nodded. "I think I know who you mean."

"Well, he, uh, set this up."

"Okay. Okay. So, uh, what are you doing in my office?"

"Sorry?" The question was so bald. I was astonished as if he'd asked *Why do I hold this job, as opposed to, say, anyone else? Can you explain that, please?*

"Just a minute," he said, holding up one finger and springing from the love seat. He leaned over his desk and pushed a button. "Mike?"

"Yes."

"What's Dylan doing in my office?"

"He's the music guy."

"The music guy."

"You remember. He's got a movie."

"Ahhhh." Now Jared turned and smiled at me. This was all pleasure. A movie! How perfectly unexpected. "Who's Randy Treadmill or something?" he said to the intercom.

"He's that guy you met when you were talking about the thing." Click, buzz. "On the boat."

"*Ahhhh.* Okay. Okay." He released the intercom. There was a hierarchy of remembering here, I understood. Mike remembered for Jared the sort of things Jared had once remembered for someone else, on his way up through the ranks. Someday Mike would have someone remembering things for him as well, and be free to abandon the skill.

Jared returned to the love seat and again pointed a finger at me, but now it was a happier finger.

"You've got a *movie,*" he said warmly.

"Yes."

"I've been wanting to hear this." He didn't know the first thing about it, I saw now. I could have offered him a comedy about a rookie vibraphonist for the Boston Pops, or a thriller about a spy who kills by ultrasonic whistle, any of the many things a *music guy* would be likely to concern himself with.

"I'm closing my eyes," said Jared. "It means I'm listening."

I was left to consider his tanned lids, immaculate desk, twin rubber tree plants. I was the ant who had to move them, apparently.

"Your movie is about—?" This was a just-because-my-eyes-are-closed-doesn't-mean-there's-no-hurry situation.

"A true story," I said.

"Okay."

"In Tennessee—"

"Tennessee?" Jared opened his eyes.

"Yes."

"What happened in Tennessee?"

I started again. "In the fifties, in Tennessee, there was this singing group called the Prisonaires. Because they were in prison. But they had a career anyway. They recorded at Sun Records, where Elvis Presley was discovered. That's the name of the movie – *The Prisonaires*."

"Did you know that both my parents came here from Tennessee?" He made it sound like Crimea, or Mars. "Or is that just some kind of coincidence?"

"I didn't know."

"Okay. Okay. Wild. What's it called?"

"*The Prisonaires*."

"Okay, tell me again."

"Let me set it up." I'd been advised to "talk in scenes." "I'd want to start the movie inside the prison. The lead Prisonaire is a guy named Johnny Bragg. He's the songwriter, the lead singer. He's been in jail for years, since he was sixteen. On trumped-up charges. So he and another convict are out in the yard, walking, in the rain, literally, and one says to the other. 'Here we are, walking in the rain, I wonder what the little girls are doing?' And Johnny Bragg starts singing the line, a mournful little song, 'Just Walkin' in the Rain.' Which became their first hit. Maybe it could be playing over the opening credits."

"That reminds me of something else."

"You're probably thinking of 'Singing in the Rain.'"

"Oh yeah, sure. He wrote *that*?"

"Different song."

"Okay, let me get this: he's wrongfully imprisoned. What's the charge?"

"Well, actually it was six convictions for rape. Six ninety-nine-year sentences, with no possibility of parole."

"Ouch."

"The cops set him up. He was an arrogant, good-looking kid, and they had it in for him. They pinned a bunch of unsolved rapes on him."

"Brad Pitt, Matthew McConaughey."

"I forgot to say black."

"These are *black people*?"

"Yes."

"Okay." Jared waved his hands, reluctantly brushing Pitt from the room. "Start again with black people. How does he get out of jail?"

"Well, he doesn't. I mean, he does later, but not right away. He starts a singing group in jail, prison, the Prisonaires. That's the gimmick – they're still in prison. They're let out for recording sessions and live performances."

"I don't get it. In or out?"

"That's the movie. The Prisonaires were so famous in Tennessee that the governor was under pressure from both sides – to free them, to keep them locked up as an example. A few got pardons, but Bragg was still locked inside. It's a great story, full of dramatic highs and lows."

"You're freaking me out."

"I am?"

"Because we don't make movies with dramatic highs and lows."

"Sorry?"

"Just kidding, man."

It was becoming possible I'd pitch *myself* across the gap between our love seats and throttle Jared.

"Look, if I could just describe it without any interruptions I think I could make you see."

"Dylan, that's not nice."

"It's just – I'm dying to tell you this story."

"I *like* you, mister."

I waited until it was clear he had nothing to add, then said, "Thank you."

"Five minutes." He spread his fingers to show me *five*, then stretched back and closed his eyes again.

"The Prisonaires are one of the great unknown stories in pop-culture history," I said. The language was dead on my tongue, but I blundered on. "Five black guys in prison in the 1950s, some serving hundred-year sentences, some on briefer stretches, all victims of prejudice and economic injustice in the Jim Crow South. Five jailbirds who form a singing group just for the love of the music. But they're so good they sing themselves into an audition. The warden issues special passes just so they can visit Sun Studios – this is in 1953, the same point when a weird little kid named Elvis Presley is hanging around Sun, trying to get a session. But the star of the movie is Johnny Bragg, the lead singer, the lead Prisonaire. When Bragg was sixteen he got railroaded – a woman with a grudge, maybe jealous because he was playing the field, called the cops on him. She screamed rape. And the white cops pinned six convictions on him, just to clear their books. Six unsolved cases, wham. Johnny Bragg gets six hundred years in prison." Nearly everything I had was cribbed out of Colin Escott's liner notes from the Prisonaires CD, or fantasized out of my own musings on a handful of newspaper clippings I'd unearthed myself. But it was enough. I was beginning to inspire myself, to remember what I'd had in mind in the first place, the screenplay I ought to have been researching and writing for the past year. "On the early-morning bus ride to Sun Studios Bragg looks out his window and sees an empty drive-in movie theater, and he says 'Wow, look at that crazy cemetery.' He's twenty-six – been in prison for ten years."

"Bad deal," mused Jared.

"So they record. Cut a single, two sides. Elvis Presley is *there*. In the studio, hanging around. Just a kid they tolerate around the place. He and Bragg make friends, this is all true, by the way. Great chance for a cameo, like when Val Kilmer plays Elvis in *Mystery Train*."

"Never saw it."

"It's okay, not great. Anyway, Bragg and the Prisonaires cut a record, two sides, and go back to the joint. End of story, right? Except the song, 'Just Walkin' in the Rain,' is a hit. A big hit, people calling in requests to radio stations. Meanwhile, the Prisonaires are back inside. They don't have radios, they don't know, but then they start getting letters in the prison, letters from strangers. They're becoming stars. And the prison officials start getting involved. You've got the warden on the phone to the governor, everybody trying to figure out how to handle this thing, whether to encourage it, how to spin the story."

Jared nodded and rocked slightly, seeming to approve, perhaps envisioning white actors in supporting roles, Gene Hackman, Martin Landau, Geoffrey Rush.

"The authorities decide to go the liberal route, and claim the Prisonaires as a sterling example of rehabilitation. They start letting them out to make radio appearances, do live shows, cut more sides at Sun. There's a lot of sentiment building up, people calling for pardons. Not least the Prisonaires themselves – they cut a song extolling the governor, called 'Frank Clement, He's a Mighty Man.' Basically just a raw bid for mercy. Not every-body's happy though. The same heavy dudes that set Bragg up in the first place haven't forgotten him. They're biding their time, waiting for the Prisonaires to stumble. When the gov-ernor's up for reelection things start getting interesting. These guys are becoming a political football. You can just picture the racial politics involved."

"I'm thinking KKK, that's what I'm thinking."

"Uh, yeah. Just about. The thing about Tennessee in the fifties, Jared, is that the Klan didn't always necessarily wear a hood." I was winging it here. But that was okay. The facts would surely have to be bent to make a movie. This was what I'd come here to do: bend these facts into Hollywood's ear. "So the governor's under pressure on both sides, he's been encour-aging these boys, raising their hopes. He begins making plans to release the Prisonaires, talking about them on the radio, milking it for publicity. And his Republican opponent is work-ing the other angle, turning it into a scare story. 'The good citizens of Tennessee better hope that not all of its convicted killers can sing' – shit like that."

"Wow. This is good stuff."

"Let me describe one scene for you. I see this as a real cen-terpiece. There are photographs of a Prisonaires show from just before the first pardons – remember, these guys have families, they've left women behind, and the only time they get out is onstage. They can't *mingle*. There's probably armed guards at the edge of the stage, that sort of thing. These pictures, I should have brought them along, they'll blow your mind, Jared." By force of will I was leveraging the Prisonaires' reality, their sweat and pain and love, into this pallid room, into Jared's pallid mind. I'd make it stick, here where nothing stuck. I understood now that I was born for pitching. I had only to be let into the room. "It's like the Beatles at Shea Stadium, Jared. Or Elvis. Women weeping, breaking down. But these aren't just a bunch of teenage girls. They're the Prisonaires' mothers, *grand*mothers, aunts, girlfriends holding babies. They're falling apart, tearing up handkerchiefs, crawling on the floor while these guys sing. The music is so beautiful, it's just tearing people's hearts out. Maybe you'd even have the girl who set Johnny Bragg up, probably she'd be there too. She's sorry for what she did, she's still in love. And she's in this crowd of women, just falling to *pieces*."

"Holy shit."

"That's just half of it. When this crying wave hits the audience, the Prisonaires lose it too. They try to go on singing but they can't. They're separated from these women, from their *mothers*, everyone, by the distance of the stage. And they start bawling too. They're clinging to each other, clinging to microphones and chairs. Trying to reach out, but the guards push them back. It's like, I don't know, like *Guernica*, Jared. It's a scene you don't forget."

"I can really see this." Jared sounded astonished at his own powers of visualization.

"Of course you can. Okay, so, back up: the governor. He's getting reports on this stuff. He's riding a tiger and he's afraid it's going to eat him alive. So he springs a couple of the guys. His opponents are roasting him alive, but he springs them anyway. And that's when a plan emerges. The governor's got a crafty little aide, a Kissinger type, who suggests they leave Johnny Bragg inside. Bragg's the one carrying the heavy sentence, and he's the songwriter, the lead voice – the genius. Split the band away from him and maybe the story can be allowed to die out."

"No."

"It's horrible, but *yes*. That's how they play it. They pardon *all four* of the other Prisonaires, one by one. Everybody's waiting for Bragg to come out and join them. Looks like a happy ending, but it's too good to be true. The governor's enemies on the right have him in a box. So he makes a show of being tough on crime by leaving Bragg inside. The warden cuts off

his privileges. The hope is that without the music, this thing is
destined to blow over."

"*Jee*sus."

Jesus, yes. Where was I unearthing *this* crap? I was pitching
the Oliver Stone version.

"But Bragg doesn't quit making music. With all his Prisonaires on the outside, he forms a new prison group, the
Marigolds. Years are going by here, you understand. They're
squeezing the life out of this man. In '56 Johnnie Ray records
a cover of 'Just Walkin' in the Rain,' and Bragg gets a check in
prison for fourteen hundred dollars – he tells them just to put it
in the commissary, he thinks it's for *fourteen* dollars. He's never
seen so much money in his life. But he's got no way to spend it.
The Marigolds record a few numbers for Excello Records, but
nothing really hits."

"What's with *Marigolds*?"

"There was a craze for flower groups, the Clovers, the Posies,
stuff like that. Just like everybody had to be bugs a few years
later – the Crickets, the Beatles."

"Ah."

"Bragg doesn't get parole until '59, *six years* after the Prisonaires' first hit. And then he only lasts a year before they set
him up for another fall. He's charged with robbery and attempted murder – for stealing *two dollars and fifty cents*. Pathetic. White
women come forward again, claiming he tried to attack them.
He's a magnet for these kinds of accusations. It's classic race
panic, and Bragg's this symbol that pushes everyone's buttons.
The man must have had some kind of presence, some pride
when he walked down the street, that these white authorities
couldn't abide. They just had to put him back inside, it was
their way of coping."

"I don't know if you'll like this but I'm totally picturing
Denzel Washington."

"Listen: that year Elvis Presley, fresh out of the army,
detours his trip home to visit the state prison to hang out with
Bragg. Picture it, the same weird little kid who was hanging
around the studio admiring the Prisonaires' harmonies is now
the biggest entertainer on the *planet*. And he remembers Bragg,
it *matters* to Elvis. The thirty-year-old black con and the King.

The visit gets publicity, but only for Elvis. No one remembers Bragg's case anymore, and the Prisonaires are a distant memory. Elvis offers to pay for a lawyer, but Bragg says it's okay, he's cut a deal. There's nothing on paper, no proof, but Bragg's promised the warden not to push the case to the Supreme Court in return for a promise he'd be out in nine months."

I paused, then, to set it up.

"Yeah?"

"They kept him another *seven years*."

"You're killing me, Dylan."

"It goes on and on. In the sixties he re-forms the Prisonaires again, this time with a white guy in the group – it's the era of integration now. But the other prisoners don't like it, he gets attacked in the yard. Later he gets out again and marries a white woman, and the cops arrest him for walking down the street with her—"

"Stop, okay? Stop. Don't tell me any more."

Jared had been growing steadily more agitated for some time, and now he sprang from his seat, bugged his eyes, and paced to the desk.

"Is something the matter?"

"Everything's great, Dylan. It's just – who else knows about this?"

"You're the first." I assumed this was the answer Jared had to hear. Needless to say, the Prisonaires story had only been sitting around for thirty-odd years, waiting to be plucked up. It didn't belong to me. For all I knew another writer was turning in a polished third draft of his version in the office next door.

I dared ask, "You like it?"

"Are you kidding? It's pure dynamite. I'm just thinking, okay? I've got to think. This is Friday, right?"

"Uh, yeah."

"Okay, practically speaking, that means I'm not going to find anybody until Monday."

"I'm not sure I understand."

"Where are you going from here?"

I suspected *ForbiddenCon* wasn't a reply Jared would easily make sense of. It wasn't that easy for me to make sense of myself. "Back to my hotel."

"Don't shit me."

"I'm not."

"Because a part of me, wow, a part of me doesn't want to let you out of my office until I know what we're doing with this, until I get *something* from you that I can take into a meeting and a promise you'll give me a couple of days from the weekend. Forty-eight hours at least. Do you want a tissue, mister?"

"Sure." I'd tear-streaked my face, evoking Johnny Bragg's dilemma. I wonder how many of Jared's pitches wept in this office. Maybe all of us, by the end.

Jared plopped his tissue box on my love seat, then leaned over his desk, onto the intercom.

"Mike?"

"Yes?"

"Mike, I just heard something *great*. This is what I'm always telling you – you never know how it's going to happen. Some boat-guy's friend just walks into my office and it's this writer Dylan and Dylan has something really great, really *really* great."

"That's incredible," said Mike.

"No, it's *really* incredible."

"Wow."

"Mike, I need Dylan's agent *right now*."

"Sure."

Jared turned from the desk. "I know this is moving fast but I just want to say, Dylan, you and I are going to be putting our kids through college on this."

"Okay." I blew my nose.

"If I can't make this movie I'm going to kill myself."

"I guess that means you have to make the movie."

"That's exactly what it means. Holy shit." He was amazed at himself, understandably. Large events were occurring, and he was at their center. "I need something on paper."

"I don't have much written down," I bluffed.

"I need to be able to explain. I have to make other people get it. I need something on paper, like what you said. What you said was so amazing. It has to be like that."

"It wouldn't take long."

"You're saying there's *nothing*?"

"Not yet."

"This is bad, Dylan. I really, really need this so I can make someone else see."

The intercom clicked. "Jared?"

"What?"

"I don't have an agent for Dylan."

"I thought I told you always to get contact information. You remember me telling you that?"

"It's my fault," I stage-whispered, wanting to protect Mike. Jared released the intercom. "I'm not into games," he said.

"Neither am I. Just let me call my agent first, okay?" I had no agent, nor the remotest notion where I'd begin looking for one. "He doesn't actually know a lot about this whole thing."

"If you think I'm letting you walk out of my office with this movie in your head you're *crazy*. I need something from you, Dylan. Don't screw me, man. This is my movie. I *feel* this one."

"It's great," I said, holding up my hands, hoping to slow the madness. "We're both excited. Just tell me what should happen next."

"Call your agent from here."

"What?"

He held up both hands. "Sit at my desk. I promise I won't listen. I'll go out in the hall." He paced madly. "Just sit and call him from here."

"I—"

"I'm giving you my office, man. Go. Sit."

There was no refusing. I took his chair. He shut himself out in Mike's antechamber, first pointing at me from behind the half-closed door. "Tell him I'm holding you hostage until I have something I can take into a meeting."

"Okay."

When he'd sealed the door I dialed my home number. It rang through to the machine, of course. Abby was at school. I hung up without leaving a message, then retrieved my address book and rang Randolph Treadwell at the *Weekly*. I got him.

"Help," I said.

"You had the meeting?"

"I'm *in* the meeting. He left the room so I could call my agent, only I don't have an agent. I'm at his desk."

"Interesting." Randolph's voice was neutral.

"Is Jared always so, uh, volatile?"

"I don't really know him that well. Why?"

"He's seems to think we're about to have a baby together. A solid-gold baby."

"That's the way these things go," said Randolph, unimpressed. "It's sort of like a faucet. If it's on, it gushes. Now you have to keep it open."

"Thanks for the advice."

"You want to come by the office after this? How long are you in town?"

"I have to go see my dad, in Anaheim."

"What's he doing in Anaheim?"

Jared barreled through the door. "I gotta go." I hung up the phone.

"What's the ending?" said Jared.

"Sorry?"

"I was trying to do it for Mike, the whole thing, the black guys, the jail, Elvis. And I forgot if you told me the ending."

"I . . . think we didn't get to the ending," I said carefully.

"And?"

"Well, Johnny Bragg was in and out of prison a couple more times, I think. He made music whenever he could. No big hits, though."

"The Prisonaires?"

"They died, I think."

"Could we have, like, a big *comeback*?"

I shrugged a *why not?* I couldn't bring myself to pronounce the words, though. Was there any aspect of Johnny Bragg's story I hadn't dishonored by my pitch? What further harm would a little comeback bring? Or a big one?

"What about Elvis? Elvis is really important to this whole thing. That was a really great part, when Elvis visits and you were crying, remember?"

Maybe Elvis could return and bust the warden in the jaw, then personally break Bragg out of prison. Or the two of them, Bragg and Presley, could be shackled together at the ankles and sent to break up rocks. The singing would be amazing, anyway.

"Well, the story doesn't really have a big ending," I said. "It just sort of goes on and on. I'm sure we can figure out a good place to end it, though. Maybe Johnny Bragg walking through the gates, a free man. The last time."

"It has to be good."

"It can be good."

"Do they catch the guys who really did it?"

"Did what?"

"You know, killed all those women."

"There aren't any dead women. There wasn't a big legal showdown or anything. Eventually he was just old and they stopped picking on him, I guess."

"How old?"

I'd wondered when this might come up. "He might even still be alive," I said. At the time of Colin Escott's liner note, nine years ago, Johnny Bragg was still alive and giving interviews. His anecdotes were the source for half my pitch. For years I'd been planning a visit to Memphis to try and interview him myself. That visit waited, with so many other speculative projects, for an entity like Dreamworks to bankroll. Anyway, that was my excuse.

"*Alive?*"

"It's possible."

"*Possible?*"

Yes! Alive! Possible! I wanted to scream. "He'd be in his seventies."

"You don't know?"

"I'll find out."

"This is a serious problem, Dylan." Jared raked his hand through his hair and frowned, under stress I couldn't possibly understand. "Can I have my desk back, please?"

"What do you want me to do?" I asked as we swapped places.

Scowling, he settled back, crossed his legs, and with two fingers kneaded the bridge of his nose and then the periphery of his jaw. He appeared to be recovering from a sort of bender, *coming down* as after an orgasm or a hit of crack. I wondered how often he indulged.

"You just came in here and pitched me someone's life story, a living person," he said, not angrily, but with deep regret. "Well, we'd have to option life rights. That can get *really* sticky."

"He'd want it told," I suggested.

"Yeah, yeah, of course. I don't know about the ending, though, Dylan. I'm not happy about that ending."

He spoke as though *The Prisonaires* was already filmed and edited and he'd just screened it and been disappointed. Now we were left with the sorry task of mopping up, cutting our losses. "It's so vague, he gets out, he goes back, the band never reunites. And I kept expecting something to happen with that woman, the one in the audience, you know? The crying one."

Inescapably, absurdly, I fell to the same tone. "I guess we could end it sooner. After the first parole."

"Oh, I doubt that would work."

"Okay," I said, helpless.

"Listen, I don't want to – I don't want to tell anyone about this thing until we pull it together. It should be *perfect*. A slam dunk. You and I should both think really hard about the third-act problems and do *nothing* until we've cracked them. If I bring this upstairs I want it to be airtight, you know?"

"That makes sense."

"Did you talk to your agent?"

"He, uh, feels the same way, actually."

"Of course he does. He knows how these things work."

"So—" I was baffled. "What happens next?"

"The question is what *you* do next. This is all in *your* hands."

"Uh, okay."

"I'm not easily discouraged, you know. I believe in you, mister."

"Thanks."

"There's nothing wrong with taking some time, by the way. This isn't going anywhere. It'll happen when it's meant to happen."

"Okay."

"So, do you have a driver? Because I need to have you out of my office now."

"I can call—"

"Yes, but use Mike's phone."

In the middle chamber I handed Nicholas Brawley's card to Mike and asked him to call.

"Jared was really knocked out," Mike whispered, eyes wide at what I'd accomplished inside.

"I think he'll recover," I said.

I waited with my overnight bag in the shady lot for a long fifteen minutes before Nicholas Brawley's cab pulled up again at the gate. The man with the Oscar never came back. Brawley's radio was still tuned to MEGA 100, and the station was broadcasting my old nemesis of a theme song, Wild Cherry's "Play That Funky Music." Of course, the thirty-five-year-old rock critic knew what the thirteen-year-old scrap of prey on the sidewalks outside Intermediate School 293 never did: Wild Cherry was a bunch of *white guys*. The tune which had been enlisted as an indictment of my teenage existence was in fact a Midwestern rock band's rueful self-parody. I'd wondered many times since then whether knowing would have helped. Probably not. Anyway, it struck me now in a different light, as being yet another bit of personal meaning which had been taken from me, stripped off like clothes I'd only borrowed or stolen. I had maybe the least persuasive case for self-pity of any human soul on the planet. Or anyway, the most hilarious.

CHAPTER 3

ABRAHAM AND FRANCESCA stood together in the lobby of the Anaheim Marriott, still as sculpture. All around them the lobby boiled with arrivals, misshapen travelers clad in black and purple, peering nervously side to side as though concerned with the impression they made as they wheeled suitcases in agitated confusion to the check-in desk. Others lurched or darted through the vast open space of the lobby, gathering briefly in groups of four or five to hug and talk, to crinkle brochures with circled program items, or present one another with buttons or ribbons to affix to suspenders or knapsack straps. Some wolfed sandwiches, licking gummy fingers unselfconsciously. Many wore plastic-frame eyeglasses or floppy hats or molded jewelry, others T-shirts with proud enigmas emblazoned: MORE THAN HUMAN, DONATE YOUR BODY TO SCIENCE FICTION, I USED TO BE A MILLIONAIRE THEN MY MOTHER THREW OUT MY COMIC BOOK COLLECTION. Photocopied signs, taped inelegantly to corridors and glass doors, offered suite numbers for hotel parties, advertised special events, and directed attendees to the registration table or the art show or the first aid station. Certain laminated name badges were labeled PRO or VOLUNTEER. Voices rose and were lost in a babble of others – monotonous harangues, kooky laughter, anxious questions, hysterical reunions. Forbidden-Con 7 was under way in all its glory. I only had to figure out what it was, or else not bother. I didn't sense it needed me to know.

Francesca saw me first. "There you are!" she cried out. Abraham nodded and they surged toward me as I came through the revolving door. I hurried forward, trying to save them the trouble. "You're late!" said Francesca. "We're practically going to miss Abe's *panel*."

I'd promised to meet them in the lobby at three – it was almost four. Nicholas Brawley had laughed and shaken his head when I gave him the destination. "You should have rented a car," he said, and by the time we'd crossed the ocean of suburb between Hollywood and Anaheim I saw his point. The fare was $114.00. Now, however, stepping into the lobby of the convention hotel, I considered the even greater conceptual distance I'd covered, moving from Jared Orthman's office to ForbiddenCon. Brawley's fare was a bargain.

"Dylan," said my father. We embraced, and I felt him sigh against my body. Then I turned and dipped to Francesca, just in time to be enveloped in her swarming attack, not soon enough to plan where on my exposed surface the lipstick would be delivered. It landed north-northwest of my mouth, a misaligned mustache in beet purple. I swabbed it with my thumb and said, "Sorry I'm late."

Francesca's badge was unadorned, while Abraham's bore a special purple ribbon, reading GUEST OF HONOR.

"They need Abraham in the greenroom," she said gravely.

"Lead the way," I said.

"That's all you have?" said Abraham, looking at my bag. He seemed disappointed. "You're staying the night?"

"Of course."

"You're registered already," said Francesca. "Zelmo took care of everything." She scrabbled in her purse as we moved through the lobby. "Here's for your room. It works like a credit card – you *swipe*. The key's for the minibar."

"I'll be hitting it hard," I joked, taking the keys.

"Oh, you won't have time," said Francesca. "Zelmo Swift, the committee chair, is taking us to dinner." She goggled her eyes at the honor.

"He knows you're coming," added Abraham. "I asked and was told it's fine."

"You're being foolish, darling," said Francesca. "You're the guest of honor, why wouldn't your family be invited?"

"It's an extra body at dinner. I asked." He turned to me. "We'll talk there if Zelmo lets us get in a word. Now I have to do this thing. I hope you won't mind sitting."

"Mind?" said Francesca, taking my arm. "He'll be proud!"

My father had lived alone for fourteen years after I left Dean Street for college in Vermont. Little changed in those years – he'd gone on painting paperback-book art to cover his mortgage and shopping, and gone on pouring every spare hour on the clock and spare ounce of energy in his frame into his epic, endless, unseen film. In 1989, at last granting the absurdity of having three floors to himself, he'd converted the brownstone to two duplexes, adding a small kitchen to the second floor and renting out the parlor level, with the basement, to a young family. What remained untouched was the upstairs studio, the monk's quarters where he daubed out days in black paint on celluloid. The neighborhood, in fits and starts, gentrified around him, Isabel Vendle's curse or blessing realized in lag time. For Abraham it was primarily a matter of raised property taxes. He'd never asked what the rental market would bear – the duplex was always leased at a bargain.

There were never women, that I heard of. If Abraham knew how to seek for that part of his life, after Rachel, he didn't know how to mention it. Then he'd come to the attention of Francesca Cassini, a fifty-eight-year-old receptionist working in the offices of Ballantine Books. This man slumping into the offices with his latest jacket art tucked into a pebbly black pressed-board portfolio tied together with black laces, this man slumping from the elevator dressed humbly, in his Art Students League proletarian garb, fingertips slightly stained with paint, his demeanor mordant, as ever – this man had caught the eye of the fresh widow from Bay Ridge. A woman who, despite her immigrant's name, had lived all her life among the postwar generation of New York Jews, Francesca spoke in their manner and recognized them as one recognizes oneself. She'd lost a Jewish husband six months earlier, a career accountant, a man bent, I imagined, over a lifelong column of figures likely as dear to him as the world's longest abstract film in progress was to my father. Abraham, jacket-art celebrity, butt of corridor jokes for his Bartelbyesque mien, didn't stand a chance. If ever a man cried for Francesca's salvaging, here he was. She'd announced herself. She'd attached herself. One winter I visited Brooklyn and there she was, moved into the Dean Street house. I couldn't complain. Francesca organized my father, and she seemed, in a peculiar way, to make him happy. She made him visible to himself, by her contrast.

The greenroom had been set up in a small conference room off the lobby, guarded from the ordinary public by a volunteer at the door. In breathless tones Francesca explained we were a guest of honor's entourage, and we were allowed into the sanctum. It held two urns containing coffee and water for tea, and a sectioned plastic dish full of cubed cheddar and Triscuits. A pair of volunteers sat behind a tray of blank badges and their plastic holders. From them Francesca demanded a pass "for Abraham Ebdus's son," then clipped the result to my shirt pocket.

It wasn't clear what we were waiting for. My father stood, stalled in consternation, in the center of the room, while Francesca dithered around the edges.

"Mr. Ebdus?" ventured a volunteer.

"Yes?"

"The other program participants went upstairs. For your panel. I think it's beginning now."

"*Without* him?" said Francesca.

"The Nebraska Room, I think. Nebraska West."

We hurried out. "I told you we could go direct," said Abraham to Francesca as we went up the wide central stair to the mezzanine.

"Zelmo said meet at the greenroom."

Abraham just shook his head.

Everyone moved awkwardly in this space, drifting as though rudderless, then abruptly accelerating, in explosions of tiny steps. Crossing paths they'd glare, mutter, wait for apologies. Through this fitful human sea we made our way to Nebraska Ballroom West. A sign taped to the door announced the program as "The Career of Abraham Ebdus," as though this were self-explanatory. I supposed it was, or would be by the time the panel accomplished its work.

We entered at the back of the room. At the front, four figures already occupied the elevated dais, behind table microphones and sweating pitchers of ice water. The dais was covered in maroon bunting which matched the acoustic padding of the ballroom's walls and the thin upholstery of the stackable chairs that were arranged in rows, wall to wall. A crowd of perhaps fifty or sixty sat, attentive and respectful, scratching, coughing, crossing and uncrossing legs, wrinkling papers.

"Good of Abraham to honor us with his presence," said one of the panelists into his microphone, with heavy sarcasm. It drew a burst of relieved laughter from the audience, then a scattering of applause.

"Up," egged Francesca, and my father obeyed. She and I took seats at the aisle, Francesca clutching my arm in her excitement.

The moderator, who'd wisecracked at our entry into the room, was a balding, sixtyish man, distinguishable at this distance from Abraham himself primarily by a garish blue ascot. He introduced himself as Sidney Blumlein, formerly art director for Ballantine, and if not exactly Abraham Ebdus's discoverer then at least his main employer and patron during what he called *the crucial first decade* of my father's work. "I've also been his apologist for longer than he'd want me to remind you," Blumlein continued. "I'm not ashamed to say I protected his art from editorial meddling a dozen times, two dozen. And I talked Abe out of refusing his first Hugo." Another warm chuckle from the crowd. "But truly, it was always an honor."

The others introduced themselves: first Buddy Green, who blinked through thick glasses and couldn't have been more than eighteen or nineteen, editor of an online zine called *Ebdus Collector*, dedicated to the purchase of the rare original painted boards of my father's designs. I'd blundered across Green's Web site a few times, Googling the name Ebdus to search my own archived journalism. Next was R. Fred Vundane, a tiny, withered man in a Vandyke beard and mad-scientist glasses, author of twenty-eight novels, including *Neural Circus*, the very first for which my father had painted a jacket. Then Paul Pflug, another paperback painter, a fiftyish biker-type, fat in leather pants, with a blond ponytail and eyes concealed by dark wraparounds. Pflug seated himself at the far edge of the dais, leaving an empty chair and unfilled water glass between himself and Vundane.

The tributes and anecdotes weren't so terribly interesting that I couldn't mostly study my father and his reactions. I didn't recall ever seeing him this way, onstage, at a distance, held in a collective gaze. The result was a kind of nakedness I realized now he'd always avoided. Green spoke gushingly in a high whine, claiming Ebdus as the successor in a line of science-fiction illustrators from Virgil Finlay through Richard Powers

– names which meant less than nothing to me – and it was evident Abraham took pleasure in it, however masochistically. Vundane spoke with aggrieved vanity – perhaps he yearned for a panel on "The Works of Vundane" – about Ebdus's deep and uncommon insight into the surrealist nature of his, Vundane's, writing. And when Pflug's turn came he reminisced, gruffly, about meeting my father at the beginning of his career, and claimed Abraham's seriousness, his regard for standards, as an example which had altered the course of his, Pflug's, career.

Abraham didn't speak, just nodded as the others alternated on the microphones. But his distaste for whatever it was Vundane and Pflug had accomplished – or failed to – was painfully obvious. For that matter, it was unmistakable that *nobody* on the dais liked Pflug. I wondered how he'd come to be invited.

"I've told this story many times," said Buddy Green. "I was trying to trace the provenance of the original art for the Belmont Specials – his first seventeen paintings. They weren't in the hands of any of the major collectors. They weren't in the hands of any of the minor collectors. Unfortunately, they weren't in *my* hands. I kept writing to the Belmont people and they said they didn't know what I was talking about. I thought they were *stonewalling*. So, being a little slow on the uptake, it finally occurred to me to ask Abraham. And he explained, like it was no big deal, that he *destroyed* them. He couldn't imagine anyone cared."

Abraham's eyes scoured the crowd, looking for me, I permitted myself to imagine. I wondered how it felt to hear those called *his first seventeen paintings*.

"It's true," said Sidney Blumlein, with great avuncular gusto. "When I hired him away from Belmont, Abe was *systematically* destroying the work."

This drew oohs and aahs, a kind of titillated awe from the crowd.

"This man is the only one your father respects," whispered Francesca. "None of the others. Not even Zelmo."

"Zelmo?"

"The chair. I mean, of the whole convention. You'll meet him at dinner. He's a very important lawyer."

"Ah."

Now the microphone was retaken by Blumlein, whom Francesca had claimed as Abraham's only friend on the panel. Being moderator, Blumlein took it upon himself to prize open the jaws of the clam – to find a way to force Abraham Ebdus to acknowledge and address his admirers.

"For more than two decades Abe has graced our field, and I do mean graced. All well and good. But at this time of celebration there's no reason to pussyfoot around the question – he's done so at a remove. His background isn't science fiction, and in that he's an exception from the vast majority of professionals at this gathering, at *any* gathering in our field. We're fans, our interests begin in the pulp-magazine tradition, however we might like to hope we've elevated it."

Pflug sneered. Vundane took a pitcher and topped off his untouched glass.

The audience was stilled, silenced from its murmurs of approval and recognition, perhaps less certain now that everything they were hearing fell safely in the vein of an Elk Lodge testimonial dinner.

"Abraham Ebdus, let's not kid ourselves, had no interest in *elevating* it. He was looking to make a buck to support his art – what he regarded as his real art. As perhaps some of you, perhaps *many* of you may know, Abe is a filmmaker, an *experimental* filmmaker, of terrific seriousness and devotion. This is how he spends his days, when he's not painting jackets for books. It has nothing to do with science fiction. What's miraculous – what we're all here to celebrate – is that being a *real* artist, one of depth and profundity, Abe brought to the books a visionary intensity that *did* elevate. That contained beauty and strangeness. Because he couldn't help himself."

I saw how well Sidney Blumlein knew my father. He was urging Abraham into the weird light of this roomful of celebrants, baiting him with the possibility of an audience *worth* addressing. I didn't know whether I wanted him to succeed.

"This is what, Abe? Only your fifth or sixth time at a convention?"

My father hunched, seeming to wish he could reply with his shoulders. Finally he leaned into the microphone and said, "I haven't counted."

"I first dragged you to a LunaCon, in New York, in the early eighties. You weren't happy."

"No, it wasn't to my taste," said Abraham reluctantly.

The crowd tittered.

"And wouldn't it be fair to say, Abe, you rarely if ever read the books under your jackets?"

Now a collective gasp.

"Oh, I've never done," said Abraham. "I say it without apology. Mr. Vundane, your book, what was the title?"

"*Neural Circus*," supplied R. Fred Vundane, his jaw so clenched it mashed the vowels.

"Yes, *Neural Circus*. I was always stopped by that title. It seemed, I'm sorry, vaguely distasteful to me. You speak of surrealists – I suppose you mean the poets. It feels a very poor shade of symbolist imagery, actually. Rimbaud, maybe? No, I was asked to envision other worlds, and I did. Any congruence with the work is happenstance."

I'd read R. Fred's book. I recalled a troupe of genetically altered acrobats residing in a hollowed asteroid.

Blumlein rode in to the rescue now, perhaps pitying Vundane, who'd shrunk even smaller in his chair. "This is just an example, I think, of the wider context, the *erudition*, that Abe brings to what he touches. In our field he's a comet streaking past, whom we've managed to lure into our orbit. A fellow traveler, like a Stanley Kubrick or a Stanislaw Lem. He disdains our vocabulary even as he reinvents it to suit his own impulses."

"I have to interrupt, Sidney, to say you're overstating the value of what I do." Here was a subject to rouse Abraham's passion. "You throw names, Kubrick, Lem. And Mr. Green, god bless him, throws Virgil Finlay, whom I've never had the good fortune to encounter. Let *me* throw a few names. Ernst, Tanguy, Matta, Kandinsky. Once in a while, the early Pollock or Rothko. If I've accomplished one thing, it's been to give a rough education in contemporary painting, or what was contemporary painting in 1950. The intersection of late surrealism and early abstract expressionism. Period. It's derivative, every last brushstroke. All quoted. Nothing to do with outer space, nothing *remotely*. Honestly, if you people hadn't put such a seal on yourselves, if you'd visit a museum even once, you'd know you're celebrating a second-rate *thief*."

"You stopped at pop art?" asked Blumlein.

"Please. You have Mr. Pflug for that. That's all there *was* when I began doing jackets – pop art."

Blumlein and Ebdus had begun to seem a kind of vaudeville act, scripted at the expense of the fall guys who'd made the mistake of joining them onstage. The audience ate it up.

"Yet here you are, Abe, among us. LunaCon wasn't to your liking, but you've spent a career among us, sharing your gift. You're the *guest of honor*."

"Look, that's fair. You want an explanation. It isn't pretty. If I were a stronger person I *wouldn't* be here. I'm tempted by flattery, so I come. My work on film is hardly known. It's *unknown*. You people have been very kind, too kind. I've grown fond, despite myself. My companion enjoys travel. There isn't one explanation, there are several."

"Do you feel a part of the field, warts and all?"

Abraham shrugged. "It's a bohemian demimonde, like any other. There are similar convocations in the world of so-called experimental film, but I've always declined to go. Some attend imagining they can further themselves. But the work, the *true* work, is of course carried on elsewhere. Perhaps for me the stakes there are too high, so I accept your invitations instead. I don't ponder these things. An event like this is an accident, not necessarily a happy one. I frankly marvel at the oddness of a room gathered in honor of a forgotten man, a nobody. Perhaps I can wake you from the trance you're in, but I doubt it."

Fifty people laughed in delighted recognition, and a light spontaneous applause broke out. I heard a woman in the row ahead whisper appreciatively, "He always says that."

"I'm ashamed of myself," said my father.

The applause grew. Buddy Green shot upright from his chair and led the clapping. Only Pflug refused the consensus, turning in his chair.

"I've wasted my life."

This was the last thing I made out before my father was drowned in the ovation. A two-way masochism was at work here, made possible by the total insularity of the gathering. The *bohemian demimonde,* as Abraham called it. My father was their pet heretic, their designated griever for lost or abandoned possibility. The way he brandished his failure thrilled this crowd, and they'd obviously known it was coming. By accepting his contempt like a lash on their backs, the Elk Lodge of ForbiddenCon 7 could feel ratified in their unworthy worthiness, their good sense of humor about themselves and their chosen deficiencies.

And yet I felt his not entirely withheld affection too. Through his eyes I could even share it. I thought of my namesake's "Chimes of Freedom" – *tolling for the aching whose wounds cannot be nursed, for the countless confused accused misused strung-out ones and worse, and for every hung-up person in the whole wide universe!* Certainly I'd witnessed gatherings of rock critics or college-radio DJs, on panels at the South by Southwest conference or the CMJ, which were no less self-congratulatorily marginal. Only the costumes were different. I flashed on a vision of a world dotted with conferences, convocations, and "Cons" of all types, each an engine for converting feelings of inferiority and self-loathing into their opposites.

The panel was over. Another man had made his way to the front and taken the left-hand microphone from Sidney Blumlein. Now he tapped it repeatedly to get our attention. The new arrival was as eccentrically dressed as anyone in the room, but to an entirely different effect. His clean blue pinstripe shirt with white collar and red bow tie, natty mustache and slicked hair – all suggested a Republican senator who'd run a calculatedly old-timey campaign bankrolled by dark and secretive private interests. His voice was incredibly loud.

"This is my first chance to welcome you to ForbiddenCon 7," he barked. "What a beginning, hey? Mr. Ebdus is too modest so I'll remind you myself, we have the privilege of a special screening of a portion of his film, tomorrow at ten in Wyoming Ballroom B. Really, don't miss this, it's a rare opportunity."

"Him," whispered Francesca. She tugged my arm. "He loves your father."

It's *you* who loves him, I thought but didn't say. You're projecting, Francesca, you see it everywhere. Seated beside her, the Cumulus of Love, I felt enveloped in perfume and emotion.

Nevertheless, I contemplated this bow-tied man at the microphone, the one who stirred my father's girlfriend to such a peculiar excitement.

"One more big hand, ladies and gentlemen, for our artist guest of honor, Abe Ebdus!"

It was my first glimpse of the man Francesca had called *Zelmo the Chair.* The important lawyer. An unlikely emissary for secrets pertaining to my whole existence, but he had a few.

CHAPTER 4

THE RESTAURANT, Bongiorno's, was bad and didn't know it. Everything was presented with a passive-aggressive flourish, as though we probably weren't savvy enough to appreciate the oregano-heavy garlic bread, the individual bowls for olive pits, the starched napkins stuffed into our wineglasses, or the waiter's strained enunciation of a long list of specials. Zelmo Swift seized control of the wine list and addressed everyone by name, making sure we took the whole episode personally. "This is on me, not ForbiddenCon," he stressed. "They wouldn't know food if it bit them on the ass. They're happy with that crap in the hotel. I know how gruesome that whole scene can get, so I always try to take the guests out once."

"Nice," I lied. At the table Zelmo still barked, his voice shockingly large. And he was master of the sudden conversational stop which demands tribute, his whole face and chest near to bursting with his readiness to resume once he'd been endorsed with a *No kidding?* or *You devil, you!*

"Dinner and real conversation," he said now. "Real *life*. That hotel is full of *mummies*. God love 'em."

Yes, and aren't you the King of the Mummies? I wanted to ask. But I understood it was precisely Zelmo's superiority to the gathering at the Marriott that our candlelit dinner was meant to authenticate.

"Also, I knew *Madame Cassini* would appreciate the best Italian food in southern California."

Francesca, seated to Zelmo's right, twinkled at the flattery. I was pretty sure her Italian heritage went not much deeper than knowing the difference between a Neapolitan slice and a Sicilian square in the pizzerias of outermost Brooklyn. But then I was pretty sure this wouldn't be the best Italian food in southern California. Maybe in Anaheim.

Zelmo's costume and manner had initially disguised the fact that he was, like me, and like Jared Orthman, in his thirties. It was the second time in a long day I'd been forced to see that my dress and affect, contrasted with peers in other professions, was less that of a grown, employed man than of a gas-station attendant or homeless person. The scruffy credibility my gear signified in my native habitat was lost on the Jareds and Zelmos, my antique wire-frame glasses only suggesting I couldn't afford contacts. Los Angeles held this lesson around every corner, I suspected. Berkeley, still in its dream bubble of the sixties, never did.

The wine arrived, and Zelmo tasted it. "That's the one," he proclaimed. Then he confided in me specially: "You'll *love* this." Apparently the son wouldn't be allowed to float in a funk through the meal. I required winning over.

My father sat beside me, separated from Zelmo by Frances-ca. Inserted between Zelmo and myself sat Zelmo's date, Leslie Cunningham. That Leslie in her gray suit perfectly resembled an actress playing a legal intern on a certain television show didn't prevent Zelmo's announcing that she actually was a legal intern, one who worked in Zelmo's firm. At Bongiorno's we were past irony's county line. I didn't trouble myself to wonder what nestled behind the trim tailoring; I refused to desire Zelmo's woman. In Berkeley I wouldn't have glanced at her, I told myself. She'd have been a bank teller, an office manager, just another style-deaf California blonde. I also didn't trouble wondering what she was doing on Zelmo's arm, figuring the *best things in life are free*, but, as well, *you can leave that to the birds and bees*.

The women on either side of Zelmo bubbled along on his stream. My father sat in grave silence. I suppose we made two of a kind, only he'd earned his supper by two decades of *service to the field*. I was expected to at least act impressed and grateful. It was Abraham's trademark, I'd learned at the panel, that he wouldn't.

The sommelier filled our glasses. I had mine to my lips when Zelmo said: "A toast."

"To you!" said Francesca. "Your generosity!"

Zelmo shook his head. "I have a toast. When I invited Abe to be ForbiddenCon 7's artist guest of honor, I could have hoped the man would be as wonderful as his work. He is. But how could I have known he'd bring along a beautiful, magical lady! Francesca and Abraham, your story touches me. To have found one another, so late in life." Zelmo was nearly bellowing by the time he raised his glass to the table's center. "*To the human heart!*" Diners at other tables glanced to see what the matter was.

We clinked, a plate of fried calamari was set down, and the celebrated couple fell to some low squabbling. Zelmo put his arm across Leslie Cunningham's shoulders and leaned to face me. "So how was it growing up in the home of the great man?"

I'm sure the look on my face was awful, and Zelmo said, "You don't have to answer that. Abraham's a tough bastard. That's the only way anything gets done in this world. Too few people understand what toughness is. Nobody back at that hotel has any idea." He laughed. "Leslie here doesn't know why I bother running the convention year after year. She wouldn't set *foot* in a place like that. Isn't that right?"

"I don't like science fiction," she obliged.

"Well, I grew up *loving* it, honey. I didn't discriminate. *Star Wars*, *Star Trek*, I loved it all. Abraham wouldn't want to hear it, but it's true. Later, I developed taste. That's how it happens, Les – it *develops*, like film. And in the great men of the field I saw the same toughness that got *me* where *I* am. Only nobody pays your father six hundred thou a year – do they?"

"No," I agreed, just to kick him loose again.

"I wanted to give something back. So I created Forbidden-Con. It's my puppy. Seven years. You think I need this, dealing with the committee, those types? They hate me but they *need* me. A night like this is what makes it worthwhile." He was still making certain I knew he mostly despised his puppy.

"Why ForbiddenCon?" I asked.

"You'll find this hard to believe, but ours is the *classiest* of the conventions. Real talent goes begging at a majority of these things. Your father, he'd be pearls before swine."

"I mean why the name? What's forbidden?"

"It stands for things hidden, occult, revealed. The rare, the taboo, the seldom seen. Elusive or neglected wisdom. Acquired tastes, like caviar, or single-malt scotch."

"I see."

"Also it's a reference to *Forbidden Planet*, the greatest

science-fiction film bar none. Many people would catch that implication."

"Ah."

"I go all out. You think Fred Vundane has been to a convention in the last twenty years? He couldn't afford the badge to get in, let alone the plane ticket. I had him flown out here, just for the privilege of Abe saying he never read the book."

"A painful moment," I suggested.

Zelmo waved his hand. "A man like your father should have whatever he wants."

I couldn't disagree, but I wasn't sure Vundane's public shaming had been high on the list.

"What do you do?" asked Leslie, leaping into the breach.

Zelmo took charge of this, too. "Dylan's a writer," he said proudly. "A journalist."

"I write about music," I said. "Lately I package collections for Remnant Records."

I gazed into Leslie's blue, stupefied eyes. I wished to have met her in a singles bar on my last night on earth, not in this moronic conversation.

"Remnant's a reissue label. I put together collections on various themes, write the liner notes, stuff like that."

"Give us an example," said Zelmo, gesturing with his wineglass munificently, as though if I said the right words he'd whip out his checkbook and bankroll something. Again I was pitching.

"Well, *The Falsetto Box* is one you might have seen. It got some press. Four CDs of, you know, the history of falsetto soul – Smokey Robinson, Curtis Mayfield, Eddie Holman. And some unexpected stuff. Van Morrison. Prince."

"We missed that," said Zelmo, speaking for Leslie. "What's another one?"

"Some of it's pretty gimmicky," I admitted. "Remnant has sort of a novelty slant. So, uh, one example is we did a disc called *Your So-Called Friends* – all the songs that have that phrase."

"I don't understand," said Leslie flatly.

"It's just a vernacular phrase that shows up in different lyrics – *so-called friends*. Like, *you and your so-called friends*. Elvis sings it in 'High Heel Sneakers,' Gladys Knight in 'Come See About Me,' Albert King in 'Don't Burn Down the Bridge,' and so on. It's like a meme, a word virus that carries a certain idea or emotion . . ." I trailed off, humiliated.

Our entrées were set in front of us. "I'll want to hear more about this," Zelmo warned, wagging a finger at me.

But the lawyer was too busy presiding over the women's meals, and I slipped his bonds for the time being. Instead I turned to my father, and over our twin plates of spaghetti and meatballs – had Abraham and I had the same instinct, to deflate the pomposity of Bongiorno's list of specials with the down-scale entrée? – we at last shared a moment of privacy.

"Are you enjoying yourself?" he asked.

"Sure. You?"

He only raised his eyebrows. "Before I forget, this is something I wanted you to read." He palmed me a triple-folded sheet from his inner jacket pocket and passed it to me covertly, at the level of the table. I unfolded it in my lap. It was a photocopy of a clipping from *Artforum*. "Epic Crawl: The Hidden Journey of an American Titan," by Willard Amato. It began:

> *What chance that the most dedicated abstract painter in the United States abandoned canvas in 1972? Or last showed in 1967, in a two-man show of figurative work which was barely reviewed? As likely that the most profound avant-garde film-maker of our time would never receive a single screening in his native burg of New York, or that the last monumental modernist artifact should be eked out secretly, in an unnameable medium, through the long heyday of modernism's toppling. Each of these improbabilities leads to the same place, an attic studio in Boerum Hill, Brooklyn, where—*

"Read it later," he begged. "Keep the copy, I've got others."

So the forgotten man, the nobody, wasn't quite content to be. It wasn't news that Abraham's aspirations still burned, but the clipping was a surprise. I stuffed it into my pocket.

"Tell me, how is Abby?"

"She's okay."

"Too bad she couldn't be along." I suddenly saw our table

in another light: two couples and a broken third. I had no idea where Abby was tonight.

"She's got school," I said, hearing my own defensiveness, unable to stop it.

Francesca overheard and announced, "I wish we could have seen her, Dylan. She's such a sweet girl!" This drew Zelmo and Leslie's attention. "She's a black American," Francesca explained, wide-eyed in sincerity. Francesca and Abby had met just once, when Abby and I passed through New York on our way to a music conference in Montreal. "You should meet her," she gasped to Leslie. "Such lovely *skin*." Francesca's good intentions vaporized conversation. We were left seated at our pasta and veal like obedient soldiers.

"Still in school?" said Zelmo at last, with pious sympathy: yes, my absent black girlfriend was underage too. Count a grown-up, employable blonde in the same category as bow ties, contact lenses, and wing tips: appurtenances Dylan Ebdus was not yet mature enough to brandish.

"Graduate school," I said. "She's completing her dissertation."

"That's wonderful," said Zelmo, turning it into a congratulation to Abby's race that she should be in such a position. I understood it was impossible to squirm from beneath Zelmo's patronage. Artists were his broken, defective flock, and he'd herd as many as he could into the safety of his care – a plate of meatballs and a ticket to ForbiddenCon. And black people were pretty much artists by definition.

"Darling," said Francesca to Abraham. "Tell him about his friend's father."

"Eh?"

"That poor man down the street, Abe. You said he'd want to know."

Abraham nodded. "Your old friend Mingus – you remember his father, Barry? Our neighbor?"

Barrett Rude Junior, I corrected silently. Francesca's logic was endearingly bare: *Dylan has a liking for black Americans* led directly to *That poor man down the street*. I promised myself I'd be patient, though hearing Abraham begin so ploddingly made me want to scream. Our neighbor! Mr. Rogers has neighbors – we had a *block*. I merely *grew up* in that house, I wanted to say. I merely wrote the man's biography in my liner note to the Distinctions' box set. But the first I wouldn't mention because Abraham would feel it as a rebuke. And the latter he didn't know of, because I hadn't mentioned it or sent him a copy.

Barrett Rude Junior couldn't be dead, I was certain of that. I'd have heard. *Rolling Stone* would have called on me to write the obit – my guess was they'd ask for about four hundred words.

"His kidneys collapsed," said Abraham simply. "Awful. They came in an ambulance. He was on a machine to keep him alive."

The subject was too remote, and perhaps too vivid, for Zelmo Swift. He threw another conversational gambit at Leslie and Francesca, and my father and I were left to ourselves.

"He'd been alone in the place for weeks, basically dying there. Nobody on the street had any idea. He's lived among us so long, but since the shooting, he's very rarely out of the house."

Abraham and I had never discussed what he called *the shoot-ing*, either in the two weeks of summer that remained before I decamped to Vermont for college, or after. Mingus and Barrett had left my name out of any conversations with the police. My presence in their house that day had been kept secret from anyone but themselves, so far as I knew.

I recalled for the thousandth time those heaps of white powder – *of course* his kidneys collapsed. What had they been waiting for? I began writing those four hundred words in my head.

"At that point a miracle occurred. Your friend Mingus was found. In a prison upstate. They got a court order, and he was released to a hospital, to give a kidney."

"*What?*"

"They made a special provision – Mingus was the only possible donor. He saved his father's life by submitting to the operation. And was returned to prison."

I brought my wineglass up, a phantom toast, then sucked down what remained inside. Behind the glass my head was heating, and my throat tightening, so I nearly choked on the mouthful of Burgundy.

"So, Mingus is back inside," I said.

"You thought he wasn't?"

"Last I knew, Arthur said he was out. But that was maybe ten years ago, more. I don't know what I thought, honestly."

"Barry is a very sweet man," said Francesca, leaning in, selecting her moment. "Very quiet. I think he's awfully sad."

"You know him?" I managed. Why shouldn't she? It all seemed equally likely now. A mist fogged my glasses.

She nodded at Abraham. "Your father and I bring him food sometimes. Soup, chicken, whatever we've got extra. He doesn't eat. Sometimes he just sits, out on the stoop. Sometimes he sits in the *rain*. The people on the block don't know him. Nobody talks to him. Only your father."

"Excuse me," I said, and tossed my napkin on my chair. I was able to reach the men's toilet before I wept or vomited into my meatballs. I was unwilling to brandish this new misery of mine before the lawyer who appreciated single-malt scotch and *Forbidden Planet*. Let my tears remain occult, elusive, seldom seen, ineligible for display in Zelmo's Museum of the Pathetic alongside R. Fred Vundane.

He saved his father's life by submitting to the operation. Every once in a while, every decade or so, I was forced to know that Dean Street still existed. That Mingus Rude wasn't a person I'd only imagined into being. I took a minute to be shamed and then I pushed Mingus back to where he'd been, where he always was whether I bothered to contemplate him or not, among the millions of destroyed men who were not my brothers.

Then I rinsed my glasses, blew my nose, and returned to the table, where through the latter courses I ignored my father and Francesca, though they were my only reason for being there. Instead I did my honest best to get potted on expensive cognac and to demolish Leslie Cunningham with my wit and charm, my roguish innuendo. I think I might even have made an impression on her, but it was all wasted on Zelmo Swift. I would have had to bend her over the table to dent his implacability.

Zelmo took me aside as we rose from the table. My father had wandered off to the men's room. "You're staying for the film tomorrow?"

"Of course."

"It means a lot to your dad."

It must be hard to strangle a man using a bow tie. That might be the reason for them. "I'll try not to do anything embarrassing," I said.

Zelmo frowned as if to suggest he hadn't been worried, but now would reconsider. "What time is your flight?"

"Right after."

"LAX?"

"No, my flight's out of Disneyland. Goofy Air." The joke soured in my mouth; it was indebted to one of Abby's, earlier this endless day.

"Har har. I'll drive you, if you'll let me."

Maybe I'd had more to drink than I realized, but this confused me. "I can take a cab," I said angrily.

"Let me save you the fare. We can talk."

Then Francesca was beside me, whispering. "Go with him, Dylan."

"Talk about what?"

"*Shhhh,*" said Francesca.

I lay on one of the Marriott's twin doubles in my underwear and spun channels, watched crocodiles fucking and Lenny Kravitz. Twice I rolled over to the phone and punched in my number in Berkeley; twice I hung up on my own voice on the machine. I tried to focus my eyes on the *Artforum* photocopy.

—*Ebdus abjures the comparison to the Wittgenstein-like protagonist of Thomas Bernhard's* Correction, *who labors for years in the forest constructing a mysterious, unseen "cone," just as he rejects any conceptual or philosophical reduction of the essentially material, "painterly" nature of his exploration. All in Ebdus's work proceeds from the purely physical nature of pigment on celluloid, and of light through the gate of a projector. A more fertile comparison might be made to the decades-long, meditative (not to say obsessive) journey of modernist composer Conlon Nancarrow, who during a blacklist-inspired exile in Mexico explored the unique compositional possibilities of the player piano, developing*

a unique and painstaking method of hand-punching the rolls
which operate the mechanical keyboard. Two or three years of
Nancarrow's effort was required to produce a five- or ten-minute
composition, a rate only marginally slower than that of Ebdus in
his painted film . . .

I was glad for my father, but my attention wasn't held. My
sick heart swirled with distraction. When I closed my eyes it felt
as if Mingus Rude was in the room, perhaps on the second bed
or in the bathtub. I borrowed from some grisly urban legend an
image of a man packed in ice, robbed of his kidney by a gang
of organ bandits. Alternately, despite a room party chattering
and clunking through the wall, and the fact of my own father
in a suite five floors above, I felt the possibility that my hotel
room was detached in the void, a plush sarcophagus with cable
television, drifting in space. This second hallucination jolted
me from my daze on the bedspread, to reach for the key to the
minibar.

I'd emptied my pockets on the dresser. Now I saw what was
arrayed there. Beside the minibar key, the room's keycard, and
some crumpled dollars, lay Aaron X. Doily's ring. I'd pocketed
it that morning, to rescue it from Abby's interrogation of my
stuff.

I wondered if the ring still worked, and, if it did, whether
its powers had changed again. Before I was done wondering
I'd pulled on my pants and slipped the keycard into my pocket
and the ring onto my finger. In bare feet I crossed the carpet
to the door, and out into the corridor, to stand blinking in the
bright light.

I couldn't see my hands or feet, but then I was drunk too.
It wasn't until the elevator door opened and I stepped into its
mirrored interior that I was certain. I was alone there, and the
elevator's cab appeared empty. I pressed my hands to the mirrors
and blew breath around them, saw invisible fingers outlined in
visible steam. No matter that I'd left the ring alone for years:
this was still its power. Mine, when I chose to wear it.

Upstairs, I'd lain tripping on misery for what felt like hours.
So I expected the lobby to be empty. Instead it was full of
gabbling Forbiddenoids. So was the hotel's bar. I crept in, easily

dodging the usual collisions. I'd become a skilled invisible man ten years before, and the expertise was ready in me.

The convention's denizens surrounded the bar's round tables in gathered chairs, groups of ten or fifteen. Their conversations had a sprung, argumentative quality, like regurgitated panel discussions. But they were human; they imbibed, galed with laughter. Some would probably pair off tonight, like the crocodiles. I was glad to be invisible. The bar itself, an island in the center, was mostly empty. I overturned a glass of melted ice at one end to make a diversion, then, as the bartender groused over to swab it up, snuck behind him to grab a third-full bottle of Maker's Mark. As I clutched it to my chest it was enclosed in my transparency. I tiptoed back through the lobby. Paul Pflug was there, pinned on a couch between identical women in leather bustiers, and high-laced boots not so unlike Abby's. I toasted him with the invisible bottle, then brought the whiskey up to my room, to render invisible by other means.

Ten was too early, but at least the room was dark. My father dithered angrily, threading the projector, insisting on doing it himself, while the pair of hotel staff who'd wheeled it into the room were exiled to one side. I sat with Francesca in the front row, unable to completely avoid the knowledge that only a scattered fifteen or twenty filled the seats behind us, in a room which wanted a hundred. The audience waited patiently, more patiently than I. Some drew orange juice from small boxes through straws, others munched Danish. Zelmo wasn't in evidence, not yet.

Under my starchy lids a film of hangover already played. I'd barely showered and made it out of the room in time to find Wyoming Ballroom B. I was relying on coffee and a bagel on the plane, for now an Advil from Francesca's purse. My floppy bag was repacked and stuffed under my chair, Aaron Doily's ring returned to my pocket. The emptied bottle of Maker's Mark I'd hidden in the minibar – it took some jostling to get it inside.

"I'll show two sequences," my father explained, beginning without any warning. "The first is from 1979 to 1981 and lasts twenty-one minutes. The second is more recent, from 1998. About ten minutes, I think. If it's all right I'll leave any remarks or questions for the end."

No one objected. No one but myself or Francesca could have known a reason to. The small population of hardcore Ebdus fans shifted in their chairs with that rote hushed excitement which precedes the start of any film, even one shown at ten in the morning in the Wyoming Ballroom of the Anaheim Marriott. They had no idea.

I cared about the film. What choice did I have? I'd cohabited with that presence longer than any other, apart from my father himself. In my childhood life the film was a sort of crippled, mute god, one nursed upstairs like a demented relative. I knew the twenty-one-minute 1979–81 section well – I'd attended its one other public screening, at the Pacific Film Archive in Berkeley, four years ago, and watched it twice in practice runs during the same week. It was a sequence Abraham thought particularly definitive. A landscape lit by an unseen moon, the horizon splitting the screen, the ground brighter than the sky – though Abraham would have rejected the terms "landscape," "horizon," and "ground." Nevertheless: the sky gray-black, the ground gray-gray. The effect more or less that of a thousand late-period Rothkos, stacked in time, and vibrating in project-ed light. The years 1979 to 1981 were just two in a half-dozen when Abraham had painted this one image – black and gray wrestling in fierce tandem. The ground might rise, or roll slightly, as though an ocean had swelled and waved. The black might leak from the sky and briefly roll across the lower frame – the moments when it did were shocking action in the dazzling, dancing stillness. Just once a red-and-yellow pulse moved like an occluded sun behind the black, then dissolved in shards. Had Abraham secretly gotten his ashes hauled that particular week, so long ago? I'd never dared ask.

As it happened, I was reasonably sure that the twenty-one-minute segment included my sole contribution, a single frame I'd forged one day after school, during my senior year. I'd come home to find Abraham out, perhaps shopping. Later I couldn't remember the exact circumstances, only the compulsion which had come over me, to sneak into his studio and paint the frame.

Abraham's brushes were wet – he'd just been working. The empty frame was centered in the sprockets, and I would only have to ratchet it one position farther to conceal my addition. The chance was handed to me on a platter, but still I barely dared. With a loaded brush tip I trembled over the frame, not setting the pigment down: the irreversible act. I was terrified of *authority* – not Abraham's, but my own.

I painted it – laid down black, laid down gray. Then broke out in a fearful sweat and fled the scene. I spent a week waiting to be accused, and wasn't. Whether I was caught I'd never know. My father was more than capable of detecting the forged frame and opting not to speak. Leaving it in or splicing it out, but saying nothing. Now, though, I permitted myself to imagine he'd left it in. One twenty-fourth of a second in twenty-five years: mine.

Now I cadged a painkiller from Francesca and tried to ignore the pressure of my dehydrated brain against the top of my eyeballs. The room was silent apart from the film's clicking passage and the whine of the projector's fan. It was hard to give the film its due (whatever that was), between hangover and my sense of Abraham, back with the projector, watching us watch from across a distance of empty seats. Hard not to feel his disappointment in this venue on the back of my neck. I waited for that one strange flare of yellow and red: there it was. Twenty-one minutes passed.

"This is how your father tortures these people who love him," whispered Francesca. "By subjecting them to such darkness."

I didn't reply. I could have used even more darkness at the moment.

The second excerpt was a surprise. A dispatch from the frontier: my father had discovered a green triangle with blunt-ed corners, one trying and failing to fall sideways against the phantasmic, blurred horizon.

The triangle occupied perhaps a quarter of the frame's area. It trembled, tipped a degree, nearly kissed earth, jumped back. Progress was illusion: two steps forward, two steps back. Impossible, though, not to root for it. To feel it groping like a foot for purchase. Daring, hesitating, failing.

I was unexpectedly moved, forgot the room, forgot my headache, suddenly wept for the triangle's efforts, a tragedy in no
acts. Francesca handed me a tissue from her purse. Prisonaires,
triangles, I was a pushover these days. Then it was done, and
the lights came on. No one clapped – they'd forgotten how, or
perhaps the film had persuaded them to fear that their hands,
urged together, would fail to meet.

Zelmo Swift appeared at the front and taught us to be brave:
a clapping sound could indeed be produced. He led the way. We
applauded and my father came to the front, was seated before
another microphone, though he hardly needed it to be heard in
the sparse room. The few questions that came were either timid
or inane. Abraham took them politely.

"Have you ever considered adding a soundtrack?"

"You mean conversation? Or music?"

"Uh, music. It would give you something to listen to."

"Yes, it would do that. And then, yes. We'd be listening to
music." He paused. "It's something to think about."

Another asked about the progress of the film since the second
excerpt. What did it look like now?

"I find a paraphrase almost impossible. Some progress has
been made. You'd see a superficial resemblance to this sequence,
I think."

"Is the triangle—" This is what the questioner had really
wanted to ask. "Is the triangle, uh, *lower*? Has it finished
falling?"

"Ah," said Abraham. He paused a while. "The green, yes. It
continues in its struggle. More or less as you saw."

There was a hush within a hush.

"Will it *ever*—?" someone managed. The question on everyone's lips. That unfinished falling had broken a lot of hearts,
not only mine.

"I prefer not to speculate," said Abraham. "That's the daily
task, in my view. A refusal to speculate, only encounter. Only
understand."

Zelmo, waiting in the wings, could stand it no longer. He
swept up the microphone. "In other words, folks, *stay tuned*.
Abraham Ebdus isn't *done* yet. Pretty amazing." Yes, the film
had gone into extra innings, but Zelmo the Chair, Zelmo the

Connoisseur, he wasn't one of those philistines getting a head start to the parking lot, no sir.

With that the spell was broken. My father's fans drifted from the ballroom, checking their pocket schedules. Maybe somewhere in the building R. Fred Vundane was seated on another panel, if they were lucky. Abraham hurried back to prevent the hotel's employee from rewinding the film incorrectly, and Zelmo and Francesca surrounded me again.

"You've got a plane to catch," Zelmo said merrily.

"There's plenty of time."

"Sure, but my car's waiting downstairs. So—"

"You better go, dear," said Francesca.

I was too blurry to fight. Zelmo was a thug by nature, and Francesca a thug of love, and together, in the name of convenience and some irritating secret agenda, they would cheat me of a half hour more in my father's company. He'd fly back to Brooklyn and another year or decade would go by. But I'd made no use of the visit so far, and there wasn't a lot of potential in half an hour at the Marriott, not with Zelmo and Francesca and my hangover all circling, making their claims. I slung my bag over my shoulder.

"Son."

"Dad."

"It was good to see you. This—" He waved. "Impossible."

"The new segment was beautiful."

He closed his eyes. "Thank you."

We embraced again, two bird-men briefly touching on a branch. I'd showered but already reeked again of the liquor working through my pores. I wondered if my father thought I'd come to Los Angeles in the middle of a breakup, or a breakdown. I wondered if he'd be right to wonder.

Then I smudged Francesca's face and was escorted downstairs, through the lobby, and into the backseat of Zelmo Swift's chauffeured, window-tinted limousine.

Disneyland was distantly visible from the gray suburban freeway strip, a clutch of spires like a sinking ship in the industrial sea.

"You don't like me," announced Zelmo, with no regard for the driver's hearing. On the leather-plush seat there was plenty of room between myself and the lawyer. I suppose it seemed I wanted to climb out the window.

"What do you want me to say?" I needed orange juice, a toothbrush, a blood transfusion, a Bloody Mary, Abigale Ponders, Leslie Cunningham, a Thneed, someone to watch over me, a miracle every day – anything but a moment of truth between myself and Zelmo Swift. I needed a *volume knob* on Zelmo Swift.

"Nothing. I'm doing this out of respect for your father and Francesca." He took an envelope from his jacket and placed it beside my hand.

"What is it?"

"An accident. You'll understand when you look. I go all out for my guests, Dylan. Whatever you might think of Forbidden-Con, it's a moment in their lives, I like to make it a big one. We usually do a 'This Is Your Life, Abraham Ebdus!' kind of thing at the Saturday banquet. Surprise appearances from the past, very sentimental."

I opened the envelope. A single sheet, two typed paragraphs. Some legal secretary's notes, unsigned. Nothing official, but dry legalese aspiring to the official, language dead with indifference to its subject.

Ebdus, Rachel Abramovitz, conviction for forgery, conspiracy, Owensville Virginia, 10/18/78, sentence suspended. Subsequent arrest and indictment, Lexington, Kentucky, 5/9/79, accomplice armed robbery; bail flight, whereabouts unknown; warrant issued 7/22/79.

And:

Ebdus, Rachel A., last verifiable address, 2/75: #1 Rural Route 8, Bloomington, Indiana, 44605.

"I hope you don't feel I was prying," said Zelmo. "We have an excellent research staff at my firm. What they discover is out of my hands."

"Why am I seeing this?" What I meant, really, was: *Why am I learning this from you? Why in your limousine, Zelmo?*

He understood. "Abraham wanted me to destroy it. He wasn't interested. Francesca spoke to me privately."

"So Francesca's wishes prevailed over my father's?"

"She's well intentioned, Dylan. She thought you had a right." His voice rose to a declamatory, courtroom-finale level. "You shouldn't be furious with her. It's difficult coming into a family, knowing what's right to do."

I glanced at the sheet again, and felt Zelmo's eyes on me. I wanted to fly at him in my rage, but I sat. *Fuck you looking at?* I wanted to ask, then throw him in a yoke.

But I sat, a white boy saying nothing.

"Forget it, if you want," said Zelmo. "I'll destroy the traces."

"I don't care what you do. Just don't bother Abraham with it again."

"Assuredly."

I put the sheet in the envelope, the envelope in my bag. We fell to silence, Zelmo gratefully for once. I wondered if he'd ever been so little rewarded for what he regarded as his generosity.

Still, it was hardly his fault a legal researcher in his firm knew more about my life than I did.

Destroy the traces. I'd never tried to do that. Instead I'd lived in their midst for thirty years, oblivious, a blind man fancying himself invisible.

CHAPTER 5

PERHAPS EVERY MALE animal has an idea what he'll do with himself the evening of the day he comes home to a newly empty house – rooms which show signs, as mine did, of a hurried start to permanent departure. Perhaps every man has a consoling, self-abnegating fantasy lined up for such a moment, a rabbit hole down which to plunge. Anyhow, I did. I only had to stretch out on my daybed for a few hours, dozing slightly as light turned to dark in the trees outside, the jewel-case shambles of Abby's tantrum still decorating the floor at my feet, to have my chance. Once night fell I only needed to change my shirt, splash water on my face, and walk a few blocks south through the cool evening to put my plan under way. My scheme of self-wreckage was that near at hand, that much in my back pocket all the time.

Shaman's Brigadoon, on San Pablo Avenue, was a Berkeley institution, a dingy, poster-layered blues-and-folk nightclub where for some thirty-odd years black musicians in dark suits, narrow ties, and freshly blocked fedoras came to sit on a tiny stage and perform for an audience of white people wearing berets, fezzes, ponchos, and dashikis. As a music journalist known to Shaman's longtime floor manager I could rely on being waved in free of charge. I always fulfilled the two-drink minimum at the candle-in-mason-jar tables, though – it was worth it for a seat nearer the stage, and lately for the sweet, slow-cooking flirtation I'd been engaged in with one of their typically zaftig young cocktail waitresses, a wide-faced, green-eyed, cigarette-raspy blonde seemingly just arrived from Surferville, named Katha.

Katha had been born in the late seventies but her flippant smile, easy banter, and the pitch of her sturdy hips as she moved with a tray, all were film-noir vintage, whether she knew it or not. Though I gobbled her up with my eyes, she was only an easy, impersonal icon of sexual cheer in my life the first dozen times she waited my table. I took her friendly provocations for nothing more than an aspect of her art, and tipped accordingly.

As has sometimes been the case for me, it was one woman who focused my attention on the reality of another. "You and that girl really get a kick out of each other, don't you?" Abby said one night in May, as we walked home from a Suzzy Roche show.

"She's got a Drew Barrymore smile," I joshed, denying by not denying.

"She's got Drew Barrymore *jugs*," said Abby, and punched me on the arm. We laughed, chummy, jaded cohorts in my self-deception. And that was the last night Abby and I went together to a show at Shaman's Brigadoon.

My next visit I learned Katha's last name, and a few other things. Katha Purly only looked nineteen – she was twenty-one. Despite appearances, she wasn't up from some beach town, but down, from Walla Walla, Washington. Flying in the teeth of cliché, she was an aspiring singer-songwriter waitressing at a joint where she hoped someday to headline. She lived in a commune in Emeryville, along with two of the other waitresses from Shaman's who'd come south with Katha at the same time. No, the three weren't a band, just friends. I couldn't keep from asking the questions but after I learned the answers I pretended I didn't know them. My sincerity had almost spoiled our breezy, effortless repartee, but on my next visit we fought our way back. And that was where we'd left it, until this night.

Onstage was a trio of African musicians, an organist, xylophonist, and bongo player, billed as the Kenya Orchestra Vandals. They weren't creating a lot of excitement, and I wondered if a major portion of the orchestra hadn't been detained at the Nairobi airport. There were free tables near the riser, but I didn't sit as close as I could have. Instead I picked the quietest corner of Katha's section.

"Hiya, buster," she said, and dropped a menu on my table.

"Katha, Katha, Katha."

"What's the matter?"

"Nothing at all. Just saying your name. It sounds like panting, actually."

"I guess, if you're a dog. You drinking?"

She brought me scotch and I pretended to admire the band.

Whenever she was near enough I made jokes about Walla Walla and tried to make her sit at my table for a cigarette break. Once I succeeded, I said: "So what are you doing later, anyway?"

"Who, *me?*" Katha's tone of delighted surprise was all I wished to inspire in her, or for that matter in any other living human, ever again. When two bodies felt the raw uncanny instinct to be joined, and before any damage had been exchanged, it was so easy for one to make the other smile.

"You. You and your so-called friends. You and what army."

She squinted. "What about the horse I rode in on?"

"The horse especially."

"You want to *party* with me, Dylan?"

"I want to hear you play your guitar."

I felt her hesitation, avoiding a trap. *I will not trap you ever or tonight*, I willed.

"I'm not off until one-thirty," she said.

I shrugged and she began to know that I was serious.

"Some people are showing up later," she said, precisely vague. "But if you don't mind coming along we could get some hanging-out time."

I wasn't much into the Kenyans, so I took a walk to the marina. Mexicans fished off the pier by night, hunched against the indifferent skyline, the Orwellian Transamerica pyramid. I went as far as the pier's crumbled tip, where lovers walked, though I couldn't decide whether to count myself as one.

Then ten blocks back to Shaman's, to an alley door Katha had told me to use. A rap beat pulsed from a small boom box on a kitchen shelf, playing Digital Underground's "Foghorn Leghorn," a song which happened to include a few sampled bars of Doofus Funkstrong's "Bump Suit." You could hear Barrett Rude Junior's tenor moan deep in the sample, if you listened hard. The lights in the kitchen were up, the chairs in the darkened front room already turned on the tables. Katha and one of her friends counted the till, mumbling numbers aloud like a prayer, hurrying through the work. The third girl had drawn lines of cocaine on the counter with a kitchen knife.

"Deirdre," said the girl with the knife, and handed me a rolled bill. Hair had fallen to cover her face as she concentrated over the drug and now she swept it back behind her ear.

"Dylan. Thanks."

"You know Katha—?" She left it for me to fill in.

"Just from here."

"Cool."

The quick onset of alliances were the stuff of these girls' days, that was the impression Deirdre gave. She'd make a place for me, *mildly weird older guy*, if I'd make a place for myself. So it was here, as elsewhere, Gowanus, Hollywood, ForbiddenCon 7, other secret zones of belonging. Entry points between zones are hidden until they aren't, until they become as obvious as a lit kitchen door in a club's alley, behind which three young women from Walla Walla pool an evening's tips. And as so often in my experience, passage between was eased by alcohol or marijuana or cocaine, those boundary medicines. Line, Mr. Mildly Weird Older? *Of course* I'd like a line, and to cross one too, please. How could I *not* find myself doing Barrett Rude Junior's drug before this weekend was behind me? That was precisely what I'd come here to do, without knowing it. It wasn't that I didn't want Katha. I wanted her badly, but now I'd sensed that the price for having her would be a reschooling in the provisionality of my being, in the futility of my illusions of control. And I wanted to pay that price as much as I wanted Katha herself.

"You really write for *Rolling Stone*?"

"I have."

"Who'd you meet?"

"Uh?"

"Like, did you ever meet Sheryl Crow?" The questions were flat, unashamed.

"Nope."

"R.E.M.?"

"I was backstage with R.E.M. once, at the Oakland Coliseum." How to explain that I'd spent the time talking to the dB's – the opening act?

"What are they like?"

"Well, Michael Stipe was sucking from an oxygen tank after the show."

"Wow."

Katha was at the wheel of her Ford Falcon, Deirdre beside

her, up front. I was being interviewed by Jane, third and young-est, in the backseat, as we whistled down San Pablo Avenue into Emeryville. A bag of bottles from Shaman's sat on the seat between us. Velocity, the company of girls as brash as Frank Sinatra and Gene Kelly in *Anchors Aweigh*, and revelatory after-hours views of streets I took for granted in daytime, these were the intoxicants I was high on, as much as the cocaine. Or at least I couldn't parse my other thrillments from the drug. Katha hadn't spoken to me directly, back in Shaman's kitchen, only taken the rolled bill from me with a wry, welcoming smile before doing a line herself. And she ignored me in the car, left me to Jane's questions. That was another thrillment. The silence seemed consent that we'd taken a step. That this night was already earned. We could rest the banter for now.

We slowed in front of a big, turreted, three-story Victorian, set back from the street and with a low white fence around its weedy yard. Bare bulbs and postered white walls blazed from behind curtains of bedsheet and hippie tapestry, so the com-mune stood out like a piñata from the two-story cookie-box apartments which slumbered on all sides. The cars parked on the street included two that weren't going anywhere, and one that looked lived in. As my eyes focused I made out a black man in a white undershirt, seated in a lawn chair under the carport of one of the neighboring apartments, and crumpling a paper bag around a bottle. His gaze followed the sputtering progress of the Falcon into the alley beside the commune, impassively.

"You wanna meet Matt?" Jane asked, as Katha parked.

"That's just her polite way of saying goodbye," said Deirdre from the front. "Jane and Matt pretty much just fuck all the time."

"*Shut up!*" said Jane, and slapped at Deirdre's head.

"You can't deny it because you know it's true."

On the porch Katha smiled at me again, as though she knew she was handling a man in a trance. "Go ahead," she said. "My room's on the second floor. You'll find it."

Jane and Matt lived in the attic, reachable only by ladder from the commune's third-floor landing. When Jane summoned him Matt didn't come down, just peeked his bare-chested torso over the edge of the loft. Despite a Christian beard he also wasn't past nineteen.

"Hey," he said.

"Dylan knows R.E.M.," Jane told him. "He's Katha's friend."

"Cool," said Matt, blinking, waiting, if I believed Deirdre, to fuck.

"Okay, bye," said Jane to me, shy now for the first time. She climbed the ladder, squirrel-like.

I turned back down the grand ramshackle staircase, which was lit by a bare violet bulb. Music seeped from behind various doors, and the air of the house was stale with fumes – laundry, cigarettes, old beer. This was my chance: I could have crept past the second floor, found my way out and to a cab on San Pablo. I didn't.

Katha's two rooms formed a suite at the back of the second floor, and with their built-in bay-window seats and ornate ceilings and mosaic parquet they would have been grand rooms in a grand house, if the house were anywhere but Emeryville. As it was, the ceiling was water-stained, the parquet warped, and I was sure the landlord was grateful to have tenants to fill the place, even if they mostly used strings of Christmas lights for lamps. Katha's guitar case leaned against a wall near a CD boom box; a shelfless, doorless closet was heaped with clothes. The smaller second room was empty except for a tapestry-draped single mattress. There was nothing at all on the walls.

In the main room Deirdre kneeled on the floor, slicing more coke, on a mirror now, with a taped blade. Katha, tucked into one of the bay windows, spoke on a telephone, low murmuring not audible over the Beck on the boom box. Another couple sat, knees up, on a futon against the wall, a light-skinned black with a large Afro, faint mustache, and mild eyes, and his girlfriend, a somewhat older-looking woman with choppy short black-dyed hair who, when she spoke, disconcertingly revealed a German accent. Sprawled in a butterfly chair was a Mexican-appearing teenager, fifteen or sixteen at most, gangly in oversized hip-hop trousers, his hair in a blue handkerchief. Deirdre didn't offer any introductions. Sultry and hollow, she seemed a player in a Warhol film of the mind. Rolando and Dunja, the couple on the futon, gave their names and smiled pleasantly. The teen in the butterfly chair said, "Yo," and presented for a black-power handclasp. I took his hand and he chewed his name: *Marty* or *Mardy* or *Marly*, I couldn't be sure.

It was the least of the uncertainties which gave shape to my long night in Katha Purly's rooms. Katha's slighting me in the shuttered nightclub and again in the car had turned into a policy. We weren't together in any sense that I could tell. I did coke and talked with Deirdre and Rolando and Dunja. Maybe-Marty refused, his expression haughty, full of childish disdain, like a housecat preening to avenge an indignity. Maybe-Marty was silent, though when the last track of the Beck ended he moved over and found N.W.A.'s *Straight Outta Compton* in Katha's small collection, then twisted the volume up. The rest of us raised our voices to be heard. Asking some innocent question I unleashed talkative Dunja, who was, it turned out, an *Israeli* German, raised both in Germany and on a kibbutz. Her life wasn't a history lesson or an allegory to her, only a story. I listened, marveling that I had followed my waitress crush to a ghetto mansion in Emeryville to sit, cross-legged and stoned in Christmas-bulb light, learning of a sixteen-year-old German girl's losing her virginity on a moonlit Middle Eastern soccer field to an émigré Russian engineer. Meanwhile, elsewhere in California, Abby slept or didn't sleep, and in Anaheim, my father had a few hours earlier been treated to his banquet.

Katha made a couple of calls and left the room. She returned, perhaps half an hour later, with a six-pack of Corona, and trailed by someone she introduced as Peter. Peter was twentyish as well, demure and chubby, maybe gay, I thought. Katha took a line of coke, but Peter waved it off, instead helped himself to a beer. He seemed to know the others, or anyhow he was comfortable with Deirdre and Rolando, and began explaining to them how he'd had a fight with his roommate and now refused to return – that was where Katha had gone, to pick him up. Meanwhile Dunja went on telling me of kibbutz days, her cokey tales like an encyclopedia entry, devoid of highs or lows. Katha offered me a beer, the first words she'd spoken to me inside the commune. I took one, just to rinse my gummy throat. It was sweet and sharp, a treat I hadn't anticipated.

Maybe-Marty did some shy, tentative break-dancing in the corner near the boom box. No one watched. The time was three in the morning.

I leaned away from Dunja and the others, to Katha. She still sat to one side, distracted – on duty, it seemed to me.

"Play your guitar," I said.

"You want to hear me play?"

"Something you wrote."

We moved off, sat in one of the bays. Under a humming, sneaker-draped streetlamp the street was dead calm, poverty calm. The lights were out even in the lived-in car. Katha told Maybe-Marty to turn the music down – not off, just down – and he did, then flopped back in his butterfly chair. The others, Deirdre, Peter, Dunja, and Rolando, paid us no attention, went on murmuring. Rolando rubbed Dunja's shoulders; she talked with her eyes shut. I saw Peter had changed his mind, accepted a line. The supply was low. Deirdre shaved the mirror in an obsessive, mechanical action. Katha tuned her guitar, not looking at me.

She began suddenly. Her voice was deep and gorgeous, the lyric remorseless:

> Psychedelic twitches in my mood
> I'm getting down I'm gonna have to get high soon
> I didn't mean to smoke your last cigarette
> I love you baby but sometimes I forget
> It was the drugs that made me lose my mind
> It was the drugs that made me so unkind
> It was the drugs
> That made me love you in the first place

And:

> Last thing I remembered before I passed out
> Were your needful eyes staring from across the couch
> I never look at you like that
> I guess I don't need you, I just need you to need me back
> It was the drugs that made me lose my mind
> It was the drugs that me so unkind

It was the drugs
That made me want you in the first place

Maybe-Marty's hip-hop selections throbbed on in the silences. The talk had quelled, though. Katha tuned again, then began a simple blues. She bluffed some verses, humming, but sang the refrain clear.

I don't need you to tell me I'm alone
don't you think I know I have no home?
I just want to call my mother on the phone
I just want to call my mother on the phone

"That's new," she said, interrupting herself.

Peter got up sobbing, both hands on his face, and left the room. To my dismay, Katha put down her guitar and followed him into the hall. Dunja too, jumped up and went after them.

Maybe-Marty turned up the music.

Rolando switched to kneading Deirdre's shoulders, which I wanted not to resent. Deirdre had been doing an awful lot of coke and reminded me more of an anorexic raccoon than anything alluring, but the dishonorable truth was I yearned to be touching one of the women by now, and I felt a little bitter about Rolando's access. I wandered over for another beer and peeked into the violet-hued stairwell, but it was vacant. I heard thin trails of music from other floors, nothing I was tempted to follow. I ducked back inside.

"Yo."

It was Maybe-Marty. I'd gotten used to pretending he wasn't in the room, the universal strategy here, it seemed.

He'd switched off the music. "You wanna hear my shit?"

"Sure," I said, helpless.

"Okay, but hole on, I gotta get set."

"Okay."

I sat against the wall near the boom box. In the silence I could hear Deirdre's breath sighing from her as Rolando labored over her shoulder blades. Maybe-Marty shrugged his wrists together and cocked his head, then planted one foot ahead of the other and dipped his knee like Elvis onstage. He pushed the words out in a stream, his high voice slurring the syllables, popping for emphasis on the p's and g's.

> Check it out like this and then like that
> Li'l gangsta M-Dog with that smoov-ass rap—

"Hole on, hole on, I gotta start over." He spread his hands in an appeal, as though he'd been challenged. When he resumed he went on tossing out poses, but his eyes were closed in shy concentration.

> Check it out like this and then like that
> Li'l gangsta M-Dog with that smoov-ass rap
> Y'know it goes like this and then like this
> 'Cause when I bus' my gat I never miss
> I'm good in the hood with my homie Raf
> So if you step in our path you might get blown in half
> Don't laugh 'cause I'm ill from Emeryville
> Where if you don't survive then your memory will

"How you like that?" he said defiantly.

"Let's hear it again," I said.

He rewound into his starting pose, absolutely ready to oblige. The second run-through was more confident and precise, and fiercer, or mock-fiercer. Maybe-Marty looked younger each minute to me, twelve or thirteen now, despite *gangstas* and *gats*.

I'd spent fifteen or twenty years being angry at rappers, black and white equally, for their pretense, for claiming the right to wear street experiences, real or feigned, like badges, when mine were unshown. I'd spent fifteen or twenty years senselessly furious at them one and all for not being DJ Stone and the Flamboyan Crew in the yard of P.S. 38, for being ahistorical and a lie, for being ignorant of Staggerlee and the Five Royales, for not knowing what I knew. M-Dog, with his bashful Mexican face and utterly derivative rhymes, couldn't offend me this way. Perhaps Katha would have said it was the drugs, but I adored him. He'd never lived in a rapless world, I understood. M-Dog's cobbling a rhyme of his own wasn't pretense – and now it seemed terrible that I'd ever been so punishing in my judgments. His reaching for this language was as elemental as wishing to be able to roof a spaldeen.

At some point Katha had returned, and when M-Dog finished again she said, "That's great, you wrote that?"

"Me and my homeboy worked it out, yeah."

"It's nice."

"There ain't nothing on paper," he said, eager to be understood. "I got it all up in my head."

Katha took my hand. Something had changed. I'd done something right, soliciting M-Dog's performance – or at least admiring it, as I had. It was as though Maybe-Marty's presentation was what we'd been waiting for this night, as though it had broken some stalemate and freed Katha's movement toward me. Perhaps the change was in myself. I felt now that instead of being sharpened to the icy edge of cocaine, I'd been bathed in some river of love – as if I'd taken ecstasy, a drug whose effects I'd only imagined, often resentfully, with the same sort of grudgingness M-Dog's rhymes had just overwhelmed in me.

Katha and I returned to our bay, without the guitar. Maybe-Marty put on another disc. Showtime was over.

"What's up with Peter?" I whispered.

"He's in *love*," said Katha. Her tone suggested that to be so was a rare and passing condition, to be met with both skepticism and sympathy. "Dunja's putting him to bed."

"That sounds nice," I said, surprising myself. It did sound nice.

She was willing now to hear a little smutty implication in that, one I'd only half intended. "I'll chase everyone out of here soon."

I nodded at the empty side room, suggesting the mattress there. "We could just disappear. Let them go on with the party."

"No, that bed is – not for that."

"Not for what?"

"Not for anything but my little sister."

"What sister?" I asked, stupidly.

"She's still with our foster parents, in Washington. Sometimes I bring her down for a weekend. I'm trying to get her transferred to a school here, but she's only fourteen."

"If she's fourteen shouldn't she stay with your parents?"

"It'd be better for her here."

This level pronouncement finished the topic. I sipped my beer while Katha sent Maybe-Marty home, and dislodged Deirdre and Rolando from the futon where they were still engaged in a long massage, Deirdre's head curled down between her knees, as though Rolando had committed to smoothing the long night's worth of cocaine shivers from her body with his palms. After they'd slumped from the room, Katha, undaunted by the obvious, put on Van Morrison's *Astral Weeks*. I was grateful, but also afraid of that album's particular scalpel-like quality. I was near enough to bare as it was.

Now we were alone. Katha lit a joint from the tip of her cigarette and handed it to me. She closed the door and we moved to the futon.

"So, what are you doing here, Dylan?"

I'm here to party with you? I thought. No words came out.

"What about that lady you're with?"

"You mean Abby?"

"If Abby's your beautiful black girlfriend, yeah. I see her on Telegraph Avenue, you know."

"You do?"

"Just going into bookstores, whatever. She doesn't know me."

"She's in a hurry," I said, picturing Abby moving on that crowded street, past the teen beggars in their hundred-dollar leathers – if I ran it like a video clip in my mind's eye, the soundtrack might be Central Line's "Walking into Sunshine" or some other not remotely depressing disco cut. Meanwhile in Emeryville it was darkest before dawn, and Van Morrison and the sacred fumes of sex and marijuana beckoned me into the slipstream.

"She looks kind of *angry* to me," said Katha, startling and delighting me. "But it's none of my business."

"It's okay," I said, marveling that she'd said it. "Maybe she is. Sometimes it's hard to figure out what a person is like, when you're up close."

"I don't know what that means."

"Like your song." I was shameless. "Sometimes you understand all at once, in a flash." I was so grateful to Katha for calling Abby angry. I wanted to reward her, stroke her, call blessings of orgasms down upon her for pardoning my bungled life with that passing observation.

Years ago, I'd read a novel, a thriller in which glamorous people destroyed themselves by sexual intrigue. One character was another's shoals, that was what I'd remembered about the book – and the character who'd wrecked the other had explained how she was infinitely dangerous because she was *damaged*. This character's damage made her an involuntary criminal, the book seemed to say. Her damage – orphanhood, abuse, I couldn't remember what it was – made her unfit to mix with those who'd been luckier, who'd squeaked through life innocent of such knowledge. The story was enthralling bunk, impossible not to finish even as I'd loathed it for its implicit assertion that the undamaged ought to bolt their doors against *the damaged ones*, who would hurt them if they could, who couldn't help wishing to. When I read the book, I'd never met anyone undamaged. I still think I never have.

Suddenly Katha Purly seemed to me a refutation of that book, refutation I hadn't known I'd needed until this instant. I'd raged against the silly, trashy novel because of the nerve it twinged – my shame at my own hurt, my fear that it made me an untouchable, poisonous to others. Katha made nonsense of that. I'd thought I was following a dangerous angel to her lair, that I'd been drawn by some offer of destruction. But Katha was only an ordinary angel. Her sister's room was evidence, and so was M-Dog, and so was Peter. But the best evidence was my own presence here. She'd taken me in when I'd needed her to.

Katha was only as good as her damage. It formed the substance of what she knew. What made me dangerous, or at least awful, wasn't my damage, but the way I'd denied it. What I'd left undone. Katha sheltered her sister and M-Dog, Mingus surrendered a kidney, and Abraham and Francesca brought Barrett Rude Junior soup and chicken. In my visionary state I could see the Tupperware containers, could see a skeletal Barry as he smeared hot mustard on a fridge-gummed thigh or drumstick. Meanwhile, Abby and I conducted a witty war to prove which of us was truly depressed. Shunning my damage I'd starved my life, it seemed now. I was lost in feints and skirmishes three thousand miles from the homefront. Katha had a bed made, waiting for her sister in Walla Walla – I had *The Falsetto Box* and *Your So-Called Friends*.

When, ten months before, I'd delivered my Subtle Distinctions box-set liner note to Rhodes Blemner of Remnant, he'd let two weeks pass without calling to confirm he'd received it. Finally I cracked, and called him myself.

"You got it?"

"Sure, I got it."

"What's the matter?"

"Nothing's the matter. We'll run the note in the box, I sent it to the art department. It's scheduled."

"How'd you like it?"

"It's not your best work, Dylan." Rhodes had perfected a lethal hippie frankness, after the manner of his heroes, from Bill Graham to R. Crumb. "I was disappointed, given how you pushed so hard for the reissue. It wasn't what I expected."

"I think it's *exactly* my best work."

"Well, it conveys the impression you think that. It's full of big thoughts, if that's what you mean. But I personally think it's also full of shit. Beginning with the quotes up front, all that Brian Eno stuff, which I cut."

"Fuck you, Rhodes. Send it back to me."

"We'll run it. What do I know? You'll win a Grammy, that's my prediction. For best hot air."

I defended. "I had to create a context—"

"It's a false context. The piece reads as if you sat in a small room listening to nothing but Distinctions records for a year and then *postulated* the history of black music. It reads like you were avoiding something. Maybe you were avoiding your research. You quote *Cash box*, for crying out loud. That's like something one of these British writers would do – write a note on living musicians and quote an interview somebody gave to *Cash box* in 1974."

Now, here on Katha's futon, layering pot over coke at the outer reaches of a binge which felt stolen from time, my hand beginning to explore the waitress's knee in automatic lust, Rhodes Blemner's cavil to my liner note seemed completely of a piece with every other revelation. My failure to provide

Jared Orthman an end to the Prisonaires' story held the same message for me as M-Dog's rhymes, as Katha's sister's empty room, as my father's green triangle – I was halted in a motion half-completed. My facts were no good. I'd been scooped by Zelmo Swift's interns, out-researched by Francesca's soup. *The man himself is still alive*, I'd written, but I hadn't believed it, had to be told again and again by the Jareds and Rhodeses and Zelmos. The man himself, and his son too, even if they only had one pair of kidneys between them.

Katha and I talked and kissed while my thoughts raced, and until they didn't. My waitress and I had months of teasing in the bank, and we drew on them now. On the sticky tapestry-covered futon, in the streetlamp light which streaked the wall above our heads, with Van Morrison moaning Celtic inspiration, our addled bodies pushed and gnawed at one another. Hot blunt hands got stuck under blue-jean waistbands until we sighed and tugged apart the snaps. Katha's flesh was smooth and sheeny, so rubbery I wondered if it was somehow an effect of drug-dust between my fingers and her skin. She was plush and uncreased, like a marzipan animal. An elegant margin of hairs rode the curve from her navel into her pubic tangle.

I paused where I always do, melancholy at the threshold, a make-out man. Thinking, *We could stop here. This could be fine, this could be enough*. I'm often more certain I want to be held than engulfed.

"I've got something," whispered Katha. "I'll be right back."

"Okay," I said.

My blondes had always been those Leslie Cunninghams, striding the world undamaged, or seeming so, impassive goddesses who regarded me dubiously. Or Heather Windle, or the Solver girls, forever circling away on bikes and skates, forever packing and moving from the neighborhood of me. Now I had my blonde in Katha Purly. At last one had given herself to me, completely and without bargaining, but she was different, realer, rich with damage. This was an ordinary, rapid-fading epiphany, the last of my dozens: my young waitress wasn't a fantasy because nobody was. People were actual, every last one of them. Likely even the Solver girls, wherever they were.

I had my blonde now, yes, but I couldn't stay hard inside her.

It was the drugs – I couldn't feel myself inside her from within the condom she'd unrolled. But Katha Purly was unbearably generous with me. In the pale daylight now infecting the room, long-shadowing the crumbs in the stale corners and the silent boom box, the streets below noising to dawn life, the house around us still and full of sleeping bodies like an interstellar ship, Katha touched herself, gorgeously gave herself the orgasm I'd wanted to provide, made her own face and throat flush red, temples pink beneath pale eyebrows, while exhorting me to give tribute onto her superb pooled chest, championing me with her voice, cooing me forward. I managed to do it, just.

When I woke it was in sweat, sun blazing over me and Katha in that barren room, our bodies peeled out of their embrace to opposite sides, sheets squirmed down around our ankles. Katha woke a little and said I could stay, but I couldn't. I dressed and left, walked home into Berkeley along San Pablo Avenue. It was ten in the morning. I couldn't stay at Katha Purly because Katha Purly wasn't, after all, a place. Neither, for that matter, was Abigale Ponders. Or California itself, not for me. They weren't Dean Street, specifically, weren't Gowanus, and that was where I was going. I had to get back to where I once belonged. I phoned an airline and booked a coast-to-coast flight, then showered, then slept. When I woke the second time I packed another bag, and again I took along the ring.

CHAPTER 6

I REMEMBER ALMOST nothing of the few weeks which remained of summer between Barrett Rude Senior's death by shooting and my Greyhound ride from the city to begin my first term at Camden College. The tragedy became the communal property of Dean Street, of course, and my own close knowledge of it was a secret. So my sense of it was soon blunted into the pell-mell of general gossip. I spared little sympathy for Mingus, who was under arrest and being charged as an adult; I was a fierce rocket of denial awaiting escape velocity from the scene. The killing only gave a clear name and shape to my fog of reasons for wanting to leave Brooklyn. Anyway, I was scared of Mingus. He'd killed someone with a gun. That hadn't happened before. This was 1981, before drive-bys made shootings commonplace. It was still a time of knives and baseball bats, of homemade nunchucks, of yokes. I'd seen guns brandished, but never fired.

Vermont was my antidote. I'd only been there once since my thirteen-year-old Fresh Air Fund voyage, and that just seven months earlier, in late January, for my entrance interview at Camden. Still, though the green hills of the Vermont landscape were fresh-quilted with snow, whiter than any I'd seen, and the wind on the vacant campus bit through my fake down coat, I felt stirrings everywhere of Heather Windle-ghosts, of my dragonfly-and-swimsuit summer. I bought a single cardboard-and-cellophane-boxed leaf of maple-sugar candy in the bus depot in Camden Town and when I melted it on my tongue as Heather had once taught me to do I got the most innocent and yearning erection I'd had in four years.

Camden College wasn't Heather Windle's Vermont, though. At Camden Heather would have been a townie, a girl glimpsed at the Brass Cat or Peanut's, one of those small-town bars Camden students sometimes dared themselves to frequent on their sorties from the idyllic walled preserve, the bucolic acres of the campus itself. Inside that trimmed-green sanctuary was a sort of collective solipsistic laboratory, where high-strung urban children were allowed to play however they liked. Dressed in leather and fur and batik they and I – for I was briefly one of them – roamed an environment one part New England farmland, complete with white clapboard dorms, twisted apple trees bearing inedible fruit, low lichen-covered Frostian stone walls wending nowhere through the woods, and tattered cemetery plots with burial dates in the 1700s: one part experimental arts college, founded in the 1920s by passionate Red-leaning patrons, and legendary for its modern dancers and faculty-student marriages; and one part lunatic preserve for wayward children of privilege, those too familiar with psych counseling and rehab to follow older siblings to Harvard or Yale, and which recapitulated in junior form the tribal rituals of Mediterranean resorts and East Hampton summers and the VIP room of Studio 54.

I understood none of this. I was class-dumb, protected from any understanding of money by my father's artisan-elitism and, paradoxically, by Rachel's radical populist pride: I'd been raised by a monk and a hippie, each of whom stood willfully outside any hierarchy of class. The desires our little family couldn't afford to indulge had never seemed important, only snobbish and silly and somehow misplaced, like Thurston Howell's priorities on *Gilligan's Island*. Besides, I'd had as much or more money than most kids I'd known in Brooklyn, if somewhat less than the majority of my Manhattan schoolmates at Stuyvesant, so figured I was somewhere in the middle. Yeah, sure, that was it: I was *middle* class.

The truth was, few Camden students had ever set foot inside a public school, much less attended one. And I'd never set a foot inside Brooklyn Friends or Packer Collegiate or Saint Ann's. A handful of students formerly from those schools, Brooklyn Heights kids mostly, were introduced to me by others, in those first weeks, as being "from Brooklyn too," yet they were strangers, and when I admitted that I'd gone to P.S. 38 and I.S. 293 they knew, better than anyone else at Camden, what a freak I was to be in their midst here. Across this gulf of experience my new acquaintances and I stared, as though at denizens of a looking-glass world.

In a gesture which could be taken for either a muddled kind-ness or a cruel segregation, I'd been given a roommate who was also on financial aid. Matthew Schrafft was from Keene, New Hampshire, a town much like Camden, only lacking a glamor-ous college. He'd attended Manhattan prep schools until sixth grade, but his family's fortunes had tumbled, his father aban-doning a career as a junior producer at CBS News in order to live in a small town and write a novel. For this reason I suspect Matthew felt dangerously near to being a townie. We became friends, and it was a solace that my roommate and friend was, like myself, sometimes to be found on the wrong side of the dining hall's counters, wearing a white apron, spooning hot waffles and sausages and eggs from steel vats onto our fellow students' trays. Food server was one of the less hidden or euphemistic work-study jobs – those other charity cases who were tucked away quietly research-assisting or working in the alumnus office could afford to pity Matthew and me as they lined up for their meals.

Matthew and I had also been awarded an unusual housing arrangement, for a pair of freshmen: Oswald House Apartment. Oswald was famously the rowdiest and druggiest of the dor-mitories which surrounded the Commons. Each of these eight clapboard buildings included one central "apartment": a suite of connected rooms with a fireplace and a private bathroom. These upscale digs were ordinarily reserved for a graduate stu-dent or visiting professor, only no one expecting a moment's peace would have accepted placement in Oswald. The floors in the living room there reeked continuously of cleanser-scrubbed beer spills, the carpet was riddled with burns, the doors decked with thumbtacked porn and spiky, punk-style graffiti. Oswald House was like a pirate ship sailing the apple-strewn lawn, one which blared Grateful Dead more or less around the clock in late summer, when speakers could be mounted facing outward in first-story windows and students sprawled on the grass. The Oswald Apartment had been the domain of a legendary pair of bearded, Belushi-esque partyers, and I think the Housing Office had a notion that by replacing these ringleaders with two fresh-faced, short-haired scholarship students they'd effected a kind of heart transplant on Oswald – that Matthew and I would temper the place from the inside out. That wasn't exactly how it worked out, but I'm sure the established Oswaldites were every bit as dispirited to see us moving into the Apartment that September as the administration might have wished.

Matthew and I ironized our discomfort by sublimating it in culture. Devo, a band I'd never cared for in high school, became an emblem of our difference, not only from the Camden hippies, but also from the chic, Bowie-loving punk types who had subscriptions to *Interview* and vacationed in Paris. Devo expanded the nerd-brainiac ethos of a band like Talking Heads in a usefully hostile direction. Loving Devo, it was possible to indulge our class resentment by masking it as anticapitalist satire. They became an adjective: Certain things were awfully *Devo* around this school, weren't they?

One balmy afternoon that first week in Vermont, still stunned at catapulting out of our high-school lives and knowing no one, Matthew and I attended an out-of-doors afternoon talk by Richard Brodeur, the new president of Camden. Brodeur seemed as terrified of the place as we were. Like Matthew's father, he'd thrown over a corporate career for something more *real*, and his descriptions of why he'd wanted to preside at Camden sounded a tad defensive. In fact, Brodeur was an efficiency expert brought in to repair damage done by a charismatic and tolerant seventies type. Nobody but us gullible freshmen had bothered to attend his talk.

"There's a story I like to tell," said Brodeur. "When I was a boy I used to love pizza, and whenever my father took me to the pizzeria I'd order two slices. And I'd sit and he'd watch me wolfing down the first slice with my eyes on the second. I wasn't even *tasting* that first slice. And one day my father said to me, 'Son, you need to learn that while you're eating the first slice of pizza, *eat the first slice*. Because right now you're eating the second slice before you've finished the first.' And a year ago I realized that I needed that lesson again. I took a look at my life and realized I had my eye on the *second* slice of pizza."

The parable wasn't completely lost on me, though I couldn't keep from recalling the day Robert Woolfolk and his little friend had tried to mug me for my pizza on Smith Street. I wondered if Richard Brodeur knew of any approach to the problem of the *one* slice. I suspected not.

Afterward Matthew and I drifted back to the Commons lawn, where, beyond the outermost row of dorms, the mowed rim plunged out of sight – the place was known as the End of the World. There a gaggle of our housemates tapped an early keg. We lined up for plastic cups of frothy beer, against a backdrop of green hills dimpled with sunset shadows.

"What did you take away from that?" said Matthew.

"When you think you're eating the first slice, you might really be eating the second slice?"

"Something like that. Anyway, it made me hungry."

This would be a running joke: when he and I began sleeping in late in the Apartment and missing classes we called it *eating the first slice*. My career at Camden, as it turned out, wouldn't involve a second.

That week we experienced our first of the famous Friday-night parties. Dorms were provided with a booming sound system, and plastic cups and kegs of beer from the food service – the administration had a stake in keeping its tender wards out of Vermont bars on weekend nights. Camden, truthfully, wasn't an accidental hothouse, but a deliberate one, an experiment like the Biosphere. So by eleven o'clock two or three hundred of us throbbed in one mass to Rick James's "Super Freak" on the sticky living-room floor of Fish House, another party dorm only slightly less notorious than Oswald. That easy appropriation of dance-floor funk was a first taste, for me, of something I desperately wanted to understand: the suburban obliviousness of these white children to the intricate boundaries of race and music which were my inheritance and obsession. Nobody here cared – it was only a danceable song. The Rick James was followed by David Bowie, the Bowie by Orchestral Manoeuvres in the Dark, and the OMD by Aretha Franklin. I threw myself into the dance, briefly freed.

A couple of hours later Matthew and I brought two girls back to the End of the World. Now the mowed edge plunged into mist-laced darkness, the nickname explained. Aimee Dunst and Moira Hogarth were, like us, freshman roommates, and suitably punkish, with eye shadow and gelled hair. Matthew had met them in a class on Milton and Blake. We four had talked or tried to talk in the spilling craze of the party, the penumbra of retching and squirming bodies, then ferried our plastic cups of grapefruit juice and vodka out into the chirping dark.

Aimee was from Lyme, Connecticut, and Moira was from Palatine, a suburb of Chicago. Hardly anyone, I'd learned, was really from a city. If they said Los Angeles or Chicago or New York they meant Burbank or Palatine or Mount Kisko.

As a trick of flirting I'd been boasting of my inner-city knowledge, turning discomfort inside out.

"Were you ever mugged?" asked Aimee.

Aimee, like anyone who ever asked me this question before or since, was thinking of a stickup in an alleyway, an adult transaction, a transaction of strangers. She was thinking of *Death Wish* and *Kojak*. The nearest I'd come was Robert Woolfolk's holdup of the drug dealer. That event was beyond explanation.

"I was yoked," I said instead. "Ever been yoked?"

"What's that?"

"I'd have to show you."

They giggled, and Matthew stared, not knowing any more than they did.

"I don't know," said Aimee, trailing backward, her footfalls stumbling.

"Okay, forget it."

"Do me," said Moira, boldly.

"You sure?"

"Uh huh."

"It doesn't really hurt. But you should put down your drink." We nestled plastic cups in dewy grass. Straightening too quickly, I grew dizzy. The Vermont oxygen was like another drink, a chaser.

"*Fuck* you lookin' at?"

All three turned their heads, fooled by my sudden volume and hostility. But we were alone there, at the End of the World. It was the only place I could ever have put on my mummery, my minstrel show.

I kept my eyes locked on Moira. The others were irrelevant.

"That's right, girl. Don't look around, I'm talkin' to you. Fuck you think you lookin' at?"

"Stop," said Aimee. Moira just stared back, rattled but defiant.

"See, that's all right. I don't mean nothing. Come over here for a minute." I pointed to the ground at my feet. "What, you afraid? I ain't gonna do nothin'. Just let me talk to you for a minute." My drunken self was astounded at how well I knew the drill. These words had never come from my mouth.

Moira stepped closer, taking the dare, Bacall to my Bogey. I might have liked to quit already, but the script demanded I play it all the way. There was rage nestled in the script, urgency I'd never tapped.

"See, I'm your friend, right? You know I like you." I threw an arm around Moira's shoulders and tugged her close. "You got a dollar you could lend me?"

"Don't give it to him!" howled Matthew, getting the joke now. Only it was barely a joke.

"No," said Moira.

Trapping Moira gently as possible in the triangle of fist-elbow-shoulder, I dipped her, as I'd been dipped a hundred times. Not far. To my chest. "You sure? Lemme check your pockets for a minute." I frisked the front pockets of her corduroys, found bills and plucked them out. Then Moira twisted against me and I took pity and loosed my hold. She sprang back angrily toward the others.

I raised the curled bills. "It's just a loan, you could trust me. You know we was just foolin' around, right?"

Moira rushed and tackled me into the grass. I felt the fury in her body at being handled as I'd handled her, a fury I knew precisely, from her side. But she was also drunk and excited and putting our hips back in conjunction. Yoking Moira, I'd also chosen her. A thick shock of sex was in the air – as it had been on the dance floor at Fish House. It was everywhere at Camden, only waiting for anyone to slice off a portion for themselves, and now Moira and I had done so. In all of high school I'd never kissed a girl without long spoken preliminaries, yet here it was simple. When she grabbed the bills in my hand I grabbed her hand and we returned the money to the pocket of her corduroys together, rolling on the wet lawn, kissing wildly, missing one another's faces, kissing ears and hair. Beyond where we lay, Matthew and Aimee had gone past the End of the World and vanished in the dark.

What I could never have explained to Moira was that the sexual component of a yoking was present before she and I enacted it, was buried in the practice, as I knew it, at its roots.

Moira Hogarth and I spent that night in her and Aimee's room in Worthell House, while Aimee and Matthew took Oswald Apartment. Moira and I were a couple for two weeks from that night – an eternity at Camden, where rehearsals of adulthood were rendered miniature by a compression of time and space. A whole relationship could be enacted in a weekend, wounds nursed before the next Friday night. In our case, by Halloween Moira and I wouldn't be speaking. Then again, by Thanksgiving we were confidantes, whispering and laughing our way across Commons and spending nights in bed together so that everyone was certain we were a couple though we were in fact sleeping with others. Then before the end of the term we'd fucked and fallen out again. And so on: there was nothing notable, at that school, in the close recycling of the same few sympathetic souls. There were too few to waste.

My yoking of Moira, out at the End of the World, became the origin of a scheme: I'd throw Brooklyn down like a dare. I needed something. I'd been set up to feel like a square at Camden, where my short haircut and cardigan-and-loafer style, so decisively David Byrneish or *Quadrophenia* mod at Stuyvesant, only looked ordinarily preppy to those who'd actually been to prep school. But nobody could question my street credibility here, where nobody had any street credibility whatsoever. I earned my stripe at Camden by playing a walking artifact of the ghetto. I pretended to be ignorant of what Baja and Aspen were, or why schoolmates named Trudeau or Westinghouse might be particularly well-heeled. I smoked Kools, I wore a Kangol cap, I called my friends "Yo" – and this, long enough before the Beastie Boys made it widely familiar, was funny enough to a couple of Oswald House upperclassmen, a pair of hipsterish coke dealers named Runyon Kent and Bee Prudhomme, that they made a version of it my nickname: I was *Yoyo* to them. Basically, I turned myself into a cartoon of Mingus. The shtick was a splendid container for my self-loathing, and for my hostility toward my classmates. And it made me popular.

I became adept at beguiling and mocking the wealthy, right to the point of their tolerance. I cadged, shamed them into floating me meals and haircuts and cartons of Kools, flattered and appalled them by mentioning what they'd already spent years preparing to spend lifetimes never discussing – their money, the trust funds that kept them in BMWs and design-er clothes and brunches and dinners at Le Cheval whenever the dining-hall fare didn't thrill them, the checks which kept coming though there was nothing, really nothing, to purchase in rural Vermont. Except drugs. And drugs were the other way I earned my stripe.

Camden provided us with free beer and movies and contra-ception and psychotherapy. These were spoken of, joked about freely. But the school provided other things, not named, which were free as well, like a class called Unorthodox Music, run by a benevolent white-haired professor named Dr. Shakti, and widely known to be a guaranteed pass no matter how rarely you attended, or the books and cassettes which could be boost-ed hand over fist from the campus store because someone had decreed that nobody's transcript ought to be blemished with accusations – presumably the administration quietly compen-sated the vendor's losses. Of course, our parents would have laughed bitterly to hear these things called "free": the costs were folded into the absurd and famous tuition, our experience made seamless. Camden was so lush with privileges that it was easy to overlook the fact that a handful of us weren't rich. We all rode in the first-class compartment, even if some of us also swabbed the deck.

As for drugs, the school didn't actually supply them, but the blind eye they'd turned was understood as another privilege. Dealers like Runyon and Bee operated with abandon. Joints were smoked openly on Commons lawn, and parties at Pelt House were famous for acid punch concocted in an in-house lab. William S. Burroughs was nominated as commencement speaker, and during screenings of *Eraserhead* or *The Man Who*

Fell to Earth a cloud of smoke rose through the projector beam in the tiny campus auditorium. Though it was considered polite to shut your door while doing a line of coke or meth few bothered to rehang mirrors afterward, and some kept them propped on crates as permanent coffee tables, much like Barrett Rude Junior.

I was a skunk for coke. It was part of my act. Afternoons when we should have been in class or the library Matthew and I played basketball with Runyon and Bee, out at the largely unused court which was carved deep into the woods at the edge of campus, beyond the unused soccer field – Camden was an unathletic place. Runyon and Bee enjoyed the way I tried to juke and fake, all the moves I'd absorbed and never dared attempt in the gymnasiums of my youth. Matthew and I became Runyon and Bee's adoptees, their mascots. Like them we wore Wayfarer sunglasses on the court, played slack or nonexistent defense, and, between half-court games, snorted and smoked in the pine-carpeted shade at the perimeter of the asphalt. That I couldn't pay for my share was irritating or endearing to the dealers, depending on their mood, but hardly important. Evenings I hung around Runyon and Bee's rooms upstairs, and when another student casually drifted by to cop a quarter gram I'd be included in the obligatory tasting. Once I earned my keep by typing a paper Runyon had written on *As I Lay Dying*; it was shockingly riddled with grammatical errors. I rewrote it, as I suspect he'd hoped I would, and we got an A together.

Three or four afternoons that autumn, high on something at an uncommonly early hour, and cut loose from whomever I'd partied with, Moira or Matthew or the dealers upstairs, unable to stem whatever it was that surged in me, I went into the woods and flew. I no longer had the costume, and I wasn't really Aeroman anymore, just a kid from the city uncorked in the woods and venting crazy energy by soaring between branches. That I wasn't Aeroman was probably why it was possible, after so long, to fly. I'd never flown in Brooklyn, not apart from one spaldeen catch. I'd been physically cowardly, but also too burdened with what I needed Aeroman to accomplish, with notions of heroism and rescue. Here there was no one to rescue from anything, unless it was all of us from ourselves, and a flying eighteen-year-old couldn't have attempted that. So instead I wandered into the trees east of the End of the World, below the soccer field and the basketball court, screwed Aaron Doily's ring on my finger, found a high rock to leap from, and rode air. To rise slightly above the campus, to glimpse the stopped clock on the Commons tower from afar, was to attempt to believe in my luck, in my improbable, intoxicating escape from Dean Street. I tried to make the hills real by confronting them alone and head-on, make the branches mine by grazing them with my fingertips. I don't know if it worked or not. I've never been certain I could taste freedom, not for longer than the fading buzz of a line or the duration of a given song. And a song, when you press *repeat*, rarely sounds the same. Still, white powder, menthol fume, pine breeze – those flying afternoons my nostrils seemed reversed, so I could smell backward to my own minty-fresh brain.

One of those afternoons, having landed, I was startled in my stroll back up through the trees to Commons lawn by Junie Alteck. Junie was a sylphlike Oswald hippie, a durable partyer who could be found decorating Bee's room late, after others had folded their tents. We suspected Bee slept with her but he'd never admitted it. Runyon liked to call her "Aspect." She'd been walking alone in the woods. I understood from her expression that I'd been spotted.

"What were you doing?" she said dazedly.

"Performance-art project," I said.

"Oh."

"Pretty good, huh?"

"Uh, yeah!"

Cocaine and black slang and headfakes and flying: everything unsafe all my life was safe here, suddenly, and why not. Camden was designed to feel safe. It was in that state of mind, late one evening in the first days of December, that I took the call at the Oswald pay phone, from Arthur Lomb.

CHAPTER 7

ARTHUR'S STORY TUMBLED out in a hurry. The odd entrepreneurial partnership forged between Lomb, Woolfolk, and Rude in the last months before the shooting had survived Mingus's conviction for voluntary manslaughter, and his sentencing, in October, to ten years at Elmira, a prison upstate. The result was an even odder partnership: Arthur and Robert. They'd taken the money I'd paid for the comic books and the ring, and the rest they'd scraped together and bought their quarter kilogram. Then successfully dealt it. Barry being a primary customer, I also understood. And Arthur and Robert had kept from consuming the profits, held enough in reserve to cop another quarter kee and begin again. Only now they'd fallen out. Robert had come around Arthur's place with a pair of cohorts from the Gowanus Houses, demanding money, and Arthur's mother had freaked out and called the police. Now Robert had promised Arthur he would kill him if he didn't produce a certain sum by a certain time, only Arthur couldn't go alone to Gowanus to deal the stash, not with Robert's friends knowing his white face and the stash he'd be carrying; meanwhile Barry had taken a trip over Thanksgiving, to visit a doctor in Philadelphia, and not returned—

I stopped him, not needing to hear more. In fact, it mattered to me that I seem uninterested in the details of that distant morass.

"No Mingus to protect you," I said, with satisfaction.

In reply came only Arthur's breathing on the line, and I detected a little phantom of fake-asthmatic seizure in his genuine panic.

"Buy a Greyhound ticket," I said. "We'll unload the stuff in a couple of days, no problem. You'll come back with his money."

It didn't take much to persuade Arthur. The next day, a Tuesday, the first light snow of the season drifted down as I waited at the depot in Camden Town. The bus curled in the wide lot, making virgin treadmarks in the fresh accumulation. It sighed to a stop and the driver emerged to pop the undercarriage, but Arthur hadn't stowed anything. He tiptoed through the snow with an Adidas gym bag slung on the shoulder of his inadequate bomber jacket, blowing into cupped hands and looking bewildered.

"This is your school?"

"This is the town. School's three miles out."

He regarded me blankly.

"It's an easy hitch," I boasted. This was another secret perk: someone from the school, an upperclassman or a graduate student with a car, sometimes even a professor, invariably recognized the style of dress which distinguished you from a local and picked you up on the side of Route 9A, to ferry you from the dying industrial center of Camden, past the strip malls which had vampired the town's life, and into the woods, up the long driveway behind the college's gates. I wanted Arthur cowed by the full effect. I hoisted his Adidas bag and we trudged across a Dunkin' Donuts lot, to the gray-sleeted roadway.

As it happened, the car which stopped for us belonged to Richard Brodeur, president. Maybe he'd gone into town for a slice of pizza. As we climbed into the car I introduced Arthur as a friend visiting from New York. Brodeur greeted him uneasily, and reminded me of the official policy requiring overnight guests in dorms to register with the office. And of the three-day limit for such visits. I assured him we'd comply. Brodeur seemed aged from the man I'd seen deliver the pizza speech – I wondered if his first three months at Camden could have been as full as mine. I felt sorry for him, actually. Picking us up on the road seemed evidence of a desolate wish to be liked, to find a place for himself in the casual atmosphere, one he hadn't found, yet.

Snow bunched at the windshield's edges, smashed into crumbling pillars by the wipers, and flakes swam up madly to speckle the glass.

"Are you in college, Arthur?"

"Nah. Uh, I'm going to Brooklyn. City, I mean. But I, uh, gotta pick up a couple of credits first. So I'm taking the year off."

This contradictory blurt didn't leave a lot of room for a follow-up. Brodeur smiled and said, "You're a bit underdressed for this Vermont weather, aren't you?"

"Nah, I'm cool," said Arthur. "Sir."

Brodeur drove us all the way to the door of Oswald Apartment, when anyone else would have dropped a rider just past the guard's booth. I had a ridiculous impulse to invite him in. I wondered if he'd been inside a student's dorm room in his time here – probably not. And Matthew would be impressed. It would have been a very *Devo* move. It wasn't likely any drug paraphernalia or stolen campus property was sitting out in plain view, but I figured I couldn't take the chance and let the whim pass.

"Enjoy your time here, Arthur. Maybe you'll want to transfer."

"Uh, yeah, cool. Thanks."

In the space of two days Arthur Lomb was locally famous. If I was the Cat in the Hat, I'd now revealed the more unlikely Cat hidden under my headgear. With his baggy jeans and fat laces and clumsy patois, his constant references to rap and graffiti, and his unvarnished, bug-eyed awe at the place he'd come to, Arthur struck my Camden friends as riotous confirmation that whatever it was I alluded to, with my ghetto shtick, I wasn't completely kidding. Ironically, Arthur struck them as something *real*. When he insisted on counting their money before handing over the drugs – he and I and Matthew had spent the waning hours of that first afternoon divvying Arthur's quarter kee into Camden-sized portions in folded paper sleeves – they were titillated out of themselves by his street sincerity. An actual drug dealer had come to campus at last. And though Arthur was the joke, he also got it, and pushed its limits. No one could have said who was laughing harder at the other's expense.

Arthur's third day on campus Runyon and Bee drove us to Camden Town's hardware store, where we boosted a batch of Krylon and Red Devil. The four of us spent the small hours of that night spray-painting the sides of Oswald, then the campus pub and the arts complex for good measure. Arthur and I adorned the buildings with "authentic" Brooklyn graffiti, reproducing tags of FMD and DMD members, the gangs who'd *toyed* our own feeble tags out of existence. Those runes meant nothing here, though if we'd dared appropriate them on Brooklyn walls we'd have soon afterward seen the inside of the emergency room at Long Island College Hospital. Runyon and Bee wrote KING FELIX in erratic block letters a few times – the name was a private running joke of theirs – but after they saw our dexterity with the spray cans they mostly didn't bother.

Arthur must have felt as though he'd been dropped into a *Saturday Night Live* skit: "Samurai Drug Dealer," or maybe "Cokeheads in Vermont." I dedicated myself to acting as though I'd fit in this atmosphere all along, as if I found it unremarkable, needing to make sure Arthur got the message: Dylan Ebdus had been a sort of prince in pauper's clothing on Dean Street, waiting to assume his rightful place. I assuredly didn't want to discuss what had happened between Mingus and Barry and Senior. I refused to reminisce, or even acknowledge how long I'd known Arthur. I doubt I mentioned Abraham, unless it was to scoff at how little my father knew of my life at this school. Abraham, who was of course footing the bill – but that was an inconvenient detail.

Friday we woke to find we'd scrawled the tags of our enemies all among the pastoral buildings. It was actually shocking to see the fresh red paint against the white clapboard in the morning light, as though Arthur and I had imported our urban nightmares in some sleepwalkers' compulsion. The dining hall was buzzing with theories as to who'd done it, but Runyon and Bee, in whispered voices, persuaded me it was no big deal. We'd redecorated our playpen, that was all. Camden was ours to deface.

Arthur should have been put on a bus back to New York that day, to honor the rule, but the rule was far from our minds. I wanted him to see a Friday-night party – tonight's was at Crumbly House – and, though word had spread among the campus cokeheads that I was holding a fire sale out of Oswald Apartment, and Arthur had already covered Robert Woolfolk's payment, we needed another big night, a party night, to shift the last of his stash.

We had the Apartment mostly to ourselves. Matthew

had lately been sleeping with his sophomore girlfriend in an off-campus house in North Camden, and Arthur had taken Matthew's place in the bedroom in the rear of the suite. My bed was in the big common room, with the fireplace and couch. That afternoon Arthur and I lounged stuporously in that front room as the thin December light dimmed in the bare apple trees outside, the two of us recovering from the night before, waiting for the night to come. Arthur didn't like the Devo and Wire and Residents records Matthew and I had in constant rotation those days, and he'd dug deep in Matthew's collection to find something he liked better: Genesis's *The Lamb Lies Down on Broadway.* We slumped in the dark, me on my bed and Arthur on the couch, and the hysterical symphonic glamour of that music seemed to speak for the rich absurdity of our circumstance so well it felt as though we'd never need to utter a word again.

The first knock on the door wasn't a customer for Arthur's wares but a member of the cleaning staff, a woman I'd seen a dozen times before but without any name that I knew. Pale and thick and stooped, she seemed to me a kind of crone, though she was surely no older than forty. It was her job to scour the Oswald bathrooms, most of which were common spaces, adjoining public corridors. But once a week she had to clean the private bathroom in our apartment, and so we let her in. With barely a nod at Arthur she vanished through Matthew's room, into the back of the suite. I flipped the record and sagged back on my bed.

The woman was typical of an army of gray locals who maintained the buildings and grounds at Camden. They had none of the color or defiance of the usual townies, but were true servants, perfecting the art of deference to the point of invisibility. We knew the names of a few of the older men, those who'd served for twenty-five or thirty years and, having seen generations not only of students but professors come and go, achieved talismanic status. They had snaggly grins and names like Scrumpy or Red and were hailed as they bumped past on a mower or snowplow. But the toilet-scrubbing, Morlockian women never spoke. Runyon liked to call them *little people,* and I once saw him raise a beer and say, "I'd like to thank all the little people, especially the one that mopped the puke off the landing Saturday morning while I was still blissfully passed out."

Before the album side was finished playing I had to rouse myself to answer another knock. Now it was Karen Rothenberg and Euclid Barnes. Karen and Euclid were friends of Moira's, from Worthell House, and I suppose they were mine also. Now they were also customers – had been, already, during the three-day binge surrounding Arthur's arrival. Euclid was a tall, soft junior with loose dark bangs that tumbled into his eyes. He was resignedly, mopily gay, never found anyone to have sex with, complaining bitterly of his isolation in Vermont. Karen was his protector and solicitor, a dark-haired, heavy girl who wore gothy makeup and affected a jaded exhaustion. In relentlessly pitching Euclid at various boys it seemed to me Karen was really protecting herself from a terror of her own desires. One desultory three A.M., weeks ago – which was to say, in Camden time, eons past – I'd fended off a double advance from Karen and Euclid. Now they were both openly obsessed with Arthur, the wild child of Brooklyn.

Euclid shook out of his pea coat and threw it over a chair, then immediately began fumbling with his cigarettes. "What *are* you listening to?" he said.

"Genesis," I said.

"Nonsense, this sounds nothing like Genesis. Take it off."

"Where's Moira?" said Karen.

"I don't know," I said.

"She said she'd meet us here."

"Okay, but I didn't hear about it."

Karen plopped herself on the couch at Arthur's feet, startling him from his doze. This spree might be more wearing for him than I'd realized.

"I'm absolutely tapped," Euclid muttered around his cigarette. He tossed four twenties onto the dresser. "My parents are late with a check, blame them. This has to be the last."

"We're almost out anyway," I said. Arthur was sitting up, rubbing his eyes.

Euclid frowned, disapproving my unworldliness. "Isn't there always more?" His eyes slid to Arthur, now understood to be cocaine's personal escort in its inevitable passage from New York to Camden. For the first time it occurred to me this needn't be a one-time thing. I'd thought of my dealerhood as a kind of paraphrase, a larkish appropriation of Runyon and Bee, upstairs. But then maybe Runyon and Bee had been ironic when they began too.

"This music is agony. It sounds like *troll* music."

"What's troll music?" said Arthur.

"It's the music trolls listen to," said Euclid. He shook his head to show that if you didn't understand this it couldn't be explained. "I always predicted Dylan and Matthew would succumb to the pressure of living in Oswald, but I'm sorry to see it happen so quickly."

"This place is a hotbed of trolls," I agreed.

"Ooh, play this, I like this," said Karen, sing-songing for her pleasure like a child. She'd been flipping through a pile of LPs and now held up the Psychedelic Furs.

"Dang, I hate that shit," said Arthur with dopey sincerity, and we all laughed.

"Do it yourself," I told Karen. She replaced one record with the other, then cranked the volume. Richard Butler snarled *Yaaah fall in love* and as if on that cue Moira came in without knocking and joined us there as we sat, all of us on my bed now, while Arthur sliced lines of coke on a duct-taped scrap of sheet steel Matthew and I had liberated from the welding studios. In four days Arthur had come a long way toward the Camden manner of dealing cocaine, the casual sampling which surrounded every act of throwing down bills as Euclid had just done. In Arthur's idiom the dealer was meant to be above partying with his customers, but that distinction was meaningless here.

I was happy to see Moira. The binge with Arthur and Runyon and Bee had been boyish, and I missed her. I was glad she'd invited herself with Euclid and Karen, glad she'd known to enter without knocking. In fact, as she slid in beside me, under that roar of guitars which made conversation unnecessary, I decided I probably loved her, that I'd need to be more than her confidante. In fact it would be two nights later, after Arthur had finally gone, that Moira and I slept together again, a costly mistake in a December of costly mistakes. Now I just smiled, assuming she felt what I did.

We all did lines. When Arthur objected that we'd given away too much I silenced him by buying an eighth myself with my share of our profits. In fact, everything I did was meant to chagrin Arthur. That I treated him so casually as my sidekick masked an obsession with Arthur's witnessing eyes. While we did the lines Euclid and Karen plied Arthur with questions: Why were the laces on his shoes never done up? How he could walk with his jeans so low? Was anyone ever tempted to pull them down around his ankles? When Arthur looked to me for help in his bafflement, I looked away, pulled Moira closer, only laughed. See me get the girls, Arthur, and get the friends, and get the jokes, see how hip I am – if you'd grasped how I was on the brighter path all along you never would have thrown me over for Mingus. You and Mingus never would have thrown me over for one another. Arthur and I were still playing chess, two wretched nerds on his Pacific Street stoop, and now I'd toppled his queen but let him go on playing, hobbled and bound to lose. See, see? In another day or two I'd exile Arthur back to Brooklyn, to Robert Woolfolk. But first he had to take a good look at what he'd lost and I'd won.

It was five o'clock. The first wave of students would be lining up with their trays in the dining hall. The party at Crumbly wouldn't be under way for hours but it was already dark and we were high and the music was loud. Our party was under way. Probably we'd skip dinner. If we were hungry Karen Rothenberg would be willing to drive us into town, we'd pile into her Toyota. Soon others would attach to our core, be led into the Apartment for drugs. We'd see Matthew, surely, and his new girlfriend, though she was a bore and making Matthew boring too, that was the consensus. We'd visit Runyon and Bee upstairs, tip back their six-foot Lucite bong. Our ranks would grow, then split like a paramecium, we'd drink flavorless drinks, see all our friends and enemies, visit the dance floor, transmute yet remain ourselves. At some point Euclid would commit a sulky pass at Arthur, humiliating them both. Consoling Euclid would be a rich drama, occupying us deep into the dawn hours. Anyone could see it all coming and no one could possibly stop it and that was the beautiful thing. Friday night was open wide and writ in stone.

The cleaning woman barreled out with her body protecting her yellow bucket of cleaning supplies like a tiny fullback. She must have been cowering in the bathroom, her work completed, listening as the party developed, praying we'd disperse for dinner. Then, as the minutes ticked past, it would have dawned, with horror, that we weren't going anywhere, that she had no alternative but to make her mad run. To get from Matthew's room out of the apartment she needed to thread between the five of us arrayed on the bed and the couch, and sidestep a heap of LPs Karen had spread across the floor. This she did very nimbly, with the harried grace of prey. She might have muttered *Excuse me*, but not audibly. Whether she'd understood the references in our talk, or the scrape of razor against steel, she evidenced understanding by her fear, the way she'd dunned her rabbity eyes against seeing as she passed through.

Then she was gone, leaving us shocked into silence under the buzz-saw music.

Karen dropped the rolled dollar she'd held and covered her mouth in theatrical astonishment.

Euclid spoke first: "*What. Was. That.*"

"Ho, snap," said Arthur. "That's fucked up."

"I totally forgot she was there," I whispered to no one in particular, my mind reeling at the insane mistake.

"Did she see?" said Karen, her black-ringed eyes wide like a bird's.

"Of *course* she saw," said Moira. "What do you *think*?"

We knew what we thought, but none of us knew what it meant. A famous Camden story – I was certain Moira at least also knew it – concerned a student dealer at Fish House, a few years earlier, who'd been discreetly warned by the school of an imminent bust by the Vermont Police. A sympathetic faculty member had suggested the dealer lock his door and take a long weekend off campus. The point being: Camden had a monumental stake in protecting us from tangles with the law. Talented and eccentric children shouldn't be judged by society's harsh adult standards. Let them be eased through their difficult years – this was the deal implicit in the huge tuition, and in the school's quarantine deep in the woods.

So what did it mean if one of the *little people* knew I dealt coke from Oswald Apartment? Maybe nothing. She might not tell. She might not have caught the full implication, anyhow, might not have seen money change hands. It was easy to imagine nothing crucial had occurred, only something freakish and funny. I could hear Runyon's voice in my head, urging me to understand it that way. I tried not to race through recollection of the words we'd said aloud, the words she might have overheard.

"Well, I consider it appalling," said Euclid, breaking the long silence. "The notion of keeping a cleaning woman locked in your bathroom as some kind of sexual pawn. I can't imagine how you thought you'd get away with it."

"Ew, she was definitely *not* my sexual pawn," I said.

"Of course she was," said Euclid. "You and Arthur both, you're animals. It's lucky we created a diversion so she could escape. Were you even intending to give her any food? Were you even intending to give her any *drugs*?"

"Hey, man," said Arthur, getting with the joke now. "Everybody pays."

"I wouldn't have it any other way," said Euclid.

"Well, I'm glad she's gone," said Karen. "Because I have to pee."

"That would have been a shock," said Moira.

"Go see if she built a fire," directed Euclid. "She probably tried to send smoke signals, to others of her kind."

"Maybe she ate the soap," suggested Arthur.

The scandal passed, and we resumed our evening's plot. When Matthew appeared, we recounted the story, competing to exaggerate the details: the woman's demented scurry, Karen's nearly wetting her pants, Arthur certain it was narcs and ready to swallow his stash. The five of us were still laughing about it over ten o'clock cassoulet at Le Cheval, courtesy of Karen Rothenberg's mother's MasterCard. The next day I described the incident to Runyon, who, as I'd expected, waved it off. And so it was forgotten.

Two weeks later Arthur's visit was a distant memory for us all, folded behind a dozen other dramas. Moira and I had had our third fling and imploded in misunderstanding, each hurt in a way we could never have articulated, each consoled by newer friends. And as the campus, wreathed in cold and dark, prepared to shut down for the long winter break, the whole term just past dwindled into twee irrelevance. Where were you spending January, that was the question now. Mustique? Steamboat? Well, I was going to Dean Street, but never mind. The future hurtled toward us – who would be our new lovers, in February, when we returned? We had our eyes on a few alluring prospects, ones we'd somehow overlooked the first time. The past term was already mute, and our glories and mistakes there were mute as well.

That was how it felt the afternoon of my conference with my faculty advisor, Tom Sweden, the last day of classes. Sweden was also my sculpture teacher, and he was a typical Camden sculptor, a gruff, inarticulate chain-smoker in a permanent proletarian costume of work boots and plaster-clogged jeans, a bit of a Marlboro Man. We didn't like one another – I had as much use for his romance of faux poverty and mock illiteracy as he did for mine of faux privilege and mock sophistication. Yet somehow I'd imagined my wit and vigor put Sweden on my side of a line dividing the hipster students and teachers from the square administration. I don't really know why I thought this, except that I was drunk on college.

Sweden was seated in his wreck of an office in the basement of the arts complex, ringed in a chaos of scrap dowels, overrun ashtrays, and unsorted paperwork. When I arrived, ten minutes late, he was already scowling at a sheaf of pink forms, final evaluations from each of my four classes that term. So he knew, as I did, that I'd failed sociology outright and taken an incomplete from my English professor.

"This ain't so great," he said, wrinkling the papers.

"I'll take care of the incomplete," I said, approaching the meeting like a negotiation. "I've got the paper half-written." I didn't have it begun.

Sweden rubbed his bristly chin with stained fingers. Like Brando, he was superior to the part he was playing, and it pained him. He couldn't fit his deep thoughts to the banal language at hand, so he only frowned.

"I was just more *excited* about sculpture this term," I said, trying flattery.

"Yeah, but . . ." He trailed off, leaving us both guessing.

"And I passed Unorthodox Music," I pointed out.

Sweden raised an eyebrow. "Dr. Shakti?"

"Yes."

"Yeah, but that ain't really a class, is it?"

If Sweden didn't know he was the only one on campus. I kept silent.

"Was there anything . . ." Sweden kept glancing at the door. "Was there anything, ah, *bothering* you this term, Dylan?"

"No, I just think it was a period of adjustment and I'll probably focus better when I come back. On classes and stuff. But nothing's wrong."

He scratched his chin again. Perhaps my little speech was enough to get us both out of the conference – he seemed to be weighing this. Then there came a knock on his door.

"Yeah, come in." Sweden sounded disgruntled, but not surprised.

It was Richard Brodeur, president.

"I thought I'd just run these over myself," he said, showing Sweden a clutch of folders. Sweden grunted, gestured at his desk. Brodeur dropped the folders into the mess there.

"Richard, uh, Dylan Ebdus," mumbled Sweden, painfully reluctant with his lines. "We're just, uh, having ourselves a conference here."

Brodeur reached for my hand and, as he gripped it, looked deep into my eyes. "Yes," he said gently. "We've met."

"Sure, hi," I said.

"Gave you a lift on 9A, didn't I? In the snow."

"Yes," I said.

"How's your friend?"

"Fine, I think. Fine."

"Well, look, I shouldn't interrupt," said Brodeur abruptly to Sweden. "Those papers aren't urgent. Get to them whenever."

"Right," grimaced Sweden.

There was nothing to interrupt. With Brodeur gone Sweden

had little to say. He managed to wish me a happy holiday, and good luck with the paper. He had to light a cigarette before he succeeded in telling me to *take care, man*. That was apparently all he'd wanted to get across.

The letter arrived less than a week later, in Brooklyn. It was addressed to my father. We were at the breakfast table when Abraham turned it over to me, replaced in its torn envelope, with no more than a dry, "This is for you, I believe." But the letter had come the day before – Abraham had taken it upstairs and contemplated it for an afternoon and evening before decid-ing to say nothing.

The letter was on Camden's embossed cream stationery and bore Richard Brodeur's signature. It explained regretfully that for my violations of the school's policies on overnight guests and narcotics possession, I was subject to a mandatory one-term leave of absence, followed by a student council hearing. More to the point, really, my scholarship had been suspended because of my failure to sustain a minimum threshold of aca-demic excellence. After a specified period I would be invited to *reapply* for the scholarship.

The legend of the dealer at Fish House who'd been warned to close up shop wasn't misleading, not really. Yes, Camden College could, and would, protect itself from the Vermont narcotics squad. It could also protect itself from me and Arthur Lomb. I stuffed the letter into my jeans, eyes cast low to dodge Abraham's. My father went on clinking saucers and scraping toast, then in a flurry of excitement, read me an obituary of Louis Aragon, French Poet, eighty-five. With that I could have been off, up Nevins to the 4 train, my knapsack loaded with undone homework and photocopied flyers for Stuyvesant bands. Dean Street was intact as I'd left it, the letter in my pocket the only evidence I'd been anywhere else.

CHAPTER 8

THE UNIVERSITY OF CALIFORNIA at Berkeley would still have me. That was far enough to suit my mood, a distance from which Vermont receded into that gnarled mass of old states no one on the bright coast could ever be bothered to tell apart. My Camden credits were useless in the transfer, so I began again as a freshman with a clean slate, so-called. More like a clean chip of slate on my shoulder. The school was Camden's reverse – an Asian, Mexican, black, and white sea of students, a bayside city in place of Camden's evergreen art-school hot-house. At Camden, classes had been ten or twelve around a long oak table, all bantering and debating, all preening and being acknowledged. Here a professor muttered into a microphone on a far-off platform while a stadium of freshmen jotted notes, arms synchronized like assembly-line robots. For the first time in my life I learned to study.

The best thing for miles around was the campus radio station, KALX. The gang of DJs there had been freed by the station's open format to obsess in any direction they liked, and the results were splendidly motley. Many DJs had been allowed to keep their slots for years past graduation – it was this exception to the usual rule which gave KALX its special depth, the depth of an anarchic family, the members all with nicknames to distinguish their shows: Marshall Stax, Gale Warning, Commander Chris, and Sex For Teens were a few of my favorites. Their charismatic, caustic, and homely voices punctuated the seasonless Berkeley days and nights. In my dorm room, on the twelfth floor of an ugly high-rise, above the sightline of the palm trees which dotted a path to the bay, their voices were my only regular company.

The source was a tiny building on Bowditch Street, white cinder block with the station's call letters painted in a blue stripe. KALX was iceberglike, mostly submerged – the booths and record collection were in the basement, upstairs just a spare office, desks with rotary telephones, and a waiting room full of thrift-store couches leaking foam through cigarette burns. I visited at the first chance, volunteering to man phones during a fund-raising marathon. My shift was in the earliest hours of the morning, and the DJ looked at me like I was a loser for taking it. He explained the drill: for pledging more than twenty-five dollars a caller could visit the station and claim a T-shirt; for more than fifty I could gift them with one of the lousy records clogging the station's in box. Through the shift I took fifteen or twenty calls. I listened to the DJ's voice piped from below as he grudgingly fit the fund drive into his format, but I wasn't admitted into that basement chapel.

Afterward I asked about becoming a DJ and was given little encouragement. It took a hundred hours of dull volunteer work to get on the list for training. Then the waiting list, for even the meagerest twilight slot on the roster, was usually a year. I'd be trained by other DJs, who'd prefer if I didn't waste their time – I should be serious, or not bother. KALX was, true to Berkeley's ideals, a real volunteer collective, but managed without any Berkeley sanctimony or mysticism, instead with a stoical punk exhaustion. This was March of 1983. By the end of that year I'd claimed a show, from two to six Thursday mornings. I kept the slot for three years. That was a trifle by KALX's standards, but it was as large a commitment as I'd managed in my new grown-up life.

I called myself Running Crab. If I'd had a vague suspicion that in transferring to Berkeley I'd mimicked Rachel in her long-ago westward dash, now I bitterly joked with myself that she'd be within hearing range of my broadcasts. She could wonder who he was, her phantom double. I played Ian Dury's "Reasons to Be Cheerful, Part 3," a Monty Pythonesque white rap, at the start of every show, and declared it my anthem. But my bitterness, like my playlist, was soon hung out to dry. My show was bad. However many favorite songs I'd thought I had, they looked threadbare after a few repetitions. I was trying to make an impression, to stake a personality, as Matthew Schrafft and I had by wearing Devo on our sleeves.

It was impossible to hide from the fact: those lonely hours before dawn were either void or mirror. I was talking to nobody, or myself. So I began again, in a mode of fumbling and discovery. Before each show I excavated forgotten albums from the station's musty library, and on-air I stirred my own curiosity, played cuts I'd never heard and always wondered about. What I cared for, when I permitted myself to know it, was doo-wop, rhythm and blues, and soul. Stax and Motown, but also Hi and Excello and King and Kent, the further reaches. Otis Redding and Gladys Knight but also Maxine Brown and Syl Johnson. And groups – I loved harmony groups. I loved the Subtle Distinctions.

I turned myself into a vinyl hawk, scouring record shops for out-of-print LPs, studying them with Talmudic intensity. The music I loved would all be dug out of studio archives and put onto CD within a few years, but then it was still scratchy and moldy and entirely my own. I read Peter Guralnick and Charlie Gillett and Greg Shaw and forgot which opinions were received and which were mine, and then I made them all mine by playing the records, by playing the records, by playing the records – I learned to shut up and play the records. I'd intersperse the music not with my own comments but with readings from the vintage liner notes on the LP jackets, like Richard Robinson's for Howard Tate's *Get It While You Can*:

> Yes, Howard is black underground, white folks only admitted by insight. He's got the true emotion of soul which is only out of sight because you're not listening with your heart. That's what Howard and his music are all about: the indifferent earth and the long crawl between breaking day and darkening night.

Who could top that, who would want to try? I'd read a liner note, then play a side at a time. For in KALX's basement I discovered I had all the time in the world. There I learned that to find one's art is to kill time dead with a single shot. I felt akin to Abraham. I built a path of two- and three-minute cuts through the night like my father in his cold studio daubing paint on a ladder of film.

The station wasn't a social place. Staff meetings were gruffly efficient, and the DJs made a hermetic community at best. You might bond with those whose shows bookended your own, literally in passing. But I befriended a group of current and former

DJs who played softball together. They called themselves the People's League. We gathered every Sunday at a place called the Deaf School Field for a ramshackle co-ed game with no balls and strikes, no score kept, and plenty of beer and grilled food. Ten years of lunging at spaldeens with a broomstick had made me a pretty good hitter, though one exclusively capable of line drives up the middle. The other DJs mocked me for my predictability: everything looped over the second baseman's head.

It wasn't easy to explain to them the narrow, flattened diamond of Dean Street, with car handles on either side for first and third and a distant manhole for second. To pull a ball in Brooklyn was to smash a parlor window and end the game. The DJs were from California and had never played in a street. As it happened, the Deaf School Field's irregular shape gave it a cavernous left field, while a stand of trees in center made my tic an advantage: the league's sluggers boomed three-hundred-foot fly outs to left, while my drives scooted into the glade and were lost. As the center fielder beat in the carpet of eucalyptus, searching for the ball, I'd dash around the bases for an easy home run. Once, with a girl there I wanted to impress, I hit four tree-assisted home runs in a single afternoon. It might have been the happiest day of my life. Certainly it would have been if Mingus Rude had been there to witness it.

My People's League heroics were accomplished without help from Aaron Doily's ring. The thing was shelved. I'd forgotten my identity as the world's most pathetic superhero, become a Californian instead. I had California girlfriends, a California apartment, and, after I'd dropped out of classes from sheer disinterest, a California newspaper career, as music critic for the *Alameda Harbinger*, the job an extension of some work I'd done revamping KALX's moribund gazette. It was three years before I reached for the ring, took Aeroman out of mothballs. What happened was I got yoked, on a bus.

I'd taken Lucinda Hoekke to see Jonathan Richman at Floyd's, a tiny stage in downtown Oakland. Lucinda was a transferred sophomore from St. John's in Annapolis, a KALX groupie; this windy night in March was our third date. After the show we boarded a lonely bus on Broadway, pointed back into Berkeley,

and sat too near the rear. I may have been trying to show Lucinda Hoekke or myself that I wasn't afraid of the sole other rider,
a tall black kid slouched in the corner, down coat puffed from
beneath his arms like water wings. So we took a twin seat, our
backs to him. Between woolen hat and striped scarf I sported
heavy, black-rimmed glasses, a Buddy Holly/Elvis Costello
prop signifying rock hipness. That's what they signified to me.
To the kid I surely looked like a caricatured victim: Woody
Allen had stepped onto his bus. He threw the yoke on general
principles, tipped my jaw with his elbow just long enough to
show it could be done.

"I'm just messin' with you, yo. This your girl?"

Lucinda blinked. The windows might as well have been
painted black. The bus whirred down the avenue, the driver
impassive in his cage. My face grew red.

"You got a dollar you could lend me?"

The script was identical coast to coast. Maybe I had it written on my back. I grabbed Lucinda's mittened hand and drew
her up to the front. We sat across from the driver, who barely
glanced.

"Are you going to tell him?" whispered Lucinda.

I shushed her.

"See, you don't gotta be like that," called the kid in the
back. "You can't even *talk* to me, man?"

He pulled the cord, then stepped through the back stairwell,
loudly smacking the bus's side panel in farewell. We rode on in
silence, the driver and I complicit in shame, Lucinda cowed. I
saw incomprehension in her eyes: Had we been *mugged*? Why
was I enraged – why did I seem angry at *her*? The conundrum
was unaltered since I'd met it last, on some pavement in the
vicinity of I.S. 293. A yoking was a koan – it could perplex
forever and never be solved. What it had to teach couldn't be
named. I never called Lucinda Hoekke again. I also never wore
those glasses after that night.

Aeroman's costume was long gone, moldering in some police
evidence crate, or disposed of. Just as well. This time I favored
something less flamboyant, away from the caped Superman or
Omega the Unknown model, nearer to those masked, nattily

dressed urban avenger types, the Spirit or the Green Hornet. The change represented an incorporation of my recent fondness for forties and fifties film noir, allied with a general sense of embarrassment at the candy-striped Marvel costumes, which in my mind were now bundled in a seventies-style trash heap with Kiss and T. Rex and the uniforms of the Houston Astros. Our capes – Mingus's, Aaron Doily's, mine – had never helped with flying anyway. So I began shopping in Berkeley consignment shops for a really fine vintage two-piece with narrow lapels, something dashing and memorable and worthy of Aeroman's high intentions: brown sharkskin, maybe, or forest green. Then I discovered the search was unnecessary: Aeroman no longer had an appearance, was no longer capable of dressing up, or down. The ring had changed since my soaring in the Camden woods.

I learned it in open air, in twilight, no mirrors nearby. I'd climbed Berkeley's hills, to a bluff where I could gaze on the rooftops of luxury homes braced on stilts against the grade, the green steppes above campus, including the Deaf School Field and the skirt of flatlands that spread to the marina. I'd gone into the woods to bolster courage, remind myself of the only flight I'd experienced worth recalling, not on city streets where the action was but alone among trees and ponds. I thought I'd work my way down the hill, perhaps light on the Deaf School Field to begin with. And I wasn't stalking injustice tonight. I didn't have a costume or plan of attack. This was just practice.

I only had to don the ring to instantly feel the difference. The ring wasn't drawn to the air – that part of it was dead. Now it didn't confer flying, but something else. My hand was invisible. So was the rest of me, that I could see. I stumbled on the rocky path there, tangling invisible feet as I twisted around, trying for a glimpse of myself, anywhere. As long as I wore the ring there wasn't a glimpse to be had. I could scuff earth with my shoe, I could cough or yell and be heard, could feel my own breath against my palm, could lick a fingertip and feel saliva evaporate in the bay wind. I merely couldn't be seen.

I don't know why it changed. I've wondered if it was a California thing, the ring's nature linked to geophysical forces and altered by its transportation there. Or it might be some passage of age – the ring's, not my own, since Aaron Doily had flown, albeit lamely, in his fifties. In the end I accepted it on personal terms. When I was twelve and the ring first came into my hand I believed that flying was the denominator, the bottom line of superheroic being: any superhero flew, even if they had to cheat by vaulting or floating on bubbles of conjured force or riding in hovercraft. So it was a flying ring. By the time I wore it again on that Berkeley hill I knew differently. Invisibility was what every superhero *really* had in common. After all, who'd ever seen one?

In truth, if it was still a flying ring I might never have tangled with Oakland, might only have flown in the hills and retired the ring again. My cowardice was ritual by now. The fury at being yoked on the bus in front of Lucinda Hoekke might have been expiated by a bit of zipping around, a refreshment of my irrelevant secret power. But this change in the ring seemed a message that Aeroman had grown up. Invisibility was sly and urban and might just do the trick. I was made ready for something.

As I stood dazzled by my transparency, a small bird, a sparrow, attempting to land on what must have appeared to be an empty bluff, swept from the sky and punched me in the temple, hard. We both fell. I crumpled to my hands and knees in panic, not sure the surprise attack wouldn't continue until I spotted the stunned bird lying on its side in the dust. I thought it had killed itself against me, then it began whirring feet and wings, swimming a tiny circle before righting, to stand, head cocked. I pulled the ring from my finger and looked at my palms, found them scraped pink. When I touched my temple I found blood in my hair – my own, not the sparrow's.

The bird stared. It didn't seem entirely surprised I'd become visible. I suppose it had proved my existence by other means. It hopped a short distance, examined me again. Then – satisfied? stupefied? pissed off? – it turned, and we each walked, not flew, from the site of the encounter.

CHAPTER 9

THE FIRST CDS came in long boxes, to stack in the bins left behind by the vinyl CDs had displaced. The great first wave of box sets were disguised as vinyl too: discs or cassettes, either might lurk in packaging which mimicked a carton of LPs. It might even be LPs – you read the fine print to know. Rick Rubin put guitars in a rap, and MTV put the rap on television. His group, Run-DMC, found their best success with a cover of Aerosmith's "Walk This Way," only Aerosmith was brought in for the chorus, as rappers didn't sing. Cocaine bifurcated, and blacks were awarded crack, beneficiary of the best marketing campaign since – LSD? The Ayatollah Khomeini? In Berkeley, deep in the decade of Reagan, students at Malcolm X Elementary took their lunch hour in Ho Chi Minh Park.

My epic project that year, never to be completed, was something called *Liner Notes: The Box Set*. The container would be one of those LP-square boxes so beloved by collectors like myself. Inside, loose sheets bearing the greatest liner notes of all time, in fine reproductions of the original designs. They'd include chestnuts by Samuel Charters, Nat Hentoff, Ralph Gleason, and Andrew Loog Oldham, as well as notes written by musicians themselves: John Fahey, Donald Fagen, Bill Evans. Landmarks like Paul Nelson on the Velvets' *Live 69/70*, Greil Marcus on *The Basement Tapes*, Lester Bangs on the Godz. Joe Strummer on Lee Dorsey, Kris Kristofferson on Steve Goodman, Dylan on Eric Von Schmidt. James Baldwin on James Brown, LeRoi Jones on Coltrane, Hubert Humphrey on Tommy James and the Shondells. The Shaggs' father on the Shaggs, Charles Mingus's psychiatrist on *The Black Saint and the Sinner Lady*. Above all, the uncanny found poetry of the endorsements I'd been reading aloud over the KALX airwaves, like Deanie Parker's for Albert King:

> *If you've ever been hurt by your main squeeze, deceived by your best friend, or down to your last dime and ready to call it quits,*

Albert King has the solution if you have the time to listen.
Maybe you're just curious . . . he'll get through to you . . . put
Albert on your turntable . . . put your needle in the groove . . .
now drown yourself in the . . . blues.

That it might be regarded as a disappointment to find not a single note of actual music inside *Liner Notes: The Box Set* never dawned on me. I can't say why, exactly, except that a wish to place the writing on a par with the music was the purloined letter of intent at the project's center. People like to be fooled, and they like to fool themselves. I was twenty-three, and believed to my heart that music fandom needed *Liner Notes: The Box Set*. Similarly, I persuaded myself that the crack epidemic, then reaching its local pitch in Oakland and Emeryville, was a job for Aeroman.

I went where scared me the most. That was a bar on Shattuck Avenue near Sixtieth Street, called Bosun's Locker, a place where *everyone knew* it was easy to score and an excellent place not to be *caught dead* if you were white. Edgy groups of young black men could be seen milling on the sidewalks there, in a way which reminded me, when I'd glimpsed it from a passing bus, of the corners near the Wyckoff Gardens or Gowanus Houses, back in Brooklyn. Drive-by shootings were now a famous problem in the poorer suburbs of the Bay Area, Richmond, and El Cerrito, but I was a typical New York expatriate, still without a driver's license, and the suburbs surrounding Berkeley on three sides felt impossibly remote. Besides, I found it hard to envision how an invisible man would halt a drive-by shooting. He'd need an invisible car. I went to the place *I could walk to* that scared me the most, and that was the big gloomy pool joint on Shattuck.

I walked in visible at seven on a Tuesday night, fingering the ring in my pocket. I was sure I could get myself mugged – by now I was sure of nothing so much as that. And sure that with the ring I could free myself of a mugging as well. But contriving to rescue the same old whiteboy wasn't right. Aeroman's vanity required somebody to protect. Maybe in some recess of my mind it was a Rude, Mingus or Barrett Junior, someone I'd abandoned. But maybe Rachel too. For Mingus had abandoned me as I'd abandoned him, and I think I had the two, abandoning and being abandoned, confused. This was the fog I carried with me into Bosun's Locker, and the reason my invisible adventure was destined to be so foggy. But I wasn't invisible, yet.

Every head turned, though that was only four. The muttonchopped bartender, large enough to be his own bouncer, two fiftyish pool shooters weighing angles on the farthest of three tables, and a boy, or man – he was my age, and I believed I was a man, then – seated at the bar's corner. He wore a tan suede-front cardigan under a wool coat, and a Kangol cap, the costume of a player. I was the only white face. Nobody spoke, or anyway nothing I could make out over the jukebox cut, the Blue Notes, Teddy Pendergrass intoning *Bad luck, that's what you got—*

"Help you?"

"Anchor Steam, please."

"Bud, Miller, Heineken."

"Okay, uh, Heineken."

My bar companion had been staring, so I raised my bottle before I sipped from it. There were five stools between us. He turned his head to the window as if sickened, and nodded to the music, not me.

I went over. "Hey—"

"Yo, don't be steppin' up on me."

"I just wanted to ask—"

"I'm only saying don't be steppin' up, shock a brother like that."

"Can I ask—"

"Nah, man, just get away from me."

I went back to my seat. A minute later he slid over to me. "What you wanna ax me, man?"

"I'm looking to get high," I said.

He wrinkled his nose. "Fuck you on about, man?"

The word *crack* felt too on the nose. *Newsweek* and *60 Minutes* were those days likening crack to the plagues of the Middle Ages. "I want to freebase," I said. "I'm looking to score some rock."

"Yo, shut the fuck up. The fuck you think I could help you *score some rock?*"

"Sorry."

"You lookin' for trouble, man?"

Well, I was, wasn't I? This was the essential point. In this moment he'd seen me clearly.

"No," I said.

"You wouldn't come around here if you wasn't looking for trouble." But he grinned. "Listen, man, feebase and rock two diffint things entily." Despite *feebase* and *diffint* and *entily*, he genuinely wanted me to understand.

"Sorry," I said again.

He looked to see who might be watching, then offered a handclasp. I took it.

"What your name?"

"Dee," I said.

Again he glanced around the room. Nobody was in earshot, bartender giving berth, pool shooters oblivious. "You could just call me OJJJ." *Oh-Jay-Jay-Jay.* I supposed OJ and OJJ had been spoken for, in OJJJ's neck of the woods.

"You cool?" he asked me. "You my boy?"

"Sure." I wondered if he thought I was a cop, and if so, why he didn't ask that.

"You wanna get high?"

"I've got money."

He winced, leaned in closer. "Dang, man, shut up. You don't need money you want OJJJ get you high. Just ax."

"Okay."

"Aight." We clasped hands again. OJJJ fought the urge to glance over his shoulder at the window every few seconds, lost, won, lost again. Meanwhile, I caught the bartender checking us out, squinting his distrust. My imagination wrote a voice-over: *What's OJJJ doing with that white boy?* I was certain anyone here was a regular. And that anyone would audition me for cop. In fact, according to what I soon read in the *Oakland Tribune*, the bartender had never seen OJJJ before in his life and never wondered for a moment if I was a cop. That wasn't how I struck anyone, apparently.

OJJJ led me into the bathroom, past the pool table, the

shooters who still didn't think us worth a look. The place was utilitarian, with a steel trough urinal, and a floor pitched around a central drain, for easy sluicing. Graffiti hadn't completely blackened the lime walls. The stall doors had been taken off, but we hid in a stall, each with our back to the divider. It stank of ammonia there, nothing worse. Then OJJJ opened his coat to pull out a glass pipe and I did smell something worse: the acridity of his sweat, infusing the layers of his fancy sweater. I wondered how many days it had been since OJJJ had bathed, or even gone home, wherever home was. Later I'd know it was the chemistry of his fear.

Now his acridity mingled with the tang of crack, seared in a glass pipe lined with a tiny copper screen. I watched OJJJ and tried to do as he did. I'd never smoked cocaine, only seen it done by Barrett Junior. I think OJJJ knew he was teaching me, and was glad to be. I think it gave him courage. He showed me what was a *rock* and what was a *pebble* and a *twig*. He and I smoked a few of these and once or twice I felt I grasped it, felt the cold rush threading me. But the nature of the high was elusive, impossible to savor, only chase. Then OJJJ took the pipe and showed me the *big rock* he'd been saving. I watched him smoke it and then he asked to see my money. I offered him forty dollars and he told me to hold it, that we'd need it where we were going, if I wanted to come. I saw he wanted me to. I wondered when I was going to become invisible.

There were women at the bar when we came out, made up for the night, and as we passed one of them said to OJJJ, "Hey, where you goin', pretty man?"

"Aw, shut up, bitch."

The bartender shook his walrus head, but we were gone, we didn't care what he thought. OJJJ led me around the corner, down the dark residential block. The poorest parts of Oakland looked the same to me as the rich parts, like suburbs, lawns and driveways, nobody on the sidewalks. Only the cars told the tale of what was inside. The cars on Sixtieth Street were twenty years old, Cadillacs with rotted vinyl roofs, Olds and Chryslers calicoed with rust and mismatched fenders.

OJJJ had been charging ahead, egging me to follow. He seemed to want to keep some momentum, sparked by his hit off the big rock. Midway down the block, he halted. Hand in pocket, I tickled the ring. OJJJ nodded at a free-standing garage, with pink siding to twin it with the home on the left. Yellow light and bass beats leaked from beneath the wide door.

"Ready?"

"Sure, yeah."

Up the drive we found our way to a side door. OJJJ rapped and the door opened on a chain. A face looked us over.

"Yo, it's me."

"Who that? OJJJ?" The voice came from somewhere behind the silent face, which only peered at us.

"Shut up – let me in."

"What's up with your boy?" said the peering face at the chain.

OJJJ nodded at me. "He cool."

"Don't keep my man OJJJ standing," said the hidden voice. The door shut again long enough to free the chain, and then we pushed inside. A yellow party bulb cast its glow over a loose ring of men on folding chairs, around the grinning coils of a space heater. The four of them were more than OJJJ had expected – one more in particular. OJJJ turned back for the door the instant he saw the man he hadn't wanted to see, but it was too late, we were in, and the door was blocked.

The man stood and smiled at OJJJ and held out his hand. OJJJ ignored it, didn't face him directly, but turned to another in the circle and made a wheedling appeal. "*Damn*, you let Horton come here just to set me up? That ain't *right*."

"Horton said how you took him off, OJJJ." The same voice had invited us in. "That ain't seem exactually right to us."

"Shut *up*, man. Fuck you even *listen* a ill thug like Horton?"

Horton let his hand fall. "I ain't no thug like you, boy."

"You come round here to take us off, OJJJ? Who your ghost-face friend?"

With that OJJJ had reached the limits of language – that was what his grimace seemed to say as he tugged the pistol from the interior pocket of the coat, from which the glass pipe had come and returned. It was a snub revolver, as dated as the cars on the street. OJJJ might have bought it at the same thrift shop where he'd bought the suede-front, if thrift shops sold pistols.

He fired it, or anyway it fired, on its way out of the coat, shattering plasterboard panels on the ceiling. Dust rained, chairs clattered, the report seemed to ruin my eardrums, only they lived to pulse in pain with the music. Between the first shot and the next every man had time to shout *fuck*, but after the second anything was drowned by Horton's bellowing. Blood seeped through Horton's interlaced fingers as they gripped his knee, and as in a child's game he moaned, "You got me, you got me, you got me!"

I put on the ring and became invisible. No one noticed. OJJJ stood inert, enthralled by the work he'd done on Horton's knee, but the gun went on moving, jerking back and forth, shaking in tensed fingers, not firing for now. Someone chanted *shit*, *shit*, *shit*. I moved to OJJJ and in the great act of physical courage to that point in my life kneed him in the balls and twisted the gun from his hand – he doubled and vomited so quickly it was as though I'd relieved him of the task of withholding the bile, as though vomiting had been his purpose here from the start.

The pistol was gulped into my invisibility for an instant, but it seared my hand, heated from the combustion of firing – it was a primitive thing, barely more than a nugget of steel and dynamite made for flaring fire in a certain direction, for giving out its jolt, and it had done its work and was a coal. It burned me and I dropped it. Only it wasn't done. It fired once more as it cracked to the floor, then spun there to a stop in OJJJ's splash of thin green puke. The third bullet found OJJJ's neck. He gulped and flopped backward and grasped his neck as Horton had his knee, and as he gulped his body flopped and spasmed, and his mouth shaped words which likely didn't exist. Or if they did he couldn't say them. That bullet shut him up.

Me, I ran, I booked. I was ten or twelve blocks down Shattuck, past whining sirens, when I smashed face-first into the shoulder of a tall black woman who'd lurched into my path and realized that the series of magnificent collisions I'd barely avoided were the fault of my invisibility. She was twisted around by the impact, and I staggered and nearly fell. As I recovered I wriggled the ring into my palm. When the woman spotted me she swung out in instinctive anger and boxed me in the eye with a heavy jeweled ring, which served nicely as brass knuckles. "Watch where you're going, child!" I couldn't blame her and couldn't explain, only rasp bewilderment. I put my hand to my eye and ran again, Doily's ring in my pocket now. The sparrow on the hilltop had borne a message for me, if only I'd listened: nature, or at least birds and women, abhorred the invisible man.

Orthan Jamaal Jonas Jackson survived. His and Horton Cantrell's stable condition at Herrick Hospital's intensive care unit was reported on the city page of the *Oakland Tribune* the next morning. The item, headed TWO WOUNDED IN NORTH OAKLAND, included a tantalizing note that the police were searching for a white gunman. Both victims were familiar to the police, bore a record of detainments and, in Cantrell's case, a conviction and suspended sentence for narcotics possession. Neither faced charges in the current investigation. The item was perfunctory, giving no sense of the architecture of the incident, the fact that Cantrell and Jackson had begun as foes before being wounded by the same weapon. It wasn't, probably, the most compelling of stories. The milieu was familiar, drugs and guns, and had it ended there the eyes of the world might have remained glazed over.

But Thursday the story had grown, and graduated to the front page. MYSTERY SHOOTER DESCRIBED AS URBAN AVENGER, that was the hook. The two victims had given witness now, and, with the brothers Kenneth and Dorey Hammond, owners of the house and garage, all on the scene concurred: the mystery white boy had come in with gun blazing, having trailed their distant cousin and good friend Orthan Jackson from Bosun's Locker. The bartender weighed in with a description of my *scrawny, nervous demeanor*, confirmed that I'd been behaving strangely and had approached OJJJ first. OJJJ, who'd been photographed in hospital gown and a bulging white patch from ear to clavicle, explained that he knew I'd been looking for trouble from the start. Though he hadn't been fooled for a moment, I'd been pretending to be a nark, had inquired about the local dealers. He should have known, he said, that I was *another crazy white motherf****r gaming to cap some n****rs*. If it was the journalist, Vance Christmas, who in the following

paragraph coined the phrase "Oakland's Bernhard Goetz,"
OJJJ had led him there deftly enough. Vance Christmas would
have had to be no journalist at all not to coin it. Goetz was still
very much in the air those days.

I moped around KALX for hours before doing that night's
show, a mechanically thorough tribute to Bobby "Blue" Bland
I'd prepared weeks before. The grim purple welt on my eyelid
I explained, to those who asked, by recounting the collision
on Shattuck, leaving out the part about invisibility. My time
in the Hammond garage itself had left me unmarked. After the
show, I bought the Friday papers. I scanned the *Tribune*, found
it mercifully clear of reference to the Tuesday-night shooting.
Then I curled in a ball and slept until dark.

This false calm lasted until Sunday, when Vance Christmas
had his way with me on the weekend op-ed page. EAST BAY
AVENGER, LIKE NEW YORK SUBWAY SHOOTER BERNHARD GOETZ,
BETRAYS A LYNCH-MOB SENTIMENT NEVER FAR FROM SURFACE
took its inspiration from a scattering of letters in support of
the mysterious white gunman the *Tribune* had received since its
Wednesday coverage. The long piece began as a psychological
exposé of Goetz, New York's soft-spoken would-be quadruple
murderer. It was an aging story, but Christmas gave it fresh life
and a local angle by cobbling the bartender's and OJJJ's quotes
into a speculative portrait of an "East Bay Avenger" cut from
Goetz's cloth. There was no mention of what Horton Cantrell
and the Hammonds (the fourth man had vanished from the
story entirely) might have been doing in the garage, apart from
waiting for OJJJ, and for their *fateful moment of terror* at the hands
of the *warped vigilante*. The initial encounter at Bosun's Locker
was given peculiar emphasis. Christmas wondered: Had the
Avenger any idea that Bosun's Locker was the same bar where
Bobby Seale and Huey Newton once sat together drafting the
Black Panther Manifesto? (I hadn't.) This led to a digression
on the poor state of black radicalism, the rise of drug lords
and gangstas in the Panthers' former place of pride in the community. Had white scaremongering – and episodes like Goetz
and the Avenger – been partly the cause of the substitution?
Christmas's conclusion was a pregnant *perhaps*.

The *Oakland Tribune* was a black-owned paper, in a city with a black mayor, and when on Monday I telephoned the news-paper from a pay phone in the Cal Students Union building and asked the switchboard for Vance Christmas, the Panther-obsessed journalist, I expected a black man's voice on the line. His name sounded black to me. But Christmas was white, I could tell immediately by his voice. I told him he had the story wrong.

"Hmmm, yeah, how's that?" He was chewing something.

"Orthan Jackson fired the gun."

Christmas wasn't terribly interested. "He shot himself?"

"It fell."

"Right, huh, and what's your name?"

"I can't tell you my name."

He was quiet for a moment. "So how would you know this?"

"I'm in a position to know."

"Why would I believe you knew anything?" There wasn't any note of hostility – it was a sincere question.

"The gun fell in vomit," I said. There'd been no mention in any article, that I'd seen. "Check the police report."

"Would you hold for a minute?"

"No. Give me your direct line and I'll call back."

He asked for ten minutes. I hung up, bought a blueberry smoothie from a cart on Bancroft, found another phone booth and called again.

Now Christmas said: "I'm listening."

"They're dealers." In my mind I was on a tight clock: as in a million movies, police experts were tracing the call to this booth, and soon SWAT teams would swarm the building. I only wanted to say enough to put an end to it – or I told myself that was all I wanted.

"Sure," he said gently. "They're known dealers, you're right. The question is, what are you?"

"I only wanted to help. OJJJ was messed up on crack, and I think he'd been stealing from those guys. He might have been planning to start shooting before we went in."

"Who were you trying to help?"

"Help catch them," I said impatiently.

"By killing them?"

"I didn't shoot anyone. I'd never fire a gun."

"You mean, like Batman?"

"What?"

"That's what Batman always vowed: that he'd never fire a gun."

This stopped me. I tried to picture Vance Christmas, but nothing came. I suppose we were each trying to picture the other. His breathing was calm on the line while he waited for me to speak again – perhaps he knew he had me hooked – but I could hear something like a frantic whisper in the background: a pencil's soft scribbling on a page.

No, I wanted to say, *Batman's DC, and I like Marvel. DC sucks.*

"So you really didn't mean things to turn out the way they did." Christmas didn't force the tone of sympathy. He seemed to be musing on the misinterpretation which had snared us both. "That's why you called, to set things straight."

"Sure."

"You don't hate black people, then?"

For a moment, it nearly poured out of me: the yearning to compensate for "Play That Funky Music," the desolation which had once birthed Aeroman and now brought him back to life. But that path from Dean Street to Bosun's Locker was too much. I only said, "No."

"It must be pretty strange to find yourself in this position, huh?"

Now I felt I was being patronized. "What I'm trying to do isn't easy," I said. "I screwed up, that's all."

"You've had better days."

"Plenty."

"A history of successes, then?"

Vance Christmas had begun to remind me of a computer program designed to mimic a psychiatrist, or a scratch on my cornea: he'd follow anywhere. So I led. "When it goes well, someone like you wouldn't even learn about it," I said. "The satisfaction is in helping."

"You eschew publicity."

"Ordinarily I do."

"Well, I'm lucky," he said. "You've given me a big exclusive."

"Don't call me the East Bay Avenger."

"What can I call you?"

"Aeroman."

"A-R-R-O-"

"No, no." I spelled it for him.

"When is your next scheduled, uh, event?" he asked.

"I go where I'm needed."

"Wow, yeah. Of course. Listen, do you have an, um, a dis-tinctive *appearance*? I mean, would a person know you if they saw you?"

"Definitely not."

"And you wouldn't be someone already known in the community? Like the way, you know, Clark Kent or Bruce Wayne are."

"No."

"Not a name I'd know? Because it's funny, but your voice seems familiar."

My heart began pounding. Could Vance Christmas be a night-owl KALX listener? Again I tried to see him: racial muckraker, Batman fan — how old was he? Once I'd had the thought I couldn't bring myself to utter another word. So I hung up the phone. I'd said too much, stayed on too long, as it was. But no SWAT team ringed the Student Union, and I figured I'd gotten away with it.

Christmas's exclusive ran above Tuesday's fold. None of my attributed quotes were outright lies, but their context was awfully bad: "I GO WHERE I'M NEEDED"/AVENGER TO TRIB: I'LL STRIKE AGAIN. Oakland, according to Christmas, ought to brace itself, for a fantasizing madman was running amok. I'd bragged of a legacy of covert attacks, reserving a righteous vigilante authority while admitting to a slight "screwup" in this case. I denied my hatred of blacks — sure. Still, I took "sat-isfaction." And, though I'd acted as judge and jury in accusing Jackson and Cantrell of being "dealers," the story's new wrin-kle was a report I'd been using crack in the Bosun's Locker restroom prior to the shooting. Aeroman's name didn't appear — it might be the only word I'd uttered which didn't. Perhaps that was Christmas's bait. He'd sensed my eagerness on that point, and hoped I'd call in again to push for the correction. He was almost right.

Wednesday it crossed the Bay. An *Examiner* editorial scold-
ed Avenger and Christmas alike for creating a sideshow, one
dwarfed by the real crisis engulfing Oakland. Meanwhile, Herb
Caen's column asked: "Oakland's East Bay Avenger and Taxi
Driver's Travis Bickle . . . have they ever been photographed
together? . . . Just wondering . . ." Those were the mentions
I found, before I lost heart and quit looking. There may have
been others.

Christmas hadn't forgotten the name Aeroman. On the
contrary, he'd taken it and done some good work with a micro-
fiche. A week later, after I'd begun to believe the story's coals
were damp, the *Tribune*'s front page boasted an NYPD mug
shot: Mingus Rude, front and profile. They'd been taken later
that distant Sunday afternoon, the day of the shooting – this
was Mingus caught exactly where I'd left him. AVENGER LINK
TO NEW YORK KILLER? was the slug along the top.

Mingus was still in prison at Elmira, I learned from the
paper. His first parole hearing came in three months, and he'd
been nowhere near Bosun's Locker anytime lately. Nevertheless, exclusive sources pointed to a connection. Aeroman's name
was still coyly withheld. Instead, Vance Christmas proposed it
as a puzzle, and the paper had put up a reward for the solution: a thousand dollars to anyone who could connect the dots
between a six-year-old incident in the Walt Whitman housing
projects in Fort Greene, Brooklyn, and the fresh atrocity on
Sixtieth Street, between this pathetic black face in lockup and
our elusive white maniac on the loose. Had Rude taken a fall
for the Avenger, so long ago?

Christmas had called me out, but I was staying in. The
reward was one I wouldn't collect, the question one I couldn't
begin to answer. I retired the ring. My Bosun's Locker jaunt
was essentially the last time I touched it, until that morning
when Abigale Ponders plucked it out of a mess of memorabilia
and returned it to my attention.

CHAPTER 10

ARTHUR LOMB ASKED me to meet him at a restaurant called Berlin, on Smith at the corner of Baltic. The place was one of a run of glossy new restaurants and boutiques on the old Hispanic strip, dotted in among the botanicas and social clubs, and the shuttered outlets full of dusty plastic furniture and out-of-date appliances. Abraham had tried to explain it a dozen times, but there was no understanding until I saw with my own eyes: impoverished Smith Street had been converted to an upscale playground. I suppose it was susceptible to such quick colonization precisely because so many stores had been boarded and dark. The street would be barely recognizable for how chic it had become, except the Puerto Ricans and Dominicans had stuck around. They were refugees in their own land, seated on milk cartons sipping from paper bags, wheeling groceries home from Met Food, beckoning across the street from third-floor sills, trying to pretend gentrification hadn't landed like a bomb.

Arthur wasn't at Berlin when I arrived. It was eleven in the morning and I was the first customer. The place showed evidence of a fresh, expensive renovation, one hip to the virtues of a century-old shopfront. They'd preserved the tin ceiling and exposed and varnished the brickwork on each side wall. The floor was glistening blond hardwood, quite new.

The maître d' had been smoking at the back bar when I entered, but he stubbed it quickly, and faked a smile. He was tall and slouchy, a little glum for so early in the day. He offered me a window table and a minimalist menu: one soup, one sandwich, one crepe, today's oyster. I still felt the effects of my two-nights-before binge with Katha Purly, and of my over-feeding, last night on arrival from La Guardia, at the hands of Francesca Cassini. When the maître d' returned I only asked for a cappuccino, and studied him more closely. The shock of black hair was gone, trimmed close and salted white, but it was Euclid Barnes.

He went and worked the foam-hissing machine himself.

When he set the coffee down he caught me looking, and looked back.

"Do I know you?"

"Dylan Ebdus."

He blinked.

"We went to school together."

"Dylan from Camden?"

"Right."

"I never thought I'd see *you* again."

I didn't point out that he was working in my backyard, my stomping ground. I'd visited Boerum Hill three or four times in nearly two decades, and the place wasn't mine anymore, obviously.

"Are you in touch with anyone from before?" I asked. I realized I was a little dumb at seeing Euclid again – at being served a cappuccino by Euclid Barnes at a fancy café a block from Intermediate School 293.

"God, I don't know. *Every*one, *no* one, you know how it happens."

"Sure," I said, though of course I didn't. I'd never heard from any Camdenites again. Moira Hogarth and I had been off speaking terms at the end of that one semester.

"Can I sit down?" Euclid asked.

"Please."

"Smoke?"

"Go ahead."

He was dressed in a black turtleneck, a bit hot for this September, which had been warm on both coasts. He tugged it from his neck and I saw how soft the skin around his throat had become: Euclid was nearly chinless. Apart from that, and from a deep weariness around his eyes, he'd retained his mournful glamour, had gained, even, for the way flesh had slightly sunk from his high cheekbones. The sparkle of beard at his lips showed gray, as mine did when I let it appear.

Seeing him, a flood of useless memories returned, hard on top of those I'd just triggered walking the distance from Abraham's house to Smith Street. It was of course Dean Street that had provoked the deepest calamity of resonances. But I'd come here to invite those. Euclid was an unexpected factor.

He stared at me as he lit a cigarette. "What happened to you?"

I understood what he meant. "I dropped out."

"I remember you but I don't," he admitted.

"The feeling's mutual," I said, though it wasn't as hard for me, I knew. In my life Camden was a singular episode, a window in time. Euclid had been there for four years, among cohorts from his boarding-school life, and others he'd carried on knowing after. I was a blip.

"I transferred to Berkeley," I told him. "Then stayed in California. I'm just visiting back here."

"What do you do?"

I was briefly tempted to claim I was writing a movie for Dreamworks. "I'm a journalist," I said. "Mostly music stuff."

"Smart boy."

"And you? You own this place, or just run it?"

"Why own a restaurant when you can wait tables?"

"Ah."

"I used to get shifts at Balthazar, but a certain person decided I wasn't charming anymore, and I got canned."

"So you moved out here?"

"Christ, I haven't been able to afford Manhattan for years. I can barely hack Boerum Hill."

Of course. From my lousy vantage I'd seen the wealth at Camden as an edifice, seamless, without variations. But it wasn't. It was a milieu, a money style, sustained even in cases where money itself was gone. Euclid's parents' checks were always late, I remembered now.

"This neighborhood's gotten pretty swanky," I said, still playing possum.

"I hate it, it's too trendy. In just like six months everybody came and spoiled it. Smith Street just got listed in some German tourist book as 'the new Williamsburg.' They're like real estate *vampires*."

"You're part of the old guard around here."

"I'm *old*, anyhow. Thanks for noticing."

"This place looks like it opened yesterday."

"This place is a fucking *fake*," he stage-whispered. Since I'd ordered nothing the chef had wandered from the back and taken

Euclid's place at the bar, but Euclid wasn't really concerned about being heard by the chef. "The owner's the landlord," he explained. "He owns the whole block. He saw his tenants were all getting two stars from Eric Asimov in the *Times* and thought he'd make a killing with his low overhead. He's just some fat local fuck. Everybody in this community despises him."

By *community* I understood Euclid meant the true foodies, chefs who'd risked their careers to open doors in this hinterland.

"What are you doing here, anyway?" he asked.

"Meeting an old friend. He's late."

Perhaps Euclid saw some expression cross my face, for now he remembered. "You're *from* Brooklyn, aren't you?"

"Right around here." I did feel weirdly bitter, but it was hardly Euclid's fault. My possessive feelings were silly. I saw meanings encoded everywhere on these streets, like the DMD and FMD tags still visible where they'd been sprayed twenty years before. I saw the changes here in terms of Rachel's war on the notion of gentrification, which had been conducted mostly in the battlefield of my skull. I walked an invisible map of incidents, shakedowns, hurled eggs, pizza muggings, my own stations of the cross. But imagining those terms should be relevant to the hipsters who'd colonized this place was like imagining that "Play That Funky Music" heard on a taxicab's radio was a message of guilt and shame intended for my ears. No, Isabel Vendle was dead and forgotten, and Rachel was gone. Euclid's Boerum Hill was the real one. The fact that I could see Gowanus glinting under the veneer wasn't important, wasn't anything more than interesting.

"How's Karen Rothenberg?" I asked, shifting to safer ground.

Euclid goggled. "She quit calling when she came back from Minneapolis – rehab. Now she's got this custom hat shop on Ludlow Street. They look like hemorrhoids, if you ask me. But Dashiell Marks – you remember Dashiell?"

I lied and said I did.

"Dashiell got Karen's hats listed on the Best Bets page of *New York* magazine, so everything's hunky-dory."

Euclid liked reminiscing. He lit the next cigarette from the butt of the last and told me of other classmates, rehearsing

grievances which seemed as fresh as if he'd left Vermont yesterday. In the gush of names I learned that Junie Alteck art-directed
Cypress Hill and Redman videos, Bee Prudhomme had been
knifed to death by a lover in a ski chalet outside Helsinki, and
Moira Hogarth was a performance artist known for being cen-
sured by a Midwestern senator.

Then Euclid began stubbing his cigarette and waving off the
smoke and standing from the table, all at the same time. Arthur
Lomb had come through the door, and now I understood why
out of the host of Smith Street eateries Arthur had picked Berlin
for our meeting. It was like him to underplay and show off at
the same time. Arthur wasn't so much fat as leadenly fleshy,
along the coke-bottle lines of his growth spurt at seventeen.
Still, I could see why, without anything to suggest a connection
to that distant week of cocaine trafficking in Vermont, Euclid
hadn't recognized my old friend as his loathsome employer.

The ashtray palmed unconvincingly away, Euclid scuttled
into the back, and I saw what ten or fifteen years of waiting
tables had done to the fragile homosexual prince I'd been so
intimidated by, that first year of college. At Camden Euclid
hadn't asked to be liked, but he'd yearned to be pitied. I'd never
managed before now.

Chunky, bearded Arthur Lomb scowled at Euclid's retreat-
ing back, then brushed real and imaginary ashes from Euclid's
place at my table, and sat.

"You don't want to nosh? It's on me."

"I heard it's your place."

"Right, I'm bleeding cash all over the place. What's a little
more?"

"I'm good, I want to hit the road." My rental car was sitting
on Dean Street. I was anxious on behalf of its disc player.

I'd invited Arthur to drive up to the Watertown prison with
me, to visit Mingus. He'd declined. He'd already visited, earlier
in the summer. But he wanted to see me, and proposed we drop
in on Junior together. That was our mission this morning, and
now that I'd put aside the distraction of Euclid I was impatient
to have it done.

"Okay, after you," said Arthur. "Coffee's on my tab, kids,"
he shouted into the back.

I took my package and we stepped together onto Smith, the block Euclid claimed all belonged to Arthur: a smashed barbershop with an old glass pole, a botanica, window full of votive candles and folk art, with ghetto apartments above it, and four or five of the understated, sexy little bistros Berlin was meant to undercut. The aesthetic was awfully precise, cute serifs hand-painted on tiny signs or directly onto the discreetly curtained windows. In acts of kitsch or voodoo they'd appropriated local-historical monikers: Breuklyn, Schermerhorn, Pierrepont. One called itself the Gowanus Tart Works, exhuming the name Isabel Vendle had worked so hard to bury.

"Fuck you talking to my faggot waiter for?"

Arthur wore a Yankees cap. I still hadn't forgiven him his flip-flop from Mets fandom when we were twelve. That betrayal stood, in my mind, for Arthur's easy adaptation to black style, his glomming onto Mingus Rude. The same inhibition that stuck me to the losing Mets had barred me from the minstrelsy which would have allowed me to follow Mingus where he was going.

It was a form of autism, a failure at social mimicry, that had kept me from the adaptations which made Arthur more Brooklyn than me, in the end. I'd had to hide in books, Manhattanize, depart. So it only followed that Arthur Lomb would still be here, gobbling up Smith Street's commercial real estate just in time to cash in on the yuppie entrepreneurs, a *fat local fuck*.

It was too much trouble to blow Arthur's mind making him recall that the faggot waiter had once fondled his then skinny, narcotized ass in a dorm stairwell in Vermont. Lomb and Barnes could recover their small history, or not, without my help. I had no difficulty keeping secrets from Arthur. I'd done it my whole life, in the case of the ring.

I said, "He told me you own the block."

"I've got five buildings, sure. You believe what they tell you, I'm Smith's Don Corleone."

I wondered if it mattered to Arthur that his holdings were around the corner from our old school. Probably not. Probably you had to leave and come back, as I had, to feel the juxtaposition, the crush of time, as we now retraced our sixth-grade walks home to Arthur's chessmen and graham crackers. Once upon a time me and Arthur Lomb cornering Smith onto Dean were merely the most yokeable pair of humans on the planet.

The evening before I'd been given a Francesca Cassini–guided tour of my own life. *"Imagine the two of you alone in this big house!"* she'd cried repeatedly, and I wanted to reply: *I don't have to!* She'd rounded up some fugitive snapshots of myself and Abraham and created a new family album, one to follow the last of those Rachel had assembled and abandoned, the ones showing me in my mother's arms, and Abraham, younger than I'd ever seen him, standing at his easel before paintings that were sold or lost before I or the film was conceived. Francesca's album gathered school photos, my desperate grins against powder-blue backdrops, as well as a few from my Fresh Air summer, me and Heather Windle, pond-wet hair twisted into horns. The last pages showed Abraham and Francesca on an Italian holiday, my father shading his eyes on hotel terraces, restaurant patios, in vineyards. This was a satisfactory conclusion to the tale which preceded it – the two men alone in the house.

More interesting to me were the new paintings, ten or so, hung in the corridor and stairwell. These were on boards, like my father's jacket art. The style had no relation to his book designs, though. It recalled the paintings on those easels, and others, the nudes. These weren't nudes but portraits: small, penetrating studies of Francesca with her glasses off. They weren't flattering, but they weren't exposés, either. What struck me was the lack of any strain to make the paintings differ. Several were nearly identical. In that sense they resembled the film, or, anyway, were indebted to the film in their diaristic patience. *Something here might or might not change,* they seemed to say. *I have no particular stake one way or another, but if it occurs I will be here to record it.*

I couldn't ask my father about them that night, couldn't get words in edgewise. Francesca was overexcited at my being in the house, and her chatter was something all three of us could only wait out. My father went to bed. Francesca ran a while before exhausting herself. Once she did, I rang my own number twice, checked my messages. There were none from Abby.

Francesca slept in. I'd asked Abraham to wake me for my date with Arthur at Berlin. He and I sat alone with coffee, but I couldn't remember anymore what I'd meant to ask about the portraits. I told him I liked them.

"Thank you."

"Are you going to try to show them?"

"I never think of it."

"You still work on the film?"

Abraham shot me a look of stern Buster Keaton panic. "Of course, Dylan. Every day."

The abandoned house wasn't abandoned. I had to count stoops from Henry's yard to know which it was. Brickwork all along the block was repainted, the brownstone lintels and steps refreshed, the gatework repaired and reblacked – the block was like a set for an idealized movie that fudged poverty into sepia quaintness. Even the slate was straight and neat, repainted like the brick, where it hadn't been replaced with poured concrete.

I was gazing dizzily at the cornices, wondering how many rotting spaldeens still clogged gutters, when Arthur called to me; I'd drifted past him. He'd stopped to talk with a black woman on Henry's stoop, or what had been Henry's stoop, and though like Euclid she was no longer skinny, I knew the woman was Marilla. Her braids had grown long, and were bundled in a nest atop her head. She had a morning drink in a brown bag by her side on the bottom step.

"You remember Dylan?"

"What you talking about, Artie? I knew Dylan before I *even* knew you."

The claims of provenance poured from us, like vows to a great cause. If Marilla hadn't said it, I might have. It was barely different from writing, as I once had, *No one who's ever heard Little Willie John's "Fever" ever need bother with subsequent recordings of the song.* Maybe I'd first found it on Dean Street, my rage for authenticity.

"You a big old *man*, Dylan. Where you been at?"

"I live in California," I said.

"La-La went to California. You ever seen her?"

"No," I said, my voice almost failing me. "I never ran into

La-La." I considered the joke of *La-La in La-La Land*, figured it wouldn't go over.

"No?"

"It's a big place."

"I got to see that for myself one day."

Marilla wasn't the least surprised to see me, only that it had been a while. I gathered she hadn't left the block, that Arthur might be an adventurer who'd roamed far, by her measure. I wanted to convey my astonishment that she was still here, that after where I'd been she could still recognize me, but nothing I babbled about Berkeley or Vermont, about Jared Orthman's office or ForbiddenCon 7, could have conveyed anything except, well, babble. My astonishment, really, was at my own denial of this place. Standing here with Arthur and Marilla it felt that to stay was the obvious thing.

"Henry still live here?" I croaked.

"He comes around," said Marilla. "You should see these white people stare at us on his own street. They want to call the police and Henry *is* the damn police."

"The new type of people in the neighborhood don't really get the whole stoop-sitting thing," said Arthur apologetically.

"Henry's a cop?" I asked.

"Actually, *Alberto's* a cop, Henry's an assistant D.A." Arthur mused on this. "Pretty much everybody's either in jail or a cop. Except for you and Dylan, Marilla."

"I know some people who *should* be in jail."

Arthur laughed. "We're going to see Junior, Marilla."

"Junior? Damn. He first on the list."

Rhodes Blemner's art director had gotten a startlingly early photograph from the Michael Ochs Archive for the cover of Remnant's *Bothered Blue* box, one I'd never seen until finished copies of the set's first pressing had arrived at my Berkeley doorstep a few weeks before, shipped direct from the Canadian factory. It showed Barrett Rude Junior at a microphone in the Sigma studio, ringed by admiring Distinctions, one hand to his ear, mouth bellowed wide like a bragging Ali. From the look it was one of their first sessions together, the Distinctions still awed by the jewel that had dropped into their setting.

I wonder if a stranger could have squared that broad, strong face and those neat fingernails and geometric 'Fro, that sharp-knotted tie against paper-white shirt, the whole authority and predatory ease of the thirtysomething Barrett Rude Junior, with the Fu Manchu mustached, yellow-clawed, shrunken-apple-form who accepted the box as a gift from me now. It wasn't that he should look as good – *nobody* had ever looked as good as the man on the box. But I don't know how I could have fathomed time's work on Barry's face without my advantage of knowing son and grandfather. That was the gap the man and the box spanned. The singer in the photograph was Mingus at eighteen, on a good day. As for the man clutching the gift, shaking my hand, nails scoring my palm – well, if it was less than a revelation it was more than a joke, the line that came into my head: *Junior was Senior now.* He even wore Senior's Star of David necklace, webbed in white at the gap in his robe. When I saw him lower his eyes to the box and discover himself I wanted to tear the thing from his hands and toss it in the street, only it was too late.

"I wrote the notes," I said.

"Oh?"

"Inside, there's a book, a little essay about your career. I wrote it. I hope you like it." I somehow hadn't until this moment weighed the odds of Barrett Rude Junior reading my tribute. Now there were a few sentences I might prefer his eyes glossed over. Again, too late.

"I like it *already*, baby," said Barry. He put the box on the couch beside him where he sat. He'd ushered us in, no more surprised than Marilla had been. The apartment was barely changed, only corroded by twenty years of neglect. Barry took up a considerably lesser portion of it. I'd swear certain LPs were right where I'd last seen them, in piles on the floor by the stereo, half out of their sleeves.

"See, Arthur," he said, taking just a glance from the television, which was tuned to *Judge Judy*. The television was new, and I sensed it got more use these days than the stereo. "I always told you Little Dee would do us proud."

"Sure," said Arthur. "Here, Barry, I brought you something too." He slapped at his pockets until he found it: a fresh pack of

Kools, which he tossed to Barry's lap. "You know that warning about how smoking is bad for your health? Very few people realize I actually *wrote* those words."

"Y'all a couple of gifted children, I'll give you that."

"Of course, they changed them all around, took out most of my best stuff."

"That's their prerogative, though, isn't it, Arthur?"

"Yeah."

"You got to *grant* them their pre*rog*ative."

"I guess so."

"I heard *that*." Barry reached to graze fingertips with Arthur, still not neglecting the television show. He'd pushed the cigarettes off with the box set.

"You want to hear the CDs?" I said stupidly. "They sound really great." Barry's publishing stake meant he'd see some money from the box, eventually. It should add to the trickle of royalties which presumably kept him in the house. Maybe I was wrong to think he should be proud of the monument too. Maybe the Barry I wanted to be able to give the box to was the Barry of 1975. That man, like the one in the photograph, was as inaccessible to Barry now as he was to me.

"I know what all them old records sound like."

"Yeah, but—"

"I'll check them out some other time, man." He spoke slowly and carefully, and I knew I should drop it. "I don't have no CD player, anyhow."

I just nodded.

"You know that Fran, that girl your old man took with?" Changing the subject, his voice grew gentle again. "She's all right. She's been looking out for me, you know."

"I heard."

"He's lucky, find a girl like that."

"I know." Everyone agreed, from A to Zelmo. I only hoped Abraham did too. It was then that I remembered what I'd wanted to ask my father about the new paintings. Were the portraits of Francesca an excuse to stare, to try to see through the skin of his new situation, this woman who'd taken Rachel's long-abandoned place? Was he trying to fathom Francesca? Or had she asked him to paint her, requested he look with that intensity? Who'd sought the confrontation the portraits recorded?

There was a long silence, filled by the television's yammer. I began to think of the rental car again, and the road I meant to cover this day. My heart was bogging on Dean Street, but it was Mingus I had to see.

Barrett Rude Junior focused his eyes on mine for the first time in nearly twenty years, perhaps reading my mind. His gaze at last pierced the caul that had covered it even when he'd found us at his door, and through his short inspection of the photograph and words on the box set's cover.

"What brings you round to see this old washed-up singer, Little Dylan?" he said. He gave *washed-up singer* some of his old melodic juice, and I felt a twinge in my saliva glands, as though I'd dipped my tongue to cocaine.

"I just wanted to give you the records," I said. I couldn't call them *CDs* now.

"You done that," he said, a little coldly.

"And we're going up to visit Mingus. I mean, I am."

"Huh." Barry clouded. He grimaced in concentration at something in Judge Judy's realm, perhaps a ruling going the wrong way. Someone had to keep a watch on such stuff.

"Maybe if you've got any message for him—"

Barry chopped with a clawed hand. Mingus in Watertown was too distant, that was what the gesture seemed to say. Dean Street was real, Francesca and Arthur were real and worth acknowledging. One brought soup, the other cigarettes. Judge Judy was real enough: she was in front of his eyes. I'd come and proposed that Barry consider California and 1967 and Watertown and those were all too remote, too tiresome.

"You know I'm watching my morning shows," he said, addressing Arthur. "I'm not awake yet, man. Come around tonight and we'll party."

"Okay, but Dylan's gotta head," said Arthur. "He just wanted to say hello."

"Tell the boy I'm watching my morning shows."

Arthur walked me to my car, and apologized. "I should have

told you not to mention Mingus," he said. "It sort of shuts him down."

"What did Mingus do to him?"

"It's not that simple."

I'd stashed my bag in the rental's trunk already, and said my goodbyes, promising Abraham and Francesca I'd spend a day with them on the other end of my jaunt upstate, before I returned to California. I was ready to go.

"Here," said Arthur. He frisked himself again and produced an unsealed envelope full of cash, evidently counted in advance. He slapped it into my hand. "You can't give it to them directly, they can't have money inside. You have to contribute it to their commissary accounts, then they, you know, take it out in cigarettes, or whatever. Hundred apiece."

"Who's *they*?"

"You know how I was saying to Marilla it seems like everybody's in jail?"

"Sure."

"Robert Woolfolk's inside too. Watertown, same joint as Mingus."

CHAPTER 11

I WAS AN AMATEUR here, as much a neophyte crossing these thresholds as I'd been in L.A., penetrating Jared Orthman's sanctum. Only now I was an amateur among professionals. All the black and Hispanic moms and grandmoms, all the stolid grown-up homeboys visiting homeboys, all but me knew how to visit a prison. Their expertise began to be shown just past the parking area, still well outside the outermost ring of wire, where taxicabs from the Watertown train station and the Greyhound terminal turned in a circle, where the chartered bus from New York, full of prisoners' families, off-loaded and waited, the driver smoking hand-rolled cigarettes and picking tobacco from his teeth. There the visitors fell into a line, to trudge through a long shack, a small aluminum trailer on concrete blocks. It had been raining the afternoon before, as I drove out of the city, raining when I took my motel room just outside downtown, raining just a bit more this morning, as I breakfasted on sausage patties at a Denny's. Now gray-green clouds wheeled above the prison and were mirrored in the puddled gravel at our feet. No one but me glanced up at the sky or down at the ground as I hurried in to take a place. Inside the trailer three guards — *correctional officers*, they were called — ran a bureaucratic outpost, one where we displayed ID, signed this form, then that one, giving address, stating relationship to prisoner, avowing comprehension of rules, etcetera. All but me knew the prisoner's number they'd come to visit. I knew only Mingus's name, causing a bored captain to have to flip open a fat binder to locate the corresponding digits. The bathroom in the trailer was our last chance to pee. Everyone took it, knowing the drill. I took my cue, fell in line. The trailer's single pay phone was the last we'd see, and it too was in continuous use. I thought of calling home, trying for Abby. But the line of callers was too long.

The drill the visitors knew was above all that of waiting, in total deference. Complaint had been worn out of them some time ago. We waited in one secured zone after another, as we progressed by degrees inside the Watertown facility. First, approved by some unseen hand, we were taken from the trailer, along concrete paths marked with fluorescent orange-and-yellow paint. I found it impossible not to fear being rifle-shot from a high tower for crossing the painted stripes, for we were now under the gaze of the concrete towers, having put the trailer and parking lot, the whole of Watertown out of sight behind us. Then we passed through what was called an "A/B door" – a metal cage, wired so door A and door B couldn't be unlocked at the same time. After we were inspected from within a windowed office there came a joltingly loud buzz to switch the circuit. Bolts slammed through the door behind us, and the door ahead opened to permit us to pass from the box.

With that we were inside, sort of. The prison wasn't, as I'd pictured, a single edifice, a stone Gormenghast or iron Death-star, but a sprawled compound of structures and fences and gates, a bleak ranch for human livestock. Between everything, safe zones, moats of speckless concrete, protected by razor wire. And, through doors unlocked for us by gray-clad, dronelike officers, the interiors were dully institutional, like 1960s-era school buildings or hospital emergency rooms, full of mint-green tile and wooden paneling worn to matte. Each place we encountered in this visitor's gauntlet felt provisional, refitted for this temporary use, though they'd likely been used this way for years.

I later understood each prisoner had to be located, cleared, brought to the visiting room hidden deep inside the walls – there was no motive for the guards to finish processing us until the prisoner had been escorted to wait for us in that room. This was a place of canceled time: it had no value. We weren't customers, to be pleased or reassured. Yet for all the waiting, I was always guiltily startled when my name was finally called, was always gazing in the wrong direction, distracted by the stuff pinned to the walls, yellowed notices, ten-year-old memos requiring *block sergeants to remain at posts until the arrival of replacement block sergeants* or forbidding *visitors skirts higher than 2 inches above the knees* or "*bear midriff*," advertisements for shuttle services and child care, twelve-step and pregnancy clinic solicitations, and a long, hypnotic list, photocopied into a runic blur, of commissary items: toothpaste $1.39, comb 19¢, ketchup packet 19¢, jar chicken $1.79, jar lima beans 89¢, jar instant coffee $1.59, peanut butter $1.39, conditioner $1.29, hairnet 29¢, bun 25¢, chocolate bun 30¢, and on and on from there – the list was schemeless, incantatory, horrible.

"Ebdus."

"Yes."

"Belt and shoes off, contents of pockets in the wooden box."

I waddled up, the only one who needed to be told.

"All in the box."

I scooped out my pockets, offered them my shoes and belt.

"No pens."

I shrugged helplessly.

"You can throw it out here."

"Sure." I put my ballpoint in the green steel garbage pail. Other visitors streamed through the metal detector while I fidgeted with my crap.

"What's this ring?"

"Wedding ring."

"Why ain't you wearing it?"

"Uh, it's my mother's wedding ring. I just carry it around, it doesn't fit." Don't make me put it on, I prayed. The officer squinted, frowned, let it pass. Something else was more interesting.

"What's that?"

"What?"

She pointed to a single pale-orange conical earplug which had sprung to the top of the change and rental-car keys I'd heaped into the wooden tray along with the ring. The plug had unsquished, breathed open as foam shapes will do.

"Earplug," I said.

"What for?"

I considered the appearance of the earplug, the vaguely sexual fitted form, through the officer's eyes. "For the airplane," I said.

She looked at it closely. Now I wondered if it more resembled drug paraphernalia.

"That's for an *airplane*?"

"For blocking out the sound of the engines. So I can sleep."

"Just one?"

"I guess I lost the other one."

"Huh."

I'd never pondered the bourgeois implications of an earplug. The officer scowled, but placed my tray full of stuff on the far side of the barrier. "Give me your right hand, sir." From a stamp pad she marked my knuckles with some invisible stuff. "Take your box, sir."

Once through, I began slipping into my shoes, repocketing my stuff.

"Sir, not here."

"What?"

"You can't stay in this area. Take your box to the bench in there."

Five of us were called, to have our hands examined with a black-light wand that exposed a purplish emblem. The keys on the fistlike ring at the escort officer's belt varied in size and shape, some as modern as my rental car's ignition key, others as medieval as those wielded by the *Wizard of Id*'s bailiff. As our group strode the corridor I learned another subtle art, of slowing so that the officer, who'd lingered to relock the door behind us, had time to overtake us and open the door ahead.

I tried to absorb the others' expert docility, as a balm. We were being transformed into inmates, I began to understand, as our reward for asking to go inside. We'd crossed seven or eight levels of lock-in before I was led to meet Mingus Rude in the visitor's room, a bleach-redolent chamber of pale blue tile. There, we were sealed from one another by a Plexiglas window covered with minute scratchiti, and allowed to converse on telephones.

He had to speak for both of us, at first. I couldn't find a word.

"D-Man. I can't believe it's you, shit."

I nodded.

"Check you out. Boy done growed up. Hah!"

I'd journeyed back, from that distance at which Mingus had sometimes seemed an implausibility, a myth. Now he was before me, in the all-too-human flesh. His skin was skull-tight, the whites of his eyes sickly yellow, he wore his father's ridiculous

Fu Manchu mustache and a filthy red sweatshirt, his wide grin revealed a chipped incisor, his raised eyebrows a thin scar seaming his eyelid. Still, I persuaded myself he didn't look bad, or so different from the man I remembered. In Junior's photograph on the *Bothered Blue* cover I'd seen a resemblance to Mingus, but now, despite the mustache, I didn't see Mingus in terms of his father. Mingus was only Mingus, the rejected idol of my entire youth, my best friend, my lover. Seated across from him, I knew he'd already grown into a man at some point before the last time I'd seen him, the day of the shooting. I hated to recall the boy I'd encountered in the mirror when I first arrived at my Camden dorm – the frightened boy, desperate to impress with his fresh punk haircut, who'd go on to spend his life pretending not to have seen and known so much.

"I can't believe it. Where you *been*, son?"

He spoke as though resuming where we'd left it, my year before graduation from Stuyvesant. As though I'd been at high school in Manhattan these decades, and now we only hadn't run into one another, to exchange a quick handclasp on Dean Street, for a few long months.

So where *had* I been? I answered, "California."

"Yeah, yeah, I heard from your pops you was out that way. Someday I got to get out there myself – *the Golden State*, damn." Like Marilla, Mingus merely hadn't gotten around to it. "Dillinger's gone way out west, checkin' out the Golden State. Yet despite how the boy's livin' large, he don't diminishize his roots, he comes back to *represent*."

Mingus was authoring a romance, wrapping my awkwardness in his old raconteur's warmth. It was nonsense and a gift I took gladly. No mention of the special nature of the setting for our reunion, though his jive happened to be piped over an intercom. The setting didn't bear mentioning. His smile's warmth, the way he beamed himself across that thickness of Plexiglas, suggested a capacity for a binocular vision which excluded surroundings. Recalling how the city had reeled from us as we stood on the Brooklyn Bridge's walkway gazing at spray-painted stone, I thought now that that had always been one of Mingus's talents.

"Arthur couldn't come," I said, as if Arthur were the

unfaithful one. "He sent up some money for the commissary, though."

"Arthur's always lookin' out for a brother," said Mingus. He didn't mean to sting me, only to bathe Arthur, too, in beatific gratitude. "I know I let Arturo down a bunch of times, but my man always picks up the phone."

"I count on him for news of you," I lied. I hadn't been any more in touch with Arthur than I had with Mingus. And I hadn't heard news of Mingus until Abraham and Francesca raised the subject in Anaheim, at dinner with Zelmo Swift.

"Little brother's doing fine for himself, too," said Mingus, freeing me from this line of talk. "Done got fat and happy."

"Well, fat."

Mingus wheezed, too much laughter for the joke. "Ho *snap*," he said, putting on a show. "I *heard* that. I been tellin' the boy he got to shed some poundage he wants to snag himself a *wife*."

The word was peculiarly silencing: heading to forty, we'd fallen laps behind life's course. We had no wives. Mingus, at least, had an excuse for why he hadn't been dating lately. About Abby there was nothing I could say that wouldn't sound self-pitying or fatuous. I felt the distance between Dean Street and my Berkeley life as an unbridgeable gulf.

At the lapse I tuned in the murmur around us: one-sided talk into the visitors' telephones, the unselfconscious yakking of two corrections officers at the door, and, from one of the booths, a voice gummy with weeping.

"I saw Junior," I said.

"At the house?"

"Yesterday. With Arthur."

"My old man," said Mingus. He spoke simply now, his gaze shy. "He's hanging in there."

"It was good to see him," I said.

"He must have been glad to see you."

I couldn't fathom a reply, so we fell to silence a second time. Mingus had abandoned his patois, and the trumped-up garrulity that had gone with it. I was ashamed to want it back.

Mingus smoothed his long contrails of mustache, stroked his chin. There were flecks of spittle on his side of the glass between us, evidence of his actor's enthusiasm, now gone. I met his rheumy eyes and saw a stranger. I could no more ask Mingus who he'd become – whether incarceration had broken him the first time, at eighteen, or what had led him back inside after his first release, or what his life had meant to him in the time between his two sentences – than I could imagine how to confess myself to him. I was helpless to say who I'd become in California, or to let him know I remembered everything between us despite it all.

"Arthur says Robert's inside too," I said, despising myself for the false casualness, for my use of *inside*. My heart was thudding now.

"Plenty of brothers you'd recall from the old days inside now," said Mingus. There might have been rebuke in his words, I wasn't certain. "Donald, Herbert, whole bunch of them."

I didn't remember Donald or Herbert. Perhaps Mingus knew this.

"You and Robert see a whole lot of each other?" Dopey questions poured from me, helplessly.

"I put myself out for Robert until I couldn't *afford* to no more." Now there came a steely note of institutional savvy in Mingus's voice, and his gaze blinked from mine. "Our boy Robert put himself in the way of some trouble. They had to shift him into protective custody."

"Oh."

"I told him but the poor-ass snake can't listen."

To divert the anger that seemed to be unstoppering, I said, "Actually, Arthur sent cash for both of you."

"Put mine to Robert's name, Boy could use it."

"Really?"

"It's not too late for him to pay his debt down. Anyway, I'm in a protest with these motherfuckers, they took my stamps."

"Stamps?"

"For letters. Postage stamps, man."

"What happened?"

"I had thirty dollars of stamps in my bunk down at Auburn. When they moved me up here they were supposed to be trans-ferred—" Here Mingus launched into a torturous account of a paperwork error. The Watertown facility prohibited stamps because they resembled paper money, could be used as scrip.

The postage had been meant to be dissolved into Mingus's commissary account, had been placed instead with belongings to be returned to him after release. Mingus filed protest forms, but the seized stamps were stranded in a limbo between the two prisons, the two sets of rules. Mingus retailed this story with a joy-in-persecution that could only be called Kafkaesque. In a world of deprivations, I suppose the smallest might become a fetish. It made my head hurt. I wanted to scream *Forget the stamps, for God's sake I'll buy you thirty dollars' worth of stamps if you want!* But the stamps were Mingus's cause, and so he railed on. What was thirty dollars compared to a cause? Too, in this place a talker's gifts were only encouraged in one direction, to stanch the wound which bled hours, days, years. I tried not to lose patience with the monologue.

"I brought you something else," I said, when Mingus paused for breath.

He scowled confusion.

I dug in my pocket as discreetly as I could. "I've been keeping it for you," I said, and pushed the ring to the edge of the Plexiglas, like a checker I wanted Mingus to king.

"Put that away," he said. He waved, a low flat gesture which seemed to say *Keep it under the table.* "They'll confiscate it."

I covered the ring with my palm. Still, I couldn't keep from avowing my mission of rescue. "This is why I came – I mean, I wanted to see you. But the ring belongs to you."

"It never did."

"It does now, then."

"Shit."

Mingus had grown cold and wary, as though I'd asked him to recall things he couldn't afford to.

"How can I get it in to you?" I said, thinking moronically, *If I'd known about the hermetic seal, I'd have baked a cake.*

"Put it away."

"You could use it to break out of this place," I said quietly.

His laugh now was bitter, and authentic.

"Why not?"

"You couldn't even use that thing to break *into* this place."

The rest, until my time was up, was small talk. Mingus wanted news of my father, so I described the honor he'd received in Anaheim. I mentioned Abby, omitted her color. We even talked over the stamps again. Mingus asked questions and didn't listen to my answers. A wall had fallen between us. Afterward, I was led out, my knuckles inspected again for the phosphorescent stamp of a free man. On my way out I deposited two hundred dollars into Robert Woolfolk's commissary account, keeping my promise.

CHAPTER 12

INVISIBLE IN TWILIGHT, my eyes picked out stuff I'd missed the first time crossing the yard.

On concrete clean of the slightest scrap of litter or leaf, a single latex glove, flipped inside out in the haste of its removal.

Pinned to the fence, a hand-painted sign: DON'T FEED THE CATS!

Past the fence, shadow-blobbed trees. Sensuous unreachable hills. The moon a pale disk snuck into sky before sunset.

It wasn't either day or night when I crept back inside the gates of Watertown Correctional, but something in between: daynight, the hour of the changing of the guards.

I'd only had to lay on my motel bedspread flipping cable channels for half an hour – Mets game; *Emeril*; *Sunburn*, with Farrah Fawcett and Charles Grodin; and *Teddy Pendergrass: Behind the Music* – before Mingus's words penetrated my brain in their full profundity: *You couldn't even break* into *this place*. I'd heard them as merely scoffing, when in fact they spoke of my whole life's flinching from what mattered most – not California, dummy, but Brooklyn. Not Camden College, but Intermediate School 293. Not Talking Heads, but Al Green. "No way out but in" (cf. Timothy Leary, 1967). "The old way out is now the new way in" (cf. Go-Betweens, *Spring Hill Fair*, 1984). Behind the Music, sure. But I needed to go behind the walls. My first pass at the prison had been too cursory, a tourist's, as ever. I had to earn Mingus's escape with my own willingness to go inside, to show it could be done. I'd known Aeroman had one last mission: now I saw it couldn't be conducted by surrogate. I'd wear the ring myself, once more.

This certainty came like a fever. The motel room seemed to pitch, the walls to crawl, like Ray Milland's in *The Lost Weekend*. I broke a sweat, felt my bowels loosen dangerously. Lying still, apart from the twitching of my thumb on the remote, I sought a channel to distract me from my intent, uselessly. So I sprang from the bed, rinsed the clammy perspiration from my throat, and spent five minutes or so under the motel sink's fluorescent, trying to stare myself out of what I was about to do. Then I repacked my small bag and checked out.

I hid my rental car in the stadium-sized lot of a shopping mall at the edge of town, camouflaging it in a sea of like models. Recalling the metal detectors, I slid off my belt and watch and left them under my seat, then locked my wallet in the glove compartment, not wanting to carry it inside, either. I also removed the car's key from its bulky ring and tucked it into my shoe, like sixth-grade mugging money. Finally I slid on Aaron Doily's ring and walked invisible out of the mall lot, then made my way to the prison along two miles of well-groomed highway shoulder, past signs reading DO NOT STOP FOR HITCHHIKERS.

CO parking was down the hill, behind the trailer where I'd begun my first voyage inside, earlier that day. There, the evening shift trickled in, one or two at a time, in ten-year-old compacts and pickup trucks, to receive perfunctory badge checks at a manned booth, and a glance into bag lunches for signs of contraband. I had no trouble slipping past the cyclone-fence gate behind a Datsun – it felt as though a visible man could have done it, cloaked in haze and exhaust. My guide-Datsun took its place in a scattering of cars. Its driver was a pearishly short man with Elvis sideburns, wearing a Bills jersey. He paused in his open door for long-sighing finish of a smoke before crushing the butt into the gravel lot, then headed for the entrance. I fell in close behind him, matching my invisible footfalls to his own crunching steps. I staggered slightly, and recalled the special nature of invisible clumsiness, the inner-ear panic that seemed to go with appearancelessness. Aping Mr. Pear's low-center-of-gravity lope helped me find my rudder, though.

The officers had their own A/B door, where they scrutinized one another through a glass partition. This required a hairbreadth maneuver: ducking through, I was almost clipped by the B door, and in hustling to avoid it grazed the heel of Pear's shoe with my Converse high-top's toe, nearly giving him what in grade school we would have called *a flat tire*. Pear whirled. I backed to the gate, clammed my mouth. Pear squinted, saw nothing, believed his eyes, carried on. I let out breath. The prison groaned and hummed, deep in the floors, and the air was full of a distant cascade of clanking – enough to cover an invisible man's inopportune gasps for air.

So I trailed my unknowing escort across the moon-pale yard. We passed into a low bunker showing lit offices behind unbarred windows, a building I hadn't glimpsed in my official visit, one with no cell blocks that I could see. Pear turned through an unlocked doorway, headed for a door marked MEN'S LOCKERS. It was there I realized he'd played his full part, that I had no reason to follow him farther. I'd need to find other bodies to trail – it would have been impossible dumb luck if Pear had happened to lead me to the exact block where Mingus was celled.

I parted from him there, and wandered through into the offices. The air here was free of the tang of authoritarian fear I'd smelled in the visitors' hall. Instead the place was as innocuous as a smalltown Department of Motor Vehicles. Two COs flirted at a coffee machine, the woman with a black crew cut, but zaftig in her uniform. Two more sat with clipboards, yawning at paperwork. Another pair, one slurping a Coke, the other tapping down a pack of cigarettes, watched a clock-radio-sized television, showing late innings of the same Mets game I'd glimpsed in my motel. Lime-green walls were disguised with school photos, newspaper cartoons, garage calendars. Ten years ago they might have featured pinups, but the presence of female guards prevented that. I supposed there were still pinups in the men's lockers, though.

While I stood flattened just through the doorway, Pear, now in his well-ironed grays, and belt loaded with baton and keys, waddled into the room.

"Yo, Stamos," said the CO standing by the coffee machine.

"Yo," said Pear-Stamos. "Whatchoo doing?"

The guards were all Caucasian. Yet even here, podunk nowhere, everything was *yo, yo, yo.*

"Looking for you," said the male guard, and now his female companion peeled away from the coffee machine with something like a look of disgust. "Metzger wants us up at the shoe for deadlock. Crappy birthday to you."

"With ice cream on top," said Stamos in a dead voice.

"Be careful what you wish for."

"Christ almighty, don't let me get shitted tonight."

"I'll protect you, sweetheart."

Stamos and his friend shook their heads as they departed the oasis of the offices, bound for whatever grim duty *the shoe* represented. "Force be with you," said another from his desk, waving farewell without looking up.

I let Stamos go. I wasn't hugely fond of him, anyway. I assumed I'd be able to shadow one or another CO making rounds through any given building if I was patient enough to hover at locked doors, and cool enough to suck in my breath and still my heartbeat while I waited for keys to turn, for my chance to glide through on their heels. My problem was how to locate Mingus in the small dystopian city of the prison, where the streets had no names – at least, no street signs.

His coordinates might be on those clipboards, or in a binder like the one the guard in the trailer had flipped through. So I began ghosting among the desks to peer over shoulders at exposed paperwork, even rifling through pages on vacant desks when I thought I could afford to. Nothing was revealed. The one column book I found was filled not with names but with timed entries in indecipherable jargon: *4:00 secure ATT/4:25 Sgt. Martine on G-Building LFF/6:30 Inmate Legman, Douglas 86B5978 requests mattress cover per RLH Orderly*, etcetera. On another desk I spotted a copy of *CPO Family*, trade journal of the Correctional Peace Officers Foundation, its lead feature titled simply "Outnumbered!"

Then I saw a stack of folders marked with inmate names and numbers, on a low shelf away from the desks, top pages fluttering in breeze from an open window. If invisibility was good for nothing else it had freed an old infantile delight at making things spill: with the breeze for an excuse, I splashed those folders wide over the linoleum.

"Jesus, crap," said the Force-Be-With-You CO, who was nearest.

Flirting Woman stood at her desk to gawk at the mess.

"Clean it up, Sweeney," Star Wars told her.

"Clean it up yourself."

"Nah, I'm going up to the gallery. You should have filed that crap last week."

"It's not my crap, it's Zaretti's."

"Sure, but it was you used astral projection to knock it off the shelf, just to jerk my chain. Take it upstairs already. And shut that draft, we're all getting the flu."

Surprising me, Sweeney did as she was told. Kneeling, her grays cinching to unveil a margin of floral-print underwear, she scooted the folders into rough order before I'd had a look at them. I battled an urge to spin the last papers from the floor in imaginary gusts, to cavort with their files and cause merry chaos in this dead zone, to show them the invisible-man's mania I felt throbbing inside. Instead I waited while grumbling Sweeney bundled the stack into her arms. Star Wars ignored her. A tinny Mets announcer was the only peep over the ventilator's rumble. When Sweeney took the files from the room I trailed her like a stalker, following the decorated panties, that spot of brightness.

The room Sweeney led me to, a private office full of filing cabinets behind a pebbled-glass door, also held a large wooden desk with a telephone, and a few framed citations and news-paper photos – it might be the warden's office, if I believed in such things as wardens. I remembered my surprise, as a Brook-lyn kid, discovering that the small towns in Vermont actually harbored sheriffs, when that was for me as corny and fictional an honorific as *knight* or *caveman*. A warden was a figure from a Lenny Bruce routine, or a Slick Rick rhyme. So, say, the *lieutenant CO's* office. Sweeney snapped on the light and began tugging open long drawers and replacing those files in alpha-betical sequence by prisoner's name and I knew I'd blundered into what I sought – only right at the moment I wasn't interest-ed anymore. I hewed close to Sweeney, closer than I needed, pretending for a moment I wasn't lost deep within a prison. Sweeney was a little stocky, but I loved her. I loved her purely for being female in this man-built, man-patrolled hell, and for letting me see London, for showing me France.

This was new for me. I'd never once explored invisibility's

perverse opportunities – never been one for strip clubs or porn, let alone window peeping. I identified with the figure of the subway frotteur about as much as I did with Bernhard Goetz. Now, here to renounce and abandon the ring and my secret powers, and alone in this upstairs office with a woman, a weird last-minute greed came to me, and I practically mounted Sweeney's substantial thigh as I leaned close to capture a whiff of her hair's perfume. She hummed Cher's "Believe" to herself, and farted too, but these couldn't deter me. I imagined whispering *Be still, Sweeney, don't scream, and let the invisible hands of the invisible man invade your mannish uniform.* I had a hard-on, now inches from Sweeney's gray polyester ass, a better one than I'd managed with dear Katha. The onset of this lust was surely one final denial that I was going to do what I was already in the middle of doing – that my lonely life and Mingus's had come to this. It was a call to a life unlike the one I'd lived, one full of women and foolishness, one troubled by less troublesome forms of trouble. Fuck all this dire manly courage! Fuck going "inside" barbwire boundaries and ancient conundrums! *Fuck prisons, let's fuck! Sweeney, let me take you from all this.*

Sweeney rolled out the R–S–T drawer and there it was: Rude, Mingus Wright, 62G7634. And that was all it took to deflate me. I might have been a moment or two from asinine calamity, from letting Sweeney feel my breath or erection against her. Now I backed to a corner and watched her complete the task of filing. Sweeney was blithe, unaware of our close call, still humming atonal disco. When she clicked off the overhead on her way out, I left it off. Enough light leaked in from the yard's floodlamps for me to find the drawer again, and the file inside the drawer.

I sat at the desk and had a look.

The file was fifteen, maybe twenty sheets thick. The first and by far most substantial document dated to 1978 – the year Mingus began at Sarah J. Hale, while I was still behind at I.S. 293 – on stationery headed by Frank J. Macchiarola, Chancellor of Schools.

PSYCHOLOGICAL EVALUATION: The overall test results suggest

a young man of very superior intellectual capacity whose
verbal skills are considerably more effective than his practical
problem-solving skills. Some limitations in attention,
concentration, and awareness . . . It may be speculated
that these limitations are the result of distracting feelings,
tensions, and inner upsets. Projectives testing reveals a mildly
suspicious young man who tends to view the world in a
guarded manner, tends to deny his affective needs but who is
then vulnerable to emotional stress—

And:

DEVELOPMENTAL: Mingus was a full-term baby. A breech
delivery, he was born fighting, and knocked the instrument
from the doctor's hand—

And:

INTERVIEW: Mingus feels he does not understand what has
happened to him. He stated that as far as he can remember his
problems started when he was in preschool—

And:

He has problems because of the "gang" elements in and
around his school. He has little social life and finds it hard to
explain what he does with his time—

And:

TEST RESULTS: Mingus entered the test situation readily.
There was noted, however, a tinge of mild annoyance with
the evaluation process connoting an attitude of condescending
disinterest . . . effectiveness varies from the Low Average to
the Very Superior range with the exception of a Deficient
score in a rote copying task which is seen as spurious in that
he appeared not to be applying his full efforts—

And:

His thinking tends toward secretive and foreboding themes
(i.e., on card V a camouflaged butterfly against a tree, card
III two people working over a pot, a witches' brew, card IV
a dragon with wings coming down on you) . . . suggestive of
an apprehensive and at times suspicious view of his experience
and surroundings—

And:

Mingus's typical style and manner is likely to dispose
him toward sarcasm and verbal bouts of a negativistic and
oppositional posture to do combat with authority figures in a
covert manner—

The jargon described a Mingus I barely recognized, sulking
under the shrink's gaze – in those same days he ebulliently
commanded my world, out on Dean Street. I flipped to the
end of the document, and underneath found Mingus's "yellow
sheet," his at-a-glance arrest and conviction record. First, five
or six graffiti detainments, from our high-school days. Before
Ed Koch's graffiti-specific laws, arresting officers had been
reduced to euphemistic charges:

3/2/78:   Criminal Mischief, Criminal Trespass
4/14/78: Criminal Mischief, Criminal Trespass
9/27/79: Criminal Mischief, Loitering, Possession of
          Burglar Tools

And so on. Those burglar's tools were presumably bolt cutters, for breaking into the train yards. No mention of Mingus's
leaping, costumed, from a tree in the Walt Whitman Houses
courtyard – he'd been released to Junior's recognizance that
night. His teenage jeopardy was all graffiti related. To that
point Mingus had had the freedom to smoke and snort in his
own home, when it was being forced onto the street that led to
possession arrests.

Those would come, soon enough. First, the parade of
scofflaw-charge dismissals ran over this cliff:

8/16/81: Murder 2, Handgun Possession

And its disposition:

10/23/81: Felony Conviction, Involuntary Manslaughter

The long shadow of Senior's slaying was a six-year silence on the yellow sheet, before the resumption, in 1987, of Mingus's arrests. By that time the street had undergone its crack revolution:

11/23/87: Criminal Possession of Controlled Substance
(stimulant)

This was successively shrunk by some bored typist with a fondness for capitals:

10/3/88: CPCS (stimulant), Simple Misdem.
2/12/89: CPCS (stim.) Misdm.
6/3/89: CPCS (stim.) Misdm.

The sequence was interrupted by the now-expanded penal code:

8/8/89: Possession of Graffiti Instruments

And then:

4/5/90: Larceny 1

Time after time in those court-swamped years Mingus had been held beyond the length of his sentence while awaiting trial at Rikers, and so been sprung on conviction, his time served. In the years between Elmira and his current bid he'd never left the city, never been exiled upstate. Elsewhere, his charges had been dismissed. Perhaps *superior verbal skills* – what I knew as his famous persuasiveness – had kept him afloat. Anyway, no one could claim he'd not received his warnings:

8/5/92: CPCS (stim.) Misdm.

1/30/94: CPCS (stim.) Misdm., Possession of Paraphernalia

Again it had the quality of a train wreck or cliff plummet, to see where this orderly conga line of misdemeanors was headed:

8/11/94: Felony Possession of a Stimulant with Intent to Sell, Handgun Possession

And the punch line:

Felony Conviction, 4-to-Life.

With that, Mingus's yellow sheet had run out. It was as though the state had been nibbling him, tasting him, before committing to a mortal bite.

The rest were documents generated by his present incarceration: his initial classification, dooming him to high-security institutions, based on the previous manslaughter conviction – first Auburn, and then, after his own transfer request, here to Watertown. I'd later understand that he'd swum against a tide: inmates from the city usually pushed southward, trying to shrink the distance for their visitors.

Here too were carbons of infraction tickets Mingus had been written by the COs on the galleries – his "small beefs." I puzzled the handwriting on a few before growing numb:

Inmate refused to come out of cell for inspection

Contrabanned materials, magic marker

Inmate cooking soup with heating element

Drawn on t-shirt

Excessive news paper

Inmate climbs on bunk, states he is Superman

Contraband materials, pipe

So there it was: the inadequate liner note to Mingus Rude's whole existence. I memorized his block and gallery numbers and replaced the file in the drawer. Then, before resuming my spook's jaunt through the facility, I sat at the desk and was tempted by the telephone there. Perhaps it was a lingering whiff of my encounter with Sweeney, perhaps another stalling action, but I yearned for Abby.

I'd grown so accustomed to the empty ringing, though, and the blurred click of my machine's pickup, that it was a shock when she actually answered.

"Abby?" I said, to her hello.

"Yes."

"You're home."

"Well, I'm in your apartment," she said cautiously.

"Is that an important distinction?"

"I'm just pointing out that you're *not*." She let this sink in briefly, before asking: "Still enjoying Disneyworld?"

"Disneyland. But no. I mean, I'm not there."

She waited. I slowly grasped that all the time I'd been ringing the apartment in search of Abby, she might have been doing the same in search of me, with the same result.

"I'm not in Anaheim," I said. "I came back to Brooklyn."

"Is your father sick?"

At first I was stumped. It took a moment to grasp that this was Abby's most generous guess to explain my absence. She'd spared me her worse ones.

"No . . . no," I said.

"So you're on some pathetic *Iron John* quest, huh? In the woods beating on a drum?"

"Not exactly."

"Searching for the guy with the Afro pick?"

"Maybe sort of."

"Why are you whispering?"

"I can't really talk now," I said. "I actually wasn't expecting you to pick up." I wanted to add *I've been calling a lot*, but it was too late for that. I kept an eye on the murky light which penetrated the door's pebbly glass, fearing patrollers in the corridor. Anyone alerted by my murmurs would have seen the phone's cord hammocked between the handset on the desk and a receiver glommed into invisibility close at my head.

"You don't really want to talk to me now, is that what you're saying, Dylan?"

"I'm sorry."

I heard her consider my silence. "You're in a bad place, aren't you?" Her tone was gentler, barely. "Our big talk really fucked you up."

"I'm in a bad place," I said, agreeing with the part that was obvious.

"I believe you."

"Thank you," I said quietly.

"I guess you'll call again when you can really talk."

"Yes."

"Okay, then. I suppose I can wait."

"Thank you," I said again.

"I'm staying here now," she said. "Call anytime." She was babying me, easing us both off the phone.

"Abby—"

"Yes?"

I wanted to say something before we were done, wanted to have something to say. But where would I begin? Instead I defaulted, to a factoid I'd been holding in reserve for her to admire, the sort of talk we'd enjoyed in better days. "You know how I was always wondering about the Four Tops, about why they didn't ever break up or get new members, after all those decades? When every other vocal group fell apart?"

"Yeah?"

"Here's the thing, I found out the reason, it's kind of incredible. I forgot to tell you. The reason the Four Tops never broke up is they all go to the same synagogue. They're Jewish. Isn't that kind of moving?"

"That's what you called to say? The Four Tops are Jewish?"

"Well—"

"Dylan, I thought you always said that the fact that you happened to be Jewish was, like, the *least* defining thing about you."

"Well, sure. But, it's a . . . a pretty amazing thing to know about the Four Tops."

"Hmmm. I guess getting enthralled with negritude still beats self-reflection every time, huh? They must surely have a couple of those *black Jewish girls* hidden away in Crown Heights somewhere. Good luck on your quest, soul brother."

With that she clicked off the line. It wasn't the worst finish I could imagine, only a tad one-sided.

And with that, I had nothing left but my purpose here. Or take Abby's word and call it a *quest*: go to Mingus.

CHAPTER 13

HE NEVER WANTED to be King of the A, the CC, or King of any of the IRT lines, never wanted to be King of any line at all. It wasn't like that for Dose: counting tags, bragging, marking turf. No, you might strike deals with the crews who fought dumb wars for dominance – Dose finally joined FMD as a matter of least resistance – but this was only to free you to practice your art. The days of Mono and Lee and Super Strut – the legends who'd operated in a wide-open Gotham that needed to be taught what a tag or throw-up or top-to-bottom was, what graffiti was in the first place apart from primordial bathroom-wall gags and faggot phone numbers – were over. Gone. A million kids tagged and nobody knew the stories. The kids might figure it was always this way: eat and breathe, watch TV, join crews, do tags.

You needed a feel for the lonely art. It was the line and the language of a fuzzy-gushy flow of pigment settling into vibrant evidence against stone or steel that Dose hungered for. The line and the language, the startlement a perfect tag carved into the city's face. Let alone a blazing top-to-bottom car rocketing through a station: holy shit! This world might be a dungeon these days, but a few voices called out to a few others. Graffiti never was a popular movement, despite a fog of pretenders. Like Jackie Wilson to Sam Cooke to Otis Redding to Barrett Rude Junior, the real stuff formed a most rarefied continuum, a constellation.

Barry might not understand, but Dose knew his own art brought them, father and son, closer.

Cocaine might do the same thing – Barry seemed to think so, by the way he welcomed Dose to it.

A drug was a long study, nothing to take lightly. You might die before grasping what it had to tell you.

His father Barry and his friend Dylan – they couldn't know how alike Dose saw them, in the end. He felt the weight of their high expectations, of Dose, and of the world. Pops and

Dillinger were dreamers, it made them shy. Weak. He wished to protect them from knowledge that would crush them, even if at times it seemed that might be any knowledge at all. Stuff Mingus knew just because his eyes were open. When he abandoned Dylan to his fate at I.S. 293, it wasn't in ignorance. The opposite: he couldn't bear knowing the grievance Dylan was destined to absorb, couldn't face his own inability to stem it. Certain days he wanted to ring the doorbell and roar at Abraham: *Send the whiteboy to Brooklyn Friends School already! Get him clear of there!*

And flying? He'd mainly just tried not to disappoint.

Black Panther, Luke Cage, Arrowman, sure. Like what Gowanus needed was a black superhero.

Dose read between the comic-book panels, where Dylan failed to, and knew they were only extras in this urban scene. A soon-to-be-canceled title.

Half the yoke artists they clocked were chumps Dose knew from around the projects anyway.

Barry and Dylan, both lingered in a romance of Dean Street. Dose saw the block for the fragile island it was, at sea in the larger neighborhood – knew it as a flying man might, aerial view. He saw Nevins and Hoyt and where they led. Nobody, apart from maybe Marilla, knew how Dose protected the block from thirsty brothers from Wyckoff Gardens and Gowanus Houses, from Robert Woolfolk's young uncles and their like. Nobody knew how he sheltered the Dean kids, even Alberto and Lonnie, even chest-puffing Henry, from being beaten, from having skateboards and bikes ripped off countless times. Defended the brownstones from the gang on Bergen and Third, who pried basement-window bars with car jacks and slipped inside. Selling them herb, he'd overheard and petitioned against their plotting on the renovators: *Ain't nothing to steal, man! You think those white folks got cash? They a lot of hippies, man! Had a choice you think they'd settle* here?

A fair question, actually. Did the renovators think this was Park Slope? Or what?

Why should Dose have to carry them?

Abraham and Dylan was one thing, but some of those brownstoners, David Upfield, Isabel Vendle, the Roths, wouldn't look him or Junior in the eye, seemed to begrudge their place on the street. Upfield, out there each day in his Red Sox cap and handlebar mustache, picking litter from his yard. Glaring at PRs on crates in front of Ramirez's store, like they were ever going to quit tossing bottle caps and empty packets of plantain chips in his forsythia.

Possibly it was shifting from Philly that made him alert to the lines of force. Shedding Boy Scout uniform, football jersey, he'd had to tear down and start over. The whole middle-class assumption that was untenable here.

Junior could stay indoors and buff gold records. You, you were going to have to be able to move along the sidewalk.

There were mornings he just took off down Montague Street, strolled though the crowds of Heights kids rushing to make the bell at Packer and Saint Ann's, to steal away and get high at the Bridge's pilings. No teachers or school guards, no Dylan, no Arthur, no Robert. He'd be deaf to the call. No Flamboyan Crew, not today. No Savage Homicides, who wanted him to run Red Hook way, no Tomahawks, who wanted him to run Atlantic Terminals. Gone, all gone, like smoke to the Bridge's span, while he sat in the city scrap yard among the crumpled cop-car fenders and smashed parking meters and the heap of Board of Ed typewriter carcasses, keys gnarled in a knot at the platen, as if trying to blurt some unsayable word. Gone. Junior gone, Senior gone, Mingus gone.

Senior, he was more like Dose, in a way. Though rabid like a mongoose, he had eyes.

A few times Dose trailed Senior up Nevins for his parole dates, then afterward, to the Avery Bookstore on Livingston Street, where, in the aisle between the astrology magazines and civil-service test books, Senior spent an hour pawing through a bin of mildewed sixties *Playboys*, until the old Jew told him he had to buy something or get out.

One day Senior pinched his arm in the hallway of their basement apartment, said, *I feel you in my footsteps, son, hope you're learning something.*

What he recalls of the Sunday of the shooting, though, is abysmal shame, wanting to hide the white boy's eyes.

Remorse in him wasn't what they'd said it ought to be. If he mentally rewound, it was only to bag Senior by night, entrap him with the whores on Pacific, put a silver one through that vampire heart.

Really, though, his grandfather wasn't worth the bullet. If Dose could have somehow wielded a scalpel instead of the .45, he'd have bisected *Senior* from *Junior*. He'd meant to save his father. That would have been worth the bid he'd drawn.

Spofford.

Barry missed Dose's arraignment and bail hearing. He'd fled the scene, it turned out, returned with Senior's body to North Carolina, and left Dean Street behind, the apartment with its stained floor, coke dust melting into the cushions. Nobody arranges for Dose's release, nobody's got the money – what's Arthur Lomb going to do, *deal* to put up a bond? Take up a collection on Nevins? Ask his horrified mom?

Nobody knew Dose had turned eighteen. So he was first thrown into a dormitory at Spofford Juvenile, up in the Bronx, alongside thirteen-year-old heroin runners, fourteen-year-old transvestites, child child-molesters. He met a couple of slayers, neither even pubescent. They'd killed other kids. Dose already shaved, and he'd shot an old man. Spofford's boys treated him like an elder statesman. Ten days later somebody in Philly pulled up his birth certificate and the mistake was repaired. He was shifted to Rikers.

Nevertheless, if he flashes to August '81, it's Spofford he recalls: a twelve-year-old bunkmate from Bed-Stuy who heard voices he described as "Bugs Bunny in my head," who'd kidnapped a third-grade white girl from the yard at P.S. 38 and in the brick-strewn lots behind BAM and the LIRR terminal pulled off both their clothes and forced her to eat his feces, and who now spent nights keening for his mommy. Nobody mocked Bugs – his night song might have been on all their behalfs.

Rikers.

His knowledge overwritten a dozen times, Dose can no longer retrieve a first impression of this place. Mastering the island is one of his life's accomplishments, for what it's worth. So, likely he's purged the terror of his first glimpses by necessity. Building 6, sick with the special panic of the newly incarcerated: Dose is *always already* an old hand here.

There's nothing worse than scared homies, seeking to prove they're hard. You'd opt for a bid at any upstate prison over a spell in 6, once you saw how it worked. Upstate, men eased into sentences. Less uncertainty, fewer fresh crackheads, a general attitude of take your bid and do it, no unnecessary beefs. In Building 6, waves came in off the street. Young chumps, steeling for what they imagined they faced upstate, and making Rikers worse than any upstate yard. Word went out: better get yourself a reputation as a hard case, straight out the gate. So they'd play razor tag in the long unpatrolled hallway to the commissary. The bubble – the COs' glassed-in station – was so distant from the action it was humorous.

Everyone knew the adolescents were scarier than any grown man.

The fear method spares courthouse time. Every brother lands in Building 6 swearing to request a jury trial this time, vowing never to plea out again. Can't abide another conviction on the record – *Anyway, yo, I'm innocent!* Then, after six months of dodging homies slicing on each other in the commissary line, your court-appointed mentions a deal. Felony parole and time served, or one-to-five upstate, and you take it. The risk of a dime-to-life, a Rockefeller bid, is too much. Surprise: you're busted down again.

Nothing serves the system more than the system frying out of control around the edges.

Touring the island from every vantage, Dose has seen its works, like a clock pried open. When crackheads first get inside, they aim for a bunk and nobody lets them settle. Reeking, skinny, they'll never get over, never convince anyone of anything. Older hard cases or young studs, anyone says the same thing: *Damn, motherfucker, you stink!*

Get with them derelicts, boy, don't sleep here!

You've been the one carrying your blanket to the derelict quadrant, exiled to Rikers' own Bowery to bunk with the leather-scabbed, finger-split winos. Crushed men, eyes flickery from decades of cringing.

Next you get the whole Horatio Alger bit. Guys taking interest in their appearance for the first time – they've never before had an hour to themselves, never gotten clean, never went a day without drugs. Walk in howling for a hit of rock, but it's not coming. That first lockup is a glimpse in the mirror. The older men have ways, ideologies – jailhouse lawyer, Muslim, player or pimp, or the national gangs, Latin Kings, Ñetas, Bloods – and every soul's got a rap, talking endlessly about respect. Nobody's without a hustle or an affiliation, even as they speak of self-preservation by relying on nobody. Maintaining your space, staying out of debt. No arrears to anyone, that's the universal principle. So naturally everyone's trying to loan you cigarettes the first day, two-to-one interest: that's arrears, son.

Every body's got a layer of muscle too. Then there's you, scrawny freak from the street, ninety pounds once you beat the cold turkey.

You're thinking no arrears but the Rikers barber gives you a good haircut and then whispers *You owe me half a pack, brother*, and you don't even argue, you're just grateful, because you looked so screwed up before he fixed you.

Rikers provides the first audition: What's your hustle to be? Watches? Faggots? Drugs? Or just broker advice and cigarettes, narrate stories that don't ever finish, Jailhouse Scheherazade?

This island's best scam Dose stumbled into, though, his first time, between sentencing and transfer upstate. That September, with a nod to Senior's ghost, Dose had checked *Hebrew* on his intake form. The CO didn't blink, just told him when and where services were held. Dose forgot it completely until the winter holidays, when he was issued a box of kosher matzo at dinner and allowed to take it back into the dorms. Some rabbinical authority must have leaned hard to get this perk grandfathered in – whatever the source, the matzo's an absurd windfall, each day a full box that could keep him snacking a week.

Dose's bunkmate that December was a hard-ass he knew from the neighborhood, a cat he used to see looming around the Albee Square Mall, selling cakes and pushing pamphlets, dressed like Malcolm X. Just a bullshit Five Percenter out on the street, the dude had actually taken to the study of Islam when he got inside: every five in the morning he and his homies are in the dayroom going *Allah, Allah* on their knees. Now it's Ramadan, and the motherfucker is starving, since during festival week the Muslims can't eat before sundown. At Rikers this means missing all three meals, sitting on your bunk while everyone else is taken out for the five o'clock dinner. So Dose slips him a box of the matzo, and then another for his friends – he's got a supply under his bunk by now – which wins those cats over quick. He doesn't even ask for packs in return, figuring he'll have the Nation watching his back from now on. So a fake black Jew plays Santa Claus to a bunch of famished Muslims: Rikers logic.

Elmira.

Each institution carries previous incarnations, like sluggish rivers with another century's silt at their bottoms. Correctional reforms, innovations in prisonology tested and discarded, all these old uses for the same walls leave vibes. Everyone knows Sing Sing's the juice house, home of the chair, even when capital punishment was abolished the place just has death-row radiation in its steel. Auburn and Philadelphia's Eastern State are the birthplaces of solitary, stone tombs for driving men into self-hells – though the new supermaxes are working to make Auburn look silly.

Attica's just bat shit, like *Apocalypse Now*.

Elmira was once juvenile detention, and though it's official-ly phased out, they still lean to the young there, like they're doing you a favor. More lately it's replaced Sing Sing as the state's reception center, where you're tested and classified for placement elsewhere. Your educational level, plus your score on a gross aptitude test, determines what you'll be paid the entire time you're employed inside – forty cents, seventy cents an hour. You might be a janitor or trusty, hand out the soap on the block, for ten years, based on an hour's scrutiny here. Then, having been scoured for hints of gang colors, you're scattered to the far corners, away from any suspected homeboys. Men serve whole terms at Elmira, not uncommonly; nevertheless, this presumption of just passing through, combined with an air of boys' prison, makes Elmira You-Ain't-Seen-Nothing-Yet

House. There's an undertone of *Shut up, boy, count yourself lucky you here.* As though it could get any worse.

Dose spent four years inside Elmira's walls, like turning the pockets of his youthful self inside out. As on Dean Street, he made himself an old hand, an inside-track man, overnight. He was extravagant with lore, goofy with it, telling men twice his age how to operate the system he'd hardly seen firsthand. All Dose needed to know, really, he learned his first day on Elmira's yard, at the bench, when he found the free weights fused to the crossbar, so they couldn't be stolen or used to crush a skull. In other words, you'd best have gotten pumped quickly at Rikers or you wouldn't even be able to budge the set here. Plus if you weren't already a certain size the dudes around the bench won't let you near it. So much for the illusion your fate was yet untold. Any forking path was further behind you on your journey, further back than you dared guess.

Career.

At Elmira Dose turned himself into a jailhouse artist. Like Rikers matzos, the career was a thing he stumbled into. At a table in the dayroom, he'd been curled in an introspective shell around a series of notebook pages, sketching, in blue ballpoint, elaborately rendered designs for train cars of the mind, in blazing colors supplied only *by* the mind. He'd been working the hardest at a top-to-bottom with a Valentine's theme: goopy bulging hearts speared by feathered arrows, shot by a Porky Pig cherub in Nike high-tops.

A stony-eyed brother in net muscle shirt and doo-rag, one Dose had so far assiduously avoided, suddenly lurched at his shoulder, startling him. The brother pushed a forefinger at the Valentine page.

"Yo, that shit's *nice.*"

"Thanks."

"You could do me something like that? For my girl?"

"Sure, I guess."

"Put me and her name together. From Raf to Junebug."

"Sure."

"Put it around the edge of a paper, man. So I can write inside."

"Yeah, sure."

"How much?"

Dose shrugged.

"Four packs," grunted Raf.

Raf was one of those who, having likely neglected or even slapped around his girl in his free life, became a romantic inside. What, apart from love talk, flowery letters, promises of marriage, did a man have to offer, if he wished to keep a woman visiting, or from making time with Jody or running away with his kid? Raf had gone through his little vocabulary of woo in a phone call or two, so gestures like the decorated stationery were increasingly urgent. Possibly he felt Junebug turning from him. Possibly her visits had slowed. He commissioned from Dose a series of ornately inscribed love cards, graffiti Hallmark.

One evening Dose had the wit to say: "This one's free, man."

Raf narrowed his eyes: *No arrears* was the message flashing in them. *Don't play me, man.*

"Just don't mail it right away, okay? Show it around to the brothers." Raf sat at the Bloods' table at dinner, an unapproachable zone of latent violence. "Say who did it for you."

Raf smiled now, getting it. "Aight, Dog. I could do that f'you."

Dose hadn't taken long to see that the hand-drawn posters and logos and primitive porn Scotch-taped to so many bunk walls were the work of just a few prisoners, and the rest of the population customers of those few. No reason not to crack this wider market – his cards for Raf were head and shoulders above the usual crap, which mostly resembled tracings from 1950s comic books. Graffiti stylings, those were what elicited the oohs and ahs.

Sure enough, a little promotional savvy brought the flood. Dose found himself doodling borders for any number of love letters – the sheer flood of woo being pointlessly pitched from behind stone walls and steel bars could make you dizzy if you dwelled on it. Every one of these retrofitted paramours was a former ho-slappin' mack daddy, now down on one knee. Dose tried not to learn too much about who was really getting mail back, or visitors, or even their phone calls answered.

But Valentines were only a feature of the market: Dose did hand-over-fist business in cardboard frames for photographs of loved ones, and burner-style name tags on notebook sheets for personalizing bunk spaces – anyone who saw one would say *Yo, I gotta get down with that*, and get in line during next rec. He manufactured custom porn, homemade Tijuana Bibles featuring, for instance, Crockett and Tubbs nailing Madonna, whatever the customer wanted, the customer was always right. He drew prototypes for tattoos, which ballpoint-pen tattooists transferred to biceps and thighs and chests. Dose would see men he didn't know in the commissary line, wearing his tags on their bodies. Call him King of Elmira. Sometimes it threw him back to Boy Scout days, as if he could get a merit badge for Tit Art or Tattoo.

A Puerto Rican kid asked Dose to personalize one of the system's standard-issue white T-shirts. He wanted a cartoon of himself, palms turned outward in an expression of helplessness, and the slogan TEN TO LIFE?!? Sad but true, the kid wished to wear it, so Dose knocked it out, bestowed the kid big oval Felix the Cat eyes, not bad if he said so himself. The next day an older black CO named Carroll, ordinarily a stand-up dude, appeared at Dose's cell.

"Stand out for search," said Carroll.

"What up, man?"

"Put a sock in it and stand out."

Carroll emerged from his bunk search with all of Dose's art supplies, plus ten packs of coffin nails Dose had stockpiled. "I have to seize these materials and write you up," he said. "Holding more than six packs is an infraction."

"Dang, take the butts, but that's my drawing shit."

"Listen, Rude. You make this shirt?" Carroll showed Ten-to-Life's T, which he'd had balled in his back pocket.

"What if I did?"

Carroll shook his jowly head, weary with all he'd seen in his days. "You're risking seven years for attempted escape for altering a garment."

Dose started over, assembling new materials on credit, and leaving all garments unaltered this time around. The second assault on his enterprise came a few weeks after he resumed, at the hands of the Astacio brothers: two older Hispanic jailhouse artists, either real brothers or not, maybe cousins. No one knew, though both were short and chubby, and both wore their hair in a net with an oily knot at the neck. The Astacios worked in a truly pathetic Coney Island-tattoo style, their lettering of any slogans or monikers as crude as a woodcut. Without troubling to notice, Dose had been suffocating their livelihood, so the brothers began stepping up on him, in the food line, in the commissary line, on the yard. They'd growl animalistically, something about quit stealing their customers – as if Dose was expected to screen requests: *You don't happen to be clientele of the esteemed Astacios?*, some shit like that. Dose only pretended not to understand, like they were speaking Spanish. Then Ramon Astacio stepped up on him at a urinal, in an abruptly vacated F-gallery shower.

Ramon hemmed in near to Dose, now seeming not to have the use of language at all, only body English. He opened his smile and showed why: he was twirling a razor blade in his mouth, flipping it with his tongue like a cheerleader knuckling a baton.

Dose flipped, a year's accumulated fear brimming in him, the first rage he'd opened himself to feel since expelling the bullet in Senior's direction. He threw an elbow and hung Ramon on the jaw, causing him to bite on the ritually displayed blade. The move was triumphant and a mistake. As in a yoking, there were rules to follow, an art of encounters. Threat had a rhetoric. Ramon might have a mouthful of his own blood, but Dose had surrendered the rudder of the moment.

A man didn't just hit another man unless he could go all the way and kill him, and this was not the place Dose had staked out for himself.

Now he rushed from the shower, past Noel, the other brother, sentry at the door.

At dinner that night Ramon was absent and the word buzzing through the hall was he was getting his mouth sewn. Noel sat at the Ñetas' table and he and some of the Ñetas were offering heavy glares. Dose knew he would have to move eventually and saw no margin in waiting, so he went right at the unthinkable, and approached the Bloods' table. Not directly to Raf, but to the place where King Blood sat. It took gulping back his heartbeat to do it.

"I want to apologize for disturbing your meal," he told King Blood. "But I've got trouble and I have to ask if I could speak to Raf."

King Blood didn't look from his tray, as if they were all working from a script too familiar to bother dramatizing.

"This a question of mercy, or you looking to do business?"

"Business," said Dose.

"Go ahead," said King Blood, only after an appreciable pause, time enough for any pair of eyes in the room to see it was Dose who'd come to them and been made to wait trembling for an answer.

So it was that Raf became Dose's protector and broker, taking fifty percent out of any payment, and stockpiling a certain vein of big-titted poster work for private dispersal among the Bloods network. In an unseen deal some top-level Blood had a word with some top-level Ñeta and the Astacios melted away. The brothers only shot Dose dartlike glances when they were certain no one saw, Ramon salaciously licking his teeth with his scarred tongue, wanting Dose to see the badge he'd awarded and consider its implications.

But Raf was big and strong, and devoted, and so Dose's safety at Elmira was secured. Dose was one of his several mules; the others dealt "trees" – tight-rolled cheeba sticks, cut with mentholated tobacco to stretch the ingredient – and he would slip Dose a fistful of these once in a while, a small perk. Dose had arrived at a policy of no dope inside, witnessing the rapid spiral of arrears this led to, but getting stoned on the gratis trees was a safe exception. Raf also turned out not to be so faithful to the recipient of his incessant Valentines that he didn't want his dick sucked a couple of times, and then to suck Dose's in return once they trusted one another. The Bloods had a broom closet permanently bought for more or less this exact purpose. Dose learned to admire how Raf could want to stretch a suck-job out to defeat time, like relishing a shaggy-dog story. If he even came to crave it a little, in both directions, find himself as entranced by the tensing in Raf's lifter's thighs as he was by the avidity of a mouth, that was fine, neither here nor there, not particularly telling. If there was one thing Dose had learned from his father — the Love Man resting on his laurels, lazily taking what came to the house, Horatio's women or, on occasion, Horatio — it was that it wasn't a big deal to suck a little dick now and then, so long as nobody girled you out. That had been Dose's understanding the day Barrett Rude Junior walked in on his son with Dylan Ebdus: there were more things under the sun than what cats might get up to with one another if there were no women on the scene.

Not that Dose spent a lot of time thinking of Dean Street, or of the days before Senior had come to the house, with Barry still in full polymorphous splendor, before things got paranoiac and eerie all over, in the basement and upstairs and out on the street. In those days when it still seemed Barry might resume making music, might fall in with that crowd of funk superheroes.

The four-track the secret machine under the floorboards, not the .45.

In that brief margin between renouncing his Boy Scout uniform and taking up with FMD and Robert Woolfolk, and spurning Dylan Ebdus, or being spurned by him, whichever it was, Dose could still be enticed by the simplest games, stoopball, wallball, skully, boosting skin mags from the newsstand on the triangle at Flatbush and Atlantic, committing each syllable of Sugarhill Gang's "Eighth Wonder" or Kurtis Blow's "The Breaks" to subvocal memory.

Or lie in a breeze from the backyard window and page through *The Inhumans*, waiting for their mute leader Black Bolt to open his mouth and bring it all crumbling down, with one shattering doomsday utterance: the bridge, the towers, the schools, all the public concrete Mono and Lee and Dose had tagged with spray paint for future demolition.

When Black Bolt at last sang it would level the city and there'd be only the subway running underneath through its theorem of tunnels, the one true neighborhood.

Dose could lie on his bedspread in the rotten-ailanthus breeze and dream it for hours.

Or, alternately, rush onto the street on the broilingest of days to join in directing, with a tin can open at both ends, a stream from a wrenched hydrant through the window of a passing car. Driver hectically rolling it if he saw what was in store, never fast enough.

But the stories you told yourself – which you pretended to recall as if they'd happened every afternoon of an infinite summer – were really a pocketful of days distorted into legend, another jailhouse exaggeration, like the dimensions of those ballpoint-crosshatched tits or of the purported mountains of blow you once used to enjoy, or how you'd bellowed an avenger's roar when you squeezed the trigger of a pistol you'd actually brandished in self-pissing terror. How often had that hydrant even been opened? Did you jet water through a car window, what, twice at best? Summer burned just a few afternoons long, in the end.

As for flying, Dose never even glanced at the sky. Flying was a summer within a summer, a whim. So why think of it at all?

CHAPTER 14

IN THE YEARS between Elmira and Watertown Dose's life on the street was a shadow, a pale dream between bids.

One release blurred into another, a Twilight Zone recurrence of being dropped by the Rikers shuttle at Queensboro Plaza. There the bus stopped under the el tracks and the driver doled out subway tokens, one per man, the system's laconic parting gift. Up on the platform, Dose would wait in the middle of a gaggle of freaked-out felons, each pretending not to be in the company of the others, each with panic in their eyes. The releasees chewed gum frantically, spit, tugged too-tight street clothes over new biceps and pecs, every last one of them as conspicuously ill-armored for this world as lobsters loosed in an open field.

From Queensboro Plaza Dose made his way back. He'd ride the 7 to Grand Central and change for an express to Nevins if he was feeling bold, hoping to see some fresh top-to-bottom work on the trains, hoping to run into someone he knew. On more sheepish days he'd walk the two blocks to Queens Plaza instead, for the G's slog through Greenpoint, Bed-Stuy, Fort Greene, thirteen subway stops nobody used, an hour in the tunnels to calm your thoughts.

Sing a song of returning: *Ya miss me, sucker? Well I'm back!*

Back in the New York groove, sure.

On discharge from Elmira Dose aimed, by prearrangement, for Arthur Lomb's crib on Smith Street. Barry had rented the basement rooms; no question of a homecoming there. His first season of freedom Dose worked for a hippie contractor named Glenray Schurz, replacing window frames in the rotting brownstones, complicit in renovation, making Boerum Hill of Gowanus. Those early days Dose visited Barry at lunchtimes, still covered with plaster dust, his particle mask around his neck. He'd stop in with a bag of sandwiches from Buggy's, the hot mustard Barry used to adore. Only now Barry never ate a bite. Dose sat on the couch with him, trying to know his father, but they'd hardly talk. Just watch TV, *Phil Donahue*, *Mission Impossible*, or Sunday afternoons sit and groan at the Jets blowing another tackle.

Outside the block was dead, no kids at all.

Henry every once in a while saying *yo* in a suit and tie.

Barry putting the sandwich in the refrigerator and twisting the cap off his malt-liquor lunch while the fridge door was open.

He'd see his father on the street too, on Atlantic, at the Times Plaza Hotel. There Dose would choose not to be seen, just witness, as Barry hung at the entrance waiting for a deal to unfold.

Later, when Dose had returned inside and been released again, his cycling through Rikers under way, crackhead days birthing crackhead months birthing crackhead years, years spent *on a mission*, Arthur Lomb grew too uptight to offer his couch. Arthur would spot Dose coming a mile off on the street and pull his wallet out, stuff a five-spot into his palm for their handclasp when they collided, pity money Dose had become too unproud to refuse. Those days, dropped at Queens Plaza, Dose wouldn't head back to Gowanus, not to Brooklyn at all. He'd shortcut to Manhattan, Washington Square, seeking cats he recognized, or word of a club or a private affair, and by after-hours be crashing with some woman desperate enough to join his desperate ride, foolish enough not to see where it went: a trail of her pawned possessions, like bread crumbs, pointing to the day of his next arrest.

The song of returning blurred into a mumble, all you recalled were a few phrases from the chorus: *I ain't never going in the joint again, damn straight!*

Girl, you like to party?

Later still, near the finish, before he'd found his way to Lady's apartment in the Gowanus Houses, Dose would begin his time of freedom as he knew it was fated to end: nights at the disused public swimming pool on Thompson Street. There he'd hide and sleep beneath the pool's platform, in a crawl space through a curled-aside section of Cyclone fence, one no derelicts had claimed, likely because John Gotti's social club was just up the block.

Nothing but a crackhead and a booster, then. Just boosting day and night, harder work than anyone knew, racking CDs, racking clothes, racking belts and shoes and small electronics, until there weren't any stores left open to boost from. Then find an all-night restaurant and try to steal tips off the counter.

Living dawn to dusk, pawn to pipe.

There was only one rescue possible in those years, and that was arrest. Dose came to yearn for it like a changing of seasons, his chance to quit starving in plain sight. He'd smoke himself to ninety pounds, then eighty, become a scarecrow man sleeping in gutters, and begin to beg for recapture: *God's sake, throw me in Rikers before I die!*

Invisible in a throng of invisible men, Dose had to step out to get what he needed. Solicit an undercover, or work a routine, the same spot every day, a marathon in the alley behind Tower Records or the doorway of OK Harris Gallery, until someone finally requested the police buff this broken human signature from the urban façade.

Wherever you wandered in Dinkins's boroughs, then Giuliani's, this archipelago city was always changed after your intervals on Rikers, the exile island.

Fuck did the graffiti go?

What was happening when a motherfucker can't even light up a joint on Eighth Street?

Not to call yourself a zombie. But you did stalk an unreal city.

Windsor Weather Stripping.

It was Arthur who set Dose up with Glenray Schurz, brought Dose around to the hippie commune on Pacific, one of the last left in the neighborhood now. Schurz was bearded, pinwheel-eyed, but in overalls and no shirt showed only gristle and vein, a vegetarian strongman. Schurz had been a furniture builder, Utopian Woodstock style. Then, coming to Brooklyn, a cabinetmaker, taking kitchen jobs in the neighboring brownstones. Only it was too much hassle finally, the ceaseless answering to housewives' magazine fantasies. Schurz hit on a simpler life: applying Windsor Weather Stripping to the air-leaky sashes of the decaying row-house windows, the double-hung frames which dated to the 1860s and 1880s – work as repetitive as changing tires, but the renovators were at his mercy. The shade of Isabel Vendle could lure them to the neighborhood, beguile them into perilous mortgages, but no Vendleghost nor anybody else would be there to soothe them after the first winter's Brooklyn Union Gas bills came in: Yikes! Then they'd sheepishly ask around and be told: *Windsor Weather Stripping. There's this carpenter guy on Pacific who'll lay it in, forty dollars a window plus materials, pays for itself in six months. He's a bit seedy and a bit creepy but—*

So Dose became Schurz's assistant. Twice a week they'd gather a load at the mom-and-pop factory down Fourth Avenue that manufactured the zinc linings. Quick run next to Brook Lumber for fresh bullnose molding to replace the bad strips they'd surely find on the job. Then in, often under the flitty eyes of a woman alone at the house, her husband having struck the deal – she likely thinking *Did he have to bring an ahem? Should I hide my purse?* – to set up their little industrial operation. First unhang the window, lay sash weights and pulleys to one side. Then cut zinc to fit the frame. Router grooves in top and bottom sashes. Line zinc into the header and the sill while the sashes were free. Then the tricky part, which if a renovator attempted himself always proved their dependence on Schurz's expertise: rehanging those ancient sash weights into the air pockets concealed at each side of the frame, so the windows were balanced on their pulleys. Pity the soul who let a weight slip from his fingers to thud to the bottom of the pocket. They'd have to demolish a molding to fish it free again.

Oriented correctly, the two sashes sealed, the zinc airtight at the seam. On a good day they'd get through eight frames. Dose detected Schurz's secret satisfaction at the job well done, though Schurz did nothing but sneer at the work as corrupt and at those who'd hired him as bourgeois pigs.

Glenray's communal housemates were ceding their neighborhood to the yuppies as much as the blacks and PRs. In a gentrification some white people – say Glenray, or Abraham Ebdus, or Arthur's mom – might only bridge to another kind.

Some of the latter of whom were not above niggerfying the former.

Sometimes one of their clientele recognized Dose and just noted it with their eyebrows. Life's eternal lesson: people return in new guises.

You learned it and taught it at the same time.

One day Dose passed Abraham Ebdus on the street and looked away.

On a few occasions, busting through hundred-year-old plaster and lattice Glenray and Dose discovered stashes of browned newspapers left by long-dead laborers, baseball scores and ship sinkings from the century's start. Once they found a sealed bottle of brandy tucked deep in a wall, its label so dark it was only readable like a photographic negative. On their break they sat on the building's stoop and swapped the dust-shouldered bottle like it was Night Train. The stuff was sweet and thick and moldy, mustified by time.

Elsewhere they'd find just pencil marks, names and dates left by the workers who preceded them, *Jno. Willson 2.16.09*. Then Dose would take Glenray's carpenter's pencil and tag *Dose 1987*, a little enigma to send down history's line before they sealed the wall.

On other breaks Dose and Glenray climbed fire escapes to rooftops, and smoked the commune's petty-cash sinsemilla. They'd gaze out past Wyckoff Gardens, past the F-train platform where it camelbacked over the canal, gaze out toward Coney and the alleged ocean. Dose never spoke of knowing the scheme of streets from the air.

Glenray said: "That Ulano factory is giving us all testicle cancer. If someday it burns down in the dead of night you'll know it was me."

Glenray said: "I'd like to build a yurt on top of the Brooklyn House of Detention."

Glenray said: "Your old man opened for the Stones? Your old man's a fucking god, man."

Glenray said: "Once I was on mescaline and I whacked off into a liverwurst sandwich, just because I read about it in a book."

And one day Glenray said: "It's weird, I've got a million

connections for brown leafy drugs but none at all for white powdery drugs, which I am totally in the mood for right now. Any chance you could help me with that, Mingus?"

On a mission.

All he ever got out of recovery – Alcoholics Anonymous, group therapy at Rikers – was a name for what it felt like when he was on the street and pushing toward the next high: Dose was *on a mission*. The term encompassed the thousand-and-one things he'd find himself doing, his crafty diversity of scuffles and scams, scalping tickets at the Garden, racking art books at St. Marks and shifting them at the Strand, pawning some girl's hair dryer or clock, or just slumping around Washington Square watching for some dealer he knew enough to persuade to allow him to shift some rock in return for a rock commission. These might seem to be many activities but were all only one thing, Dose on a mission: intent, monomaniacal, autistic in craving.

His weirdest brush with recovery wasn't either in the city or inside, but in Hudson, a dying industrial river town upstate, at a program called NewGap. One January night he'd taken refuge from subzero in a city shelter where a social-services worker was scouting. Dose began talking with her for the cup of coffee, and found himself inking block letters on a form. Next thing he knew he was whisked on a bus to the crumbling-brick facility, a refitted TB asylum. The NewGap regimen consisted of some unholy blend of Gordon Liddy fascism and Werner Erhard brainwash, its inductees reconfigured at every level of the social self in order to break self-loathing habituation. Dose and the other "freshmen" were denied the use of speech without written permission, through an elaborate system of note-scribbling and hand-raising, a vast twenty-four-seven parlor game with drill sergeants barking fury at the slightest mistake.

Dose played the game for two weeks. The day he went AWOL he found his way to Hudson's crackhouse within an hour of hitting the streets, radar working fine after building up his strength on NewGap meals. Invariably, those years, any town had its own microcosmic crackidemic: dealers, whores, every element that the rest of the country righteously decried as big-city symptoms were right up their armpit anywhere you troubled to look.

Indeed, it was in Hudson where Dose met with what he'd always consider his all-time-low glimpse of degradation. In the city proper it was not unknown to hear a dealer humiliate a desperate crackhead, one pleading for free rock: *Yo, you want a rock you could suck my dick for it.* If it was a cracked-out woman, the dealer might or might not be for real; if it was a man, it was for the laugh, to see the flicker of shame in the human skeleton before giving the charity or kicking him out. Nevertheless, however much debasement might be the real language of the encounter, garbing it in sex kept the players in that drama above a certain threshold, in the realm of greed, desire, human things. Dose understood this when he saw what he saw in Hudson: how much lower one human being could wish to take another.

"You need a rock, man?" the Hudson dealer had told the crackhead in question. "See that roach over there?"

Dose saw it, bigger than a roach in fact. A doleful waterbug, shining yellow-brown under a shattered sink. Dose saw the begging crackhead see it too.

"Eat that bug, I give it to you."

The skeleton had reached for the waterbug, nabbed it, gulped. And been given his hit, to the cackling enjoyment of the dealer and others. Dose only turned his eye, bewildered at what had so suddenly been flayed from all their souls. They were each dead there in that paint-peeling room, and only Dose knew.

When Hudson cops caught Dose in a sweep they didn't arrest him, only put him on a Greyhound back to the city. A month or two later, after his next city arrest, Dose sat on a Rikers bunk and told the Hudson story. Incredibly, one of his listeners offered triangulation. They'd seen the same once, the eat-a-bug shtick, on a jaunt down in Florida.

All agreed: such grim hick shit would never go over here. New Yorkers had too much self-respect for that.

Lady's.

That night in June in Barry's front room was the first and

only time Dose ever saw Lady out of her own crib. You'd be stretching to call it a party: Dose and his father, plus Horatio, Lady, and some skinny crabby other girl who struggled to keep her head up.

Dose had full-circled with Barry, to sharing the pipe.

If crackheads were an extended family, as hateful with one another as true relations, why exclude his father?

Smoke scribbled in the air between them, like exhausted language, Senior's unmentioned name etched in fume.

Once in a blue moon Dose brushed dust off an album jacket and placed the tonearm over a groove Barry hadn't aired in ten years – Esther Phillips, Donny Hathaway – treasures moldering in disuse. The evening when Dose met her, though, there in the half-light of Barrett Rude Junior's parlor sarcophagus, Lady had already been at the old vinyl and made a selection – *Curtis Live*, "Stare and Stare," "Stone Junkie," Mayfield laughing in falsetto at his drummer's stuttering breaks.

Lady featured the hugest capacity Dose had seen. He never knew anyone could smoke more rock than him, let alone a woman. She partied three, four days in a row, hardly nodded, and never more so than that first time, beginning after Barry kicked them out, four in the morning. Horatio and the floppy girl went up Nevins to the IRT, and Lady led Dose to her crib in the Gowanus Houses, a public housing apartment turned crack den.

Her true name was Veronica Worrell, though he never heard it from her lips. She offered what everyone called her: Lady. The name encoded her formal airs, a tinge of severity. She was nobody's girl and nobody's mother, but everyone's Lady, well known as such.

If walking down Dean with her that night Dose might have mistaken what kind of pickup she'd made, what it was Lady had spotted in his eyes, seeing her crib dispelled any uncertainty. Her door opened to the Hoyt Street face of the projects, in sight of traffic, cars rolling by with the booming systems, backbeat rattling windows, the cops cruising too, ominously hushed in their Giuliani Task Force vans. Lady kept a lookout, a crack-head schooled in two hand signals, all they could keep track of: fist for a white man, or an unfamiliar black, a maybe-cop, open hand for a recognized customer or any obvious pipehead, too young or skeletal to be a threat.

He didn't know it but Dose had come in for his last mission, homing like a pigeon.

The place was a factory geared for one purpose, support of Lady's own habit. The volume of enterprise out of a three-bedroom public unit was staggering, a feat to make Henry Ford or Andy Warhol envious. Any space was rentable, not only bedrooms to girls for turning tricks, kitchen to dealers cutting up their shit, but closets for stashing quantities in transit, corridors and couches for slumping against. You might not sleep anymore – many didn't. Dose couldn't recall authentic sleep by the end of two months at Lady's. But if you didn't sleep you nodded, if you didn't nod you rested with your eyes open. At Lady's, you paid to rest.

Dose paid the only way he could, by bringing people back to Lady's crib. If they bought product he was settling his debt. This was Lady's specialty, her adding-machine brain. Even as she smoked more than he thought a human body could tolerate, Dose never knew her to drop a digit in her calculations. She'd tell him when he was ahead enough to earn a rock. Or more, ahead enough to be allowed to pitch some rock himself. He remade himself as an entrepreneur four or five times in his months under Lady, taking vials of product onto Hoyt or up to Fulton, to the Albee Square Mall, or just into the courtyard in the project's interior. Then he'd fail, smoke it all, not be able to afford another vial, and when he'd nod he'd be in debt for the extent of wall he took up. It was a tough system, but fair. Nothing could be held against Lady, she was so obviously looking out for her people, the pipeheads. Nobody stole your shoes or your clothes when you closed your eyes at Lady's.

This was the true love affair, Dose misunderstood no longer. Lady saw into his soul and found an appetite for rock there, all the way down to the bottom.

That was his last summer, a long nod against her corridor wall. And smoking until by arrest he was thinner than he'd ever been, maybe seventy pounds light.

Let's get small, everybody get small.

That same June, on Smith Street, one measly block away, Sans Famille, the first of the area's upscale French restaurants, opened its doors. The bistro drew a star from the *Times*, the first tick of Smith's gentrification time bomb, precursor to the cafés and boutiques which would leverage out botanicas and social clubs, precursor to Arthur Lomb's counterfeit Berlin.

Sans Famille's busboys and dishwashers weren't unwitting of the action on Hoyt. More than a few made their way to Lady's threshold on their city-regulated ten-minute breaks.

Once he proved himself untrustworthy for taking vials on the street, Dose accepted his obvious fate, the slot for which Lady might have pegged him the moment they met. He ran her door. Not the lookout window, he'd not plummeted to that ignoramus level. He was a dealer still, just one trusted to go no farther than his hand could reach through the security-chained door. Money in and product out, Dose touched it all as it passed and kept barely anything.

He unchained the door for the cops when they came. They came just in time. He was going to die if he kept Lady's pace.

The gun was nobody's in particular, hidden in a drawer, but it stuck to him. Dose had to be philosophical. It was in the nature of an arrest situation that a floating gun attached to the individual bearing a manslaughter rap.

He'd been six months at Rikers and was up to a hundred and thirty pounds when he pled out and was moved upstate to Auburn, then Watertown.

Auburn.

His first tour, Dose had been prodigal, an advance man for a generation destined inside. Now it wasn't just Rikers which brimmed with faces from the neighborhood or the yards. It was the big upstate houses like Auburn, too, as though the system was inadvertently reassembling the city and its factions here, 1977 trapped in the amber of incarceration. Writers were reunited with their crews, none having seen each other since back in the day, since they'd spun from teenage affiliations into lives more burdened and serious. Yet those adult lives seemed stripped away by their failure. What remained were thirty-year-old teenagers joshing in prison: *Ho, shit, man, it's you! This my boy Pietro, from DMD!* Or: *Damn, I used to see your shit on the 6 line, you were with Rolling Thunder Crew, right?*

Lines of enmity dissolved. Any connection was a good one, here in the woods. Dose met a couple of boys from a once-upon-a-time-terrifying Coney Island gang. Some summer ago, Dose and two others from FMD had gotten on the Coney crew's bad side by making a dumb mistake: they'd tagged inside a bunch of apparently clean D-train cars in a yard's dim moonlight, using black ink from heavy-flowing fat mops. When the trains ran the next day, Dose and his mates saw with horror what moonlight hadn't revealed: the D-train interiors had already been covered with the Coney Island crew's clunky tags in pink ink. Black now overlapped the pink everywhere. How to explain the pink hadn't even been *visible*? Impossible. They thought Dose had deliberately backgrounded them. Dose spent that summer watching over his shoulder for the Coney gang, marked as prey.

Now it was all hunky-dory, good for a laugh. Dose was one of the famous names, so the Coney crew recalled the incident as evidence they'd once been significant writers.

Dose was ambulatory history, and brothers wished to claim some for themselves.

"Yo, Dog, you remember me? I wrote *Kansur 82*, you used to background me all the time."

"Sure, sure, I remember you," Dose would say, if he was in a generous mood.

Other times he'd withhold the glory of being linked to his name, just to see their frustration: "Why would I trouble to background you, blood? What was you to me?"

"I was a toy, I know – you was right to go over my tags."

Dose would deny it, tormenting their minds: "You claiming you got up somewhere before me?"

"You used to go over me!" the younger writer would insist.

"Nah, man. You used to go *under* me."

Surgery.

Of course it would be Horatio, clownier than ever, who turned up in Auburn's visitor's room talking around the subject, not saying what he meant. Barry was illing – well, Dose knew that already. No, *truly* illing, like in the Long Island College emergency room a couple of times. His father *needed* Dose now, in some way Horatio wouldn't explain. Dose agreed without understanding what he'd agreed to.

A week later he was escorted to Auburn's infirmary for consultation with a surgeon who acted like Doolittle among the savages, brow furrowed in reproach even as he spoke at moron rpm. Did Dose grasp what he was offering? Yes, sure, though he hadn't until then. There was no certainty it would work, Doolittle warned. Tests were required, to check the match. His and his father's candidacy had to be examined. Dose, old hand in passivity by now, submitted to three weeks of fluid donations, spinal, bile, and shit. The results: Dose was a hundredth-percentile shoo-in to rescue his father's putrefying blood.

Doolittle, chafing at being instrument of a back-channel exception, prison strings pulled by Andre Deehorn and others in the Philly scene, advised Dose against the procedure. The kidney could fail within five to ten years – that was a *successful* outcome.

Dose would have given heart, or hands, or eyes.

Recovery took six days in Albany Presbyterian Hospital. Dose and his father lay in side-by-side narcotic slumber, with a holstered guard in the room patently thrilled with the assignment, full of *Playboy* dreams of nurses.

The day before he was returned inside, with both Dose and Barry up and running, having demonstrated renal function to Doolittle's satisfaction, the four of them – son and father in cotton pajamas, and Horatio, and the guard – escaped through fire doors to the hospital's roof.

There they smoked a joint Horatio'd smuggled in, conducting their own tests on that new kidney – what else was it for?

There, as they squinted in the glare off Albany's toy skyline, his father's fund of disappointment was proven bottomless. Barry could help himself to Dose's extra kidney and still not meet his eyes.

When he learned how famous the organ donation made him at Auburn, Dose wanted no part of it, and requested the transfer to Watertown, to finish his bid in anonymous peace.

Watertown.

Dose shed it all. No jailhouse artistry, he'd left that behind years back – a million guys could execute the graffiti style now. He had no illusions about stockpiling cigarettes. Old-school eminence held nothing he wanted, it signified zip to the time he had to do, played no real factor in the endurance of the mind. Claiming this or that alliance outside – *Yo, I know that dude, younger brother of Fitty Cents, that nigger's King of Wyckoff Gardens, he gonna set me up when I'm sprung* – looked thinner every day. Duck ensnarements and arrears at any level, this was Dose's campaign. Beguiling COs was of use only if you wanted something a CO could give you. They could give you nothing. A protector like Raf mattered only until you understood there was nothing to protect.

Invisibility, intangibility, Teflon eyes.

Yet he had one last error of affiliation in him.

Robert Woolfolk was the same hectic proposition he'd ever been, only stretched and torn by fifteen years more on the street and inside. Gold-toothed, arm-crook scarred from vein hunts, one ear nipped, Robert staggered on, decades beyond adventures that ought to have been his finish if he hadn't had so many lives, like Wile E. Coyote still climbing out of the crater and dusting himself off, rubbing his hands and grinning in conspiratorial glee. You wanted to put the man to bed.

Dean Street had come to Watertown, like a radio signal wandering through space, a hit song from 1976 become sole sign of life in the galaxy.

So Dose took him under his wing, as though he had one.

Robert Woolfolk was dealing trees within a few weeks of appearing at Watertown, against Dose's advice. If you wished to smoke, smoke. Be a customer, laying low. Nope: Woolfolk began dealing two-for-ones, betting against guys' commissary checks coming in on time, juggling debt. Then slicing trees open and stretching them with stale tobacco. This was tolerable, a line Dose had seen men walk for years, a line he'd walked a few times himself, merely to keep himself amused at Rikers.

Then Robert found the market in spitback sacks, and lost his interest in trees.

A spitback sack was a parcel of liquid drugs. Methadone,

smuggled from the dispensary by signed-in junkies, by the method of concealing a few fingers of a Saran Wrap glove in the throat or the cheek to catch the spitback. This art, of pretending to swallow yet retaining the drug in the slippery sack, wasn't simple. Not every junkie who wished to mule could be trained into it. Those few were a commodity. A finger of ninety-percent methadone sold for six packs of smokes. This was a trade all contained inside the walls, no outside connection necessary, no dependence on the gangs.

Who you stole your mules from – now that involved a degree of difficulty apparently beyond Robert Woolfolk's finesse.

The day the Latin Kings stepped up on Dose in the yard he felt the charge in the air a minute before it happened. He'd become a barometric instrument of a prison's weather without even noticing. Those bumping on either side against him were men he'd ignored and been ignored by for years, but the new intimacy was undeniable, three years of flinched glances gone up in smoke.

It was the old story, weary beyond telling, Robert in arrears on all sides, and Dose to answer for it, and it all went down as scripted since One Million B.C.

Except for one thing.

That one day, Dylan Ebdus came and offered a ring.

CHAPTER 15

I ASKED MINGUS the time: a quarter to one. I'd been seated on the gallery floor for five hours, my shoulder wedged against a thin lip of wall between Mingus's cell and the next, my temple close at the bars, and his close beside mine, so we could talk. I felt our ears graze once or twice. I'd shown myself just once, slipping the ring loose and then vanishing again, when I explained how I'd snuck in and found him. We conversed in low murmurs, which drowned in the cavernous block's slurred surf of illegal radios, inmate talk, ventilation. As the block dimmed to a murmur itself, we whispered.

In the last hours it was Mingus who spoke. I listened, and tried not to drown along with our talk. I'd never been invisible for so many hours, for one thing. Seated on the chill concrete, I felt a recurrence of my childhood micropsia, a night terror I thought I'd left behind at age eleven or twelve, in my bedroom on Dean Street: the sensation that my body was reduced to speck size in a universe pounding with gravitational force, a void crushing against me on all sides. The ailanthus branches brushing the back windows had seemed to me then like the spiraled arms of distant galaxies. Later, in the years after I retired the ring, I'd blamed my inability to fly from a rooftop, my preference to look away from the sky, on the micropsia hallucinations. Now they'd returned to undermine my heroism in the prison. My heroism was used up. I had only enough left to flee the place, and fling Aaron Doily's curse once and for all into the brush at the side of the highway, then reclaim my rental car and vanish gratefully into the ordinary angst I'd earned as a grown-up Californian. I was an author of liner notes, an inadequate boyfriend. How could I have thrown over these attainments for this chimera of rescue? All I felt was the submarine pressure of the room, the special claustrophobia of a cathedral vault parceled into rat cages. The room had climate, a muggy stink of curdled human years. After lights-out, a planetarium show of cigarette ends pulsed on the galleries above and around us, reproachful failing stars. Go, they said.

I suppose I was trying not to drown, too, in the beauty of Mingus's voice, as it reeled through jivish yarn spinning to the brokenest kind of confession, the kind which didn't know it was broken at all. Mingus had borne his own life a hundred or a million moments longer than I could bear to. I tried not to drown in the consolation and guilt of having him back and being an instant from losing him again, of being about to steal invisibly away.

The ring was useless to him. So Mingus wished me to understand. He explained how he was doing good time, hadn't been written up in years, despite Robert's tangling with the Latin Kings. He'd felt a prospect of mercy in his last review, and might be near release, in a year, two. Perhaps the kidney had made an impression on the board. Anyhow, the life of an escapee and permanent fugitive, visible or not, held no allure.

When Mingus made me know what he wanted, it felt that he'd had it in mind from the start, that he'd begun bringing me along ten hours earlier in the visitor's room. I'd offered a way to spare Robert Woolfolk falling into the Kings' hands. It wasn't a *shoe* I'd heard mentioned in the offices, but a *SHU* – a special housing unit, protective custody for those either threatening the safety of the regular population, or needing protection from it. There our homeboy from Gowanus was celled. I'd take the ring to him – Mingus would tell me how to find my way there, and where guards could be found napping on cots, with stealable keys. Like hitting a broomstick home run, Mingus knew I could do it. Mingus knew I would.

I had a few questions before I left him. Before I decided whether or not to fail him – I had scant interest in the SHU and Robert Woolfolk. Either way, I was nearly done here, the Proust's madeleine of "Play That Funky Music" eaten. I had just crumbs to savor.

"Mingus," I said, "did you have any idea how often I was getting yoked?"

"You mean brothers putting you in a headlock?"

It was a point of clarification, not mockery. He didn't mean to shame me by contrasting my complaint with his withheld lamentations. He hadn't asked for pity, not once. I'd shamed myself, but I still wanted an answer.

"Putting me in a headlock and frisking me for money," I said. "Sometimes practically every day for the three years I was at I.S. 293. Calling me a whiteboy."

"Them niggers took me off a few times too." He took my inquiry more seriously than I probably deserved. "Dudes from Gowanus Houses, Whitman, Atlantic Terminals, man, they were always robbing, grubbing, didn't know any different. At Manhattan clubs everybody'd say look out for them crazy Brooklyn homeboys, those motherfuckers are just stick-up kids, always waving a piece."

Fair enough. I'd been a crash-test dummy for real crime, nothing personal.

"Wasn't so much a black-white thing," Mingus went on. "Those motherfuckers were just *thirsty people*."

Thirsty people. That about said it. Now I was meant to go to the thirstiest – thirsty for my bicycle, thirsty for my terror – and free him from his cell.

"Mingus?"

"Yeah?" I heard in his voice that he was as tired as I was. He'd given me my task, now I should go. He'd been talking all night, trying not to disappoint, working to shelter my ludicrous expectations, to make something of my incursion here that we could both live with. He'd come this far, to Watertown, out of easy visiting range of the city, in order to stop carrying Barry, Arthur, anyone else. How far should he have to carry me tonight?

"Did you ever yoke a whiteboy?"

He dredged his last reply from some weary place, yet I caught a note of puzzlement, in his tone, at what he found. "Yeah," he said. "Once. I mean, I didn't throw a headlock. Nobody had to."

"How?"

"Me and some homies from Terminals wanted to score some cheeba. Brother said we should go up to Montague and take money off some Packer boys or whatnot. We cornered a couple of kids with braces, on the Promenade, broad daylight. I hung in the background, just looking ill while them other brothers checked their pockets. But I knew I was doing what it took."

"Which was – what?"

"What I said. I went to the Heights, I made the mean face."
He pressed close to the bars, and the dim gallery light, pruned
his chin and brow for demonstration: *the mean face*. A Sylvester
the Cat scowl, yet the volt of panic it struck in me was one of
my life's companions.

What age is a black boy when he learns he's scary?

Mingus showed it for an instant, then backed into shadow.

I think I went a little crazy when I wandered from there. Invisibility and Mingus's voice had flayed me bare. I had no secrets to
conceal. I had no *mean face*, or any face at all: no wonder Zelmo
Swift had treated me like a moron child! Zelmo Swift and Jared
Orthman made adequate nemeses for a man without a face to
turn to the world. I felt I couldn't leave the Watertown facility
without completing my mission, and yet couldn't imagine sur-
rendering the ring – it had become a part of me, become the
truth about me. So for a while I split the difference, and mean-
dered. In fact, I made my way to where Mingus had claimed
I could acquire keys to the SHU, only I didn't tell myself this
was what I was doing. I moved recklessly, reeling past COs
who opened doors for me, a live disturbance in the air waves, a
poltergeist sick with ambivalence. It was easy to steal a fat ring
of keys. I used them heedlessly, rattling through options until I
fumbled the right key into a lock. I left doors swinging behind
me as I moved through the compound. Maybe I thought they'd
remain open for me when I needed to retrace my steps, maybe
I only thought they ought to be open. I wasn't thinking – my
brain was invisible to itself.

I passed back through the yard. Now the moon was gone.
Like a puppet under Mingus's guidance I found the SHU, a
squat three-story building, more a hospital annex than an arm
of the prison proper. The look didn't suit my mood. The beast
at the heart of the maze ought to be captive in an open-air cage,
or at the bottom of a pit, staked to a post. The SHU looked
soft. They might as well have cordoned the Lord of Elbows,
He Who Can Throw A Spaldeen Sideways, in a gingerbread
house, where he could gnaw his way free.

I let myself in. The lower level housed a special ward for incarcerated paraplegics – dying AIDS junkies, spinal gunshot victims with maximum-security designations. On the second floor, protective custody, the rooms were Inspector Clouseau loony bins: barred windows, knobless doors with slots for the exchange, I supposed, of trays or papers. There, Robert Wool-folk and I had a tiled corridor to ourselves.

I needed to raise my voice to wake him.

"Will Fuck!" I called.

I removed the ring and stood where he could see me in the light, then came nearer to the mesh grille of his door.

"Dylan?"

"Yes, Robert."

"Fuck *you* doing here?"

It was him, Robert Woolfolk, figment of my hatred turned real once more. With his jumpsuit and shaved head, and the long, disgust-lined sneer of his features, his eternal Mean Face, he resembled Scatman Crothers come for the garbage. Those limbs, now draped in prisoner's orange, had tangled with Rachel's on Bergen Street. I despised and envied him for having been embraced by her fists.

"Mingus sent me," I mumbled.

"You must of thought I was sleeping, right?"

"You were sleeping."

"Nah, I *ack* like that, but I was awake. Nobody could sneak up on me, man."

"Whatever," I said.

"You know what I was doing?"

This wasn't the conversation I'd intended. "What?" I said.

"Writing rhymes in my mind. I wrote a whole album in my mind. None a these fools know what I'm doing, think I'm crazy 'cause I always got my eyes closed, my head be nodding – I'm a be bust out with this shit someday, shock all they world."

Bust out sooner than you know, I thought.

"You want to hear?"

"Uh, sure."

You know my name, read it off the liner notes

Pussy rappers with vagina throats
Get snatched out they designer coats
For trying to float concrete boats in the Gowanus
Talk about a battle but they really don't want this—

His delivery was gruff and leaden, the lyrics growled incoher-
ently – or perhaps the incoherence was in me.

Maybe your queer ass better wait till the fear pass
'Cause I could see your teeth chatter thru your jaw like it was
clear glass—

"Robert, stop."

"What?"

"I don't have time." I pushed the ring at his eyes, impatient.
I'd wanted him to ask for it (*Yo, let me see that ring for a minute,*
let me take it around the block, what, you don't trust me?). Now the
game was over.

"You remember this?" I asked.

"Ho, shit. That's G's."

I hadn't been able to get Mingus to accept the ring as belonging to him, but Robert made the call instantly. There was odd
satisfaction in this. "Right," I said. "He told me to bring it to
you."

"Ho, shit."

"You can use it to get out." I pushed it through the slot,
to plop into his cupped hands. The instant it was free of my
fingers I felt a tidal panic wipe all giddiness from me: I was
drunk on nothing now. I had to go from here.

"Why don't G want it for himself?" Robert asked.

"He wanted you to have it."

"How's it work?"

"You'll figure it out."

Robert puzzled on this briefly, then his mind slid to another
question. "Yo, Dylan, man, you got keys?"

"I need them."

"Unlock this shit, though."

I stared at him, for what must have been a long moment.

"Yo, Dylan?"

"What?"

"*Fuck* you, motherfucker."

Prisons slept. I had transit of the Watertown facility by now – three, four in the morning, whichever it was. The familiar music of clanking deadbolts and jangling keys alerted no one. I was only certain the A/B doors were my limit, a test I couldn't pass visible. In my previous plan – just hours old, though it felt like another world – I'd intended to ask Mingus to wait a few days before using the ring, to give me a head start in getting clear. I doubted I'd get the same consideration from Robert. Anyway, I hadn't asked for it.

I held to that previous plan nevertheless, which consisted of getting as near to the visitors' room as I could. If I had to be found inside the compound, I figured innocence by association was my best hope – a civilian, I'd go to where civilians could be found, from time to time. There I'd wait out the last few hours of the night, then try to blend in with the morning's first wave of visitors, maybe claim to have accidentally blundered through the wrong door. I still hadn't scrubbed my ultraviolet-inked knuckles, and could reasonably hope the mark would still register in the COs' scanners. I'd offer that up, with my whiteness, as sign I wasn't part of the population. And, after all, I wasn't. They'd have to let me go.

I reentered the green-tile pavilion which led to the visitors' room, found my way to a corridor I'd passed through, one in sight, through wide Plexiglas windows, of the chamber where I'd removed my belt and shoes and had my earplug puzzled over. There I found a doorless room, really only a vestibule leading nowhere, with a pair of bright-lit Pepsi machines, another vending machine offering cellophane-wrapped Oreos and Cheez-Its at the end of corkscrew spirals, and a high-mounted television set, angled as though for a bedridden patient.

I slid the ring of keys into the dust deep between the feet of the Cheez-Its machine. They'd be retrievable if I needed them, but should I be caught, they'd hardly aid my case. Then I slumped inside the doorway, tucked my feet close, drew myself out of sight of the corridor from every angle I could calculate. Exhaustion was toxic, and my head began to nod. Not nodding in time – I wasn't composing and committing to memory a lost masterpiece of a rap album, only nodding off. Anyone could sneak up on me who liked to. The black eye of the television glared down, but it wasn't intelligible, wasn't Vader or Big Brother. There was no authority here, malign or otherwise. The Pepsi machine glowed, but no one was home.

I woke, to bright sunlight and an aching urge to pee, to find the Plexiglas window across the corridor full not of sluggish morning visitors but an agitated glut of COs, Watertown city policemen, and a handful of other middle-aged white men in dark suits, a few of them jotting on stenographer's pads. Then I was startled by someone nearer: a young CO in the vestibule with me, back turned as he fed dollars into the machine, one after another, and gathered an armload of Pepsi. The rolling clunk of a can into the machine's gullet was what had jerked me awake. The CO hadn't spotted me, but turned now, abruptly.

"I, uh, dropped some change," I said, blinking awake, and pawing with my hands on the floor.

"How the hell'd you even get in here?"

"Through that door," I bluffed. "It was open."

"Holy Hell, if Talbot saw you!"

"It was Talbot who told me I could come in here," I tried. "I think I'm a little confused. Where's the bathroom, anyway?"

Now the CO squinted down at me, sensing something irregular. He had to straighten his shoulders, and reorganize the freight of soda cans in his crooked elbow. He was the youngest I'd seen, evidently a gofer, though his belt was laden with keys, plastic baton, and, I was pleased to see, ultra violet scanner.

"You're a newspaperman, right?" he asked.

"Surely you remember me, young man." I stood, brushed myself off, and affected a transatlantic tone of befuddled impatience, casting myself as Cary Grant, him as Ralph Bellamy.

"What's your name again, though?"

I searched and came out with: "Vance Christmas." He was the only newspaperman I could think of in my condition, besides Jimmy Olsen. I supposed Christmas deserved any belated trouble Aeroman could bring him.

"Right, yeah, but from where?"

"Albany," I said. "I'm with the, uh, *Albany Herald-Ledger.* You know, we're doing a special feature on the state of the prisons."

"But you came in with those other guys, right?" The fog of uncertainty between us was an irritation to this man, my diffident captor – he wanted me to supply a right answer as badly as I wanted to supply one, so he could resume his uncontroversial errand.

"Sure, Talbot invited me to tag along," I said. I supposed *those other guys* were the ones just on the other side of the window. If I was made to join them perhaps I would be allowed to tag along and, eventually, shuffle out. "Because of the special feature thingee, the supplement." This fiction was becoming distractingly real to me – I imagined a shattering exposé, Pulitzers for the underdog *Herald-Ledger* – so I neglected to wonder why reporters, real reporters, were here in the first place.

I'd made a mistake, though, in trying a second time to claim the unseen Talbot's blessings. Gofer squinted harder, and arranged the cans of soda along the top of the machine to free his hands. He rubbed the crook of his arm to restore feeling to the chilled flesh, and cleared his throat, reassembling dignity and command.

"Can I see some I.D.?"

"Look, listen," I said, lowering my voice. "I didn't really come in with those other guys."

"How'd you get here, then?"

"I spent the night. I came in as a visitor, yesterday – here, check my hand stamp, you'll see."

"Well, I don't know about that . . ." He seemed about to panic and seek help. We were still unnoticed by the congregation in the search room. This was my margin, my breath, and it was rapidly vanishing.

"Listen, wait," I said. "I really am a reporter for the *Albany Tribune.*" Had I bollixed my credential? No matter: "I persuaded a couple of guards to smuggle me in here – you know Stamos and Sweeney?"

"Yeah?"

"I didn't want to get them in trouble, that's why I was stalling. They let me stow away, for my investigation."

"*Stamos* did that?"

"Yup."

"Christ, they're idiots!"

"I know, I know."

"Talbot's going to *murder* them."

"Maybe not, if you can get me out of here. Just slip me back through to the lot. I'll never involve any of your names, I promise you that."

"Jeez Louise!"

"Check my hand."

Shaking his head, Gofer unclipped his scanner and shone it on my knuckles. The purple emblem seemed to hover, a tiny hologram.

I tried to hustle him past deliberation, by acting as if he'd already agreed. "Let's make a move now, they're not looking."

"Jeez—"

"Only I really need to stop in the bathroom, I was stuck there all night."

"Oh, brother."

When I emerged from the men's toilet Gofer regarded me pityingly, my threat all dissipated now. "Guess it was unlucky for you this whole thing went down today," he said.

"*Crazy* unlucky," I agreed.

"Teach you to try that again."

"Indeed. Never."

"It's not funny."

"I'm not laughing."

At the A/B doors I whispered, "Probably you should just say I left something in my car." Gofer made a face, then leaned through a sliding window.

"This guy's got to go back to the lot," he said, his tone morose, like a bullied boy. "I'm taking him out."

"Okay," came the bleary reply. The cage's bolts slammed open and shut, each in turn, and we moved through.

"Hey, so what exactly *did* go down in there?" I asked Gofer at the entrance to the lot. The dawn's early light, still combing through the treeline, shocked my crummy orbs. I caught a whiff of myself, an ordinary all-night stink. Three disgruntled crows jogged across the gravel as we approached, then flapped aloft to barely clear the razor curls atop the Cyclone fence, and winged for the highway and the strip mall beyond it. The birds made shabby harbingers of my freedom: the prospect of my rental car's AC, some McDonald's coffee.

"Holy Moses," said Gofer, incredulous I'd been so near yet missed the breaking story. "Nothing apart from a fellow up in the SHU fooled an officer into opening his door, made a run for it. I guess he had some stolen keys, so we've got a whole headache about it now. Talbot's having a cow."

"Guy escaped?" I was blessed, I understood now, in being one headache too many this morning. Hence my easy ticket out. No one, least of all Gofer, wished to see Talbot further inflamed. I couldn't have scripted Robert Woolfolk's role better if I'd tried.

"Killed himself."

"What?" I blurted.

Gofer shut his eyes and stuck out his tongue.

"They killed *him*, you mean."

"Nope." He staged-whispered for effect. "Suicide. Got loose, then did away with himself, poor crazy son of a gun."

"Why would he kill himself if he got free?"

Gofer shrugged. "This fellow leaped off a gun tower, highest point on the yard. Gunnery officer said he was hooting like an eagle. He hit a sloped concrete embankment, landed sideways, I guess. It was pretty sickening. They were taking pictures out there but nobody's going to use them. Craziest thing I've ever seen – his arms got tangled under his body, so he sort of crumpled up and broke in half as he slid down that bank. Didn't even look human by the time he came to a stop."

CHAPTER 16

THE HOAGY CARMICHAEL ROOM, a mock Midwestern parlor with carpet and furniture and vitrines full of Carmichael's own scrapbook memorabilia, was open only by appointment, but I was able to make one on the spot. I didn't sense the room's keepers had too much demand. The formalities were only to be certain no intruder seated themselves at Hoagy's upright piano and started playing, or swiped hand-scrawled notes from Bix Beiderbecke or Governor Ronald Reagan. The key-bearer was a middle-aged secretary down the corridor, in the Archives of Traditional Music, there in Morrison Hall. She hovered nervously beside me in the room, until I persuaded her I was a good bet. Then I was left alone, to balm my soul in contemplation of the original sheet music for "Ole Buttermilk Sky" and "My Resistance Is Low" and a ribbon-bound screenplay of *To Have and Have Not* autographed by Bogart, Faulkner, and Hawks. Afterward I went to the listening room and spent some time on headphones, exploring lost acetates, rare masters of Carmichael's music. The Collegians, Carmichael's Indiana University fraternity band, had recorded a stomp called "March of the Hooligans" – careening hot jazz with a fiddle solo to peg it as Hoosier. I played that tinny, miraculous bit of schoolboy art five or six times, then returned to dwell some more in the Zen garden of the room.

I'd driven all day and far into Sunday night from the mall lot in Watertown, committing topological penance across western New York and into Pennsylvania, on a flat, three-lane interstate which judged or forgave nothing, only left me wholly to my own judgment. Now I understood: I'd wakened Aeroman to kill Robert Woolfolk. It was a collaboration that had taken Mingus and the ring and my half-conscious hatred years to devise, though the seed of inspiration had been unmistakable, in Aaron X. Doily's plunge into the Pacific Street vest-pocket park, twenty-three years ago – what goes up comes down. Aeroman was nothing if not a black body on the ground. I hadn't even played fair and told Robert of the ring's switch to invisibility. I wondered if he'd discovered it. I wondered if the guards on the tower had only told themselves they'd seen the man who screamed like a raptor on his way down, if there'd been anything to see until he'd smashed to pieces on the embankment.

For so long I'd thought Abraham's legacy was mine: to retreat upstairs, unable or unwilling to sing or fly, only to compile and collect, to sculpt statues of my lost friends, life's real actors, in my Fortress of Solitude. To see the world in a liner note: I am the DJ, I am what I play. But here I'd catapulted across the country in an airplane seat, a deranged arrow-man of pure intention, to uncover Mingus and Robert at Watertown – they hadn't asked me to come. Maybe I'd underrated the Rachel in me, the Running Crab ready to destroy and bolt, to overturn lives and go on the lam.

So now I had to move on the ground, touch the earth. I needed to follow her crab footprints exactly, make no mistake in whom I was tracking this time. I drove just over the limit, anonymous in the flow, but inside the space of the car I was a vigilante, a low rider. I drove without music, my CD wallet on the backseat, untouched – no soundtrack to prettify the ugly scene of me. I stopped only to stretch my legs, gas up, and piss, and to make a handful of calls, letting Abraham and Francesca know I wouldn't be returning to Brooklyn, contacting the airline to cancel a ticket and the rental office to say I'd be returning the car to Berkeley in a few days, not La Guardia tomorrow. No one was pleased, but I didn't give anyone a choice in the matter. I didn't call Abby, because I didn't have anything to tell her, not yet.

I lost my wits on the road at around three. The sporadic lights coming the other way seemed always about to veer into mine, despite the wide grassy divider between us. I found a Howard Johnson's then, at the entrance to Ohio, and slept for a few queasy hours, showered, hit the road again. I made Indiana by midmorning – a left turn at Indianapolis, past Larry Bird's auto dealership, south to Bloomington. Campus parking was a bitch, so I settled for a faculty spot. I'd killed a man last night – I could stand a campus parking ticket.

At a terminal in the library I made my discovery: my quarry

not only still lived in Bloomington, he worked on campus. I wouldn't even have to repark my car. The researcher at Zelmo Swift's law firm had traced Running Crab's last known address to Bloomington, 1975, before she'd dropped off the map after bail flight in Lexington, Kentucky. But Abraham had refused even to look inside Zelmo's manila folder of "This Is Your Life!" data, and neither Zelmo Swift nor Francesca Cassini could have known, as I did, another name to use to pick up the Bloomington trail.

The Archives of Traditional Music and the Carmichael Collection shared Morrison Hall with a portion of IU's English and psych departments, and with the Kinsey Institute for Research in Sex, Gender, and Reproduction, which occupied two of the hall's upper floors. It was at the Kinsey Institute that I'd located Croft Vendle. He worked in their Office of Public Affairs. I called him from a phone in the library, and he told me to come by.

When I arrived, the Kinsey secretary explained that Croft was on a call. So I sat in a waiting room and read brochures. From the evidence, the institute was still struggling to defend its first, half-refused gift of knowledge to the American mind, and teetering always on the brink of exile from the campus by Indiana's priggish legislature. The walls around me held the single biggest repository of "erotic materials" in the world, Alfred Kinsey having forged deals with police departments all over the country to quietly cart away seized materials, sparing the expense of their storage or destruction. For all this, the offices were homey, walls lined with neat-framed fifties-vintage smut, black-and-white photos as sunny as Topps baseball-card photography. Beside the receptionist's desk hung an honorific row of studio portraits of past directors, beginning with bow-tied Alfred himself, and continuing through a charming sequence, leading to the present day, of thoughtful eyeglass-frame-gnawing psychologists, gentle stewards of freaky reality.

Croft was a man I barely recognized, in a rust corduroy two-piece, maroon tie, and milk-chocolate Earth shoes. His ruddy features swarmed with wiry silver beard, all trimmed to an exact length, even where it sprouted from his ears. He resembled a diet or exercise guru, someone usually seen only in running shorts but temporarily got up in a suit for a book-plugging appearance on *Today*. It was a shock. In my mind's eye only Abraham aged; Rachel and her lover were still verdant, in 1974 bodies forever.

"I've got this call on hold," Croft said apologetically, gesturing back toward his office. His voice was helium-high, another thing I didn't remember. He seemed to take my appearance more in stride, despite my hints of road-weary desperado: three-day beard and sunburned forearm, Vietnam-vet walleye. Perhaps he'd been expecting me for years. "It's this wealthy gay collector in Los Angeles, he's been dangling this donation for months, a stash of Japanese erotica, thousands of pieces. I've got him on the brink, but it's taking some real hand-holding."

"No problem," I said. "I can wait." I wondered if Erlan Hagopian's Rachel-paintings would find their way here someday. Maybe they already had.

"I was thinking if you're free you'd come out to the farm for dinner," he said. "So we can talk."

"Number 1, Rural Route 8?" I asked.

Croft's eyes widened. "We call it Watermelon Sugar Farm, but yeah. Bring your car out front at five and I'll lead you. Place can be difficult to find – kind of a backroads, no-map-to-the-territory deal."

"Okay."

"Cool," he said. "I'd better get back to this call. If you're just killing the afternoon I could get Susie, she's our intern, to give you the full Kinsey tour."

"That's okay."

I'd noted the Hoagy option on the way through Morrison's lobby, and suspected that better fit my mood. So Croft went to his phone call, I to "March of the Hooligans."

"Just one thing I want to show you," said Croft. "Then we ought to go for a walk around the property, before the light's gone. It's a rare night."

Croft, piloting a decrepit Peugeot, had led me along a serpentine country road, through hamlets and farmland and well into the woods, before we'd turned onto a well-maintained dirt road with w. SUGAR marked on the mailbox. There we'd rumbled past a few rotting Volkswagen Beetle exoskeletons, field grass swum up through their engines, to stop in front of a hand-hewn cabin, with an ancient paint job mostly blistered off its plank exterior. I thought it leaned dangerously, but we headed for the half-open door. Beside it, an upright manual lawnmower was rusted to sculpture beside a primitive stone well, each having surrendered, like the Beetles, to the field grass.

"You live here?" I asked. I withheld the question that went with it: Was Croft the only one left on the property? The scene was Walden-pretty, but a little desolate, regarded on civilization's terms.

"God, no, the homes are down the hill, in the woods. We've got a hundred and sixty acres. This place was the old communal cookhouse, back when we all ate together. Plus a winter sleeping bunk for the folks in tepees. This was some time ago, though. Nobody uses this for anything anymore, except the bees."

I suppose there was never a reason for tearing down a cabin or scrapping a stopped automobile, if you had all those acres. Particularly if your models of exterior decoration were author photos of Richard Brautigan, at the door of a Kaczynskian Montana shack.

Inside was an abandoned kitchen: an old range, its enamel webbed like the glaze of a Renaissance painting, a long, stained butcherblock which could have been salvaged for installation in a loft in Emeryville or Gowanus, and a double-basined sink with an old plastic bucket below, in place of plumbing. What Croft had called a sleeping bunk sagged so low over the stove it threatened to kiss it. I picked out wood rot and insect eggs, a hollow-log scent. Croft clambered over some barrel staves and steel drums, into the corner beneath the loft, and from a shelf full of water-swollen hardcover books plucked up a mechanical something and curled it under his arm. When he crawled back through the wreckage, he presented it to me: a manual typewriter. The double ribbon, black-over-red, which had produced the reverb of crimson in Running Crab's postcard font, was still strung between the spools, though the spools themselves were thick with corrosion, going nowhere in a hurry.

Any stray tendril of fantasy that Croft was about to produce Rachel in the flesh, that she dwelled incognito like a Weatherman or Symbionese soccer mom in one of those homes in the woods, evaporated now, even before he spoke.

"We kept it in the Bug, when we drove out to the coast. We'd write you a postcard each time we stopped for gas, or to get stoned."

"You wrote them, or she did?"

"I had to kind of push her, but she helped. I think she was ashamed, you know? Later it was just me. After she was gone." I held the melted typewriter in my two hands, like a beggar with his hat. Croft brushed at the sodden chunks of rust it had deposited on the sleeve of his corduroy jacket.

"You want it?" he asked.

"No." I wanted my cleaning deposit back when I returned the rental, that's what I wanted.

"Let's go for a walk."

The dirt road curved out of the open field at the property's entrance, down the hill and to the woods. We left the cars, strolled into the glade, the cool forest, too steep and irregular to ever have been farmed. The sun gone from sight below the hill's line, the birch trunks and pale ferns seemed bioluminescent, charged with the day's light. Our footfalls whispered unreplied on the private road's fresh layer of sharp, gray gravel. The woods were an engine of silence, pumping it to the sky.

Around each turn lay a house. Wooden two-story buildings, seven or eight total, each with their thoughtful trace of Buckminster Fuller or Christopher Alexander – circular rooms with skylight domes, greenhouse windows, breezeways attaching a low annex or small studio. Each house with a car or two in the drive, a few with smoke unfolding from a chimney. Here and there bicycles, chain saws, snowshoes, mulching piles, splintery blast marks of log splitting, ax wedged in a stump. The Watermelon Sugars were home, their kitchens lit. From the distance of the road, though, we granted their privacy as we passed. I was humbled, as I ought to have been, to see what varieties of life could hide between the arrogant, oblivious coasts.

"Rachel and Jeremy were probably the biggest challenge this

community ever faced," said Croft in his squeaky alto. "Confronting them helped us grow up, so I guess we owe them a lot. I'll never forget that night, we held hands in a circle around them and told them they had to go. I just about shit my pants. Jeremy had already punched me a couple of times, but I was too embarrassed to admit it to anyone. Turned out he'd punched a lot of people."

"I don't know who Jeremy is," I said.

"Somebody told me he died a couple of years ago. He was basically just this really charismatic, really violent guy from Kentucky who used us as his playground for a few months. His favorite game was to scare guys by getting them really high, then talk about how he'd once killed a man outside a bar with a single blow to the throat. He had a lot of those biker horror stories. Right after the throat story he'd move in on the guy's girlfriend. Everyone was sort of passive, you know, like 'If she wants to be with Jeremy, that's cool, maybe she'll bring him some peace.' Rach was actually the only person who really stood up to him."

"He took her away from you?" I asked. It was growing darker, and I'd been momentarily transfixed by the scene in a bright-lit kitchen window – a middle-aged woman, her hair as gray as Croft's, sliced tomatoes at a counter, while behind her, two blond daughters, bright and shiny as Solver girls, played a dual-remote video game, some dungeon or deep-seascape glowing unearthly blue on a screen. But they couldn't see me, and I felt like Frankenstein's monster, peeping at the humans. So I turned away.

"Oh, we weren't spending much time together at that point. Rachel was her own problem, a lot of people weren't completely thrilled about my bringing her out here. She had that New York sarcastic thing that burst a lot of people's balloons." He laughed. "I mean, she sort of ran rings around people, truth be told. She ran rings around me. Plus she wasn't happy here. She's wasn't all that happy, period, or she would never have gone with Jeremy. I think she regretted leaving New York."

"Did she talk about – Abraham?"

"Well, she was pretty ashamed," Croft said. It was the same word he'd used to explain why he'd had to force her to write the postcards. I supposed it was true, the right word. I decided to quit fishing for more.

Croft went on. "Mostly I just remember this one day, I tried to get her to come looking for mushrooms with me. She hated that kind of thing, she thought it was stupid. This was after Jeremy showed up too. I was just trying to reach out, you know, make some connection, because she seemed so balled up. So she had this routine, every time I tried to get her to do anything outdoors she'd say, 'I wonder what's playing at the Thalia.' Like I should know what she was missing, from her life before. She'd say, 'Maybe it's *The Thirty-nine Steps*, or *A Thousand Clowns*,' or whatever. So this particular day she said yes, I don't know why. It had just rained for three days, and we went hunting for fresh morels." Croft gestured at the forest floor, and I understood he meant *here*. More or less right around here. "Not that she picked mushrooms. She was chain-smoking – she couldn't drive, either, she constantly forced me to run her into town for cigarettes. Anyway, she walked with me, smoking like a fiend, and when she started in about the Thalia she said, 'Maybe they're showing *Beat the Devil*,' and I said, 'What's so great about *Beat the Devil*?' and she told me the plot of that fucking movie for an hour. I mean, doing Peter Lorre's voice and everything, all the lines – she had the whole thing memorized."

I didn't reach for music until I was out of Indiana. First Croft and I reclaimed our cars, and he showed me his house, another beauty nestled at the end of the drive, where the Watermelon Sugar property nearly ran out. A fire lane cut across another twelve acres, then opened onto the interstate, up from Louisville, Kentucky. If the wind blew right you could hear the trucks. It was then that Croft mentioned, just an afterthought, that the farm was in the fight of its life, against a creature less chimerical than Rachel and Jeremy. The legislature meant to extend the highway across the property, a four-billion-dollar contract for local construction – one which, Croft said, would cut only ten minutes off the trip to Chicago. We considered this together, tipping our ears to catch the distant whine of tractor trailers. Then he showed me inside, and we lit his kitchen, and he made me a plate of spaghetti. He offered a guest-room bed, but I wanted to drive. He told me I could use his phone and I nearly did, then decided I'd call Abby from somewhere west of here, somewhere nearer to home, when I'd sorted out more of all I'd have to explain.

At the door Croft hugged me, awkwardly, and I hugged him back, awkwardly. There was nothing to accept or refuse in the embrace. Isabel Vendle's nephew wasn't the mother I never had, any more than a rotting typewriter was. He wasn't the father I never had, either. Abraham was the father I never had, and Rachel was the mother I never had, and Gowanus or Boerum Hill was the home I never had, everything was only itself however many names it carried, and so I hugged Croft and I went out to pilot my car through the woods, back to the serpentine road. I was lost a few times on the way to Bloomington, but I never stopped and asked for directions. There was no one to ask. And I wasn't in a hurry.

It was after midnight when I skirted Gary, Indiana, birth-place of the Jackson Five. In Illinois I stopped for gas and noticed the wallet of discs on the backseat. Once on the road I groped one into the mouth of the car's player, the first to fall into my hand – Brian Eno's *Another Green World*. Prog rock – troll music, Euclid Barnes would have called it. I'd listened to this record my whole life since discovering it in the cut-out bin on the eighth floor of Abraham and Straus, at the dying record store there, behind the stamp and coin collecting department. Using Brooklyn skills, I'd boosted another copy, a commercial cassette, from the Main Street record shop of Camden Town, then played it endlessly one night as I made love to Moira Hogarth. I adored the record's harmless spookiness: Eno's key-board washes, John Cale's sawing cello, Robert Fripp's teardrop fretwork. And I always associated it with driving, with miles rushing beneath headlights and my eyes. I associated it with one drive in particular.

This was the winter of my expulsion from Camden Col-lege. After Richard Brodeur's letter, I'd been forced to return to the campus once more, to collect my belongings – books, bedclothes, stereo – all crated in the attic of Oswald House. So Abraham had, in his typical, infuriating, silent way, driven me north, in a borrowed car. The school was closed then, for the long, fuel-conserving winter break. Still, at my insistence, Abraham had waited in the car, while I found a security guard who could unlock the dorm's attic. I didn't want my father to set foot on the grounds.

Returning, we'd driven through a Massachusetts blizzard, wind swirling flakes in a tunnel of white around the mole-eye of our windshield. Our silence was total. My shame at Abraham's presumed disappointment could only be stemmed by stony, preemptive fury of my own. When the storm was at its height, our car inching through the polar cyclone, navigating by the taillights of a wavering truck whose treads ground a path through the slurry, I'd reached into the backseat, into a carton of books and cassettes and, as tonight, pulled out the Eno, and put it into the car's player. The music made an ideal soundtrack to the blizzard's unreality. I suppose Abraham was actually struggling with a vivid amount of danger, but *Another Green World*'s supernatural placidity seemed to acknowledge his effort and to calm us at the same time. Eno sang *I can't see the lines I used to think I could read between*—

Earlier, the first years of high school, when the Clash and Ramones were first thrilling me and Gabriel Stern and Timothy Vandertooth, I'd bring a record home and play it for Abraham and ask him, "Do you hear it? How great it is? There's never been music like this!"

"Sure," he'd say. "It's wonderful."

"But do you *really* hear what I'm hearing? Can you hear the same song I do?"

"Of course," he'd say, leaving me perfectly unsatisfied, leaving the mystery unplumbed: *Could my father hear my music?* By my college years, though, I'd never have asked, even if we weren't on that dour voyage home. Those lines of inquiry were shut down, so I barely troubled to speculate what *Another Green World* might mean to Abraham, whether he felt it shaping our pummel through the snow. Eno sang, *You'd be surprised at my degree of uncertainty*—

I considered now that what I once loved in this record, and certain others – *Remain in Light*, "O Superman," *Horses* – was the middle space they conjured and dwelled in, a bohemian demimonde, a hippie dream. And that same space, that unlikely proposition, was what I'd eventually come to hate and be embarrassed by, what I'd had to refuse in favor of soul, in favor of Barrett Rude Junior and his defiant, unsubtle pain. I'd needed music that would tell it like it is, like I'd learned it to be, in the inner city. *Another Green World* was like Abraham's film: too fragile, too yokeable – I wanted a tougher song than that. I knew stuff B. Eno and A. Ebdus didn't, and I couldn't afford to carry them or their naïveté, any more than Mingus could afford to carry me or mine.

The collapsing middle was what Running Crab had fled out of. It was the same space the communists and gays and painters of celluloid imagined they'd found in Gowanus, only to be unwitting wedges for realtors, a racial wrecking ball. A gentrification was the scar left by a dream, Utopia the show which always closed on opening night. And it wasn't so different from the space Abraham raged not to find opening to welcome his film, a space the width of a dwindled summer, a place where Mingus Rude always grooved fat spaldeen pitches, born home runs.

We all pined for those middle spaces, those summer hours when Josephine Baker lay waste to Paris, when "Bothered Blue" peaked on the charts, when a teenaged Elvis, still dreaming of his own first session, sat in the Sun Studios watching the Prisonaires, when a top-to-bottom burner blazed through a subway station, renovating the world for an instant, when schoolyard turntables were powered by a cord run from a streetlamp, when juice just *flowed*. I'd come to Indiana not to see a typewriter, or meet Croft, but to walk that back road in dusk and see the middle space the Watermelon Sugars had wrested from the world, before the makers of highways wrested it back, just as I'd gone to Katha's house to see the pallet she kept for her sister, to hear M–Dog's rhymes. A middle space opened and closed like a glance, you'd miss it if you blinked. Maybe Camden had been one once too, before it was poisoned with cash. It bore the traces. In the same spirit, on Rachel's principles, I'd been pushed out like a blind finger, to probe a nonexistent space, a whiteboy integrating public schools which were just then being abandoned, which were becoming only rehearsals for prison. Her mistake was so beautiful, so stupid, so American. It terrified my small mind, it always had. Abraham had the better idea, to try to carve the middle space on a daily basis, alone in his room. If the green triangle never fell to earth before he died and left the film unfinished, it would never have fallen – wasn't that so? Wasn't it?

Brian Eno sang *How can moments go so slowly?* as we drove through the storm. Abraham and I let ourselves be swept through the blurred tunnel, beyond rescue but calm for an instant, settled in our task, a father driving a son home to Dean Street. There was no Mingus Rude or Barrett Rude Junior with us there, no Running Crab postcard or letter from Camden College pushed through the slot. We were in a middle space then, in a cone of white, father and son moving forward at a certain speed. Side-by-side, not truly quiet but quiescent, two gnarls of human scribble, human cipher, human dream.

ACKNOWLEDGMENTS

Just Walking in the Rain by Jay Warner, unread by D. Ebdus, is a responsible account of the Prisonaires.

"It Was the Drugs," lyrics by Chrissie McClean.

Among too many to thank, I must at least mention Elizabeth Gaffney, Lynn Nottage, Sarah Crichton, David Gates (the man in the abandoned house), Christopher Sorrentino, Lorin Stein, Julia Rosenberg, Walter Donohue, Zoë Rosenfeld, Bill Thomas, Richard Parks, and Yaddo.

Above all, Christina Palacio, Karl Rusnak, Dione Ruffin, and my brother, Blake.

ABOUT THE INTRODUCER

CHARLES YU is the author of four books, including *Interior Chinatown*, which won the National Book Award for Fiction, and the novel *How to Live Safely in a Science Fictional Universe* (a *New York Times* Notable Book and a *Time* magazine best book of the year). His fiction and nonfiction have appeared in *The New Yorker*, *The New York Times*, *The Atlantic*, *Harper's*, and *Wired*, among other publications.

CHINUA ACHEBE
The African Trilogy
Things Fall Apart

ISABEL ALLENDE
The House of the Spirits

MARTIN AMIS
London Fields

IVO ANDRIĆ
The Bridge on the Drina

ISAAC ASIMOV
Foundation
Foundation and Empire
Second Foundation
(in 1 vol.)

MARGARET ATWOOD
The Handmaid's Tale

JAMES BALDWIN
The Fire Next Time,
Nobody Knows My Name,
No Name in the Street,
The Devil Finds Work
(in 1 vol.)
Giovanni's Room
Go Tell It on the Mountain

JOHN BANVILLE
The Book of Evidence
The Sea
(in 1 vol.)

JULIAN BARNES
Flaubert's Parrot
A History of the World in
10½ Chapters (in 1 vol.)

GIORGIO BASSANI
The Garden of the Finzi-Continis

SIMONE DE BEAUVOIR
The Second Sex

SAMUEL BECKETT
Molloy, Malone Dies,
The Unnamable

SAUL BELLOW
The Adventures of Augie March

JORGE LUIS BORGES
Ficciones

ELIZABETH BOWEN
Collected Stories

RAY BRADBURY
The Stories of Ray Bradbury

MIKHAIL BULGAKOV
The Master and Margarita
The White Guard

A. S. BYATT
Possession

JAMES M. CAIN
The Postman Always Rings Twice
Double Indemnity
Mildred Pierce
Selected Stories
(1 vol. US only)

ITALO CALVINO
If on a winter's night a traveler

ALBERT CAMUS
The Outsider (UK)
The Stranger (US)
The Plague, The Fall,
Exile and the Kingdom,
and Selected Essays
(in 1 vol.)

PETER CAREY
Oscar and Lucinda
True History of the Kelly Gang
(in 1 vol.)

ANGELA CARTER
The Bloody Chamber,
Wise Children,
Fireworks
(in 1 vol.)

WILLA CATHER
Death Comes for the Archbishop
(US only)
My Ántonia
O Pioneers!

RAYMOND CHANDLER
The novels (2 vols)
Collected Stories

G. K. CHESTERTON
The Everyman Chesterton

KATE CHOPIN
The Awakening

SANDRA CISNEROS
The House on Mango Street